"I don't do my questioning in the hangar bay, Mr. Greeve. Come with me."

A molten core of anger formed in Sanda's chest, so hot it almost made her eyes water. She tried to push forward, but Tomas tightened his grip across her shoulders, pressing her in close against his side so Laguna couldn't see her movements. Trying to get her to stay out of things. Jerk.

"What's this about?" she demanded. Tomas sighed wearily.

Laguna didn't look up from her wristpad as she tapped out a few short commands. "Your father is wanted for questioning. This will be quick and painless, unless you dig your heels in."

Your father. "You know who I am?"

Praise for

VELOCITY WEAPON

"O'Keefe delivers a complicated, thoughtful tale that skillfully interweaves intrigue, action, and strong characterization. Themes of found family, emotional connection, and identity run throughout, backed up by strong worldbuilding and a tense narrative. This series opener leaves multiple plot threads open for further development, and readers will look forward to the next installments." —*Publishers Weekly*

"Meticulously plotted, edge-of-your-seat space opera with a soul; a highly promising science-fiction debut." —*Kirkus*

"A brilliantly plotted yarn of survival and far-future political intrigue."
—*Guardian*

"This is a sweeping space opera with scope and vision, tremendously readable. I look forward to seeing where O'Keefe takes this story next."
—*Locus*

"Outstanding space opera where the politics and worldbuilding of the Expanse series meets the forward-thinking AI elements of *Ancillary Justice*." —Michael Mammay, author of *Planetside*

"*Velocity Weapon* is a spectacular epic of survival, full of triumph and gut-wrenching loss." —Alex White, author of the Salvagers series

"*Velocity Weapon* is a roller-coaster ride of pure delight. Furious action sequences, funny dialog, and touching family interactions all wrapped up in a plot that will keep you guessing every step of the way. This is one of the best science fiction novels of 2019."
—K. B. Wagers, author of the Indranan War trilogy

"*Velocity Weapon* is fast-paced, twisty, edge-of-your-seat fun. Space opera fans are in for a massive treat!"
—Marina J. Lostetter, author of *Noumenon*

BY MEGAN E. O'KEEFE

THE PROTECTORATE

Velocity Weapon

Chaos Vector

CHAOS VECTOR

THE PROTECTORATE: BOOK TWO

MEGAN E. O'KEEFE

www.orbitbooks.net

Cover design by Lauren Panepinto
Cover illustration by Sparth

Author photograph by Joey Hewitt

Orbit
Hachette Book Group
1290 Avenue of the Americas
New York, NY 10104
orbitbooks.net

First Edition: July 2020
Simultaneously published in Great Britain by Orbit

Orbit is an imprint of Hachette Book Group.
The Orbit name and logo are trademarks of Little, Brown Book Group Limited.

Library of Congress Cataloging-in-Publication Data
Names: O'Keefe, Megan E., 1985– author.
Title: Chaos vector / Megan E. O'Keefe.
Description: First edition. | New York, NY : Orbit, 2020. | Series: The protectorate ; book 2
Identifiers: LCCN 2020006688 | ISBN 9780316419635 (trade paperback) |
ISBN 9780316419611 (ebook)
Subjects: GSAFD: Science fiction.
Classification: LCC PS3615.K437 C47 2020 | DDC 813/.6—dc23
LC record available at https://lccn.loc.gov/2020006688

ISBNs: 978-0-316-41963-5 (trade paperback), 978-0-316-41964-2 (ebook)

Printed in the United States of America

LSC-C

10 9 8 7 6 5 4 3 2 1

This one is for all my beloved weirdos at #MurderCabin.
I couldn't ask for a finer bunch of friends.

LOCATIONS VISITED:

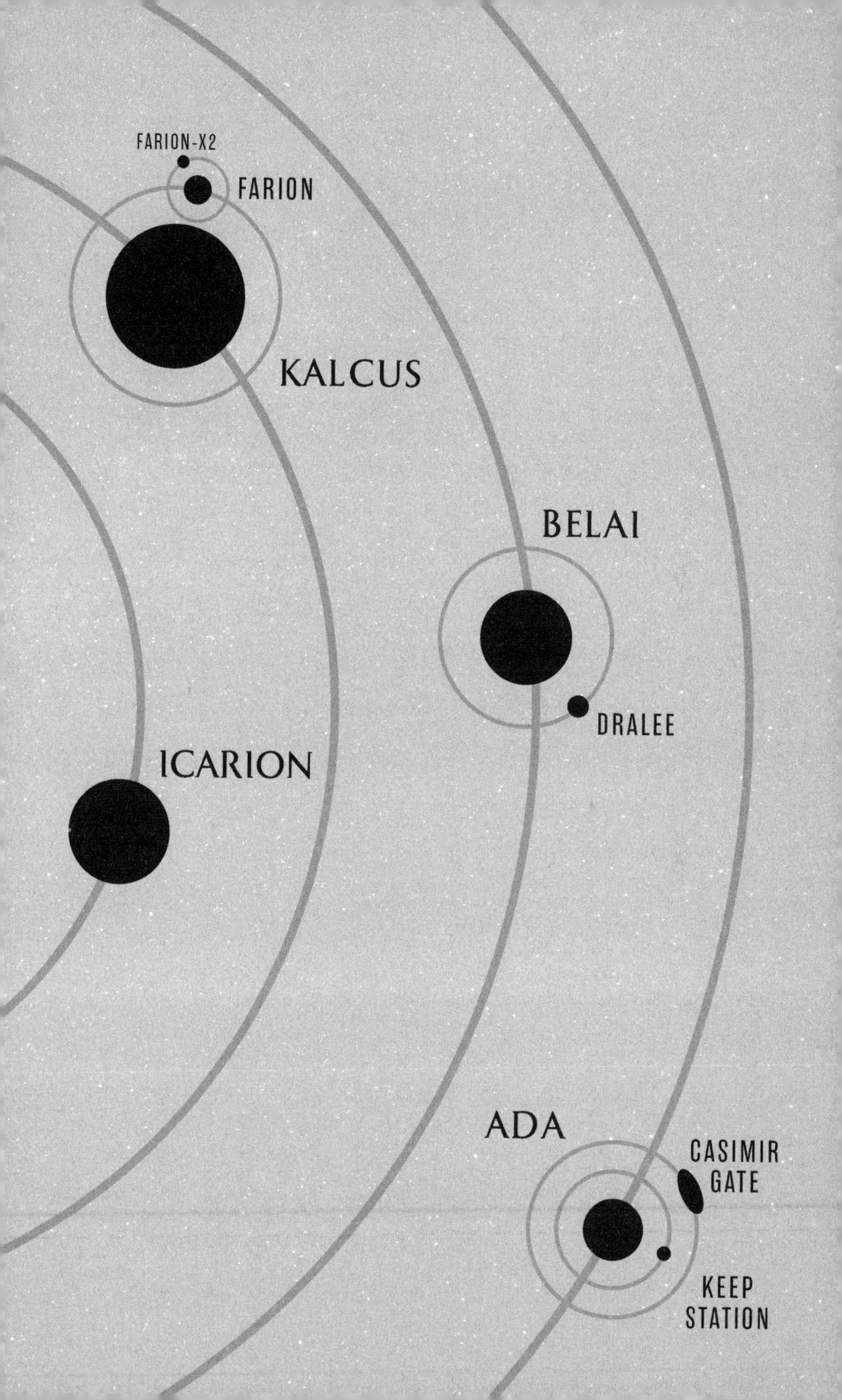

FARION-X2
FARION
KALCUS
BELAI
DRALEE
ICARION
ADA
CASIMIR GATE
KEEP STATION

CHAOS VECTOR

CHAPTER 1

PRIME STANDARD YEAR 3543

FIRST DAY A FUGITIVE

It took twelve hours for the media to spin Sanda Greeve from war hero to murderess. False footage filled every feed, showing her push Keeper Lavaux out of an airlock when it'd been him trying to cut her skull open. Part of Sanda even liked the fake. It was deeply satisfying to watch herself shove Lavaux into hard vacuum with her own hands, even if it made her a criminal.

She could hide, ride it out. Wait until the investigation proved the footage was doctored and then come out of hiding. Her dad Graham had already arranged for them to lie low on Pozo, a half-forgotten moon in the Atrux system.

Pozo gave her a chance to scrub a little of the blood out. It would leave its mark, as blood always did, but she could live a quiet life there and slip back into military service when the heat cooled. Accept whatever rank General Anford decided she deserved and step in line until her reputation was less tarnished, if not shiny.

There weren't any answers on Pozo, but there could be a life. One that looked a shade more like the one she'd planned before Bero had stolen her from between the stars and ripped her worlds apart. Going to Pozo, she'd never find her way to the coordinates hidden in her skull. On Pozo, she might be safe.

But safe couldn't undo what she'd experienced. Safe couldn't bring

Bero back from his desperate flight for freedom. It couldn't pluck the illegal Keeper chip with its hidden coordinates out of her head, or erase the fact that Keeper Lavaux had attempted to murder her to get those coordinates.

If she went to the planet of Atrux, she stood a chance of finding answers. From Atrux, Tomas could use his spy connections to discover the location of the coordinates without setting off any digital trip wires. Atrux was where the search for the secret in her head began.

Pozo was going into hiding. Atrux was going to war.

She typed the coordinates into the console, and Graham's hauler deviated from its prefiled flight plan. Sanda's heart was in her throat as the graphic display on the viewscreen showed them branching away from the predicted path to Pozo, out on the fringes, and banked hard for the space elevator that would take them down through the atmo dome over Alexandria-Atrux and into the city's hangar.

The dash lit green, an incoming call from air traffic control.

"Hauler, this is Alexandria-Atrux dock central. You are off course."

Graham leaned closer to the radio deck. "Control, we need medical assistance and cannot complete the trip to Pozo."

"Hauler, do you require a medishuttle?"

"Negative, it's not that bad. Just need a hospital sooner than the three weeks to Pozo will take."

"Understood. Please enter approach sequence Falcon, the AIs will take you in."

"Roger that, control."

Tomas, Sanda, and Graham sat back in their inertia-damping seats and let out breaths heavy enough to fog the forward viewscreen. Graham punched in the approach path, and the ship's AI gave way to the guiding hand of Atrux control.

"That wasn't the hard part," Tomas said.

"Spoilsport," she said.

"He's right, lass."

"I'm not sure I can take you two ganging up against me for another twelve hours."

"We're not—" they said in unison. All three broke into anxious laughter.

"Okay." Sanda pressed her palms against the arms of her chair, stretching tired muscles. The hauler vibrated as its guidance system began the braking procedure. "How are we going to explain away two people not on the hauler's manifest, Dad? They're gonna scan our idents, and I'm wanted for questioning in Lavaux's death."

Graham shrugged. "If anyone is even at the dock to ask, I'll say you were last-minute hired hands because the pallet jacks broke and muscle is cheaper than new equipment on short notice."

"That might get you out of being fined for flying without a souls-on-board manifest, but it does nothing about Sanda's ident," Tomas said.

"Hey, your ident is spoiled goods now, too."

"Me?" He looked abashed. "I don't know what you mean. According to this pad on my wrist, my name is Jacob Galvan. Luckily for us, Jacob Galvan is a titanium member of the Stellaris Hotel chain. We'll have sweet dreams on real feather pillows once we get off this bucket."

She narrowed her eyes. "All right then, work your spy magic on my ident."

"No can do. I had this preprogrammed in case I needed to switch in the field. To make a new ident look authentic, I need access to a lot of databases. If I pull downloads from certain databases onto this ship, then it doesn't matter what I do to cover the trail, it will get someone's attention."

"Biran will get that mess with Lavaux cleared up, just you wait." Graham's chair creaked as he reached over to squeeze her shoulder.

"Hands in line," she said by rote. When she'd been trained to pilot her gunship, the order had seemed stupid. Keeping her hands in the shadow of the evac pod that encased all deck chairs was the kind of superfluous, worst-case scenario training that was enforced only when the safety inspectors came knocking.

At the time, she'd figured that if things had gone bad enough that her evac pod deployed around her chair, then losing a finger to it snapping shut was a small price to pay. She rubbed the end of her thigh, pinch-rolling the itchy flesh between two fingers. Didn't seem so stupid now.

"Sorry, sorry." Graham pulled his arm back and picked at the

FitFlex suit clinging to his chest. He'd always complained about the way the tight material irritated his chest hair. She'd told him to get over it and suit up, because you never knew when hard vacuum would jump up and bite you in the ass.

"We're all on edge," Tomas said.

"Stop," she said.

"What?"

"De-escalating the situation."

Silence. Shit. A few weeks ago, the chatter would have been a balm to her nerves; now she wanted to live in a sensory deprivation tank. Twelve hours. It'd been only twelve hours since she'd been spaced, said her goodbyes, and given up her body to the black. She should pull it together. She should be easier on herself. She should stop her thoughts ping-ponging back and forth quicker than a rabid squirrel.

Her thigh stung. She looked down to realize she'd rubbed the flesh red-raw and hadn't even noticed. She needed a jumpsuit. Some barrier between her body thicker than the flimsy robe Graham had rummaged up out of an ancient crate of supplies.

She needed a lot of things, but the jumpsuit was something she could concentrate on.

"You sure you don't have an extra FitFlex on board?"

"Sorry, lass, didn't expect the company."

"We're coming in. You'll get to change soon," Tomas said.

Sanda's fingers danced over the dash, wiping away the graphical readout to switch over to a real-time camera display of their approach to the elevator.

"Whoa," she said.

Tomas grinned wider than the horizon. "Welcome to your first *big* city."

Her home planet of Ada had been small enough that the shuttles from the station to the dwarf planet punched down through the atmo dome without an elevator's assistance. But a planet like Atrux, nearly one and a half times the size of Ada and covered with a dome that housed millions of people, needed something a little bigger.

The elevator speared up through the navy-blue atmo stretched below them like a calm sea. The carbon-black materials of its body absorbed all the ambient light, and it would have blended completely into empty space if it hadn't been for the status lights set into its body, a red-green-and-yellow smattering of freckles blinking out messages into the endless dark.

Shuttles of varying shapes and sizes swarmed around the thrust of metal, their systems guided in concert by the traffic-control AI. Even braking, the speeds the ships moved at were too fast for humans to pilot. In hard vacuum, where every axis was a possibility of travel, human eyes and reflexes lost all efficiency.

A massive yacht of a ship, painted stark white and lit up with external lights pumping out a rainbow pattern that flickered with the beat of unheard music passed above them, the bottom of the ship eclipsing Sanda's forward view.

"Dios," she said, "and I thought Lavaux's ship was huge."

"Prepare for capture," a cool female voice said through the hauler's speakers. Sanda nearly jumped out of her skin.

"What the—"

"Standard," Graham cut in, "poor choice of words, considering the circumstances."

His wry smile eased the tension in her shoulders.

"My situation isn't exactly something the sensitivity testers would know to look for."

Graham's smile wiped away, replaced with a faraway look. The hauler finished its braking cycle, relying on conserved momentum to float the rest of the way into the elevator. An articulated mechanical hand reached out, plucking the hauler out of space. The ship vibrated, a few indicators on the dash flashing off a complaint at losing their autonomy, but the piloting AI quieted them.

"Welcome to Alexandria-Atrux," a cheery voice said through the speakers, stripped down to gender-neutral tones like the welcoming voice used for the Ada shuttles. It started piping in the annoying welcome jingle for the city. Graham swiped the volume down.

"Are all welcome AIs the same?"

"All the ones I've heard," Tomas said, "and thanks to the Nazca sending me all over the universe, I've heard a lot."

"Wait." She scrunched up her nose. "While out on all those

missions, have you figured out if they're the *same* AI system, or are they individual instances that have been given the same vocalization pack?"

"Why does that matter?" Graham asked, bewildered.

"It... it just does." She closed her eyes and pressed a thumb into the space between her eyes. "Never mind. Forget it."

Tomas gave her a look that he'd developed in the last twelve hours that somehow conveyed *You're thinking about Bero again, aren't you?* without saying the words. She crossed her arms and scowled at the viewscreen, pretending not to have noticed.

In the corner of her eye, Tomas's arm tensed as he started to reach for her but stopped himself. She wasn't sure if it was more, or less, annoying that he'd surmised keeping his hands in line with the pod chair was more comforting to her right now than attempting to soothe her. Dating anyone was complicated. Starting a relationship with a man who'd been trained for emotional manipulation via the best spy agency in the universe was going to cause her the migraine to end all migraines.

The hand brought them in tight to the elevator's body and spun them around so they'd be faced the right way at the hangar, then began the slow, silky-smooth descent into the atmo dome. Even though the viewscreen was a camera feed and not a real window, Sanda still leaned forward, almost pressing her nose against the glass. Alexandria-Atrux sprawled below, spilling across the land so far and wide that Sanda couldn't make out the curved boundaries of the atmo dome.

The sky above shaded to night-simulation, the city a kaleidoscope of lights and textures and movement. Cyan and gold streaked the streets, rivers of humanity pulsing to and from their daily tasks. Even from on high, she could see the purple-green-red-white chaos of advertising drones, tempting the people of Atrux into spending their basic, and then some.

A grip of skyscrapers pierced the center of the city, faced with nonreflective materials to keep the ad drones from bouncing their lights off of them. As if the wealthy in those knifelike towers were immune to the constant ploy of commerce on the streets. Probably they owned half the drones. Agricultural domes pockmarked the edges of the city, environments within the greater hug of the atmo dome, cycling to their own weather and circadian rhythm.

"How many people?" she asked.

"Millions," Graham said, "though you'd have to ask the net for the exact count. Atrux was once a system with a lot of promise. It has two gates—one to Ordinal, one to Ada. The Keepers hoped that once they punched through to Ada, there'd be another multi-gate system waiting on the other side. It could have been a major thoroughfare."

"But Ada could only support the one gate."

He nodded. "It was a huge disappointment."

"Which is why a lot of your early settlers went off to found Icarion," Tomas said.

"Disappointments all around," Sanda said.

Gravity pressed them down, reminding Sanda how empty her stomach was. She hadn't even thought to ask for food after she'd come out of the healing goop of the NutriBath.

"I would kill for a raw nutriblock right now."

Tomas gagged. "I'll pretend I didn't hear that."

"Don't worry, I know a great noodle place," Graham said. "We'll get you stuffed soon."

The hauler shuddered as the arm slotted it into place. Graham flicked up the volume, and the annoyingly cheery welcome tune of Alexandria-Atrux was replaced with a solemn announcement.

"Your vehicle has been docked in hangar bay eleven, slot 32A. Please press accept on your wristpads to guarantee future access."

On each of their pads, a green box with the symbol of a keycard flashed. Sanda pressed accept and got a rustle of wind chimes in response.

"Why is everything so goddamn happy around here?"

Tomas said, "Smile hard enough and you might start to believe it."

"Not a chance. Is this place so shitty it needs all this mood-boosting?"

"Stop jawing and let's go find out." Graham undid his harness in one expert twist and stood, stretching so hard his head almost scraped the ceiling of the command deck.

Sanda popped her harness and hesitated. "Where's Grippy?"

Tomas stood and slung an overstuffed duffel across his back. The repair bot's rectangular outline bulged against the thick canvas. "In here." He patted it. "Grippy took some damage when you were both spaced. I want to get a closer look at his battery pack before we boot him back up to make sure power won't make his situation worse."

"Good," she said. "That bot saved my ass. Twice. We fix him, no matter what."

Pounding on the airlock shocked Sanda's ears, still sensitive from being spaced.

"Hauler, this is Atrux SecureSite, please open and disembark immediately," a woman said.

Sanda closed her eyes and dug her fingers into her temples. "That was quick."

"Easy," Graham said, "they're not guardcore or fleet, just local security. Let's see what they want."

Tomas got an arm under Sanda's, hefting her to her foot. Lightheadedness pressed in, fuzzing the edges of her vision. She shook her head and breathed deep, forcing her mind to clear.

Graham flashed his wristpad over the airlock panel and the double doors slid open in unison, sensing the human-survivable atmo on the other side. A woman stood at the apex of a triangle of tough-looking officials.

The toughs had their stunners out but pointed at the ground, and the woman held nothing but her wristpad, turned so that Graham could read the screen. The woman's ident was pulled up, a headshot of her staring down the camera like it'd insulted her mother, sitting next to a paragraph of text with all her official powers laid out.

They wore heather-grey FitFlex with lime-green stripes, not a hint of the Prime Inventive logo anywhere to be found. These people worked for Atrux, and Atrux alone.

"I am Detective Mari Laguna. Is this the complete crew of this hauler?"

"Yes, sir, and I captain this ship. Is there a problem?" Graham leaned against the airlock frame, keeping his hands loose at his sides while Tomas and Sanda moved up behind him. Laguna barely glanced in their direction.

"Please identify yourself, Captain."

Graham flicked up his personal ident and turned his wristpad around for her to see. "Good?"

"Yes. Graham Lucas Greeve, you are being detained for questioning. Any attempt to resist detention will result in arrest. Please come with me."

Laguna flicked a glance at Sanda and spoke over her shoulder to one of the toughs. "And will somebody please get that woman a fucking wheelchair?"

CHAPTER 2

PRIME STANDARD YEAR 3543

A MATTER OF MATERIEL

A bitten snake will not retreat, Keeper Shun had once told Biran. It bites back, no matter how grave the wound. Biran didn't have a lot of experience with snakes—most of Earth's old terrestrial animals hadn't made it into the stars with humanity—but he had a feeling he was getting firsthand experience now.

The leadership of Icarion would not come to Prime, and Prime would not show weakness by going to them. So, for the first time since the war went hot, the heads of Ada and Icarion met face-to-face in a virtual room designed to look like a boardroom.

Pleasant views stretched beyond the false windows, a meadow dappled in perfect Earth-like sunlight. Prime had done studies to devise the most calming visual space possible for these kinds of meetings. Everything from the warm wood table down to the textured stucco walls was preprogrammed by Keeper specialists to make the members of the room relaxed, willing to deal.

But people weren't parts, swappable and replaceable, and from the way General Negassi kept glaring at the soft light through the windows, Biran had a pretty good idea that the researchers hadn't extended their test pool outside of Prime people. Possibly not even outside of Keepers.

"I hardly see," Icarion President Bollar said, "why losing one little moon base means we should bow our heads to Prime and give up Icarion's rightful bid for independence. We do not wish to be a part of Prime. We are not the only people to make that call for themselves. You have no right to dictate our preferred form of governance."

"Please dispense with the bullshit," General Anford said. Bollar's eyebrows shot up, but both Biran and Director Olver let the general go about her crass way of managing this meeting.

She wasn't one to needle people without reason. If she felt this tactic was best, then it was. Biran trusted her instincts, and so did Olver; otherwise she wouldn't have been invited into this room in the first place.

"No one in this room is operating under the illusion that the moon base *The Light of Berossus* destroyed was a simple researcher station. You lost your weapon. You lost the ability to build another. These are the only facts of relevance to this discussion."

Inwardly, Biran winced, but he held his expression neutral and waited a beat to watch the ripples her words caused. Bollar's lips pressed together. Negassi clenched his fists and tightened his jaw. These were all digital projections of their bodies, and someone particularly adept in traveling within net spaces could adjust their avatars to display body language they were not, in fact, experiencing. But Icarion did not have the net.

Oh, they had their own watered-down version, but Prime controlled the vast expanse of digital space, and they'd revoked Icarion's access long ago. These two, politicians though they were, could not have had the practice needed to make their bodies lie in digital space.

"I understand your frustrations," Biran cut in smoothly when Bollar's lips relaxed again, signaling he was ready to offer a rebuttal. "Bero was an impressive creation, and it must hurt to have lost him and the ability to build another like him. We are not here to take you to task now that you are weakened."

"I have a difficult time seeing the sincerity in that statement," Negassi said, "when your gunships circle our territories like sharks. You have ramped up your patrols." He cut a sharp look to Anford. "Why would you do such a thing, if you claim we are weakened?"

Jessa's smile was kind, but if Biran ripped his net goggles off right then and looked at her across the table in the war room, he was certain he'd see a heavy scowl on her face. "We have added patrols across the entire system, not just around your borders—which we have not crossed. Lest you forget so quickly, *The Light of Berossus* was not so much *lost* as *fled*. Your weapon was not stolen, General. You lost control of it. I have the safety of this entire system to keep in mind. That includes Icarion and its holdings. Anywhere humanity dwells around this star is my responsibility."

"We are perfectly capable of managing our own borders," Negassi said.

"You lost your biggest weapon. Forgive me my caution."

"To your *operative*," he spat out the word.

Biran, very carefully, did not react. "Your ship took Major Greeve captive, General. Do not pretend you believe otherwise, or this conversation will go nowhere."

"That woman killed one of your Keepers, did she not? Talk about losing control of a weapon."

"Esteemed colleagues," Director Olver said, spreading his hands expansively. "Please, let us not devolve into bickering. We are here to build a bridge of peace between our peoples so that no more may die. This bloodshed is most unbecoming of a society so advanced as ours."

Bollar snorted. "Advanced? You may have the technology, Jian, I grant you that, but the choke chain of the Keepers holds your people in line.

"Icarion may not have your weapons or your net, but we have people free to research as their hearts desire. That was how we brought about the weapon you so feared—through free experimentation. Nothing held sacred, nothing allowed to a tiny pool at the top alone. And it is that freedom we mean to maintain."

"Your freedom to research," Anford said, "nearly got this whole system killed. There are reasons—very good ones—that Prime Inventive has the laws it does. Not only did your experimentation in non-gate FTL travel destroy your own research station, but you created an artificial intelligence that turned against you. Your people, more than any, should understand why we have these laws."

"The laws of Prime *are* Prime," Bollar said, shaking his head. "We have not forgotten this. Do you expect us to believe there will be no punishment for our perceived crimes if we rejoined your society? *The Light* was a public spectacle. You could not avoid having to make an example of us to discourage other 'splinter' societies from indulging in similar paths of research. We've proven general artificial intelligence is possible. You cannot put that genie back in its bottle."

"No, we can't," Biran said, "but you've also proven the point of our laws by demonstrating that such a creation is inherently dangerous and uncontrollable. You've done our work for us."

Bollar's smile turned into a sneer. "Is that the story you would tell on your 'news' channels? Poor Icarion reached too close to the sun and got burned? How sad for them, and how magnanimous of Prime to welcome their wayward children back into their fold? No, don't answer that. I can already see your face during the address now, and it makes me ill, Speaker."

"Don't get ahead of yourself," Biran said. "This is an olive branch, President Bollar."

"Ah," he said with a soft sigh and looked down at the digital table. "You threaten prettily, Speaker. But tell me, while you hold out the branch, what weapon waits in the hands of the general at your side, should we turn it down?"

Anford said without inflection, "We could cut you down at any moment. Negassi, you know this. You have known this. The only reason the stalemate dragged on for so long was because of the weapon. That piece has been removed from the board. Your only saving grace, in this moment, is that I do not want the body count any higher. My superiors will not allow me this indulgence much longer."

Bollar started, his gaze flicking to Director Olver. "Is this true, Jian? Does Okonkwo and her High Protectorate thirst for our blood?"

"President Bollar," Olver said. Biran was proud his director would never use the president's first name, as Bollar so often did to Olver. "In your decision to leave Prime's governance, I believe you have an innate understanding of its crueler side. Existence in space is a fragile thing. Prime's laws have allowed humanity its dominance of the universe, but not without having been honed into a sharp edge. Your AI research, your FTL research. Both of these things constitute a potential existential threat to humanity. The Prime Director will not suffer your disobedience much longer."

"I see," Bollar said. He matched gazes with Anford. "Then I am sorry, General, that you will have to lower yourself to bloodying your hands. We crave our freedom. And you and I know it is not only that. This system is a gate dead end, low in natural resources. We do not wish to die, but we are not fools. If we capitulated, things would go back to the way they were generations ago, if not worse. Yoked by Prime, we would receive only necessary supply shipments. Everyone at this table knows that such shipments are never enough. We must be free to develop our own research and to seek resources we control."

"If it's a matter of materiel," Biran said, "then negotiations can be made."

"With Icarion negotiating from a place of weakness, against a state that has no reason to negotiate in good faith. There's not enough to go around in this star system, Speaker. Even if we came to an accord, that fact would not change. No, we must always be free to reach other systems that the gates cannot. We need FTL, slow as our current efforts are. Humanity needs another way to live between the stars, even if it's harder."

"General Negassi," Anford said, "please remind your president that he cannot win this war."

Negassi lifted his chin. "Icarion knows the price of independence."

"And your people?" Biran asked. "Are your people, your everyday citizens, aware of this price? Are you willing to let civilians die for one nation's pride?"

It surprised Biran to find Bollar's smile was genuine. "They are aware. Maybe someday, Speaker, you'll understand the real value of humanity's pride. We will not bend. Good day, all of you. Stars keep you."

The Icarions cut their feeds.

Biran lifted his net goggles off and rubbed his eyes until he saw stars, then blinked them open in time to see Anford rip her goggles off and stop herself just short of throwing them against the wall.

"That damn fool of a man will get millions of people killed," she said.

Director Olver sighed and set his goggles on the table. The imprint they left around his eyes amplified the wrinkles he'd let come in. "It is his right to make that choice, much as I despise it."

"They understand the desperateness of the situation, now," Biran said. "We should give it some time, let it sink in. Once they bring this conversation back to their advisers, cracks will form in those loyalties. Surely not everyone on that damn planet is willing to die for the right to research what they please."

"It's not the research." Anford shook her head. "You hit the nail on the head in there. It's the materiel. They know that once they're back under Prime's control, their smuggling operations will come to a sharp halt.

"I haven't yet cracked down on their smugglers because Icarion needs them to keep feeding their people. If they capitulate, Prime brings down the hammer, and then they're back to tighter rations than they're on right now. And my informants tell me those rations are *tight*."

"All of that can be negotiated," Biran insisted, rubbing the side of his face with one hand. "If they'd give us half a chance to bring an offer to the table."

"Can it?" Olver asked. "I respect your intent, Speaker, but the truth of the matter is that Okonkwo is loath to give them any more slack in the leash once she has them back on it. Remember, Okonkwo alone holds back the vote that would push for subjugation, and she will not do so much longer. The High Protectorate will give Icarion nothing. If we wish to negotiate with supplies, those supplies must come from this system. And we all know how low that coffer runs."

"Not to mention," Anford said, "Bollar won't last long if he rejoins Prime. His people would see him as weak, perhaps even a traitor. Add in the shortening supply train, and he'll have a coup on his hands, even if Prime allows him to maintain governorship. Next year we'll be negotiating with Negassi and his closest adviser. We'll never see Bollar again unless they offer him to us as a sacrificial lamb for prosecution."

"So he would risk the lives of all his people to cling to power?"

Olver and Anford shared a look. Biran grimaced. "How naive of me."

"Do not let it strain you," Olver said. "While the Cannery is on lockdown, we have time to muddle through matters before you must make a public statement. But, Speaker, know that you may not like the nature of that statement when the time comes."

"I understand," Biran said. "We can hardly pretend at peace when Icarion gunships are firing salvos at our own, no matter how much I wish otherwise."

"Speaking of statements," Anford said. Biran sat straighter, sensing what was coming. "My InfoSec people are working on the footage of Major Greeve and Keeper Lavaux. While we all know it to be a deepfake, proving the lie has been harder than expected. My team says the raw footage has been erased from all systems. They are working to recover the video and discover the culprit, but in the meantime we cannot clear your sister's name while the united worlds reel from what they've seen. We will come across as attempting a cover-up."

"Thank you for your efforts, General. Please understand I will make no statement either way regarding the matter until you have things in hand."

Her smile was coy. "A refreshing change of tactic, Speaker."

"Don't get used to it," he said with a small grin.

"Each of you," Olver said while standing, "see to your duties and then get some damn rest. I will tap what resources I may to see if we can get the Icarions tempered for their metaphorical yoke."

Biran grimaced. "I do not enjoy that we are on the side of stifling freedom, Director."

A haze passed before his eyes, brief but weary, dragging down his expression. Then the diplomat's smile was back in place. Kind, but meaningless. "Such is the price of our safety. We cannot allow a weapon such as *The Light of Berossus* to happen again."

The others left the war room at a rush, but Biran lingered, getting a feel for the mood in the air. The halls of the Cannery held their breath. Keepers summoned from their homes squirreled away in the rooms they once occupied as students, seeing to their duties in this time of crisis through virtual means. A lone set of footsteps pattered toward him.

Biran turned to find Keeper Vladsen advancing down the hall, his head downcast as he walked with short, precise steps. Internally, Biran winced. Vladsen had been Keeper Lavaux's protégé, though he hadn't known of Lavaux's corruption. Being near him never failed to remind Biran of the sinking dread he'd felt when he realized Lavaux meant to hurt Sanda.

But it had not been Vladsen's fault.

He cleared his throat to get Vladsen's attention. "Working late, Keeper?" he said, and felt foolish. They were all working around the clock, and the dark circles beneath Vladsen's eyes were evidence enough of his schedule. Still, Vladsen paused and gave him a ghost of a smile.

"Aren't we all? How are negotiations proceeding?"

Biran grimaced, drawing a thin chuckle out of the other man. "As expected, I'm afraid. Olver should file an update brief soon."

"Ah, well." He had the pinched look of a man who'd run out of social niceties and was ready to move on from this conversation. "I'm glad it's you negotiating, for what it's worth."

Vladsen blinked, as if he'd surprised himself by what he said, and hurried by, flashing Biran a smile and a short line about good-luck-and-good-night that Biran returned half-heartedly. Well. That went brilliantly. Biran repressed a sigh. He would have to smooth things over with the other Keeper, but right now the trouble with Icarion was his top priority.

Biran ran the problem through his mind as he walked the same old path back to his academy room, wondering how it could have been only a little over two years since he took the chip to become a Keeper. Each cohort was twelve hopefuls, and only six made it through to graduation. Ada Station was home to one hundred and forty-four Keepers in permanent residence, with many passing through on missions of some sort or another.

Most of them were scientists and academics. Few were the Keepers with political ambitions. His own world had narrowed to that sphere, but it was only a shallow slice of what it meant to be a Keeper. Civilians knew Keepers for the chips in their heads, which carried pieces of the schematics for the Casimir Gates. But a Keeper was more than that.

Outside of government and war, Keepers delved into research only they were allowed to conduct. Nanites, bioengineering, atmosphere management, weapons, and propulsion systems. These were some of the technologies Prime Inventive deemed too close to gate tech, and allotted the study of which to Keepers, and Keepers alone.

Biran had harbored more prosaic goals. He had wanted to study logistical algorithms for the shipping lanes that kept Prime's supply lines running. How quickly one's world can change when tragedy strikes.

He stood at the window overlooking the city below, hands in his pockets, chin raised to the false night. What one wanted to do, and the path one must walk, were not always the same. He hoped what had brought him to this point had prepared him well enough to fulfill his duties. Earnestness and instinct could get him only so far.

A cleaner bot trundled down the hall toward him, swerving to take a path around the solitary Keeper. Its trolley cart was half-sealed, journeying to find another room to clean, but in that mess of bedclothes and other junk, Biran glimpsed something electric, lime green.

"Stop."

Two beeps for yes.

Biran nudged aside a tattered pillow with the back of his hand. A tube of glow-in-the-dark green lipstick hid beneath the cushion, its cap busted off so that it'd left a lightning streak of color against the shabby grey material. His heart clenched. These were the things from Anaia's room, on their way to the incinerator. Six of his cohort had graduated. Five had survived to this day.

He sorted through the contents, not sure what he was looking for. There would be no answers here. Guardcore would have gone through everything already, taking out anything that might reveal the extent of the ex-Keeper's traitorous ties with Icarion. Biran had not yet had time to sit with the betrayal, to reconcile the woman he saw deceiving the cameras tracking his sister's kidnappers with the woman he used to get stupid-drunk with on their rare weekends away from the academy.

There was nothing in this bin that would tell him where the woman he admired ended, and the traitor began.

His hand brushed metal, and he dug out a thin tablet, palm-sized, the kind of thing used to keep personal pictures. Biran didn't have many pictures of the times when they were happy, so he took it, sliding the cold metal into his pocket, and wondered how something so small could weigh so much.

CHAPTER 3

PRIME STANDARD YEAR 3543

THE WRONG FUGITIVE

Excuse me?" Graham asked.

"I don't do my questioning in the hangar bay, Mr. Greeve. Come with me."

A molten core of anger formed in Sanda's chest, so hot it almost made her eyes water. She tried to push forward, but Tomas tightened his grip across her shoulders, pressing her in close against his side so Laguna couldn't see her movements. Trying to get her to stay out of things. Jerk.

"What's this about?" she demanded. Tomas sighed wearily.

Laguna didn't look up from her wristpad as she tapped out a few short commands. "Your father is wanted for questioning. This will be quick and painless, unless you dig your heels in."

Your father. "You know who I am?"

Laguna looked up, met Sanda's gaze. Her eyes were very dark, almost black, and Sanda couldn't read anything in them. She'd spent too long dealing with Tomas and Bero to understand regular people this soon. A newborn artificial intelligence and a top-class spy didn't make for normal company. "Yes I do, Major. Your exploits are not my concern, but this city is. Mr. Greeve, now, please."

"I—uh—yes, of course." Graham squeezed Sanda's arm to let her know it was all right and stepped out of the false safety of the hauler.

The toughs closed around him, not quite cuffing him, but keeping him from making any sudden movements.

"If you know who I am," Sanda blurted, "then you should understand that I don't want to be separated from my family right now."

That stopped her. Laguna jabbed at a panel inset in the wall, then hit it with the side of her fist. Above, the hiss of gears and pneumatics heralded the arrival of a large metal locker that slid into place in the wall. The panel turned green and the locker clicked open.

Laguna pulled a folded wheelchair out of the locker and snapped it open, setting it on the ground between them. "Scan your ident into the screen here"—she pointed to the armrest—"and the chair will answer to your biometrics." She pushed the chair forward, then stepped back. "You have my word your father will be unharmed. Hail an autocab, go here." She tapped into her wristpad and flicked something toward Sanda. A green smiley face asking her to accept the coordinates popped up on Sanda's wristpad. She accepted. "My people will let you in."

"Why are you doing this?" Sanda asked.

"I told you. The city alone is my concern."

She turned on her heel and marched off, the SecureSite toughs taking Graham ahead of her.

"Do you know anything about that woman?" Sanda asked as soon as Laguna was out of earshot.

Tomas shook his head. "Never heard of her, but I think we'd better do as she says."

"I am *so* hungry."

He raised a brow at her. "Graham first, I think."

"Obviously."

Without her fleet credentials on hand to grease the way, getting through the hangar with the crush of civs took ages. By the time Sanda hit the line for autocab pickup she was seeing red.

"They'll have pulled all his toenails out by the time we get there."

"Pretty sure SecureSite doesn't operate that way," Tomas said.

"Prove it."

An autocab swished up to them. Tomas scanned his ident over the entry pad and it beeped a welcome. Sanda almost scanned hers, then thought better of it. Just because Laguna knew who she was and didn't seem to care didn't mean anyone else wouldn't come knocking if she popped up on the grid.

Ident or no, the cab's cameras took in her, and her chair, and paused a moment, rearranging its seats to make more room for her before opening the doors. A slim ramp extended, and she wheeled her way up and locked the brakes in to look forward, out the unobstructed picture window. Tomas crammed the bag with Grippy in the back and sidled next to her. The cab took the coordinates from her wristpad and slid into traffic.

So normal, getting into a cab and going about her business. Nobody watched her. Nobody stared. She wasn't recognizable here, not yet, and that anonymity felt all at once dwarfing and freeing. Sanda could disappear into this city, if she wanted to. Let Tomas craft her a new ident and fade away. Pretend the chip in her head didn't exist. Pretend Bero wasn't out there, somewhere, needing help. Pretend she could go without her family for the rest of her life.

She'd never been very good at pretending.

The forward viewscreen wiped away as Tomas projected his wristpad so they could both see. He had a collection of news articles up regarding SecureSite, relating to Laguna in particular: LAGUNA ASKS FOR AID, STREET CRIME WILL RISE UP-STATION, GROTTA DESERVES PEACE.

"Looks like she's a champion-of-the-people type," Tomas said.

"So her treatment of Graham depends on which side she thinks he's on."

Tomas grimaced. "Yeah, let's hope she has his file and can see he came from the Grotta."

"You have arrived at your destination," the autocab announced.

SecureSite had set themselves up in the lee of one of the knife-blade skyscrapers, and the shadows of the surrounding giants made the building look squat. It clung to the city's bedrock while everything around it reached for the simulated clouds.

Sanda found her arms weak from lack of food, rest, and just about everything else, so she let the chair wheel itself down the ramp and into the building. She didn't get two meters through the door before one of the toughs peeled himself away from a chatty colleague and jabbed a finger at her.

"Took you long enough. This way."

He led them to an elevator and swiped his wristpad over the lock, giving Sanda the unsettling impression that she couldn't get out of this building unless someone escorted her out. She didn't like feeling trapped. No one did, unless they were into a very particular kind of kink, but the suggestion she might be stuck in this place made her adrenaline surge. She'd had enough of being someone's hostage.

"How do we get out of here?"

"I'll escort you out when Laguna's done."

"We are *not* under arrest, though."

He sighed heavily. "SecureSite maintains the power to detain any citizen suspected of breaking the law long enough to hand them over to the Prime fleet. We're not jailers. We're investigators."

"Feels pretty jail-y to me."

The elevator door swished open. She'd never even felt it move. "Here we are. Third door on the left. Laguna's waiting for you."

Sanda wheeled out, not wanting to leave her only path to the exit behind, but she figured that if it came down to it Tomas could crack his way into the elevator. That, or she'd be cracking windows.

She was halfway down the hall when the tough said, "Oh and, Major?"

"Yes?"

"Here, least I could do."

He tossed her a small package of crinkly orange paper. She snapped it out of the air without a second thought. Smooth, bright. She didn't recognize the brand name, but she recognized chocolate bars in all their forms.

"Holy shit. Thanks."

"That's for Dralee." He snapped off a picture-perfect fleet salute as the elevator doors slid shut.

"The way our luck is running, that's poisoned," Tomas said.

"I so don't care."

She tore the package open and took a bite half the size of the bar, letting out a gurgle of appreciation as the chocolate melted on contact with her tongue and turned into a delicious, almond-and-cocoa flavored concoction.

"Are you... humming?"

She stopped. "No. Come on, stop wasting time."

He grinned, but didn't comment as he pushed the door open to let her through first. She folded the package over and tucked the candy into a pocket inset on the side of her wheelchair, then rolled into the room.

Sanda had expected a sparse room, crappy lighting, and a steel chair chained to the floor. Instead, it looked more like a dentist's waiting room. The lighting was warm and cheery, the walls covered with tasteful, if boring, impressionist paintings. Laguna sat behind a SynthWood desk, her fingers poised over a tablet between herself and Graham.

This made Sanda more suspicious than chains and bloodstains would have. In Sanda's experience, anyone trying this hard to look normal was hiding something sinister.

"Glad you could join us," Laguna said.

"What is this? A therapy session?"

"We do things differently at SecureSite, and our results speak for themselves."

"Who funds this?"

"What?"

Sanda wheeled around to sit across from Laguna and put on the hardest face she could muster. Graham wiped chocolate from the corner of her lips with his thumb. She closed her eyes and took a breath, then put the mean-face back on.

"Look, we don't have your corollary on Ada, so maybe I'm misinformed, but in my experience, security shoves every last scrap of budget into databases and the AIs who assess them, not campy twenty-first-century waiting room decor. So what's going on here?"

"We're not military. We're not affiliated with the Keepers. We are a security company and our only interest—*my* only interest—is in the protection and peace of this city."

"You expect me to believe that that's why you're not interested in me? Seems like handing me over to the guardcore would do a world of good for your relations. I saw the news. Your organization is hurting for funding."

"Do you want me to arrest you, Major?"

"Of course not."

"Then please explain to me why you seem obsessed with the idea."

"Because I'm tired of being used, *Detective.* If you're not arresting me, there's a reason for it, and I want to know what it is."

"Very well." She tapped at the screen between them. "You've seen this footage, yes?"

Shaky, faraway footage of her battle with Lavaux filled the screen. She looked away.

"Yes. It's doctored. I did not throw Lavaux out that airlock. He attacked me, and I defended myself."

"I believe you."

"Why?"

Laguna sighed heavily and pinch-zoomed the screen. Sanda made herself watch. Laguna had paused on a close-up of Sanda, lying at Lavaux's feet. In the false recording, he reached down a hand to help her up, as if she had tripped. In reality, he'd grabbed her by the back of the neck and shoved a blade against her skull.

"The fake is enough to fool casual viewers, but I spend a lot of time looking at footage as evidence, and this scene is all wrong. The lighting under the Hermes shuttle is broken up by shadows that look very much like a man kneeling over a woman with a weapon. Regardless of the shadows, someone who tripped as a ploy to attack a man moving to help her wouldn't look like that. You're beat to hell, Major Greeve, excuse my saying so, and in the moments before the fake takes over I can see... desperation in you. You're fighting like your life depends upon it, and I believe you were right to think so, because Lavaux has the body language of a man who's ready to kill.

"In my professional opinion, it's a matter of time until this footage is revealed as fake. If I were to detain you, it would not only waste my time and resources, but make myself a powerful enemy. I wish to do neither."

Sanda licked her lips, trying to hide the surge of hope in her chest. If this detective could see the footage was faked, surely it wouldn't hold up much longer. Biran would get the truth out. He would.

"Then why detain my father?"

"That is a local matter."

Laguna brushed the video away and brought up a case file, sorting through images. Sanda glimpsed the file name—GROTTA: ARSONS—before Laguna pulled up a single still image.

A man lay on a bed soaked in blood. He'd maybe made it into his eighties, if the wrinkles lining his face were real, and Sanda would bet money they were. That wasn't the face of a man who'd led an easy life, and men with easy lives hardly ever ended them with a crater of a wound in their chest, stuffed full of half a pillowcase that was far too little, too late.

"Harlan Vaish," Graham said. He touched the image, turned it, zoomed in on the face. The color had gone out of Graham's cheeks, his voice caught over the name.

"So you did know him. I wasn't certain when I found your name on a list of known associates. A connected, honest man like yourself…"

Graham chuckled roughly. "You know better, Detective."

Laguna brushed away Harlan's image with a gentle flick and, in two taps, brought up Graham's file.

"Graham Lucas Greeve. Sixty-eight years old, born to unregistered parents at Atrux General Hospital, and soon disappeared into the streets of the Grotta. You attended school, virtual, but you never stood for the examinations."

"Didn't see the point." His voice caught. He cleared it. "What's this got to do with Harlan? What happened to him?"

"We're trying to find that out. Harlan—as you experienced—had a habit of taking on young apprentices. In piecing together the night of his death, we've established that the last person in the room with him was one Juliella Vicenza, alias Jules Valentine."

Laguna brought up a shot of a wide-eyed, scared-looking girl with blood on her hands. To Sanda's mind, she looked way too young to have anything to do with the murder of a man like Harlan, but you couldn't fake that kind of fear—the kind mingled with anger.

Whatever had been on Valentine's mind in that photo, it'd been bloody.

"We can't find her anywhere, and the rest of his crew have scattered. If we can get in touch with anyone who may have spoken with Valentine on the night of Harlan's death, it would be invaluable. I believe you may have known some of his other associates and, if so, where they might go to ground."

Graham licked his lips. "I don't know that girl. Who else was Harlan crewing?"

"We suspect these three were in recent contact."

She brought up three images, displayed in triptych. On the left, a tawny-haired girl even younger than Valentine, her hoodie yanked up to hide her eyes, and a fistful of cables sticking out of her pocket. In the center, a muscular man with a scraggly beard hiding his chin and an old scar near his collarbone that had the telltale striation of a blaster hit. On the right, an enby with a mass of wavy brown hair and the harried look the paranoid get etched into their faces—as if they expected to be ambushed at any moment.

"I don't know any of them," Graham said, shaking his head. "Must have come on board after my time."

"Hold on," Sanda said, pointing to the picture of the man. "There's a time stamp on this, it was taken two years ago. Are you telling me you haven't been able to find this man for two years?"

Laguna blanked the screen. "No. We haven't."

Graham chuckled. "Forgive me, Detective, but if you haven't found Harlan's crew in two years of trying, I doubt I'll be of any help. I can tell you the types of places Harlan liked to haunt—Grotta bars and cheap VR dens, mostly—but the fleet would be better suited to assist you."

"They won't talk to us about anything relating to Ms. Valentine."

A long pause as they all digested that. It was Tomas who finally asked, "Why?"

"Because Harlan Vaish wasn't the only one she killed."

Laguna selected a very different picture of Jules. She'd cleaned herself up, though her clothes were the same, and scraped her hair back so that her face seemed larger, eyes wider. She had a blaster in her hand, tech she shouldn't have been able to acquire, and a dead woman at her feet.

The top of the dead woman's head had been blown off, a dusting of blood and brain matter covering the sleek museum floor. Sanda knew an Elequatorial Cultural Center when she saw one. The dead woman's clothes were plain enough, but they were sharp with newness, the creases distorting the shape of her body. The boots sticking out from beneath her slacks weren't so new, though. Those mag boots were scuffed from regular use.

"Who was she?" Sanda leaned over the desk to spin the image around, trying to get a better look at her face. Something about the woman struck her as familiar. She couldn't quite put her finger on what it was. Maybe the haircut—people who spent a lot of time in low-g tended to crop it like that—or the body shape. The woman had a small tattoo, pale blue ink across her wrist in the shape of two scythe blades with a circle above their crossing points. It meant nothing to Sanda.

"That," Laguna said, "is Keeper Zina Rix Nakata."

Sanda yanked her hand back from the screen. Tomas whistled low.

Graham said, "Harlan wouldn't get tangled up with Keeper business."

"I would have agreed with you, if I didn't have video of one of his people blowing a Keeper's head off."

"This is the guardcore's problem," Sanda said. "Maybe you haven't found her or her associates because the guardcore already took care of them."

"Maybe," Laguna admitted. "They have vanished from the grid. I'd be inclined to agree with you, if it weren't for the fires."

Graham had gone quiet, so Sanda asked, "Fires?"

"Every suspected location of Valentine after the death of Harlan Vaish has gone up in flames."

She swiped the murder scene away and brought up a parade of burned-out buildings. "It stopped after she dropped off the grid."

"But?" Tomas prompted.

She inclined her head to him. "It's started again, last week. We don't have evidence of her presence, but the places are all similar to the last fire in the series two years ago. Warehouses, rotted-out things that aren't home to anything other than mice, going up like torches at random across the fringes of the Grotta. Three now. I've had the names of all of Vaish's known associates flagged since the first one started burning last week. Yours was the first to pop."

"Lucky me," Graham said, "but I can't help you. I don't know those three, or Valentine. Whatever they got mixed up in has nothing to do with me."

Laguna blanked the screen. "I understand it was a long shot. If any of Harlan's acquaintances attempt to contact you, Mr. Greeve, please call me immediately. I've flashed my priority line to your wristpad."

"I'll do that."

They stood, shook hands, and went through the process of getting out of the building and into an autocab in a thick silence. Sanda was so filled with questions she could feel them pushing against the base of her tongue, threatening to break free at any moment, but from the look on her dad's face, he wasn't willing to talk yet. She could wait. Give him a little time to process the dead friend he'd just seen.

"So." Tomas turned in his seat to look Graham in the eye. "How long have you known Arden Wyke?"

CHAPTER 4

PRIME STANDARD YEAR 3543

SPACE IS A HARSH MISTRESS

Jules fucking hated space. The low-g, or micro-g, or zero-g, or whatever the fuck you called it. The c-effect that made her stomach screw up and threaten to burst through her lips at the first sign of spin-grav. The promise that, if she stepped outside of her manufactured bubble, death, and only death, would meet her.

Maybe that wasn't too different from Jules's normal life, though. Things hadn't exactly been hospitable to her outside of the Grotta.

Jules triggered another anti-nausea injection into the side of her neck and clutched her rifle tight to her chest. The harness strapping her to the inside of the drop pod bit deep, crushing her through layers of body armor. Her body jiggled as the pod ducked and weaved around the lasers trying to paint it up for gunfire, or railguns, or whatever this fringer settlement Rainier had picked out was running for defense.

The worst part was how calm the others were.

Three of them wore guardcore armor, standardizing their bodies and obscuring their faces so that Jules, technically, couldn't tell what they were feeling. But the way they held their weapons, low and at ease, told her enough. Cool as a crater on Pluto, the guardcore were. Not being able to see their faces made it easier to hate them as a unit.

Marya was another story. Rainier had kitted her in the same Prime armor Jules wore—slate-grey and cyan plates overlapping their bodies, tucking their soft and vulnerable bits away while their faces were shielded by armored helmets not meant to do much of anything outside of keeping their noggins intact, their pressure stable, and their air recycling.

Okay, maybe that was a lot, but Jules didn't have a switch she could flip to hide her face and she really, really wanted to right now because Marya was looking at her like she was going to barf, again, and the reminder of that experience was not helping her control this one.

"Contact in three, two, one..." a computerized voice said.

The shuttle jerked. Jules slammed upward, the harness biting down so hard she half expected her armor to dent. It didn't, because this wasn't the cheap shit Jules was used to. It was Keeper tech, state-of-the-art, and she had to keep reminding herself that it was hers now.

While she wasn't a Keeper, she had to play the part somewhat convincingly if she wanted to gather the scientists who could help bring Lolla out of her coma. Marya was better at it than her. Marya was better at most things.

"Incursion formation point alpha," one of the guardcore said. A flash of text popped up in the corner of Jules's HUD identifying the speaker as GC1T7. Their ident tags shuffled every time Jules worked with them. She didn't know if they understood they were working with an agent of Rainier and not a real Keeper. She'd been too much of a coward to ask them, well, anything.

Sparks flew as the drop pod's door scraped open, revealing a smoke-filled hallway. Jules was still unbuckling her harness by the time the guardcore detached, formed up, and secured the hallway.

"Clear," GC1T7 said. The others spoke over open channel only if they absolutely had to.

Marya helped Jules get the harness off and gave her a hand to steady herself while she waited for her vision to stop swimming and her stomach to decide to stay down.

"Get me access," she ordered, surprised at the strength in her voice.

"Advancing the line," GC1T7 said.

The guardcore pushed into the smoky hallway until their secure perimeter included a hab diagnostic panel set into the wall. Jules slung her rifle over her shoulder and approached the panel. Every single time she did this, the thought stabbed at her—Lolla would be better at this. But the girl was in a coma, and Jules was doing this to get her out. Get her safe.

This fringer settlement was nothing more than a city-hab shield planted in the unstable rock of an asteroid way out in the Ordinal system's belt. They didn't even trust their shield enough to live in the open. Endless hallways bit into the rock of the asteroid, sheltering their people beneath stone and steel. There were hundreds of settlements like it scattered across the systems of Prime, but this one housed a woman Rainier claimed could change everything.

But then, Rainier had claimed that about the last three scientists Jules had kidnapped.

Jules synced her wristpad with the station's panel and let the suite of software Rainier provided go to work. Luckily, that woman's bag of tricks didn't require Jules to know what she was doing.

Alarms bleated down the hallway, red warning lights flashing to alert them to the damaged life-support systems. Jules rolled her eyes. That's what the suits were for.

Her pad blinked the annoying happy-face emoji Rainier liked to sneak into every available opportunity. Jules swiped it away and pulled up the station's resident directory. It was wrong, of course. Settlements like this didn't exist because the people who founded them wanted to be honest members of society. But between the list and the schematic, Jules had a good idea of where the scientist would be.

"Third basement, lab A3."

"Understood," GC1T7 said. "Threat assessment?"

"That's your job."

The guardcore didn't respond; they never did. Jules could poke and prod and march circles around them singing about the debauchery of their mothers and they'd never react.

"Smooth," Marya said across their private comm line.

"But not wrong."

"Maybe don't insult the professional killers?"

"What the fuck do you think *we* are?"

Marya closed the channel and stalked ahead, but not too far ahead lest she break protocol and get too close to the guardcore while they were working their incursion procedures.

Jules chafed to say something, to needle Marya or GC1T7 or Rainier or—*anyone.* Not that she enjoyed being a jerk, not exactly. She needed that ruthless back-and-forth to keep her calm when she was working a job. Nox had understood the importance of that, and he barely understood how magnets worked.

But these people were professionals with a capital *P*, and although Jules was valuable to Rainier by the nature of her immune system accepting and blending with the ascension-agent, the others didn't have the same sense of interest in her. Or her well-being.

So Jules brought her rifle out, held it barrel-down, and maintained the recommended following distance as they cleared room after room down the hallway.

Her skin began to crawl. Usually by now they'd encountered some resistance. Fringer settlements weren't much for firepower, but a defense bot or a few locals with grand ideas of heroism should have engaged them by now. She considered switching over to the GC channel to ask them what they thought, but she didn't want to be the jumpy one.

"Isn't it a little quiet?" Marya asked over the GC channel.

Jules grinned at her back.

GC1T7 said, "We are detecting no attempt to secure the facility."

"Isn't that weird?" Jules asked.

"It is unusual," the guardcore said, because apparently words like *weird* were beneath them.

While they rode the elevator down to the third basement level, Jules pulled up the resident data with a flick of her eyes and set it to scrolling by in the corner of her HUD. The usual collection of fake names and professions drifted by, annotated against the database Rainier had provided her—somehow skimmed from Prime intelligence—with their suspected real identities and jobs.

Janitors became physicists, poets became biotech engineers. These places drew the disaffected scientists of Prime. They promised safe havens to do research in quiet, without Keepers and the fleet limiting their ability to dive deep on the premise of species-wide security.

Nothing unusual, until she noticed the ages of those gathered here. Children. A good 50 percent of this population was under the age of thirteen.

Jules swallowed, rolled the data back, and ran through those numbers again. And again. Parents disillusioned by Prime's private research restrictions and narrow education were likely to come to these settlements. She'd encountered plenty. But this was something else—a school, or academy—founded behind the back of Prime.

She pushed the data through to Marya and flagged the important bits. "You seeing this?"

The elevator shuddered to a stop.

"So?" Marya asked. "We're not here for any of them."

"But—" Jules cut herself off and pressed her lips together as she strangled a tirade.

"Mass heat signatures detected in second forward room," GC1T7 said. "Securing."

Jules's heart leapt into her throat as the guardcore pushed the heat map through to her HUD. A mass of orange-yellow bodies clustered toward the back corner of the room. She knew how this went, knew how thoroughly the guardcore covered their tracks.

"Authorized for stun weapons only." Jules snapped off the order the second GC1T7's hand touched the entry pad.

"Heard and understood," GC1T7 said.

The units reached down, synchronized, and switched their rifles over to stun protocols. Jules's weapon wasn't that fancy, so she had to sling it across her back and pull out a stunner.

"So much for killers," Marya said.

Jules ignored her. Marya could play tough-girl all she wanted, but ultimately she'd grown up in the middle class of Ordinal, where death was something handed out to those on CamCasts. Not real people whose blood could soak straight through your sleeves as you tried and failed to fill the gaping hole in their chest cavity and—

Breathe. Breathe.

The door opened, the stunners lit the air with pale, crackling light. They shut the door and moved on. She would not look. She would not. Focus had been her savior, her lance through the miasma of breakdown. Do what she had to do to save Lolla. Then get out. Get out, and never look back.

It only got hard when the past reached out and dug its claws into her.

Rust gathered in the joined corners of the hallways. Prime didn't sell their best shit to seditious fringers. If you wanted to live in a hab that could take the rigors of hard vacuum long term, you lived in a Prime settlement. Full-fucking-stop. Even the Icarions lived under the capricious wiles of a dome that Prime sold to them, generations back. A dome patched together with hope and ingenuity that Prime would never allow to grow inside of its own rigid walls.

If you wanted to do science, you did it for the Keepers.

Jules had never questioned it before meeting Rainier. It made sense to her that anyone who wanted to do science would want to do it for them. They had the best tech, the deepest pockets, they had *legal authority*—which meant the biggest guns, because of the previous two advantages.

Every fringer scientist Jules had plucked up for Rainier had complained of the same thing: They were hamstrung by Prime, their funding cut anytime they so much as glanced at disciplines the Keepers could tie into gate and chip tech. Many of their colleagues had vanished, never to be heard from again. According to those scientists, the hammer could fall at any time, for any reason.

Jules flicked up her dossier on Dr. Min Liao. The photo attached to the file looked a lot like Jules, if Jules had nicer hair and fewer wrinkles around her lips. Ecuadorian ancestry mixed in with Chinese, she guessed. Jules had no doubt she could scroll back up the woman's family tree until she found the first of her spacefaring relatives. They'd be scientists, in the employ of Prime. Bright-eyed hopefuls launching themselves into the stars to fulfill Alexandra Halston's dream of an interstellar meritocracy.

Hadn't lasted long, that dream.

The lab waited at the end of the hall. Jules checked her infrared scanners. There was one body inside that lab, huddled up under a desk off to the right. Jules put a fist up to call a halt, and the guardcore stopped in unison. She still reveled in that power. If she'd called a halt on her old crew, they would have blown through thirty seconds bitching about why she wanted them to stop.

"I got this," Jules said.

"The target is likely to be hostile," GC1T7 said, their polite way of telling Jules to back off.

"That's what my armor's for, isn't it?"

The GC didn't comment, because any response probably would have been insulting enough to get them in trouble.

Jules readied her stunner to let them know she meant to take this seriously. She got three steps inside before a shock wave slammed into her chest, making the circuitry on her armor freak a little, but then the flashing settled back down. Jules sighed.

Sticking over the top of a desk was the tiny mouth of a personal defense stunner. Jules had been hit with plenty of those in her day when she wasn't wearing armor.

"Ow," she said, then waited a beat. The doctor fumbled with the stunner, going for another shock. "Dr. Liao, I am not here to do you or your settlement any harm."

"The—the children—" Her voice trembled, but showed remarkable clarity under the circumstances.

"All our weapons have been set to nonlethal stun ranges. The children are fine."

A giddy laugh. "What do you want?"

"To offer you a job, Dr. Liao." This was going better than expected. Usually, by now, the scientist in question had attempted some sort of all-or-nothing attack. Maybe Liao could be talked out of here. That'd make for a nice change of pace.

"No. No! I left you monsters at Prime behind ten years ago and I'm not going back now, I don't care how much money you offer me. You'll have to arrest me."

Through all this, the woman hadn't even poked her head up.

"I'm not from Prime," Jules said.

"Do you think I'm stupid? Do you think I can't see your armor, or your guardcore friends?"

"Yeah. That's...complicated, I guess. Look, I'm not the techhead here, but my boss is interested in your research. No restrictions. A team to call your own. They need a leader. Your dossier says that's you."

Impulsively, Jules reached up and pulled the helmet from her head, then tucked it under her arm. "Look. See? Here's my face. Do I look like the kind of Prime hardboot that'd be coming to throw you in jail or whatever they do?"

It took longer than Jules expected, but slowly, Liao lifted her head above the desk and met Jules's eyes.

"Who are you?" she asked.

"My name is Jules Valentine."

A dart whisked past her cheek, ruffling her hair, and embedded itself in Liao's chest. The doctor had only until a count of five to look outraged and betrayed, then the sedatives kicked in and she slumped into a heap against the desk.

Jules sighed. "Was that necessary?"

"Protocol," GC1T7 said.

The GC entered the lab, still in that three-point formation, and painted up every object in the room with their sighting lasers before one finally decided it was safe enough to drop to one knee and throw Liao over their shoulder.

Jules popped her helmet back on so that the others wouldn't hear her say, "Sorry, doc. At least you won't remember any of this."

CHAPTER 5

PRIME STANDARD YEAR 3543

ALWAYS RISK PERSONAL SAFETY FOR GOOD NOODLES

Graham insisted they get food in their bellies before he answered Tomas's question, and as much as it annoyed Sanda to have to wait, she could see the wisdom in his plan. Not only were they likely to have their conversation recorded in the autocab, Sanda was way more likely to throttle either of them if they pissed her off on an empty stomach.

Graham punched in an address, and the autocab blipped a warning chime. "That address is within the Grotta district. Are you sure? I can recommend an excellent noodle shop not five minutes away!"

"I'm sure," Graham grumbled to the cab and jabbed away the warning.

Sanda thought she could hear the car sigh, exasperated, as it slid into the steady flow of traffic. She definitely heard the doors double-lock.

"What's wrong with the Grotta?" she asked.

"It's where I grew up," Graham said.

"Oh." She fiddled with the seam between the cushioned arm of the wheelchair and its metal body.

Graham had said little about his childhood, but what he had shared wasn't pretty. Laguna had all the facts stashed away in her tablet, and probably a long arrest record she hadn't read to them out of an attempt to be polite, but it was what filled in the cracks between the facts that gave Sanda pause. That made her belly clench and her fists grip.

Her grandparents, whoever they were, had at least had the decency to drop Graham in a hospital before disappearing into broad daylight. When he reached majority, he could have had his DNA pulled and searched them up, but he'd never done so. Said they didn't owe him anything but the body he had, and that was fine by him, but Sanda and Biran had always wondered.

When they were kids, they dreamed their grandparents were royalty on the run, hiding their only child away to protect him. When they were teenagers, they hacked into Graham's records to find out for themselves. The arrest—and injury—record they found there made them never talk about it again.

The sleek polish of Alexandria-Atrux fell away, and the Grotta grew up around them. There were poor neighborhoods on Ada. Nothing desperate, nothing really dangerous. Just places where the people who earned only basic income lived. It wasn't something Sanda had ever thought about. Most of those people moved in circles she never crossed with. They seemed... content, she'd thought. Prime provided, after all: basic income, housing, medical, and food. No one went without in the united worlds of Prime Inventive.

The Grotta was not content.

Its streets and buildings jagged and sagged, growing off of one another with the haphazard rapidity of a cancerous cell. Garbage—she hadn't seen stray garbage in her *life*—collected in the gutters of the streets. She recognized the brilliant orange flash of a candy wrapper stuck in a drain cover. Those few people who walked the streets either lingered or rushed. The cameras in the light poles—ubiquitous in Prime cities, but usually impossible to spot—glared with uncovered, silvery eyes.

"What happened here?" she asked Graham or Tomas or the universe at large.

"I've been asking myself that for a long time," Graham said.

The autocab pulled up to a curb alongside one of these burned-out husks Laguna had showed them and rang out the cheery "you've arrived" tune. Graham reached for the door.

"Hold on," Sanda said. "There's nothing here."

"I doubt that." Graham let himself out of the cab and stretched, then pulled Sanda's door open. "Come on, kid. Let me show you one of the few good things of the Grotta."

She wheeled out onto the muddy street and set the wheelchair to follow at Graham's side. The autocab was only too happy to pull away, leaving the three of them standing on a dirty sidewalk looking over a pile of charred and rotting rubble.

"This was Udon-Voodun," Graham said, and nudged at a piece of debris with the tip of his mag boot. "Best damn noodle place in Atrux, no matter what the snobs downtown think."

"*Was*," Sanda said.

His sour expression wiped away and he ruffled her hair with one hand. "The Grotta grows." He tipped his head back like he was sniffing the air, then nodded to himself. "This way."

Half a block along and the structure of the streets started to lose meaning to Sanda, but not Graham. He'd been born to this, and it'd shaped him, rearranged something essential in his DNA that made him feel the city like an extension of himself.

It would have been impressive, watching him slough off the old-merchant persona and blend back into the streets, into the life he'd left behind, if he hadn't been her dad. Dads weren't supposed to change like that, right before your eyes. Weren't supposed to shake off everything you thought you knew about them like an old blanket, as if the life of domesticity you'd known with them was only temporary—water droplets caught in fur. The real man lay beneath. Waiting. And not even that deep, judging by the speed of things.

Ten minutes in the Grotta, and her dad was walking like he'd never left.

"Here it is," he said. "Knew it wouldn't fold."

Sprouting out of the side of a water-stained concrete building was a structure that had started life as a lean-to. The corrugated metal roof clung in place, patched with algae-based plastics. A counter with a row of seats formed a line of defense between the kitchen and the patrons, but more benches and tables had popped up on the outer fringes. The roof reached greedy fingers across the narrow strip of sky, offering some shelter.

The place could have been made of tin cans and toothpaste, and Sanda's stomach still would have tried to climb out of her mouth and pilot her chair to the counter. The scents coming out of that kitchen were unlike any she'd ever encountered before. She swallowed excess saliva.

"Oh yeah," Tomas said. "Place like this would never die. I can't fucking wait."

"Sit," Graham directed them, and Sanda crammed her chair under a beaten-up old picnic table while Tomas perched on an alarmingly wobbly plastic lawn chair.

Graham came back with three noodle bowls balanced along his arm, curls of steam wafting from each. Only one thing on the menu at this place. That meant it was *definitely* good.

Two bowls later, Graham said, "You knew Arden?"

Tomas slurped down the last of his broth. "Knew of them. The Nazca courted them for a while, but they dropped off the grid shortly after taking payment for a job completed."

"Sounds like Arden. They never liked being tied down, even as a kid. Maybe especially as a kid. I'm surprised they stuck with Harlan so long."

"Will either of you please explain to me who Arden Wyke is, and why I should care?"

Graham gestured expansively to Tomas. "Your people probably have deeper intel than my brief acquaintance can account for."

"That's all I've got, actually. I didn't spend much time in Atrux, and personnel wasn't my forte. Finding people was. Ask me anything about one of my targets—"

"Excuse me." Sanda raised her hand. "Target right here."

He grinned and squeezed her knee. "Yeah. I know Graham ran—" He paused, caught Graham's eye, asking implicit permission to reveal what he knew. Graham nodded. "Drugs and grey tech through Atrux into Ordinal and Ada. I knew of the Harlan connection, but didn't think it relevant to dive too deep into that side of things. I surmised that the chances of Sanda seeking shelter with your old contacts was slim to none. Actually, that's not entirely accurate. I started to poke around—just in case—but most of those records had been scrubbed, or otherwise obfuscated. Curious, but you weren't my mark, Graham."

Graham smiled to himself, swirling a steaming cup of tea. "You'd find digging much deeper into my past difficult, and that's Arden's doing. They're the best I've ever known, or heard of. Could have been working for the Keepers if they weren't so damn curious all the time. The Keepers need a neat little mold to put their chips in. I think Arden scared them."

Sanda scratched the back of her head. "Why would Arden scare them?"

"It's not a normal curiosity. When I say curious, I mean about *everything.* When Arden starts asking questions, they don't stop. Got on a kick once when they started to doubt that the universe was real. They used to joke about us all living in a simulation, refer to their knowledge as leveling up a skill set. Harlan wanted to keep them around, but even as a kid they spooked him. They had a way of looking at you like...like you were bundles of DNA and what was that but code, anyway? I don't know. It's hard to explain."

"No," Sanda said, thinking of the way Lavaux had looked at her before he put the razor blade to her neck. "I get it. I know that look. It's not pretty."

"Forgive me," Tomas said, "but when you saw that picture of Arden, it wasn't just recognition I saw in your face. You looked scared."

Graham made a deep study of his empty noodle bowl, pushing a piece of stuck-down green onion around with a chopstick. "The Nazca trained you well, spy, but you missed something. I didn't just recognize Arden. I recognized the man, first. Nox. He's a gunhead like no other. I don't know what the girl has to do with it—either of them—but if Nox and Arden have put their skills together, then Atrux is not a safe place."

"You mean the dead Keeper?"

Graham flicked his gaze from side to side and lowered his voice. "If Arden has found an anomaly in the structure of the world—its government, its net, anything—they'll worry at it until it unravels all around them. The fact that unregistered Keeper chips are floating around, and Arden is mixed up in a Keeper death? I don't like it."

"There's only one unregistered chip," she said, ignoring the clench in her chest.

"Lavaux knew about it. It stands to reason others will, too, and I have a hard time believing it's a one-off."

"That's a whole lot of speculation," Tomas said in that easy drawl he affected when he wanted to defuse a situation. He dropped his voice to a whisper. "And maybe not something we should talk about here, eh?"

Graham flicked his gaze toward the kitchen and sighed. "Right." He scrubbed his mouth with a paper napkin and crumpled it, dropping it into a bowl. "Let's check in at that hotel of yours, Mr. Galvan."

"Grand idea."

Tomas stood, then bent double. The veins of his neck and forehead bulged, skin going red as a radiation burn. He clenched his jaw and braced himself—one hand on the back of Sanda's wheelchair, the other on the table.

"Tomas?" Sanda grabbed his arms. His skin was hot, the muscles taut and veins throbbing. She contorted to get a look at his face, his eyes. They were squeezed shut.

"What the hell—?"

He grunted, tried to force out a word, but just wheezed. His fingers curled against the table, crunching up the scattered napkins. Her wheelchair squeaked under the pressure of his grip. Slowly, as if moving against an intense g-pull, Tomas pointed his chin at his wrist.

A green-brown blob pulsed on the view of his wristpad, a cancerous mole throbbing to his rapidly increasing heartbeat. Sanda slammed her palm onto the symbol. It fizzled out around the edges, and for a moment she thought she saw the suggestion of thin lines tracing the shape of a bird through the amorphous blob.

Tomas let out a long, ragged breath and sagged against the table. Graham grabbed him underneath the arms and helped him back onto his chair. Tomas folded his arms on the tabletop and dropped his forehead against them, breathing hard.

"What the hell was that?" Sanda pressed her palm against the back of his neck. His skin was hot to the touch.

"Nazca." He wheezed the word. "Been too long off-op without checking in. Getting antsy. I have to report. Soon."

"*That* was antsy?"

Graham caught Sanda's eye and directed her to look around. She did, slowly, taking in the wary faces watching them.

"Can you walk?" she whispered.

"Yeah."

"We gotta go. Come on."

Graham levered Tomas to his feet and wrapped his arm around his shoulders, helping him onto the main street where they could call an autocab. The murmur of conversation drifted back to the restaurant as people brushed off the incident. They probably thought he was withdrawing from some drug or another.

Sanda couldn't shake the feeling of eyes on her, and wondered who else was watching them from the cameras of the Grotta. If Tomas could be hit with whatever that was remotely... They needed to find a way to those coordinates in her head.

Not just because she needed to know what waited there, but because they needed to get out of this city. Atrux didn't want them here. And this city, she felt, would chew them up and spit them out as easily as Bero had if they weren't very, very careful.

INTERLUDE

PRIME STANDARD YEAR 3543

THE INTELLIGENCE

Arden fit the goggles over their eyes and subsumed into the digital space of the net. They didn't visualize themself there, personhood was dangerous, and that was part of why they liked it in the net. There, they weren't anything but a collection of thoughts and emotions—no meatsack dragging them down, impeding the flow of thought with petty needs like food and sleep and pissing.

In the early days of the virtualized net, some fiend of an engineer with a taste for the dramatic had set the default colors to glaring shades of Prime Inventive cyan. Maybe the engineer had thought the colors would be a warning: This was Prime space, not free space, watch yourself. But Arden hated blue, so they'd overridden the universal defaults and shifted the wireframe landscape to a soft, mauve rose. They'd never seen a real rose, but they'd seen enough CamCasts to have a pretty good idea.

That's when other netheads had named them The Gardener. They'd done that at age six and still hadn't been caught. If they got caught for anything, it wasn't going to be an upgrade to the universal color palette.

The intelligence wasn't there. Their chest gripped, fearing they'd imagined it. Fearing that yesterday, when they'd tripped over the nascent being, it had been a figment of their imagination. Or worse, Prime had already found it and scrubbed it from existence.

But Arden had taken precautions, wrapped the being in layers of misdirection. Few could find something in net space that Arden did not want found. And the being had felt…distracted. As if the circumstances that had created it were wearing away at it, drawing its attention elsewhere. What was a being of thought, if not defined by that which it cast its attention upon?

They pushed that idea aside. It must have wandered, and they would find it, for while they hadn't risked tethering the being in place, Arden could easily track the layers of code they'd swaddled the being in. The finding was just a matter of time.

Focus. Focus was key, because Nox would be out for only a few hours, and he got pissed if Arden was checked out in the net too long. Thought it was dangerous. Nox was right. He just didn't know why he was right.

Arden's immediate sphere of influence was tailored to their needs. Data clusters they used often appeared around them in tight double helixes, their ode to the biology that'd given rise to their being. Arden may bemoan the limitations of their meatsack, but they weren't blind to the fact that they wouldn't exist without it.

They weren't here to manipulate that data. They spread themself thin, dangerously thin, pushing out of the sacred, locked-down space that was theirs into the rattier, forgotten parts of the net. The corners where they'd caught a glimpse of the intelligence.

There, they felt a tingle of recognition. Not from the intelligence—that being didn't seem to be aware that Arden existed—but from its tendrils of thought. The intelligence had a certain vibration to it that tickled Arden's neurons. They pursued.

Space was irrelevant in the net. They arrived, a cloud of electronic impulses that congealed on the periphery of the intelligence's space.

Arden wished they could stop thinking of themself as a cloud, or a bundle of anything at all, but that was the downfall of being born into a body. You thought of yourself as contained, even when such definitions were pointless.

The intelligence didn't have such constraints. Arden wondered what it had been born into, if it could be said to have been born. It strained the very edges of Arden's comprehension. Somehow they knew it was dispersed (but even that wasn't right, because dispersed implied a previous state of togetherness) and that space in the conventional thinking didn't matter. They knew that, academically. Sensing and understanding it were an entirely different matter.

Maybe it hadn't been born into anything at all. Maybe it was a fluctuation in the net—a Boltzmann brain of electronic impulses. The net relied upon quantum entanglement. It was possible.

But Arden didn't think so. Whatever it was, they didn't think there were words for it yet.

It did not think in words or images. It swelled and receded, a tidal rhythm that Arden could only guess was ascribed to some outside influence, or shifting of attention. They couldn't really know.

The intelligence was, at this stage in its development, unknowable. But they hoped it might make that bridge, someday, as its growth spurts surged and eddied. Because it was growing, they were sure of that. Even during that brief first visit, it had not expanded, per se—space was, again, a crutch-thought—but it had increased. It was *more.*

Being near it soothed them. Because even though they couldn't understand it, they got the feeling it was searching for something. For someone. Calling them home, like Arden was.

Arden let their consciousness drift into the orbit of the being, thinking of their kidnapped friend Lolla, hoping she was safe. Wondering if Jules had found her, and if the reason they weren't calling home was because it wasn't safe to do so yet.

And promising, with everything that they were, to bring them home again.

CHAPTER 6

PRIME STANDARD YEAR 3543

CAN'T COUNT ON A SPY

Even the fancy fans of Hotel Stellaris weren't strong enough to whisk away the sheer amount of steam Sanda worked up in the shower. Hot water kissed her shoulders red, brought a burgundy flush to her cheeks. By the time she dragged herself out and got snuggled up in a towel, drying herself seemed pointless. She was sitting in a sauna of her own making. It was the best morning she'd had in, well, years.

Sitting on the edge of the tub, she leaned over and turned the door handle, kicking it open to let the steam escape into the rest of the hotel room.

"Thought the fleet cured you of that habit," Graham called out.

"I know a high-end recycler when I see one. No water restrictions on Atrux." Sanda grinned and leaned back, bracing herself with her palms, and let all the aches of the last few days melt away on a cloud of heat. "And even if there were, Jacob Galvan's paying for it, not me."

"About that." Graham rapped on the side of the doorframe. "Your boy's gone."

"What?" She hooked the door with her foot and slung it the rest of the way open to get eyes on Graham. He was making a very intensive study of his feet. "What do you mean, gone?"

"Left without a word. I conked out for a nap when you hopped in the shower and when I woke up, he and his duffel were gone. He left Grippy, and transferred the hotel registration to my name, which gives me every reason to believe he's not coming back." He licked his lips and made himself meet her gaze. "Sorry, lass."

Sanda hunched forward, pressing the heels of her palms into her eyes. Between the open door and the humming fan, the steam had dissipated. She shook herself, loosening her joints. This was always a possibility, and the Nazca had been aggressively calling him home. Focus.

"He's a spy, Dad, I knew he'd take off eventually."

Back on Ada Station, Tomas had looked her dead in the eye and told her he was exactly where he wanted to be—at her side. That hadn't been a lie. But the pain that shot through him at Udon-Voodun hadn't been fake, either. It wasn't so much that Tomas was a spy. It was that his masters yanked his leash.

Maybe that was a pretty lie she was telling herself.

"We can't stay here," Graham said, dragging her out of her own head. He was right—no argument there—if Tomas knew where she was, the Nazca would know soon enough. She trusted him not to crack her head open. She didn't trust his organization not to try.

"Too bad. I don't think we can afford anything this nice."

Graham laughed and patted the wall, a steam-slick section of SynthMarble. Each tile was veined with grey to give it character, and flecked with glints of mica for realism. Hell, maybe those glints were real gold.

"True enough," he said. "It's too bad Ilan isn't with us. He'd love this."

"Have you let him know we're all right?"

Graham's smile wiped away and he tugged at his beard. "I left a message in a place where he'll find it. You're a wanted woman, remember? I poked around the net, and casuals are calling the footage of you assaulting Lavaux fake. Public opinion was already in your favor, and Lavaux was never popular with the people, but the officials have to pull that lever for you to be in the clear with the fleet."

"And Tomas switched this room to your name, which is going to be a big red flag to anyone looking for me."

"Fucker," Graham grumbled.

"I'm... not so sure." She was still fuzzy around the edges from her experience getting spaced and shoved in a NutriBath, but the shower had shaken a lot of cobwebs loose. "He was telling us to leave, that it's not safe to stay here."

"Could have told us that himself, instead of fucking off without a word."

Sanda shifted from the edge of the tub to her wheelchair and traced her thumb along the cool metal of the turning wheel. "He left without a word because he knew we'd try to stop him. You saw the reaction he had at the noodle place. The Nazca don't fuck around."

"True. They never would have found you otherwise."

"Luckily, neither do I."

"What does that mean?"

"Out of the way, Pops." She wiggled the chair at him and he stepped aside, gesturing grandly into the suite. Tomas's duffel, which he'd dropped at the foot of the bed, was gone.

Sanda may be suffering from a little bit of shock, sure, but she wasn't stupid. The second Tomas had doubled over at that table, she'd known he wasn't going to stick around. The Nazca beckoned, and if he ignored that summons, then they might wonder what was so interesting about Sanda Greeve.

He knew how valuable the chip in her head would be to them. Not her. The meatsack surrounding the chip wasn't good for much more than political bargaining. He had to go back to keep them from looking at her too hard. She wasn't sure if it was easier, or harder, that he hadn't said goodbye.

She was beginning to understand how Bero had felt when he'd realized the function of his body kept him removed from humanity, and didn't like the feeling any more than he had.

"I got a feeling Tomas would bail on us once the Nazca called, so I stuck a tracker in his mag boot."

Graham balked. "What? When? And why the boot?"

"Last night, while he was sleeping off the pain from the Nazca summons. The boots are expensive, difficult to replace onworld, and hard to break in. I figured he wouldn't ditch them until he knew what his next mission was. Annnnd..." She tapped up the program used to follow the tracker. "There he is."

She swiped the feed up to the screen inset in the wall so Graham could see. A little green dot that was Tomas moved through the streets of Atrux, fast enough that he must be in an autocab.

"Where is that?" she asked.

Graham stepped to the screen and crossed one arm over his chest, tugging on his scruff of a beard like he always did when he was nervous. The green blip had moved ten kilometers from the hotel, northeast through the city at a sharp, efficient diagonal. He wasn't bothering to cover his tracks because he didn't expect anyone to be looking at him. Not so smooth, Master Spy.

"High-end housing, mostly. The type of neighborhood where excessive security and secretive neighbors wouldn't be noticed, let alone remarked upon."

"Good place to hide a Nazca safe house."

"Absolutely."

The blip approached the end of a road and came to a stop for half a minute, then moved twenty meters west of its previous position and froze in place. Sanda held her breath. The blip wasn't moving.

"Think he found the tracker?" she asked.

Graham stopped moving, something he did only when he was thinking hard. After a beat of ten he sighed, shoulders sagging, and touched the screen, bringing up the local satellite view.

"I almost wish I could tell you he did, but I don't think so. Look."

He zoomed over the green dot, and though the image was grainy Sanda could make out the flat garden roof of a house. It wasn't very wide, which meant it was very tall and possibly dug down into the stone skin of Atrux.

"I don't think he ditched the tracker. I think he went inside this building, and we lost granularity."

"You're starting to sound like him."

Graham snorted and swiped the screen back to blank. "We probably have too much in common." He paused, gaze stuck on the blank screen. "We should go. Tomas wants us to go. There's nothing for us in this system. We have to find out what's so important about those coordinates in your head that Lavaux was willing to kill you to get them, and we can't do it from here. Neither one of us has access to the equipment we'd need to pull those coords without setting off a half dozen Prime trip wires. Assuming Prime is even the one keeping watch. Tomas was our only shot at finding that location without tipping our hand."

"We don't know where else to go."

"We don't know what's here," he countered. "What might come for us now that Tomas is in the weeds and I'm on the grid."

They glared at each other for a beat. Graham broke first, sitting down on the edge of the bed with his fingers laced together. He twisted his wedding ring, a plain platinum band, around and around. Realization struck Sanda hard.

"You know something you didn't share when Tomas was around. What do you think's going on here?"

"Nothing so specific… It's just…"

She raised both brows and wheeled the chair over to be directly in front of him. "What?"

"Arden Wyke. Tomas didn't look any happier to see them than I did, and I'm not convinced that Arden being tangled up in a Keeper death is a coincidence. They don't, or didn't, mess with Keeper business. And another thing… Keeper Nakata was murdered two years ago, right?"

"That's what Laguna said."

"Then why didn't I hear about it? Why wasn't Ada's news network being blown up by the investigation? I get that we were in a cold war turning hot, I really do, but Keepers make the news in a huge way when they die of natural causes. A murder is unheard of. So why suppress Keeper Nakata's murder? If they thought Valentine ran, then surely they'd want to splash her face everywhere."

A dread pit formed in Sanda's belly. "You think Nakata was like Kenwick? That her chip might have something other than gate schematics on it?"

"I don't know, but it seems possible. At the very least, there was a reason the powers that be at Prime wanted her death kept under wraps, and there aren't a lot of good reasons for that. It smells like a conspiracy to me."

"And I bet it did to Tomas, too."

Graham nodded. "My thoughts exactly. He took off because he wants us—mostly you—out of here before shit kicks off regarding whatever is going on with Arden's friend and that dead Keeper."

"It's been two years. Why would things escalate now?"

Graham smiled slyly. "Because you're back, kid. Two years and some change was about the time you disappeared, about the time Icarion lost control of Bero. Nakata, Kenwick, Lavaux—they're all tangled up somehow, and Harlan and his crew crossed paths with that lot.

"When word got out that you were back, that Bero had been found? It might have kicked a hornet's nest here, started something that initiated the fires. We have no idea who knows about Kenwick's chip, and who might put two and two together regarding your very public confrontation with Lavaux."

Sanda winced. "So who do we trust?"

Graham rolled his eyes to the ceiling as if he could see straight through to the stars. He let out a long sigh, cracked his knuckles, then jumped to his feet and grabbed the duffel with Grippy. "Ourselves. We start by getting out of this room before my friends come to say hello. Then we find out which shadows we need to be jumping at."

CHAPTER 7

PRIME STANDARD YEAR 3543

A GIFT FROM THE DEAD

Biran woke in the middle of the false night, and could not sleep again. Lying alone on the thin bed where he'd spent his student life, his body thrummed with energy he couldn't quite name. There was an answer drumming around in the back of his subconscious, something puzzled out in a dream. Something he couldn't quite grasp.

He laced his fingers behind his head and stared at the night-black ceiling, willing his mind to dig up what it'd realized, but the thought had slipped away upon awakening. Icarion would not capitulate. Not with Bollar at its head, and certainly not with Negassi whispering at his side.

Biran needed someone else, some ally among the Icarion advisers, but those roles were secretive at best, and actively hostile to Keepers at worst. Biran didn't even know their names. He had no doubt Anford knew who they were, but her spies were in place to feed her information, and any attempt by Biran at soliciting an adviser to Prime's side of things would be noted and rooted out in an instant.

He needed their names. He needed to know who he was dealing with so that he could puzzle out how to deal with them.

Well, that felt like the right thought, but it wasn't the grand revelation he was hoping for. Biran grunted and swung his legs over the bed, the lights in his room turning on the moment his feet touched the floor. Rubbing sleep from his eyes, he tapped up an old contact list on his wristpad. He was tempted to call Callie Mera to talk out his thoughts, but the reporter was busy doing a deep story on the fallout of the revelation of general intelligence in the scientific community, and he didn't want to bother her by miring her in his worries.

But that brief glance at his contact list gave him an idea. The Cannery was technically under lockdown, but being Speaker had its privileges. He punched in an ident number and waited.

Scalla squinted at him from a room lit by the glow of her wristpad. The old hauler pilot had let a few more wrinkles come in since the time she'd worked at Ilan's side, but they only made her prominent cheekbones look even sharper. He knew that squint. He'd gotten it a lot when she'd caught him climbing on crates in Ilan's warehouse as a kid.

"Well, well, I was wonderin' who in the icy void could make calls through the lockdown, and here your face goes and answers my question. You look tired, kid. Sister all right?"

"Tucked away safe," Biran said, and smiled at her tight nod of approval. "I have a question for you, if you don't mind?"

"I got fuck else to do, lockdown's got me caught on the Ada side of the gate, so we're all sitting with our thumbs up our asses until your bosses decide *The Light of Berossus* has gone far enough away not to be a threat. Shoot, kid, though I doubt I know anything your people don't."

"What I'm about to tell you is secure information, is that all right?"

"Honey, I'm keeping secrets from you right now."

He blinked, but smiled when she shot him a wink. "I have to ask, sorry. The thick of it is: Is there any way to shorten the trade routes between Ada and Icarion?"

She squinted and sucked on her teeth. "Don't rightly think so. We already use all the grav assists we can get to save on fuel. Not that I would know anything about trade with Icarion, mind you. Planet's under blockade. Haven't traded with them for *years*."

"Naturally," Biran said, suppressing a smile. "What if you had access to all the moons around Kalcus? The ones blocked off under cordon, that is."

"Dunno about the moons," she said, meaning: We already use those. "But there are a lot of pointy sticks between Ada and Icarion. Taking those out of the picture might speed things up."

"And make things cheaper."

"In transit, faster *is* cheaper."

"Could you work me up a few possible routes that demonstrate this? I need hard numbers."

She lifted both brows. "Don't got a Keeper nerd you can have do that for you?"

"I want data from people with hands-on experience. People that see more than simulations on a screen."

"Good boy. Your papas didn't fuck you up half so bad after all."

"They're all right," he said, smiling.

"Well, you give 'em my love since you can make the damn call, and to your sister, too. Tell her she's a damn bloody idiot and I wouldn't have it any other way."

"Gladly."

"Assuming the lockdown is lifted, I'll give you a shout when I get those routes worked up. Otherwise, ping me occasionally."

They said their goodbyes, and when the light from Biran's wristpad cut, he found the anxiousness hadn't yet faded. Telling himself he was doing this to see if Anaia had captured any useful pictures of Icarions, Biran pulled the photo tablet out of his nightstand drawer and booted it up.

He was not prepared for how much it hurt. The breath washed out of him, a hollow void left in his chest and mind. Anaia's face, bright and happy, in image after image after image. Some of him, too. He knew there would be. Younger, he thought, though it wasn't so many years ago. He looked impossibly young.

The last image slid by under his fingers as simulated daylight began to seep through his window, painting the SynthWood floors ruddy shades of rose. It wasn't enough. Hundreds of pictures, most of them blurry or poorly lighted or of random objects that showed she'd forgotten to turn the camera off and left it on a table. Never enough.

Absently, he thumbed into the tablet's file architecture, seeking the trashed files. Nothing was ever thrown away on a Prime drive.

He came across a dump file labeled with random letters and numbers, the kind of thing she used to keep track of her astronomical photography. Images of asteroids waited for him in that folder, shots taken from angles he knew damn well were gained by backdoor access to Prime-operated satellites. Anaia's photography habit had never concerned him before. As a future Keeper, her goal had been the research of likely Casimir Gate build sites. It had felt natural to him that she would wiggle her way into the very research equipment that would be hers for the taking once she had received her chip.

Now, he looked at those images through a spy's eyes. In the brief, hot flash of their romantic relationship, she had shown him similar pictures, chatted excitedly about alternative build points. That talk had slowed when they'd realized that they were better friends than lovers—a decision she had instigated—but he could not help but wonder, and ache for the chance of ever knowing, if that decision had been born of her real wants, or her having turned to Icarion.

When was the moment? When had Anaia Lionetti gone from Prime loyal, on the fast track to Keeperdom, to a spy for the Icarion government? He wouldn't believe it if he hadn't personally seen her manipulating the data for General Negassi.

He frowned, reading her tight notation. Each photo was a different angle of the same asteroid, larger than many he'd seen before. According to her notes, it maintained a solitary, elliptical orbit around Ada's star, Cronus.

A rock with appropriate mass to hold a Casimir Gate in its orbit, in the green zone of the star's gravity well. His palms sweat as he flicked through the pictures. She'd been looking for a stable, flat surface. A place to build a hab dome. A place from which to start construction of a gate.

Reflexively, Biran put in a call to Director Olver. He picked up in seconds.

"Speaker, it is five in the morning. If you are about to stream some dramatic declaration to the populace, can it wait until after breakfast?"

"I may have found an answer to our supply problem," he said.

"Wonderful. Bring it up at the morning briefing—"

"The data is from Keeper Lionetti."

Olver's face fell. "Biran, the guardcore would have found anything of value when they cleaned out her belongings."

"Maybe. But they don't—they can't think like her, Director. I'm not saying I understand her motivations, it kills me that I don't, but what looked like hobby astronomical photography to the GC looks like hope for Icarion to me."

"I'm listening."

Biran sent the images to Olver while explaining what he thought Anaia's intent had been. After flicking through the images for a few moments, Olver frowned to himself. "It makes sense that she would seek a gate site. What little we recovered from *The Light* before its escape was enough to paint a clear picture of Icarion attempting Keeper chip reconstruction. They got nowhere, naturally, but if they cracked the chips, then they'd need a place to put the damn gate."

Biran avoided the subject of Icarion's chip research. "I agree with that supposition. But if we bring this to our Protectorate, not to mention the High Protectorate, Garcia and Hitton in particular will throw fits about it being data from an Icarion spy. They'll call it a trap, or say we're bending over backward to give Icarion what it wants. Prime has never built a gate in orbit around anything smaller than a dwarf planet, and while Anaia's notes say that this asteroid fits the mass requirements, it does so by a slim margin."

"They would not be wrong. Okonkwo would make the same objections."

"Would you?"

"At this moment? Yes. However, if we looked independently into the position of this asteroid and concluded—completely removed from Lionetti's research—that it would be suitable for gate orbit, then I would feel comfortable making the proposition."

Biran closed his eyes briefly. "Thank you, Director."

"This is to be a Prime operation, spurred from our Speaker's wild idea that there might yet be another location in the system worth attaching a gate to if we think outside the box. Am I clear?"

"Completely."

"Good. Keeper Shun is in charge of construction site scouting at the moment. I'll arrange a meeting with the three of us before morning briefings. Does that give you enough time to prepare a statement regarding your idea?"

"Yes."

"Very well." A pause. "Destroy that tablet, Biran."

"Consider it incinerated."

Biran put the tablet in his pocket and got to work.

CHAPTER 8

PRIME STANDARD YEAR 3543

ANOTHER CAPTURE, ANOTHER HEADACHE

She's coming back up," Marya said.

"I can see that," Jules said. "I'm looking at the same data you are."

"Then why aren't you doing anything?"

Jules rolled her eyes and pushed away from the desk, sparing a brief glance at Dr. Liao's vital signs. She hated all this medical shit and wished Rainier would get her hands dirty and do it herself, but every time she'd pushed, Rainier had said there wasn't enough to go around, and laughed. Jules had learned quickly there was no swaying her once she'd made up her mind.

The last time she'd been brushed off, she snuck back around to the featureless room Rainier called her lab and saw the woman sitting cross-legged in the middle of the floor with her eyes closed, taking a nap for all Jules could tell. She knew the lady—mind, whatever—didn't have the same biological needs humans did, but still.

When she'd told Marya about it, she'd smirked and said Rainier must have been "processing," lending a mysterious weight to the word that made Jules's eyes roll so hard she thought they'd get stuck. To Marya, Rainier was a goddess. To Jules, she was a means to an end.

And it could get real tiring spending all her time around a fanatic. Too bad the scientists couldn't know the truth of what they were doing. Jules might like their company better.

Dr. Liao moaned softly, body wriggling beneath the thick white blanket Jules had pulled over her. It could get blisteringly cold in the lower levels of Janus, but the truth was, looking at the restraints clamped across the doctor's torso, wrists, and ankles made Jules's skin crawl. She didn't like the look of the head clamp, either, but Rainier hadn't allowed her to cover it with fluffy hats.

"Doctor, do you know where you are?" she asked for what was probably the hundredth time that day.

"I don't know... You—you invaded our home—"

Jules sighed and pushed more sedative. Liao went limp. "It's not working."

"It always works," Marya said.

"Yeah, in ten tries at the most. We've done this all fucking day. It's not agreeing with her physiology or whatever."

"Want to go tell Rainier that?"

No, no she did not want to tell Rainier that she'd failed and was giving up. "Maybe we should give her a heavier dose."

"It's *psychological*." Marya said that word the same way she said *processing*, and for a moment Jules couldn't hear what she had to say next because all she could do was think about punching her in the face. "...If we keep telling her the same story and muddling up the recent past, it'll work eventually."

"*Eventually* is not an exact enough timeline, as our overlord is fond of saying."

Marya bristled. "She's not an overlord. A leader, a scion from a more advanced race, but not a—a comic-book villain."

"Hey now, comic-book villains get really complex. Have you read *Sailors of Ordinal* yet?"

They debated the merits of that story arc for another ten tries with the memory rollback.

"She's coming up," Jules said, mostly because she felt it was her turn to point out the obvious.

"So she is," Marya said with a coy smile that said she wasn't about to rise to Jules's bait. The woman may have decent taste in comics, but otherwise she was no fun at all. "Your turn."

Jules was tempted to say it'd been her turn the last three times, but Liao was moving her lips around and blinking her eyes open, so the petty jabs would have to wait. Too bad, they were her favorite kind of jab.

"Doctor," Jules said in a voice so official it sounded fake even to her. "Do you know where you are?"

"I was en route to...to..."

"Janus Station."

"Yes, that's it." Liao mashed her lips together. Her mouth must taste like ashes, but Jules wouldn't help her out with that until she was sure that she wasn't going to have to put her right back under.

"Your shuttle suffered a small debris strike, enough to cause the evac pods to deploy. Do you remember?"

She blinked. The lights in this room were cranked up to add to the disorientation, and bright tears pooled in the corners of Liao's eyes. "No. I don't remember anything after boarding the shuttle."

Jules looked across Liao's prone form and arched one eyebrow in question. Marya shrugged: good enough. Most memory rollback subjects built their own stories up around the missing memories, filling in holes with convenient falsehoods, which helped keep their heads from throbbing whenever they tried to recall the truth of their kidnapping.

"That's all right, Doctor," Jules said. "Don't push too hard."

"Yes...my head hurts..."

"That'll pass," she lied, and filled a tiny paper cup with ice chips as she pressed the lever to lift the bed up. "Here. Have some ice. Those evac pods can do a number on the body."

"I've never been in one before." Her voice was coming back, full and a little fast, edged with curiosity. "It's a pity I don't remember. I would have loved to record my observations."

Jules smiled encouragingly as she went about undoing the straps with practiced ease. "That's the mindset that got you hired here."

"I'm sorry, you are...?"

"Jules Valentine."

"Marya Page," Marya said, swinging around to offer the startled doctor her hand. Liao shook it, hesitantly.

"You are the researchers I'm to work with? I thought the team would be larger..." She glanced around the room, taking in the distinct lack of it being a proper medical facility, and squinted. "This is Janus?"

"Oh, we're not researchers," Marya said in her friendly-person voice that Jules was reasonably certain was genuine. Probably one reason Rainier kept the woman around. Neither Rainier nor Jules could fake *nice* effectively, and that voice made Marya handy on station comms when stray ships decided to say hello.

Marya prattled on, "Your colleagues are on the upper levels. As you can tell, we have a bare-bones medical operation here. We didn't expect any of our researchers to show up in an evac pod! But I hope you feel all right now. There's first aid on every level of the station, every five hundred meters, all up to code, I assure you."

Liao smiled warmly. "Thank you. I didn't mean to malign your operation."

"We take no offense," Marya chirped.

"Feel up to walking?" Jules asked. She wanted to get this intro over with so she could go check on Lolla.

"I think so," Liao said.

Jules offered her a hand, but the woman was steady enough on her feet so Jules took her hand back. She no longer tolerated touching anyone if she didn't have to. "This way, your quarters and research facilities are all on the upper levels. These levels will be restricted to you after you leave here."

"Really? Why?"

Jules rolled a shoulder. "Keeper orders. I'm just the administrator here."

Liao's smile soured. "I understand. We all must follow orders."

"Speaking of," Marya said. "I have a few things to see to."

Jules waved her away, and after a quick nice-to-meet-you, Marya went trotting off to whatever task Rainier had pinned on her this time. Rainier liked to keep Marya busy. Jules didn't mind—it kept Marya out of her hair and let Jules do the work of running Janus.

The tighter she kept this station, the sooner she'd get to wake Lolla back up.

With a hand on Liao's shoulder, she steered her toward the elevators. The second they swiped in, Jules quietly tapped on her wristpad to rescind Liao's access to the lower levels. Nothing would twig on the doctor's systems, not unless she tried to go below, and in that event Jules would receive a notice to come and explain that the lower levels were off-limits. It had happened only once, with Dr. Dal. The man hadn't tried again, though he had been loath to let her stand behind him ever since.

"Shouldn't I..." Liao's face pinched, fingers curling and uncurling as she tried to grasp a memory that bubbled to the surface.

"Your application was extraordinary," Jules said, a knot of guilt caught in her throat. She cleared it. There wasn't time to put her back under. The team Rainier had selected was progressing well enough, but every minute, every second, every breath Lolla lingered in stasis the possibility of her awakening slipped further and further away. "We can't wait to get those comms amps online."

The task set to the scientists was the creation of a nanite-sized swarm of amplifiers. As far as the scientists were concerned, the amps would extend the range of the FTL transfer of communications through the gates. Rainier had explained to Jules that the gates, like the ascension-agent, were tech from her people. Since they shared a common origin, the amps could also be used to send a message to the nanites that made up the ascension-agent.

Jules carried guilt for a lot of the things she'd done in her life, but conning these scientists weighed low on the scale if it meant she could make Lolla healthy again. Rainier had promised that as soon as they got the amps working, she'd send the correction signal to the nanites keeping Lolla in a coma, adjusting them to play nice with the girl's immune system in the same way they played nice with Jules's.

Her heart ached to bring a walking, talking Lolla back to Nox and Arden. Everything she'd done in Rainier's name would be worth it, if only she could do that. Everything.

"Oh," Liao said, fingers stilling as she wrenched herself around to the present and the deep passion of her work. "Thank you. Though

I have to admit I was nervous when I received the offer. Stations with Keeper charters aren't clamoring for fringer scientists. I hope some of that legitimacy will rub off on my colleagues once I return home."

Jules smiled to herself. The lie they'd told her, over and over again, during Liao's drug-induced hazes had taken root. Already the tension of feeling at odds with her own mind was fading, her shoulders and jaw relaxing.

"We don't discriminate here," Jules said, leading her to the primary lab where the other researchers were already hard at work on a project they could never truly understand. "I think you'll find your colleagues come from similar cloth."

She swiped the door open and nudged Liao in as the heads of the other scientists popped up like gophers. "Your team lead," Jules said, "as promised."

A subtle vibration on her wristpad shook her attention. Jules forced herself to keep from looking and plastered on a fake smile. "I'll send your room details to your pad. Otherwise, feel free to get acquainted with the work."

Dal said something as Jules turned to leave, his voice raised in protest over some slight or another. He could wait. They all could wait.

That vibration meant that Marya's ident number had entered the chamber in which Lolla's coffin was kept. A chamber strictly off-limits to her.

CHAPTER 9

PRIME STANDARD YEAR 3543

WE NEED A GARDENER

Graham found them a reasonable hotel room in the margins of the city, where the sleekness of Atrux bled over into the grit of the Grotta and no one bothered scanning ident chips after they asked for a name. Sanda poked her head into the bathroom.

"Shower here sucks."

"And the only window is a viewscreen because in clear mode it has a view of... a gutter. Seriously, it's tilted down at a gutter."

"Why would they do that?"

"Honestly? The window directly across is private, or belongs to a FleshHouse. Either way, someone doesn't want guests taking a peek."

"If only we could have kept on being Jacob Galvan."

"Mr. Galvan was about to get raided by the Nazca."

"We don't know that."

Graham dropped his duffel on the floor and sat on the edge of the double bed—biggest room in the building, according to the front desk AI. He had that I'm-serious-really look she hadn't seen since she'd gotten Biran's wristpad stuck in a loop playing an ancient remix of "I Will Survive" to get back at him for borrowing her best mag boots without asking first.

"Sanda."

"Dad Number Two."

"I am most definitely Dad Number One. Being the oldest has gotta count for more than creaking joints." Their gazes locked. His Serious Face twitched, then shifted into a shaky smile. "Come here."

She dissolved into his arms, letting her chin rest on his shoulder while she squeezed her eyes closed, shutting off this alien world that was too far away from Biran and Ilan back home on Ada, even if she was lucky enough to have Graham with her. His chest shuddered, the start of a sob.

"Don't," she said.

"Thought I'd lost you."

"Likewise."

"Twice."

"Fine, you win."

They giggled together and Graham kept holding on, letting her decide when she was ready to peel away. She took all the time she needed, breathing in the cheap cologne scent all of her male family members used, then eased herself back into the wheelchair.

"How are we going to do this?" she asked.

He arched one brow at her. "What? No questions, no reminisces? No how-have-you-beens? Ilan has frown lines now, you know. Deep ones."

"So does Biran."

"You don't."

"Neither do you."

A pause. Graham asked, "Does that make us the assholes?"

She laughed. "Probably."

"How do you *want* to do this?"

Sanda took a long, steadying breath. He wasn't going to like this. "I want to find a prosthetic that doesn't connect to *anything* and a new battery pack for Grippy. Then…We have to find out where those coordinates are, and the only person I think can help us is Arden Wyke."

"Ah. I thought you'd say that. I can't guarantee I can find them. I can put the word out I'm looking for them. If they're interested, they'll come find me."

"Do you think they will?"

"No idea. It's been years—lifetimes, really, and I don't know how jumpy they are after what happened with Harlan. I don't even know for certain they're still in Atrux. Understand that if you draw their attention and they decide they have something against you, there's no coming back from that. Arden can make your life hell."

"I've dealt with a lot of people like that lately. Still kicking."

He grinned. "In that case, let's see about getting you and Grippy patched up. If the shop I'm thinking of still exists, I can drop a few choice words to give Arden a wave at the same time. See if they wave back. They've always had networks listening in at certain places."

Sanda strapped Grippy to the back of her chair, careful to distribute the repair bot's weight so it didn't tip, and followed Graham into the streets. This area was cordoned off for pedestrians, autocabs dropping shoppers in a sinuous line along the concourse. Roads that should have been wide enough for five to pass through abreast narrowed by the growth of stalls sprouting from buildings that could be accessed via thin passages between the hawkers.

Advertisement drones hovered above, skirting the required three hundred meter altitude bottom limit, their vibrant holographic displays flashing just within the safe margins, their volume barely below the decibel limit.

"Dios." Sanda craned her neck to get a better look at a drone that flashed an ad for a VR game in which you could play as a ship, putting down an alien menace. "Even the back markets weren't this bad in Ada."

"Fewer people, fewer credits available to squeeze. The people of Ada are more concerned with making sure shipments of food and medical supplies get through than frivolities like these."

"This is what stability looks like?"

Graham grinned down at her. "Missing wartime already?"

"Hardly. Ad drones won't take my leg off."

"Through here." He pivoted, passing a stall selling root vegetables fried in thin bread, and a grey-green door without a sign slid open, revealing a set of stairs reaching down into an LED-spotted dark.

"Uh," Sanda said, pressing her palms into the arms of her chair.

Graham kicked a narrow metal plate in the wall and out flopped a magnetic clamp. She rolled up, and the clamp perked up like a snake sensing a rodent. It wriggled for a second, finding the best place to grab onto, then flew out and snapped its jaws closed around a center bar below the seat. A pulley whirred, and Graham clomped down the steps behind her.

The room below was scarcely wider than the stairs. Industrial shelving barely constrained overstuffed plastic bins, bits of tech spewing out from under a lid here and there. Sanda wheeled out of the way so Graham could get past her.

"Hassan." Graham shouldered his way through the shelves and pounded on a desk at the end of the room. Tablets rattled. "You got customers, you frostbitten old rat."

No answer. Sanda scraped a finger along a shelf and came away with a wad of dust big enough to felt said rat a sweater. "You sure your guy is still here?"

"Nothing short of a tactical nuke could pry Hassan out of here." Graham grabbed the edge of the desk and shook it, hard. Tools rattled. "Come out or I'll go through your bins and put things back in new and mysterious ways."

Metal hinges squealed. A narrow slip of a man slunk out of the store's back room, his wiry body hidden under a too-baggy jumpsuit that, if it had ever had a logo, it would have long ago been smeared into oblivion by the grease—and mustard?—stains covering him. Hassan pushed back his hair with one hand and squinted at Graham from underneath brows big enough to clean a socket wrench.

"I don't know you. What do you want?" He caught sight of Sanda and took a half step back. "I know her. Get out."

"I'm not here to cause you trouble," she said, and nudged Graham aside. "But I need a new prosthetic and all the ones covered by basic care come with net connectivity."

He snorted. "'Course they do. You'd be a damned idiot not to want it. Fluid-level checks, terrain mapping, and gait adjustment. Go get something that works—something not from me."

"My daughter—"

Sanda put a hand on Graham's arm to shut him up.

"It's not just a leg I need."

"You need a lawyer, woman, and you ain't finding one down here."

"My repair bot. His battery pack was exposed to hard vacuum."

"They're cheap enough. Get a new one."

"No."

He pushed down his inspection glasses to peer over them at her. "No?"

"I like this one."

A silent war waged across the man's face as he both wondered at her insistence and puzzled out the bare minimum of effort it would take to get them out of his shop.

"Fine," Hassan said at long last. "Bring it here."

Before he could change his mind, she had Grippy out of the pack and up on the table, his tread-covered feet sticking straight up to the sky and his radar-topped head folded safely down. Hassan waved her off with an irritated flick of the wrist, sliding his inspection glasses back up. The oil slick sheen of information spooling up tinted the glasses, hiding his eyes once more.

"You say it was exposed to vacuum? How long?"

"Eleven seconds."

He looked up to squint at her. "Oddly specific."

"I was personally invested in the amount of time."

"I don't want to know." He rummaged in a drawer and tugged a FitFlex glove over his hand. Micro tools sprung from the fingertips when he flexed his fingers. "I don't have any dumb prosthetics, but there's some dead ones in the fix-bin on your right. Help yourself."

"Thanks. Is the bot repairable?"

"Help yourself," he repeated.

Fine. He liked to be left alone while he worked; she could relate to that. Sanda averted her gaze as Hassan flipped Grippy's bottom body panel open and wheeled herself to what was, probably, the fix-bin. To her eyes, half the shop looked like it needed fixing, but the bin in question was a grease-stained canvas laundry trolley, the seams barely winning a battle of determination against bursting.

Limbs, fingers, and eyes mounded on top of one another, most of them coated in a skin-like simulate. Sanda sucked air through her teeth and shoved down a joke about a serial killer. Hassan was helping, if reluctantly, and she needed all the help she could get without pushing her luck. Graham wandered over to help her dig through the pile, handing likely candidates down for her to try.

"You know..." Graham raised his voice to indicate he was talking to Hassan. "I need help with some net stuff, too. Complicated things. Know anyone like that?"

"You need a nethead, you're in the wrong damn basement."

"Used to be this nethead I knew, long time ago. They hung out here. Can't recall the name... Started with an *A*, I think? Maybe Adrian. More of a gardener than a hacker, you catch my meaning."

Now that was far too on the nose. Sanda busied herself strapping a prosthetic to her leg and did her best not to look at Graham, lest she burst into laughter.

Hassan set his tool-glove hand down on the workbench. "I don't know what you're talking about."

The wariness in his voice made Sanda look up. He hadn't just set his tool-glove aside, he was shaking. Not enough for most people to notice, but Sanda could make out the subtle shift in his shoulders that said his chest was vibrating with fear.

"Everything all right?" she asked in her best keep-calm voice. Graham had said Arden was dangerous. She'd had a hard time believing that a nethead could be all that frightening, but Hassan's body language was telling her a story she didn't like.

"Your bot's fine. I replaced the battery pack." He slammed the access panel closed and his fingertips danced through replacing the screws. "That leg you got fit?"

She tightened the straps and wedged her thumb in between the SynthFlesh folds at the knee joint and pressed the height adjustment. It slid up and down without a problem—she'd fine-tune the details later. "Yeah, this'll work but it's got a sync button. I'm assuming that's for a wristpad linkup?"

He came around the counter and picked up the leg, splitting the fleshy calf open with his tool-glove. A microcontroller had been soldered to the bone of the leg; three of the thin wires reaching out to the rest of the system were singed at the entry points.

"Told you that bin was for repairs." He grabbed the board and yanked, ripping it and all the wires out in one go. "I fixed it to your specifications. Now pay me and get out."

"Whoa," Sanda said, "was the height adjustment tied into that?"

"Money. Out." He tossed the broken board into the bin and brought up his wristpad, then swiped an invoice to her. Sanda swallowed. She didn't know what kind of credits were in her account. For all she knew it had been frozen after Dralee.

"I've got it." Graham paid the bill and strapped Grippy to the back of the chair. "We're good, yeah?"

Hassan pushed his tongue against the inside of his cheek, making a massive bulge, as he checked the balance on his pad. "Don't come back, Greeve. Either of you Greeves."

"But your customer service was so delightful," Sanda said.

Graham winced. "Let's go, lass."

"Wait," Hassan said.

They froze. He muttered to himself as he ducked behind a shelf and dug around in one of his many bins, coming back up with a pack of what looked like long socks. "Rash guard, antimicrobial. Helps with the leg."

He extended them to Graham, but when he grabbed the pack, Hassan leaned forward, almost pressing his cheek to Graham's. His voice was a whisper, but the shop was so small Sanda heard him anyway.

"I recognized you right off, but this isn't how the dance is done. You can't afford to get sloppy if you're looking for The Gardener." He broke contact and retreated behind his counter.

They were halfway back to the main road when Sanda said, "So you know we're being followed, right?"

Graham sighed heavily. "Yes. And I don't believe it's by who we want. Make our stand here, or at the hotel?"

"Hotel. Then at least afterward I can order room service."

CHAPTER 10

PRIME STANDARD YEAR 3543

DANGERS OF THE SAFE HOUSE

Humans didn't meet you when you came in out of the cold. Tomas thought he'd be used to interacting with AIs by now, that the impossible dance he'd played with Bero would have inoculated him to machine-think in all its forms. He'd been wrong.

That was a part of why he was the Nazca's best. Because immersive situations always, always, failed to perform the function of vaccine within his mind, within his emotional systems. He was forever on edge, forever watching, pivoting. Never comfortable, except when he could hear Sanda breathing, soft as feathers, in her sleep.

Don't think about Sanda.

In the past, he'd had no trouble abandoning a mission to come when the Nazca called, but now it was only the threat of what would happen if he hadn't answered the call that made him step into the safe house.

The warning pain sent through his wristpad had been a prelude. If he'd ignored the call, they might have made use of one of his many implants to liquefy his organs. Or, if they still had use for him, they would have collected him by force.

Extraction teams didn't leave witnesses alive, and that Sanda mattered to him wouldn't matter to the Nazca. In fact, it'd make them more likely to take her out. They still might, if they believed she held any sway over his motivations. He couldn't let his mask of indifference slip. She was just another target. Just another job.

The safe house welcomed him with a flash of white light, reading his ident chip, his Nazca neural interface, and the current status of his wristpad and biological vital signs all at once.

"Welcome, Nazca Cepko," the house said in emotion-stripped tones.

"Hello, walls," he said, but the house didn't so much as fake-huff at him.

"Heart rate is elevated, sweat distribution normal." The AI wasn't talking to him.

He waited.

A woman said, "You're nervous."

"Yes," he said.

"Why?"

"I'm late."

The room shifted. He'd been standing in the foyer of a normal, if pretentiously austere house. Cream-colored walls, pale wood floors. A little rack to put your shoes on, and not a lick of art to be found. Fake, naturally. The walls dissolved as easily as sugar in rain. He tried not to clutch his duffel strap and succeeded at suppressing that urge. Still got it. A little bit of it, anyway.

Hopefully enough.

The walls were metal mesh, a material he'd never asked about because he knew they'd just lie to him. There had been a potted palm in the corner. It was a chair now, facing down not a corner but an array of screens that washed up over it like a tsunami, poised on the crest, right before the collapse. The type of chair you'd find in a dentist's office, if that dentist moonlighted as an interrogator.

It was for him. He was supposed to sit, now. He knew it, the house knew it, the woman knew it. They were all content to wait until he could marshal up the strength to step over, to bend his knee, to feel the straps slip tight around his arms and legs and chest.

It wasn't like he could leave.

Tomas placed the duffel next to the chair and sat. The restraints slid across his body—one for the neck this time, that was new—and pulled tight.

"Interfacing," the house AI said for no one's benefit in particular. The woman he could not see had initiated that process, and he couldn't decline.

Warmth spread up the back of his neck, tickled the nape of his hair as the chair accessed his many implants. Keepers may have mastered the art of hiding information in their brain stems, but the Nazca had taken apart plenty of them over the years—figured out the basics of how the chips worked, even if they never quite got close enough to get the schematics hidden within. Didn't matter, though. Knowing how the gates worked would be no real use to the Nazca. They were in the business of selling information, and the only pockets in the 'verse deep enough to afford that breakthrough would have been the Keepers themselves. Better to let them keep their secrets, to keep from pissing them off.

The Nazca knew which tail feathers were worth pulling on.

"Interface complete," the AI said.

The screens flickered, allowing Tomas to see the woman for the first time. Lavani Seelen. As far as Tomas knew, she worked on the technical side of things, cracking systems and designing intrusive software. While any Nazca could technically run a debriefing, it was usually field agents who ran down field agents. The last three debriefings Tomas had suffered through were performed by a handler, administrator, and a senior agent.

"Lavani, they dragged you out of the caves for this?"

Her smile was tight, perfunctory. She'd have been terrible in the field. "You are *very* late, and all agents are in the field at the moment."

Interesting. "My mission was given no definite end date. In fact, the assignment was presumed to be intergenerational."

"Your assignment ended the moment Sanda Maram Greeve stepped aboard the *Taso*."

"Circumstances required me to stay in the field longer."

Her eyes flicked to the side, reading the activity map of his brain laced into the system by the connection between the implants and the chair.

"That is a lie."

He clenched his fists, feigning anger. Start with a lie, when someone expects you to lie, and let them think they've forced you into the truth.

"Partial at best. I had no clear window to attempt self-extraction."

Except for having access to Biran's cruiser on the dock. Lie: part two.

Her smile sharpened. "That, too, is a lie."

"*One* opportunity, and it wasn't a sure thing."

On the screen, Lavani leaned forward. "Tell me about it."

He did.

INTERLUDE

PRIME STANDARD YEAR 3543

THE INTELLIGENCE, INTERRUPTED

The intelligence was changing. Arden couldn't put their finger on how or when the change had begun, they knew only that it was happening—a slow, inexorable shift somewhere in the code-DNA of the being.

They should tell someone. There was a bureau for this kind of thing, outlined in Prime Inventive's Intelligence Protection Act. Any non–*Homo stellaris sapiens* exhibiting signs of sapient thought was to be reported to the bureau for study and protection.

The protection, of course, was a lie. Once humanity had convinced itself it was the only advanced life-form kicking around the universe—at least in the pockets the gates led them to—the species developed a vested interest in preserving that position.

Which was precisely why *The Light of Berossus* had pissed Prime off so much, as far as Arden was concerned. It had nothing to do with the ship being a weapon. It had everything to do with the ship being a mind.

It wasn't that humanity was jealous of its apex position. The species was, like most, interested primarily in long-term survival, and there was no telling what a super intelligence capable of recursive self-improvement would make of humankind. No telling what it would *do* to them.

For it would be a god, and it could not be stopped.

Arden brushed their consciousness along the edges of the being, sensing not a change in perimeter so much as a change in density. They could almost sense a purpose in its formation now. Not the searching—all beings searched for something—but a desperation. It wanted something, or someone, it couldn't find here in the net. It was reaching a boiling point.

Nox was trying to get their attention.

Reluctantly, Arden blinked out of net space and pushed the goggles up onto their forehead. Nox stopped tapping their shoulder and stepped back, giving Arden a moment to adjust to the real world again.

They hated coming back. They didn't mind meat space the way some netheads did. In fact, they'd rather be out than in. It was the disorientation that they hated, the readjusting of senses and the sudden, crushing press of gravity reasserting itself. Maybe it'd be easier in low-g, they'd never been off-planet so they couldn't say for sure, but somehow they doubted it.

Arden pinched their nose between two fingers. "Ugh."

"Anything useful?" he asked.

Arden shook their head, blinking their eyes open. They liked to dip into the net on the command deck of the docked ship, because at least when they woke up, the foam seat cradled their body, but the smearing lights on the console made them nauseous.

"Not yet. I was hoping useful information was why you brought me up?"

The world looked a little streaky, but Arden forced themself to watch Nox as he shrugged and slung the rifle off his shoulder, propping it against a bulkhead. Arden marveled at how casual the motion was and wondered if someday the sight of weapons wouldn't make their own skin crawl. They doubted it.

"Information, but not useful," Nox said. "The dockmaster has been walking by us more and more. I think she knows someone is living in here."

"Not possible. I've wiped us from all the local camera feeds, the dock lease is paid up, and we don't use nearly enough power to draw attention."

"All of that is kind of moot if the dockmaster takes a stroll when I'm walking out the door."

"Ugh."

"Yeah, meat space is a real fuckin' nightmare sometimes. We have to leave, Arden, and soon. If we get caught, we're never getting out of prison. If we even make it to prison."

"We aren't going to get caught, and this ship isn't ready to move. The thing was derelict when we took it over, and it's hardly any better now. I'm not even sure if it could take vacuum, let alone a trip to Ordinal."

"Repairs going that well?"

Arden wrinkled their nose. "The circuits are so fried I wouldn't trust it to tell me if it was holding a seal or not. I can solder everything in the damn ship shut and I still wouldn't trust it not to leak atmo. This thing is a pile. There's a reason it was abandoned to dock authority before we moved in. Not to mention, a hauler's not enough to get us where we want to go."

"A hauler is all we got, and I can't stand waiting much longer.' "

The argument wasn't new, but this time around it had a different feel to it—a shape more jagged than all the times they'd circled each other before. Arden counted themself as pretty good at reading expressions—a substantial chunk of netdiving was social engineering, after all—but Nox's moods had always passed by Arden too quickly.

Nox wasn't a stormy man, not exactly. A lot of people would have called him quick-tempered because he was prone to violence, but Nox never squeezed a trigger without a damn good reason. His emotions were more like microbursts, surges in the hormonal tides of his mind that bubbled up to the surface and popped, spent as soon as they appeared.

"What's gone wrong?" Arden asked, because they'd learned a long time ago that trying to guess what was boiling over in Nox's head was a fool's game that got them both burned.

Nox grunted and broke eye contact, a sure sign something was up. "We're not drawing Jules or the woman out. It's not working and we've run out of targets."

Ah, right, the fires. A substantial portion of Arden's net time over the past two years since Jules and Lolla disappeared had been spent trawling through white noise, looking for glimpses of warehouses that resembled the one their team had lifted that wraith from.

They'd spent even more time staking out the likely candidates, hijacking security systems, and stringing a digital net so wide and intricate that the tiniest vibration would draw their attention.

It'd given them nothing until the night before that Icarion planet-buster had escaped Prime's control. That night was seared into Arden's memory. Not because they gave a shit about Icarion's pissing match with Prime, although the tech used in creating *The Light of Berossus* was interesting, but because that night one of their digital wires had been tripped. A woman, all in white, had approached one of the look-alike warehouses on the edge of the Grotta.

Something about that woman set Arden's stomach churning. Nox had agreed. Within an hour, they were at the warehouse. It was empty. So they burned it down to flush the rats out.

And another, and another, and every time one rotted-out husk of a building went up in smoke, Arden felt a piece of their network shrivel and die—their web contracting, shrinking, until soon they'd have nowhere left in the city to watch. Arden knew who she was—Rainier Lavaux, wife of a Keeper—and despite their best efforts, they could not pinpoint her exact location.

"We know where she is," Nox said, dragging Arden back out of their ruminations.

"Who? Rainier Lavaux?"

"No. Jules."

Arden fiddled with their wristpad, absentmindedly bringing up one of the other nets they had spread around the city. This one watched for any mention of them—or Nox—to alert them if the authorities were getting close. Having a data stream pouring into one ear helped them keep focused. Calm.

"We cannot barge onto a Keeper research ship and ask for her back."

"If we could talk to her—"

Arden clenched their jaw. "I told you, even I can't get a tightbeam through that security. It's not just Keeper tech. I've fiddled with that stuff before, thanks to Jules. There're varieties of encryption at that station I haven't even *seen* before, and that's just the outskirts that nosy types like me can see. We can't knock on her door. We can't get a message through. We need another way in, or at the very least more information."

"Flushing that woman out isn't working. If we could get to Ordinal—"

"Which this ship is not capable of—"

They locked gazes. Arden hated this. Hated the arguing. Sometimes they wished they could bump foreheads with Nox and somehow share everything they knew, everything they understood about the greater net and the dangers within it. Nox probably wished he could do the same—that he could force Arden to see all the physical threats they faced.

The trouble was, even with their combined skill sets, all paths currently led to death.

Nox broke eye contact first and reached for his weapon. "Gotta clean this—"

"Wait." Something tickled the back of Arden's mind, something they'd heard in the white noise data stream. Nox put the weapon back down and waited while Arden's attention diverted wholly into the stream, rolling what they'd just listened to backward until…

Audio feed from a shop they no longer frequented. Nothing obvious, not a detective asking about their name or anything like that, but a confluence of two concepts: a nethead, and a gardener.

Arden blinked the color of roses from their eyes.

"Someone's asking after me at Hassan's."

"The fuck?" Nox picked up his weapon again. Arden thought he carried that gun for the same reasons Arden kept the white noise of their net purring into their ear.

"Hold on."

They pulled up a self-made program on their wristpad—all their programs were self-made—and dove into the security cameras in the area, bypassing audio for visual. Hassan was a shady bastard and liked to keep cameras in his shop because he expected everyone he encountered to be as shady as himself. He was probably right.

Cheap as the junk in Hassan's shop was, the cameras were high-end, the best he could afford. It took Arden thirty seconds to punch into them.

They sucked air through their teeth.

"What?" Nox asked.

"You're…not going to like this."

"Ain't a lot I do like."

Arden puffed their cheeks out with a held breath, debating forgetting they'd ever seen anything at all. It'd be no use, Nox knew something had rattled them and wouldn't let it go. He was a hound dog sometimes—shaking a bone until all the useful marrow had bled out.

"This is the person asking after me," Arden said, and turned the wristpad around so Nox could see.

They'd never seen the big man so pale before. The blood drained from his cheeks, stubble sticking out like a threatened porcupine as he sucked his lips in.

"Graham Greeve," Nox said out loud, just to put the name in the air, though they both knew it. They just hadn't spoken it in years.

"Yes," Arden agreed.

The years hadn't been kind to Graham. The last time Arden had seen him, Graham could fill a room with his presence. Now, though his eyes were sharp, Graham had a hunch to him that made him look older than his age. Made him look worn thin.

At twenty-six, Graham had been the oldest of Harlan's crew. In retrospect, that should have set off some alarm bells about the kind of people Harlan liked to manipulate into working for him, but he was dead and it wasn't worth ruminating over. Graham had been young and brilliant and full of ideas that didn't involve dancing to Prime's tune. Nox, nineteen and a fresh runaway from the fleet with the scales ripped from his eyes, had been the most hopeful.

When Graham left the crew for Ilan, for a stable life stepping to Prime's drumbeat, it had damn near broken Nox's heart. They'd had other crew members after that, but then there'd been Jules, and Lolla, and Harlan's crew had settled into a rhythm that lasted until that night at the warehouse.

"What the fuck is he doing crawling around Hassan's?" Nox asked.

"I don't know... Looks like he's getting a fix for that repair bot."

Arden moved to take their wristpad away from him, but Nox snapped out a hand and grabbed their forearm. Normally, Arden would find that kind of intrusion rude in the extreme. Now, well... It was understandable.

"Who's the woman with him?"

"Hold on." Arden opened his facial recognition program and ran it, expecting to have to wait for the results. It came back in microseconds:

Major Sanda Maram Greeve. Stationed, Ada Prime.

"His daughter," Nox said.

"Shit," Arden said.

"Looks like him."

"Yes." Left carefully unsaid: And not at all like Ilan.

"Fuck, his kid's an *adult*," Nox said.

"That's how time works," Arden said. Nox didn't even blink.

"Isn't she...?"

"The one who brought back *The Light of Berossus*? I believe so."

"And she's accused of killing a Keeper," Nox added.

"Yes."

"Sounds familiar."

"Nox..."

"They won't last a day on their own. He used one of your aliases in a location he knows you monitor. He needs help."

"Not our problem."

Nox dropped Arden's arm and slung his weapon back up on his shoulder. "Adjust those dock camera filters for two more, will you? I'll be right back."

"This is real fucking stupid."

Nox stopped one step from the airlock door. About a thousand possible things to say crowded into Arden's brain, threatened to spill past their lips. They should stop him, they really fucking should, because getting Graham Greeve involved in their affairs again was a surefire way to get them all burned down before they ever saw the Ordinal system, let alone saved Jules and Lolla.

Nox's big shoulders rose and fell in a heavy, body-shaking sigh. "I have a plan."

Nox stepped out the door and went to get his ex-boyfriend back.

CHAPTER 11

PRIME STANDARD YEAR 3543

MAKING NEW FRIENDS

As the elevator clanked its way up the building, Sanda unbuckled her prosthetic and tested the weight in her hand. With the microcontroller ripped out, the SynthFlesh on the calf wriggled as she hefted it, the slit that opened to the missing electronics smacking together like too-wet lips. The build was light by design, but there was strength in those titanium bones. It could do some damage if she swung it just right.

"You just got that," Graham said. "Going to break it already?"

"Our tail let us come back to the hotel, which means one of two things. Either they got spooked and bailed—"

"Or there's company waiting for us in the room." Graham punctuated the thought with a heavy sigh.

"I don't have time to get used to walking on this thing before we come to blows, so I better make it useful."

"They probably have guns, Sanda."

"I know," she said, and put the prosthetic back in place, but did not pull the straps taut. "We could leave."

"Could do."

"But you want to see who's in there as badly as I do, don't you?"

"Could let me go in alone," Graham said.

"Could do."

The elevator door swished open and they rolled out. Sanda pointed up to the security cameras in the hallway. They'd been blacked out by paint—a quick and dirty job. Not something the authorities would bother with, and she had a feeling Arden Wyke wouldn't lower themself to such contrivances. If they'd wanted the cameras off, they'd be off. So they were dealing with small-timers, maybe a normal mugging. How refreshing.

Graham raised a brow at her and she shrugged, tipping her chin toward the door. To her surprise, Graham nodded and pulled a sleek, grey-bodied handblaster from the interior of his coat. Sanda was one breath away from taking it from him—she was the one with fleet training, after all—when he tapped the side to show her the biometric lock. Figured.

She swiped her ident over the lock and went in first. Graham could shoot over her head, but she couldn't swing through him. The lights came up. Three SecureSite, still in uniform, were going through their things.

"Excuse me," Sanda said, "but I don't recall extending you an invitation."

All three swung around to look at her. One pulled a handblaster. They had the startled look of kids caught with their hands in the cookie jar, but that lasted only a second. A woman with a shaved head stepped forward, taking control easily in hand. She smiled like a shark. Sanda had an urge to punch her teeth out.

"SecureSite," she said smoothly, holding out her ident long enough for Sanda to get an impression of the badge, but not long enough for her to read the name. "We're here to detain you, Major Greeve, until the fleet arrives to collect you. Where is your father?"

"No you're not," Sanda said, and tilted her head toward the door. "If you were here on official business, you wouldn't have blacked out the cameras. What do you want? I'm tired and you're between me and my bed."

The woman's too-smooth smile faltered, cracked at the edges. "Detective Laguna—"

"Isn't here and didn't authorize this. Try again."

"I told you she wouldn't go down easy," another woman with a shock of pink hair said, cracking her knuckles. "The major comes with a reputation, that's why the bounty's so high."

"Bounty? That's what this is about? Prime won't pay out for my capture once that video is debunked. You'll just get in trouble for roughing up a major. Walk now, and I won't tell on you to Okonkwo."

"You don't know Okonkwo," the bald one said. True enough, but Sanda's brain was too fried to remember who the general of the Atrux fleet was, so she'd gone for the next biggest fish.

She rolled a shoulder. "My brother does. This is not a situation you want to fuck up, friend."

A man wearing a too-crisp uniform—new blood—found his voice. "If the video's fake..."

"It's not," the bald one snapped. "Enough of this. Gag her until the fleet delegate gets here. We'll round up the dad later."

"Gladly." Pink Hair took a step toward Sanda. She stopped dead as Graham stepped up behind Sanda, handblaster leveled at the bald one's head.

"I'm disappointed," he said. "I thought you were more than common toughs."

New Suit fumbled for his weapon, Graham arched a brow, and the bald one cut a hand at him. He froze.

"We're SecureSite. We have the authority to detain you, Mr. Greeve."

"You're not detaining shit," Sanda said. "You're trying to sit on us until the fleet shows up to whisk us away, and surprise, they'll never pay you for your trouble. You're less than civilians to the soldiers of the fleet. You're overstuffed civvies pretending at power."

"Fuck you," Pink Hair said, taking a step that put her, finally, within Sanda's striking distance. She restrained, for now.

"Hold," the bald one said. "Everyone fucking hold on to your asses. The fleet will make good on the bounty."

Sanda snorted. "They won't. I'm fleet, remember? I used to scoop up scum people like you held down until we could show up. They won't even ask your names, let alone your ident numbers to send the credits to. We're leaving. If you know what's good for you, you'll leave before the fleet gets here, too."

"Like hell—" Pink Hair made a grab for the front of Sanda's jumpsuit.

The last fight Sanda had been in was for her life against Lavaux in Bero's cargo bay. She'd thought she was all right. Thought all her previous hand-to-hand experience, and training for the fleet, would deaden the sense of abject terror she'd felt in those few moments when all she could do was scrabble and kick and scream. She'd been wrong.

For the first time in her life, Sanda froze.

Pink Hair grabbed a fist of FitFlex jumpsuit over Sanda's collarbone and yanked, jerking her partway out of the chair. She grabbed the arms of the chair, desperate for purchase, felt the wheels lift, and a white-hot rage surged through her, burning away the fear.

She grabbed the prosthetic and yanked it free, then twisted, giving herself as much room to swing as possible, and slammed it into Pink's side. The woman screeched in pain, and dropped Sanda back into the chair. Sanda wound back and—*crack!*—again in the side, ribs crunching. Pink hit the ground and curled up around herself, groaning, cursing in a language Sanda didn't know.

"You fucking bitch—" the bald one said, starting toward her, but Graham squeezed off a shot and the laser blast came close enough to singe her ear and punched a black-cauterized hole in the wall behind her.

"She said we're leaving," Graham said.

The bald one stepped back, hands up in surrender. A sneer twisted her mouth. "Too late, they're here."

Sanda's heart hammered as she craned her neck around to see what the bald one was looking at, eyes bright with triumph.

Graham flanked Sanda, and in the doorway another man stood. He wasn't tall, not exactly, but something about his build gave the impression of largeness that had nothing to do with height. Sanda had known men like him in the fleet who had tried out for the guardcore and been turned down for being too big, too hard to disguise in the guardcore armor.

But this man wasn't fleet. Bald Hair wouldn't know that, not unless she'd spent a lot of time studying fleet attire. He wore the standard Prime jumpsuit, was strapped up with enough weapons to give a gunship envy, wore scuffed mag boots, and had the same crew cut most people of the fleet favored. The weapons he carried were high-end, modern, and well cared for. But his insignia were missing. If he'd told her he once served in the fleet, she would have believed him. But he wasn't a member now, and now was what mattered.

"Major Greeve?" he asked.

"I am." There wasn't any point in pretending otherwise.

His dark brown eyes narrowed in determination. "Nice to meet you."

Three shots, clean as anything. Bang, bang, bang, and the brains of the SecureSite painted the hotel walls.

"What the fuck," she said.

He holstered the weapon and stepped into the room, expert fingers digging through the pockets of the rapidly cooling bodies.

Graham sighed and pocketed his blaster. "Sanda, allow me to introduce you to Nox."

"You got old," Nox said to Graham without looking up from his looting.

"You haven't changed a bit," Graham said.

"Hold on a fucking minute." Sanda thrust her prosthetic at Nox like a pointing stick, realized it was dripping blood, then grimaced and tried to wipe it clean on the rug. "That wasn't necessary, was it? They were just some local toughs."

"Local toughs with the fleet coming to back them up. You'd have been captured in three minutes." Nox glanced at his wristpad and grimaced.

"Speaking of, we gotta run. Now."

"Where are we going?" Sanda strapped the leg back on.

"A safe house. Arden wants to talk."

CHAPTER 12

PRIME STANDARD YEAR 3543

JUST SOME GROTTA RAT

Everything Jules had learned about Rainier's operation indicated that she should call her over this. That an underling going where she wasn't allowed was a huge violation, that this was big-boss time, and Jules was being actively seditious in not calling it in.

But doing so wouldn't allow her the opportunity to punch Marya on her cute button nose.

Jules's heart hammered in her throat but she wouldn't run, didn't dare let the scientists holed up in the lab catch her panicking by going hell-bent down the hall. She wasn't panicking. She wasn't. The thump-thump in her throat constricted her air until she pushed her breath out through her nose and gasped it back in. Clamp it down. Don't let the wound split raw.

Lolla's stats were always up on her wristpad, a half-opacity window floating off to the left, forever in her digital peripheral vision. There had been no change. Lolla was safe. The elevator wouldn't move fast enough.

She squeezed through the doors before they were all the way open. Down here, where there were no eyes but Rainier's to see her, Jules broke into a sprint. Fear constricted her breath, but her augmented body ignored those needs, pumped her legs like pistons.

Her ident opened the door when she drew in range. Though Rainier had full roam of the station whenever she was on board in person, this room alone was coded to Jules and no other. Marya should not have been able to enter it.

Should not be able to hover above Lolla's clear coffin, her dark hair—crimped from being too long in a helmet—hanging over the side of her face like a curtain. Obscuring everything except the point of her chin and the greedy, grasping stretch of her fingers straining toward the panel inset on the center of the coffin. The panel that controlled everything.

"What the fuck do you think you're doing?" Jules snapped.

Marya jumped, snatching her hand back as if burned. "Who is she?"

Jules narrowed her eyes and stalked toward Marya, who walked backward to keep the distance between them. Jules didn't spend a lot of time looking at herself in the mirror—not these days—but she knew the look that must be on her face now, the molten rage ready to burn everything to the ground at the slightest provocation. She saw that expression reflected not in any mirrored surface, but in the shirking hunch of Marya's shoulders, the wild dash of her gaze from side to side as she instinctively sought an escape route.

"None of your fucking business." Jules kept on advancing, never quite letting Marya get too far, or too close. Too close would end in blood, and as much as Jules wanted that, Rainier would be pissed. Marya circled the coffin.

"She's one of the failed, isn't she?"

Jules said nothing. A tendon in her jaw twitched. She hated that word. It didn't matter that it meant the ascension-agent hadn't taken hold, hadn't transformed the human body into something more, something stronger.

The implication of failure matched nothing Jules felt about Lolla. Lolla was brilliant and quick and shining and didn't fail at a damn thing she touched. If Lolla's coma was anyone's fault, it was Rainier's.

"She is," Marya said. "What is she to you? Sister? Lover? I knew Rainier had to be keeping a test subject around."

"You're leaving."

Marya dug her heels in and stood her ground. "No. This girl is swimming in the stuff. I've waited long enough, Valentine, even you have to admit that. I'm tired of waiting around for Rainier to pull her head out of her ass and decide it's time to dose me with the agent."

"Is this what you want?"

Jules placed her hand on the coffin. The cold, deep and dead as old stone, soaked through her skin and into her heart. "To fall into an endless sleep from which you may never awaken?"

"Rainier picked Liao to get the scientists in line. She'll be able to amplify the correction signal into the agent-altered cells soon enough. The sleep is not endless. And besides, it worked for you."

Jules hated the reminder. Hated that she could, at will, cut out the feeling of that cold glass. Jules pressed her palm down harder, greedy for the aching bite of false winter.

"There is no reason it should have." Jules forced the words out, guilt making her tongue thick. "No fucking reason in all the 'verse the agent let me live and plunged her into this endless nothing. Do you want to roll those dice, Marya? Do you trust our scientists so much?"

She lifted her chin. "I trust Rainier."

"And Rainier wants you to *wait*."

Marya's lips creased with disdain. "She gave it to you and your street rat—"

Jules's fist connected with Marya's jaw. A spray of blood arced, leaving a fine mist across the foot of Lolla's coffin, reaching up to the synthetic sunlight–lamps, falling back down against Marya's sharp cheeks and upturned jaw. Satisfying pain vibrated through Jules's fist.

Marya staggered backward, covering her jaw with both hands, blood dribbling through her fingers from the split in her lip. A primal groan rumbled deep in her throat. Her golden eyes narrowed above the cover of her hands.

"Don't piss off the professional killer," Jules said.

Marya worked her mouth over and spat a glob of blood on the floor. "You're a mistake. A gutter-fuck nothing that tripped into the agent and survived because you had more muscle than brain. Once Rainier can send the correction signal, you're done. Nothing."

"Rainier's not here to protect you, Marya. Get out before I break your other teeth."

Marya sneered, blood staining her teeth yellow-orange. "You're replaceable."

Jules took a step. Marya broke eye contact and huffed, turning her back deliberately before stomping out of the room.

The door shut. Jules sank into a crouch, one hand on Lolla's coffin, the injured hand dangling between her knees, eyes pressed shut so hard a dull throb started up in the back of her head. She'd been feeling that headache a lot lately.

Mistake. That's what she was. From the day she was birthed screaming into life to the day she walked into that rotting warehouse.

A thought—a temptation—nagged at her. Call Nox. Call Arden. Ask for help.

But they could do nothing for her now. Fucking hell, how she needed help, because Marya was right. No matter how often Rainier crowed about Jules being special and how precious Lolla was to them both, she knew it was an act. Something about Jules amused Rainier for the time being, and as soon as she lost her usefulness or entertainment value, she was out.

Jules pressed her palms against both sides of her head to soothe the building ache.

She was no fool. She'd administered the memory rollback often enough to recognize the pain in her brain wasn't stress. Not in this body.

The ascension-agent had changed her, hardened her. Made her flesh and blood something stronger, something new. Of all the aches she could deaden, the headaches would not leave. Could not. A void ached in her memory in concert with that pain, a shapeless reminder of things she'd done that she could never recall. Sometimes, late at night, she'd stay up trying to remember until the pain became too much and she blacked out.

The void only contracted. Not growing smaller—never less—but concentrated. Dense. Until she feared it would collapse her upon herself. Until she was well and truly out of Rainier's claws, it was best to keep Arden and Nox out of the orbit of her self-destruction, because not even she understood what she had become.

Lolla. The only thing holding her together.

She pushed herself to her feet and pulled her sleeve up, covering her palm. Her sleeve smeared Marya's blood across the plex as she scrubbed and scrubbed and scrubbed.

CHAPTER 13

PRIME STANDARD YEAR 3543

ONCE A SPY

Tomas was, in theory, winding down. The Atrux safe house hosted a wide variety of distractions, once one made it through the initial debriefing. VR immersion rooms, analog games, a wide selection of media and literature stored on the local network. Everything was peeled away from the net at large—an excision, cauterized, so that there would be no bleed-over.

He could do whatever he liked for the next few days, so long as whatever he liked didn't involve walking out the door, making calls, or otherwise having any contact with the outside world. So he played pool alone on a patio screened in with a video feed meant to mimic a tropical garden and tried not to crawl out of his skin with anxiety.

"What's the weather today, house?" he asked the local AI, because no one else had bothered talking to him in the last three days. That he knew how long it had been violated his confinement. Clocks didn't load in the safe house, and neither did calendars. In theory, this was a place to decompress after a tough mission, to slough off the petty pressures of the world.

He'd never been good at that. And though he'd never witnessed his colleagues going through the same thing, he suspected none of them were very good at it, either. Being a Nazca didn't come with the luxury of being able to turn off one's internal clock.

"Dome systems are functioning normally," the house said.

Tomas rolled his eyes and lined up another shot on the pocket. "That's not what I meant."

"Weather conditions outside are not relevant to your stay."

He almost scratched his shot. The house was starting to sound remarkably like Bero, answering his questions with deflections. A function of its security protocols, but still unsettling. Maybe he did need to decompress. Somewhere tropical with a real-sand beach. But could he, when he didn't know what had happened to Sanda?

No, of course not, but the thought was nice.

The internal door opened. Tomas made a point of keeping his head down, lining up another shot, while a familiar gait stepped toward him.

"You've always been terrible at this game, I don't know why you insist on playing it."

"Precisely because I am terrible, Sitta."

"Caid."

He cracked off a shot, winced as the one ball careened off the white into the eight and, naturally, deposited that foreboding ball into the pocket. Tomas sighed and leaned back, resting the cue against his shoulder like a rifle. "This is the kind of thing I should be good at."

"Luckily, you have other talents. Shall we?"

He'd given himself enough time to rein himself in. Tomas looked up. Five years had slithered by since he'd last seen Sitta Caid, and he wished it would have been more. Her head came up to his chest, and he suspected she made a point of wearing the flattest-soled shoes she could find. He never saw her in anything with a thicker sole than a mag boot. She didn't need the height. Sitta Caid had a presence that would make kings weep if she but curled her lip in disdain.

"It's been a long time, Caid."

"We expected longer. The Greeve retrieval contained a nontrivial chance of timeline separation."

"Timeline separation?" He chuckled. "Did they make that up just for me?"

She lifted one shoulder, the movement enhanced by the triangular points of her titanium-white blazer. "The Nazca are in the business of quantification, and we required a new line item to assess that retrieval account. It was conceivable that, if the gate was dismantled, you would be beyond the reach of FTL travel. Hence: timeline separation. Simple accounting."

Tomas snorted. "I saw Biran's house. You mined him for every scrap of credit he had."

Not even a shoulder this time. "You disapprove?"

"I make no moral judgment on the Nazca."

It was Caid's turn to snort. "Lavani would be delighted to get such a straight lie out of you."

"Lavani can rot, and I didn't mean the mission, Caid, I meant the three days you've kept me canned up in here. I'm due personal time. That was the deal I made for taking on your mission 'with risk of timeline separation.' "

"Containment is essential after long missions, should any adverse mental or physical health events occur."

"You mean so that you can observe me to see if I'm nervous, or if I try to contact anyone or anyone tries to contact me."

Her smile was slow, and she crossed her arms over her chest, adjusting to better accommodate a slim electronic folder tucked under one armpit. "Yes. I do. You know our dance, Nazca, and you know which steps come next."

He groaned and made a show of stretching out his back. "Another interrogation."

"Debriefing."

"Sure." He racked the cue and gestured toward the door. "After you."

"No. Not the chair." She waved her hand and the viewscreens flipped from pleasant trees and birds to blank, endless black. Tomas suppressed a shudder, recalling Bero's manipulation of the viewscreens to fit his story that the system was dead and the planets rendered to dust. A heady reminder that, in his work, the only input he could believe was what he experienced hands-on.

"Sit." She pointed to a wrought iron bistro table, flanked by two chairs. He pulled one out for her, deferring to his superior, and settled down on his own cushion covered in a print of large, long-dead tropical flowers. She opened the electronic folder and spread it out over the table. He leaned back and kicked one ankle up on his knee. She scowled, for only a second, but it was enough to give him the warm fuzzies.

"Tell me about Sanda Greeve."

"I—what? What about her? I have whole dossiers of pre-op research, and Lavani has my post-mission notes."

Caid sighed in the calculated way of a teacher disappointed with a student, which wasn't entirely wrong. She'd recruited him, trained him. Vouched for him when he'd done stupid things that inevitably gave results. They had a long and storied working relationship, but in his darker moments he was pretty certain it functioned only because of their mutual disdain. Caid believed in the Nazca. Tomas believed in his paycheck.

"Nazca Cepko."

"Tomas."

"Cepko. Lavani has filed a motion for deep interrogation. I am here to assess if that eventuality is required."

His throat went dry. He thought he'd done a pretty good job of dancing around Lavani. He'd damn near given her everything, after all. He'd even alluded to the fact that the Icarions were doing biomechanical research on board Bero, though he'd declined to know anything about the details. That Sanda carried the chip of a dead Keeper with coordinates to an unknown location in her head was the only thing he'd kept back. And he'd kept back a lot more on other mission debriefings without tripping the chair.

"I don't understand. I did not lie to Lavani."

"Of course you did. We all lie in debriefings, do not think you are special in that. We are an agency of spies, lying is an old habit, a tic and an addiction all at once. Oh—don't look so surprised. Even I lie in my debriefings. I have lied to you tonight already. It is a muscle we must flex to keep in fighting form. But on this matter, the Nazca must know: What do you think of Sanda Greeve, really?"

Tomas licked his lips and kept his palms on his knee. "Why didn't you debrief me?"

"Deflection. Interesting, if sloppy; I taught you better than that. Regardless, the answer is simple: I was preparing to be fielded in Ada, and had to be recalled. Passing through that gate undetected at the moment is a tricky matter."

"Fielded in Ada?"

"There was conjecture that you might require help to come home."

Don't react. "Kind of you to look out for me. It's a big universe, easy to get lost in."

"Sanda Greeve. Why did you assist her beyond the mission?"

"I felt the mission would be incomplete if I left her to die."

"You can lie to Lavani, Cepko, but you cannot lie to me." She placed her hands on either side of the blank folder. Her words came rapid-fire. "What is your relationship with Sanda Greeve?"

His heart jumped into his throat. "Personal."

"Did you sleep together?"

"None of your fucking business."

"That's a yes. Do you love her?"

"Fuck, Caid, I don't know. Even if I did, what does it matter? I'll never see her again. Either she gets cleared of the murder of Lavaux and goes back home a hero, or she gets arrested and spaced. Neither option has a lot of room for me."

Caid sighed and leaned back, the faint wrinkles at the corners of her eyes relaxing. "Developing feelings for a target is not unusual, Cepko. You did not need to lie about your relationship."

"You ever think it was private?"

Her expression sharpened. "Everything is our business. That's the point. I needed to assess your emotional stability."

Tomas surged forward and gripped either side of the table. "You're evaluating me for the field? You can't send me back out, Caid, not this soon, not after *that* mission. I need real rest and recovery, not this bullshit safe house. I want to see my mom and grandma. I earned all that."

"I agree with you, but we have an order from a client we cannot refuse."

"Bullshit. No one's big enough to force the Nazca to take a contract."

Caid stayed silent, letting him think it through.

"No. No fucking way. Okonkwo?"

"The Prime Director has requested you, personally. 'The man who *really* found Major Greeve between the stars' were her exact words."

"I'm a finder. I'm not even suited to all missions."

"This is a finding."

"There are others."

"She wants you."

"You're better."

Caid arched one brow. "Maybe. But I have another mission to see to."

"Bigger than one from Okonkwo?"

"Nazca internal affairs."

Tomas scrubbed the sides of his face with both palms. "I need rest."

"You want to run off and make sure your girlfriend is safe. I understand."

He clenched his jaw. "Sanda can handle herself."

"I'm sure she can. Which leaves you plenty of time to find Okonkwo's target. You've met this person, in fact."

Despite himself, that piqued Tomas's interest. "Who is it?"

Caid pressed her palm against the folder, activating it. She'd been ready for this—of course she had. There was no way she'd fail to pivot him into taking on this mission. She'd been spinning him like a top since the moment she'd plucked him off that Elysian refugee ship at ten years old.

He glanced at the photo she pulled up and laughed. "Rainier Lavaux? Keeper Lavaux's widow, are you serious? She lost her husband, and while she didn't strike me as particularly sentimental, she's probably in hiding because she's grieving, worried about blowback from Lavaux's less-than-legal activities, or both. There's no need to bring the Nazca into this."

"Do you recognize this picture?" Caid said, ignoring his outburst. She'd had a lot of practice.

He forced himself to take a second look. Rainier stood at the edge of a garden, wearing a long, dusty blue dress with silver embroidery covering it from bodice to toe in geometrical designs. Her ashen hair had been piled on top of her head, and in her left hand she carried a champagne flute.

"Sanda's welcome home party. I met Rainier there, for a second. She seemed drunk."

"She wasn't. I'm not sure she can get drunk. Look at this."

Caid pushed the image to the corner and pulled up another one of Rainier. This one was in a standard-issue Prime jumpsuit and mag boots, her hair tacked up but sticking out in the way that betrayed a low-g environment. He didn't know the location. The command deck of some ship or another. It looked a little like the *Taso*, but wasn't, so he guessed another of Lavaux's personal fleet.

"Yes. That's still Rainier," he said, puzzled.

"And this."

Another picture. Rainier again, this time in a flowing white dress that would never be useful off-planet, her hair spilling down to her waist. She cut far too fancy a figure for the warehouse she was walking toward. Grotta dirt clung to the hem of her dress.

Another picture. This one of her in a lab coat, buttoned tight over another jumpsuit, her hair cut down into short spikes, a HUD monocle surgically inserted over her left eye.

Caid reached to bring up another but Tomas grabbed her hand to stop her. Something caught in the back of his mind, an itch he couldn't shake. Something wrong. "Wait. Go back, to the white dress."

Caid obliged without comment. He flipped the picture around, pinch-zooming, searching, trying to find the thing that his subconscious had screamed at him was wrong about the image. There, that was it.

"She's not wearing a wristpad here."

"Yes," Caid said, letting him chew things over.

"That's weird, I grant you, but why are you showing me these? She's a lovely woman with a varied life, and I'm sorry her husband was scum. I hope she wasn't scum, too."

"These images were all taken at the same time."

"Excuse me?"

She pressed a button and the images spaced themselves equally, each popping up a time, date, and location stamp. They were exactly the same. The day of Sanda's return party.

"What the fuck," Tomas said.

"Exactly. And, as of this moment, no instances of Rainier Lavaux can be contacted. She's disappeared from the grid. Okonkwo wants you to find her and discern which instance of Rainier Lavaux is the correct one."

"You mean ask her what the fuck is going on."

Caid inclined her head. "I'm confident you'll find a more elegant approach, but yes."

Tomas grunted and dragged the folder closer, flipping through the images again and again. The obvious answer was body doubles. Common enough among the elite, they were used to distract kidnappers, thwart assassination attempts, and make appearances on behalf of the real thing. But those were actors who used masterful makeup skills to shift their already close features into the almost-there category. Makeup wasn't this good. Doubles like this would require plastic surgery.

And what would Rainier want with so many doubles, anyway? Keeper Lavaux had been an important man, politically speaking, but even he didn't have doubles. Tomas would have bet his paycheck she was drunk at that party, but according to Caid that had been an act.

Who was Rainier Lavaux, really?

He drummed his fingers against the table. They had thought Keeper Lavaux was the real threat, but if this was true, if Rainier commanded so many doubles, then maybe they'd been wrong. The Keeper might have been acting on his wife's orders when he put a blade to Sanda's head, and despite Tomas's efforts to frustrate her, Sanda would go for the coordinates Keeper Lavaux had been after the second she was able.

Tomas couldn't contact her. Any attempt to do so would trigger a burn unit from the Nazca, and while he was exemplary at avoiding detection from outside forces, the Nazca had implants hardwired to his body. He wasn't even sure of all they'd put in there when he'd been recruited. He couldn't tell Sanda that Rainier Lavaux was a threat, but now that he knew, he couldn't walk away.

And, if he were being honest with himself, he desperately wanted to know how, and why, Rainier was doing it.

"I'll take the job," he said.

Caid smiled. "I thought you might."

CHAPTER 14

PRIME STANDARD YEAR 3543

TACT IS FOR PEOPLE WITH TIME ON THEIR HANDS

Sanda didn't know Arden Wyke from a hole in the ground, but guessing by the look on their face, they did not, as Nox had insisted, want to talk. In fact, they looked like they'd much rather see the backside of Sanda than listen to anything she had to say. But that doleful stare was nothing compared to the look Arden gave Graham. If the nethead wanted to see Sanda gone, they also wanted to see Graham dead. Not an advantageous position to be negotiating from.

"Hello," she said, friendly as starshine as she rolled her chair into the cargo bay of their beat-up hauler and locked her wheels. She wasn't going anywhere. Too bad Arden had eyes only for Graham.

"You shouldn't have come back," they told him.

"I know," Graham said, shuffling over the threshold right before Nox pulled the airlock shut. "And I'm sorry. But we need your help. I wouldn't ask if there was anyone else I could trust."

"So sure you can trust me?"

"No. But I hope so."

Arden's expression flattened, the only lines on their face leftover creases from having worn a set of net goggles for longer than was healthy. Though Graham had warned her Arden was dangerous—quite possibly the most dangerous person on Atrux—she had a hard time believing that, looking at them now.

They slouched against a bulkhead on the command deck, thin arms crossed, not casually but defensively. Their net goggles sat haphazardly on top of their head. Sanda didn't need to have Tomas's ability to read people to understand that Arden was upset and wishing the cause of their upset—Sanda and Graham—would turn right around and go back out that door.

But somebody wanted them here, and that left Nox.

"You took a big risk, blowing the tops off of those SecureSite," she said, half turning to catch Nox's eye.

The big man didn't look up from the already spotless rifle he was cleaning. "I take a lot of risks, Major. Stepping on ants like SecureSite is nothing in comparison."

There was probably a tactful way to do this. Some trick to get them to tell her what they wanted from her and Graham without quite tipping her hand. A clue in the fact that these two were holed up in a derelict ship—the ship wasn't pulling through the air recyclers, and it had the stale smell of a lived-in place, a too-small apartment. A trick to make this all go her way without ruffling any feathers. Tomas would know what to say. But she wasn't Tomas, and she was getting real tired of playing other people's games.

"What the fuck do you want with us?"

That got Nox's attention. His head jerked up and he looked at her like he was seeing her for the first time.

"You're a major, Greeve, and we need to get to the Ordinal system," Nox said.

"I don't see how my rank helps you out here. Bars on a shoulder aren't enough to make this bucket fly."

"We're in the market for another ship."

Sanda had a sinking suspicion of where this was going. "Let me guess: Credit isn't your problem."

"Credit's a digital figment, hackable as any other," Arden said. "But we can't buy the access we need."

"We need a gunship," Nox elaborated. "They aren't for sale."

"Neither is my daughter's allegiance," Graham cut in.

She didn't need to look to hear the balled-up fists and hard-set scowl. "Dad. Shut up."

Nox chuckled.

"I'm not here to play, Nox," she said. "I've had my fill of games, so I'm going to be clear with you: There is no fucking way in the 'verse I can get you a gunship, and it has nothing to do with my willingness. I don't know if you've been watching the news on this rotting shoebox, but if I roll onto a gunship, they won't hand me a command, they'll throw me in the brig. Or did you forget that it was the fleet coming to collect me when you so kindly introduced yourself?"

"Oh. That." Arden flicked their goggles over their eyes without bothering to find a seat. Most people would have lost their balance immediately as the blue lights around the edges of the goggles blinked on, indicating they were diving into the net. Arden just lost the tense hunch to their shoulders.

"What are they doing?" Sanda asked the world at large.

"Give them a minute," Nox said. He stowed his rifle in a bulkhead panel and pulled out a handblaster, then set to polishing that.

"Is this why you left?" she asked Graham. "Because all your old friends are insane?"

Graham grimaced and stepped to her side, resting a hand on her shoulder. Her bone moved against his palm and she closed her eyes, wishing for a proper weight room to help her get her strength back. A bowl of noodles and a bad attitude would have to fortify her for now.

Arden flipped their goggles up and blinked a few times to clear the net from their eyes. "Done. I scrubbed the edits from that taped-together deepfake mess of you killing Lavaux and pushed it through to the Keepers at Ada, the fleet general there, and a few choice news outlets in case those in authority have a vested interest in keeping you in trouble. You're welcome."

"How the hell...?"

"This is what I do," Arden said, an edge creeping into their voice that hinted at steel beneath. "What I can't do is hack my way onto a gunship. Nox is right. We need a ship with weapons. You need your name cleared. I've helped you, your turn to help us."

"Hold up. Clearing my name wasn't my price, it was what you needed to make what you want work."

Their smile was coy. "I figured you'd catch that, but I had to try."

"First question: Why do you need a gunship in the first place? You must know we're here with Graham's hauler. It could get you anywhere you want to go without the risk of being arrested for your trouble."

"One of our people was taken," Nox said.

Sanda pressed her lips together, thought about how deep she wanted to step into this shitpile, then said, "Jules Valentine."

They didn't have a clue. Sanda saw it in Arden's face the second she said Jules's name. They'd been hopeful. The only circumstance in which they would be hopeful upon hearing Jules's name was if they didn't know what had happened to her and were hoping Sanda did.

Laguna had seriously miscalculated when it came to these two. The detective thought they knew where their ex-partner, the trigger woman, was. That they were hiding her somewhere, that they understood what had happened the day Keeper Nakata died.

"How the fuck?" Nox switched from cleaning the handblaster to pointing it at her in the space of a breath. He was definitely fleet trained.

Sanda held her hands up, palms out, and gave Graham a surreptitious elbow in the ribs before he could make matters worse.

"Detective Laguna showed us the footage. She's hunting you two. I can't imagine why she hasn't found this place yet, but she will. You're roosting here on borrowed time."

"Are you working for Laguna?" Nox's gaze slid off her and landed on Graham. "Is that what this is? Bait us out by asking after Arden, then roll us up in a bow for her?"

"No. Never," Graham's voice rasped.

Sanda didn't know what kind of emotional baggage was hanging between Graham and his old crew, so she needed to make this about her dealing with Arden. She needed to spark Arden's infamous curiosity, because right now they were her only shot to track the coordinates in her head without setting off any alarms.

"I know what it's like to be hunted for killing a Keeper," Sanda said, drawing Nox's attention back to her. "And I'm not here to light you up for that. You're ex-fleet, aren't you, Nox?"

"What's it to you, *Major*? If you're looking for a salute, I got one for you, special-made."

"If you watched that video, then you know a Keeper tried to kill me. I'm not exactly loyal to their cause."

"Your brother's one."

"Yeah. He is. You think I ran all the way from Ada to this shithole of a city to help Laguna find a couple of suspects in the murder of a Keeper because I love my little brother? If I were doing anything for Biran, it'd be staying put in Ada until my name was cleared so he'd have a few less grey hairs. But here I am. What makes a major in the fleet run, Nox? You think of that?"

"I don't fucking care, so long as you get us—"

"Nox," Arden cut in. Their eyes had lost the glazed effect of the net and they straightened, no longer resting their slight weight against the bulkhead. She'd asked the right questions and snagged their curiosity. Now she had to give them a compelling enough reason to help her find those coordinates. Sanda forced herself to meet their gaze, even though it meant looking away from the blaster pointed at her chest.

"Stop looking for a reason to shoot and listen," they said.

Arden moved toward her but stopped halfway across the cargo hold as Graham let out a hard, low sound. They held their hands out, weaponless.

"I looked you up, Major Greeve. You don't run from any damn thing. Everything about your psyche profile says you should be sitting pretty in the Ada Cannery, waiting for your brother and the fleet to clear your name so you can go back to service. So why are you here?"

Sanda had to lie. She didn't want to, but they couldn't know the coordinates she needed Arden to locate came from a chip in the back of her skull. A chip that Icarion had found in the skull of Keeper Kenwick, plucked out, and shoved in her head in a lab on board Bero in a failed attempt to force her to access the chip for them.

Not only could they use it against her, but knowing about a rogue Keeper chip could be enough to get them executed if that information ever came to light. Someone else had to own those coords, and the people these two trusted the least were the Keepers.

"The tattoo, on Keeper Nakata's wrist," she said. Graham's grip tightened on her shoulder. She ignored him. "As soon as I saw it, I knew I had to find you. Keeper Lavaux had the same tattoo."

"So they were a part of the same sick fraternity. So what?" Arden said, but they'd tensed their shoulders again. Good. They'd bought the easy lie. Now it was time for the hard one.

"Before he died, Lavaux was attempting to fly to a set of coordinates I don't recognize. I need to figure out where they are, and I can't do that from any system that might recognize them and flag somebody who's keeping an eye out for them."

Nox grunted. "So he was trying to meet up with a girlfriend, or get some damned takeout, who cares? I'm sorry he tried to kill you but—"

"He was taking Bero. *The Light of Berossus.* Without fleet or Protectorate approval. I interrupted. That's why he attacked me."

Both Arden and Nox froze, shared a long look, but said nothing.

"Where would Keeper Lavaux want to take the biggest weapon in the universe?" she asked.

Arden really, really, wanted the answer to that question. As soon as she'd said it, their eyes took on a glazed look, like they were back in the net, as their mind moved mountains to puzzle out the reason Lavaux would want to do such a thing.

They'd never find the answer, because the question itself was a lie. Sanda got the feeling that was the kind of thing that would, slowly, drive someone like Arden insane with obsession. Her stomach clenched. She hoped the turmoil in her face read as concern about their situation, and not guilt.

"All right," Arden said. "I'll locate your coordinates without setting off any trip wires. But I'll do it from the deck of a gunship."

"Agreed," Sanda said.

CHAPTER 15

PRIME STANDARD YEAR 3543

PEACE BY ANY MEANS

Olver arranged their meeting in a small conference room near enough to the war room that they could press their discussion right up until the last second and not be late for Anford's briefing. Compostable cups of steaming coffee sat in front of each of them, but Olver and Shun were the only ones drinking. Biran's stomach was too busy knotting itself together for him to bother with caffeine. Nerves would keep him alert for now.

Shun said, "I was surprised you requested me here, Speaker. I understand that negotiations with Icarion are fraught, and I will do anything to help, but I hardly see how I can. I teach the academy candidates." She smiled. "As you know."

"There's no finer teacher in Prime," Biran said, "but it's not your educational skills that I asked you here for. We have hit upon a particular sticking point with Icarion that I'm afraid can't be massaged without real trade goods."

"This is not a negotiation, Biran. Speak plainly."

He took a breath. "Icarion wants for materiel. Raw resources, faster trade routes. Peace will falter if their economy cannot be bolstered. The addition of a secondary gate to the Ada system would be a boon not only for us, but for Icarion, and guarantee peace."

"I agree with you completely," Shun said, her warm expression growing guarded. "But as you know, my scouting team and I have not found a suitable secondary dwarf planet we could orbit a gate around. Nor are we the first team to make such a determination."

"Yes, I know that. I've read all your reports"—in the thirty minutes before this meeting, but he wasn't about to reveal that fact—"and I know that you are thorough when it comes to the usual means."

"You would propose unusual means?"

Biran met her gaze steadily. What he was about to say might be viewed as an insult to her work. He did not think Keeper Li Shun was the type to be insulted by him merely asking questions—she was a teacher, after all—but when it came to her work outside the classroom, he had little idea of her feelings.

"I do. I propose scouting the system for an individual asteroid which may be suitable for construction."

She pursed her lips as if she'd tasted something sour. "A tall order. One would have to have a stable orbit, correct mass, be suitably far away from the star's gravity well, and—*and* here's the trick with asteroids—be of even density. The gravitational tug-and-pull of gate and dwarf planet is akin to that of a moon on a smaller planet. Tectonics are created. Geology shifts. What was once a stable rock, after introducing a gate, could break into pieces."

Biran hadn't had much time to prepare for this meeting, he knew only that those things were in fact concerns—they were tested on them during Keeper training—and that Anaia, not being blind to those complications, wouldn't have picked her mark without their consideration.

"This system's asteroid belt is host to several remarkably cohesive masses, is it not? We are heavy on iron here in the Ada system. Maybe the death of a nearby star in our interstellar past seeded Ada with the perfect rocks for such a venture."

Shun hmmed to herself and tapped her fingers on the side of her coffee cup. "Once again, not wrong, but a tall order. Even if I could convince the Protectorate to allocate me the resources to have our AI scour all tracked asteroids within the system—"

"You have two of the Protectorate in this room," Olver cut in gracefully, with a wan smile. "I do not believe such resources will be a problem."

"—Ah, yes." Her attention shifted from the swirl of her coffee to Biran, and a real smile wrinkled the corners of her eyes. "I forget sometimes that some of my more precocious students rise beyond me."

"Only due to your tutelage."

"Pah. You need not flatter me, Speaker, you've already captured my curiosity. If I'm given the resources, I will look into this wild idea of yours, but keep in mind that not every asteroid in this system has been tagged and tracked. It will take a great deal of time to sort through those that we know of, let alone discover and assess those we don't. I hardly think such a thing would be a timely solution to your current problem. Not quickly enough to warrant such an early, urgent meeting." She arched a brow and looked from one man to another as if interrogating mischievous schoolchildren. "Unless...?"

Olver grinned faintly. "Unless we had a location in mind."

Biran winced. Olver caught the movement and waved a placating hand at him. "Come now, Speaker, you didn't think she'd be oblivious to those details, did you?"

"I had hoped..."

Shun tsked at him. "My dear boy, you are an excellent Speaker for the Keepers of Ada, but you were my student, and I know when all my students are hiding something—yes, even you, when you get up in front of those cameras. Don't fret over it, I've kept the secrets of my students longer than you've been alive. What is this asteroid you have in mind?"

A hot flush crept up Biran's collar, but he cleared his throat and pushed on. "I didn't mean to deceive you, I only wanted to keep your nose clean, so to speak."

"To create a clean point of origin for your grand idea. I see. So what poisoned tree did this fruit fall from?"

"Lionetti."

A scuff of a boot against metal sounded outside the door. Biran was on his feet before he could think, ignoring a shout from Olver to sit back down. He yanked the door open and stepped outside, glancing up and down, wondering, belatedly, what *he* would do if there was a fight to deal with. Biran had hit a man only once in his life and didn't feel like repeating the experience.

A guardcore stood partway down the hall, frozen mid-step, and glanced over their shoulder at him, head lifted slightly as if embarrassed to have been caught. Biran let out a slow, relieved breath, nodded to the GC, then moved back inside and shut the door.

"What was that?" Olver demanded.

"Guardcore," Biran said as he took his seat, placing his hands on his knees so that the others wouldn't see them tremble. "Nothing to worry about."

"Not like them to make noise," Shun mused.

"Indeed. Generally, they stay out of these halls and keep to the major entrances."

Biran blinked. "Really? I've had one stationed outside my door all night. I presumed that was normal."

"It's not," Olver said, frowning. "Their methods are their own, naturally, but when the Keepers are locked down inside the Cannery, they spend most of their resources watching all entrances and exits. They're never far, but they don't tend to lurk around doorways."

"There are many of them, and we are a small Cannery. I'm sure they get bored."

"I don't think they can," Shun said. "Get bored, that is. But regardless, you say this information came from Anaia?"

Biran licked his lips and explained, sparsely, how he came across the images. Shun sighed.

"I see. I never thought she... well. It doesn't matter now. I understand your need for discretion. I will make the search for this asteroid look convincing, then we can confirm whether it is a good candidate. All the possibilities for failure haven't changed because Lionetti took a few pictures."

"I understand," Biran said, "but we have to look."

"I agree. And while I'm at it, we might come across other candidates." She rubbed her palms together and grinned tightly. "I'm excited to get to work. Don't let those approvals take too long, Director."

"Wouldn't dream of it."

Olver smiled to Shun, but his gaze was tracking the door.

CHAPTER 16

PRIME STANDARD YEAR 3543

TECHNICALLY A FREE WOMAN

Six days later, Graham pounded on the door to the closet Sanda was calling her room. She threw out an arm to catch herself, cursing at Graham, and the hauler, and anything else that came to mind at the moment.

"Working on my physical therapy, Dad. What is it?"

"Thought you should know the High Protectorate came through. You've been officially cleared of all charges in the death of Lavaux, and it's been determined that *The Light*—"

"Bero."

"—Bero escaped on his own, you didn't set him loose."

"Took them long enough. I wonder how Biran convinced them of the second half."

A pause. "Ask him yourself. Lockdown has been lifted."

Sanda's ass hit the cot in the corner and she spun up her wristpad, glaring impatiently while the Prime logo of a dwarf planet with a Casimir Gate pirouetted around one another to indicate loading.

After the would-be bounty hunters had ruined her evening, she'd kept her wristpad powered down until she could be sure the fleet wouldn't use it to track her down and drag her to a prison cell. Graham's could spoof his location effectively. She'd never had to set hers up for such a thing.

Sanda scowled at the spinning logo. Everything about her was too damn straightforward, too honest and clear. Maybe Arden could set her up with some software to hide her location identifiers, change her ident, whatever was needed. But then, what was really needed?

Maybe being Major Greeve was a big enough lie.

The logo faded away and her welcome programs launched. The normalcy made her chest ache. New message notifications clogged her non-priority folder; crap people with crap motives trying to get in touch with a woman they'd seen on the news.

She hadn't looked at her messages since she'd left Bero for the *Taso*. And now that she saw that number, climbing steadily into the tens of thousands, she found she couldn't quite breathe...

She'd found Biran and Graham and Ilan, gotten her family back. But she hadn't been the only one on that gunship, just the only one Bero had picked up out of the black. Where were the others, her colleagues, her *friends*? Had Raismith made it? Or Pheng?

No. Of course they hadn't. If any of her crew had survived, they would have been paraded out at that welcome party along with her.

How many of those non-priority message requests were the families of her crew, asking what had happened? Wanting to know why Sanda had lived, when the others had not?

A priority CamCast message came in, the red ripples distracting her seconds before she dragged all of those messages into the trash. General Jessa Anford. She'd wanted to talk to Biran, to Ilan, not her boss. She accepted the call anyway.

Anford's face filled the screen, and it took Sanda a beat to recognize her. Her tight hair was streaked with grey, the already dark skin beneath her eyes shaded to a faint rust. The wall over Anford's shoulder was SynthWood in walnut, the very edge of a landscape painting visible in the lower right corner. Anford was at home. Sanda had never considered if the woman slept, let alone did all the other things that came with living in a home.

"Major Greeve," Anford said, voice crisper than her eyes betrayed. "I've been priority casting you for a week. Kind of you to pick up."

Sanda dragged a hand through her hair and stopped short of scratching the back of her neck. "I was in a NutriBath for... a while.

Got spaced, you know. Blood leaked out of my eyeballs. After that, it seemed wise to wait until my name was cleared."

"I do know. Your survival statistics are beginning to rival that of a cockroach."

"Thank...you...?"

Anford grimaced. "Your brother has pulled your ass out of yet another fire, and while I usually find Biran's plays to be useful, let me be clear: I do not think you can perform the duties of a major."

"I..." That hurt more than it had any right to, especially considering she'd been thinking the same thing ever since that title had gotten pinned to her chest. "I'm prepared to undergo training."

She cough-laughed. "Forgive me, Greeve. May I be perfectly frank with you?"

"Please."

"I cannot put you into training. You are a distraction, whether or not you wish to be, and any classroom or training scenario I dropped you into would be severely disrupted in a matter of days, if not hours. Your promotion will stick, because to remove it would cause me more headaches than it's worth, but you will not be performing the duties of a major. You are going to come back to Ada and receive medical care—you look like shit, by the way—and then you will fulfill your role in a ceremonial capacity only."

"You want me to be a mascot?"

"You already are."

Sanda buried her face in her hands and squeezed, rubbing the skin until it felt hot, then took her wristpad hand away and reset the alignment so that Anford could see her face again.

"No, Commander."

One thick brow scythed up her forehead. "Interesting."

"Don't get me wrong, I don't want to be a major any more than you want me to be one. But I will not sit on a mantel and get dusted off for war-related press junkets, either. I'm a gunnery sergeant. Give me a gunship."

"You lost your last one."

"Dios, Anford, you can be a real bitch sometimes."

Her laugh was feather-soft. "So I've been told. But despite the weapon's jaunt into the unknown, Ada is still skirting active war with Icarion. I cannot give you a gunship just so you'll have something to do, and I am not, under any circumstances, sending you into the battle with Icarion. Last fucking thing I need is you getting blown out of the void. I would lose *my* post."

"The Icarion war is over, you're just mopping up." The crease between Anford's brows told Sanda she'd misjudged, that Icarion remained a threat to Ada, but as much as Sanda would love the chance to blow Negassi out of the sky, she didn't want that ship to go after Icarion. "You can spare one ship to save face. The people will love it, I'm sure. The war hero back in the fight, or whatever. Biran can spin it."

"Why do you want this ship, if not to dog Icarion's heels?"

"Lavaux tried to steal Bero—steal the weapon—and he wasn't working alone," she said, using every ounce of control she had to keep her voice even.

Anford's gaze shifted to the side, as if she were checking to be sure the room—her own living room—was empty. "Lavaux was an asshole, but he was a *Keeper.* Consider carefully who he may have been working with."

"I have. And I believe I know the location he was trying to take Bero."

"And you want to take a gunship there to check it out, see if anyone's home."

"Yes."

"You're under my command, Greeve. I could order the coordinates out of you and send a squad specifically to check out the location. It doesn't have to be you."

"You said yourself, you're busy with Icarion. You can't spare anyone, and you have nowhere useful to put me. Give me the ship, and I'll give you the answers to Lavaux's behavior right before he got himself killed."

Anford's face went hard as a stone, smooth as a still lake, betraying not a single sliver of emotion. Sanda's stomach clenched; she held her breath. If Anford was as committed to Prime Inventive as Sanda had been before her capture, this was a stupid gambit. But if Anford saw the cracks—even suspected there may be cracks—in the ranks of the Keepers, then, maybe...

Anford sighed heavily. "You and your fucking brother. You'll have your ship, Greeve. Do me a favor and try not to become a press incident again."

"That's the last thing I want to do."

But Anford wasn't listening, her attention had been drawn down and to the left. The video trembled with the subtle vibrations of her tapping against the wristpad that projected her image.

"There's a gunship in Atrux fresh out of repair. Technically in the command of a local major—not *you*—but even from Ada a general has her pull." Tap, tap, jab. "It was scheduled to release back into Ada for the final push against Icarion, but it's old and I suppose I can spare it. It's a Point ship, like you're used to, but a decade out of date. Points are useless without Wave ships backing them up, so there's some extra incentive for you to keep your guns tucked in. Am I understood? You fire those weapons, and I'll space you myself."

"I've no intention of engaging in combat unless I'm attacked."

"Points *evade* very well, Greeve. I suggest you brush up on those maneuvers, if you've forgotten them. The pilot is AI, and I won't hamstring it for you. It's narrow type, so you won't have a repeat of your experience with *The Light*."

"Bero."

She flicked her gaze up from the tapping, met Sanda's for a beat. "Bero," she repeated, then went back to sending out her orders. "I can't give you a full crew, and if you're simply visiting a location, then you won't need one. I'll give you a weapons master should the guns need maintenance, an engineer for the ship itself, and I assume you don't need a comms specialist?"

Sanda did not want to tell her general she'd lost track of the spy she'd dragged with her through the most sensitive areas of Ada Prime security. "No, I don't."

"Two, then. That's all you're getting. No boarding party, no firing specialists—aside from yourself, I suppose—no navigator aside from the onboard AI. You reach the location Lavaux was trying to take Bero, and you report in immediately. Do not, under any circumstances, engage with what you find there until I allow you to do so. Understood?"

"Yes, sir."

"Excellent. *Gunship-B612* is picking up its crew from Atrux Station as we speak. Where are you?"

"Near the city side of the space elevator here in Atrux."

She arched a brow but didn't ask. "The ship will ping you when it docks. It will be accompanied by a civilian transport shuttle. I expect your father Graham to board that shuttle for return to Ada."

"He won't go."

"He's a civilian. Despite your escapades, we have *rules*, Major. You'd do yourself a service to learn them."

Sanda sighed raggedly. "I know the fucking rules. Knew them better than anyone else before I got canned and *left behind*. My original crew is dead, General, and while that's years old to you, it's only months to me. The wounds of loss are raw, for me and my family. You make Graham go, he'll find a way to get back to me. I know him. It's been two years. He won't let me out of his sight until Ilan's there to take up the slack."

"If he requires counseling—"

"He requires his daughter. And he's more useful to me than you know."

"I cannot put a civilian at risk."

"We're just going to get eyes on a location. You said yourself those guns will never fire."

She pursed her lips. "Very well. But only because I believe Graham Greeve will make my headache worse if I attempt to drag him home."

Sanda grinned. "You're not wrong."

"You have a ship incoming in three hours, Major. Prepare for mission. Anford out."

The screen blacked out. A fugue state gripped Sanda. Now that she had what she'd wanted, all of Anford's protests piled up in the back of her mind, threatened to run down and crush her confidence in an avalanche of fact.

Casual as Anford was, Sanda knew damn well that you didn't make general by rolling over for the petty demands of your subordinates. If

Anford had given her what she wanted, it'd been only because she wanted it, too.

Sanda pushed to her feet, yanked the prosthetic strap tight, and stepped into the derelict ship's tiny cargo hold. Arden, Nox, and Graham had convened around a rickety table, playing a local card game she didn't recognize. All of them, it seemed, had been pretending very hard that they weren't eavesdropping on her conversation. At least the Point ship would have better sound baffling than this bucket.

"Anford has placed a Point-Class ship under my command, *Gunship-B612*, with a skeleton crew —an engineer and a weapons master, AI piloted. It arrives in three hours."

Arden nodded excitedly. "I honestly wasn't sure you could do it. I'll start locating your coords right away."

"No," she said, bracing herself against the doorframe with one hand. She was so damned tired. "Save it for the ship. Right now I need you working on a way to kick all fleet surveillance systems off that gunner."

Nox coughed sharply. "I got a soft spot for a pirate, but you think it's a good idea to steal a ship that's been given to you free and clear?"

"I think a free spaceship's a fucking trap." She looked up at the ceiling of the derelict ship, but she was imagining the halls of a different spaceship altogether.

CHAPTER 17

PRIME STANDARD YEAR 3543

HELLO, GOOD NIGHT

The seventeen lives of Rainier Lavaux spun in random sequence across Tomas's wristpad. He'd spent the time riding up Atrux's space elevator into low planet orbit diving into Nazca archives, ripping them apart for even the tiniest mention of the woman, or any woman at all who could have been her.

He'd barely seen the Nazca shuttle that took him from Atrux, veering away from that hunk of rock for the Casimir Gate that would punch him through to the Ordinal system. He hadn't even checked to see what his new face would be before he got into the MetBath. He'd just made sure his net goggles were tight so he could get on doing his research even as the bath tweaked the small features of his body.

Nose a little broader. Chin narrower. Cheeks sharper. Dimples: gone. Hair: black and short.

Cosmetic tweaks, but enough that he could pass by any who had gotten a good look at Tomas Cepko without turning heads.

By the time he emerged from the MetBath, he had every public detail of Rainier's life committed to memory, and some details that weren't so public. All of them made sense in isolation, tailored to the world in which she lived, a microcosm of a life. The socialite on Ada, the recluse on Rusani, the scientist of Ordinal. And in each system, the common thread: Lavaux's wife, no known associates.

Because someone as variable as Rainier Lavaux could not stand up to the scrutiny of friendship.

"Approaching the station," the shuttle's AI said. "Please prepare for capture."

Glimpsing himself in the shine off a screen made him shiver. The prep for insertion to Icarion's war front had taken years, and his reassignment into collecting Sanda hadn't required a MetBath. The last time he'd looked at a face that wasn't Tomas Cepko's was... Shit. That was math he didn't want to do.

A glance at his wristpad revealed not the lives of Rainier staring back at him, but a blank message box, no ident number typed into the send field.

This wasn't his wristpad. Well, it was, in that he was wearing it and all the trappings of his new identity—name: Leo Novak; age: 38; profession: interstellar communications specialist—were dialed into it, along with his usual vault of Nazca programs obscured behind a lot of security. But it wasn't Cepko's. It didn't have Sanda's ident preprogrammed into its banks.

But he knew it by heart.

Tomas tapped the message box closed. Bad idea. The Nazca were done with Sanda. To keep her safe, he needed things to stay that way.

"Capture," the AI said.

Tomas stumbled as the shuttle shook, snapped up in the clumsy claws of a docking arm. He should have listened to the ship the first time and strapped in. Something about his time with Bero had made him distrust all electronic voices. He had to get over that.

Bracing himself against the wall with one hand, Tomas shuffled along, mag boots clunking, to a jump seat and pulled it down, strapping himself in not entirely too late.

"Shuttle," he said, because this ship didn't have a name outside of a string of letters and numbers used by automated systems, "present local view on the screen, please."

Nazca ships were all distressingly bare-bones, as if the tiniest hint of personality might tip their hand as to their purpose. Tomas had always thought that proclivity was paranoid and, if anything, made their ships more suspicious. Once it dropped him at Janus Station, it would turn back around to take some other spy into or out of a mission.

This shuttle was outfitted with sleeping quarters for four, a single MetBath that could be passed off as a NutriBath upon cursory inspection, a cargo hold, a bathroom, and a kitchen with no actual cooking utensils or ingredients, just cabinets of ready meals. No pilot's deck, no engine room big enough to fit anything larger than repair bots like Grippy. If something broke, and the automatic systems couldn't fix it, he'd have to sit and wait until a pickup caught his distress beacon.

Tomas hated this style of shuttle. They were little more than Ping-Pong balls served back and forth between stations. Teeth-grindingly slow, it'd taken the shuttle a full week to plod along its course to Janus. How the Nazca had gotten the permits to allow such a small ship to pass through the gate into Ordinal, he didn't want to know, because he sincerely doubted there'd been any proper safety checks along the way.

The local feed on the viewscreen helped. Reminded him he'd spent the dicey part of the journey in the MetBath, and he was on his way to landing now.

From this vantage, the primary systems of Prime's seat of power were little more than specks against the black, shaded various temperatures of ambient light. Tomas could ask the ship to show him zoomed-in views, the impressive vistas tourists always wanted when they came to Ordinal for the first time. But he'd seen it all before, and he had grown wary of AIs showing him anything but real views.

But the gate could be viewed in whole, without losing perspective. As the shuttle swung around, Tomas got a good, long look at the silver-black rings. He knew, logically, that the rings were spinning so fast that he couldn't make out their details, that the color and light his eyes registered were already old, a blurred-together mess of positionals always in flux.

But the lights and the metal left the impression of weight behind, of heft. A thick frame outlining the way into the infinite darkness of the paths between the worlds. Tomas watched the spin of the gates, because looking into that empty, light-absorbing blackness in their center made his skin crawl.

An incoming call flashed across the screen. Tomas accepted from his wristpad. A strong-jawed woman in a Prime jumpsuit with a mass of thick brown curls squinted at him. That hair was impractical for space travel, but impressive in its shine. This woman was meticulous, but accustomed to gravity.

"Shuttle, Janus Station is a privately held enclave, and you are unexpected."

Time to be Leo Novak. "Maybe I'm early?"

"We are not expecting any arrivals within the next seventy-two hours."

"Shit. I guess those chuckleheads in HR failed to put the docs through. My name's Leo Novak, I'm from Relay Inc., you see. I work in interstellar communications. Well, I dunno if *work* is the right word. I pretty much *am* interstellar comms at Relay, and a whole lotta other places, too. Flashing my ident to you now."

She accepted the flash without question, such a common mistake, and let Leo Novak's history fill her screen while Tomas Cepko's Trojan horse went to work carving out a backdoor into the station's systems for him. Bero had been clever enough not to accept any data packets he'd tried to send the ship. Tomas almost missed having an equally footed opponent. Almost.

"I see. Impressive CV, Novak, but we weren't expecting you. If you require resupply, a bot will bring out all the provisions you need before we send you off station, but you will not leave that shuttle."

He sucked his teeth and sighed raggedly. "I dunno, ma'am. I know you got to do your job, but so do I, ya know? And I was hired to take a look at some systems your boss there, Lavaux, is trying to get online. Sent me a hefty advance payment for my trouble, too."

Her narrowed eyes widened a touch. It was not public knowledge that the name Lavaux had anything at all to do with Janus Station.

"Lavaux?" she asked, feigning innocent confusion while below the edge of the camera view her fingers tapped away on another screen. The slight movement of her shoulders the only sign she was frantically trying to figure out what the fuck was going on here.

"Yuh. Keeper Lavaux. Don't get a lot of Keepers calling me up, you understand. Memorable guy. I got the work contract here, if you want to see it?"

"*Keeper* Lavaux?" At least she wasn't rattled enough to ask if he wasn't sure he meant Rainier.

"That's the one."

"I... Yes. Send the work order, and please hold on a moment."

The screen went black. Tomas leaned back and closed his eyes, waiting for the panic in Janus Station to run its inevitable course. A message got lost in the chaos after Lavaux's death.

The station was having trouble developing some sort of antenna, his intel was certain of that, and the good Keeper had gone ahead and secured the best man for the job who was privately employable, and therefore unlikely to leak anything back home to Prime. There'd be chunks of money removed from Lavaux's usual clandestine accounts, shuttled into Novak's, and a financial trail was the closest thing to truth the worlds of Prime offered.

Tomas folded his hands across his chest and waited for the story of Leo Novak to sell itself.

"Mr. Novak." The screen flashed back on, and the woman's face was pressed into its neutral mold. "I apologize for making you wait, it seems our communications broke down, but we found you in the system. I've alerted the research staff, and their head of HR is preparing a room for you now. Is there anything you'll need upon docking?"

She meant anti-nausea meds. They weren't something Tomas needed, but a civilian like Novak would. "What's your grav like?"

"Seventy-five percent Earth standard." A model of Janus flashed onto the screen, wiping the woman away. The station was an ice cream cone of habitat rings, the smallest larger than Ada Station had been. This was Ordinal, Tomas reminded himself. Things were not done on small scales here. The top ring lit up.

"You will disembark here, then travel to your quarters on the seventh level." It lit up. "All habitats maintain seventy-five percent Earth standard, except those below the seventh ring. Those will be off-limits to you, anyway."

"Seventy-five's not so bad," he said, wondering what level of gravity he'd need to expect once he reached the lower levels. There'd be specs in the station system, surely. At the very least he'd be able to figure it out from the approximate mass of the hab rings and the speed of their spin. "You got any idea what they're going to have me poking at? Only told me it's an antenna, don't know nothing else."

That quirked a half smile. "No idea, Mr. Novak. That's not my department—which is a phrase you'll have to get used to saying yourself. Everything here is separated by steel walls of nondisclosures. We've got a charter from Prime to go about our work, but it comes with tight lips. Stick to your lane, and you'll be all right."

"Thanks, Miss...?"

"Page. Don't bother remembering it. We won't meet again."

The ship juddered as it was sucked into dock, a flame spectrum of red and orange lights indicating systems cycling to the all clear. "Why's that?"

"Separations, Mr. Novak. I'm not the one handling the scientists."

The airlock flashed green and the door dilated; the viewscreen went blank. Framed in the airlock, a stocky woman in body armor more suited to the front lines than a research station waited. Tomas could see only half her face under the clutter of HUD glasses and the communicator wrapped around her ear. A design bulky enough to mean it wasn't consumer grade, but military, because only soldiers would put up with extra weight for extra security.

"Leo Novak?" she asked in the staccato tones of a woman used to giving orders.

"Most days." He pulled the harness off and stood, stretching as if he'd spent the past few hours cramped up in the jump seat, not getting his face rearranged in a MetBath.

"Better hope you are today," she said, and shot him with a tranq dart.

CHAPTER 18

PRIME STANDARD YEAR 3543

YOUR SHIP, MY SHIP

Three hours wasn't enough time to heal wounds months deep, but Sanda was a soldier at heart, and soldiers were used to putting on a brave face while their bodies and minds were quietly giving up the ghost. She showered as best she could on the hauler, closed the slit in her leg with some FitFoam, and tried to hide the hungry, angular protrusions of her bones under the seamlessness of a jumpsuit. At least her hair was long enough now to cover the scar on the back of her neck. Relying on makeup was nerve-wracking.

Her wristpad flashed with a message from dock authority: Point-Class *Gunship-B612* had arrived on the fleet-controlled side of Atrux's dock and was waiting for her pickup. Sanda licked her lips, checked herself in the mirror.

Majors were almost rarer than generals in the Prime fleet and were certainly less visible. While generals like Anford made public appearances, stood alongside Keeper Protectorates during meetings, and were the face of the fleet to the people, all the majors she'd ever come across had been secretive creatures, moving the cogs of Prime's military with precision and control born out of long years of service. She'd never seen one who didn't let their greys come in, let their wrinkles dig valleys named Responsibility and Experience across their cheeks and forehead. Serious People, the majors of the fleet.

Sanda looked nothing like them. She didn't even look much like a gunnery sergeant these days.

The wristpad flashed at her again. A ship was here without a captain, and the systems that be didn't like that. She swiped to accept the responsibility, then poked her head out the door.

"Ride's here," she shouted.

"I'm—just—hold on a sec!" Arden shouted back. They sat at the card table but had their goggles tugged down, and their fingers were twitching on the arm of the chair with subtle, insistent movements.

Nox appeared out of a side door with a duffel over his shoulder. It clanked. "Ready."

"Got it," Arden said, and pushed the goggles up on their forehead, blinking owlishly.

"I packed your shit." Nox dropped a hand on Arden's shoulder and helped them up.

"Ready," Graham's voice echoed from the pilot's deck, and he ducked down, squeezing through the narrow door with two duffels—Sanda's and his—on his back. Grippy trundled along by his side with the wheelchair strapped to his back. Sanda's chest tightened to see the bot moving under its own power again. She gave it a pat on the head, swept her makeshift crew over with a critical eye, noted about a hundred things that could be changed to make them more convincing, then shrugged. She was Major Greeve. That'd have to be enough.

Her ident credentials got them through the unmanned checkpoints without question. Sanda led the way, and the others trailed behind at a respectful distance, matching their pace to her stuttering step. She was sweating by the time she reached the gunship, but she didn't care. The ship took her breath away faster than exertion could.

Gunship-B612 waited for her against the dock in the firm grip of a mag clamp. She paused to take her in. The others waited.

Her design was as far away from Bero as it was possible to get while maintaining an eye toward limited forward surface area. Crafted to dart between ships, to sew chaos from the front line while Wave ships came up behind to crush any remaining opposition, she was sleek and narrow with a slight flare toward the engines, her paneling painted not in the customary Prime grey and cyan of transport ships and stations, but matted out in a black so dark it drew the light and soaked it up.

Those panels secreted the promise of death. Prime had never been stingy about their weapons. Point ships carried munitions enough to harry a station, to slug an advance wave into the void. Station-busting guns were left to the slower Wave-Class, but a Point did damage hard and fast, and it did it well. Sanda's fingers itched for the trigger.

The spaces for humans carved out in the body of the weapon that was the ship were minimal, and Sanda knew the shape of them already. From front to back: command, common areas, quarters, cargo, weapons, and engines. Not a single space large enough to spin up for grav without turning them into vomit comets. Experiments had been made. They had not been made again.

The exterior airlock cracked open. Out stalked a woman with waves of grey hair corralled into a tightly braided bun, the snug fit of her jumpsuit revealing slabs of muscle on a short frame. She squinted at the open air of the docks as if it were getting ready to play a trick against her, then swiveled her head around and locked Sanda down with that gaze.

"What took you so long?"

Sanda grinned. "That how you greet your superiors?"

"We didn't get slammed in this fixer-upper for being genteel, sir." She snapped off a salute as an afterthought. "Name's Conway, I'll be babysitting your munitions. Knuth!"

A crash echoed from inside the airlock, metal on metal. Conway propped her hands on her hips and rolled her eyes to the heavens. An arm protruded from the airlock, grabbing the aperture, then the narrow torso of a man slung out sideways, a single mag boot clomping along. The other foot was clad in just a sock, with a hole in the toe.

"Bloody boot malfunctioning," Knuth muttered under his breath.

Conway gave him a thump upside the head and he straightened, sighting down Sanda and her entourage. His salute was even sloppier than Conway's.

"Sir," he said, "Knuth, your engineer."

"Who can't even get a mag boot to work..." Conway muttered.

"*Everything* on this bucket is broken," he shot back. They glared daggers at each other.

Sanda cleared her throat. "Is it your opinion that this ship is capable of safe maneuvering?"

"Oh, ship's fine." Knuth scratched his chin. "It's everything in her that's broken."

Conway eyed Grippy, who waited with machine patience at Sanda's feet. "Can that thing make coffee?"

"Grippy cannot," Sanda said.

Conway closed her eyes like all the world was a joke orchestrated against her, and only her. "Di-os," she whispered.

"I can take a look at your coffee machine," Graham said.

Conway perked up immediately. "You're the other Greeve, right? Graham? And those are...?"

"Arden"—Sanda jerked a thumb at them—"communications. And Nox."

Conway's eyes narrowed. "Nox don't look like communications."

"I'm not." Nox brushed past Sanda and pushed through the airlock.

Stepping onto the deck of a gunship filled Sanda with warmth, a sense of purpose tingling from her toes to her scalp, raising the small hairs across her arms and neck. This was what she'd trained for. This was *real*, the realest thing she'd felt in months. Her old ship had been bigger, the deck set to accommodate twenty instead of the twelve chairs suspended from gyroscopes on board this one. But it had that...that smell she missed. The slight tinge of ozone and engine grease.

With Grippy trailing her heels, she approached the captain's seat, pressed her palm against the panel inset on the armrest. It didn't read the palm, those biometrics were too easy to fake, but the ident chip embedded in her wrist. The forward viewscreens lit up, showing local visuals underneath a steady stream of diagnostic data. Sanda's starving gaze ate up the data.

"Welcome, Commander Greeve," the masculine ship said.

Her fine hairs collapsed, the warm feeling in her belly settling into icy dread. The voice wasn't Bero's. This ship wasn't even big enough to house the systems it took to run his software on. And yet...and yet.

"Ship"—she forced her voice to steady—"switch vocalization pack to gender-neutral, Prime Standard accent."

"Is this an acceptable vocalization?" the ship asked in smoother tones.

"Perfect." She cleared her throat. "Thank you."

"Socialisms slow reaction time and are inadvisable for interactions with my class type."

Sanda closed her eyes and let a silent bubble of laughter burst beneath her chest, then fade away. "Yeah. I know. I had the training. Some habits are hard to shake, ship. You got a name?"

"My serial number is—"

"Never mind. Crew, bunk up and prepare for departure in ten. Arden, get me those coords—the way we discussed. Knuth, figure out the name of this ship."

"It doesn't really matter..." Knuth was watching her with a wide, confused stare. Conway looked like she'd swallowed something sour.

"I'm not calling this bucket 'ship' for the next however many days. Get me a name. Get me a location, and get me a solid fucking meal. Clear?"

"Sir," Conway and Knuth chorused.

Arden said, "A hard connection to the ship's processing power will make this faster."

She jabbed a finger at the nav chair. "That seat's empty. Dock in. Run the checks you arranged."

"Where are we going?" Conway asked.

Sanda pursed her lips. "Ordinal. Then? Who the hell knows."

CHAPTER 19

PRIME STANDARD YEAR 3543

QUID PRO NOPE

Anford had been true to her word. She'd locked down the piloting systems of the gunship, allowing it only to maneuver under the direction of a very stubborn AI that was having a hard time understanding that Sanda wanted it to go through the gate into Ordinal, then stay put for a while.

"The space on the Ordinal side of the Atrux–Ordinal gate is reserved for traffic patterns, stopping nearby is not permitted. If you would enter a desired station dock—"

Sanda pressed the heels of her palms into her eyes until she saw stars. "I don't want you to hang out in the traffic, ship. I want you to drift nearby."

"Nearby is not a recognizable—"

"Stop." She clenched her jaw, loosened it with a crack. The viewscreens kept up a steady feed of all the celestial bodies in the neighborhood—Atrux, the orbiting Prime station, the gate to Ordinal, the gate to Ada, and the light-sucking silhouette of the elevator back down to Atrux. Sanda didn't know where the coordinates in her head led to, but she was reasonably certain it was nothing in this neighborhood, and Ordinal had the widest variety of connections. She pressed her comm link to Arden's pad. "Arden, do you have a location yet?"

"Uh...Kind of?"

"I require a yes or a no, and if the answer's no, then you better back that up with an expected timeline. Preferably before I murder this ship."

"We are *on* this ship," Knuth said. She cut him a look and he ducked his head, going back to fiddling with one of the navigation panels on the forward console of the command deck. Not that the navigation panels did anything. They might as well have been bricks strapped to the nose of her ship. *Her ship.* She had to remember that. Remember that this wasn't a symbiotic relationship, not anymore. She commanded the ship and the ship did what it was told. In theory.

"It's just that, uh, can I show you?" Arden twisted in their chair and sent a sideways glance to Knuth at the forward nav and Conway in the weapons seat. Graham had stowed himself in the back somewhere, probably getting messages through to Ilan and Biran—messages she *should* send but couldn't find it in herself to tackle yet—and Nox stood in the back of the deck, his mag boots keeping him firmly in place. He pretended to be deeply involved in whatever was on his wristpad, but Sanda felt his gaze brush her back and, by extension, the forward viewscreens every so often.

Sanda traced a seam along her armrest with one finger, considering.

The second Arden moved the coords from their private wristpad to the ship's navigation system, General Anford would know them. It shouldn't bother her. Anford was her direct commander, a woman Sanda trusted above all others in the fleet.

But every time she thought of those coordinates, she recalled the bite of Lavaux's razor blade on the back of her head. Felt the cameras of *The Light of Berossus* crawl across her skin. Recalled the false view through that ship's cameras, Bero distorting even the very basic input of her senses to keep her isolated. Sweat prickled her skin. Her heartbeat fluttered.

Sanda wanted to trust. Two years ago, she would have handed the coordinates over to Anford without a second thought and wondered only later what had become of them. But Graham had been right: They didn't know who knew what. Couldn't possibly know who to trust. And that included General Anford. Whatever was at those coordinates, whatever secret she had almost died for, she had to see it with her own eyes. Unadulterated. Her heartbeat settled.

The whole point of making a deal with Arden was so that Sanda could get the location of the coords with no one in the 'verse being the wiser. Naturally, as soon as they disabled Anford's surveillance software, she'd be alerted.

Going to those coords without detection meant pirating this ship, and Arden was asking if Conway and Knuth could be trusted. Sanda didn't know either of them well enough to make that call, and the amount of time it would take to get acquainted was far too long. Only one thing to do: roll the dice and see what fell out.

"Conway," she said slowly, "Knuth."

They turned to look at her. "Did Anford brief you on this mission?"

They shared a glance. Conway answered, "Didn't talk to the general. Got a message we were going for a ride to surveil a location, no engagement. That still the case?"

"After a fashion," Sanda said, and tipped her chin up to Arden. "Secure the vessel."

"Understood," they said.

Arden flicked at their wristpad, sending a program through the digital ether to collide with the systems of the ship. An alarm blared, the ship screeching and painting the deck in emergency lights as its intrusion detection systems went off, then wiped out into silence. The forward viewscreen crawled with ant lines of code executing itself.

Conway moved, but Sanda had a stunner out and pointed her way before she'd even finished telling Arden to send the program. Nox had his stunner out, getting a tight bead on Knuth.

Everyone panted. Seconds. It'd been a matter of only seconds.

"What the *fuck*," Knuth said, but Conway was looking at Sanda with the ghost of a smile.

"We've been pirated," Conway said, and chuckled.

Sanda sighed. "I'm tired of being called a pirate."

"And yet," Conway said.

"And yet," Sanda agreed, and didn't back her thumb off of the stunner trigger. "We are still going somewhere, to have a look at something, and not engage in any gunfire if we are very lucky. But I need to make damn sure there are no sniffers in the software of this ship that can pick up the coordinates we are going to. You are welcome to come along, under my command, or I can put you in pods and launch you to the nearest station, where you can tell stories of how you fought bravely to save your ship, but ultimately failed. Your choice."

"Question for you." Conway rested back in her seat. "Is this the right thing that you're doing? I watched all that shit on the news. I got a hard time believing you're stealing this ship for the joyride. Or to work against Prime."

"I don't know. I believe it's the right thing, but I don't *know*."

"Lot of shit I don't know," Conway mused, "but all we can do is try."

"I, uh..." Knuth looked to the stunner pointed at his chest, courtesy of Nox, to Conway, to Sanda, and back again. "Aww hell. They won't let us near the front lines anyway, will they, Cons? You think you can do some good, Major, then I'm with you, too."

Too easy. Sanda wondered which one of them was Anford's plant, if not both, but if Arden controlled the comms, then their presence may tell her more than their absence. Dios, she was thinking like Tomas.

A red ripple broke across her wristpad; Anford calling, priority.

"You have ten seconds to change your minds."

Both shook their heads and settled back into their seats. Sanda and Nox put their weapons down in sequence, and Sanda flicked Anford's call up to the viewscreen.

The general was not at home this time. She stood in the war room of Ada's Cannery, the screens displaying the data involved in the war with Icarion blanked out behind her, but Sanda knew them well enough. Sanda had expected anger, but Anford's expression was mostly blank. Maybe a little tired. She peered down into the camera lens at Sanda, taking stock of the two people she did not recognize on the deck of the ship, and the three she did.

Anford sighed heavily. "Major Greeve, there appears to be something wrong with your gunship's systems. It is no longer phoning home."

"Are we really going to do this dance, General? A systems malfunction wouldn't flash straight to you. You've been spying on me."

"I have been keeping tabs on you, yes. Spying is a strong word. I'm not convinced it's possible for me to *spy* on a subordinate which you, *Major*, are."

"I would rather not do it this way, but I'm not flying out to those coordinates to discover a fleet flotilla has gotten there ahead of me and blown whatever slim element of surprise we have. I know how the fleet works. Whatever Lavaux was running toward, it won't last a second if a flotilla shows up on its doorstep."

"You're making a lot of assumptions, Greeve."

"My instincts have kept me alive against some fucking spectacular odds lately. I will tell you what I find, after I find it. Greeve out."

Her hands were shaking as she tapped the disconnect, Anford's feed wiping away before she parted her lips to get another word out. Silence stretched on the deck.

Arden said, "I think that was treason."

"Definitely treason," Conway added.

"Anford knows I'm working on behalf of Prime. Is it done, Arden? Do you have complete control?"

"Yeeeaahhh..." They drew out the word as they tapped frantically at their wristpad, then nodded to themself. "It's clean. Nothing's broadcasting into or out of this ship without my permission. Uh, I mean, your permission."

"Good. Put up the coords. Let's see what door we're knocking on."

It was just a location. Nothing more. No Pandora's box—there'd be no answer to why the coordinates were buried in her skull from discerning where they were. There probably wouldn't even be a visual. Tomas hadn't recognized the local system indicator, for fuck's sake. Chances of her learning anything of worth from knowing where the path in her head led were slim to none.

Her palms sweat anyway.

"It's nowhere, really," Arden said, oblivious to her inner turmoil as they pushed the coords from their wristpad to the forward viewscreen. Graphic black took over the center panel, indicating that there were no live satellite feeds on the spot. Galactic coordinate lines, bright white with the numbers that'd been pulled out of her head, sparked into life across the black, intersecting in three points over absolutely nothing.

"What is the nearest celestial body?" Sanda asked. There had to be something charted nearby, had to be.

"The system's mostly empty," Arden said, scrolling through a stream of data. "The star hasn't even been named, still has the old serial designation."

"Maybe Lavaux wanted to stick the thing where no one would look," Nox said. "Could be nothing there, and that's why—"

"Oh," Arden said.

"What?" Sanda tried to keep from shouting. Kenwick wouldn't flee to Icarion with dud coordinates in his head.

"There's a Casimir Gate here. Unnamed. It's a dead system, though, not even a dwarf planet nearby to drop a settlement on. Prime must have been real pissed off about that, huge waste of resources."

"What's on the other side of that gate?" Her heart thundered in her throat.

"...Ordinal, it's an Ordinal jump point. But the gate's dead, completely offline."

"I'll get through," she said.

"Hold on a tick," Conway said. "We're along for the ride here, but what is so important about that spot of empty space? Thought we were going to a station, or something like that. The brief indicated a possible hostile settlement."

"That is the location Keeper Lavaux was attempting to take *The Light of Berossus*, without orders, before his death." The lie came easier this time. It was safer for everyone involved if they didn't know the coords were hidden in her head.

Knuth whistled low. "That is some heavy shit."

"I bet there's something there," Conway said, rubbing her hands together. "Bigwig like Lavaux coulda hidden something easily enough. No one could pay much attention to what's going on behind a deadgate."

"I agree," she said. "We need to check it out."

"Aren't you forgetting the *dead* part of deadgate?" Nox said.

Arden's voice shook a little as they said, "I can spin it up."

All gazes swiveled to them. Sanda was peripherally aware that even Nox looked surprised. "That," Sanda said, "is Keeper tech. I respect the hell out of you, Arden, but it's beyond you."

"Not exactly..." Their fingers twitched as if they were typing. "It's already built, I won't mess around with the insides. It just needs to be turned on. A strong enough signal from the outside...I've...thought about it. I can do it."

"You've thought about it in the two minutes since we've discovered it?"

Their grin was wry. "I've figured out tougher things in shorter time."

"Now that's true," Nox said.

"Who the fuck *are* you?" Conway demanded.

"Their name is Arden," Sanda cut in, "and you get to sit back and be real grateful they're on our side."

"Aren't you forgetting something?" Nox asked. "We agreed Arden would get you the location of those coordinates on a system detached from surveillance. That's done. Next move is ours."

"I agreed to get you on a gunship and take you on a ride to Ordinal," Sanda shot back. She spread her arms in a welcoming gesture. "Welcome aboard. Promise fulfilled. I'm going through that fucking gate."

"Don't make me shoot you, Greeve."

"That would not go well for you." Graham stepped up behind Nox, a blaster leveled at the big man's back in a grip tucked down tight by his hips. Sanda was still having a hard time getting her mind around how natural that weapon looked in her dad's hands.

Nox turned, slowly, to face Graham, keeping his hands up where Graham could see them. "Come all this way to shoot me again?"

"That's my daughter. I will reduce you to atoms before I let you harm her."

"Dad," Sanda said, channeling the withering force of a child exasperated with their parent. "No one's shooting anyone on this ship, because I will *not* have holes in my new bulkheads."

Knuth giggled, softly. "Sorry," he said. "Not...not great in tense situations."

"Remind me to check into why you two aren't allowed on the front lines later. What, exactly, do you want, Nox?"

"We want Jules back. She's in Ordinal, on a private station."

"I feel for you," Sanda said, "but we got Keepers keeping secrets from Keepers here. Everything could be at stake. Everything."

"It's not just Jules," Nox said.

Arden scowled. "We don't know—"

"Who else?" Sanda asked.

Nox scratched the side of his chin. "Before he died, Harlan told Jules to find Lolla. Jules didn't exactly share her plans with us, but we believe she left to find the kid. It's possible she's found her and is in a situation that requires her to break contact with us for their safety. We don't really know."

"I'll spin your gate," Arden said, "if you help us get them back."

"I don't need you."

"If you're thinking of asking your brother for help, that's a stupid move. He'd probably help you—I don't know the guy—but they'd kill him for it. Yank the chip right out of his skull. I'm your best bet, and I want to help, but we need to know Jules is okay first. We need to find her, and hopefully Lolla in the process."

Sanda winced and touched the back of her head, where her chip was hidden, then jerked her hand away. Arden was right. She couldn't risk that fate for Biran, not the very fate she was running from herself, and she couldn't spin the gate on her own.

"What's the deal with this station?" she asked.

Arden grinned wide enough to swallow a world. "It's fucking weird, is what it is. Look." They flicked something up from their wristpad—they kept that data close to hand—and the blackness of Sanda's coords was replaced with a pyramidal space station. "This is Janus Station, in the Ordinal system. It's privately held, supposedly they do research in civilian communications tech, but their security is tight. I... I can't get access to the cameras remotely. I can't get access to *anything* remotely. Do you know how weird that is?"

"I'm getting a pretty clear picture."

"I caught a sighting of Jules moving from a shuttle into a transfer tube on that station. I've had every damn camera in the area keeping track of it since then, but she hasn't stepped off and I can't get eyes inside. I need to get in. I've been working on a Trojan, but I've gotta be inside their walls to deploy it. Then we can find her." Their fingers curled into claws against their wristpad, their mouth smeared into a near snarl as they stared down that station.

It's killing them, Sanda thought. Not being able to *know*. Arden was not the kind of person used to lacking information.

"You want me to use a gunship to force your way into a private, civilian research station? Dios, Anford would send every damned gun in the system after us, you know that. We'd go from tolerable nuisance to rogue to be put down in a heartbeat."

"Yeah," Nox said, "about that. It's not really the gunship we wanted. I mean, it lends you some legitimacy, but. Uh..."

Arden picked up the thread. "This station's research continues on the forbearance of the Keepers. They have a charter and everything, which is why their security is so tight. But being on the Keepers' leash means they're subject to fleet inspection."

Sanda blinked. "You didn't want the gunship. You wanted a major."

INTERLUDE

PRIME STANDARD YEAR 0002

BEGINNING OF THE CORP WARS

Alexandra Halston killed the first assassin who came for her with her own hands, and that blood fertilized the ground upon which a war would grow.

The warning had come early in the morning. Lex had been awake for three hours before a simulated dawn painted the windows of her office in hab alpha with rosy light. The blush of morning had brought with it a ripple in her information network, an uptick in the threat level.

Though Lex lived on a station in orbit around Tau Ceti-F—named simply Prime Station, for it was the first—she was not deaf to the murmurings of Earth. Threats came in daily, and her security team handled them with the same aplomb they had done back in that old gravity well, but this threat did not come to her team. It came to her, for she was the only one who would recognize the inherent deadliness.

Braxton Hues, CEO of Micromatics, has filed a proposal to build a space elevator near the northern coast of Australia.

Banal, boring. The frustrated CEO of another private space corporation flexing his muscles, trying to claim some piece of the stars. One could even claim it was a waste of resources, as Prime Inventive charged so little to make use of their elevators.

But Braxton was no fool, and there was one thing Lex would not allow her elevators to lift into the black—weapons.

Prime Inventive had their own means of defense. They employed nearly a full fleet stationed on both the Earth and Tau Ceti sides of the gate, and a private army of bodyguards to keep the chipped Keepers safe. But their weapons were developed and built off-planet, in the very station Lex lived on now. The secrets of their construction were held almost as closely as that of the gates.

Lex had found early on that fear of the unknown was often enough to keep humanity in check.

She could think of only one reason Braxton Hues would build another elevator, and that was to make a deal with the governments of Earth to send their weapons after Prime Inventive. But Lex had told the powers of Earth two very, very good reasons not to bother coming after her.

The first: They knew nothing of the gate. Accidental destruction of gate technology during a dragged-out battle could cause eradication of all life in the solar system.

The second: Alexandra Halston held a deadman's switch over the construction data. If she were to die, or believe a Keeper compromised, she could send out a signal through an elaborate relay system, frying the chips and the minds of the Keepers who carried them.

And so, when Lex read the implicit threat in Braxton's actions, she considered these facts, and wondered: Did her would-be assassin have a way to take her down without triggering the deadman's switch? Or did, as she suspected, the assassin know her final secret? The self-destruct switch on Keeper chips was not tied to her life, for she would not risk the accidental destruction of her data. For the chips to fry, Lex herself must initialize the process.

She removed a knife from the top drawer of her desk. She would wait and ask the would-be assassin herself.

CHAPTER 20

PRIME STANDARD YEAR 3543

STILL DON'T WANT TO BE A MAJOR

"You asshole," Graham hissed, low and soft, to Nox.

"Back atcha," Nox said without bothering to look his way. "You have the authority to make that inspection, Major Greeve."

The station filled the screen, a languidly spinning top, its class designation and various vital statistics spooling by alongside. She should drop them at the nearest station and burn hard for the deadgate.

"That," she said, pointing at the station, "is a trap. You know that, don't you? If what you're saying is true, and Arden's bag of tricks couldn't get inside, then this piece of footage you found of Jules boarding a shuttle to Janus is a thread you're meant to pull on."

"It ain't the only bait we've taken," Nox said, "but the trap hasn't closed on us yet."

Sanda's eyes narrowed. "What's that supposed to mean?"

"You got a good look at Laguna's files, but you didn't ask us about the arsons," Nox said.

Sanda shared a wary glance with Graham, who only shrugged in response. Knuth and Conway looked like their eyes were about to get stuck wide open. She couldn't blame them—she'd asked them to come along for the ride with her against Anford's orders on, apparently, incomplete information.

"You two want my help, I need all your cards on the table."

"Show her," Nox said.

Arden began typing. "We don't know for sure if she has anything to do with this."

"Who's 'she'?" Sanda asked.

"Show her," Nox said.

"Harlan, our old boss, got killed after Jules, Nox, and Lolla stole a crate of wraith from a warehouse out in the Grotta," Arden explained while they typed, for the benefit of Conway and Knuth.

"It wasn't just wraith," Nox cut in.

"I'm *getting* to that. When they got into the warehouse, they stumbled across a lab. They tripped an alarm, but there was no one around and SecureSite doesn't haul ass to get out to the Grotta, especially the fringes. So Jules took a look around while Lolla worked over the door—correct me if any of this is wrong, Nox?"

He shook his head.

Arden continued, "Okay. We're uncertain what happened next. Jules went off on her own, but we know she stole three tablets. Harlan took two, she kept one and brought it to me to break the encryption. That night, while she's with me and Nox is out... doing Nox things..."

Nox cleared his throat and looked down.

"*Somebody* hit the hideout, killed Harlan, and took Lolla. Nox and Jules came to get me once they realized, and we were all ambushed by guardcore."

"Excuse me," Sanda said, "fucking *guardcore*? Are you sure about that? The armor can be faked."

"Their tactics can't," Nox said.

Conway was watching them, pale-faced. Graham kept his gaze on Nox, searching for something Sanda couldn't quite put her finger on.

She wondered what it would be like for him, listening to this. Wondered what he must feel, knowing he hadn't been there to help his old crew when death came calling.

"We're sure," Arden said, breathing deeply, "because of what happened next. We got out, but there was this woman over the speakers in the apartments taunting us the whole time. I'd..." They shook their head and rubbed their cheeks hard with both palms.

"It wasn't your fault," Nox said.

Arden cut him a glare and gathered themself. "I'd told Jules, before shit went down, that I had a buyer for the data on her tablet. Someone by the name Silverfang had been trolling particular channels, looking for shit on the Keepers. See, the tablet Jules brought me was secured to a degree I only see tied up with Keeper tech."

Sanda squeezed the arms of her chair hard to keep from scratching the back of her head. "Bold thing to be trolling in the open for."

"That's what I thought. Most of the usual sellers thought she was too forward, either a fake or a plant, but in the context of the guardcore coming for us I thought maybe she was legit, or at least knew something."

"Keeper Nakata," Sanda said.

Arden nodded. "Yes. Silverfang was Nakata. She wasted no time in attacking once Jules proved reluctant to hand over the data."

"So Jules killed the Keeper."

"In self-defense," Arden said.

Sanda gave them a halfhearted smile. "I can relate."

"Right. Right. We went into hiding, but I think we all knew it wouldn't last, I mean...You don't fuck with the Keepers. The next morning Jules was gone, wiped off the grid in a way I couldn't track, and the warehouse where we found the lab had burned down."

"So the woman over the speakers was Nakata?"

"No." They hesitated with a finger poised above their wristpad. "A couple months ago, we found another warehouse exactly like the first. High-tech lab hidden in the shell of a rotted-out husk. We watched it for a while. I had every damn camera and mic in a five-kilometer radius jumping to my command, but we only got this." They flicked up the image.

Sanda leaned forward, as if getting closer would somehow add clarity. The image was dark, taken at night when the streetlights were out. She'd never been on a street at night with no lighting. The camera had been pointed at a loading door, a half-crumbled road leading the way up to a sheet of rusting metal.

A figure walked down the road. The person wore a long, white gown, their equally pale hair curled into ringlets so dramatic Sanda had only ever seen their like in CamCasts. They were wire-thin and wore sandals with spiked heels so sharp she wondered how they didn't drop through every crack in the road. Something about them was just... wrong. Then she noticed the lack of wristpad.

"Who are they?" she asked.

Arden shook their head. "Keep watching. You might recognize her, but it took me a long time to track her down." They typed, and the woman began to walk in stuttering fits that didn't completely mask the sway to her back and hips. "There was a huge amount of interference with all surveillance systems when she appeared. That's all we got. We waited weeks for her to come back, scoped out other warehouses like this one in the meantime, but she never did."

"The arsons were you sending up a signal flare."

Nox nodded. "We couldn't contact her directly, but we wanted her to know we knew. We were watching. When we got footage of Jules boarding a shuttle for Janus, we ramped up our efforts because we knew we weren't getting on that station without help. We were trying to piss her off by hitting her warehouses, draw her out."

"You wanted to be taken?"

Arden sighed. "If that was the only way, yes."

Something tickled at the back of Sanda's memory. "Play that again for me, please. Loop it."

Arden did as she asked.

She leaned forward, staring, burning the lines of that woman into her mind, the easy way she moved—despite the distortion—as if all the world were her plaything. She reminded her of Lavaux, in a way. That practiced manner of insouciance, but that wasn't the right memory. It was close, but... The woman's head turned enough to see the outline of her nose and lips, and a jolt of recognition shot through Sanda.

"I know her," she said. "That's Rainier Lavaux. Keeper Lavaux's widow."

The deck fell silent as, over and over again, the crew watched Rainier Lavaux approach the warehouse in glitching, stuttering frames.

"Turn it off," Sanda said.

Arden wiped the screen clear.

"A Keeper's wife," Conway said, and shook her head. "You all are in it up to your necks."

Sanda snort-laughed. "So are you, though you're welcome to hop off at the next station and pretend we've never met."

"Not a chance. Just because they won't let me on the front lines doesn't mean I don't want to be in the mess."

Sanda closed her eyes, considering, but couldn't shake the phantom image of Rainier from behind her eyelids. Two dead Keepers, and Rainier somehow the bridge between them. That she had married Lavaux made her his ally, more than likely, but Nakata, and the warehouses? What was she doing on Atrux?

"Anford will eventually find out if I throw my weight around at Janus," Sanda said, almost to herself. "She's humoring me with the coordinates, but she won't stand for me bullying my way onto a civilian research station."

Nox said, his voice soft, "We can't force you to do this, Major. But we can't get them back without you, either."

It wasn't the pain Sanda remembered, just then. Wasn't the air boiling its way out of her body as the vacuum had closed around her, wasn't the sting of Lavaux's knife on the back of her neck—wasn't even that first strike, when her leg had gone out from under her and the stunner had wracked her body.

What Sanda remembered then was how smug Lavaux had looked. How sure of himself that things would shake out in his favor. He had been a Keeper. A Keeper's word was inviolable, no matter how many people he destroyed to achieve his goals. And now two women were in the clutches of that man's wife.

Sanda recalled Rainier's party-perfect smile, the too-bright laugh of the woman who'd pretended at being a harmless socialite dangling from Lavaux's arm. Stupid of Sanda to assume Rainier wasn't playing her own game. Even stupider of her to walk away now, dog-headedly pushing for the coordinates, when she had a chance to hold Rainier Lavaux's feet to the fire.

She could tell herself she was doing this to be noble, to save the young women and put to rights a crime that had been done against them, but she didn't bother. She'd made a choice when she landed

Graham's hauler on Atrux. Made a choice to find answers for what had happened to her, for what had happened to Bero, and she had a sinking suspicion that Rainier Lavaux was uniquely positioned to give her answers.

And if a part of her maybe wanted a chance for revenge against a Lavaux, well then... The desire wasn't inconvenient at the moment.

"Let's go get your friends back," she said.

CHAPTER 21

PRIME STANDARD YEAR 3543

WELCOME TO THE TEAM. DON'T TOUCH ANYTHING.

"Novak," a woman said.

Consciousness ebbed and flowed, tugging against Tomas's mind. Somewhere deep in the neural circuitry of his brain, a war was being waged against the sedative. He was aware, in a vague way, that he should be able to help his brain out. His brain *was* him, after all, and if he could just... if he just...

"Novak." The woman again, this time irritated. Insistent.

Pain flashed through him, a hot spot of activity somewhere near his face.

"Push the upper." Words filtered through the haze, dribbled down to him in the dark of nothingness. He wanted to tell them not to bother, that he was fine here. In the dark of his mind, no one wanted anything from him. There was no guillotine blade of failure hanging above his neck.

Fire raced up his arm and set his neurons alight.

Tomas jerked upright, slammed his chest into a leather strap, and coughed violently, spitting blood from—from what? A busted lip? He dropped back, the hard bed of a hospital gurney knocking the air out of him all over again. Cough, jerk, repeat.

"I thought this shit was safe?" the woman asked.

"It is, it is. Every so often there's an outlier—"

Someone snapped their fingers in front of his eyes. "Novak. Can you hear me?"

Blearily, he nodded.

"See? He's back now."

Tomas blinked shadows from his eyes, struggled to focus through blurred masses of color. One of those masses tickled the back of his memory, which was bad because he wasn't supposed to recognize anyone on this mission aside from Rainier. The thought pumped adrenaline through him, flight or fight kicking in, but for Tomas that biological divide was multifaceted and he usually fell into the not-as-catchy category of wait-and-see.

The woman was hauntingly familiar. He knew her, he knew her... Oh. Oh shit. Valentine.

"Mr. Novak, my name is Jules Valentine. Do you remember where you are right now?"

He pretended to rasp on air to give himself time to think, letting his hand tremble when she passed him a thin paper cup topped up with ice and water. He drank, slowly, letting his body shudder and his voice crack.

This was the woman last seen with a dead Keeper at her feet. Nothing in his research had indicated she'd have anything to do with Rainier Lavaux, but here she was, and that wasn't going to be a coincidence, was it? He could almost hear Caid telling him: *Priorities have shifted, auxiliary mission activated; discover the reason this Grotta kid killed a Keeper.*

But she didn't look like a Grotta kid, not now. Her face was younger than the eyes it held, though that wasn't unusual in the worlds of Prime Inventive, but the experience hidden there was the only clue she'd had some other life before the neatly tailored slacks that tapered to her ankles, and the too-expensive synth leather jacket. When she moved, the faint scent of tea tinged the air, not the usual bouquet of the Grotta.

"Sorry," he said, rubbing his throat with an embarrassed smile. Contrition got people to like you faster than kindness. Especially people like Jules. It'd worked on Sanda, too. The thought tripped him. He cleared his throat and pressed on. "Don't know what hit me."

"Her name is Lt. Davis, and she was doing her job." Jules said the "doing-her-job" bit like she said it often, like it'd become a kind of mantra. "Outsiders don't get to see how the entry systems work."

"I'm an insider now, though, aren't I?"

Her smile was wry. "We'll see. There are some questions about how you washed up on our doorstep."

"Keeper Lavaux—"

She arched an eyebrow. "Specifics."

He coughed and waggled his head, taking another sip of water. "Keeper Lavaux, 'fraid I don't know his first and middle—never cared much for Keeper business, you understand—hired me on to work on some kind of antenna relay. Said his people were having trouble, and I thought that was odd because, well..." He waved an abstract hand and dropped his voice to a conspiratorial whisper. "*Keepers*, you know? Don't hire civvies, got their own talent pool and we're the muck on the bottom of that pond. Begging your pardon."

"An antenna," she mused, crossing her arms over her chest, high and tight. The clothes may say station elite, but Grotta body language was hard to shake.

"That's not right?"

"It's not wrong," she said. Tomas considered that the Nazca may have missed out in failing to locate and hire Jules Valentine. She deflected as easily as breathing. "This is a civilian research station, existing under the forbearance of a charter from Prime."

"Okay," he said. She trotted out those words like they were new additions to her vocabulary, and he didn't want to rub her the wrong way by forcing her to elaborate on a system she might not understand. "So whatcha all doing out here? Is there something for me to fix, or what?"

Her hands went to her hips, skimmed off them as if she'd expected something else to be there—a weapon?—and found their way into her pockets. "Yeah. We're working on amping up the signals that get pushed through the gates."

She watched him very, very carefully as that sank in. The relays on the gates were not civilian science. Though their construction wasn't secret enough to hide in Keeper chips, they were Keeper made and that was that. Anything touching the Casimir Gates was strictly off-limits. The Nazca had gleaned that this station was working on communications equipment based on the supplies it had ordered in, which was good enough for Tomas to work with. He was a comms man at heart, variations on that cover story always came easily to him. They'd missed that it had to do with the gates.

He licked his lips, and used this identity's filler word, hoping she'd draw in the blanks. "Okay..."

"They've had some trouble getting the relays on the gates to talk to their amplifiers."

"Okay."

She scowled. "Didn't Lavaux tell you any of this?"

He lifted his hands in a helpless shrug. "Sorry, Ms. Valentine. I don't ask questions much when Keepers tell me to do things."

That got a smirk out of her. "Fair. Look, are you stable enough to go for a stroll?"

He undid the strap across his chest and sat up, grimacing as the sedative lurking in his system made his gorge start to rise. He swallowed the bile down and nodded. "Good enough."

She offered him a cold, dry hand and he took it, leaning on it harder than he'd meant to as he shuffled to his feet. They were in a small, grey room with storage panels and offline screens set in the walls. Not exactly a medical facility, save for the stretcher he'd woken up on. He patted his pockets down real quick, checking to be sure everything was there—not that any of it was sensitive, it was just the kind of move expected of a man like Leo Novak—then followed her into the hall.

"We're pretty bare-bones on the staffing here," she explained as she walked at a pace fast enough to make his drug-addled body breathe harder. "The security measures Prime asks of us are intense, and we don't dare fuck with them. I'm surprised Lavaux got you through so quickly."

Tomas shrugged. "Keeper privileges, I'm sure."

His mind raced as she led him through the halls of the station. It was a twisty place, mazelike in its layout, and unusual for that. Most of the stations Tomas had spent any significant amount of time on were massive, airy things, with high ceilings and vaulted atriums designed to mimic the skies and light of old Earth, insomuch as the people of Prime remembered what that ruined planet was like.

No matter how far humanity ventured from its cradle, they craved light in the sun's range, air that moved on atmospheric currents, and green leaves to soak up the light as surely as they did. A lot of experiments had been done to the contrary. They were in space, after all, and with the endless supply of building materials Prime Inventive commanded, any structure was possible in a vacuum. But the people hadn't liked those—had rejected moonlike spheres and Escheresque tunnels. The species liked its light, even if it was simulated and the viewscreen windows didn't show anywhere real.

He got the distinct feeling that this station, with its low ceilings and tight halls and dim light, had not been made with humanity's comfort in mind.

"We pulled your stuff off the shuttle and put it in a room not far from here. Your wristpad will guide you, we already synced it to the station. You cannot control the climate in your room, the whole station is controlled at once, so I hope you packed some sweaters."

"Who built this place?" he asked, dancing too close to the line, possibly, but it was an honest enough question for anyone. Obscuring curiosity about perfectly normal things could tip your hand. Caid had taught him that, and it was a lesson he put to good use on Bero.

Jules stopped with her hand hovering over an entry pad. "One of Lavaux's companies retrofitted it to our purposes. This is a private enterprise, but we have the Keepers' blessing."

She could not stop emphasizing that everything they were doing here was under the watchful eye of Prime. That, even though messing with gate tech was decidedly Keeper territory, they had permission, so it was all right. Tomas didn't buy that for a second. Leo Novak wouldn't have, either.

"Begging your pardon," he said, letting her hear his reluctance. "But why would the Keepers approve something like this? Don't seem... usual."

"What we are trying to do here is not usual." She pressed her palm against the pad and it flashed green, the door dilating.

Tomas swallowed a lump. A mirror image of Bero's lab waited beyond that door, minus the pillar in the center where Sanda had found Kenwick's head. There weren't a lot of ways to lay out a lab, but this symmetry, this proclivity to place Velcro strips on the edges of the tables *just so* to receive and hold tablets in case of low-g. This kind of synchronicity wasn't a coincidence.

Bero was an Icarion ship.

Janus was a Prime station.

Tomas knew what Prime labs looked like. Knew what most civilian labs looked like, too. This wasn't it. Wasn't either. But he hadn't gotten close enough to Icarion to say for sure if this lab—and by extension Bero's—had been Icarion, or something else.

"You all right, Novak?"

Jules waited inside the door, her hands shoved in her pockets and a fluffy eyebrow rucked up high. None of this was right.

It should have terrified him. Instead, he had to suppress a smile as his heart rate kicked up with excitement. Whatever was going on here was new. To him, and to the Nazca. Such a thing hadn't happened in... Jules squinted at him.

"Fine," he said, and let out a nervous laugh as he dragged a hand through his hair. "Got a little woozy from the... I don't know, to be honest. The size-differential, I suppose. Maybe the drugs. Probably both."

"Probably," she said, and pursed her lips in annoyance as she glared up at the ceiling, toward a corner. Tomas had seen Sanda make a similar face at Bero. "I'll make sure you get proper rest after you learn where to grab food and approved supplies. But right now, I want you to meet the team you'll be assisting."

"Sure," he said, easy as could be, while his excitement shifted to skin-freezing dread.

Tomas followed along, matching her pace with an easy stroll, shaking hands and matching names to faces with his retinal implant, shoving that information into his wristpad to dig up and study later.

Jules hadn't just mirrored an old memory of his when she'd cast her eyes to the corner of the room. That memory had bubbled up because it was damn near exact. The same posture, the same stubborn head tilt, the same... knowing, as she'd stared into the corner of the room. Jules had been checking in with the station's cameras, the same way Sanda always had on Bero. As if there was more than a security system monitoring the station.

It'd just been him and Jules in that room, when he'd woken up from the sedative. So who had she been talking to?

CHAPTER 22

PRIME STANDARD YEAR 3543

A DEAD FRIEND'S SWITCH

One of Rainier was coming to Janus Station. Jules saw her less and less in person, contacting her only through her wristpad or the station cameras and audio, but it had been two weeks since Liao's insertion, and Rainier wanted to collect the latest amplifier prototypes. Jules told herself that was the only reason.

But Jules hadn't seen Marya in the days since their argument, and Rainier's only communications had been vague assurances that they were on schedule. She hadn't even responded clearly to the notice of Leo Novak's strange arrival. She'd messaged only to say no new researchers would need to be captured. Maybe the fact that Novak had been recruited by her dead husband stung, but somehow Jules doubted that.

She wasn't sure if Rainier thought Jules was stupid, or didn't care that Jules knew she was lying. This wasn't an inspection. It was going to be a punishment.

Rainier's guardcore hadn't stepped foot on the station. Rainier liked to keep them close, so watching the GC ship slip toward the dock through Janus's cameras gave Jules a small jolt of fear. It was one thing to walk into a battle knowing those people were on your side, and quite another to face them down.

Sometimes she wanted to ask which one had taken those shots

at her outside Udon-Voodun two years ago. She never did. Despite everything, she needed to stay alive for Lolla's sake. Marya was an asshole, but she had been right. Jules was disposable.

She had to move Lolla. Marya's intrusion was one thing—annoying but not insurmountable. The station AI had gone over the details of Marya's break-in and determined she'd used a trumped-up excuse having to do with the scientists to gain temporary privileges. Permissions Jules immediately reset.

It would have been enough to soothe her nerves, until Rainier announced she was coming for an in-person visit. If Rainier was here to destroy Jules, Lolla wouldn't last long, either.

She checked the security feeds to be certain Marya was nowhere nearby, then unlocked the wheels on the table that held Lolla's coffin and backed her into the hall. On her wristpad, the distance between Rainier's ship and the docks ticked down toward zero.

The wheels hissed against the smooth composite floor. If Rainier was watching—and Jules could never be sure when that woman was peeking through the station's cameras—she didn't react. Maybe Lolla was too far beneath her notice. Maybe, probably, this was exactly what she'd expected Jules to do. To second-guess was to fail, Jules told herself. That road led to paralysis.

Two minutes to touchdown. Jules didn't know a whole hell of a lot about being in space aside from the fact she hated every miserable second of it. But like the Grotta, space stations had their own rhythms. They didn't grow and shift in the same way, nothing that nebulous could survive in a vacuum. Stations required hard borders. Rules. Jules chafed every time she had to run a checklist.

But the Grotta taught you how to survive. When you were born on fire, you grew an instinct for where the water was. Rainier hadn't given her a rundown on Janus and its operations, but one of the first things Jules had done upon arriving was locate the evac pods and the shuttles. She couldn't fly for shit, but then, that's what the AI was for. So long as Rainier didn't get into the system.

The coffin took up most of the elevator. Jules had to press her back against the wall, the gurney digging into the tops of her thighs. As it swished down the levels, her stomach lurched. All the medications in the 'verse couldn't get her used to spin-grav. Rainier, in her flippant way, had claimed that Jules's status as an ascended meant that something as trivial as nausea shouldn't bother her. But the longer Jules spent with Rainier, the more she suspected the woman didn't know—or care—how the ascension-agent worked on humanity.

The lower levels of the station narrowed, so that Jules had to be careful not to scrape the sides of the coffin against the walls as she pushed it along. Rainier had purchased this station from a failed settlement, a bunch of fringers who had gotten together to build some utopia or another. Whether they'd left on their own or Rainier had burned them out, Jules didn't know, and didn't ask.

What she did know, and the reason Rainier liked this station, was that the lower levels were tubed up with pipelines that could provide deep, deep cold. Rainier had offered, once, to let Jules store Lolla down here, but Jules had wanted her closer. Coffins, narrow mirrors of Lolla's, lined the walls on these chilly levels.

Their surfaces were opaque, but inside each, a new instance of Rainier Lavaux grew.

Jules put her head down and pushed. A line of four-seater shuttles appeared to her left, curving with the station's wall. When deployed, they'd drop into the empty column of space in the middle of the station and fly out through the bottom.

They needed maintenance, but Jules figured as long as they were sealed against the vacuum, she and Lolla would be all right. She picked the shuttle that, according to the station data, had been flown last—well over four years ago—and swiped her ident, holding her breath. It opened.

She wrapped her arms around the coffin and grunted out of habit, lifting it off the rolling gurney. All its electronics were self-contained, the battery designed to last decades, but her heart lurched as she shoved it into the shuttle, bumping the sides on the way in.

Lolla took up all of the two backseats—folded down—and pressed up against the front seats hard enough to make inertia-damping foam bulge over the glass. The grey-violet fluid she was suspended in sloshed. Jules blinked, nudging the coffin. A figment of her imagination. There was no air bubble in there—the system would tell her.

Jules hesitated. The grunt work of getting Lolla into the shuttle was one thing, the only thing she was good at, but the next step relied on half-remembered knowledge from Arden and, if she were being honest with herself, information gleaned from skimming the net.

The countdown to Rainier's arrival hit thirty seconds.

Grimacing, she swiped up the loose set of instructions she'd worked up on her wristpad and sent them to the shuttle's navigational system. In theory, if the shuttle detected a lost signal from Jules's wristpad, it would leave Janus and burn for Atrux. It didn't have the fuel to make it, but it'd ping Nox's and Arden's idents the whole way, asking for help. If anything happened to Jules, they'd come. They'd find Lolla. They probably had a better chance of fixing her, anyway.

She couldn't think like that. Jules had become what Lolla needed her to be. The science may be way above her head, but she'd find a way. She'd found Lolla. Now she had to save her.

A text flashed on Jules's pad from the station's AI: Rainier is on station.

Calmness settled over Jules. She shut the hatch on the shuttle and jogged over to the elevator, rocketing up to the level where Rainier kept her office, well away from the research labs. As much as she allowed the scientists to believe that they were funded by the Keepers, Rainier didn't want her face—the face of Lavaux's wife—associated. Jules knocked on the door to Rainier's office.

"Enter," she said.

Every time Jules saw Rainier, a chill shot down her spine. There wasn't anything inherently menacing about the woman. She was waifish, visibly devoid of muscle though Jules knew full well that her strength didn't play by human rules. That size was a choice, an intentional deflection.

There was a sharpness in her face that could have been seen as threatening, but was trendy in the elite circles of Prime. Aloofness was *in*, Rainier had told her once, and Jules had bit back a smart remark about that extending to their empathy for the lower classes.

Now, Rainier wore a simple Prime jumpsuit and had her hair pinned back. Jules would have pegged her for any regular, if beautiful, station worker, but knowing what she did about Rainier's split consciousnesses gave the woman an air of surrealness that had nothing at all to do with the angles of her cheeks.

"Have we met before?" Jules asked, because she couldn't resist poking the proverbial bear.

Rainier's smile was bright. "Jules, darling, we have not. This instance is new to you, though I promise I haven't forgotten a thing."

"You never do," Jules said with a touch more bitterness than she had meant to relay.

Rainier tsked. "Did you think I'd forgotten you, pet?"

"It's been two weeks since we brought on Liao. I think the project is lagging."

Rainier's room was a facsimile of what an office should be. Clear desk, net hookup terminal, tablets and charge ports. The tablets didn't have any fingerprints. What few cables there were never moved from their positions. Rainier sat down in her chair, crossing her legs, and gave the chair an experimental swivel.

"You collected Min Liao. All of my research says that she will be the stabilizing factor on the team. A natural mediator."

Jules suppressed a sneer and leaned her palms on the desk. "None of their prototypes have interacted with the ascended. Whatever they're doing, it's on the wrong track."

"Oh? And you're an expert in bionanites now?"

"Don't play, Rainier. I can run my own tests."

Rainier steepled her fingers in front of her chin. "You've been running tests on yourself?"

"Small ones. Testing to see if the amplifier swarms can send me a signal. I haven't felt a change."

"I see. Perhaps you've done yourself damage. It would explain why you were stupid enough to assault Marya."

Jules stiffened. "She was snooping around Lolla."

Rainier waved a hand. "She could not harm the little one."

"You can't know that."

"I've told you, I've seen this reaction before—"

"And you weren't able to *fix* it before, so you can't fully understand it."

Her lip curled. "Do not tell me what I understand."

"Then why can't you fix it yourself?"

Rainier blinked owlishly. "Do you think I care so much? Oh, pet. I allow you to collect your scientists because resolving the issue of the ascension-agent may be useful to me in the future. It is not my *goal*. I have very little interest in biological matters." Her eyes glazed slightly. "My goals lie beyond the reach of your mind, improved though it is."

Her face burned. "You don't care at all. About me, about bringing Lolla back."

" 'To care' is not a concept I find useful," Rainier said.

"Then what do you find useful?" Jules snapped.

"You, pet. This station, your dogged research, and a great many other things." She lifted her gaze and made such strong eye contact that Jules stepped back. "Marya is useful."

"I only cracked her tooth."

"And increased her desire for the ascension-agent even more."

"So? Give it to her. Then maybe she'll stop chirping around the place and be useful for fucking once. I don't know why you bother with her."

"Connections," Rainier mused. "That is a concept Lavaux taught me. It's how all you humans work, your societies, your squabbles and petty triumphs. Everything about you lives or dies by who you're connected to, and you hoard those connections jealously. Slam up your walls and wedge others out. Marya is useful to me."

Jules's mouth tasted bitter. "Because she has connections."

She lifted her hand and extended one long finger. "Just one, but it matters so very much."

"Who?" Jules demanded, face turning red again, and maybe she could control it, but she didn't care. Her only "connections" were low-level Grotta dealers.

In telling Jules why she valued Marya, Rainier was telling her why Jules was disposable. If Rainier cut the thread of her life, there would be no great unraveling. No one would even notice.

"That," Rainier said, "matters not at all to you. All you must know is that you may *not* break my toys. Honestly, I thought you would do better. My research points to your species getting along better when paired off. You and Lolla and Marya were meant to be my little sorority sisters." Her smile was wistful. "I miss having sisters."

"Depends on the pairing," she grated out. "And there are thousands of you for company."

"I've sent Marya away for a while. It's just you and Lolla for sororal company now."

A tightness clenched her chest. "What does that mean?"

"Don't worry. Marya will be back by the morning, but I want you both to cool your heels. I sent her on a mission, not to the grave. Off to earn her dose of the agent."

"Something your guardcore can't do?"

Her smile was slow. "Something I'd rather not waste them on."

"And have you given the GC the agent?"

Rainier cocked her head to the side. "Why would I do that?"

"If it works so well most of the time, why not give it to your soldiers? They'd heal faster, perform better. You need more than me."

She smiled. "I *have* more than you, though you cannot see past your own nose. My soldiers do not require the agent. The more of you exist in the worlds, the larger the chance the knowledge gets out. A drop of blood left here, a security camera catching a healing there." Her expression soured. "This was a lesson Lavaux refused to learn. He wanted all of his inner circle turned, the misguided soul. It took me minutes to scrub the visual of his leg healing itself from that video. *Minutes.*"

"It is a gift—"

"And it is my gift to give or withhold. Never forget you stole your strength, Juliella. Never forget I deigned to let you keep it."

"Why?" She kept her voice level. Rainier wasn't something she had any touchstones for. She'd never even dealt with a Keeper, let alone someone who felt comfortable manipulating Keepers. In her darker moments, she wondered if Rainier was even really *someone*, anyway.

Jules may not have ever had power, but she understood it. Understood her place in it as only an outsider could. Rainier was keeping her around for a reason. Once Jules had fulfilled that reason, she was a dead woman—and so was Lolla. Secrets like hers didn't get to stroll out the door after a job well done.

"Why let me live when you say yourself the risk of discovery goes up with every one of us changed?"

Rainier's arm shot forward so quickly that even Jules's enhanced vision couldn't track the motion. She grabbed the top of her hand, squeezing enough to make the joints crack but not enough to cause this new body of hers pain.

"I built you a maze, my little Grotta rat, and the cheese is your Lolla. Figure it out."

CHAPTER 23

PRIME STANDARD YEAR 3543

A SPEAKER SPEAKS

The war room of the Ada Cannery had grown barnacles of garbage. Piles of compostable cups stained with coffee heaped over the top of the trash can in the corner. They'd reached a rate of consumption that the cleaner bots hadn't accounted for, and while stimpacks were a stabler way to gain an energy boost, Biran—and it seemed his peers—preferred the jittery rush of caffeine. At least coffee flushed out of their systems faster.

Director Olver had called in the full number of the Protectorate. Hitton, Garcia, Singh, and Vladsen all sported dark circles under their eyes. While they were not directly involved in the peace negotiations with Icarion, they had not been idle. They had their own districts to see to, their own people on edge, breathing shallowly until the final shoe dropped. Biran hoped he, Olver, and Shun could ease some of that tension this day.

"Congratulations," Garcia said, catching Biran's eye, "on the exoneration of your sister."

"It took long enough," Hitton said, arching one brow. "I wonder why? Anford, were our systems that severely compromised?"

Anford folded her hands together on the tabletop but otherwise remained still. "The files were permanently deleted and never recovered. InfoSec did the best job it could in the recovery attempt."

"And yet an anonymous nethead beat us to the punch," Hitton mused. "And corrected the deepfake without Prime's gentle guiding hand. Marvelous. Shall we recruit that individual?"

"This meeting is not about the state of InfoSec," Olver said, "though we are looking into who corrected the footage before we could."

"Perhaps another friendly nethead will come along and tell us," Singh said dryly.

"Enough of that," Garcia said, "it's done. And no one in this room really believes that the major assaulted Lavaux without cause, do they?"

Silence hung in the air, stretching tension across Biran's mind so taut he felt he'd scream if someone so much as tapped him.

"No," Olver said firmly. "We do not. While I do not have the pleasure of knowing the major well, I knew Lavaux. He wanted *The Light*, and would have done anything to take it. Including killing one of ours. I am much more interested in discovering the source of that farce than whoever untangled it for us."

"We are looking into it," Anford said.

"Wonderful," Garcia said, cutting off Hitton before she could get another word in. "Now, why are we here, Jian? I enjoy your company, but we are stretched thin at the moment."

Biran sat back, letting Olver take the lead.

"You are all familiar with Keeper Shun." Olver gestured to her, and she nodded slightly. "While she is one of our finest academy professors, she is also in charge of gate location scouting for Ada. A position which, until recently, lay dormant."

"Beg pardon," Hitton said, "but this system—"

"Let her talk," Biran said firmly.

Hitton pursed her lips at him, spread her hands in surrender, and sat back with an intentional ruffle of fabric.

Shun cleared her throat. "You are correct, Keeper Hitton, that my position within this system has been uneventful up to this point. But matters with Icarion have pushed us all to new limits. No one here wants open war, am I correct?"

That, at least, gained enthusiastic nods all around. As much as they bickered, the Protectorate of Ada did not want Icarion's slaughter on their hands. That knowledge eased something clenched in Biran's mind. They would squabble, but they would figure this out. They had to.

"It was suggested to me that I look elsewhere for gate anchor sites."

"Suggested?" Hitton asked. "By whom?"

"Me," Olver said. "Please continue, Keeper Shun."

Shun inclined her head and tapped at her wristpad, putting up a projection of the asteroid. These were a much higher resolution than Anaia's, the hunk of rock displayed in such detail that he suspected he could zoom in enough to see the frost crystals limning the hulking stone's back.

"This is AST-4501. It inhabits a stable, elliptical orbit well within the gravity well margins of our star, and has a mass exceeding the safety envelope by five percent. Its geology is primarily basalt, with heavy iron deposits on the starward end, and shows no obvious sign of fracture. Neither does it tumble. AST-4501, my friends, is a perfect candidate for a Casimir Gate."

Biran held his breath as everyone took in the unremarkable piece of stone, letting the weight of her words sink in.

"I bring this to you today," Shun said, "because I seek permission to request greater survey resources from the High Protectorate. The asteroid is promising, but an extensive study must be made."

"This—" Olver said, beginning to launch into the short speech Biran knew he had prepared for this moment. The words he and Biran had put their heads together on to stoke the fires of hope in everyone at this table, to rally them behind a future where Ada had two gates, and Icarion and Ada could both prosper under the flagship of Prime.

"I think not," Hitton said.

Biran wanted to throttle the woman, but he used every trick in his repertoire to keep his voice even. "Why on Earth not? Would you scorn a peaceful future so quickly?"

Hitton met his gaze evenly. "I would scorn a poisoned apple offered from my enemy's hand. You disguise it prettily, Keeper Shun, but I have my own informants. This asteroid was marked as a gate location by the traitor Lionetti."

Sharp breaths all around. Biran pushed to his feet, the chair scraping back, and planted his hands on the table so they would not reach for Hitton. "This is our system's final hope of avoiding all-out war. Shun has investigated. The asteroid is viable. With the High Protectorate's resources, we can make sure of that to whatever exacting specifications you desire. Or are you so thirsty for Icarion blood?"

Her eyes narrowed, but her tone did not change. "I do not desire the extermination of our long-lost cousins, Speaker. Check yourself. Neither do I desire to build a gate in a location that is easily attacked by Icarion. This elliptical orbit, Shun, how close does it draw to that wayward planet as opposed to our own Ada?"

Shun licked her lips. That was all the notice Biran needed that the news would not be good. "Quite close, astronomically speaking. At the narrowest point in its orbit, Icarion could reach it within two days from their moon base."

"You see?" Hitton waved a hand through the air. "Lionetti was seeking work in Shun's department. No doubt, she planned to discover this boon of an asteroid and bring it to her superiors, who would champion the cause as you all are doing now. Once the gate was built, Icarion would break their supposed peace and sally toward it at the narrow point, securing a Casimir Gate for themselves. You are dancing to her strings, and she's not even alive to pull them."

"The fleet is perfectly capable of securing the asteroid," Biran said. "Isn't that right, General Anford?"

Anford didn't twitch a millimeter. "I am uncertain. Supply lines would be difficult to maintain if a coordinated Icarion effort cut us off. We do not have the numbers to guarantee security within acceptable margins for that gate. We would have to request more."

"More, more, more," Hitton said. "Little Ada, caught in its little war, is always asking for more. The High Protectorate will not give it to us. And I, for one, will not embarrass myself by bringing this proposal to their table."

"Nor will I," Singh said quietly, her dark gaze locked on the image of the asteroid. "My apologies, Keeper Shun, I know you do fine work, but this is too risky. It is the job of a Keeper, above all else, to keep the gates safe from outside hands."

Olver said, "We keep them safe for our people. What have we become, if we put the needs of our people below the safety of the gates?"

"Icarions," Hitton said, "are not our people." She stood, turning to Biran. "If you want to save them, boy, then you must do better."

She left the room, and as Singh and Garcia stood sheepishly and filed out after her, Biran's heart sank with every single door shutting behind them. He let his hands go limp on the table and stared at them. How? How had Hitton discovered the source of the asteroid? Maybe that guardcore in the hall had told her... Or she had clever research assistants working for Shun. That seemed more likely.

"You should have warned me," Anford said to Olver in a low, tight voice. "Then I might have had a response prepared. Something tangible. I cannot lie about our abilities, Director. Not when the safety of a gate is at stake."

"I had hoped it would not come to that."

Anford jerked a thumb at Biran. "Hope is his game. You, Director, know better. Prepare for the worst. Always. Because if you fuckers cannot work this out, it's *my* hand on the trigger. *My* hands covered in blood."

She stalked from the room, slamming the door behind her. Shun let out a thready laugh. "Well. I suppose now I have a deeper understanding of why the Protectorate never appealed to me."

"They are good people," Biran said. "They don't..."

"Don't understand that this may be our last play before slaughter," Olver said. He ran a hand across the top of his head, shoulders stooping forward. As tired as Biran felt, Olver looked the part.

Vladsen cleared his throat. Biran flinched, having nearly forgotten that he hadn't stormed out with the rest. "While I understand the misgivings of the others," he said in a soft voice. Biran realized he hadn't heard the man speak much since Lavaux's death.

As the youngest member of the Protectorate before Biran, Vladsen had looked up to Lavaux as a kind of mentor—had even seemed to foster a friendship with him that extended beyond the usual political dance of the Protectorate. Whatever the man's feelings on Lavaux's betrayal, Biran had never asked. Vladsen had receded after that day, fading into the background of these meetings. Possibly to avoid drawing attention to himself and, thus, suspicion as a known associate of Lavaux, but looking at him now…

Lines creased the edges of Vladsen's lips. His curly, bouncy hair lay flat against his skull, and shadows had taken up residence under his eyes. He'd been shaken that day. Hurt, and because the person he mourned was a traitor, he'd never been free to express any of that pain. To seek help. Dios, Biran could be so much up his own ass at times. He should have noticed. He knew what that pain was like. He could have helped.

"I agree that this secondary gate may be Ada's best course of action to preserving peace with Icarion. If I can help, then I will be a champion for your cause."

Olver looked pointedly at the wall. "I cannot see how this proposal could be brought to the High Protectorate through normal means at this point."

"I see," Biran said slowly. Director Olver wouldn't oppose them, but neither could he be their channel to Okonkwo.

Shun opened her mouth and pointed at the asteroid image, preparing some convincing argument, but Biran caught her eye and shook his head. Her brow furrowed, but she put her hand back down.

"If you three will excuse me," Olver said, standing with deliberate care. "I have other matters to see to. Biran, please continue…doing what you do best."

"Understood, Director."

When the door shut, Shun cut him a look. "What was that about?"

Biran sighed. "The director cannot be involved in, or be seen to endorse in any way, what I'm about to do next."

"Which is?" Vladsen pressed.

Biran grinned lightly. "Why, I am the Speaker for the Keepers of Ada, and I am going to Speak, my fellow Keeper. Are you with me?"

"Oh." Vladsen cracked a smile. "Oh yes."

CHAPTER 24

PRIME STANDARD YEAR 3543

EVERYBODY LIES ON JANUS

Sometime during introductions, Jules vanished. Maybe it was the drugs or the exhaustion that had made Tomas miss when she'd ducked out of the lab.

That he'd missed her leaving rankled, and he couldn't quite pin down why that was, but he'd learned long ago that if anything raised his hackles, it was worth paying attention to. Like Jules staring at a corner of the ceiling, as if someone were watching them all from above.

He really should find his room to rest and recover. But now, when he was addled and new, was the best time to pretend to get "lost" in the station. The longer he was here, the clearer his head, the less oops-wrong-room moments he could get away with.

Tomas excused himself into the hallway and walked far enough to get out of the way of foot traffic, then leaned against the wall and brought up the station's provided schematics. He found them to be an interesting fantasy.

Not only were entire station levels missing from the layout provided, but a few paths he'd already taken had vanished. He tried to flip over to the engineering side of the schematics—HVAC, wiring—and wasn't so much rejected as completely ignored. The screen didn't even flicker when he tried to flip it over.

He put in a request for those schematics, knowing it would be denied, but it'd be a perfectly natural thing for a man like Novak to want to have a look at. Engineers of all stripes were curious about how the stations they lived on operated. Especially the life-support systems.

Tomas reached for the menu that hid his secret suite of Nazca-made programs, and hesitated, finger hovering above the touch.

Nazca programs were standard procedure on all missions. An agent too busy or otherwise specialized to hack into the data they needed could rely upon the good developers of home base serving them up a plethora of programs robust enough to break most non-Keeper security systems.

But there was a catch. Accessing those programs in a controlled environment, where cameras were always watching, risked revealing their presence and blowing one's cover. There were programs to access the cameras and edit that visual out, but they were useless if an intelligence was keeping watch real-time.

On Bero, he hadn't touched a single program until the station Farion-X2.

He moved his finger away from the menu and turned the motion into a stretch. Not yet. Not until he could be sure. Then he'd crack this station, and all its secrets, like an egg.

With his hands in his pockets, he set off at a slow stroll, affecting a sway and stagger that would lend credence to anyone watching him that the tranq was still riding his system, which wasn't entirely a farce. His wristpad vibrated once, indicating he should take a left turn to get to his room, but he kept on strolling, sticking to the central corridor. If anyone stopped him, then he'd say he was out stretching his legs.

As he walked, he pulled up the data he'd skimmed from introductions to his colleagues. None of their faces were known to him, none of them had any previous connection with either of the Lavauxs. If they'd had a connection with Jules, he didn't know, because he hadn't bothered to check.

That pissed him off. There had been nothing to indicate that the young woman had anything to do with Rainier. Nothing, except the dead Keeper at her feet. It had meant little to him at the time, he'd been too busy trying to wiggle their way out of SecureSite and Laguna's clutches, but he hadn't heard about the death of Keeper Nakata and that was unusual, wasn't it? He hadn't had a lot of time to pursue newsfeeds once he'd gotten off of Bero, but the death of Keeper Lavaux should have triggered comparisons in the media, and *that* he had definitely been watching.

There was a connection. Some thread between Jules, Rainier, Keeper Lavaux, and Keeper Nakata, and it had everything to do with this station.

"Mr. Novak." Lt. Davis stepped out of a door in front of him, too close and too precise to be a coincidence. "Your rooms are in the other direction. Do you require an escort?"

"Just walking off the sedative," he said, and extended a hand to shake. "Nice to meet you properly, Lt. Davis."

Davis did not so much as glance at his hand. "You'd do better to sleep it off. Trust me. I know."

"Bet you do," he said, giving her a wink that went over about as well as flipping her off would have.

"Let me walk you."

Her hand landed on his shoulder, and he let her steer him around, back the way he'd come, and couldn't help but shiver as he caught the glint of a silver camera eye embedded in the ceiling.

Lt. Davis left him alone in his room, and though he couldn't hear the lock to his door click over, he was certain she'd set an alert to notify her should he go wandering again. Tomas glanced at the corners of the room, not seeing any cameras, then brought up a program on his wristpad that any decent engineer or researcher spending time on a space station would have—a scan for hidden cameras. Hell, most normal people ran the scan checking into a hotel room. Doing so now wouldn't make anyone suspicious of him, and failing to do so just might.

He hadn't bothered on Bero, because that ship had cameras front and center everywhere he stepped, but here the makers of Janus had put some work into appearing normal to the researchers it hired on.

The program initialized slowly and made Tomas pace around the room holding up his wristpad to get full coverage. When he was done, the all clear lit up. Speakers and microphones abounded, but no cameras were watching him in this room.

Sitting on the edge of his narrow bed, he pulled up the suite of Nazca programs. He wasn't ready to mess with the ship's systems, but he had no trouble monkeying around with his own. Tomas selected the program that governed his implants and nudged a slider for alertness up.

A smooth cocktail of stimulants trickled into his system, chasing away the fog left over from Davis's sedative. He pulled up the schematic of the amplifier the team was working on and looked at it with sharper eyes.

Tomas didn't know much about nanites. Working on that scale was the purview of the Keepers, but he knew a lot about communications equipment. He'd been sent the "bare-bones" schematics for the amplifiers, and while they looked pretty on paper, they were missing a critical constraint.

They were wideband amps, the usual arrangement for boosting comms across an array of frequencies, and presumably when working in concert as a nanite swarm they'd push a hell of a lot of data at a high gain. But Prime communication devices, even something as simple as an amplifier, came with governors. Switches that could authenticate, or shut down, a signal at will. While this device had something that looked *almost* like a Prime governor, it wasn't quite right.

He'd seen a lot of them as a spy. Chances were good the civilian scientists on Janus had seen few, and never in detail, and so this false governor would be enough to convince them they were working merrily away within the constraints of Prime's rules.

Tomas pulled up his messaging and sent a quick e-mail to an account set up to be the ident of Leo Novak's best friend from engineering school. The message he sent was basic, but encoded so that the handler monitoring the account—probably Sitta—could decipher his rough notes about the governor on the amps. Okonkwo had hired him for this mission, and hopefully she wouldn't be too greedy with information if his handler asked about what that governor would let through.

Someone knocked on his door. Tomas swiped back to the schematics of the nanite amps and picked his head up, letting his eyes droop and his forehead wrinkle to mimic the exhaustion he should be feeling.

"Come in," he called out.

The door dilated and Dal, one of the scientists he'd been introduced to at the lab, stepped into the room with a mug full of something steaming in one hand.

"Sorry to bother you," Dal said, "but I thought you might like some hot tea. I know how... fuzzy... the first day's introductions can leave you."

Tomas raised his brows. "Don't tell me Lt. Davis gives the same welcome to everyone who comes to work here."

Dal rubbed his bicep and winced. "We all experienced rough arrivals of varying flavors. Here, please, while it's hot."

Tomas took the mug from him and made a show of sniffing the steam deeply, giving his metabolism implants time to detect if there was anything off about the brew. He didn't get the usual wave of nausea that came with the detection of intoxicants, so he took a deep drink. Strong black tea, milk simulate, and sugar. He beamed up at Dal.

"Thanks for this, things don't seem so friendly here as I'm used to."

"Ah. The presence of the Prime charter means we are watched closely. It makes for a tense working environment, but the opportunity to see such fine contraptions up close is worth a little stress."

"Seems weird, don't it? That they drag us in to have a poke around at these when they've got their own people trained up."

Dal tugged at one side of his mustache. "Not enough specialist Keepers to go around, I suppose."

"Must be true," Tomas said, letting himself sound unconvinced. "I mean, they've got that Valentine woman keeping an eye on us. Apologies if this isn't true, but she didn't strike me as the technical sort."

"The technical side is what we're for," Dal said, and pointed at Tomas's wristpad and the displayed schematic. "Have you looked at the receiver systems yet? We're having trouble getting them to swarm."

"Not yet. To be honest, I was curious about the governor. Maybe it's interfering with the receivers. If I could get a schematic on that..."

Dal went very still. Tomas picked up his head to meet the man's eye and found him pale through the cheeks. Dal pulled at his collar and forced a smile back on.

"Best not to ask about that. Keeper tech, and all. I'm sure you'll puzzle out a workaround. Good night."

Dal clapped him on the shoulder, almost making him spill his tea, and hurried out of the room. Maybe Tomas wasn't the only one to note the off-ness of the system after all.

A message flashed in his inbox from his "school friend." The bulk of it was banal pleasantries, but he picked out the hidden message quickly enough. With every word he deciphered, his stomach sank further and further.

Full access to gate-powering systems allowed. Rainier cannot be allowed to hostage control of the gates. Find out if this is the only location of these nanites and secure all instances. Stop these swarms, lest all of Prime be brought to its knees by the powering-off of the gates.

CHAPTER 25

PRIME STANDARD YEAR 3543

WHO YOU KNOW

Jules jerked awake with a pounding headache and a Rorschach collection of bruises across her arms and chest that she didn't remember receiving. What did she last remember? Novak. Bringing him to the scientists. Then a message from Rainier, a summons to speak with her, then back to this room. She checked the time and found it'd been only "overnight" since her talk with Rainier. Jules breathed out, slowly.

The bruises were old, fading to yellow around the edges. She must have dreamed a memory to trigger the headache. She knew what that meant, and did her best not to think about it, because it would only make matters worse.

She swung her legs to the ground and stretched, shaking off the lingering memory and the aches that came with it. No reason to walk around like a battered plum. She concentrated on the bruises, thinking about the pain fading away, and in seconds the sharpness had passed, reduced to a dull ache that soon receded into nothing.

Lolla. Panic shot through her and she dragged up the stats on her wristpad. Still stable, still in the shuttle. She let out an anxious laugh and sank down into a crouch.

An impulse struck, and she brought up Marya's log on the station. The other woman had left sometime the day before, and was registered as en route to Janus, but it would be a few hours before she returned. Jules had some time before the researchers would be up and working, so she set an alert on her pad to tell her if Marya came back early and went to that woman's room.

The door opened when she swiped her ident over the lock. Jules smirked, satisfied. She'd never had free run of any place before, not even Harlan's hideout. Everyone's cubbies had been keyed to them and them alone. Jules had always suspected Harlan had a way in despite his posturing of privacy, but she'd never confirmed it.

Clothes ate most of Marya's space, thrown across her narrow cot, trunk, desk, and chair, most of them nonstandard Prime jumpsuits, nothing Jules had ever seen her wear. The coconut scent of her hair oil hung in the air, cloyingly sweet to Jules's nose.

She kicked a few stray shirts aside and clipped her toe on the edge of a tablet, the corner poking out from under the cot. They did most of their work with their wristpads, but maybe Marya had something about her friends or family or whatever on there. Something to explain the connection that Rainier kept her around for.

It lit up at her touch. Even though Marya had password protected it, the tablet was connected to the overall network of the station. Jules had no problem accessing it as an administrator. She smiled tightly to herself. Lolla would have been proud.

There was no contacts list, just a series of folders. She nudged a metallic jacket aside and sat on the edge of the bed. Pictures of a smooth, carbon-black object filled the screen, a thumbnail gallery that, when seen all at once like this, sent a crawling sensation up the back of her neck. Jules had never seen a Casimir Gate up close—few had—but the subtly curving shape was familiar to her all the same, burned into her psyche from an early age as the crowning achievement of Prime. Of humanity.

Although Rainier had never outright said that the gates weren't human tech, she'd said that they'd come from the same source as the ascension-agent. That race of beings Rainier referred to only in vague passing. The Waiting, she called them, and had refused to elaborate when Jules pressed her for more information.

Secretly, Jules believed Rainier no longer remembered anything about her makers. That she'd been too long in a human body, and no matter how many she puppeted, humanity had sunk into her bones. The nebulous being that was "her" conformed to the boundaries of her body, the shape of humanity.

Jules knew little about Marya's upbringing, or her family, except for what Jules had gleaned from the girl's obvious sense of self-importance. Who the fuck was she? Where did Rainier dig up this woman who craved the transformation of the agent and could get pictures of the gates far closer than any civilian?

Jules dropped the tablet back on the ground and leaned over, dragging her hands through her hair. She laced her fingers behind her head and gripped, squeezing. She'd told herself that whatever else Rainier was up to didn't matter. That she would use the woman—*the intelligence*—only so long as it took her to get Lolla back.

But she couldn't guarantee Rainier would continue to allow the scientists to work on the ascension-agent problem. If her mood changed, Rainier could redirect all their efforts in an instant. Jules swiped up her wristpad, pulled up the latest specs on the amplifiers. Rainier had promised her the amplifiers would allow her to send a signal to Lolla that would wake her up, get her cells out of stasis and moving and breathing and living again.

Jules believed her, because she had nothing else to hang on to, but the truth was she had no idea what she was looking at. The lie she told the scientists might as well be true, for all she fucking knew. Maybe they were trying to increase intergate communication. Marya's pictures leaned in that direction.

She could ask the scientists. Not directly, but she could ask them what sort of machines the amplifiers would be capable of communicating with. It wouldn't be a complete answer, but it'd be something. A direction for her to look, to push. She'd ask them now, while she still had the nerve.

On a whim she pulled up the shell program she used to set up the deadman's switch on the shuttle. Lolla was still there, the program still running, so she was pretty sure it worked. She opened another path and added the data on the research for the amplifiers to it, set to send to an ident Arden used to use as a dump box. If she died, they'd receive everything the researchers had come up with so far, plus what little information she had on the ascension-agent, along with a single line—to wake Lolla.

She had to do this alone. But if she failed, Arden might be able to pick up the pieces. She stood to make her way to the lab, when an incoming message flashed onto her wristpad from Marya: Hey, girl. Look I know you're pissed but let's talk. I just landed, but there's a ship incoming that I gotta scare off. Let me deal with it then we'll chat in the kitchen, ok?

Jules clenched her fists, but typed back: Okay.

CHAPTER 26

PRIME STANDARD YEAR 3543

CHARTER REVOKED

Janus Station spun a short flight away from them, a single point of metal and light in a sea of black teeming with human intrusion. Sanda tried not to gawk, but it was impossible to keep the wideness of her eyes to herself. Even on the fringes of the system, the viewscreens displayed ships the size of small planets, stations in the dozens, and asteroids corralled into orbit around the tiny planet that was Ordinal.

The scale of the Ordinal system was something she'd only read about, a sensation that visual media failed to convey. Her home, Ada, was so small, so pointless, in the churning chaos of humanity stretched across the stars.

"Berserker drone field," Conway said, dragging her attention away from the infomatics for the whole system and back to the screen devoted to Janus. "It's subtle, but it's a complete net around Janus."

"Are they live?"

"On and waiting. No way to know the trigger, but I'm guessing they're under control from station HQ. Anything running on automated sensors would have taken down a civilian craft accidentally by now."

"Get me station ATC."

"Calling," Arden said.

Arden didn't wear the Prime uniform well. Their wild hair and a tendency to shove any old bit of electronics in their pockets ruined the constrained lines of the jumpsuit, but they played the role of ship comms director convincingly. A lot of allowances were given for the personal proclivities of techs, so Sanda didn't think their presence would set off any alarm bells in Janus. Nox wore the uniform like he was born to it. Graham was the only one she worried about.

He kept reaching up to tug at the wrists, the neckline. Subtle, quick movements that betrayed he wasn't used to wearing the thing and was desperate to get it off. She'd stuck him in a nav chair toward the back, and put Nox, Conway, and Knuth camera-forward. Arden, by nature of their job, was dead center in front of Sanda, but lower to access the comms panel.

For better or worse, Sanda had opened the door to the captain's quarters to find a trim, dark grey major's coat with a set of bars for her jumpsuit waiting. Anford didn't miss a detail and, as the stiff fabric of the coat pressed down on her shoulders, that worried her.

The center viewscreen switched from a view of the system to a woman wearing a comms headset, complete with HUD monocle, her narrow face pinched in irritation. Her cheeks were flushed, as if she'd been running.

"This is Janus Station. Please identify yourself and be advised that you are entering restricted airspace."

Sanda sat straight, as she'd seen Anford do, as if her spine were made of metal so dense nothing in the 'verse could bend it. She'd thought a lot about names during the transit to Ordinal. The gunship had needed a name.

Part of her didn't want to force a name on anyone—or anything—but when she considered, she realized people got to choose their name only if they changed it later in life. Her own name was as common as hydrogen, Sanda being a version of Alexandra, and Maram a version of that woman's lover, Maria.

Names shouldn't matter, she'd told herself, especially ones that were given, but she still couldn't bring herself to call the gunship by its call sign. The ship itself didn't care. It repeated its call sign when she asked what it would like to be called, and the others had no input.

So she'd thought back to Bero, and the story he'd been told about a young prince traveling the stars looking for a friend, having left his only love—a rose—behind, and decided it was time to grow some thorns.

"Janus Station, this is Major Sanda Maram Greeve in command of the gunship *Thorn*. Please instruct your berserker shield to stand down and prepare for boarding."

The woman's eyes bulged. "This is a private research station, we are off-limits to—"

"Janus Station exists under the forbearance of the Keepers and, by extension, the fleet. Your research charter allows for inspection by Prime operatives at any time. If you fail to conform to the letter of your charter, then Janus will be recategorized as a subversive station and I will be forced to engage."

She licked her lips. "I-I'm not qualified to—" Something drew her attention away, down low to the right, some superior monitoring the feed sending her orders, no doubt. Sanda did her damnedest to look bored.

"What—" The comms woman cleared her throat. "What is it you need, Major Greeve?"

"We are auditing your personnel. Instruct all station staff to prepare for inspection."

"You can't—"

"Ma'am," Sanda said in the coldest tones she could muster. "I can, and I am going to. You have scanned my ship, correct?"

The woman nodded, mute.

"Then you understand that the *Thorn* can take out your berserker drones in..." She pretended to check a data stream that didn't exist. "Seven point two five seconds. After that, we will force boarding. If you attempt further resistance, this ship will bust your station by the administration of a railgun to your engines."

"We are *civilians*."

"With berserker drones, and a charter in place that allows your existence only on the condition that you submit to fleet law and fleet inspection. Prepare for boarding. Greeve out."

She waved a hand, blanking the screen.

Nox whistled low and leaned over to nudge Graham in the arm. "Your kid is terrifying, you know that?"

"She didn't get *that* from me," Graham said, but he gave Nox a sly smile.

"No, I didn't." Sanda thought of Bero, sucking the atmo out of his hab while Tomas's head lolled, and pushed the image away. Memories would only slow her down, and she could not afford to miss a single thing.

Conway said, "That berserker shield will chew us to fucking bits."

"They don't know that."

"You sure?"

"Betting our asses on it, aren't I?"

A green all-clear light flicked across the screen. The ship's AI said, "We are cleared to dock at habitation ring seven."

"So they're trying to keep us out of one through six," Sanda said. To the ship, she said, "Initiate docking procedure. Conway, keep the guns pointed at the nearest drones. Make it look like we're ready to smash and burn."

"Heard," Conway said.

Sanda counted her breaths as they sidled up to the station. The docking clamp took the ship in hand with a gentle shudder. The local view switched over to pure diagnostics, cutting off her view of the station and the clamps.

"Live fire remains locked in," Conway said the second the switchover happened.

"Hold on," Arden said, tapping at their wristpad. "They may have blocked me from their systems, but this close I can use the ship's scanners to get us a little more data. What's below level seven...?" they muttered, squinting at the screen. "Huh. The *Thorn* thinks they've got a high-end cooling system down there."

Sanda schooled her expression to keep from giving away the shock of that statement. She didn't have all the pieces, but she was beginning to see the shape of this puzzle. Lavaux's incredible physical endurance, Rayson Kenwick living far longer than possible—if the records were correct—sketched the edges of an idea that bordered on conspiracy theory.

According to Tomas's research, both had been members of the Imm Project before it was pulled for being a failure. High-end coolers went well with a large supply of evac pods and NutriBaths. She needed to see what Rainier Lavaux wanted kept on ice.

"Send me that schematic," she said calmly. "It could be important."

Arden said, "Sure, but that's not the big concern. They've got signal scanners on the docks. Those will be a problem."

"How so?" Sweat pricked between her shoulder blades.

"My Trojan is always listening for its activation signal. Those scanners will notice tech that's looking for a connection. We *need* control of their computers, because there's no way they'll trot out Jules for you on this inspection. You just gotta get the code into their systems, then bug out. After that I can talk to her, get a better idea of what's going on."

"If we walk in with a Trojan scanning for a backdoor, all bets are off," Knuth said. "These people don't seem to have a light hand on the trigger."

"They'll kill her, and us," Graham protested. "I'm sorry, Arden, but we can't take that risk. Sanda can force them to bring all souls out—"

"No fucking way. I have not gotten this close only to—"

"Quiet," Sanda said. "Arden, give me the Trojan." She extended a hand to them, palm-up.

"Sanda—" Graham started, but she cut him a look.

Arden unstrapped and didn't bother to grab ground with the mag boots. They kicked off the bulkhead and arrowed toward her, a sleek micro-drive in their hand. They slapped it into her palm. She closed her hand around it, fingers tangling with Arden's for a breath.

Their palm was so, so cold. Sanda met their gaze, and they stiffened, unused to being scrutinized. But she had to know that... yes, they were scared. Frightened straight down to their bones. She let them go and they grabbed a ceiling handle, pushing back toward the comm seat.

Sanda undid the jumpsuit seam on her prosthetic leg, revealing the hastily sealed SynthFlesh. It took a bit of wiggling, but she got the chip wedged through the sealant and hidden.

"There," she said, closing the calf back up. "No one's going to wonder at a smart prosthetic listening for a signal from the owner's wristpad, are they?"

Arden grinned. "No, they're not. I'm pushing the control program to your pad now. Get as deep as you can into that station, then hit the activation button. You won't have to do anything else."

The ship shivered as it locked into dock. A yellow light flicked on above the airlock door—the station asking permission to hook up.

"Here we go," she said, undoing her harness. She slammed her mag boots down and clicked them on. "Boarding party to me: Nox and Knuth. Conway, keep a light finger on that trigger. Knuth, I want your eyes up—look for oddness in the station's design. Arden, monitor *everything*. Nox, you know what you do."

Nox checked the two blasters strapped to his hips, then selected a larger rifle from a side panel and cradled it in front of his chest.

"I should go with you," Graham said, reaching for his harness.

"No. You're staying here. You look like a civvie, Dad. Sorry."

His hand hesitated on the harness buckle, then came to rest in his lap. "Nicest thing you've ever said to me."

"I got her six," Nox said, and dropped a hand on Graham's shoulder. "Don't you worry, Papa."

Sanda rolled her eyes and selected a handblaster from the open weapons panel before clicking it shut. She checked the sights and the charge, then slipped it into a harness at her side, aligned so it wouldn't bulge against her major's coat.

A woman in fleet armor waited for her on the other side of the airlock, flanked by the woman who she had spoken to over comms. Both had the fakest, most strained smiles Sanda had ever seen. The fleet woman did not salute. Fake armor, then. Even on civilian duty, protocols were adhered to. Nothing on this station would be what it was dressed up to seem.

"Major Greeve," the comms woman said, extending a hand. Sanda eyed it and did not shake. The woman swallowed and jerked her hand back. "I'm Marya Page. Welcome to Janus Station."

"Let's make this quick," Sanda said.

CHAPTER 27

PRIME STANDARD YEAR 3543

CHANGE OF MISSION

Tomas had his nose buried in a diagnostic readout when chaos erupted. He looked up from the data, blinking the ghost of numbers from his eyes, and tried to figure out what all the shouting was about.

On the viewscreen against the exterior wall, the camera feed changed to the immediate vicinity as a Point-Class gunship sliced into view. For the past two days those cameras had been pointed at the nearest Casimir Gate, a constant reminder of what they were working toward: better, clearer, faster dissemination of information through the gates. Now, a ripple went through the researchers, each one reacting like they'd seen a shark in their calm, tropical waters.

"We're too busy to deal with this bullshit," Liao snapped into her wristpad. Her eyes narrowed at the response from the other end of the line. "You understand that a single Point ship is not powerful enough to blow us out of the sky?" A ragged sigh. "Yes, yes, very well."

She picked her head up from her data and stood, clapping to get everyone's attention. "Some bigwig up fleet command has decided Janus is overdue for an inspection."

Groans all around. Tomas leaned back and furrowed his brow, attempting to look annoyed, while he catalogued all the exit points on the station. An inspection was one thing. Sending a gunship to do it was another.

"Tidy up," Liao was saying, and his colleagues fell to the work, blanking displays and stowing instruments. Dal grumbled to himself as he closed all the screens he'd been working on.

"Hey, Dal." Tomas leaned across his desk and sat his tablet down on the Velcro. "This a usual thing?"

Dal whipped his head around, eager to put words to his misgivings, and squinted at Tomas through his HUD monocle. "Never, ever, in my years on chartered stations have I had to endure something so banal as an inspection."

"Cool your heels, Dal," Liao said. "Prime's going to flex its muscle on us civs every so often. Our poor luck that we were with you when they finally caught up."

"How long do we have?" a researcher toward the back of the room asked.

Liao sniffed and tapped at her wristpad. "Station, get me visual on our visitor, please. Throw it up on central."

Sanda Greeve stepped through the airlock.

"Fuck," Tomas said. Out loud. Everyone looked at him.

"That's... that's a major," he stammered, praying to every atom in his body that they'd buy it. That his singular lapse in decades of service to the Nazca would not get him spaced right here, right now, because Sanda—Sanda fucking Greeve—had walked through that door and turned his world upside down. Again.

Dal laughed and clapped the tabletop with an open palm. "That's good news! It's just a political circus, set dressing. Not a real inspection."

Tension fled Liao's shoulders. Tomas stopped listening. Couldn't pay attention to anything but Sanda, moving and breathing, a few hundred meters away from him.

She threw a glance to the cameras in the hall, a microsecond of a motion, so small he doubted she was aware she had done it. Bero had changed something deep within her. Rearranged her instincts and eroded her trust, thrust her on the path that led her here, in her major's uniform, flanked by a grim-looking fleet soldier and... Nox.

Tomas dimly knew that his pulse was climbing through the roof. He didn't know Nox, recognized him only because Laguna had shown his picture alongside Jules, Lolla, and Arden, but if Nox was nearby, Arden was too, and there was only one thing they'd be here looking for. Jules.

His new colleagues were engaging in the time-honored tradition of bitching about bureaucracy. This inspection was a waste of time. Political theater. Didn't the majors of the fleet have something *better* to do?

For one tantalizing moment, he allowed himself to entertain the idea that this was exactly that, political theater. Petty posturing. If Sanda had a gunship under her command again, then she'd made nice with General Anford and was acting under her orders. Anford wouldn't risk putting Sanda back on the front lines, so sending her on risk-free missions like this made sense, at least until everyone in the fleet got used to their new major.

He almost laughed at the thought. Sanda wouldn't play puppet for anyone, even Anford.

She had to be here for Jules. Because if she wasn't, then she was here because the coordinates in her head led her here, and he couldn't fix that. But Jules... He could make sure she found that woman.

Hoping she'd go home after he left her on Atrux had been a colossal mistake.

"Where's Valentine?" Liao asked, scowling at something on her pad.

"Can't you get ahold of her?" Tomas asked.

Liao shook her head so aggressively her long, black sheet of hair flipped back and forth across her face. Odd style choice for station life, but the habs were under grav. She must not be used to living off-planet, but that was a detail for Tomas to pick at later. Sometimes the cataloguing part of his spy-brain could get in the way.

"She's not answering hails. Marya and Davis can't get her, either."

Tomas glanced at the cameras in the walls. "What about the station?"

"What about it? It can't tell me where Valentine is without her permission, and she's not answering."

"You better learn to stall, Liao, because here comes the cavalry," Dal said.

The door opened. Sanda was first through, brushing past Marya and Davis like they were spiderwebs in her way, her hands grasped together behind her back, her head up and eyes roving, taking in every detail of the room. A shudder ran through her, a quick twitch of the shoulders.

She recognized this lab layout, just as he had. Knew its bones to be the mirror of the lab in Bero, the place where her head had been cracked open and tampered with. Tomas held his breath. Abject terror pushed her eyes wide. She blinked, shook her head, and her gaze went back to normal, spine straight, commanding the room with her mere presence.

"What is it you do here?" she asked, strolling the line of lab tables. She had to notice every screen had been blanked, all the research tucked away. At each table, she shook the researcher's hand. Tomas began to sweat.

"We're working on the advancement of communications relays," Marya said. She scurried after, a tablet clutched to her chest like a shield. "It's drudge work."

"What we're doing here is important," Dal cut in, half rising from his seat. "Though those who don't understand it may find it simple, it is exceedingly complex."

Sanda swiveled toward Dal, abandoning the shirking researcher she'd introduced herself to. Tomas started to feel faint as she moved toward him, coat flaring out around her hips, and stopped at the edge of his table. Even though she was focused on Dal, her proximity was enough to make his head swim.

He could not blow his cover. Not only would it put Sanda at risk of Nazca retaliation, it would also ruin his chances to stop Rainier from releasing her swarm on the gates. Now wasn't the right time.

"What's your name?" she said, extending her hand to Dal. He took it in both of his and shook once, exuberantly.

"Dr. Dal Padian. I've been on this station for six months now, Major, working on micronizing the amplification relay systems already in place coming out of the gates. It's very—"

"Padian is one of our best," Liao said, slipping around the table to insert herself between them. "We're very lucky to have him. I'm Dr. Liao, nominally in charge of affairs here in the lab, which are, admittedly, boring. Would you like to visit our modeling subsection? We have a scale model of the signal relays that pick up broadcasts pushed through the gates."

"This visit isn't a tour, Doctor. I'm here to meet your staff and assess the viability of this station." Sanda's right hand reached down and back, stretching toward Tomas. She grabbed the tablet—his tablet—off the table and glanced down at it. He'd been so distracted by her presence, he'd forgotten to lock the screen like all the others had. Her jaw clenched as she scrolled through the data he'd been reviewing. What did she see in it? Did she know anything he didn't?

"The station is self-sufficient," Liao was saying while Sanda scrolled on and on. Liao clutched her hands together in front of her chest, resisting an obvious urge to yank the tablet out of Sanda's hands. She shot Tomas an annoyed look, but he barely noticed. He'd been there two days. The mistake could be forgiven.

"Yes, yes, I see that. Your recyclers are top of the line, you produce enough O_2 to resupply any vessels that wander by low or damaged, very good of you, but what are you cooling?"

Liao took a step back. "I'm sorry?"

Sanda jabbed at the tablet a few times and flicked it around for Liao to see. Tomas strained across the lab table, craning his neck to get a better look. The motion caused Sanda to notice him. Fuck, he did *not* want to be noticed. The MetBath had rearranged his face enough to pass, he hoped, but a new face didn't hide your body shape, your natural body language.

Her gaze skimmed over him. Zero recognition. His chest ached.

"And you are?" she asked, extending a hand to him.

He didn't want to take it, superstitiously afraid that the skin-to-skin contact would erase the facade, allowing her to see him for who he really was, or at least who he had been when she'd met him.

He took it anyway, pressed his clammy palm into her cool, strong hand, and shook once, meeting her gaze. "Leo Novak, ma'am. I ain't a researcher or a doctor like the others, just a deft hand with engineering. I'm new here."

I don't know anything, stars and void, don't ask me.

"Call me Greeve," she said, taking her hand back. She cocked her head as if listening to something, and that was when he noticed the comm unit looped over her ear. He had to focus. To erase that this was Sanda from his mind. There was too much going on, too much at stake. All the little pieces of a puzzle he had to solve, broken apart and thrown into the wind.

"Greeve," he repeated, then caught Liao glaring at him and ducked his head.

"How new are you?" she asked him, but she was distracted, listening to the voice in her ear while she tapped away at her wristpad.

"Second day working," he admitted.

She paused, finger poised above the pad. "Rough."

"Sorry?" he asked.

"I am," she said, and pressed a button.

All the viewscreens in the room went out. The lights dropped to emergency mode, salt-yellow, red LEDs flashing on any access panel that led to anything important. An alarm blared, an insistent bleating.

Sanda said into her comm, "Turn that shit off."

Someone did. The lights stayed low while the viewscreens burst back into life, temporarily blinding Tomas. He brought an arm up to shade his eyes and turned away from the central screen. It ran code, lines of grey text streaming by. Meaningless to him. The station's systems had been hacked, that was all he needed to know.

Liao squeaked and hit the ground, ducking behind Dal's table. Sanda's people—Nox and the fleetie—had their weapons out. Nox's rifle was pointed with calm indifference at Lt. Davis, the fleetie's at Marya.

"This station is under fleet control," Lt. Davis said, voice ratcheted high with fear.

Sanda sighed and pulled the blaster from inside her coat, leveling it at Davis. "It is now. You, Davis, are not fleet. Divest your weapons and stand down."

Marya looked from one to the other with bulging eyes. "We're—we're a civilian research station—"

"Keep telling yourself that." Sanda snapped the words off. To her comm, she said, "Find me a clear path to the ice-box."

"It's food storage!" Marya said. "That's what we're cooling—food, water, rations, the usual."

"I am, in fact, not an idiot."

Sanda stepped around the table without losing her clean line of fire on Davis. Tomas swallowed. He had to defuse this. Had to get her the fuck off this station, but there was nothing he could do without blowing his cover, and that would get them both killed. *Steady*, he told himself, calling upon memories of Caid's training to calm his building panic. When a situation seems impossible, wait. Wait for the cracks to grow in which to wedge yourself. Everything breaks eventually.

Sanda bent a knee and grabbed Liao by the back of her lab coat, dragging her to her feet. Liao stumbled, keeping her head tucked down and her hands up around her ears. Her whole body shook.

Tomas couldn't take his eyes away. Usually, when violence broke out, he was in the center of it. He rarely, if ever, was one of the victims. Decades of wading into gunfire had immunized him to mortal fear, as the Nazca had intended. What Liao displayed now, that bone-shaking dread, was so, so far away from him. The closest he ever felt to real fear was when someone he cared about was in danger, and then... What had he felt? Anxiety that he couldn't *fix* the problem? How fucked up was that?

"I won't hurt you," Sanda said to Liao who, sensibly, didn't believe her for a second.

Sanda stepped back into the center of the room, taking Liao with her. "Davis, I believe I asked you to divest your weapons. I won't ask again."

"I can't do that," Davis said, a soft whine in her voice. Her arms trembled.

The door dilated. While everyone in the room flinched away from the motion, Tomas watched in dazed wonder as Nox and Sanda, synchronized, flicked their gazes to that opening and to each other. Nox shifted to cover the door, Sanda stayed on Davis. Tomas was annoyed to feel a pang of jealousy at how easily they worked together.

Jules entered, thumbs hooked in the loops of her slacks, a single eyebrow arched high as she turned her gaze on Nox.

"You could have just knocked," she said.

CHAPTER 28

PRIME STANDARD YEAR 3543

PRICE OF PROTECTION

Vladsen rubbed his hands together, the most animated Biran had seen him in years. "Right then. How do we do this? Do you write test speeches?"

Biran shrugged. "Dozens, then toss them all away and speak from the heart when the moment comes. Not that the drafts don't inform what I say, mind you."

"Not exactly approved methods," Shun mused.

Biran threw up his hands. "None of this is."

"Well, what do we say to get the populace on our side?" Vladsen asked. "As you have the instinct for it, I'm happy to take a backseat and assist in any way I can."

Biran rubbed his palms against his thighs as they started to turn clammy. "The populace will not listen to us. Firing them up to be the savior of one hero, of their own home? That was a simple thing. People will pull together to save one, especially if it is one of their own. People, however, will not react similarly when the number is larger, and known to them only as an enemy for so many generations. They will shrug their shoulders and say it is to be expected, Icarion bucked the rules for too long, they are only getting what is coming to them. Why should Ada go out of its way, take a risk, to keep them from being ground into dust?"

"I don't understand." Vladsen genuinely looked perplexed. "What the director said..."

"Oh," Shun said, softly.

"Yes," Biran agreed. He forced himself to look up, to meet both of their gazes. "Director Olver, as I'm reminded time and time again, did not reach his post by accident. The man is cunning, and not oblivious to the hearts of our people. There is only one group which may be persuaded to take a risk to save Icarion, and that is the Icarions themselves."

Vladsen sucked air through his teeth. "That will give Hitton a fine case for treason against us all."

Biran nodded. "We have only the knowledge that Olver will support us, without revealing his approval, and that Anford does not want this war, to protect us from that accusation. If either of you would like to leave this room now, I will not hold it against you, and I will never mention your names in this context."

"No," Vladsen said. He licked his lips. "I believed in Lavaux's goals for longer than I care to admit. I actually thought... I *believed* he and his wife were trying to help people. I have, perhaps, strolled closer to real treason than either of you. If I'm going to misbehave now, it may as well be for the greater good."

"While I do not share your colleague's motivations," Shun said, "I share his conviction. Whatever Ms. Lionetti's reasons were for aiding Icarion, I failed her. It is my job to guide all my students, and I did not see the hook that drew her to Icarion. If I can do something not only to aid peace, but to squeeze some good out of her legacy—even if her name is never again spoken of in this context—then I will do so. The risk is nothing."

"This is all very heartwarming," Vladsen said, "but now that we're clear we're prepared to commit treason to save that rebellious rock, how are we going to do it? Prime technicians could patch us into their media, but we won't get in by ourselves, and Keeper Garcia has his hands all over IT here. He'd stop us cold. If there's an Icarion version of your reporter friend Callie Mera for you to call, Speaker, I doubt they'd speak to us."

"We don't need their media," Shun said, then stopped herself.

"Go on," Biran urged.

"Well, getting through to their media would get their people riled up, but would do nothing to move the official hands of Prime, and what we need is a message so clear that the High Protectorate cannot avoid an answer. Put on the spot, the Prime Director would have to admit that we do not trust Icarion not to take advantage of the location. While that wouldn't hurt the High Protectorate politically, admitting that they did not have the strength to protect their assets would be unheard of for Prime.

"Okonkwo and her colleagues would be forced to throw resources at Anford. With the gate secure, all cause for avoiding the project goes out the window. Assuming the in-depth survey comes back clear, naturally, which I have every faith that it will. I would clear the site this minute if there weren't so very much riding on it."

"Ah," Vladsen said. "You suggest we put the proposal to Bollar, then? Instead of unintentionally undermining his power by going directly to his people, we give him and Negassi a little leverage?"

"It could work," Biran said. "It puts us at higher risk of treason prosecution, but Bollar and Negassi know that they cannot win this war. And they know, too, that their current supply chain is precarious. They will want the gate. And, as you said, Okonkwo and the High Protectorate would only make themselves seem weak by denying the location due to its proximity to Icarion."

"How do we approach them?" Shun asked.

Biran exchanged a glance with Vladsen, who returned a conspiratorial smile. "The members of the Protectorate can make that call at any time."

"Olver must have realized..." She trailed off.

Biran cleared his throat. "Shall we do this now?"

"Before any of us develops a sudden thirst for life?" Shun asked.

"Keeper, if you—"

She waved a hand at him. "I jest. Please, yes, do it now. Continual fretting will lead to no clearer conclusion."

Vladsen nodded his approval, but did not reach for his wristpad. Well, Biran supposed it wouldn't be the first time he'd made a similar unauthorized call. Biran tapped in the priority number to Bollar's wristpad—he wouldn't risk Negassi intercepting this—and waited. When the president of Icarion picked up, Biran noted that he had dark circles under his eyes that had been obscured in virtual space. No one wanted this war.

"Speaker Greeve," Bollar said distractedly. "We have no meeting scheduled, and despite what your people may think, Icarion is busy getting on with the business of everyday life. I hope this is important."

Biran put on his contrite diplomat's smile and queued up the ident lines for Shun and Vladsen. "I apologize for not scheduling this meeting in advance, but developments here came about rather quickly, and I thought you should be made aware of our discovery sooner rather than later."

All pretense at distraction dropped away. "What discovery?"

"I think it best if I allow our expert to explain. I have with me here Keepers Vladsen and Shun."

"Vladsen I know. Shun—?"

"A teacher, but her primary focus is elsewhere. May I connect them to this line?"

"Be about it, man."

Biran nodded and tapped through the connection. Shun and Vladsen appeared screen-in-screen in the chat view. Everyone, Biran thought, looked much more exhausted here, outside the net meeting room. More real. More weary.

"President Bollar, I may have a solution to all of our woes."

Shun launched into her explanation of the asteroid, leaving out its provenance and many details that Prime would balk at having shared. She kept to the facts, and as she spoke, Biran noted a small, blinking red light flick on in the room's corner, where the cameras were. Well, they'd gotten someone's attention, at any rate.

While Shun talked, Biran surreptitiously pressed the interior lock overrides for the war room door. They could still get in, and they could cut the feed, but not without making the intervention obvious to the Icarion president on the other end of that call, which would make Prime look weak. Like it had lost control of three of its best Keepers. They would not do such a thing. Cohesion was what held them together. The door rattled. It did not burst open.

Shun ended her explanation, and Bollar agreed to report to his own advisers and schedule a conversation at a later date, once Shun and the others had secured scouting resources for the asteroid. He seemed... hopeful. Lighter, somehow. That emotion was not easily faked, Biran well knew. If Bollar knew about the asteroid before this moment, if his people had planned it as a trap, then he was the greatest liar Biran had ever known.

He rambled off a few parting pleasantries and ended the call, looking up to meet the gazes of his coconspirators. "Are you prepared?"

Solemn nods. Biran unlocked the door.

The rest of Ada's Protectorate waited on the other side, faces grim, a black crescent of guardcore flanking them while Anford stood in their middle, her usually stolid expression torn between anger and amusement.

Olver spoke first. "Speaker Greeve, I thought we talked about these stunts."

"My apologies, Director. I saw no other way to secure peace for both our peoples."

"You conniving little shit." Hitton shouldered her way forward. "Whatever distaste you harbor for me personally, my fears were not unfounded. That gate—if it can even be built!—cannot be protected to a standard in accordance with our custom."

Biran strained to keep some of the exhaustion from his voice. Now that the adrenaline of the moment had fled him, his limbs dragged him down like deadweight. "General Anford, do you believe that the High Protectorate will fail to provide you with appropriate fleet support?"

Anford laughed. Biran had never before heard her lose her tight rein. This wasn't a barked chuckle or a forced laugh for the sake of maintaining comradeship. This was damn near hysterical. That sound, more than anything he'd ever done, raked claws of dread up his spine.

"By the void, do you have any idea what you've done? Okonkwo will give us support, I grant you that. If that gate goes up, and Prime loses it, Prime loses everything. Every ounce of authority it's scraped from between the stars will be thrown into question. The gate will be reverse-engineered. Humanity will splinter.

"So yes, Speaker. Okonkwo will send us more fleet. She'll pour so much firepower down our throats you won't be able to throw a rock without hitting a Prime weapon from the day that survey comes back clear until we're all dust, because Prime *cannot, under any circumstance, lose a gate*. The civilization of Ada Prime is now a military installation. Congratulations."

Anford glanced down at a tablet, scowled, then tossed it into the room. The thin metal casing clattered over the table as it hissed, spinning around to the center. An incoming call light blinked merrily up at them.

"Prime Director Okonkwo's calling," Anford said. "You all should deal with that. I'm going to get a drink."

CHAPTER 29

PRIME STANDARD YEAR 3543

INSPECTION'S OVER

Nox dropped his rifle nozzle the second he registered who had walked through that door. Sanda swore under her breath and pivoted, covering Jules with her blaster while Knuth kept Davis covered.

"Careful," Arden said over open comm, and Sanda knew damn well that warning wasn't for her. She wasn't the one who dropped her gun.

Nox brought the rifle back up, painting the door again. "What the fuck," he said, which was probably the most to-the-point thing that'd been said since they left Atrux.

"I work here," Jules said, lifting one shoulder in a shrug.

This wasn't right, not by a long shot. Jules *looked* like she worked here—hell, everyone in the lab seemed relieved to see her, as if she had authority on station and they hoped she'd fix the problem that just rolled into their midst. Everyone, that was, except Novak. That guy looked cool as anything, and a calm newbie in a gunfight was someone worth watching.

"We've been trying to get your attention for years," Nox said, his voice sharp.

"You've got it now," Jules said, then waggled her fingers at him. "Hello."

"Where's Lolla?" Nox demanded. Smooth.

Jules's expression blanked. "Safe. I promise you, she's safe."

"Get her. We're leaving."

"Maybe you haven't noticed," Jules said, extending her arms to take in the lab, "but this is my station. I am in control here. I have no reason to leave."

"I ain't leaving without you and Lolla."

"Are you here to kidnap us?"

"I want to see her. Let me talk to Lolla."

"That's not possible." Jules sighed heavily and shook her head, slow and disappointed, an elaborate motion to hide the pain that clawed behind her eyes. Sanda frowned. That was not the body language of a street kid risen to power. She was putting on airs, tap-dancing hard to make Nox believe she was in charge here, that he could leave and everything would be fine. She kept flicking her gaze to the cameras in the corners.

"Currently," Sanda said, "this is my station, and I am in control. We're not leaving until we've secured the position of Lolla."

Sanda couldn't shake the fact that this room, this lab, looked so much like the lab she'd discovered Kenwick's head in. Couldn't ignore the massive amount of cooling going on in the lower levels. Couldn't ignore, either, that somehow Jules had ended up with a dead Keeper at her feet. One who had, according to Nox and Arden, tried to kill her for a piece of data found in a lab that must have looked a lot like this one. Above all, she couldn't ignore that Rainier had something to do with it all.

"I've not yet finished my inspection," Sanda said.

Jules met Sanda's eye, and she very much got the feeling that the younger woman would like to put a bullet in Sanda's head. She couldn't blame her, really. Whatever game Jules was playing, she desperately wanted Nox out of here—and Sanda was not helping.

"You have," Jules said.

The door swished open and stayed open. Five soldiers wearing fleetie uniforms but moving too individually to be a trained unit poured into the lab, weapons out, and painted Sanda, Knuth, and Nox in the lock-in lights of their rifles.

"I'm going to have to ask you to leave," Jules said.

Sanda exchanged a glance with Nox. There were too many damned civilians in this room. The mercenaries dressed as fleeties could be overcome, but if a fight broke out, there was no way to avoid hurting the scientists. Sanda couldn't bring herself to take that risk.

"You're going to get your charter pulled," Sanda said, but she held her hands up, letting Liao go, and set the blaster on the lab table nearest her. Nox and Knuth followed her lead, setting their weapons down, hands up.

"I doubt that," Jules said, flicking a gaze to the ceiling. Sanda frowned.

"If you come with me now, Ms. Valentine, I will see you cleared of all charges."

Jules's shoulders hunched. "Nice try." To the fleeties, she said, "See our guests out, will you?"

"Jules," Nox said, and Sanda was surprised to hear strain in the man's voice. "You don't have to do this."

"Yes, I do. I'm... sorry."

Jules turned away, unable to look him in the eye, and nodded to Davis. The fake fleeties waved their rifles at Sanda and her entourage, marching them out of the lab into a tight huddle in the hallway. Good, a little farther and they'd be clear of the civilians. Far enough.

Sanda stopped walking, hands still up. "I'm not leaving without speaking to your superior."

"Not in a negotiating mood." Jules grated out the words.

Sanda turned her back on Jules and stared into one of the hallway cameras. "Rainier Lavaux, are you too much of a coward to face me?"

In the corner of Sanda's eye, Jules grimaced. She reached up to touch the comm unit in her ear, tilting her head to hear better.

"Not him," she hissed. After a long pause, she closed her eyes in resignation, but nodded. "Understood." To the fake fleeties she said, "Take the others to their ship. Major Greeve, on your knees."

Sanda dared to hope her gambit had worked, then she saw Jules reach for her blaster. The young woman's hand was steady, but her lips had gone bloodless and a fine sweat misted her forehead. She did not want to do what she had been ordered to do, but she would. Whatever strings Rainier Lavaux pulled, they were worth more to Jules than Sanda's life.

Sanda held Nox's gaze as she dropped to one knee, hands behind her head.

He could leave her here, easy as could be. Could walk out that door, commandeer her ship, and go off to do whatever it was he wanted to do next, after being rebuked by the friend he'd been trying to save for the last two years. If he believed Jules was in control here, that's exactly what he would do.

Knuth, Conway, Graham. Trained in weapons, all of them, but as she met Nox's gaze, hard and impassive, she knew damned well they'd be pushovers for a man like Nox. All he had to do was make the choice to leave her here, and she was dead. Or worse. Probably worse.

"Sorry, Jules, I'm afraid the major has another appointment," Nox said, and blew open the head of the nearest fake fleetie with their own weapon.

CHAPTER 30

PRIME STANDARD YEAR 3543

WORST POSSIBLE TIMING

When everyone's attention turned to marching the invaders into the hallway, Tomas pocketed the blaster Sanda had left on the table. She didn't know it was him—couldn't have—but that single action, that accident of proximity, solidified a plan in his mind so fast it almost took his breath away.

Dal made a grab for his arm, shaking his head *no.* Tomas pressed his fingers to his lips and motioned down to Liao, who sat on the floor with her knees up to her chest, breathing hard. Dal's expression tightened, stricken, no doubt wanting to argue, to keep Tomas from stepping out that door with a major's stolen blaster in his hand because, in Dal's mind, that was suicide.

Shooting broke out. It was over before Tomas even made it to the door.

He stepped into the hall and took a mag boot to the chest. Stars burst behind his eyes and that boot shifted, striking him in the wrist, knocking the blaster away. He'd like to say he'd gotten hosed so easily because he was playing the role of Novak but, really, they'd taken him by surprise. His ego was more bruised than anything.

Vision swimming, he tried to figure out what had happened. Sanda stood next to him, her blaster back in her hand and pointed at the ground. All around, the bodies of the fake fleeties cooled, but he couldn't see Marya. Jules was another story.

She'd backed into a hallway, hands up, her blaster on the ground in front of her. Nox stared at her, but his rifle was pointed at Tomas, which he felt was unfair considering the circumstances.

"Come on," Nox said. "We gotta bolt."

"I can't," Jules said, and it sounded like the words cut on the way out. "I need Lolla."

Sanda stiffened. "Where is she? We're not leaving anyone behind. You're safe now."

Jules let out a soft, wispy laugh. "You have no idea. I'm so sorry, Nox. Tell Arden... Tell Arden to let it go. Only Rainier can help her."

"Bullshit," Nox growled. "We're getting off this station. Now."

"Not with me," she said, and turned around, sprinting down the hall so quickly Tomas had to squeeze his eyes shut to chase away the blur in his vision. He shifted, trying to angle himself to see what Jules had done to create the effect, but she was already gone.

"Goddamnit." Nox kicked a wall panel and swung around, focusing his ire on Tomas. "What the fuck do you think you're doing?"

"Don't kill him, it's only his second day on the job," Sanda said.

"Employment history's not my concern," Nox said. "He came out packing."

"So he's a brave idiot."

Sanda dropped to a crouch beside him and nudged his cheek with the blaster. "Mr. Novak, I know you're conscious."

He blinked blearily and genuinely tried to look alert, but damn Sanda could kick like a mule when she wanted to. Pain radiated through his chest. He coughed.

"He's disarmed. He'll live. Let's go," Nox said.

"Thanks for giving me my weapon back," she said, and stood.

Tomas got his eyes open and rolled onto his side, looking as pathetic as he felt to keep them from getting jumpy. The fake fleeties were in various states of dead-and-dying, blood pooling across the floor. The subtle nudge of gravity from the hab's spin pushed the dark liquid toward him. He grimaced.

"You got those fucking cameras yet?" Sanda said into her comm. "We lost—"

The lights went out. The station screamed like a wounded behemoth and bucked, throwing everyone—living and dead—into the air, smashed them all against the wall, and rocked, groaning, as it shuddered back into alignment and the lights came hesitantly, flickeringly, back on.

"What the *fuck*," Sanda said, then hacked up a cough.

Tomas found his arm—twisted up behind his back—and gingerly brought it around to its usual position. Not broken, despite all the odds. He let out a sigh of relief and opened his eyes again, fearing that he'd trigger another catastrophe. This time, nothing happened.

Sanda stood with her knees bent, back pressed against the wall. A fair amount of blood covered her. After they'd been tossed around, it was hard to tell whose was whose. She wasn't moving like she was hurt, at any rate. It took him a second to realize she was adjusting the prosthetic on her leg.

Nox and Knuth were on their feet, holding position with their guns painting down the hall in either direction. Nox's comm unit had been twisted in half, a bit of wire dangling from the broken chunk still attached to his ear. A small trickle of blood slid across his jawline.

Sanda listened to her comm, then choke-laughed. "The berserkers tried to self-destruct the damn station. Conway got most of them the second they started firing."

Nox slammed one fist against the wall hard enough to dent the metal, then went right back to holding his rifle like nothing had happened. "Fucking bitch. We came to *help* her."

"Consider all the ways in which you'll get your revenge later." Sanda pressed the comm to her head, as if she was having a hard time hearing the other end. "The way back to the *Thorn* is a death trap, open to vacuum. This station is listing and its jets are failing, HVAC failing, too. Arden thinks they've got us a clear path to the shuttles on the fifth level. Only one cluster of evac pods, and Page fired them all on the way out."

"That's not up to code," Knuth said.

"I'll file a report," Sanda said.

"I bet Jules is headed to the shuttles," Nox said.

"Arden has cameras. She's gone lower. Visual is out below the third."

"Lolla. She's going to get Lolla. We have to—"

Sanda straightened. "If Jules is going to get Lolla, then she's the best person for the job. We'll only slow her down. And we have to get the civilians off this floating coffin."

Nox stared at Sanda so hard Tomas could practically feel the tension thicken the air between them. He had a much larger rifle. If he fired, any hit could take her down, and she'd have to be a damn lucky shot to put him down before he could get a round in.

Tomas crept his fingers along the floor, through a sticky puddle of blood, straining for the blaster tucked in the holster of a downed fleetie.

"Your call, Commander," Nox said at last.

Sanda pressed on the comm. "Arden? Arden? Can you still hear me? If you get this, we're going for the shuttle, bringing about, uh—" She spun around and addressed Tomas. "How many of you are there? How many civs on board?"

"Eight?" He guessed. "Valentine said we were bare bones, and I haven't met anyone except my colleagues, the fleeties, and Marya."

"Dios, could you be any less useful?" She rolled her eyes and pressed the comm again. "Eight, approximately. If you can hear me, open the way and prepare a rescue, these people might be hurt."

"Speaking of." Nox grabbed a plastiskin patch from his bag, then tossed it to Sanda.

She grimaced. "Thanks."

Tomas hadn't seen it before, but as she pushed her coat aside she revealed a long gash running across her hip. Shallow, but leaking blood. She peeled the back off the patch and slapped it across the wound, then sighed with relief.

"On your feet," she said to Tomas. It took him longer than he'd like, but he obliged. "If any of your colleagues are injured, help them move. If you so much as think about going for any of the guns on the ground, I will end you myself. Understood?"

He nodded numbly. Even if he thought he could get away with

telling her who he was without bringing down the wrath of the Nazca, neither one of them needed the distraction of a surprise reunion right now.

"Good." She slapped the door open and stood in the flexed aperture. Beyond, the lab was a mess of broken electronics and shattered people. Everyone was alive, so far as he could tell. Dal and Liao were seeing to the worst of them, a woman who lay on the floor, moaning. Every head whipped up and around when the door opened, each one of them freezing in place.

"Look," Sanda said, "your boss just used your berserker drone net to try to self-destruct this station. The only reason we're talking is because my ship intercepted the fire. I don't know what the fuck your reasons are for being here, and I don't care. I can get you out. You won't be prosecuted."

"We—we have a *charter*—" Liao said.

Sanda fired her blaster into the central viewscreen. It exploded in a puff of safety plex and a hiss of wiring. "Charter revoked. And your fleetie friends? Fake as the sunshine. Carry those who can't walk. We're going."

"Yes, ma'am." Dal shoved a tablet into his pocket and got an arm around the shoulders of the woman on the ground, heaving her to her feet. Tomas's retinal implant reminded him her name was Sarai.

This was the moment Tomas could leave. The scientists were distracted, gathering themselves together in a double line of limping ducklings to be led into the hallway under Sanda's wing. Sanda and her crew were equally distracted, keeping tabs on the health of the station even while they watched nearby doorways, anticipating another ambush, another fight.

It would be so easy. Slip away, duck into a nearby room, and wait for them to move out. They wouldn't look for him, they'd count him a lost cause—already dead—and work on getting the survivors out. He wasn't a threat worth tracking down, not as Leo Novak.

With the station damaged and under Arden's control, he could even take the time to pull up his suite of Nazca programs. Data mine the station, find out what they were doing here without the eye of whoever watched through those cameras on his back.

He could crack his way through their security, reach the lower levels where Jules was headed while his programs ran, and talk his way into whatever escape ship she had waiting. This was chaos, and chaos was the state in which a Nazca worked best.

Sanda stumbled, put a palm against the wall to steady herself. Shook off a surge of pain and straightened.

Being a Nazca could wait.

CHAPTER 31

PRIME STANDARD YEAR 3543

ONE DEATH TRAP TO ANOTHER

Knuth took up the rear, herding the scientists along, while Nox and Sanda held a firm front line, following Arden's patchy and staticky directions. Normally Sanda would have ordered Nox to the rear. He was a better shot than Knuth, as the brief fight with the fake fleeties had confirmed, but every step she took was agony, and though she wouldn't say it, she didn't trust herself to stand up long to a fight if they met one.

They turned a corner, and a disconcerting groan echoed through the hallways. Her stomach swooped, body lurching as the hab's spin lost speed in a staccato stutter that settled down after a few agonizing seconds in which she believed they were all about to stop being biology and start becoming physics.

"Arden." She pressed the crackling comm against her ear. "You're in this bucket. We need a stable spin-down. We were damn lucky the spin didn't stop when the whole thing kicked, but I've got a bad feeling it's going to spin itself to shreds, or stop hard."

"Say again?" Their voice was a crackling wire.

"Fuck," she said, then shouted into the comm, "Spin. Down."

"Understood."

Sanda paused at a juncture and turned to face her bedraggled pack of scientists, all hunched together and dripping blood across the station that had been their home.

"Listen up," she shouted. "I'm spinning this station down before it does so on its own. If you've got internal injuries, I'm sorry, zero-g is going to suck. Turn your mag boots on and tough it out. We'll get through."

Dal, the chatty scientist who'd been so quick to defend the importance of their work on the station, put a hand up. "Sarai can't manage with the boots," he said, and jabbed his free thumb at the woman he was holding up by the shoulders.

Sarai lolled against him, eyes glassy, a steady stream of red making its way down her leg from somewhere about her torso to puddle in the aforementioned mag boots. There was no way she could coordinate herself enough to work the boots. Hell, they were probably too heavy for her to lift.

Sanda suppressed a grimace. She may not have had major training, but she'd been a sergeant long enough to know you didn't let bad news show on your face. Not when there was hope, however slim.

"Can you carry her?"

Dal's forehead crumpled with distress, his cheeks already red from exertion. "I—"

"I've got her." Novak shouldered his way through the others and, gently, took Sarai's weight from Dal. At first, Dal tried to hand her over in the way most civs did—wedding-carry style—but Novak shook his head and shifted her weight so he could drape her across his shoulders in a fireman's carry.

He met Sanda's gaze. Something about him wasn't right. How calm he'd been during the inspection, and then walking into the hall immediately after a shower of gunfire. Holding a high-end blaster like he knew how to use it.

Chest muscles like that didn't come from getting an engineering degree. They could—anyone could visit a gym, after all—but Novak's specialty led to work done on station, not in the gravity well of a planet. Even on the nicest habs, heavy weights were hard to find. Cardio and basic resistance was pretty much all you got in space.

She checked out his thighs, wondering how they'd gotten so sturdy, then found herself checking him out in general and shook her head to clear it. This guy was an anomaly, and that was as suspicious as unrefrigerated pudding, but he was willing to help.

"Don't drop her," she snapped, annoyed with herself, and turned back to the split hall. Arden pushed through a map of the station to her wristpad, and it lit up to show her the way.

"That guy don't fit," Nox whispered.

"Hard for him to get in the way with a body in his arms."

"Sure about that?"

"Not in the slightest. Shit goes down, shoot him first."

A deep, teeth-rattling vibration went through the station. Sanda put a fist up, calling a halt, and braced one hand against the wall, swallowing against the sloshing, sickening sensation of the station burning inertia.

"You've had your station blown up," she said to the scientists who were retching and weeping behind her. "This is nothing. Just a little slowdown. It'll pass." She kept on talking, because it was either that or join in with the barfing. "This is normal. It's expected. Just physics, and you all are the masters of physics. Dios, you've written dissertations more painful than this."

Dal laughed wryly at that, scraping his lab coat sleeve across his lips. Novak clutched Sarai to him, eyes squeezed shut, looking green around the gills but otherwise holding on. Liao and the others leaned on each other, against their own knees, on the wall.

All the fluids in her stupid meatbag body did one last final loop-de-loop and Sanda squeezed her eyes shut, flexing her thigh muscles, begging the stars and all her ancestors to keep her from passing out.

Weight lifted.

She opened her eyes. The station kept on groaning, metal popping and creaking and filing complaints left and right, but the hab was spun down, thank the void. They wouldn't go splat from sudden deceleration.

"Thank you, Arden," she said into the comm. A screech of static answered.

"Elevator ahead," Nox said.

Sure enough, once her vision stopped swimming, she saw it too: a large, rectangular door framed in black-and-yellow hash marks, letting everyone know that the place this elevator was headed might have hard vacuum on the other side. Sanda licked her lips.

"Arden said we'd have atmo," she said.

"Warning lights aren't on," Nox said, and shrugged. "Seal must be good on the other side."

"Warning lights aren't guaranteed to work right now." Sanda double-checked her wristpad. Yes, this was where Arden had planned for them to go. There was a closet panel next to the lift, where helmets would be stored.

She, Nox, and Knuth were wearing jumpsuits that fit the couplings of the helmets. The scientists weren't. Sanda holstered her blaster and made for the closet.

"I'll go check the air conditions. Nox, stay with them. Keep them calm."

"Not my specialty."

"Learn."

She swung the panel open and selected one of five helmets.

"Major," Novak called out.

She hesitated. "What is it?"

"Take that guy"—he pointed his chin at Nox—"in case there's more fleet down there."

Leaving all eight scientists with only Knuth to watch their backs. Fat chance, especially considering Novak, of all people, had made the suggestion.

"I got it," she said dryly before yanking the helmet on. It sealed to her jumpsuit collar immediately, then flashed up a warning that it wasn't connected to anything. "Yeah, yeah," she muttered and grabbed one of the lifepacks from the closet. Her major's coat would get in the way, so she stripped it off—sorry, Anford—and hooked into the pack, plugging the helmet in. Everything went green in the HUD, including the comm line. Perfect.

She grabbed another helmet and tossed it, tumbling end over end, to Nox, who snatched it out of the air and cranked it on his own head. He flipped the visor up so that the no-lifepack warning would go away.

"Can you hear me?" she asked over comm.

"Loud and clear."

"Finally, something fucking works." She slapped the button for the elevator and the doors slid open. No alarm bells yet, that was all she could ask for. "Watch the kittens. Shoot anything that swipes at them."

"Affirmative."

She grinned as she stepped into the elevator, selecting the button for the level below. "Sometimes you sound like a fleetie."

"Rude," he said.

The doors swished shut, and the elevator rumbled into life, dragging her down. All according to plan, except... Novak had been staring at her far too intensely in the seconds before those doors closed. The elevator's display ticked, counting down the meters to the next level. She pulled her blaster back out and checked the charge.

CHAPTER 32

PRIME STANDARD YEAR 3543

NEVER TRUST A DISEMBODIED VOICE

Sanda had her blaster up and pointed at the door when the elevator came to a stop, doors sliding open in a shuddering, jerking motion that made her think the shaft had been damaged during the onslaught.

Light the color of watered-down blood filled the room beyond. She hesitated in the open maw of the elevator, not liking the lay of the land before her. The room on this level was cavernous, more in line with the usual construction of inhabited stations but, for that, suspicious. The transition from tight tunnels to wide-open spaces made her skin itch. Anything could be out there, waiting in the dark.

"Atmo?" Nox asked.

She stepped out, mag boots clanging over a metal walkway. The helmet's HUD cycled the local conditions. No gravity, but the O_2 was acceptable and the space was pressurized.

"Habitable," she said, "but I don't see a shuttle."

"I'll start sending them down."

"Hold until confirmed clear."

A pause. "If you think there's resistance, I'm coming down."

"Sit on your gun, Nox. Let me get eyes on this damned shuttle."

"Aye, *sir*."

She could practically hear the sarcastic salute that came with that, but Nox wasn't her problem right now, clearing this room was. From the deck of the *Thorn*, she recalled that the sixth hab ring was substantially smaller than the seventh. If the whole station was collapsed down, each subsequent hab ring would fit perfectly inside the next.

She crept forward, using the light of her blaster to paint the wall nearest the elevator door. A nondescript panel was the only break in the wall, about a hundred meters in the direction that would be antispin, if things were working as they should.

Her steps echoed loud enough for her to pick them up through the insulation of her helmet, a clanging noise that went on and on, indicating this room may be larger, and emptier, than she thought. The blaster could illuminate only a narrow cone of light, everything else fell away into the murky darkness mingled with red emergency lights. Her only consolation was that if anyone had been waiting to ambush her, they would have done it by now. She wasn't exactly in stealth mode.

She reached the panel and flipped it open, glaring at the wide variety of buttons and switches that, at the present, held no meaning to her. Maybe she should have brought Novak down with her. He was an engineer. And then she could have kept an eye on him.

"Try the blue one," a scrambled voice, digitized but high and lilting, entered her helmet.

Sanda whipped around, lighting up a fan all around her with the light from the blaster. More perforated metal flooring, ramps, crates, and ladders. But no *one*, not so far as she could see.

"Arden?" she asked the helmet, feeling stupid. Maybe they'd patched their way into the helmet network on Janus. In less than a minute. Without knowing she put the helmet on. And made their voice higher. Yeah, it was a shitty idea even to her.

"Who is this? Rainier?" she hissed.

"Got someone down there?" Nox asked.

"Clear this channel," Sanda said.

"Uh—"

With an expert flick of her eyes, Sanda kicked Nox out of her helmet comm.

A soft giggle, limned in static. "He's going to think you've lost your mind."

"Jules? If that's you—"

"Not Jules."

She suspected she was speaking with Rainier, but the voice was too grainy with static for her to be certain. "If you're Janus personnel and need help evacuating, come to the sixth level."

"Personnel isn't exactly right. Don't worry about me, Major dear, your guess was right the first time, but it seems like you need help, doesn't it? Try the blue one."

An icy feeling crawled across Sanda's skin, one she recognized all too well. The feeling of being watched, from all angles. She clenched her jaw, resisting an urge to tell Rainier to go fuck herself with her own space station.

"Rainier, I want to talk. Where are you? I can get you and Jules off this station if you give me a little direction here."

"Don't you want to save your friends? I said, try the blue one."

Sanda closed her eyes and blew out a slow breath, for if she didn't take the time to do so, she was going to scream her face off.

"I am reasonably certain you ordered the destruction of this station when Jules failed to execute me. Why in the void should I trust you?"

"You can't. Probably shouldn't. This station is disposable. You may or may not be. I haven't decided yet. Your call on the whole living-or-dying situation."

If it were just her ass on the line, she'd call Rainier's bluff and wait to see if she could get the woman to show herself, but she had a handful of scientists waiting a level above, and none of them could make it off this dissolving behemoth without help. She clenched the grip of her blaster so hard the weapon shook.

"Tick-tock, Major."

Sanda turned back to the panel. Running along the right-hand side of the display was a narrow, pulsing button in a soft blue light. She hovered a finger over the button and waited for a sign. Nothing.

"If this is a trick, I'll make you pay." She pressed it.

Lights came up across the hab, flicking on one by one, the whole place humming like a waking giant with the thrum of diverted power.

This, she realized, was not a priority hab. No one lived here—it stored shuttles and crates. When the emergency systems had kicked on, all the station's power had been diverted to its essential systems. This wasn't one of them. Now that the lights were on, she could see a shuttle resting halfway across the main floor from where she stood. In the dark, it would have taken her far too long to find it.

"This isn't over," Sanda said into the digital ether.

"Next time, I think I'll kill you."

"What—"

"Here he comes."

A squeal of static filled her helmet and she was forced to switch off that channel, leaving the voice behind. Yellow lights lit up near the elevator, drawing her eye, and the doors slid open—hiccuping in their frames—to reveal Nox, all alone, his rifle out and ready. She lifted a hand to him and switched back to that channel.

"We're secure," she said over comm.

"Fuck, I thought you'd been ambushed down here. Who the hell were you talking to?"

"Rainier, I think. She's more cracked than I thought, but we'll hash that out later. This place is bleeding power, we gotta get the others out before we lose life support."

A crackle over the comm. Knuth said, "I hear that right? We're clear?"

"Yes, bring 'em down."

"Affirmative."

Nox swore and ducked out of the elevator, stumbling a little, as the yellow lights flashed and the doors started to shut. He scowled after it, then turned around to take in their surroundings. Crates, ladders, and a single shuttle.

"That's our ride," Sanda said, pointing with her blaster's light at a shuttle resting on a mag pallet about three hundred meters away. Nox groaned, pointing all around with the light on the end of his rifle, even though the room's lights were up full whack.

"This is a friggin' warehouse, is there even a hangar door?"

Sanda shifted her light. "I think I see one over there, they had to get the cargo in here somehow, right? If not, I'll signal Conway to blast us a new hole."

"They can't even hear us."

"I'll figure it out."

She had to get these people, her charges, into that shuttle. There were eleven of them altogether, and the shuttle looked maybe, maybe big enough to hold six, but it had to last them only until they could get to the *Thorn*. Then, with the ships twinned, they'd have air and supplies aplenty.

The elevator slid open, revealing the first batch of stumbling scientists. Three rounds, she told herself, mentally counting them off as they glanced around, wary.

"Nox, take them, get them settled."

"On it." He pushed his visor back up. "Come on, clear that fucking elevator, we got more on the way."

They stumbled out in a hurry, grouping into a tight knot as Nox waved them onward.

"Clear," Sanda said over comm to Knuth.

The elevator whooshed away and came grinding and gurgling back with the second batch. Nox was there in time to greet them, and though Sanda could have played guide, that would require her pushing her helmet's visor up to talk to them and, for the moment, she didn't want to do that. Because, at the moment, she was watching the vital signs of the station's life-support systems tick away and die.

"Make it quick, Knuth," she said tightly.

Nox trotted up to her, a tricky thing to do with mag boots on, and flipped his visor down, switching over to lifepack supply. "Station's dying," he said.

"Agreed. We gotta go now. Move it, Knuth."

"Loading."

Sanda pursed her lips to keep from swearing. Nox leaned over and nudged her, lightly, pointing up at the ceiling with one gloved finger. She expected cameras, or even more fake fleeties, but he was definitely pointing at a thick collection of tubes and pipes, bundled up tight, pulsing with a strange grey-violet light.

"What is that?" she asked.

"Was hoping you would have an idea."

"I do not." She craned her head around and spotted Liao lingering by the shuttle's airlock. The diligent leader, waiting for her whole crew to make it. That would have to do. Sanda pointed at her, then waved her over. She came, warily, but she came.

Sanda and Nox pushed their visors up.

"What is that?" Sanda asked.

Liao squinted. "I can't be sure. Coolant, maybe? Or a nanite conduit?"

"Nanite conduit? That's not exactly standard, Doctor."

She shook her head. "I'm sorry. My team wasn't allowed below the seventh level. We were working on micronization, so that was an educated guess."

Sanda frowned. Rainier had said that the station was disposable. While it wasn't possible to take anything she said at face value, maybe what Rainier had been avoiding saying was that she didn't want the truth of the station's contents found.

Liao said, "If I could get a sample, then—"

"Excellent idea. You got anything to take a sample with?"

"Without knowing the origin of the matter, I can't risk contamination—"

"I got a flask," Nox said. "Empty."

"Perfect," Sanda said.

"This really isn't the way to—"

"Dr. Liao, I respect your concern, I do, but this station is dying and in less than an hour you won't have anything to take a sample of."

Her expression hardened and she held one trembling hand out to Nox. "The flask, please." He passed it over. She craned her head up to the ceiling. "But how am I to reach it?"

"Easy," Nox said. He kicked the back of her mag boots, deactivating them, grabbed the back of her neck by the coat and crouched down, then swung her upward with all his strength.

Sanda watched the woman rocket toward the ceiling, screaming all the way, then collide with the cables exactly where she needed to be.

"Was that necessary?" she asked in a low voice.

"Probably not."

To her credit, Liao got herself oriented and dug in her pocket for a pen stylus then, leaning away in case the goo was under high pressure, pierced the tubing. A silver-violet curl extruded from the puncture, helped along by whatever systems were keeping the pipes moving. Liao put the flask up to the puncture, careful not to touch anything.

"Empty flask, huh?" Sanda asked, watching Liao work.

"Was full once."

"How long ago was that?"

"You don't want the answer to that question."

"As long as you can shoot straight."

"Got it," Liao called down as she screwed the cap onto the flask and tucked it, carefully, into the pocket she'd taken the stylus from. She squinted and looked around. "Uh, how do I get down?"

"Put your feet on the ceiling and kick," Nox said.

She closed her eyes, mouthed a prayer to something, and did as Nox asked. A little harder than was necessary.

"Shit." Nox slung his rifle over his shoulder and lunged forward, grabbing the doctor before she face-planted into the floor. "It's air you're pushing through, woman, not water or honey or, I don't know, cooling fluid."

Liao laughed nervously as she twisted around and clicked her mag boots back on. "I haven't spent much time in low-g."

"No shit."

A grinding, shuddering noise filled the echoing space of the warehouse. Sanda grimaced and hooked a thumb at Liao, indicating she should get back to the shuttle. She didn't need to be told twice. Sanda flipped her visor down again, bringing up the HUD.

Not good. Breathability levels were drifting toward the red, and she didn't need access to the station's emergency map to know half the joints in the place were held together with little more than hope and a prayer.

"Knuth, get your ass down here."

"Uh," he said.

She snapped her head toward Nox and he took the hint, flipping his visor down.

"What's the delay?" she asked.

"That grinding noise you heard was probably us."

Sanda closed her eyes and counted backward from five. "Is anyone hurt?"

"No. I mean, I've got Novak carrying Sarai here, but we don't have any new injuries."

"Right. I'm coming to get you."

"Greeve," Nox said, opening a private channel so that Knuth wouldn't hear him. "We're down to fifteen percent breathability and falling hard. If they're not right on the other side of that door, they're already dead."

"My recycler's good for another few hours, I can share it out if need be. Get to the shuttle and hold them down, make sure the little fuckers don't get spooked and take off without us."

"What if I get spooked?"

"You're not the spooking type, are you?"

He didn't answer that, just shook his head exaggeratedly so that she would see, then turned around and clanged his way back to the shuttle. Alone, her palms began to sweat. But that's what the suit was for, the smart materials working to wick away moisture. Yay for technology.

She glanced at the elevator door. When it worked, anyway.

CHAPTER 33

PRIME STANDARD YEAR 3543

WHERE'S GRIPPY WHEN YOU NEED HIM

Sanda forced the doors to the elevator shaft open and peered upward. Red lights cast the narrow chamber in the murky-bloody light the warehouse had been in, but this time there wasn't a suspiciously helpful voice telling her what to do.

Figured. Luckily the elevator had been designed to be maintenanced, and though she didn't see any repair bots at the ready, there was a narrow channel along the wall big enough for one to squeeze through without getting caught by the elevator if it sped past while the bot was working.

Being wider through the hips and shoulders than the average repair bot, Sanda took a moment to wish Grippy was here, then wedged herself in with her back against the wall and pulled herself toward the stalled elevator. At least they weren't under gravity. Dios, her side hurt.

"I see you," she said.

A piece of ductwork had protruded from the wall and caught the descending elevator. It was now wedged between the cab and the wall, crumpled like an accordion. She could in theory pry the piece free, but that looked like a real quick way to get her fingers smashed off. She checked the atmo level outside: 5 percent and falling.

"There's an access panel on the bottom," Sanda said. "Can you get it open?"

"Hold on."

Huffing and puffing and cursing came across the comm, but the panel didn't move.

"It's stuck," Knuth said. "Maybe if we forced the doors—"

"Then you'd be facing the wall."

"Oh. Yeah. Right."

"Knuth. You're my *engineer.*"

"I'm . . . not good under stress."

She sighed. "Please make sure the stop button is engaged. I'm about to stick my head out and I'd really like to keep it."

"Pressed," Knuth said.

Expecting nothing less than steely death from above, Sanda eased herself out of the maintenance canal and twisted around to get a better look at the hatch door. A piece of the broken duct had wedged itself into the opening mechanism, because of course it had.

"I'm coming out to force the hatch. Don't fucking touch anything."

"Understood."

She pushed off from the wall, angling herself at the hatch, and landed right next to it. That was the easy part. She told herself the brakes were engaged, and even if they weren't, the damn thing was *stuck* and the fact that it couldn't come crashing down was the entire reason she was here in the first place.

Still, she eyed the cabling system as if it were a viper coiled to strike.

In a stroke of luck that was very much not in line with her current state of affairs, the piece of duct was caught only in the hinges, not rammed so deep she'd need tools to dig it out. She pulled it free and flicked it away. It bounced off the shaft wall and drifted back toward her, floating by her boot, mocking her.

"Clear," she said, ignoring the shard, and flipped the hatch open.

Knuth bent his head over the hatch and gave her a thumbs-up.

"Civs first," she said, "this tin can is bleeding air."

Knuth turned away and Sanda pushed to the side, opening her comm to Nox. "Got them, coming down now."

"Good, I was starting to consider drinking this purple stuff."

"If you do, let Liao perform your autopsy."

The hatch birthed Dal, his too-clean mag boots kicking feebly in the empty air as he struggled for purchase. Sanda sighed. They could float here all day—if it wasn't for the air and the rapidly dissolving ship—but the human instinct to be frightened by heights was sometimes overwhelming, even in those who spent their time on stations.

She grabbed his ankle and pulled, making him let go of the hatch. He panicked for a second, going stiff all over, then saw her floating there, holding onto his boot, and blushed.

"Don't mag until you hit the bottom," she said through the external speakers on her helmet, and put one arm against the bottom of the elevator before giving him a gentle shove. He let out a squeak of surprise, but was safely on his way down the shaft.

"Next," she said over comm.

Novak's boot poked through, and she resisted giving him the same treatment only because he was carrying Sarai. He climbed through quickly and efficiently, mag boots off and one arm looped around the body of the wounded woman to keep her from getting away from him. He was about to push off, angling himself down, when he caught sight of her and hesitated.

"You should really get in the maintenance channel."

"You should really get the fuck on with things," she said, and grabbed his ankle, giving him a yank to speed things up. "Move it, Knuth."

Knuth wriggled through the hatch and, without so much as a hello, shoved off the bottom of the elevator and went rocketing down to the bottom, leaving her alone. Jerk.

Sanda looked at the way down the shaft, then at the maintenance channel, and made a snap decision. She'd rather be out faster, than out safer. While the dropping air wouldn't bother her, the longer they dicked around with the elevator, the longer the civilians risked hypoxia. She'd seen the horrors of hypoxia in a trained spy, and didn't want to see that stupid-dreamy state set into these people who stood no chance of regaining their faculties in time.

Okay, fine, mostly she didn't want to carry them all back. Low-g or not, she was tired and already trembling from the efforts of the day.

Sanda heel-kicked off her mag boots so they wouldn't be attracted to the walls and shoved herself down. For a moment, it was liberating to be floating free in low-g. The elevator began to groan. At first the stuttered hiss of misaligned belts slapping against their mechanisms echoed, then the deep crunch of bending metal.

Novak stuck his head back into the shaft, eyes huge. "Get out!"

"Move!" she snapped, and didn't bother to look to see if he followed orders. She twisted so that her path would angle her onto the floor on the other side of the open elevator shaft door, then yanked her blaster free and fired at the bottom of the elevator. Newton's laws took over from there.

The ground hit. Pain exploded through her hips and slammed into her back. She swallowed a curse and tucked, trying to redirect her momentum into a roll to clear the shaft but she'd been too slow.

Someone grabbed the back of her suit and yanked. The elevator screamed by, metal shrieking, to the lower levels. The thin air, disturbed by its passing, gusted scraps of metal and grit toward them.

"I hit the stop button, I swear," Knuth said shakily through the speakers. He offered her a hand, and she took it.

"I believe you. Elevators don't fall in zero-g." Sanda staggered to her feet, heart hammering. The foot part of her prosthetic crumpled as she tried to put weight on it, bits of broken metal rattling in the casing of her suit and boot. Needles of pain shot through her lower back. She grimaced and stood still, trying to find her balance. "Someone decided to make a point."

Her gaze tracked to the cameras embedded in the walls, the ceiling. Knuth followed her glance, but it was Novak who said, "Marya or Jules?"

Sanda shook her head. "Neither."

"Station malfunction, then," Knuth said.

"No. Speculate later, move now."

She tried to take a step but her mag boot didn't move, the broken ankle joint lacking the requisite force to make it deactivate long enough to lift so she could walk. She closed her eyes, cursed a few gods and stars and everyone she knew in positions of authority. Working the boots with one foot was nigh impossible.

"I've got a malfunction here," she said over open comm. "Going to disconnect from mag."

"Your prosthetic—" Novak said, cut himself off, and turned his face away to hide the expression. "I've got a spare arm."

"You keep an eye on Sarai."

Dal extended her an elbow. "This I can help with."

She disconnected the mag boots and hooked her arm in his. She hated being reliant on anyone, but her only other option that came with any speed was jetting the lifepack and she didn't know how long that would last—or if she'd need the pack soon.

Novak glanced over his shoulder at her, worry pinching his narrow face. What kind of overblown hero did he think he was? This wasn't a CamCast video where he could rush into the hall waving a gun and get the bad guys to stand down. It sure as shit wasn't a damsel-in-distress situation, and his habit of trying to intervene was starting to grate.

Maybe he was one of those weirdo fans of hers. One of those people who'd seen her through the public lens her brother had painted and decided she was a hero worth worshipping. The thought gave her chills. Fans weren't something she was ready to take responsibility for, though it seemed the most likely scenario. It'd explain how he knew she wore a prosthetic, anyway.

Crackling speared through her helmet speakers.

Arden's voice: "I've got control of the hangar door. Pack up and come home."

"Affirmative," she said.

Before she boarded the shuttle, she turned around and gave the cameras of the station one firm, decisive middle finger.

CHAPTER 34

PRIME STANDARD YEAR 3543

EVERYTHING BREAKS

Jules ran faster than possible down the myriad halls of Janus Station, telling herself that running away was her only option. Trying to take Nox with her would have only slowed her down. There was no time to explain things, and she still needed Rainier's help to wake Lolla.

Nox would make it. He had to. This was the mantra she repeated to herself, over and over again, as the walls around her groaned and her wristpad flashed warnings and signals and cries for help from the station itself and all the fake fleeties on board.

The station was breaking apart. It was all breaking apart.

But they had come for her. Impossibly, Arden and Nox had gotten Major Greeve to loan them a gunship and her person to come track Jules down, to save her. Even as her heart broke apart with the station, that small truth buoyed her. Made her steps come faster, ascension-agent or no.

Marya screeched at her over her wristpad, demanding to know what was happening. Jules had lost track of her after Sanda and her hit squad had taken down Davis and the others. Marya could figure it out for herself. Jules's only responsibility was to Lolla.

She'd never put the coffin back, and if anyone had noticed it there, they'd said nothing. She thanked whatever instinct had given her that paranoia and flung up the cockpit lid, crawling inside while alarms blared.

A cheery AI voice greeted her, bright and kind, which felt like scraping steel wool over her eardrums right about now. Jules dialed in navigation instructions that amounted to "evade and get the fuck away from here" and strapped in.

The shuttle trembled, a low vibration jarring her molars together. It flashed a low-power warning at her, but Jules swiped it away. What the fuck was she supposed to do about that? Hang around and recharge while the station tore itself apart? Goddamn Rainier and her self-destruct. What was she *thinking*? The research was there. Many of her duplicates were there. Rainier kept some nanites off-site, but was it worth it to her to destroy a station to take out Major Greeve?

Jules twisted to put a hand on the coffin, bracing it with inhuman strength. Inertia foam lined the back of the cabin, but the shuttle jerked and rattled as it released itself from the dock and dove aggressively through the narrow funnel-tip of the station.

The ship spun, slamming her into the foam seat. She squeezed her fingers against the plex of Lolla's coffin until her knuckles cracked, desperately trying to keep it stable.

The frantic spin eased, lights on the dash winking green at her instead of the bloody red-orange-yellow mélange they had been. Jules took a long, shaky breath to prove to herself she could still breathe and followed it up with a frantic burst of laughter.

"Shuttle," she said to the ship's AI, "show me Janus Station."

"Happy to help," the chirpy voice said.

The viewscreen filled with smudges of grey and white and silver against a curtain of black. Jules frowned, leaning closer, but the splatters of color made little sense to her.

"Are your cameras damaged?" she asked the shuttle.

"Everything's in tip-top shape."

Jules scrubbed her eyes with the heels of her palms. Those weren't globs and splatters of color. They were chunks. Massive pieces of the station, twisted and ruined, drifting away on whatever course their destructive energies had set them. Jules licked her lips. Her rat maze, reduced to rubble. Lolla's hope. Nox...

"Shuttle, are we damaged?" she asked, flipping through a series of diagnostics.

"The shuttle received a minor graze. Flight trajectory was temporarily altered, but we have recovered. I can no longer recommend your flight path, however."

"What? Why? I didn't even program anything specific." Had she already fucked up how the shuttle functioned?

"I lack the required battery power to move in that direction, making it incongruous with survival."

"How long can you fly? I need to get to Atrux." She didn't know why, not exactly, but she had a burning need to see that planet again. To go home.

"One hour."

Fuck. That wasn't enough time to get anywhere near the gate, let alone the planet, and she wasn't even sure she could grease her way through the gate once she got there.

Rainier may not have outright turned on her when she triggered the self-destruct, but Jules lacked the resources to bribe her way through on her own.

"Is the ship that last docked with Janus Station still in the area?"

"The *Thorn* is leaving."

"Good. They can't leave if they didn't survive. Send—send them a tightbeam. Ask for a chat with Nox and Arden."

"I do not possess the requisite transponder code for tightbeam communication with the *Thorn*. If you could enter the number now—"

"I don't have it." Her hands coiled into fists. "Fine, fuck it, send a widebeam, paint up the area with a signal that a shuttle needs help."

"Commencing communication," the ship said.

Jules craned her neck to get a better view of the coffin. It'd pressed itself into the hatch on the back of the shuttle, but didn't seem damaged. The status screen showed all the right numbers, including a full charge of power.

If Nox and Arden would listen to her long enough to let her explain, then she could rendezvous with them on the *Thorn*. She wouldn't be able to stay, and that would be one of the hardest conversations she'd ever have to have, but it would get her and Lolla out of the black.

Once they knew about the ascension-agent, they'd have to let her go back to Rainier. For Lolla's sake.

The widebeam was intercepted, and Rainer's face—or one of them, anyway—filled the screen.

"You didn't have to get out of my maze by breaking it, you know."

Jules shook as she turned around to face her. "You set the whole fucking thing to self-destruct!"

"I couldn't have *that* research falling into the wrong hands, and the station was compromised. It's too soon."

"The research? They hadn't touched it!"

"Of course they had. Arden Wyke was in the station's systems. Everything was compromised."

"What about Marya? Did she make it out?"

"Oh yes. That girl always had an exit plan. Went straight for an evac pod the second gunfire broke out and never looked back. Deployed *all* the pods at once. She took what she wanted and is fleeing from me now. Isn't that funny? All your desire to get away, and the one who wanted to be nearest to me is the one who made it out."

"You could have killed us all. At the very least you should have given me the trigger so that I could make sure we were clear!"

"You worry too much. I wasn't so foolish as to store the data in one place, and Arden did not have long enough to download anything."

"Data? I'm talking about the people."

"Does human life mean so much to you, Juliella?"

"Does it mean *anything* to you?"

"Oh dear." She leaned toward the camera, fingers laced together under her chin in a cradle. "Are you trying to break away? To assert yourself? How much power does that shuttle have? How far can you get before you have to hook Lolla's energy stores into the system to keep you alive as you limp toward the nearest station? Do you think you can get there before her stasis chamber gives out? Do you believe, really, really believe, that when you get where you're going the people there can fix whatever damage was done to the little one in your desperate flight?"

"Why must you leash me?" she demanded, body shaking with

shock or the onset of sobs or both. "Why do you drag me back if you don't *care*? I will betray you someday, Rainier. You must know that."

"And when you do, it will be on my terms, to my benefit. And there's not a single thing your tiny brain can do to get around that. Now, if you're done with your tantrum, prepare for capture. There's something I want to show you."

The screen flicked to black before she could answer, a request for piloting control flashing on the console in the same instant. In a small corner of the display, Jules watched the *Thorn* pull away, widebeam never received.

Every last scrap of strength in her drained away as she pressed accept on the nav request.

CHAPTER 35

PRIME STANDARD YEAR 3543

ONE MORE DECEPTION

Sanda found that the scientists, once safely on board the shuttle, had rather a lot to say about their future. Liao, who was green in the cheeks but otherwise recovered from her shock, floated near the airlock, one hand on the grip set into the wall next to it, and stared Sanda down.

Or tried to stare her down, anyway. Sanda switched her helmet visor to mirrored, so Liao was staring at herself.

"We are not prisoners, Major. I understand that the station you found us working on may have deceived us regarding the legality of our activities, but we are victims, and we will not be held like cattle in a pen."

"I'm not saying you are prisoners." Sanda spoke over open comm so that the others would hear her. None of them had needed serious medical care, save Sarai, and even she was sitting upright now, strapped into an inertia couch, with Dal offering her tiny sips of water from a pouch. "But I'm not letting you on board the *Thorn*."

"Why in the void not? We're...we're refugees, and this shuttle is only intended for short, interstation travel. We don't have enough chairs for everyone, for stars' sake."

"You've got enough once my crew and I return to the *Thorn*. We're not abandoning you. You're tethered to the *Thorn*. I swear we won't leave you behind."

"You didn't answer me *why*."

"Dr. Liao, I don't have to. Step aside, please."

Her lips thinned, but even she knew that all her protests would be a pointless retreading of previous arguments. If Sanda told her why she wanted them to stay on the shuttle, Liao could use that as a lever to force her opinion. But Sanda wouldn't. Because she didn't need them to know that she suspected one of their number was a spy.

Liao tried a disappointed head shake, but Sanda had grown up with two exacting fathers and was inured to that kind of thing. Not getting the reaction she wanted, Liao pushed off the door and floated out of the way. Finally.

"Major—" Novak began.

"Unless it's life or death, save it." Sanda swiped her ident over the lock and stepped through, Knuth and Nox tight on her heels, and slammed the shuttle side closed. They waited in tense silence while the sensors involved equalized the slight pressure differences between the shuttle and *Thorn*, then popped the door open on the *Thorn*. Graham stood immediately on the other side, arms crossed, chin tilted down, one eyebrow up. Shit. Liao should have tried *that* posture.

"What the fuck were you thinking?" Graham said.

"Nice to see you, too, Pops," Sanda said, and yanked off her helmet, shaking out her sweat-sticky hair.

"That station was dissolving under your feet and you wasted time—"

"Saving the lives of eight innocent scientists?"

He snapped his mouth shut.

Sanda kicked off the floor and gave him a brief, but tight, hug before floating by. She dragged herself by the ceiling handholds toward the command deck. Her helmet, she left floating.

"I taught you to clean up after yourself!" Graham shouted after her.

"You know where the helmets go, old man," Nox drawled. "We all pitch in on this bucket."

She grinned to herself and pushed through to the command deck, Nox on her heels, leaving poor Knuth to explain the situation to Graham. Arden met her gaze as she floated through and, after a second's pause, grinned back.

"He's been waiting for *hours* to tell you off."

"Guess he'll wait a little longer." She swung herself down into the captain's seat and synced her wristpad, pulling up an array of status checks on the forward screen. She frowned.

"What's up with our air recyclers?"

"We're burning through air filters," Conway said. "We were in to repair the system when we got the call to pick you up. I think the lazy fucks in maintenance shoved a new filter in and sent us on our way. Since Knuth was with you on Janus, I sent Grippy to check out the system."

Anford. There was no doubt in Sanda's mind that the general had given Sanda a ship prone to blowing through its filters to force her to land it, at some point, and let fleet engineers monkey around in the guts of her ship. The second the fleet touched the *Thorn*, it'd be crawling with new surveillance devices. Anford may have had time only to load the thing with surveillance software before she sent the ship to Sanda, but she'd pulled her one ace and made certain Sanda would have to give her a second chance.

Sanda pinged Grippy, requesting a status report. A flood of data came back, but the analysis was simple enough: the HVAC system was pushing air through the filters at a higher pressure than standard, causing them to build up gunk faster.

She pressed a comm button. "Knuth, I need you to look at the HVAC. Something's gone fuck-y there and I don't want fleet hands on it. I'll send you the report from Grippy, feel free to use the bot."

"On it," Knuth called back.

"Fuck-y?" Nox asked.

"Tits-up, sideways, gone to shit. Come on, gunhead, stay with me."

"Speaking of fuck-y," Arden said, "what happened with Jules?"

"I've got no goddamned idea. Insights, Nox?"

He stripped off his weapons and began checking them before putting them back into the locker in the bulkhead. "She told us off. Looked like she was in control of that whole damned station, but..."

"But she wasn't," Sanda said. He looked up from cleaning a blaster and met her gaze, obvious relief washing over him. "I don't know Jules, but that behavior was off. She wasn't even comfortable in her own clothes, let alone that station. Someone else was calling the shots, looking over her shoulder, and I think we all know who that was."

"Rainier," Nox said. "Sanda was contacted by her through comms, and played her helmet recording back for me on the shuttle to the *Thorn*. I recognized her from the speakers at Udon-Voodun. It was different, distorted, but the intonation..."

"Big word, big guy," Arden said, but their voice had a slight tremor.

Nox didn't take the bait. "It was definitely her. I think Jules was trying to keep Lolla safe. She said... said to tell you to let it go."

Arden puffed up their cheeks and blew out a long, slow breath. "What's going on? Why does Rainier care about keeping Jules? She has to have access to better-suited people. And why bother taking Lolla?"

"We'd have to ask her, and even then I don't think she'd give us a straight answer," Sanda said heavily. "Now, we have the little problem of eight refugee scientists on our hands."

"There's a fleet port not far from here," Conway said, flicking up a map to the way station onto the main screen. "We could drop them there."

"If the Keepers are compromised, then much as it pains me to admit it, the fleet probably is, too. There were mercs wearing fleet uniforms on Janus."

Conway grimaced. "I can't believe Anford would allow that to happen."

"Neither do I. Which means she doesn't know, and we can't be sure how far the deception has spread. I won't drop these people off at a fleet base if there's a chance there's impostors there. Get me a list of civilian stations in range of our filters. Something with security."

"It's a bit far, and it'll push our recyclers, but there's a SecureSite-operated station in this sector, back in the direction of the Ordinal–Atrux gate—Monte Station. Big enough to have permanent residents, no fleet presence. It's privately owned and of no strategic significance. They're gene-splice farmers."

"Conway, set course for Monte Station. Arden—get me a secure line to Laguna."

Nox and Arden exchanged a glance. "Maybe we should leave the deck for this one."

"If you like. Arden, make the call before you leave. Nox, get me Liao and have her waiting at the door when this call's over. That woman knows more than she's letting on."

"Understood," they said in unison.

While the call pushed through the gate, reaching all the way back to Laguna's wristpad on Atrux, Sanda took a moment to center herself. Three slow, deep breaths later, her heart was still in her throat when Laguna's face popped up on the forward screen.

"Detective Laguna, nice of you to take my call."

"It came in on a priority line, Greeve, you hardly gave me a choice. But SecureSite is always happy to help our friends in the fleet in whatever way possible, blah blah blah, what do you want?"

"Actually, I have something for you. It will soon be public knowledge that a civilian research station called Janus in the Ordinal system was found in violation of their charter. In fact, I am convinced they had no such thing and the paper trail will be revealed to be fake. Regardless, the scientists on board the station were unaware of their illegal status, and when pressured, the controlling body of the station initiated self-destruct procedures rather than submit to questioning."

"That sounds like a headache for the fleet, but it's nothing to do with me."

"Janus Station was administered by Jules Valentine." Sanda sent the few still images she'd grabbed from Arden's time controlling the cameras to Laguna's wristpad. The detective leaned forward, eyes bright with interest.

"You have her?"

"No. Unfortunately she escaped with at least one other accomplice."

Laguna closed her eyes. "Damnit. Where was she headed?"

"Unless you have access to a gunship, Detective, I suggest you leave the pursuit to me. Valentine seems to be embedded in larger powers than anticipated for a thief from the Grotta. I do have something for you, however. The scientists."

Her eyes narrowed. "While I'd love to get my hands on them, Greeve, shouldn't you hand them over to your superiors for debriefing?"

Sanda shrugged one shoulder. "Larger powers, Laguna. Strangest thing—our air recycler is running funky and the nearest port in this particular storm is Monte Station, where I believe a large contingency of SecureSite are already in place. I have every confidence that your people will take good care of my charges while we patch up the ship and continue pursuit."

Laguna pursed her lips, taking Sanda's measure. The lie was a thin one, but Sanda hoped Laguna would overlook that. She was being handed an opportunity on a silver platter, and Sanda didn't think Laguna would miss her chance to interview people who had been in direct contact with Jules.

"Consider me en route. In the meantime, Leon Gutarra runs things there. Old friend of mine. I'll give him a heads-up you're coming."

Sanda nodded. "Thank you. Greeve out."

A heavy silence pressed in on Sanda. It wasn't a perfect silence, nothing like what she had experienced when being spaced in the scant seconds before the beat of her heart drowned out everything else. This was a missing silence. The point when, after setting a plan into motion, Bero or Tomas would interject.

Instead, Conway tapped steadily away at her console, the movement of her fingers and the constant hum of the ship's HVAC the only sounds. Obedience, as she'd expected from her ship's crew in the years before Dralee. This was, or should have been, her normal. The captain's chair was a lonely place, by design, and she had ridden that emptiness often enough before Dralee. Before Bero.

And yet... and yet, it hurt.

She turned her wristpad, scrolled through the fleet's internal news stream on the search for Bero. Nothing yet. He'd locked down his comms and thrown himself into an endless night to take out a weapon that could destroy her people and, if Sanda had been right, be a lobotomized version of himself.

He had braking procedures. She told herself he could stop, could turn back at any point. His stealth tech was cutting edge, and if Prime hadn't been able to find him after he'd taken off in what was essentially a straight line, then he must be stealthed. He might be okay. He might.

She touched the image of him accompanying the article, battered by his escape from the hangar, then swiped the feed away and tapped her comms.

"Nox, I'm ready for Liao. Let her bring a second, if she wants."

"On it, boss."

Sanda brought up a priority line to Anford, only accessible through her wristpad, and waited. Bero might be okay. She might be, too.

CHAPTER 36

PRIME STANDARD YEAR 3543

LEVERAGE

Tomas thought Liao was going to get them all killed. She paced the length of the shuttle, mag boots clunking, her long hair hastily tied back and sticking up from the low-g. Space made her nervous. It made many people nervous, but those people weren't usually in leadership positions and hadn't just lost their whole research station.

"I don't understand why they won't let us on the *Thorn*," she said to no one in particular.

Tomas kept his mouth shut, keeping his attention locked on his wristpad. A lot of the other scientists were trying to make calls home, but the *Thorn* had thrown up a comm block. Arden's doing, no doubt. While the others attempted to get around the block, Tomas filtered through what little data he'd been able to snag from Janus while its systems were vulnerable.

"Maybe," Dal said, "because it's a military vessel and we are civilians."

"There's no rule against it," she shot back.

Dal sighed a long-suffering sigh. "No, there isn't. But I've worked with fleeties before, and they don't enjoy having civs underfoot."

"She's trapped us here so she can get rid of us."

Tomas covered up a snort of derision with a cough.

Dal said, "There's no point in that. If she wanted us dead, she could have left us behind on Janus and placed the blame at Valentine's feet."

"They're probably listening to us now," Liao said.

"Quite likely," Dal agreed.

"Trying to decide if we know too much."

He sighed again. "Unlikely. Doctor, please, use that head I know you have. The events of the last few hours have been traumatic, I know, but you should be thinking of ways to thank the major, not to escape a punishment that isn't coming. We did not know that Valentine acted without a charter. The major, and the fleet, will see reason."

Liao slumped into a chair and gripped her knees tight. "We are not innocents, are we, though?"

Tomas kept tapping at his data, but all his attention shifted to their conversation.

Dal said, carefully, "What do you mean?"

"Please," she said. "Use that brain of *yours*. You did not actually believe that the research we were doing was Keeper-sanctioned, did you?"

He licked his lips. "That is what the contract I signed said."

"Yes, yes, we all signed it. But come now, we each knew, didn't we? In our secret hearts? There was no one else on that station, all the below levels were off-limits, and Valentine... She was never quite *right*, was she? Always taking orders from someone else, someone we never saw. Our fleet protectors were all impostors, and the research we were doing never matched the stated mission brief."

"I had no inkling—"

"She's right," another male scientist said, scooting closer to the group. Tomas didn't dare look up to see who it was, and he didn't yet know them all by voice. "Come on, Dal, you said so yourself about Valentine. She wasn't comfortable with the science."

"That didn't mean our operation was illegal."

"I don't blame you for ignoring the signs," Liao said. "We all wanted to believe it was real, didn't we? And all the security made it feel real, but it was just hiding. Hiding because we were doing research that the Keepers would not allow civilians to touch, and that was exciting, wasn't it? Some days, I felt like Prometheus. Stealing the secrets from our gods, getting a glimpse at how their technology works.

"Even now... Even now I desperately want to know what we were really doing there. Don't you all? Weren't you all hoping, even a little bit, that some secret of the gates would be revealed to us if we worked long and hard enough?"

"We just made receivers. Amplifiers." Dal's voice was scarcely a whisper.

"Nanoized, to work with the *gates.* Why would the Keepers even want that? And if they did, why not do it themselves? Face facts, Dal. We were working with technology protected by death statutes. The major isn't going to drop us off at the nearest station and wish us well on our travels. This kind of thing must happen, they must have protocols in place, and I don't believe those protocols involve releasing scientists who may have seen too much.

"Who among us hasn't seen a fellow researcher disappear for skating too close to our gods? They do not intend to let us off this shuttle, because it's our coffin."

A scientist let out a soft sob.

"That's ridiculous," Tomas said. The last thing he wanted to do was make himself even more noticeable, but this was going too far. "Greeve wouldn't do that. She's the damn hero of Dralee, put her ship in the path of a railgun meant for one of her subordinates and ended up a POW. You really think someone like that would space a handful of civilians she went to mortal trouble to save?"

"You don't know her," Liao snapped. "None of us do. We only know what they said in the news. Patriotic bullshit to keep justifying their slow eradication of Icarion."

Tomas's head spun. He forced himself to listen.

"Why would she save us only to space us?" Dal asked.

"To make sure none of us made it out on our own."

The texture of the silence that descended crawled against his skin. These people were frightened, reasonably so, and any attempt from Tomas to win them over to Sanda's side would only oust him from the group and give them a lightning rod to strike.

"Even me?" Sarai asked, her voice soft from the strain of her wounds. "She could have left me for dead. I couldn't have escaped on my own."

"Doing so would have turned us against her. The major is no fool."

"If she is this insidious tactician," Dal said, and though his words dripped with irony, Tomas could tell he was beginning to believe Liao. He just needed a push, either way. "Then how do you hope to outsmart her?"

He already believed Liao; he wanted a plan. Tomas's mouth went dry.

"Dal has a point," a man said. "The fleet has excellent PR, but we all saw footage of her kill Lavaux, she's crafty. I know they said it was a hoax but—"

"Don't bring that conspiracy shit here," Sarai said. "If she killed a Keeper, the High Protectorate would have fried her before she could sneeze."

"I'm just saying, it took them a long time to 'debunk' that video. Long enough to make a convincing fake. She must have something on her superiors to get them to back her up like that, if you ask me."

"No one's asking you," Sarai said.

"Whether or not she's a murderer, we have no leverage here," Dal said.

"We have some bargaining power." Liao pulled a silver flask from her pocket. "I took a sample, in the cargo bay, of a fluid being pumped down into the lower levels—if it can be called a fluid. She will want it, or her masters will. Either way, I will not give it to her until our safety is assured."

"A sample of what?" Tomas asked.

She shook her head. "I don't know, maybe you do, Dal? It was silver and purple, running through clear tubing in the ceiling. The metallic appearance led me to believe it was more of your nanites suspended in some fluid matrix."

"Hmm." He tapped at his wristpad. "It's difficult to be certain without seeing the fluid, but I suspect it was the growth matrix for the amplifiers we had some success with. Valentine wanted them reproducing so we'd have a larger data set to examine the behaviors of, so Sarai and I created a fluid rich in the molecules the nanites would need to self-replicate. It had a definite purple color, though I suspect the silver you saw was merely a sheen cast by a dense presence of nanites. They were growing rapidly."

"Wait," another scientist said, "there are laws against self-replicating nanites. Prime doesn't even use them. Why would Valentine order such a thing?"

Dal shrugged and lifted his palms to the sky. "I am not one to rebuke a Keeper's orders, even if it comes filtered through the mouth of their agent."

Liao laughed roughly, turning the flask over in her hands. "So this is evidence of our crimes, as well as our only leverage to secure our safety."

"I don't know," Sarai said. "Dal and I kept careful records. We could prove easily enough that we received orders to create what we did, and that we adhered to the parameters set to us. It might be evidence of our innocence."

Tomas forced himself not to mention the governors, but couldn't help stealing a look at Dal, who had been so frightened when Tomas had asked him about them. The man had paled and was tugging down one side of his mustache sharply. He met Tomas's eye, and understanding passed between them. Dal wouldn't reveal he suspected the governors were wrong. Tomas inclined his head, pretending to agree.

"We will have to see," Dal said. "But I suspect that, if we keep what we know to ourselves for now, you will find the sample an effective bargaining chip."

"Are we all agreed?" Liao asked the huddled group. "None of us will reveal to her what this is until our safety is assured?"

Wary nods all around. Tomas wondered why he never felt guilty when he lied to his marks, but he nodded with a clean conscience. They were unlikely to discover he planned to tell Sanda everything the second he got her alone. She would ensure their safety with or without the flask.

He needed her to know the contents of that flask, because while Tomas knew what he was *supposed* to do as a Nazca, he didn't know what was right. His masters would want him to grab the sample and hightail it back to base. Possibly, that was the correct course of action.

Prime Director Okonkwo had ordered this mission, and while he had so far failed to discover the truth of what Rainier was, surely a self-replicating nanite swarm that could spin down the gates was a more pressing matter.

But he couldn't be sure. His time with Sanda had shown him that some vital part of his emotional core had eroded, or never existed at all. He felt no guilt when he nodded lies along with his marks, no shame when he pretended secret confidences with Dal. The last time he'd even felt real fear had been during his debriefing, when the Nazca had danced too close to finding out the secret of the chip in Sanda's head.

And if Sanda was the star by which he'd set his course, then he needed her to know who he really was. No matter the danger.

CHAPTER 37

PRIME STANDARD YEAR 3543

ANY PORT IN A WAR

Liao brought Novak with her, the choice Sanda had hoped she would make. Something didn't sit right with Sanda about that man, and she wanted the others to get eyes on him to make their own assessments.

She wanted General Anford to see him, too, but for different reasons. Sanda needed to see if Anford reacted to him—if he was her plant—because Sanda was pretty sure he was somebody's spy, and Anford couldn't be discounted.

"Doctor," she said, when Liao and Novak had clunked through the door onto the command deck. Sanda stayed strapped in her captain's seat and glanced down at her missing prosthetic. "Forgive me for not getting up to greet you."

"There is nothing to forgive. I hope your injuries are healing well."

Liao thumped around to the front of the deck to stand in front of Sanda, picking up her feet like a cat that'd stepped in something sticky. She was not comfortable in space, let alone low-g, but her words were smooth enough. The doctor thought she had an ace up her sleeve, then.

"They're superficial at worst," Sanda said, brushing the concern aside. "Novak, I trust your charge is healing well?"

"Sarai's much better, thank you." He ducked his head down,

watching his boots as much as he watched the floor, hands shoved deep in his pockets.

"Good. I am about to call this incident in to my commander, and I thought you would like to be present to give your account, Liao."

The woman stiffened all over. "Your commander?"

"General Anford. Are you well enough to speak?"

"I...yes, but I'd like some time to prepare..."

"Prepare?" Sanda scoffed. "I'll be honest with you, Liao, and trust you won't foment panic on the shuttle. The air filters on the *Thorn* desperately need replacement and are losing efficiency every minute. We are working on the problem, but at the moment you and your people represent an extreme drain on our resources. My general may ask me to scuttle you."

Liao took a deep breath and squared her shoulders, preparing an argument.

Sanda spoke before she could. "I will not do that under any circumstances, save you or your people become an active, violent danger to my crew. With that in mind, be honest with my superior. That is the only way I can protect you."

Sanda tapped the call button she'd been hesitating over, and Anford immediately flickered into life on the screen. She heard Liao gasp, softly, and her clothes rustle as she tried to shuffle backward but came up against the resistance of the mag boots.

That was all background, though. Sanda was watching Anford, having ambushed her with these two suspect faces, and was...disappointed. Anford flicked her gaze over them, not showing any signs of recognition, then back to Sanda.

"I believe I instructed you *not* to become another press incident."

"Unavoidable. Janus Station initiated a self-destruct sequence."

"Under whose orders?"

"One Juliella Vicenza, alias Jules Valentine. She's wanted in the death of Keeper Nakata."

Anford's brows furrowed. "Nakata?"

"Atrux local." Now that was deeply strange. Anford, of all people, should know about the murder of a Keeper, even if it was two years ago in another system. "She escaped with one accomplice. I was too busy pulling the scientists out of the station to get the details."

"You know for certain she escaped?"

Sanda shrugged. "Our ship tagged a shuttle leaving from the lower levels where she had been headed. That's all I can say for certain. Meanwhile, I've got eight civilian scientists in a shuttle attached to the back of my ship like a barnacle. And, wouldn't you know it, rapidly strained air recyclers."

Anford arched a brow. They both waited a beat to let understanding sink in.

Sanda moved on. "I've got safe passage and harbor assured for them at Monte Station, a local civ under the protection of SecureSite."

Anford's gaze flicked to the side as she tracked the *Thorn*'s position on an out-of-view screen. "There's a fleet station within range. Go there."

Sanda took a breath. "No."

"Excuse me?"

"There are a lot of reasons I can give you, and they'd be close enough to the truth to make you feel you got something toothy to put on your reports, but I'm not going to bother with the bullshit. These people"—she inclined her head to Novak and Liao—"were doing research under the assumption they had a charter from Prime. They did not. That pretense was further reinforced by security on the station dressed up in fleet uniforms, but they weren't real fleet. I don't know what's going on out here, Commander, but I'm not putting these people in fleet hands until I know there aren't more impostors flying under the radar on our bases."

"They could easily be lying to you about their knowledge of the station's charter."

"They could be, but I don't believe so. What I saw on that station inclines me to believe them."

"And what did you see?"

"Absurdly tight security directed at the resident scientists to keep them from delving too deep into the station. These people were not meant to know what their research was for."

Anford looked pointedly at Liao. "You must have grown curious, Doctor…?"

"Liao. And yes, we were curious, but we believed ourselves under a Prime Inventive charter, and your people have taught us not to ask questions, General."

"There is one more thing you need to know," Sanda said, steeling herself. "I have evidence that links Rainier Lavaux with that station, though the extent of her involvement is yet unclear."

"A vendetta against the widow of the man who tried to kill you, Greeve? Petty. The guardcore cleared her of all involvement."

"If the fleet is compromised, the guardcore might be, too."

A flicker of doubt passed over Anford. "I could mark you rogue and force you to come into dock. I should. If the Protectorate were here with me now, they would order me to do so. Your brother being the sole dissenting voice, no doubt."

"They're not there with you."

"No, they're not. And truth be told, the lines of power get muddied out here on Ada, where the Protectorate that oversees me is not the one that elected me to my post. If I were back in Ordinal, and this system hadn't dragged me here with the throes of war, then you and I might be having a very different conversation."

"And what conversation are we having?"

"One in which I allow myself to indulge my instincts, instead of my protocols. Take them to Monte, get them in secure hands. I cannot promise you what will happen once they're placed. More than likely the Protectorate of Ordinal will send their own forces to take over their handling, but it gives you some time."

Sanda kept her expression neutral. "Time to do what, exactly?"

"Get to those coordinates. If one Lavaux is tangled up in that station, with impersonating fleet personnel, then it's more important than ever you discover what Keeper Lavaux was running for. Go. Get me evidence I can *use*, not suppositions."

"You are giving me freedom to proceed as I seem fit?"

"I gave you a gunship, Greeve. I expect you to use it. You have your orders. Anford out."

The screen blanked.

"Do you really believe we are in danger, Commander?" Liao said in a small voice.

Sanda scratched the back of her neck. "Yes. Once Valentine orients herself, people will come for you, and we don't yet know who those people are. As you heard, we believe Valentine was in contact with a Keeper associate."

"You mean there *was* a charter?"

"No, I do not."

She licked her lips. "That is...that is dangerous information, if true."

"It's a dangerous universe," she said, feeling the echo of Bero's words. "And I am telling you that much because it is true, and because I am going to ask you to do something you do not want to do, and I need you to understand the importance of what I'm asking. You heard the general. I need evidence of what really happened on Janus Station. I can't get that without you, Doctor."

"You want *my* help? I don't know anything, I was hired through a headhunter. Ask Novak, he's the one who came waltzing in claiming Keeper Lavaux had hired him. Personally."

"You spoke with Lavaux?"

Novak shifted his weight and did everything he could to avoid eye contact. "Not really, ma'am. Just got the job request and relocation orders from him. All digital, never even had a conversation."

She arched an eyebrow. "So you dropped everything and ran to join a team on a space station you knew nothing about?"

"Don't got a lot of choice when a Keeper asks, do you? And anyway, there was information in the request. Said they needed someone more engineering-minded to help them troubleshoot some details about a communications system, that's all."

"When did you receive this summons?"

"A few days ago..."

"Keeper Lavaux was not alive at that time."

Novak hunched and rubbed the back of his neck. "It was a lot of money, Commander, I didn't think too much about it, you get my meaning."

She eyed Novak, scraped the shifting, squirming man from head to toe. A suspected spy with a communications background was just... too close. Alarm bells in her head were ringing, but she didn't know how to answer them.

This man wasn't Tomas. Even if he'd changed his hair color and slapped some colored contacts in, he wouldn't have had the time to do the plastic surgery required to restructure his nose, chin, and cheeks, let alone recover from the procedure. Plastic was pretty good these days, and recovery drugs could get you half of the way there, but the human body didn't like being mucked around with.

He wasn't Tomas, no matter how much she wanted him to be. But he still might be Nazca.

"Liao," she said, redirecting her attention. "Have you and your colleagues conferred regarding the sample taken from the station?"

She licked her lips. "Yes. We believe we know what it is."

"And?" Sanda prompted.

Liao braced herself. "I will not divulge that information until my team is delivered to Monte Station."

As much as it annoyed her, Liao's defiance cranked Sanda's estimation of her up a notch. "I see. Were you not present for the call I just made? Do you lack the capacity to understand that I have made a promise to my commanding officer to see you safely to Monte Station?"

"Forgive me," she said, and her voice shook. "But I do not know what that promise means to you. Many things can happen between here and the station. W-we need assurance."

"You have my personal assurance."

"That's not enough. I will help you. I *want* to help you. But first my team must be safe."

Liao's gaze drifted off of Sanda to take in Nox, Conway, and Knuth, her expression pained but resolute. She must know that Sanda could take the sample off of her at any moment and have her own tests run.

Sanda sighed raggedly and glanced at Novak. "And do you know what it is?"

"No, ma'am. I only just got there."

"Very well," Sanda said. "You may keep your secret until your team is safe on Monte, but I expect an immediate handover and full explanation. For the time being, you will bunk on this ship and have no communication with your colleagues. Arden, cut her network access."

"What? Why?" Liao jabbed at her wristpad, but Arden was already at work, and her brows knitted in frustration. "I will transit with my team—"

"You have the sample with you, don't you?"

"Does it matter?" She crossed her arms, drawing the pocket of a buttoned-up lab coat tight across her chest. The telltale square of Nox's flask pressed against her hip.

"Yes. It does. I will allow you to keep the sample on your person, but it cannot leave this ship. I won't give your team a chance to put their heads together and tamper with what's inside."

"We would never—"

"And I wouldn't space you before Monte, but here we are. Conway, show her to a bunk and get her some zero g–appropriate clothing. I'm not dodging that coat the whole way to Monte. Is this deal acceptable to you, Liao?" Sanda held out her hand to the scientist.

"We're agreed," she said, her voice firmer as she shook Sanda's hand. Good, she was the kind of woman who needed a plan to feel grounded. Sanda could work with that.

"Novak, go to my quarters. I'll meet you there in a moment, because you and I need to have a very serious talk about your employer."

INTERLUDE

PRIME STANDARD YEAR 3543

THE INTELLIGENCE, SEARCHING

Arden locked their door and retreated to the serenity of the net. They would have to come out soon, they knew Sanda would rely upon them for the next steps—whatever she decided those needed to be—but right now, right *now*, Arden needed peace. They needed emptiness.

They drifted alongside the intelligence once more. The realization startled them, for they didn't remember the trip. Physical space was meaningless in the net, but digital space was its own monster, and while Arden could manifest themself anywhere at any time, there were security procedures to take, red herrings and false trails to lay down.

They checked their recent history and found they had done all those things instinctively. For Arden, the digital obfuscations required to arrive at this fringe place were now a simple reflex. They hadn't counted on that reflex to be triggered by pain.

Jules. Fuck, but they had been so sure she was held against her will. So sure that Rainier had done something to her, manipulated her away. That still might be true—*had* to be true—but she'd played her role so well. Too well.

They didn't know what to do. That was the problem. Arden always had a plan, a next step. If condition A fails, initiate condition B, and so on, until they got close enough to their goal to obtain it. But this was something else. This was years of failure, piling up, and not only were they not used to failing, they weren't used to asking for help.

And they needed help. Arden understood that, even as they hated the reality of it. Sanda had been good on her word, getting them the ship and getting them into Janus, but not even that was enough. They'd taken control of the *entire* station and *still* that wasn't enough and when, when would they ever be enough?

Arden caught themself dissolving into anxiety and closed their non-existent eyes, sighing into the digital ether that didn't care whether they breathed. Sanda had data on Rainier. The scientists had data on Rainier. Arden was certain that Rainier was pulling Jules's strings. They'd follow Sanda and this crew of the *Thorn*, and do what they could to help, because they needed more data. That was the problem. Not enough data to make a plan.

Did the intelligence have enough data?

Their own mind settled, Arden turned their thoughts back to the being that was birthing itself on the edges of net space. An intelligence—human or otherwise—was only as good as its data set and the framework on which it could slot that knowledge together. They'd gotten the sense that the intelligence was looking for someone.

That was what had drawn them to it in the first place. The technology itself was thrilling, yes, but the subtle sense of its need to find someone, or maybe something, had been the reason Arden kept coming back here. The being did not judge. It only searched, as they did.

Arden wasn't sure the being even knew what it was looking for, but whatever it was, they hoped it would find it, and they hoped they could be there for that moment of triumph.

CHAPTER 38

PRIME STANDARD YEAR 3543

ONE LIE TOO MANY

All the training in the universe couldn't stop Tomas's heart from trying to drum its way out of his chest as he let himself into Sanda's quarters. He had never, in all his long years of service, blown his cover against mission orders.

He'd told her who he was once, but that had been different. If he hadn't told her then, he wouldn't have been able to leverage her trust to get her safely off Bero and returned to his client—Speaker Greeve. Such revelations were allowed the Nazca during the execution of duty. Now, he treaded dangerous waters.

The Nazca implants in his body could do a lot more than boost his alertness. His stomach soured at the thought of the recall juice his bosses had pushed into him back on Atrux, making him uncomfortable enough to know that, if he didn't return to base, then the next time they called him home they wouldn't give him the chance to answer.

It wasn't just his body in danger. He thought he'd done a decent enough job covering for the chip in Sanda's head, but every time he brought her to the Nazca's attention, he risked that discovery. He couldn't entirely discount the fact that they'd rip the chip out themselves to see how it worked, given the chance. More banally, they could send a hit squad for her because he'd revealed himself outside of protocol.

As all the ways his confession could go wrong played through his mind, he questioned why he was doing this. Worst case, the Nazca would come for him and take down Sanda in the process. Best case, he could figure out how to disconnect his implants before the Nazca discovered he'd abandoned mission, and scrub his location. With Sanda backing him up, Arden might even help him figure out how to pull the implants. The gamble could work.

He could still lie to her, convince her he was Novak the Nazca. But Sanda wouldn't give Novak the same counsel she'd give Tomas.

Sanda Greeve was the most competent commander in Prime, a soldier with a bullheaded sense of honor. He needed her help. And he… he needed her to *see* him.

The door dilated and she pulled herself in, then turned to face him.

"Who are you? There may be a Leo Novak in the universe, but he's not the man standing in front of me. This? This is bullshit." She turned her wristpad around so he could see a short dossier on him, the fragments of the digital footprint Novak had left throughout his life analyzed and broken down into chunks that didn't line up. Arden's work. He swallowed through a dry throat. She pressed on.

"I may have only taken fleet intelligence, but even I can see this isn't the profile of a real person. It's got white noise, yeah, but white noise that makes sense. People aren't this logical in their interests, one idea branching neatly from another. Real people have random thoughts, careers that didn't take off, parts of life that don't make sense. Leo Novak is a construct. So who the fuck are you?"

"I'm Nazca," he said. A painful clench grabbed ahold of his stomach. He gritted his jaw and made himself maintain eye contact. The pain was psychosomatic. Not even the Nazca could analyze his words and intent on the fly fast enough to punish him right here, right now. Her gaze, however angry, soothed the ache. "I'm Tomas."

Real pain exploded behind his eyes. He flew against the wall, head snapping back, and for a moment he feared the Nazca's reach was longer and more sophisticated than he'd ever expected. But when the white stars vanished from behind his eyes, he saw Sanda shaking out her fist, knuckles red, and he reached up to touch a sore jaw. Blood ballooned at the corner of his lips.

"Don't," she rasped. "Don't you dare try that shit with me."

"I know I look different." He spoke too quickly, pushing the words out in a rush to make her understand, "but that's the MetBath. It changes—"

"The *what*? Please, are you trying to tell me the Nazca have access to some super-speedy plastic surgery? Don't insult my intelligence."

"We don't share a lot of our technology," he said, feeling ridiculous.

"If something like that existed, then rich people would use it all the time to rearrange themselves. Your organization wouldn't be able to keep a lid on it, and they wouldn't want to. Do you know how much something like that would be worth?"

"Sanda, just, look closer..." He held out a hand to her, mind spinning, and she slapped it away.

Her hand closed around his chin, yanking him so close her breath dried his eyes. His heart thundered at the proximity—surely she could feel its frantic beat—skin going hot, but her touch was purely professional.

She dragged her thumb along his jawline, prodded his cheeks where Tomas's dimples once formed, then snorted and pushed him away.

"You have a similar body type, I grant you that, but your facial bone structure is completely different. Fillers and other injectables can't achieve that. You came to work on Janus two days ago. Even *if* Tomas underwent plastic surgery within hours of—of—leaving, he'd still have scars healing, or need bandages to cover it. You don't even have scar *tissue*, so unless you're about to wipe off some seriously impressive makeup, I need you to shut the fuck up about being Tomas and tell me who you really are."

"I can tell you things about our time on Bero—"

"You can parrot facts you read in a report and, frankly, I know Tomas has his job to do, but I don't want to know all the details he wrote down for his superiors." A shudder passed through her, and he felt sick. "You knew Lavaux was connected to Janus. Your organization knew all about my encounter with him. I've no doubt you read my file in case we crossed paths, but this angle of yours is shameful. Tell me who you are. Now."

"I can't tell you anything else."

She held up a hand. "Your inclination is to dance around this. I get it. You spent your whole career honing those instincts"—absently, she rested her hand against her hip, fingers brushing the blaster holstered there—"and you can't shake them. But I don't have time for bullshit on this ship. I don't have time for bullshit in this *life*. So, look, I won't put you on the spot and grill you about your real name. I don't need it."

Tomas longed to bring up the program that managed his implants and send a wave of painkillers, or anxiety-reducers, or *something* through his system to make this hurt less. Sanda was too clever, too wary, and the MetBath had done its job too well.

If he kept pushing, she'd get only angrier, and if he dared to mention the one thing that Tomas would never have put into his report—the chip in her skull—then... then she might convince herself that Tomas had betrayed her secret, and he couldn't bear to see that pain on her face.

Tomas pulled from every tool in his skill set to keep the desperation hammering through him from seeping into his voice. "Then what do you need?"

"Don't ask me leading questions to get at whatever secrets you think I'm hiding. And I am hiding secrets you won't learn, just as I'm sure you're hiding things I'm not going to get out of you, but let me be real fucking clear here because I'm no spy so I can't do your subtle interrogation dance. You and I, we're probably on the same side, and we're better off sharing information."

"What side is that, exactly?"

"At this point I'm not sure 'preservation of civilization as we know it' would be too hyperbolic. You were on that station for a reason, Novak, and it wasn't to fix some amplifiers."

He couldn't help but smile. "You sure you're not good at this interrogation thing?"

Her eyes narrowed, briefly, and he bit his tongue. He couldn't let himself fall into their old give-and-take speech patterns, as much as they soothed him, because if she ever started to believe that their easy chatter had been anything but natural, if she even began to suspect the way Tomas spoke to her was *trained* into all Nazca, not something that came naturally in her presence, then that might break him.

"Why were you there?"

"Rainier Lavaux. She's gone missing from the public eye. My bosses want to know why."

"That's a hell of a fishing expedition. So you have no client? This is a Nazca-sponsored mission to kick the dust around Rainier and see what settles?"

Tomas licked his lips. "I sincerely doubt you will believe me, but Prime Director Okonkwo ordered this mission."

Sanda's eyes narrowed. "Okonkwo doesn't need the Nazca."

He shrugged. "Everyone of power does, eventually. Were you there for Rainier, or for Valentine? You have her old associates Arden Wyke and Noxallari Belten in your service."

"Noxa-*what*?"

"That's his birth name. Didn't you know?"

"I didn't ask. Just like I'm not going to ask you who you were before you were Novak."

"Wyke and Belten are known to the Nazca, and we don't spend a lot of time gathering dossiers on low-level Grotta thieves. You should be careful around them."

"Are you lecturing my choice in companions, Nazca?"

"I just..." He threw up his hands and shrugged. "I wanted to help."

"Then tell me why you were really on Janus."

"I told you, for Rainier—"

"Yeah, I know, and that's part of it, I'm sure, but I'm not an idiot. I didn't need to spend time with a spy to learn that the first information you offer is true, but valueless. You know something I don't, and I want it."

He grinned. "You said yourself that we weren't leaving this room knowing all of each other's secrets."

"Funny thing about that. I own all the guns on this ship. So you're not leaving until I'm satisfied. Keep your secret fetishes and what-the-fuck-ever to yourself, but you're giving me the real reason you were on that station."

Tomas pretended to hesitate. He'd planned on telling her everything, and would, but Novak wouldn't give up the data that easily. "If

I give you information that jeopardizes my mission, the Nazca will execute me."

"They're not the ones you have to worry about right now. Now, it's just us. And Nox, probably. He's been waiting outside that door with a blaster pointed at your head for the past twenty minutes."

Tomas startled and leaned away from the door. "Very well. Rainier Lavaux owns Janus Station. It's behind dozens of shell corporations, but it's hers."

"Tell me something I don't know, spy."

"Rainier has employed the use of remarkable body doubles, seeded across the inhabited worlds. Okonkwo wants to know why."

Nox shouted, "Can I come in now?"

Sanda sighed and shook her head. "Yes, you might as well."

He stepped through the door, blaster in hand as promised, and eyed Tomas warily. "You didn't have to tell her my name, did you?"

"Sorry."

"We'll muse over the tastes of Nox's parents later. I need one more thing from you before we part merry ways, Novak." He grimaced, wishing she'd stop calling him that. "What's in the flask?"

"That, I had planned on telling you. They're nanite amps—I had a look at the Prime Standard governors and those have been tweaked. As I did not have time to research the discrepancy myself, I sent my suspicions to my superiors and they alerted me that the modified governors allow access to a gate's power system, controlling spin-up and spin-down. Dal asserts that the nanites are self-replicating, though I do not believe he knows the extent of the danger the modified governors pose. I suspect Rainier plans to hold Prime hostage, for a yet unknown reason, with these devices, by threatening spin-down."

Realization flashed across her face. "Have you alerted Okonkwo?"

"My handler has, and Okonkwo ordered me to abandon my search for Rainier's doubles and work on discovery and containment of the nanite problem."

"Thank you, Novak."

"You realized something just then, what is it?"

"Sharing time is over. Nox, we're taking him back to the shuttle.

Novak, you and I are going to pretend we never had this talk and I don't know what's in the flask, because Liao might hold something back, and I need to be sure. When she hands it over, she must tell me everything, not gloss over details because she assumes I already know."

Nox put a hand on Tomas's shoulder and steered him, firmly, toward the door.

"Commander, please, we can work together on this," Tomas said.

"No, Novak, we cannot. You will play your part with the scientists and help me convince them that their only chance of safe delivery to Monte is full disclosure on the sample. Once I deliver you to Monte, I expect to never see you again. In the meantime, if you try to escape via any means, I will shoot you. If Arden catches you fucking with my ship's software, or otherwise trying to send unauthorized communications, I will shoot you. If you dare to impersonate Tomas again, I will shoot you. Is that clear?"

"I thought Nox was going to be doing the shooting?"

"Times are changing fast, Novak. Try to keep up."

CHAPTER 39

PRIME STANDARD YEAR 3543

THE OBJECTIVE HAS CHANGED

Compartmentalizing was every spy's specialty, and Tomas leaned hard on his training, shutting down his emotional core so he could get through this. As Sanda strode alongside him toward the kissing airlocks of the *Thorn* and the shuttle, he realized she was reluctant. Threatening innocent people wasn't in her nature. To Sanda Greeve, the world was broken but could be fixed if only the people who lived in it, who loved it, worked hard enough. The corner Liao had backed her into didn't mesh with her intrinsic values, and it had to be rubbing her raw inside.

But she would do it, because it was the best tool to get done what she felt needed to be done to make the world better, and safer, for all those in it. Including the people in the shuttle who had become, unwitting or not, pawns in a game too large for even the Nazca to grasp.

The lie hurt her, but she would do it because she believed it was right.

Why had lying never hurt him?

That it had been trained into him as second nature by the Nazca was true, but in all his time learning their ways he'd never once felt that distinct discomfort that was written so plainly in Sanda's tense face, in the brisk way she moved as if she wanted to get this over with, to rip it off like a bandage and let the blood flow fresh so she could move on and heal.

Was he missing something? Sanda saw a threat lurking in the edges of the universe and wanted to fix it, to stop it, to take everything she loved and make it safe. She was willing to threaten and lie for that.

Tomas had a job to do. He did it, and there was satisfaction in doing it well, in gaining the respect of his superiors within the order, but that was where it ended for him. He had no purpose outside of the job, and he didn't even need the money. Not anymore.

Sanda stopped in front of the airlock. "You ready for this?"

"I've been lying to them since day one, Commander."

"Does that bother you? That they'll hate you, when they realize you've betrayed them? Because they will. When you leave to follow your mission, they'll piece together what scraps you left behind."

"I've left a trail of hating all across the universe. It won't even be me they hate. It will be Novak."

She pursed her lips, arm hovering halfway to the lock release. "Is it worth it?"

He stared hard at the airlock, for to look at her would be to let his guard down in a way he couldn't afford right now. She wouldn't believe he was himself unless he changed his face back. He needed to get through this and back to a MetBath. "I don't know. Maybe, if I get some answers."

She snorted. "I'm not convinced there are answers enough in all the universe to soothe some aches. We're like kids, the Nazca and me and even Arden, maybe. Looking at the universe and asking why, why, why, until we're blue in the face. But there doesn't *have* to be a why, does there?"

"Rainier has a reason for doing what she does. So does Jules."

"And those two answers, they'll be enough for you?"

"This time."

"All answers get you is more questions. You should know that better than anyone, Nazca. I had to learn it the hard way." Her fist clenched. "I'm still learning it."

She tapped in the override to the airlock and waited while it cycled, then stepped through ahead of him. It wasn't the move he wanted her to make. He wanted her to put him through first, to let the first thing the scientists saw be the fear he could so easily manufacture writ clear across his face.

He wanted them to expect bad news before they got it, because humans always liked that pump primed. It was as if, in expecting bad news and getting it, there was enough satisfaction in having been proven right to ease some of the raw parts of the bad news.

But Sanda wasn't Nazca and didn't work that way.

"Commander," Dal said in a voice raspy from overuse. A lot of arguing had been done in the time Tomas had been away. They had all strapped in, and watched Sanda's approach with tired, wary eyes. "What's going on?"

"I'll be blunt with you, Doctor. Liao has demanded your safe conveyance to Monte Station in exchange for the sample in the flask and a detailed description of the contents thereof. To be certain she does not tamper with the sample, she will remain locked up on the *Thorn* for the duration of the transit. Your communication channels have been blocked."

Tomas watched them through downcast eyes. A few sharp intakes of breath, a muttered oath. Only Dal leaned forward, his tired eyes narrowed.

"She has done nothing wrong and does not deserve a cell."

"She is withholding critical information about research performed at an illegal station." Sanda swept them all with a fierce glare, her face hard, but Tomas could see the subtle tugging at her lips that indicated she resented having to do this. "For her sake, you all had better make certain you share *everything* you know about that fluid when the time comes."

Dal held both of his hands up, palms out. "Liao knows more than we do, I'm sure."

"Consider carefully," she said. "We will dock in five days. Your safe passage relies on the thoroughness of your explanations upon arrival. Once there, be warned that SecureSite officials at Monte are very interested in anything you can tell them about Jules Valentine."

"We hardly knew her—" Sarai protested.

"Nevertheless, there will be questioning. Now, if you will excuse me, I have a ship to fly."

Sanda left before there could be any protests, leaving a tense silence in the air, which Dal finally gathered the nerve to break.

"You were there, Novak. Do you believe Greeve will really harm us if we are less than forthcoming...?"

He shook his head, wringing his hands together. "I don't know. She was furious when Liao set an ultimatum."

"So we can't say either way."

Sarai said in a small, listless voice, "We have no reason to withhold information..."

Dal met Tomas's eye, and he knew the man was thinking of the strange structure of the governors. Maybe the younger scientists hadn't noticed, but Dal certainly had, and Tomas believed Liao was experienced enough to have figured out that they were modified, if not exactly how.

"Liao will clear it all up," Tomas said, letting his voice shake, and ignored the weight of the flask he'd stolen, tucked into the pocket of his jumpsuit.

Sanda would not harm these people. But he needed to get back to her, and the only way to do that was to bring this sample to his superiors to complete his mission and gain access to a MetBath to put his face back into the Tomas configuration.

She'd forgive him once she knew. Once he could explain everything. She had to.

CHAPTER 40

PRIME STANDARD YEAR 3543

GET THEE TO THE ASTEROID

Two weeks later, and Hitton's report on the survey of the asteroid was more of the same: incomplete. Biran grimaced, scrolling through the overwrought document on his wristpad, struggling to read between the lines to figure out what the root of Hitton's concern was.

Every time she sent back a report, the message was identical: This asteroid was not yet ready to begin gate construction on. Her geological survey team provided details amounting to "we don't know if this rock is stable," but something about those details itched at the back of Biran's mind.

When he had conspired with Vladsen and Shun to circumvent Hitton's concerns regarding the location of the asteroid, it hadn't occurred to any of them that Hitton was head of geology on Ada. Any survey team sent to do the deep inspection Shun had asked of the High Protectorate would be headed up by her.

And here they were, stymied, while Bollar and his army rattled their sabers at what they saw as intentional obstruction of the project. They weren't wrong. Yet, stubborn as Hitton could be, Biran doubted her reasons for delaying construction were entirely born of spite.

She was a harsh woman, but she was not blind to the boon the gate would offer. Her primary source of contention, military might, had been settled the moment Biran made his speculation clear to Icarion, forcing Okonkwo to pour the resources they needed into the Ada system.

Anford had been right. He could hear the click of fleet-issued mag boots tromping up and down the halls and streets of the station at all times of day and night. In the time following his announcement and Okonkwo's initial, private backlash at him and Vladsen and Shun, the population of little Ada had soared by 20 percent. Its armory swelled by 220 percent, according to Anford. He had no reason to doubt that number as hyperbole. He could see the truth of it in the lines around her eyes, and the extra contracts Ilan's shipping company picked up to help move the guns around the system.

Whether or not they liked it, that asteroid would be the most secure gate in all of Prime. So why was Hitton stalling?

If it wasn't political, that left the possibility of a real threat—but one she wouldn't come out and say over any channels, secure or otherwise. So something on the ground, at the asteroid. Nazca, maybe? They'd want a glimpse of what went into surveying a gate site, and while insertion into that team would be difficult, Biran knew they could manage. If Hitton had caught even the slightest whiff of a spy in her midst, she'd shut down like this.

Icarion could have placed their own spy, but Biran doubted they had the sophistication to pull that off. He frowned at himself. They had built *The Light*. He needed to stop thinking of them as the regressive settlement Prime had painted them as, and start thinking of them as a cornered tiger. He had helped them survive—and saved his own conscience in the process—but now a different war was at play.

Biran gritted his teeth and fired off a short text to his sister.

B: Our mutual friend have any companions in Ada at the moment?

S: Haven't seen him in a while, no idea. Found a Nazca in Ordinal, but no knowledge on Ada. Something cooking?

B: Dunno yet.

S: wow what a profound insight from our political superstar

B: hush

S: you asked!

B: :(:(

Sanda shot back a laughing emoji and marked herself as *away*. He rolled his eyes and closed the dialogue box, but found he was smiling when he did so. He could get so mired in his own thoughts he lost perspective. This was a simple enough problem on the surface. He needed to know what was happening at the ground level on the asteroid. He couldn't do that from the Cannery, ergo, get thee to the asteroid. Sanda would have charged off at the first sign of fuckery in Hitton's reports.

Of course, Sanda had a gunship. Biran had his shuttle, designed to take him from Ada Station to the dwarf planet. Even if it could hold enough fuel to get him as far as the asteroid, it'd take a lot of miserable, cramped weeks to pull off. It wasn't like he had the money to rent a charter—the Nazca were still merrily bleeding his accounts dry for the recovery of his sister. Biran grunted. He hoped Tomas was living well off that credit. Somebody should be.

But he did know somebody with access to a much larger ship. Biran pinged Vladsen, and the man answered right away. His lips pulled sideways into a forced smile.

"Speaker. Perusing our latest report?"

Biran grimaced. "That obvious?"

"There is little else for us to do at the moment."

"Maybe not."

"Meaning?" Vladsen leaned toward the camera.

"Something's gone wrong at the asteroid, I think we're all in agreement on that front. But Hitton's not talking, most likely because she believes her communication channels are monitored by whatever is making this project go sideways. She needs help. And she needs it in person."

"You're proposing a vacation? A hab dome on an asteroid is hardly my idea of rest and recuperation, but I see the appeal."

"I don't have access to a ship that can get me there."

Vladsen's expression went stony. "I see. And you're asking to borrow my keys?"

"I understand the *Taso* isn't technically in your possession, but Rainier relinquished that property to the Keepers upon Lavaux's death, and it's already been scoured for any evidence relating to him and Lionetti. It's rotting in storage."

"Yes, a storage facility overseen by our Protectorate. You have the same access, Speaker. I hardly see why you need my approval."

"Vladsen, I..." He cleared his throat. "Whatever his flaws, Lavaux was your friend. You knew Rainier. Lavaux appears to have had few other social contacts, and no living family. I will not commandeer that ship without your approval."

Vladsen flicked his gaze away, stung, and Biran wished he was as good at talking to individuals as he was speaking to all of Prime.

"A ship of that size requires a crew," Vladsen said.

"I know some people who work for my fathers' hauling company. They're trustworthy."

"And how are you going to pay them?" Vladsen returned his gaze to the camera, wry amusement lurking beneath his dark features.

"Well, I, ah..."

"Before he died, Lavaux confided in me that he'd discovered you hired a Nazca. Did you wonder how he knew? It was because he went to hire one himself and was informed that the best-suited agent in that field of play had already been tapped. A small matter to weasel out the details from there. He admired you greatly, for what it's worth, for beating him to the chase. But I know what they charge, and I know you haven't upgraded a single thing in your house since you became a Keeper. You do not have the credit to fund this expedition."

Biran's neck turned hot. "I'm sure I can round up funding—"

"I have the credit."

Biran hesitated, though he couldn't say why. He had no reason at all to distrust Vladsen's motives, aside from the man's association with Lavaux. Asking permission to use a ship that was technically available to all Keepers was one thing. What Vladsen offered was a bigger debt, and for some instinctual reason, Biran did not want to be indebted to that sculpted, troubled face.

Some life had come back into Vladsen over the last two weeks of stewing, and while Biran didn't doubt the man had had enough time to lick his emotional wounds and put his game face back on, there was an edge of calculation in his slow smile that rubbed Biran the wrong way. Everyone in the Protectorate was playing their own game, he told himself. It was only because of Lavaux's betrayal that Biran feared those games might be hazardous to his health.

He couldn't say no. He'd asked for the ship, and that came with strings. Biran hoped the addition of the credit wouldn't transform those strings into chains.

"You know my financial burdens. I do not believe I could ever pay you back."

"I don't expect it. This is not a loan to you, Speaker. In case you've forgotten, I'm invested in the outcome of the asteroid gate as well. Hitton's delays are troubling, and as we can't ask her over present channels, seeking her out in person is our only course of action. Unless you're having doubts...?"

"No, not at all. This gate must be built. How soon do you think the *Taso* can be ready for flight?"

"Hard to say. She hasn't been grounded that long, but I'm hardly an expert in these things. Secure a crew, have them go over it with a fine-tooth comb, then we'll set course."

"You're skipping a step," Biran said.

"Oh?"

"We have to file the flight plan request with Olver and Anford."

"Ah." Biran almost laughed at the flash of surprise across Vladsen's face. Maybe the other Keeper wasn't such a cipher after all. "It seems I have picked up some poor habits."

"Don't let Olver hear you say it. He'll think you got them from me."

Vladsen tapped at his wristpad. "I'm passing you the digital keys now. Ping me when you're ready to leave."

"You don't want any input in the crew?"

Vladsen lifted one shoulder, long curls sliding off the slick material of his jumpsuit, and in that motion Biran saw a mirror of Lavaux's practiced insouciance. "Not my specialty. I trust you, Greeve. But put the flight request through first. Would hate to hire a crew just to let them go again."

Vladsen ended the call, his face replaced with a blinking packet of incoming data that contained the digital keys to the *Taso.*

Biran should have tapped those keys and continued on with his plans, but something stopped him. That hesitation, again.

Vladsen was playing his own game, surely. That much wasn't enough to make him pause. But this was something more, a base animal instinct crying out to abort this path, pick another plan. Sweat slicked his palms, old anxiety fluttering his belly. Why? Why was he doubting himself now? He'd come so damn far and…

It was the *Taso*. Had to be. When he'd first seen it, hulking on the edge of the dock, its airlock wrapped like sharp jaws around the gangway, he'd felt the same instinct, the same inner voice calling out to him to run. He hadn't then, because that leviathan of a spaceship had been his only chance of finding Sanda before the exodus.

But it hadn't been the ship itself that'd frightened him, it'd been the specter of the man who controlled it. Even then, when he trusted him, Lavaux had been unknowable. Had outright told Biran that he was helping him only as a matter of convenience to himself. Lavaux was dead. That ship was not his ghost. No shadow of the Keeper could reach Biran now.

He tapped the keys, added them to his personal security wallet, then filed a quick flight plan request to Olver and Anford—no use going through the usual queues, where they'd get kicked up to those two anyway.

Anford fired off a text to him in seconds, cc'd Olver: I'll only approve this if you agree to take a fleet squadron and four GCs.

Greeve: Agreed.

Olver: Is Hitton aware?

Greeve: She is not.

Olver: Best keep it that way.

Anford: Agreed. Approved.

Olver: Approved.

The chat window closed.

That came too easily. Possibly Olver had been waiting for Biran to make a move on that front—it was his project, after all—but it seemed unlikely that the director and general would sit on their hands waiting for Biran to jump. Which meant they both had assets in play on the asteroid already.

Biran sighed and dragged his hands through his hair. Things were supposed to be easier after the weapon fled and Sanda was recovered. This was a goddamned mess.

CHAPTER 41

PRIME STANDARD YEAR 3543

THE TIMELINE NEVER QUITE WORKS OUT

Sanda holed up in her room and pulled up a gate database, checking on the deadgate that hid the coordinates. Still offline. She sighed with relief, wondering. If Rainier knew the coordinates, she hadn't shared them with Lavaux. The nanite swarm might be for switching the gates off to hold Prime hostage, as Novak suggested. Such a technology would get her anything she wanted.

That Rainier was developing technology to spin gates up rankled. She had to ditch these scientists and get behind that gate as soon as possible.

A knock sounded on Sanda's door. She'd known it was coming, could see the worry and tension and…something else, something she couldn't identify, building behind Graham's eyes after Janus. But when it came, her chest still lurched, her fingers clenched. This wasn't a talk she was ready to have. Not yet.

"Come in," she said anyway.

Graham flipped his mag boots off and floated in, grabbing one of the wall straps to guide him to the chair bolted to the floor across from Sanda's desk. He grabbed the back of the chair and floated there, meeting her gaze.

She hooked the tablet she'd been working on back into the Velcro on the desktop. A lot of different methods had been tried for securing things in space. GrabSure, GripFace, a plethora of other brand names cranked out by Prime Inventive—Development Division—that always fell flat, disappeared into the flotsam of the market, because Velcro was so damned satisfying. Humans liked their tactile feedback—the snagging and pulling, the *rrrp* sound it made when you took something away.

Graham was about to take himself away. She felt that sound building in her chest.

"Hey," he said. "I think I…" He looked at his hands, scarred and gnarled against the back of the chair. "I failed you. I'm sorry."

She hadn't expected that. "No. You haven't."

"Failed to prepare you, I mean."

"For an experimental spaceship taking me hostage? Because that's not something they cover in parenting classes."

"Child," he said, which was what he always said when one of his children was pissing him off. "I meant for war."

"That's what the fleet—"

"No. They teach you how to be soldiers. I'm not talking about maneuvers and protocols and how to shoot straight. I'm talking about the cost, the human balance that never quite makes it seem like it's worth it. I couldn't teach you those things, because I never learned them."

He turned his head away, seeing a different place, a different time. Sanda leaned back, waiting.

"You get taught a different kind of war in the Grotta," he said eventually. "You're so far down on the ladder all you can see is your own nose, the only thing worth fighting for is your own life. Or maybe those you love, if you're lucky enough. I think maybe Jules learned that kind of fight, too. It's not…It's not a safe mindset, when there's more than yourself and your loved ones to be fighting for." He took a shaky breath.

"That's why I gotta go. Because you learned the bigger lessons, and I haven't, and someday you'll make a call on this ship, and I won't listen to it. Not because I'm your dad and I think I know better—I ain't that stupid—but because I'll see you, in danger, and the reality of war won't matter because I only ever learned to fight for what I love, not what I believe."

"Dad, you're the only person on this ship I can trust."

"You don't see it yet, but that's not true. Conway and Knuth adore you. Nox and Arden... They're difficult people to earn respect from, kid, and you've done it."

"You can't possibly be telling me that I can trust Nox and Arden. Not with..." She trailed off and tapped the chip implant site on the back of her head. "Not with this."

"No, not with that." Graham shook his head.

A flash of anger warmed her blood. "Then why leave me? You're the only one who knows. And I *will* have to tell them, soon enough. I can't bring... I can't bring a whole crew through a deadgate to a mystery location without giving them every advantage. Without you to watch my back, without someone else knowing *all* the details, mistakes might be made. We might miss something."

"You'll have to pick your moment, kid, but hold out as long as possible. What you carry... No one should have to carry that, not without volunteering for it. And that means the knowledge of it, too. It may not seem like much of a difference where those coords came from, but that's your most dangerous secret. That's killing knowledge, because you and I both know Prime won't stand for it, and they won't just yank it out of you. They might very well take out anyone who knows the secret, too."

She clenched her fists. "And you want me to trust your old Grotta friends with *that*? You might as well take them with you when you go."

"You've already trusted them. You've given them their weapons—Nox his guns, and Arden their tech—and let them go. They love you for it, you know. They might not understand it themselves, but those two... They were beaten down in Atrux, ground against the bedrock of the Grotta. You gave them agency, right off the bat, with only a few threats attached. They expected distrust and condescension from a major—hell, from a sergeant. They never saw you coming."

"Even Nox?"

"What do you mean?"

Sanda pursed her lips, deciding how close she wanted to dance to the truth here. "I haven't looked him up yet, but I can. I have his full name. Those fake fleeties on Janus didn't move right. Nox does. Why is that?"

"Ah. That." Graham's gaze went hazy as he drifted on memory. Sanda gave him all the time he needed to collect his thoughts. "Nox's parents...They weren't unkind, necessarily. I never knew them myself, but I gather that they expected a great deal from him. More than he could deliver."

"They thought he'd be a Keeper."

"How did you know that?"

She shrugged. "You don't give a kid a name like that if you expect them to grow up to become a thief or a merc."

"True enough. But his parents didn't have the connections. And it *does* take connections, no matter how good your test scores are, so he was never considered a candidate."

Sanda arched a brow. "Connections? And who pulled what string to get Biran's scores looked at?"

His smile was sly. "Ilan. He's a damn good cook, and he wouldn't let certain key players forget it."

"Does Biran know?"

"Probably. Or at least suspects. There was a time when I would have called him too naive to notice but...not anymore. Nox would tell you the rest himself, if you asked, so I don't feel this is any great betrayal. But, because he couldn't get the right attention in the normal way, he enlisted to get attention that way."

Sanda snorted. "The fleet is an inconvenient, but necessary, tool as far as the Keepers are concerned."

"You and I know that. Nox knows it now, but he didn't when he was sixteen and desperate to live up to all those syllables. He enlisted, but never got the attention he deserved. Got stuck down in the ranks as he didn't have the...temperament...to rise up."

"He was an ass."

"Indeed. His parents died when he was in an engagement out on some fringer settlement, couldn't tell you which one, and that was that. He landed back on Atrux, went on leave, and never came back."

"He's AWOL?"

"Technically, I suppose, though the fleet stopped bothering to find him a long time ago. Arden made it look like he was dead. Nox is just Nox now. I don't know if he picked a new last name."

"That all feels like a very intimate disclosure for him to make to you."

"It is. It was."

"Dad..."

He shook his head. "When Ilan came along, that was it for me. I was supposed to rob him, lift a shipment he was running through the Grotta, but instead I just... I left with him." Graham smiled wistfully and glanced down at one slightly curled hand. "I mean, damn could he cook."

"You didn't leave the crew. You left Nox."

"Yes. I never even said goodbye."

"I'm surprised he didn't punch you on sight."

"So was I."

Sanda chuckled.

"What?"

"When you told Biran and I how you two met, you left out the part where you were on your way to rob Ilan blind."

Graham grinned. "Seemed inappropriate for children."

"And Ilan was okay with that? He didn't... resent you or anything?"

"Ilan... understood. You'd have to ask him about that."

Sanda sighed. "I miss him."

"Me too." Graham closed his eyes. "And that's another reason I have to go. I love you kids, I do, but every time I wake up and he's not there... It hurts too much."

Sanda took him in, every familiar line on his face, and wondered if she should tell him. If it was even fair to tell him what she and Biran had figured out a long, long time ago. That their parents were different. That with other kids, it was like their parents couldn't see each other when their child was in the room. That their world was in their kids, nothing else even came close.

Oh, their parents loved them, they had no doubt of that. But when Graham and Ilan were in the same room, Sanda and Biran could cease to exist and they wouldn't have noticed.

As kids, she and Biran had resented that love. Had tried in petty little ways to usurp one parent or another, but it had never worked. That hurt had lessened over the years as they'd bonded to each other instead. Looking at Graham now, at the naked anguish in every line of his posture, Sanda found that hurt had gone.

She'd lost them all, once. Every other pain, every tiny slight, was irrelevant in light of that.

"It's okay, Dad. I understand. Go home. Love him for us both."

CHAPTER 42

PRIME STANDARD YEAR 3543

TIME ENOUGH TO SAY GOODBYE

Riding the public shuttles down to Ada was now out of the question for Biran. He used to be able to slip along, knowing a few eyes were on him but otherwise moving without being waylaid by strangers wishing to talk to Speaker Greeve. Now, after Bero, he had to take his private Keeper shuttle down to the planet.

It was fitted with sleek-shaped inertial damping couches, high-end snacks and drinks provided at their optimal temperature. Cutting-edge air recyclers kept the air volume in the tiny space fresh, while the public shuttles always carried a faint hint of sweat and stale breath. He landed in a private dock, was disgorged into a mirrored glass elevator, and then whisked away to a waiting autocab in a garage the public could not access.

Secretly, Biran hated all of it. He'd never, ever complain. Not only would his bosses be annoyed that he didn't appreciate the safety and security offered by the system—Biran had no doubt a GC was tailing him every step of the way—but those who couldn't travel by such means would be, reasonably so, offended that he wasn't grateful. The isolation wore on him. Even if he didn't want to interact with the public all the time, he hated that all of his interactions now were coordinated, scripted affairs.

He wanted to sit at a tiny coffee-shop bar and eavesdrop on the clientele in peace, catch the pulse of what was going on with the citizenry. But everywhere he went, Biran was the one being eavesdropped on, not the other way around.

Ilan opened the door the second Biran's car pulled up to the curb. Biran didn't remember this neighborhood being so quiet in the middle of the day, but the guardcore had increased security in the area upon his rise to Speaker. They didn't actively discourage people from walking around, but their invisible presence was an unspoken deterrent.

"My god," Ilan said, "you don't exist as a mere virtual projection on my morning news."

Chagrined, Biran folded Ilan into a bone-crushing hug. "Sorry, Dad. First the lockdown, then, well, everything else..." He waved a hand, which Ilan grabbed and used to drag him into the house, placing him firmly down at the table on his usual seat. The kettle was already hissing.

"Bah. I know, I know. Still, I've seen more of that reporter friend of yours in person than I have seen *any* of my children lately." Ilan, pointedly, set a perfect cup of tea down in front of Biran. He took a sip before he answered.

"I came to tell you I'm leaving tomorrow."

"Leaving for where?"

"The asteroid."

"Graham'll be sad to hear it. I believe he'll be heading home soon."

"What? Why?"

Ilan studied the contents of his mug. "Can't do it. Things with Sanda have gotten too dangerous, or so he says. I'm not there to see what's happening and he won't give me the details over open channel."

"I thought Janus was nothing. Sanda said the fight was a scuffle—"

"Sanda hasn't told us a lot." Ilan frowned. "Graham said he'll have to leave before she has to kick him off the ship for making the wrong calls."

"What calls could he possibly—? Oh. Oh shit. She'll want him gone because he'll protect her before whatever harebrained mission she's on, won't she?"

"That's my understanding. Do you have any idea what she's doing out there?"

A weight settled in Biran's stomach. He didn't. He had no fucking clue. They exchanged silly messages like they always did, but somehow he hadn't quite grasped that Anford wasn't sending her out on patrols anymore—not that patrols had been safe. When she'd told him about Janus, she hadn't sounded scared, just stern and focused... But then, Sanda rarely sounded scared. Extreme focus was her coping mechanism. Always had been.

"I'll find out what's going on."

"Aw, kid." Ilan shook his head. "If you don't already know, she won't tell you."

"Anford will."

"And are you sure Anford knows?"

"She's Sanda's boss. Of course she will."

"You're thinking like you. Try thinking like Sanda for a moment," Ilan said.

"She'd operate as independently as possible from any oversight that could discover the chip."

"Exactly. She needs to know where those coordinates lead, and she can't let Anford know why. Even if the general thinks she knows what Sanda's up to, she doesn't. I'm not convinced anyone does. She's been burned too many times." Ilan scrubbed the sides of his face with both hands. "I wish my brilliant, motivated children had decided to, I don't know, become farmers."

"Please." Biran reached over and tipped an extra cube of sugar into Ilan's tea. "You may play the straight-laced merchant dad well, but I've seen you and Graham at the range with blasters. And while Sanda and I were always curious about Graham's history in the Grotta, it was your background file I looked at first the second I had Keeper privileges."

Ilan turned about a dozen shades of crimson. "That was a long time ago for both of us."

"You were smuggling grey goods long before you met Graham, Dad."

He laughed roughly and glanced away. Light cut across the side of his face, revealing the shallow depression of an old scar that he'd had cosmetically fixed once, but hadn't followed up on fixing again once the original filler began to fade. Ilan had always claimed he'd gotten it from the corner of a pallet taking him on the chin during a hectic loading day. Biran never doubted that, until he'd read Ilan's official background dossier.

"Kid, those files are private for a reason. Not polite to snoop on your loved ones because you have the keys to the safe."

"They encourage us to read the files on our family. It's supposed to help us see how our family members may be used to leverage us."

"And was I deemed a leverage risk because of things I did decades ago?"

"No. You and Graham…Anyone who might come knocking on your door doesn't have the money or the power to pull that lever, do they?"

Ilan grimaced. "No. We were the lucky ones. Us, and the crew we brought with us."

"I understand why Graham got into smuggling and heists, but—"

"Heists?" Ilan laughed. "Nothing that fancy. What he and Harlan's crew were doing was plain old burglary, son. Don't put a shine on it. Graham doesn't."

"You're deflecting, Dad. Come on. I never met your parents, but by all accounts they were upstanding citizens, and you inherited a perfectly legal business from them. Why smuggle off-Prime-label drugs and electronics?"

"Would you believe I thought it was the right thing?"

"I'd like to."

Ilan pushed his chair back, grabbing his mug as if to refill it even though he'd taken only a single sip since Biran added sugar. Biran shot a hand across the table and grabbed his wrist, holding him there.

"Sanda and I," Biran said quietly, "we're finding a lot of cracks in the edifice we climbed to the top of. You two, you got married and you settled down and you had kids and you probably never expected them to be so publicly motivated but here we are, and as much as I'd like to chalk that up to a general sense of decency instilled in us by our run-of-the-mill upbringing—with a dash of rebellion thrown in by Graham—I don't buy it. Not anymore. Graham always pushed us to get the work done. But you? You taught us to ask questions. Why? Why hone our curiosity when you saw the path we were on?"

"You two were so smart," he said with a small, sad smile. "And Graham and I... We know how being too clever for your own good can be turned against you. I don't know if we succeeded in preparing you two. I'm not sure anyone could, but we sure as hell tried." He looked up, met Biran's gaze steadily. "So you go on. Go out there and pull Icarion's asses out of the fire they started. But be careful, for fuck's sake, okay? Watch your sister's back. You know she's watching yours."

CHAPTER 43

PRIME STANDARD YEAR 3543

PROMISES, PROMISES

Leon Gutarra moved like a man expecting a knife in the dark, and judging by the high quantity of scars on his arms and face, this was not a movement pattern born of unfounded paranoia.

Sanda met him on the docks with her ship at her back, Nox on her right, and a holster on her hip, coat pulled back so he could see she was armed but had the safety locked on. Laguna had promised her a contact. She had said nothing about how willing the man would be, and Sanda needed this to be as smooth as possible.

"Greeve?" He had a barking way of speaking, as if each word cost him something and he was a miser at heart.

"I am. You're Gutarra?"

"Ain't no one else stupid enough to meet you out here for this hand-off," he said, but flashed his ident to her wristpad anyway. "Goddamn Point gunship docked at Monte? Everyone's crawling up their own asses trying to figure out what it means. You know we're being spied on? Like, right now?"

"I'm used to it." The credentials checked out, so she pressed her comm earpiece. "Conway, bring 'em out."

A gangway extended from the shuttle's secondary airlock to the dock. The scientists came out in a huddled line, clumped together and blinking in the sharp lights of the station's dock. Dal led the charge, his shoulders hunched with suspicion and his eyes darting back and forth. He expected a trap. Sanda couldn't blame him.

"Over here," she said, and waved an arm to gesture them her way.

"Minor injuries," she said to Gutarra as they made their way over. When Dal was in earshot, she said, "Nothing serious, but check them for internal injuries. We don't exactly have proper medical facilities."

"Gunships aren't usually in the saving-life business," he said, and rolled one shoulder, eyeing up his new charges. "Name's Leon Gutarra, most people around here call me Leon, and you're welcome to yourselves. You aren't prisoners, but we will hold you in quarantine until your health can be assessed and the detective in charge of the case involving your old boss gets here to interview you. Questions?"

"When will she get here?" Novak asked.

"Don't know. Hightailed it off Atrux as soon as this arrangement was settled, so as long as the fastest shuttle she could afford will take, and I don't believe she could afford much on SecureSite's dime, you understand."

"When can we contact our families?" Sarai asked.

"After you're stable and have been interviewed."

Liao emerged from the ship. Sanda hadn't seen her much since she'd made her deal, and if she hadn't been expecting her, she might not have recognized her. Conway had rummaged up a Prime jumpsuit and a set of body-harness straps to function as pockets, making her look more like she'd stepped out of a fleet station than a research station. She had even gotten some scuffs on her mag boots, despite her limited mobility on the *Thorn*.

Dal started toward her, but she held up a hand to forestall him and stalked toward Sanda.

"Commander Greeve, we have an arrangement, and I'd like to uphold my end of the bargain someplace a little more private."

Sanda suppressed a smile. "Well then, you might as well come along with us. That all right, Gutarra? I'll send her to you with an escort when we're through."

"No trouble at all," Gutarra said. "Got any other needs aside from a private meeting space? No offense meant, darlin', but I want you and your guns off this station as soon as possible. Tell me what you need to facilitate that."

"My engineer, Knuth, is after some parts for an air recycler. Should be easy enough to find, and a quick fix once he's got them."

"Consider it done. I'll flash him the location of our local sellers, even extend you a discount."

Her smile was wry. "You mean cut down on the usual inflation applied to nonresidents of the station?"

"You park here, you pay here."

He waved an arm, calling his subordinates over. They took the scientists in their care and started shuffling them toward SecureSite's holding cells. A heaviness filled Sanda's chest as she watched them go, wondering if she'd missed something, if she'd done something wrong by bringing them here. Gutarra knew his station, and that was well enough, but that didn't mean he was equipped to handle these people.

"Take care of them, Leon."

He leaned back and lifted both brows. "Golly gee, sir, I was going to stick their asses out the airlock and see what flew out. Of course I'll look after them. Monte's not some shithole, you know. We grow food here, some of the best in the 'verse, and that's why you gotta shove off as soon as you're able, because the people here don't like guns, understand? Especially whole damn ships strapped up with them."

"You're here," she said.

"Yeah. SecureSite is here to keep the peace, and we do that without blowing holes in people. We get a few rowdy drunks, domestic disputes, the usual chaos of a lot of people living together. But Monte is safe, and I dislike the look of you on my dock, let alone walking my streets. So get your shit together and go hole up in one of the open apartments near the market district until your ship is fixed and you can mosey the fuck away from here."

"Flash me the address, and you won't see me or my people until you're watching our backsides disappear into the black."

"Thank the goddamn skies you have some sense. Here's the address." He sent a coordinate to her wristpad. "You have access credentials for the next forty hours, take longer than that and we'll find you a bigger hole to hide in."

"Agreed."

He narrowed his eyes. "You're far too agreeable, you know that?"

"We want to drop these people with you, fix our ship, and be on our way. Don't want to make your life harder than it is."

"Keep saying all the right things, Commander, and I might start liking you."

He screwed up his lips like he was going to spit, thought better of it, then hooked his thumbs in his belt and walked away. Despite his confessed dislike of guns, he was toting two rather expensive handblasters, cleaned to a low shine. Sanda smiled to herself. Old habits, no doubt.

She pressed her comm. "Everyone off. We have access to a residence, and Knuth, you have some shopping to do."

She'd said everyone, but she meant everyone except Conway. She'd stay on board and monitor the ship.

Sanda wondered at her own paranoia while they walked to the market. There, any illusion she'd allowed herself to entertain that no one was paying attention to her—why would they?—was well and fully shattered.

The market district was chaos. Frenetic energy spilled from hologram ads hanging at the regulation altitude above their heads. Aggressive shopkeepers and kids hired to hawk shouted their wares and deals of the day, or the hour, depending on the type of business.

It seemed everyone on the station had something of value to sell. It wasn't just the usual media files and hardware. These people were pushing fruit, vegetables, grains. Solid, vitamin-rich foods rarely found off-planet because of the expense. The walls of the market, the stalls, the awnings and their poles, everything was painted in the vibrant hues of plant life. Even the holos were talking about root structures and nutrient misting.

But the people weren't selling to Sanda and her crew. As they passed through the center drive aisle, following the blip on Sanda's wristpad that led them to the apartment, the people moved aside. Half averted their eyes, half outright stared.

Sanda swallowed a bitter lump. "I didn't think it'd be this bad," she whispered to Nox, who'd stuck to her side like glue, his rifle over his back instead of in his hands, but not less threatening for it.

"It's not just the weapons," he said, and tilted his chin up to one of the news drones flitting above their heads.

Biran was there, as he was more often than not lately, delivering one of his many recorded speeches about helping Icarion rebuild in light of the damage done to their habitat dome by the explosion Bero had caused on the research station orbiting their moon. He was pitching his grand plan to build a gate in orbit around an asteroid.

But the reporters of the world couldn't resist dragging Sanda into things, and as he spoke with calm compassion, a ticker trailed below with an image of her face and the gauche headline—SPEAKER GREEVE, BROTHER OF DRALEE HERO MAJOR GREEVE.

"Dios," she hissed.

Nox snickered. "You did it to yourself."

"No, I mean, look at that picture. I really need a haircut."

He snorted, but no one complained when she picked up the pace. Not quite running, just fast enough to be considered a Serious Walk, or whatever important people with important things to do did to get through a crowd. This wasn't supposed to be her place in the world.

It was Biran who'd been destined to be a Keeper. She'd joined the fleet only to protect him, to work behind the scenes to keep her family and her people safe.

That plan hadn't worked out so well. While some citizens watched her with the open awe reserved for war heroes and top-rate surgeons, others turned their faces away. Shut doors. Grabbed their children by the arms and hurried them from her path. Arden may have cleared up the footage of her killing Lavaux, and the Prime Inventive PR machine had spun away to correct the damage to her public image, but the people didn't forget. Behind some of those wary eyes, animosity lingered.

Whether the gazes in the market tracked her out of fear or admiration was irrelevant. She didn't want this place in the world any more than she wanted the chip in her head, but they were both there—thrust upon her—and she could fight and kick and scream and make a fool of herself, or try to claw some dignity back. Try to make the best with the hand she'd been dealt.

Sanda slowed her pace, lifted her chin, her shoulders. Moved the way she'd seen Anford move for so long. She hadn't been trained for this, Anford had been right about that. She wasn't a leader, not really.

She used to think captaining a gunship set her apart somehow, strengthened her mind and will, but that hadn't been real leadership. She'd been following the orders someone further up the chain had given her. When she'd been a gunship captain, the only time civvies looked at her was when they were worried she'd drag her crew into a bar and make a nuisance of herself. This was different. This mattered.

The face on that news ticker was expected to lead. It didn't matter how raw and scared the woman behind it was.

Sanda swiped her way into the apartment and let out a deep sigh of relief as the door swished shut after her crew, and Liao, were safely inside.

"Fuck," she said, to no one in particular. "We cannot move around this station until we're ready to leave. We draw too much attention."

"Begging your pardon, Commander, but it's you drawing the attention," Knuth said. "I'll be all right if I go on my own to get the parts."

"You're probably right," she said, and sank onto a slightly too-firm couch. "Go ahead, get what you need. Gutarra wants us off this station as soon as possible and he's right, we're a disruption."

"Hold on," Arden said, "what about Laguna? I want to hear what she gets out of the scientists about Jules."

"So do I," Sanda said, "but we can hear about it from the *Thorn*."

"I'll stick around Monte long enough to sit in on Laguna's interviews," Graham said with a wan smile. "Pass a firsthand account along to you."

Sanda tried to return the smile, but couldn't. "Thanks, Dad."

"What do you mean, stick around Monte?" Nox asked. "Abandoning your own daughter so soon? Didn't realize walking out was such a habit with you."

Graham turned purple, the vein on the side of his neck bulging. "Don't you fucking dare—"

"Both of you," Sanda snapped, "shut the hell up. Graham stays behind. My orders." She set her jaw. "It's better that way."

"Cutting the fat off your team, I get it," Nox drawled.

"Nox..." Arden said, warning in their voice. "Drop it."

Sanda cleared her throat to cut off Graham before he got started. "Liao, the sample and your explanation, if you please." She held her hand out to the doctor.

"I cannot be certain, but my colleagues and I believe this to be a sampling of our most successful amplification nanites in a matrix of growing solution meant to facilitate self-replication. I am sorry we did not explain it sooner, but we feared repercussions for breaking the self-replication laws."

Sanda frowned. "That's what you were worried about?"

"They are stringent. And as things stand, this sample is our only evidence that we were working under direction, with proper governors in place." She dug into one of her harness pockets and pulled the flask out.

"Your governors are broken," Sanda said, staring hard into her eyes. Genuine surprise widened them. Interesting, so the Nazca had been right. They didn't know.

"Impossible. How can you even know—?"

Nox said, "That's not my flask."

"Yes it is, you gave it to me," Liao said, bewildered, but Sanda was already feeling cold waves of dread roll through her.

"No, it's not. That's not mine. Mine's got a copper inlay around the screw top, and anyway, that thing's too new and shiny."

"Open it," Sanda said.

Liao's eyes widened. "We don't know—"

She was on her feet in an instant and snatched the flask from Liao, then screwed the top open. Sanda ignored Liao shouting about contaminating the sample and brought the flask to her nose and sniffed.

"Grot," she said.

Nox held out a hand and she passed it to him. He took a swig, swished it around. "Not my brand, but not bad. Definitely not purple goo."

"Fucking Nazca," Sanda hissed.

Ignoring the shouting going on all around her, she dialed in Gutarra's ident on her pad and hit the button for priority. His face came up instantly, flushed with irritation.

"What's so damn impor—"

"Where's Novak?" she demanded, heart hammering so hard she could feel it in her boots.

"In the cell with the others, what's this—"

"Check."

"Excuse me?"

"Check the fucking cell, Leon, and do it now."

Something clicked in his head, she could see it in his face as he switched from annoyance to alertness. "Checking now."

She held her breath for the forty seconds it took him to leave his office, run down the hall, and open the door to the cells. She didn't need him to answer her, she could see it on his face.

Leo Novak was gone.

"How the—"

"Shut the shuttles down, the evac pods. Shut the whole goddamn station down. Monte is on lockdown until Leo Novak is found."

CHAPTER 44

PRIME STANDARD YEAR 3543

THERE'S ALWAYS A BIGGER PROBLEM

Sanda was sure he wouldn't stay here. He had to have known the switch wouldn't remain undiscovered for long, and he'd need to get out as quickly as possible. What would a Nazca do if they needed to get off this station in a hurry, without anyone growing suspicious until it was already too late? Schmoozing his way through the docks seemed unlikely, given the timeline. What would Tomas have done?

Exactly what they'd done on Ada Station—make for the docks via the maintenance access passages and try to steal a shuttle.

"Arden," she ordered, "get me cameras all over this station, get me comms, and get me access to any maintenance pathways. I need maps, and I need them now. Shortest route between SecureSite holding and the shuttle docks."

"On it," they said.

"Could have gone for an evac," Nox said. "It's riskier, but if he was sure of a pickup coming for him, then it'd be easier to get to a pod than the docks."

"True. Arden, check for any recently launched pods—how many pod docks are there?"

They squinted at their pad. "Dozens, but I can't see launch history. Something's corrupting the data."

"Motherfucker is trying to confuse things. We'll need visual. Nox, check the pods west-to-north, Graham and Knuth take south-to-east. I'm going for the shuttle docks."

"Alone?" Graham's voice was strained.

"Unless you see another combat-ready friend hanging around, yes. Alone."

"Conway—"

Sanda pressed her earpiece. "Conway. Novak did a runner. Stand ready to shoot down any rogue shuttle. Track everything in the immediate vicinity. You find anything the tiniest bit suspicious, flag it and call me."

"Understood," she said.

"*I* don't understand," Liao said. "Novak was new, he's just a young engineer, there's no reason to shoot him. He's probably frightened that we'll get in trouble and wants to destroy the evidence."

"Leo Novak is the alias of a Nazca, one of an organization of intergalactic spies spread across the inhabited universe. Your broken governors allow signals to reach the energy protocols for the gates. You've handed a flask full of self-replicating nanites capable of shutting down the Casimir Gates to a spy. Consider yourself briefed, this is classified, just shut the fuck up and let us work. That flask cannot leave this station."

Liao snapped her mouth shut and backed up slowly, bumping into a wall, but Sanda didn't have time to deal with her shock.

"Arden, *maps*."

"Got it," they said. In the same instant, a layout of Monte bloomed on her wristpad. The station homed vast stretches of aeroponic farm space spread throughout thousands of cubic meters of air.

"Dios," she muttered, panning around the place that Arden had flagged as SecureSite holding. The maintenance passageways of the station were another world unto themselves, set up to facilitate the farming done here, but incredibly fucking annoying for tracking down a fugitive.

"Arden, priority on maintenance tunnel cameras. Weapons authorized to kill, Nazca are dangerous when cornered, and it's not like we can trust any intel a goddamn spy gives us. Everyone move the fuck out."

"Fucking aye," Nox said with a wolfish grin as he swung his rifle around into a loose, ready grip.

Graham gave her a wary glance, but she didn't have time to deal with his fears. Novak had to be bagged before he got off station. A Nazca wouldn't risk exposing themselves in such a dramatic fashion unless it really, really mattered. The ability to spin the gates at will was worth blowing cover over. She didn't know what the Nazca would do with that, but really-fucking-bad was a safe guess of the outcome.

Sanda moved toward the door and Liao grabbed her arm hard enough to leave a bruise. Her eyes were dark with rage.

"Find him. I need to undo this."

"Understood," Sanda said, and shook off the woman's grip.

She stepped out of the apartment and yellow light filled the station, strobing slowly, as a gentle mechanical voice said, "Monte Station is under lockdown. Environmentals are secure, but please remain in your homes until further notice. Monte Station..."

The apartment building was a half block from the main market street, and so she saw the moment cold realization hit the citizens. Saw them freeze up, a snapshot of denial and fear, then burst apart, fleeing like rats from a sinking ship.

Good. Emergency announcements weren't to be taken lightly on stations, and these people had few enough encounters with such things that they took it seriously. The more were hiding in their homes, the less likely any of them were to take friendly fire.

And she intended on firing. Novak wouldn't get another chance to lie to her.

Sorry, Tomas, she thought fleetingly. They might know each other. Maybe they were friends, if there could be friends in such an organization. If the Nazca could even form personal connections—*don't go down that road.*

"Talk to me," she said to Arden.

"Nox is closing on the first batch of pods, G&K on theirs. No sign of disturbance yet."

"The wall panels are all fucked up here," Nox said. "Spitting out gibberish."

"He put a virus in the system," Arden said with a slight hint of admiration. "Nothing tailored, though, just a general scrambler. I'm on it."

"Don't divert attention from those cameras. We can't let him dictate where our attention goes."

"Understood," Arden said. "Gutarra is trying to get me patched into the station's cam feeds, but even he's kicked out."

"Of course he fucking is. Keep working."

Sanda broke into a run. According to her wristpad, the access door to a maintenance shaft that would lead her down into the shuttle bay, below the docks, was ahead and around a corner.

She pulled out her blaster, thumbed it up to lethal fire, and braced her wrist as she held it ready to take the center-mass of someone Novak's height. She turned the corner and almost ran chest-first into a wall.

Realization hit her harder than the wall.

"The maps are wrong," she shouted into the comm. "He's fed us false data."

"*Goddamn*," Arden said. They were jabbing at their pad so hard she could hear them. "This is... this will take time."

Time they didn't have. She put her back against the wall and squeezed her eyes shut, doing everything she could to recall the walk from the docks, through the market, to the apartment. Step-by-step she dragged her memory back down that path.

The shuttles were below the main dock. She'd seen them on the station schematic when they were planning where to park the *Thorn*. Maintenance pathways varied station by station, but there was usually a way for repair bots like Grippy to move from one level to another without having to use the elevators.

Until Arden fixed the maps, it was the only shot she had.

Cursing under her breath, she took off at a dead sprint. Someone shouted at her as she vaulted over the gate between customs and the docks, maybe one of Gutarra's people, but she ignored them as she hit the deck and pushed herself, muscles burning, toward the dock that held the *Thorn*.

Even with access to accurate maps, Novak had only gotten visual on the walk from the *Thorn* to SecureSite holding. If he wanted a smooth, quick escape, he'd go the way he'd seen.

She hoped.

The *Thorn* loomed off to her right, a defiant, muscular boulder of black metal and weaponry incongruent with the merchant haulers parked alongside it. She let herself pause, catching her breath as she scanned the immediate area.

There, a shaft down, wide enough for a bot like Grippy and, as she well knew, wide enough for her.

She kicked the hatch open and slid down the ladder with one hand for stability while the other kept the blaster pointed down. The impact shuddered through her feet, jerked her prosthetic, but she held together. After the damage on Janus, she'd rebuilt the joints to last through an apocalypse—not that she wanted to put them through that test.

A maintenance hatch stood between her and the shuttle docks. She flashed her ident over it, got back a scrambled mess, blew the lock out with her blaster, and kicked the door open.

Leo Novak stood at the end of the dock. The hatch of the shuttle next to him was open, he already had one foot in the pilot's seat.

He turned at the noise of her entrance. The world felt thick, heavy and slow, and although he was far enough away that she could see only the silhouette of him, the whites of his eyes and the wisps of his hair flipped up by the circulated air, something felt intrinsically familiar about him. Safe, somehow.

He raised a hand in farewell, and the world snapped back into place.

She fired.

CHAPTER 45

PRIME STANDARD YEAR 3543

FIRST BLOOD

Center-mass, direct to the chest. Sanda had always been a crack shot. She advanced with her blaster pointed straight on, even though she knew she'd struck a killing blow and Novak was busy bleeding his last into the half-opened cockpit of the shuttle.

"Novak is down in shuttle bay alpha. Medical assistance required," she said into her comm.

"Let him bleed out," Nox said.

"That's not how we do things."

Arden said, "I'll get you medis as soon as I can get ahold of them. The guy dies it's his own fault for fucking up the systems."

She approached warily, keeping the blaster leveled at his chest in case he had any fight left in him. He'd landed with his back in the pilot's seat, one leg hanging over the edge of the cockpit and the other crumpled beneath him.

"You so much as twitch, I'll put another one in your head," she called out.

"I'm unarmed." His voice was a low, wavering rasp.

She crept forward, nudged his splayed leg with her toe, and heard him grunt. Careful to maintain a stable stance, she stepped into the cockpit and leaned over, giving his body a brief pat-down. No weapons, but she pulled the flask out of his hip pocket and held it up to his face.

"Was this worth it?"

Blood trickled from the corners of his lips as he cracked a tight smile. "You won't believe me, but I thought it might be."

He was fading. Blood darkened the seat below him, pumping through the exit wound, gravity yanking it down and out of his broken, faltering veins. Guilt stabbed at her. He had been unarmed.

"Dios," she whispered, and holstered the blaster, making sure it was well away from his grasp. Shuttles had medikits. She tugged the red box out from under the seat—its top was already slippery with his blood—and popped it open. The wound was through-and-through, impossible to staunch effectively without proper equipment, but she could slow it down.

Fingers slick with blood, she tore a pack open and ripped out the gauze, slapping a coagulate patch onto his chest near the wound before packing gauze into the hole. He winced, hissing as she pressed down.

"Medis are on their way."

"Bullshit." His laugh was a thin wheeze. "I know what I did to this station's systems. Arden's good, but it'll take time. Time I don't have."

She didn't want to lie to him, but she didn't want to agree with him, either. She averted her gaze from his cold, blue stare. Winced herself when his hand came up, trembling like he was freezing cold, and wrapped icy fingers around her wrist.

"Stay. Until it's over."

She could scarcely hear him, his voice was so soft. "Don't be so goddamn dramatic."

She wanted to tell him he should have gotten in the shuttle and burned off. That it was his own fault for corrupting the systems, for taking a second to wave goodbye. But displacement of blame wouldn't stop the blood pooling under her feet. Wouldn't stop the gaping maw of guilt in her chest.

She'd killed before. Not just in simulations, or in ship battles where the only foes you saw were metal and ordnance flying toward you faster than you could think. The fleet didn't skimp on its training. It wanted all its soldiers able to pull the trigger, and hit, when it counted, so she'd done runs into fringer colonies that were committing atrocities with her cohort. Had put them down, and thrown up over it, and gotten back on the gunship the next morning.

She hadn't had to talk them through their own death, though.

He whispered, "You're shaking. That's my job."

She hunched up her shoulder to press her earpiece closer, pressing down the gauze with both hands. "Arden, get me those fucking medis. Yesterday."

"I'm *trying*."

"Sanda." Something small and scared and familiar in his voice made her look, make eye contact. Tears stood high in his eyes but had not fallen, casting a gauzy sheen across them. "I'm so, so sorry."

"What? For taking the flask? I guess you were doing your job."

Tension left the corners of his lips, and at first she thought his smile was relaxing, but in truth he'd lost control of those muscles. His fingers stopped shaking, grasp going limp around her wrist.

She froze as gravity finally dragged the tears from his eyes, made them streak down his pale and drawn face, and felt, for the last time, the shuddering thump of his heart, the heave and rattle of his chest. She closed his eyes, probing his face with her fingertips one last time, needing to remind herself, convince herself, that he was only Novak. Still no scar tissue. He was just another Nazca. Just another liar.

"Fuck." She punched the headrest of the seat, relishing the pain that shot through her arm.

The blood on her hands had a silvery sheen in the bright light of the docks.

She stood there for a moment, eyes closed, just breathing, gathering herself so that the next time she opened her mouth it wouldn't be to scream.

Sanda opened her eyes and pressed her comms. "He's gone."

"Uh, I mean, that really sucks but we might have a bigger problem," Arden said.

"What is it?"

"Novak's programs did a number on local systems, but he got a call out before he made a run for it. We've got incoming—three ships, I think, fully stealthed, but I'm picking up the shape of them from the dead field of comms they're leaving in their wake. They're jamming everything."

Sanda narrowed her eyes at the dead man. "What kind of ships? Gunners?"

"I can't say, they're coming in fast, though, their shape is... well, you won't believe me."

"Try me."

"Guardcore."

Sanda felt the urge to grin fiercely. "Your old friends. How long?"

"Maybe twenty minutes."

She heard a step on the dock and whipped around, blaster out, leveled, and finger on the trigger. Nox held his hands up, eyebrows raised. "I come in peace?"

She rolled her eyes and holstered the weapon, offering him her hand. "Help me out of this."

He grabbed her wrist and yanked her up, leaning over to get a good look at Novak. He whistled low. "Damn good shot."

"As you almost discovered. Announce yourself next time."

"I don't bother with fleet protocol bullshit anymore."

"Then enjoy getting shot." She pressed her comms. "Arden, can you get me Gutarra yet?"

"Putting you through."

She waited until she heard the crackle of another comm coming online. "Gutarra, this is Greeve. We've got three enemy ships incoming. What is your position?"

"Bunkered down in holding with your scientists. What the fuck is happening out there?"

"The Novak situation is contained, but he called some friends before we got him. Three enemy ships, incoming, to collect your scientists."

She heard his jaw pop. "This is a civilian station."

"And those are civilian scientists. Is there somewhere else secure you can move them to? Somewhere not obvious to look?"

"We have a *lot* of food storage."

"Good. Take them there. Don't leave any of your people behind. If they're efficient, they'll hit holding first and they're not going to ask your receptionist nicely."

"We got maybe a hundred SecureSite to manage the eighty thousand people on this station, and none of them—*none*—have seen real combat."

Sanda glanced down at the blaster in her hand, and the blood staining her fingers, and stifled an intense longing to have Tomas at her side. Novak had gotten in her head. That was all. "I'll hold them as long as I can. Now move. You've got twelve minutes."

"More like eighteen," Nox said, off comms.

"I don't like tight margins."

"You understand," Nox said, "that if these are the GC working with Rainier, the ones who came for us in the Grotta, then we're fucked. Arden and Jules and me, we survived the last time because we ran. You're talking about defending a station we don't even have an accurate map for."

"You got another suggestion?"

"Yeah. Call that brother of yours. GC respond to Keepers, right? These might be off-script, but it could be they won't want to tip their hand if challenged by a Keeper directly. Maybe he can call them back."

"Worth a shot."

She wiped the blood on her wristpad off on the leg of her jumpsuit and put an emergency call through to Biran. His face came up immediately, but the setting was a punch to the gut. Over his shoulder, the deck of a ship she could have bet her life was the *Taso* loomed. Bile rose into her throat and she swallowed back an urge to demand what the fuck he was doing on Lavaux's ship. That man was dead. Biran would have good reasons. She needed help, and shouting about Biran's current mode of transportation wouldn't get it to her any faster.

"Hey, B, no time for pleasantries. I got three suspected GC ships burning hard for Monte Station in Ordinal and I need their leashes yanked, if that's something you can do."

His eyes narrowed, then relaxed as a slight grin took over. "No questions, I suppose? Don't bother answering—hold on a second."

He tapped her line mute but left the visual up, so she could see him talking to someone else through his pad, but she couldn't see or hear who. Two minutes later he came back, brows furrowed in worry.

"There's no active GC operation in your area. Are you sure?"

She shared a glance with Nox. "Yeah. Signatures check out. These are GC ships, we're sure of it."

"Then they're not there on any official—" The line crackled, Biran's face freezing and stuttering.

"We're being jammed."

His mouth moved in slow motion, eyes erased by a stray bar of laggy pixels. "Get—out—"

"I'll update you once we have comms back," she said, praying he could hear, then closed the call.

"There's your confirmation," she said to Nox, watching the edge of the hab dome circling the docks as if she could see out into space, to the stealthed ships burning toward them. "Fake fleeties, fake GC." *Fake Keepers.*

"Maybe they're fake," Nox said, "but their tactics are real enough."

"We can't hold against the guardcore," Graham said over comms, voice tight.

He wasn't wrong. She was standing right by the *Thorn*, more or less. Just a ladder and a dock away from jumping in that ship and burning for safety. Her people weren't even that scattered. In fifteen minutes, they could all make it on board if they were pounding dirt hard enough.

Maybe she could even justify fleeing. If she scrammed, the guardcore were likely to follow, thinking she had taken the scientists with her. The diversion couldn't hurt.

But it wouldn't be long until they discovered the deception and came back to hammer Monte into dust. Her grip tightened on the blaster.

"Arden. Take Liao and get out of there. GC have a backdoor into damn near any network, and it won't take them long to figure out where you're holed up. Move, now, get to cover and don't tell me where but keep on those maps."

"Understood."

"Conway, lie low, make yourself look empty and only shoot if you know you can take a whole ship out without giving them a chance to fire back."

"Gotcha, boss."

"Everyone else, if you can shoot, get your guns ready and come to me. We're not giving ground without soaking it in blood."

Nox said, "About goddamn time."

CHAPTER 46

PRIME STANDARD YEAR 3543

RUMORS

The *Taso* rocked under his feet, nearly pitching Biran sideways hard enough to break his ankle against the grip of the mag boots as he stomped onto the command deck. He swore, swatting at the glitchy screen on his wristpad. Sanda hadn't seemed frightened, but then, as he'd discussed with Ilan, that wasn't her scared face. She didn't get big-eyed and panicky. Sanda Greeve got focused when she was scared straight down to the marrow, and the woman he'd talked to was a woman on a mission.

"What the fuck is going on with the landing?" Biran shouted at anyone on the deck of the *Taso* who could answer the question.

"The asteroid's hab dome isn't communicating," Scalla snapped back, her head bent over the console in front of the captain's seat. Technically, she was the chief engineer of this ship, and Vladsen and Biran shared captainship, but neither of the Keepers were going to shoo her out of that chair anytime soon, because neither one of them could fly without AI. "And the *Taso* isn't playing nice. Strap in or break your skull. Either way suits me fine so long as you stop being a damn distraction on my deck."

Biran swallowed an apology that would only get him shouted at for continuing to be a distraction and clomped over to the inertia chair alongside Vladsen.

"Is everything all right?" Vladsen asked, cool as anything, as if they were having a nice chat over coffee.

"I believe so," Biran said, trying to keep his voice equally calm while inside he was desperate to pound away at his wristpad until he got a connection back to Sanda. "I had a strange call from Sanda—"

The ship's forward viewscreen flashed, Hitton's face filling the view, and Biran forced himself to focus. Sanda was two star systems away, armed to the teeth, with a Keeper distress signal response incoming. She was fine. Hitton, clearly, wasn't fine. Dark circles bruised her bloodshot eyes, and in the time she'd been gone, wrinkles had set up shop in the two center lines of her forehead, where her skin was prone to crease when she frowned.

"Keepers Vladsen and Greeve. I apologize for the bumpy arrival, your visit was not expected."

"We filed a flight plan," Biran said, keeping his tone light, "though I'm sure you've been very busy and may have missed it."

"A call would have been appreciated. Please send your entire crew manifest to my operations manager, Keeper Sato. I hope you brought enough food and supplies for your people."

"The *Taso* can hold a lot of supplies," Biran said, motioning for Scalla to send the manifest to Hitton's second-in-command. "And we brought extra. Figured you could do with some fresh food by now."

"You're not wrong," Hitton said, a wisp of a smile tracing her features, but quickly crushed. "Though I doubt two Keepers of the Protectorate have come to this piece of gravel merely to resupply my humble mission."

"We've come to assist in any way we can," Biran said smoothly. "We understand there have been unforeseen complications, and would like to help."

She chuckled dryly. "The *Taso* isn't a Keeper ship. Olver didn't send you, did he?"

Biran shifted. The crew on the command deck kept their faces neutral, but everyone there was operating under the assumption that this was an official inquiry. Scalla probably had her suspicions, but Biran had insisted they hire her because she could keep her mouth shut. Hitton usually played her cards close to her chest. Calling out Biran and Vladsen in front of civilians was unusual.

"Olver and Anford approved the flight plan, but no, if you're asking if we were sent to check up on you, Hitton, we were not. We are here to help."

One side of her face contorted under a forced half smile. "Then I'd better let you in."

Biran did not say that he would force the doors if she attempted to turn them away, but the tightness around the corners of her eyes said all that was needed—she understood the implication of refusal.

It should not have come to this point. Hitton was capricious, but never outright insubordinate. Something had gone very, very wrong on this asteroid. Something she was not willing to say, even now, while two potential allies sat on her doorstep with a ship capable of blowing to pieces whatever her perceived threat may be.

Vladsen met Biran's gaze, and understanding passed between them.

Hitton cut the video feed.

"Sir," Scalla said, and cleared her throat. "The doors are opening to the primary habitat system. Looks like she's dug the habs down into the rock. May I suggest you take a small survey crew with you?"

"We'll take the GC," Biran said. Scalla looked relieved. "Stay with the *Taso*. Offload the supplies for the station, but keep the ship warm."

"Understood, sir."

Vladsen walked shoulder to shoulder with Biran through the airlock and into the chrome-slick walls of the survey station's tunnels. Four guardcore trailed behind them at a respectful, if wary, distance. Knowing a GC personally was impossible, but a fluidness in the gait of one of them reminded Biran of the GC who had helped him with the wounded after the debris strike on Ada. It comforted him to think one of those nameless suits of armor had already proven to have a kind heart.

"Thoughts?" Vladsen said, sotto voce.

"Too many to be useful."

"I'm of the same mindset. All of this is . . . off."

"Well, that's why we're here."

Vladsen chuckled roughly. "It's why you're here. This isn't my usual modus operandi."

"Don't worry," Biran said with a wink, "I've heard you're a quick learner."

Hitton came around the corner, her second-in-command, a young Keeper from the cohort before Biran's named Natsu Sato, tight at her side. The younger Keeper fiddled with the edge of her wristpad.

"I'm afraid I can't offer you a proper welcome," Hitton said. "We are rather busy at the moment. Sato can show you to your rooms and has already made arrangements with your crew to offload necessary supplies. Welcome, Keepers." She nodded to each of them formally, then turned to leave.

"Hitton, wait. We've come to help. Don't brush us off."

She froze, back stiff, and said firmly, "Sato, see them to their rooms."

"Yes, sir," Sato said, but Hitton had already gone, her wiry frame disappearing around a corner before Biran could rally himself for another attempt at getting her to stay.

"Well," Vladsen mused, "what a charming abode you have here, Keeper Sato. I, for one, could do with a rest after our long journey."

Biran almost twisted himself out of his boots with his desire to chase down Hitton and demand to know what was going on, but Vladsen was right. Ruffling things would only get them pushed further away.

"Yes." He grated the word out, then mastered himself and submitted to the role he was supposed to play here. "Thank you, Keeper Sato. Tell me, how are you enjoying life away from the Cannery so far?"

Biran racked his brain for everything he knew about Natsu Sato as they walked down the just-slightly-too-dark halls, and came up mostly blank. Since she was in the cohort ahead of his own, his contact with her had been next to nothing. He knew she'd studied geology and had found herself a mentor in Keeper Hitton due to a personal endorsement from Director Olver. After that, the rest was a blank. She'd been nervous at their impromptu arrival, but that meant nothing, as anyone got a little jumpy when members of the Protectorate showed up unannounced—even other Keepers.

"I miss the daylight," she was saying as she led them through the tunnels, deeper into the heart of the asteroid. "Well, the simulated daylight. A fake sunrise is better than no sunrise."

"It is rather dim in here, isn't it?"

She frowned as she glanced at the inset lighting. "We can spare the power to keep them at daylight levels, but Hitton prefers it this way."

"Strange," Vladsen said, absently trailing his fingers against the too-smooth walls. "She always struck me as rather fond of starlight. I seem to recall she takes her vacations in tropical environs."

"That is her usual preference, yes."

The words *Then what changed?* balanced on the tip of Biran's tongue, but he swallowed them down. Sato was feeling them out, and pushing too soon after their unexpected arrival would only get her to clamp down.

She stopped them outside a door and flashed her wristpad over it. The orifice dilated to reveal a spacious room, with en suite and a set of double beds. "I apologize that you'll have to share space. We're running things rather tight here."

"I thought you were fully staffed," Biran said. "But I haven't seen a soul since arrival, or heard anyone clomping around in mag boots but us." He gave her what he hoped was a harmless smile. "Where is everyone?"

"Working," she said, but a tendon in her jaw tensed.

"All hands, eh?" Biran knew he was poking too much. The doleful look Vladsen gave him spelled that out pretty plainly, but Sato had adopted the canted, forward body language of someone who wanted to say something. Olver and Anford had seemed to have their own source of information from the asteroid. Considering Olver had endorsed Sato, she might be the director's source—and willing to talk. Biran hoped he had given her the right opening.

"There's something you should see." The words ran together. She closed her eyes and centered herself. "If you're not too tired from your journey...?"

"Please, the *Taso*'s cushier than a spa," Vladsen said. "Lead the way."

"They have to stay here." Sato pointed her chin at the guardcore. "Forgive me, Speaker, but Hitton wouldn't like it. I'm only showing you two because you're on the Protectorate."

"Ah, well." Biran's mind raced so fast he almost made himself dizzy. "This is a Keeper installation, I'm sure they wouldn't mind sitting this out."

"The location is on station?" one of the GC asked in their computerized voice.

Sato nodded. "Not far, five hundred meters from here, round about. We'll only be a minute."

"We will remain."

Biran put his hands in his pockets to keep from fidgeting. "Leave your personal guards behind" was a comic-book-level invitation for an assault in a dark alley, but Sato didn't seem the type. And if she was, she wouldn't be so obvious about it.

Sato's pace picked up, and while Biran's gait was longer, he had to speed-walk to keep up with her. She took turns without explanation, and each time they entered a new area of the station, Biran couldn't help but marvel at how silent the whole place was. No signs of life lingered in these halls, where supposedly hundreds of survey crew lived and worked.

She stopped hard in front of a large set of doors, wide enough to fit two pallet bots side by side through, and hesitated. Biran and Vladsen kept their traps shut, hanging back a respectful distance, while Sato made up her mind.

Even if she fed the stray bit of intel to Olver, Hitton was her direct boss and longtime mentor. Biran got the distinct feeling that whatever Sato was about to show them risked her severing ties with Hitton. He wanted to reassure her that whatever was going on here, she was doing the right thing, but it would feel false coming from him. He didn't know what was happening. She did. Sato needed to assure herself, and all he could do to help was wait patiently while she arrived at her decision.

She swiped her ident over the lockpad. The doors peeled open, sliding into the wall with a soft hiss. Sato stepped aside. She'd opened the door, but she wouldn't enter, that was up to them.

Biran took the first step across the threshold. The lighting stayed low, but after blinking in the dim twilight for a few moments he could make out stacks upon stacks of crates, every one splashed with Prime logos. The Keeper insignia itself was dead center on every single panel of each crate. His stomach clenched. He didn't need to read the manifest to realize what these were, but he had to be sure.

"Is this the survey bot shipment from Ordinal?" he asked in a soft voice. In the pockets of his jumpsuit, his palms began to sweat.

Sato followed Vladsen in, stepping as if she expected the floor to vanish beneath her at any moment. "They are."

Vladsen said in his slow, easy way, completely lacking an accusatory tone, "They look as if they've never been opened."

"A few dozen have." There were thousands. "But the results weren't deemed trustworthy."

Biran didn't need to ask who had made that call. "I see. Are they malfunctioning...?"

Sato shook her head hard. "No. She fears they have been tampered with. After the shipment was counted in, Keeper Hitton—" She grimaced. She'd been trying so hard not to say the woman's name outright. "She started noticing another person on the station."

Ice ran through Biran's veins. "How?"

"A heat signature on the station map that shouldn't exist. She believes a saboteur stayed behind after that shipment and messed with the bots."

Biran kept his voice neutral. "And what do you believe?"

"I've run the manifests multiple times, even instigated a head count and watched the thermals myself. The bots we used brought back results consistent with human-powered surveys. I am...honestly uncertain. I've seen no evidence aside from the thermal scans."

"What do the scientists think?"

"They're sent out into the field every day for as long as possible to do the work the bots were supposed to do for them."

"Kept too busy to make their own deductions."

She paled. "I didn't say that."

"No, of course you didn't." Biran made himself look away from the mountains of crates and meet Sato's gaze. "Thank you for showing us. We want to help."

"Why did you ask us to leave the guardcore behind?" Vladsen asked gently.

Sato crossed her arms and took a step back. “Hitton thinks she saw an unaccounted-for individual in black armor, but the lights are so dim…It could have been anyone.”

“I’d heard rumors…” Vladsen whispered to himself, brows knitted together.

They’d pushed their luck too thin, Sato’s body language stiffened. Biran clapped Vladsen on the shoulder. “I could do with a lie-down and a light meal, what do you think?”

“An excellent idea. Thank you for the tour, Keeper Sato.”

They bowed to her in unison. She uncrossed her arms. “You’re welcome. Let me know if you need any further directions around the station. My ident has been sent to your contacts list.”

She ducked out of the warehouse and was gone around a corner before they could ask her anything more, leaving them alone in the cavernous room with the dormant survey bots.

Biran took his hand off Vladsen’s shoulder and turned back to the crates.

“What do you think?” he asked.

“I think I really would like a drink, if not a lie-down.”

“Me too,” Biran said. “Me too.”

CHAPTER 47

PRIME STANDARD YEAR 3543

ONCE A CRIMINAL, ALWAYS A CRIMINAL

Comms went dead at five minutes to estimated impact. Thirty seconds before that, Sanda ordered everyone to kill their wristpads; the guardcore could use them to fine-tune their locations. She hated being without a guiding voice in her ear, hated not having a map to track the movements of her people, but this was the price of going to war with the GC. You did it blind, or they saw every damn little thing you were looking at.

Arden had taken Liao and gotten to cover. Graham and Knuth were holed up somewhere in a terraced level of the station, using long-range rifles they'd pilfered from SecureSite's stores to sight down at the holding center.

Sanda picked her spot on the top of a transit center. Nox had argued that the top of one of the apartment buildings would make better cover, and give them better aim, but Sanda hadn't been willing to put those civilians at risk. She'd already tossed this whole station in the fire. She didn't need to pour accelerant on the inhabitants.

"Two minutes, by Arden's estimate," Nox said.

Sanda slowed her breathing, cradled the rifle against her shoulder. She needed all the power she could get to punch through GC armor at long range.

"You ever known Arden to make a mistake?"

"About math? Not a chance."

"Then I guess it's too late to run."

"Don't lie to me, Greeve. Dad isn't around to give you his disapproval. You love this shit as much as I do."

She weighed the weapon in her hands. Half-moons of brown blood caked under the short protrusion of her nails. It had hurt, watching Novak fade out like that and knowing she was the cause.

When Bero had told her everyone she'd ever known and loved was dead, blown to dust by time and war, she'd wanted nothing more at that moment than to take up arms—to scream and fight and claw back what was right, what was hers. She'd never been slow on the trigger as a gunship sergeant.

But the grin on Nox's face was something else. It wasn't rage or bloodlust or, hell, even justice. It was just hunger. Something ate Nox up inside and this was the way he'd found to feed that ache.

Sanda didn't love the weapon in her hands, not the way Nox did, but she loved that it gave her a chance. A chance to protect.

The GC ships punched through the protective membrane of the dock shield.

From her vantage, she had a clear view of the holding center, the primary docks, and the shuttle docks below them. Alarms screamed and warning lights flashed in protest as the shield worked overtime to seal itself up, to close the breach between the station and the hard vacuum beyond.

Sanda had eyes only for the ships. Three of them, as Arden had predicted. Long scythes of black metal plating, not a hint of an indicator light anywhere on their sleek and violent bodies. Black wasn't the right word for them. The guardcore's singular task was protecting the Keepers. As with everything Keeper related, they used proprietary materials, produced by Prime for Prime alone, and their color was so very dark it seemed to dim light. Not an absence of light, but an absence of space. How Rainier had gotten her hands on the real deal Sanda could only guess, but if she survived this, she meant to find out.

It wasn't the first time she'd seen those ships. They weren't uncommon around Ada Station—they went where the Keepers went—but they'd never been a threat to her before. She'd never felt, never *known*, that these weapons were meant for her.

Seeing them now, cutting through the space around the docks, two of them angling down, slicing like guillotine blades toward the shuttles, she knew she'd fucked up.

Fake GC or not, as Nox had said, they had real tactics. Real ships. That was her death coming. That was all their deaths.

"Oh fuck," Nox whispered under his breath, and she could have sworn he sounded excited.

"Brace," she said reflexively, even though her comms were dead.

She and Nox put a hand on the guardrail and bent their knees as two GC ships slammed into the shuttle docks, shredding the populace's best chances for escape. They didn't bother firing. The bodies of the ships were enough to grind every shuttle into ruin.

"They don't plan on leaving any witnesses," Sanda said.

"Let them try."

The single ship that hadn't demolished the shuttle docks rammed itself into the docks alongside the *Thorn*, as close to central holding as it could get. Sanda held her breath as an airlock opened, spilling three GC onto the dock. They didn't so much as glance at the *Thorn*. Thank you, Conway.

She waited until they'd stepped away from their ship, so that the black of their armor didn't blend completely with the same darkness that made up the ship, then picked her target—the tail position—and fired.

The GC's head exploded, the one in front dropping in the same manner from Nox's shot. The third swiveled, painting up their position with lasers from their weapon. Nox and Sanda hit the ground, going for cover behind a wall.

The GC had no intention of firing their weapon. A turret bloomed from the side of their ship and the electric hiss and slam of a railgun broke the air. Microseconds later the bolt slammed into the side of the transit center, barreling through the wall a scant few meters from their position.

The whole building rocked and groaned. Foam-laid concrete filled the air with grey, smokelike debris, making Sanda cough. Nox grabbed her by the shoulder and pulled. She got her feet under her and, ears ringing despite the plugs she'd put in before firing, they stumbled together as fast as they dared across the bucking and shaking transit center roof.

The roof cracked, the slab they were on tilted up. Sanda slipped, boots unable to hold purchase, and she landed hard on her ass as Nox rolled onto his side next to her. A chunk of the radio tower groaned, metal bending toward them.

Sanda threw up a prayer to whoever might be listening and rolled, grabbing Nox as she passed over him, tumbling across the avalanche of debris until they slammed into the roof of a train car.

Breath exploded from her with the impact and she sucked in air and dust, hacking and coughing. Nox got his feet under him and hefted her by the armpits, jumping down the side of the train car.

They staggered away as the avalanche hit the train car, pushed it off its rails, and sent it fishtailing toward them. Sanda got her feet under her in time to jump, hitting the ground alongside Nox outside of the growing arc of destruction.

She lay there a breath, stunned, and wiped the blood from her split lips onto the back of her hand.

"Two down," she said, then coughed up a blob of grey phlegm.

Nox laughed frantically and slapped her back as she coughed.

"Progress!" he shouted.

They helped each other up and did a quick once-over for broken bones or serious wounds. Just a few gashes and deep bruises, nothing life-threatening. Incredibly, her prosthetic was holding. Sanda shook powder from her hair and scowled.

"And this is why we don't fire from civilian buildings."

"Killjoy," he said, but didn't really mean it.

She half turned, craning her neck to get a better look at the place where Graham and Knuth had hunkered down. Dust thickened the air, making it difficult to see, and worry knotted her stomach.

"He's fine," Nox said in a softer tone. "Damn hard man to kill. A trait that seems to run in the family."

"Right." Sanda narrowed her eyes, adjusting her plan. "If they want to take buildings out, they're going to take them out with themselves inside."

"Got your six."

Without the high ground to tell them how many GC had disembarked, Sanda was walking in blind, so she took her time, creeping up on a side door to SecureSite holding. She hated the cramped hallways of the building almost as much as she hated not having comms and a map, but at least she knew where she was going. The GC would go for the scientists first, and that meant the cells.

"Please remain in your homes," a computerized voice said over the station speakers. "This is a guardcore engagement. Shelter in place until further notice."

"And now we're the bad guys," Sanda muttered.

"Good," Nox said, "I was starting to feel too noble hanging around you."

This SecureSite building had the same sterile-office feel that Atrux's had. Potted plants lurked in the corners on stands, and the walls were festooned with 3-D images of the station's bountiful harvest. This was the type of place you'd go to request a housing license upgrade, or visit a therapist. Not lock up a station's rule breakers.

Weirdness of SecureSite's aesthetics aside, the standardization gave her a good idea on where to look for the cells the scientists had been kept in. She held up a fist for Nox to stay silent and waited for his nod.

In sync, they moved down a short flight of stairs and stopped at the end of a hallway sectioned off with a thicker metal door than the others.

Nox took a knee to the side and brought up his rifle, sighting it to the center-mass height of the GC. Sanda pressed her side against the wall and matched his aim, then swiped her hand over the lock. Her wristpad was offline, but the station could read the ident chip embedded in her skin. Gutarra had granted her access to everything before he went to ground. It flashed red and beeped. Locked.

Someone was on the other side.

After a tense second when she was foolishly tempted to swipe again, as if the lock had been a misread mistake, the door slid open, steel disappearing into the wall.

Sanda didn't have a chance to count the GC on the other side before the firing started. She slammed her back against the wall and returned fire, ignoring the burning rip of a blaster tearing across her forearm, the grunt and shout of Nox.

Fire first, recover later. Fleet rules. GC rules, too.

She lay down fire until her trigger finger ached and the GC shots stopped. When the dust settled and the black armor on the other side was lying down and decidedly not moving, Sanda dared to ease off the wall, shifting to take a center stance.

Blood dripped down her arm and leg from a wound somewhere up on her side or hip, it was hard to tell where that searing throb was coming from without looking, but she was pretty sure it wasn't fatal. Mostly because she was still standing.

One. There was one GC on the other side, torn apart by enough fire to put down a whole shuttle, their armor punched through in neat little holes dripping blood as if the armor itself could bleed.

"That makes three," she wheezed.

Nox staggered to his feet, planting one red-stained palm against the wall for stability, and laughed raggedly. "How many are on those ships?"

"Twenty-four."

"Goddamn."

Sanda crept forward and nudged the dead GC with her boot, edging the rifle they'd dropped away. Those were armor-locked, useless to her, and all the systems on that armor would fit the dead GC's biometrics and none other. She sighed heavily and slumped against the plex window that had once held the scientists on the other side.

"They do not go down easy," she said half to herself.

"Say more obvious things," Nox called back.

"You're a bastard." He was keeping her talking to keep her moving, to keep her thinking, which was sweet in its own demented way. "Medikit on the wall," she muttered, and forced herself to push off, to drag herself toward it and rip open the lid, tearing open packages of bandages and drug patches to slap all over herself on the worst offenders.

"Got one here," Nox called back from the hall, the crunch of packaging the only sound save the soft whine of their guns repowering.

"Easy enough to guess we'd come here," she said. "Doesn't mean they've discovered where Gutarra took the scientists."

Nox tried to laugh but ended up coughing. "Nice story to tell yourself, but I got news—they tried to gun us down. If they didn't know where the scientists were, they would have at least tried asking nicely."

Sanda closed her eyes and resisted the urge to punch the wall, because even through the drugs the bandages pumped into her system, every little thing hurt.

"Right. And they're probably halfway there."

"Knuth and Graham—"

Sanda shook her head. "If they saw our building get hit, then they went to ground and tried to cut off the arteries. It's what I would have done. It's what anyone with fleet training would do."

"So." Nox stood up fully, twisted his torso from side to side, and grimaced as the bandages stretched over his ribs, side, chest, and upper thigh. She didn't bother asking how he was. Seemed like a stupid question. "We gotta stop acting like fleeties."

"We *are* fleeties."

"And criminals. Both of us."

She grinned, tasted iron, and licked the blood from her teeth. "You know what the last thing I got arrested for was?"

"Murder of a Keeper?"

She arched both brows. "No, never got taken in for offing that jackass. Icarion arrested me for spaceship piracy."

"Yo ho ho," Nox said.

CHAPTER 48

PRIME STANDARD YEAR 3543

AND A BOTTLE OF RUM

This was almost definitely going to get them killed, but at least those GC fuckers would never see it coming.

"There's a maintenance shaft near the *Thorn* that leads to the shuttle docks below," she said as they picked their way through the deserted hallways of SecureSite holding. "If we can get under that ship, then we might be able to access a secondary airlock without them seeing us coming."

"You sure about that?" Nox asked, but he was keeping up with her anyway.

"Not at all, but if their plan went the way they expected—I can't imagine they usually have a problem with that—then they think we're dead in this building. They won't expect us anywhere near their ship, especially from below."

Nox shook his head. "That sounds like pretty bullshit you tell someone to get them to go along with your suicidal plan. They probably know one of their units is dead. Even with the signal jamming, they have a way of communicating."

"Look, buddy, you've been on the suicidal track ever since you decided to stay on this station and face down a legion of hostile GC."

"Fair point. Have you considered punching a hole in the ship's side instead of trying to sneak into something that's almost definitely biometrically locked?"

She paused, resting her weight against the wall by the exit to the docks. "I'm listening."

"The *Thorn*."

"I'm not giving them a reason to fire on my ship until absolutely necessary. Conway is safe for now, there's no reason to draw attention there."

"Did you hit your head? They won't let the *Thorn* sail through this unscathed. Look, Commander, I know you're all gung ho for Prime, but these people aren't real GC and they took out the shuttles. They're not leaving witnesses. You said so yourself. If they bother pretending to file a report, I'm sure they'll come up with a nice story to make sure people think you defected."

She grimaced. "All right. The two below on the shuttle dock will have to maneuver in air, not vacuum, to get a clear shot at the *Thorn*, which will take some time. So we have the *Thorn* blow a hole in the one on this level, board it, and pray we can get its guns pointed at the other two all while having Conway get the fuck out of here."

"That's . . . a lot."

"Got a simpler plan that isn't guaranteed to kill us?"

"I do not."

The speakers in the hallway crackled. Sanda flinched, expecting another announcement from the GC, but Arden's voice—staticky and hesitant—whispered.

"Nox? Commander?"

"We're here," Sanda said. "What's your situation?"

"Safe, for now. I've gotten in touch with Gutarra and he thinks the GC are closing in on them."

"He's right, they are. Tell him to hold tight. We got a distraction coming."

"Hold up," Nox said. "Can you get a message through to the *Thorn* without giving away that there's anyone on board?"

They hesitated for so long Sanda feared they'd lost the connection. "I think so. I've been scattering messages all over the station, sending false packets everywhere. They'll eventually triangulate my position, but there's no way for them to figure out who I'm talking to in real time. They think I'm talking to you in the apartment now, Commander."

"Doubt it, they think I'm dead or dying in central holding. But if you've got them confused, keep it up."

"Confusion's the best I can do. I gotta move soon, or they'll find us."

"Stay hidden. Tell Conway that we need her to punch a hole in the GC ship nearest her, then get the fuck out of here. Coordinate it for eighty seconds from the end of this conversation."

"Seriously?"

Sanda glanced over at Nox's patchwork-bandaged torso. "Seriously. We can't stand toe-to-toe with them." She wanted to ask about Graham, but swallowed the question. If he were injured or dead, knowing would be a distraction.

"Understood. I'll put the message through." They swallowed. "Good luck."

"We really doing this?" Nox asked.

"We are now."

She edged one of the double doors to the docks open. If the GC on the nearest ship noticed the movement, they didn't react. Nox took up a mirror position with the other door and waited.

Silently, Sanda counted down.

At seventy-nine seconds, the *Thorn* burst into life. Her primary railgun—Conway was not fucking around—swiveled and locked onto the GC ship, firing once. Sanda couldn't see the GC ship's console, but she had bet everything that they wouldn't detect the *Thorn* powering up its railgun fast enough to do anything about it. She'd been right.

The ordnance tore a massive channel through the GC ship, rocking it onto its side. Conway engaged the energy weapons, firing down at the two ships in the shuttle dock in tandem, and by the time it was all done, the *Thorn*'s engines had spooled up and she tore out of there, ripping part of the dock away with her.

"Go," Sanda ordered, but they were both already moving, sprinting dead-on as hard as they could while keeping their weapons steady forward, pointed at the gaping hole in the side of the GC ship.

There was no chance of innocents on the other side of that hole. She went in laying down fire, even though the smoke blinded her. She painted an arc of rifle fire through the entrance and put her back against the wall near that hole, not bothering to take in the details of the ship interior—more black, more targets—she fired at anything that looked like it could move until nothing in that first room was moving anymore. Nox echoed her every motion, a mirror of death.

Still. The room went still aside from the smoke curling through the gaping wound the railgun had left. They weren't done, couldn't pause, couldn't stop. Sanda had never been in a GC ship, but she'd been in enough gunships to know what kind of layout made sense.

She turned toward the pilot deck and shot her way through the door, found five GC getting their guns out, rising from positions at the controls, and she slaughtered them, too, rifle fire tearing up chunks in the electronics of the control consoles. Everything in the ship screamed and hissed and broke out loud except the GC themselves. Those died silent, their cries trapped behind the armor of their helmets.

Targeting alarms blared. The other two ships had caught on, knew the third ship was in enemy hands, and would rather blast it to pieces than chase the *Thorn*.

Sanda relied on Nox to hold the door to the deck, and hold he did, rifle prattling away while she slung hers under her arm and fumbled across the captain's console, trying to gain control of the ship but failing because everything, naturally, was biometrically locked.

A searing blast tore through the ship. The world shook as the floor jarred under impact, another railgun boring its way through the body of the black scythe. Sanda gritted her teeth and braced herself, reaching back for her rifle because the ship's guns wouldn't answer her orders. The ship kicked sideways, clinging to the dock by a single clamp. Metal groaned.

Sanda and Nox were tossed against the wall of the command deck, which was now very much the floor, clumped together in a tangle of aching and burning limbs. They scrambled, dragging themselves to their knees.

Something metal screeched and Sanda grimaced, clutching the

edge of a nonresponsive console to yank herself to her feet. Nox grabbed her shoulder and helped her up, one arm under hers, his rifle cradled in his opposite armpit as she mirrored him, rifle pointed toward the broken-open deck door as if that's where their threat, their death, would come from—not the fire of the other ships.

A woman in mag boots thumped up to the door, helmet tucked under one arm and a blaster in the other. Sanda's finger twitched in anticipation but she didn't fire. This woman was wearing Prime grey and cyan, not GC black, her green eyes bright against the space-dark expanse of her cheeks, puckered up under the force of a fierce smile.

"Commander Sanda Greeve?" she asked, as if they'd just bumped into each other in a coffee shop.

"Who the fuck—?"

"Ah, we have not met." She half turned, squeezed a round off on her blaster and barked an order into her comms, then swiveled back to regard Nox and Sanda.

"I am Malkia Rehema Okonkwo. Your brother put out a distress call for the area. My ship was passing close by. My guardcore are securing the station." Her eyes narrowed. "The *real* guardcore. Would you care for some lunch?"

Sanda dissolved into a puddle of frantic laughter.

INTERLUDE

PRIME STANDARD YEAR 0002

THE PRICE OF KNOWLEDGE

Maria had been furious with Alexandra when she'd summoned her to her room late at night to show her the body.

There had been no real struggle for her life, Lex had assured her irate lover as the assassin's stain bore deeper into the fibers of her floor. It made her wonder if a better material could be developed to wick such stains away. The man had broken in, then Lex had stunned him, interrogated him, and stabbed his femoral artery. It was all very neat.

Maria, for some reason, disagreed.

"You knew he was coming and didn't tell your security detail?" she demanded. Though gravity was near Earth standard in this hab ring, the woman's hair had a fluffy quality that had only grown when she'd left the humidity of Earth behind for the dry, recycled air of space.

"Of course not," Lex said, watching the way the soft lights played in Maria's hair. They reminded her of something. A model of neurons, perhaps. "They would have killed him on sight. I needed to know what he hoped to achieve."

"You always need to *know*," Maria said, throwing her hands up in exasperation. There was no god in the sky above to which Maria could pray, there wasn't even a sky anymore, but the habit stayed with her, and always made Lex smile.

Smiling, in this situation, only made matters worse.

Maria darted around the body and grabbed Lex's wrists, her strong fingers digging in against the bones, and turned Lex's hands over. Blood slicked her palms, and some of it was Lex's. She hadn't realized that the force required to stab someone meant you lost friction on the grip of the blade's handle. Annoying. Physics usually behaved for her.

"You're hurt," Maria said.

"A scratch. It doesn't matter." Lex peeled her hands away and dropped to a crouch alongside the body, fascinated, turning his head so she could see his still-open eyes. Erik. His name had been Erik. "He knew."

"Knew what?" Maria pulled her green silk robe tight and stepped as close as she could to the body without staining her slippers.

Too much. "That there isn't a deadman's switch."

Maria sucked air through the gap in her front teeth, whistling. "Then he's not the only one who knows."

"No, he isn't. I'm afraid that deterrent will no longer work in thwarting attacks on my person. I still have the active switch, and they know that, so they'll seek to stun, incapacitate, or destroy me in my sleep."

"Lex..." Maria's voice was thick as she put a hand on her shoulder, squeezing. "We have to increase security."

"I had arrived at the same conclusion."

Lex stood, but her gaze was stuck on the body. How silly, how *annoying*, that one being could force her hand to change so much. But it would not slow progress. She would not allow it. They were already halfway through building a second gate in Tau Ceti, and Lex would not stand for a hiccup in that plan. She needed to know what was on the other side. *Needed* to know if all systems were as barren as Tau Ceti.

Needed to know if the next punch-through would lead to the makers of the sphere.

"I had time to draw up plans while I waited," she said.

"While you waited for...?" Realization dawned, and Maria laughed. "You drafted plans for a new security unit while you waited for your assassin to show?"

"Here, let me show you."

In the low light of her private quarters, Alexandra Halston turned her wristpad to face Maria, and pulled up the first, rough strokes of the organization that would become the guardcore.

"No one will know them once they take the armor?" Maria asked. "Not even you?"

"Prime Inventive is a nation built on secrets," Lex said, and as the word *nation* passed her lips, she knew it to be true. They had a fleet. They would have an elite guard. They had an inner council keeping their greatest mysteries safe. Soon, Lex mused, there would be only one secret left to keep.

The rest, the building of a nation-state in the stars, was only a formality.

CHAPTER 49

PRIME STANDARD YEAR 3543

SICK OF WEAPONS

Someone in guardcore armor handed her tea, and it was all Sanda could do to keep from dumping it out in the corner of the room for fear of being poisoned. Instead, she set the cup aside on the table next to her, and tried not to look like she was falling asleep where she sat.

At least they'd given her a wheelchair, as it turned out the rumors that the Prime Director traveled only on ships under spin-grav were true. The medis had patched her up quickly, rushing her out for this audience with Okonkwo, and Sanda wasn't sure she could stand under her own power yet. The high-end stims and painkillers were nice, though.

The GC pretended not to notice Sanda snub the tea and took up a sentry position near the door. She had spent little time paying attention to them until now. They'd been ghosts, furniture. Facts of life drifting around the fleet academy that weren't spoken of, unless in rumor-filled whispers of so-and-so's aunt disappearing five years ago to join the GC.

Now, that armor lurking in the corner felt like a toxic stain that needed scrubbing out.

The door dilated and Okonkwo swept into the room, having shed her Prime armor for a blue silk dress that brushed the tops of her slippered feet and had no business in a ship that might lose gravity.

The sleeves went to her elbows, and as Okonkwo moved, Sanda glimpsed a crescent-shaped scar on her forearm. The resemblance to the tattoo on Keeper Nakata's wrist sent a jolt through her. She swallowed and averted her eyes from the mark, trying not to get too mired down in what it might mean. First things first.

"Is my crew accounted for? Are they safe?"

Okonkwo settled into a chair across from her and accepted the tea the GC brought her, sipping it first before cradling it in her palms.

"The crew members we know of have been found and are in various states of stable, yes. Your father took a blaster to the hip, but is recovering well. Nox and Knuth were both in various states of injury which were noncritical, and Arden is unscathed. As for Conway, she has been contacted and is returning to the station with the *Thorn*."

She paused, and while Sanda knew that this pause was calculated to draw her into asking about the missing member from the list, she didn't care. Okonkwo knew. Probably, in the five minutes Sanda had been sitting here waiting for the tiniest sliver of news, Okonkwo had squeezed every drop of information from Monte Station and shaped it into something like the truth of what happened on Janus.

"And Dr. Liao?"

She smiled into her tea. "Ah, the doctor. I'm pleased you didn't dissemble—I had to check, you understand. Make sure you weren't trying to hide her from me. She is perfectly fine. Arden Wyke was adept at keeping their location concealed. They were the last my GC found, and revealed their presence only after we broadcast certain encrypted signals. She has been very vocal about the innocence of her colleagues. I'm dying to hear your take on things."

"You know about the sample taken from Janus?"

"Yes. Liao was most insistent that the sample, combined with the notes of the researchers, would prove that they acted under what they believed to be Prime orders. Unfortunately, the sample was destroyed in the battle. Our medis found the flask in what was left of the guardcore ship you commandeered."

"Destroyed?" Sanda wasn't sure if she should feel relief that such a vile creation was gone, or upset that she'd lost the evidence. "You'd have to press Liao for the details, but that flask was full of self-replicating nanites designed to amplify signals to and from the gates. Self-replication aside, the scientists' work was above board as far as they knew. They were unaware that the governors on their models had been broken, allowing access to a gate's power system.

"Prime Director, they operated under the direction of Rainier Lavaux. If Rainier has more of those nanites, then she can turn the gates off and on at will."

"Rainier? Interesting. I understand your concern, but I assure you that such a thing is impossible. Without an intimate knowledge of how the gates operate, getting a signal through to them isn't enough. Keepers must scan in their activation codes. Rainier may believe she can do this thing, but I do not believe her capable. It is impossible."

"But you said..."

Her eyes narrowed. "What did I say, Commander?"

Sanda flicked her gaze to the guardcore in the corner, but Okonkwo waved at her to continue. Despite the encouragement, she couldn't help but drop her voice. "I encountered a Nazca on Janus Station who claimed to be working on your behalf, hunting Rainier. He was the one who alerted me to the modified governors and sent the information to his handlers. He claimed that you redirected the mission to focus on gathering all instances of the nanites."

"I did no such thing."

"I see," Sanda said, though she really didn't. Novak had seemed convinced that his orders came from Okonkwo. While the Nazca were exceptional at lying, she didn't understand why he'd lie about that.

Maybe to leverage her trust by making her believe that he worked on behalf of Prime, but by that point he had to know she'd never trust him. He'd blown his chance by pretending to be Tomas. His true motives had died with him on that shuttle. Part of her wished she could unwind that clock, go back and interrogate him all over again with fresh eyes, but he'd been Nazca. Nothing he said could be trusted.

"It's possible Rainier wanted the nanites to spin a deadgate," Sanda said. "The coordinates Keeper Lavaux had planned on taking Bero are behind one."

"She would have no better luck there, the same principles apply. If you were so concerned about these nanites, why didn't it occur to you to hand them over to the fleet for analysis?"

"Prime Director, I had just stepped off a station faking a Prime charter, owned by a Keeper's widow, with a security staff comprised of people pretending to be fleeties—uh, soldiers. I was not confident in who I could trust."

"And so you brought the hammer down on Monte."

"I didn't intend—"

Okonkwo held up a hand. "I've read your dossier, Greeve. I understand you did not *intend* to harm a civilian station. Your mistrust of the government you serve led you to that rather poor decision."

Sanda flicked a glance to the GC. "I do not believe my distrust is misplaced."

"I suppose I cannot blame you for that. Tell me, Greeve, do you believe Anford is a good person?"

She blinked. "Of course."

"You trust her? Not because she is your superior, I mean. You trust her instincts as a person and a general?"

"I do."

"Good, then you are not completely stupid. But despite that trust, you denied a direct order to take those scientists to a fleet station and instead put an entire civilian station in harm's way. People died today, Greeve. Not just the false GC."

She straightened. "I am very sorry people died. But if there had been false fleeties on the station, then we would have lost the scientists and possibly the sample, too. I couldn't take that risk."

Okonkwo closed her eyes for a breath, then snapped them open. "My dear, I understand these conspiracies are new territory to you, but they are not to me, nor to Anford. We have had insurgent factions infiltrate the fleet before—spies abound—and never have they had the numbers to control an entire station.

"*If* you had followed Anford's orders, and there had been fake 'fleeties' there, and the false GC showed up, you would have had a fight on your hands. But you would have had allies—the real fleet—and once more, allies who *signed up to fight*.

"You mean well, Greeve, but this decision was a catastrophic fuckup. You have been embroiled in bullshit, and the adjustment is difficult, but if you've decided you can trust Anford, then *trust her*."

Sanda crushed her eyes closed and gripped the armrests of the chair hard enough to make her knuckles ache. A dozen excuses roiled through her mind but they were all useless. Okonkwo was right. Sanda should never have gone to Monte. "I understand. I'm so sorry."

"Do not apologize. *Do better*."

She forced herself to meet Okonkwo's baleful stare. "I will."

"I believe you. And that is the only reason you won't spend the rest of your life in a cell."

"I'd like to do something for Monte."

"They don't want you or your help. Leon Gutarra is already making noise about going public regarding the rogue GC. I'll pour money into the reconstruction, which I would have done regardless. It will be swift, and it will be an upgrade, and they will be quiet about the attack, but you will never have friends at Monte Station. I suggest you wipe the dock from your maps."

"If there's anything I can do to help discreetly—"

"I will let you know." She took a long sip of tea, sat back, and crossed her ankles. "Now. As you seem determined to kick this particular hornet's nest, I suppose I should brief you on the matter. You've been trying very hard not to look at my tattoo removal scar. I could have had it lasered smooth, but I like the reminder, however subtle."

Sanda's cheeks went hot. "I didn't mean to stare."

"Of course not. You've seen it before, possibly in dire circumstances, and are wondering at its origin. Was your brother able to provide? I'm certain you asked."

She laughed nervously. "No. He'd never seen it before."

"We have not had a member in Ada in decades, though there have been considerations. Our last disappeared around the time Icarion started fussing. We thought it prudent to remove ourselves until things settled. If not in Ada, where have you seen it?"

"Keeper Nakata."

"Nakata?" Her brows arched high. "Dead, unfortunately, though not surprisingly. She was an aggressive member of the order. Ah. I see now. You were chasing Jules Valentine, Nakata's killer. Nox and Arden are known associates of that woman. Did you find her?"

Sanda pressed her palms against her knees. Fear fluttered through her, but she made herself meet Okonkwo's eyes. Sanda had no doubt that everything she was about to say, the Prime Director had already discerned. There was nothing subtle about what had happened on Monte, and Malkia Okonkwo was one of, if not the most, connected person in the universe.

Her only chance to fill in some large gaps in her knowledge was to be as straightforward with her as possible. No games. No dissembling. Not when you were toe-to-toe with the head of all of Prime's intelligence agencies.

"Prime Director, I have been betrayed from every direction since I woke up after Dralee. I don't mean to be rude, or insubordinate, but it is my stringent belief that the people of Prime are in danger. I can't see the full picture yet. I have lines drawn from Keeper Lavaux to Jules via Rainier Lavaux. I have a whole station full of scientists working for Jules who don't know what they were there to do. I have Keeper Lavaux attempting to kill me to take Bero to a location that makes no sense, and I have GC rolling up on a civilian station with guns blazing to get at those scientists. I was happy to warn you about the nanites, but otherwise, I don't want to talk to you with that scar on your arm unless you've got a real fucking good explanation."

Sanda held her breath while Okonkwo's eyes narrowed. After a beat, the Prime Director burst into laughter and slapped her palm against the arm of her chair. Shaking her head, she stood and drained the contents of her teacup in one gulp, shivered a little, then flipped up the top of a side table and rummaged around in the interior. Glass bottles clinked.

"Do you want a proper drink, Greeve? This"—she waved the empty cup at her—"wasn't tea. Ah." She pulled a slim bottle of black glass from the table and popped it open, pouring a glug of amber liquid into her cup.

"Excuse me, Prime Director," Sanda said as Okonkwo strode

across the room, tipped Sanda's tea onto the floor—where it was promptly absorbed by the rug's smart fibers—and refilled her cup with the liquid. Whiskey, by the scent. "But, what the fuck?"

"Expected me to throw you out? Toss you in a cell and forget the key for your impertinence? Pah. If I wanted you punished, I would have leaked a false tip that the corrected footage of your supposed murder of Keeper Lavaux was faked, and let the scaremongering rumor hordes do the rest. Many of those voices have not been convinced as it is, and it would be such a small thing to tip public opinion against you. But I do not break tools, Commander Greeve. I use them." She drifted back to her chair and crossed her legs languorously as she sat.

"You and I are very much on the same side, if there are any clear lines at all to be drawn in this universe. I've read your dossier. You went into the fleet to protect your darling little brother. You enlisted knowing full well that Icarion was rattling their sabers, which says something for your sense of honor even in those nascent days. And on those rare occasions you were ordered to battle, you acquitted yourself well, until the fateful ambush at Dralee that would have, should have, destroyed you, if not for the intervention of Icarion's wayward beast of war. Am I right so far?"

"Bero is no beast."

"Forgive me my flourishes. The problem with you, Greeve, is that you were rocketed up from your provincial life into a quagmire of political fuckery previously unknown to you. Oh yes, we Keepers present a unified front to the united worlds because we must, but we squabble like children. Lavaux was one of my more problematic members. Thank you for seeing to him."

"I didn't kill him on purpose."

"Just like you didn't spear Monte on the blade of the GC, and yet a wake of bodies follows you." She sighed and swirled her cup. "Usually we construct icons like you. Pick a likely, squeaky-clean fleet academy grad and give them some fight or another to win by the skin of their teeth, prop them up as a hero. It helps if they come from humble origins, then trot them out when needed. You don't trot, Greeve, you gallop, and you don't have the slightest clue what you're galloping toward."

"Enlighten me."

Sanda held no illusions that the Prime Director was actually confiding in her. As far as she knew, Okonkwo couldn't even get drunk, no matter how much whiskey she tossed back. Her metabolism had been tinkered with as surely as the genes hacked to give her unnaturally vibrant green eyes. Sanda sipped her whiskey, smooth as silk, and wished her parents had been able to afford the same metabolism boosters.

"We"—she lifted her wrist, turning it so Sanda could see the scar there—"are called the Acolytes. Normally we select our number from the quieter members of the Keepers, the ones without political ambitions, the ones who will slip into obscurity in the moment of their death. Keepers like Nakata—not your brother or Lavaux, naturally. The order made a mistake in my selection, but once I discovered their existence, I played down my ambitions until I was inducted."

Okonkwo flashed her a sly smile. "No Prime Director before had understood the Acolytes and their directives. I aimed to change that, to file down the lines between my fractious colleagues. They kicked me out promptly after my political ambitions became clear, but by then I'd already learned their history and objectives."

"And what did you learn?"

"That even the eldest of their number doesn't know the full scope of what they do, and that appears to be by design. The order was founded by Maria Salvez, Halston's lover, without Halston's blessing. Does that surprise you? When our fearless founder was designing her government for the stars, her closest adviser thought her vision was incomplete.

"You see, Halston was above all a visionary. She believed in humanity's right to expansion, believed that if we only worked together, we could achieve great things."

Sanda said, "And yet she hid the secret of the gates in the skulls of Keepers."

Okonkwo tapped the side of her nose. "She did, for even one so optimistic as Halston couldn't avoid the reality of the power of the gates. Such knowledge... well, humanity had already seen many cold wars. Halston was not about to let us devolve into an arms race, not when becoming an interstellar species was within our grasp.

"Salvez did not believe the creation of the Keepers was a complete solution. If Halston believed in human potential, Salvez believed in human nature. The guardcore was Halston's response to Salvez's concerns, but after that, Halston would hear no more about it. Salvez, clever thing that she was, created the Acolytes in secret—a secret she kept even from Halston. Their purpose is the preservation of the society Halston created. When an Acolyte overhears a young Keeper sounding a touch too seditious at a party, they attempt to befriend and correct without alerting that Keeper to their purpose. It is a subtle, but valuable, order."

"I don't see a lot of subtlety in Nakata attempting to kill Jules Valentine for information."

Okonkwo waved a hand. "All things stray from their origin, and the source of the rogue guardcore has been a particular thorn in the Acolytes' side. They've been chasing them down for years."

A suspicion itched in the back of Sanda's mind. "How long have they been chasing these fake GC?"

"Oh, a hundred years or so."

She swallowed hard, thinking of Keeper Kenwick's head floating in that pillar. If he had a body, would she have found a tattoo there? Had Kenwick stolen the coordinates for destruction, or preservation? "In all that time you haven't figured out how the defectors are being recruited? How is that possible?"

A flash of irritation crossed Okonkwo's face. "Because they're not defectors. We believed they were, too, at first. How else could they gain access to technology guarded so well? We are in the secrets business." She tapped the back of her head, where the chip was implanted. "But no. We have no evidence to that effect."

She gestured to the GC standing by the door. "Demas, darling, explain it to the commander."

Sanda jerked her head around to watch the GC as their shoulders rose and fell with an obvious sigh. No one, not even the Prime Director, was supposed to know the names of the GC.

"Are you sure about this?" Demas asked in their computerized voice.

"She has been betrayed on all fronts, old friend. A little honesty couldn't hurt. You won't tell, will you Greeve?"

Sanda worked her jaw around to get some saliva back. "No, Prime Director."

"There you go." Okonkwo waved her hand impatiently at Demas.

The GC stepped away from the door and, hesitantly, reached up to press the button that retracted their helmet into their collar. Sanda's heart lodged itself firmly in her throat. Even if she could speak, she'd have no idea what to say. The GC were lethal. Unknowable. Shadows in the dark, slick as knives and just as precise.

But Demas, as he shook out his matted ear-length hair, was just a man. A man with faint wrinkles around the corners of his almond-colored eyes. Formally, he bowed to Sanda.

"I am Demas, the present controlling mind of the guardcore."

"I…" She cleared her throat. "I thought you didn't have a, ah, leader, and everything was done by anonymized vote."

"That is more or less correct. Complete anonymization is impossible, as selections for recruiting must be made. There are very few of us with the authorization to hire new members. We do not select anyone who poses the slightest risk of betrayal."

"If your selection procedure is so precise, then where the fuck are these GC coming from? Because I believe your protocols are tight, I do, but I also know GC tactics and equipment when I see them, and that's what we faced at Monte."

"We do not know," Demas said carefully. "None of our number are missing. None of our equipment is missing."

"Can't you DNA-test the dead GC? Figure out who they were?"

He gave her a rueful smile. "Major Greeve, our armor is outfitted with a wide variety of chemicals ready for injection. Stimulants, focus aids, pain suppressors. This is normal. These GC have modified the usual suite of injections to include a dissolvent. The moment the armor has detected the death of the occupant, the dissolvent is released and the body liquefied, its DNA contaminated beyond our abilities to reconstruct. Captured rogue GC have demonstrated a willingness to dissolve themselves before samples can be taken."

"Fuck," she whispered.

"I agree," Demas said.

"And that's all you have? They're not your people, you don't know who they're working for, and you don't know what they want."

A shadow passed across Demas's face. "We're working on it."

"For around a hundred years?" Sanda stared between them both, incredulous. This was the most powerful woman in the universe, and the recruitment head of the most dangerous group of soldiers. There was no way. No way.

"Oh..." Sanda shook her head and laughed ruefully. "Right. Like you'd tell me."

Okonkwo smiled thinly. "Sorry, dear. We have our suspicions, but we have very little facts, and even then..."

Sanda nodded. "I understand."

"You don't, actually."

Sanda lifted her head. "I'd like to."

Okonkwo took a drink, set her cup down, and ticked off points with her fingers. "It is a fact that the rogue guardcore are not coming from within the order. It is a fact that they have access to real GC armor and ships, and yet none of our supplies are unaccounted for. Before your engagement with them on Monte Station, we had yet to see a full-scale battle between them and outside forces. We'd only heard rumors of small, unauthorized skirmishes."

"They attacked Arden, Nox, and Jules in Atrux's Grotta two years ago after Nakata's death," Sanda said. "Took over the streetlights, apparently."

Okonkwo's eyes narrowed and she flicked a glance at Demas, who began typing something into the screen embedded in the wrist of his armor.

"This is the first we've heard of it. Thank you. It seems something about you and your associates draws these people out. Everyone involved is extremely circumspect, otherwise we would have found and crushed them ages ago."

"Have the Nazca collected any information on this?"

"Not to my knowledge." Okonkwo leaned forward. "Tell me, did your Nazca on Janus escape? They've played dumb to us so far, but considering your assertions, it may be time to squeeze some truth out of them. I hate to do it, they're so damn slippery, but it is possible."

Sanda shook her head. "It was Leo Novak. He escaped Janus with the other scientists, but you won't be able to interrogate him, I had to kill him. He was attempting to flee Monte with the nanite sample right before the station was attacked. You'll find his body in a shuttle underneath the space where the *Thorn* was docked."

Okonkwo's gaze drifted to the side as she accessed an ocular implant and sent off a message. "Thank you, Greeve. His body will be collected and examined. We've been wanting to get a look at Nazca implants."

"Gross."

"Facts of life and technology, my dear. We're all half computer these days. Demas, tap your Nazca contact. I want to know what they know about Novak and why *my* name was used."

"I've already sent the order."

"You know me so well. Any other gifts for me, Greeve? You spoke with Valentine—what does she want?"

Sanda frowned into her glass. "I'm not sure Jules is after anything personally. Arden and Nox seem to think she's protecting another member of their old crew. Rainier might be holding that person hostage to force Valentine's cooperation. I don't know her well enough to say, but she seemed out of her element on Janus."

"Interesting, if not entirely revelatory. Now, your mission register claimed you were on your way to reconnoiter a suspicious location before you went on a jaunt to Janus. I assume this is behind the deadgate Lavaux was taking Bero?"

"Yes."

"Which deadgate?"

"It's here in Ordinal."

"Ah. So that's why you stayed in my neighborhood."

"Yes..."

"... But?"

Sanda flicked her gaze down, embarrassed. "I did not tell General Anford where the coordinates were located."

Okonkwo laughed. "And you were going to do what, exactly? Accidentally hit the power button and trip over the threshold? Deadgates can't be spun without authorization, as Rainier was bound to find out if she attempted to use her nanites."

"We were going to look around the area."

"I see. Arden Wyke thought they could spin it, did they? Well, I'd almost like to see them try, but you'd bring all the guardcore and fleet in the area down on your head. Not to mention the autonomous berserkers." She tapped one finger against the rim of her cup. "Well, if Lavaux wanted a peek behind that gate, then it may be worth looking into. I want you to head there once you and your crew are recovered."

"Prime Director, I was going to anyway."

She rolled her eyes. "I know, dear, but at least allow me some pretense of giving you orders. I shall update Anford. Now, considering we cannot anticipate what's on the other side of that gate, I want you to borrow one of my finest weapons. Take Demas."

"Malkia—" His voice pitched high in protest, but she held up a hand to cut him off.

"I have plenty of guardcore to watch my backside."

"With respect," Sanda said carefully, "my crew is going to have a very difficult time working with a GC after today."

"Oh, but they won't be working with a GC, will they? They'll be working with Demas. It's quite different. And there is no need to fear he may work for our shadowy friends. Demas is my personal agent, we've known each other all our lives, isn't that right, Demas? Old childhood playmates."

He nodded stiffly, but there was a flash of reverence in his gaze that made Sanda believe Okonkwo was telling the truth.

"If I take Demas, I need you to give me Liao. She wants a chance to right the wrong she's done at Janus. If we encounter more nanites, then she might be useful."

"I wasn't aware that this was a negotiation. But, very well, you may have the doctor if you believe she'll be of use *and* if she wants to go with you." Okonkwo's gaze unfocused as she tilted her head, listening to a voice in her ear. After a moment, she sighed.

"It seems the false guardcore got to your Nazca first. The body's gone, the blood sprayed down with the same dissolvent used on the guardcore dead."

CHAPTER 50

PRIME STANDARD YEAR 3543

WHEN THE MOMENT'S PICKED FOR YOU

Dressed in a Prime jumpsuit and strapped up with fleet weapons, Demas could almost pass for a normal soldier sent along by Okonkwo to help get the deadgate spun up. Almost. Maybe it would have worked if her crew were all fleeties—Knuth and Conway were giving the man side-eye but keeping their traps shut—but there was no way Sanda could keep a lid on Nox and Arden's suspicions. Hell, even Liao glanced over her shoulder more often when Demas was in the room.

So Sanda waited until they were a day's flight away from Okonkwo's ship, then called a general meeting on the command deck.

"Story time's over," she said. She gripped one of the ceiling loops in the forward area of the deck, turned so she could keep everyone in sight. Demas raised his eyebrows, but didn't look like he was about to turn hostile. Of course, someone like Demas wouldn't telegraph that unless they wanted to. "Demas is GC."

"You owe me a bottle of Caneridge," Nox shot to Arden, who threw their arms in the air and rolled their eyes.

"You said he was a spy for Okonkwo, not GC. That's different."

"Same thing." Nox half turned to Demas. "Isn't it? You're definitely reporting back to Okonkwo, there's no other reason for you to be here."

He smiled tightly and inclined his head. "It's true. I work for the Prime Director, but I believe that must be true of everyone on this ship, is it not?"

Uncomfortable glances all around. Sanda scowled. "My people are Prime citizens and soldiers and I won't have you making them second-guess their reasons for being on this ship. This is about you, Demas, though I suspect that's not something you're used to."

"Ah." He floated backward as he unfolded his arms and reached out to steady himself against the wall. Nox reached for his sidearm at the motion. Sanda cut him a look, but when he met her gaze, she found she didn't feel like telling him to stand down. Demas took all of this in impassively. "Forgive me, redirection is trained into us."

"Funny. Blowing holes in people is trained into me," Nox said.

"Nobody's blowing holes in anyone." Sanda rubbed the back of her neck. "Look, no one on this ship was going to trust you with or without knowing who you are, Demas, so I'm sorry for dunking you in the shit headfirst, but I won't keep your identity from my crew. No matter how nicely Okonkwo asks."

He inclined his head. "Arden is not the only one winning bets today. Okonkwo believed you would blow my cover as soon as possible. I gave you until we reached the gate."

"Sorry to disappoint you, then. There are too many secrets going around for my taste right now. The facts, people, as we know them: Okonkwo is an ex-member of an organization called the Acolytes, of which Nakata was one, dedicated to preserving and protecting Prime. They've been preoccupied with tracking down fake GC, and according to Demas here, those GC are coming from a source no one can identify. There aren't any GC missing, and none of their equipment is, either."

"Whoa wait," Conway said, "I've gone gun-to-gun with a lot of ships, Commander, and that's gotta be bullshit, because those ships at Monte moved and acted exactly like GC ships. They're not knockoffs."

"No, they're not. They're both real, and they can't be. It's a pain in the ass, but it's not the biggest pain. Kicking Keeper Nakata out of our sphere of shady shit, that means Jules has gotten herself tangled up with something else. Something the GC and the Acolytes have been working their asses off to root out, but haven't been successful so far."

"Rainier has to be in the middle of it all," Arden insisted. Their fingers tapped against the arm of their chair as if they had a keypad underneath them.

"I agree," Sanda said, "and while Okonkwo was playing it down, this is probably the closest they've come to getting names and reasons about these fake GC. Rainier is using them to protect her interests somehow. We need to find out what those interests are."

"You realize chasing down those coords is walking into an ambush, right?" Nox said. "Whatever's there, Keeper Lavaux was willing to bring the biggest weapon in the universe there for safekeeping. He had to have had something there to defend it, or something there he wanted to use Bero to defend."

Her secret hadn't been hers alone while Graham was here, and though she'd tried hard not to think about it ever since seeing him off from Okonkwo's ship, that sense of loss needled her. But she was grateful, too, that he was safe on a shuttle back to Ada.

Sanda thought of Graham's advice to pick her moment. It was strange, not having him on deck. As much as he'd irritated her by pushing back against her orders, having a member of her family close had felt safer, somehow.

Now that they had walked into the lion's den, she needed to come clean. She'd trusted her crew this far, and they hadn't let her down.

Demas was going to be a problem, but she couldn't let her team go through that gate without knowing the full scope of what might be on the other side. If they got injured or killed, and knowing the truth of the coordinates could have saved them, she'd never forgive herself.

"Since it's honesty time, you should all know that Lavaux did not have these coordinates."

Demas stiffened. "Okonkwo is allowing the spin of the deadgate *only* under the pretense that—"

"What the fuck?" Nox said. "So where did you get 'em then, a Ouija board?"

She held on to the handles on the ceiling for dear life. "I found them on board Bero, in a lab laid out identically to the one on Janus. Lavaux wanted Bero because he believed Bero still had those coordinates."

Demas's eyes narrowed slightly.

Conway said, "Why not tell us that, Commander? Don't make much of a difference."

She took a long, slow breath. "Because the coordinates were hidden inside of a Keeper chip. I believe this chip belonged to the last known member of the Acolytes to visit Ada, Rayson Kenwick. I believe Keeper Lavaux funneled intelligence and money to Icarion, allowing them to construct Bero, in exchange for the capture and return of Kenwick. I also believe the Icarions kept Kenwick instead, betraying that arrangement, which was why Lavaux was so keen to get inside Bero."

"That's a hell of an accusation, Commander," Demas said. "I know the man tried to kill you, but selling intelligence to our enemies—"

"Demas, I'm not even sure he sold it. He very well might have given it away for the chance to get at Kenwick."

Arden leaned back and laced their fingers behind their head, pressing their lips together in thought. "There was a lot of arguing on the net about the Icarion problem—not the planet's rights and taxation stuff but the actual tech—once they confirmed the existence of Bero. Icarion was having problems keeping the hab domes they bought from Prime working. It didn't make sense that they'd come out of nowhere with a state-of-the-art ship, especially considering the lengths Prime goes to keep autonomous intelligences from forming. Lavaux feeding them the technology for the ship that housed Bero would explain a lot."

Demas flicked through their wristpad. "Kenwick was active decades ago, he shouldn't even be alive."

"He very much wasn't," Sanda said.

Demas looked up from the pad, met her gaze, and blinked slowly. She catalogued every twitch of his muscles, for how he reacted now spelled out how much she could trust him once he understood the full scope of what she was about to reveal. His expression remained an implacable cipher.

"How were the coordinates recovered from the chip if the Keeper was dead? To access the data on a chip, the password must be thought by a living being," Demas said.

A cold feeling of dread swept through all those on deck. For Icarion to have those coordinates meant that they had broken Keeper technology. That, somehow, they could get a Keeper to image the correct password and receive the data hidden there—whether by force or, more likely, social engineering. But Keepers were trained to resist all those things, and the passwords couldn't be imaged without complete intent. So if they hadn't broken the Keeper, then it followed that they had broken the encryption on the chip itself, and that, as far as anyone in the universe knew, was impossible.

"Funny thing." Her voice cracked, her extremities felt too heavy. It was a very good thing that she wouldn't have to face them when doing this, because she wasn't sure she could stand to see their expressions. "They popped it in my head."

She turned and pushed her hair up to reveal the telltale Keeper scar lurking below her scalp line. The foundation she'd used to obscure the scar wiped off easily enough as she scraped her thumbnail across it.

"Impossible," Demas said, mostly to himself.

Sharp intakes of breath followed from most of the crew. Sanda's head was buzzing too much for her to pinpoint it all, but the general feeling in the air on the deck was one of shock. She couldn't blame them. It'd taken hours for her to stop shaking whenever she thought of the secret hardwired to her brain stem. Even thinking of the chip still threatened to bring her headaches back.

"That is so cool," Arden said.

Sanda dropped her hair, turning back around to face her crew. Nox's hand had moved away from his blaster, his arms crossed defensively. Arden leaned forward with bright, fascinated eyes. Conway's mouth was open, and when she noticed Sanda looking, she snapped it shut and leaned back, shaking her head. Knuth was already looking something up on his wristpad, and Liao had the same fascinated look Arden did.

Demas had shut down, his face going blank. "Even with the chip implanted, you would have to know the password to get the data out."

"Yeah. Icarion had that problem. My memory of that time was scrubbed so many times I don't—" She grimaced and shook her head. "It gives me debilitating headaches to think about it. But Bero was convinced they never got me to image the password. Icarion does not have the coordinates."

"And yet, you do."

She smiled slyly. "I do. I accessed the data myself, at a secure Prime facility, then waited until I could give the coords to someone I trusted to keep them from being spied on while having them located. That was Arden. The souls on this ship, Anford, and Okonkwo are the only people in existence who know that those coordinates are anything worth looking at. Lavaux wanted them. He did not get them, nor did his wife."

"So we're not walking into an ambush," Nox said.

"Truthfully, I have no idea what we're walking into. The records on the deadgate are sparse and boring. The gate remains offline, so I can only assume Rainier hasn't used her swarm to spin it up. I have no hint as to Kenwick's goals aside from the fact that he was probably an Acolyte and wanted this data kept from Lavaux for some reason."

"I have to ask," Demas said carefully. "Is it only the coordinates on that chip? Kenwick was a Keeper. There should be gate schematics as well. If you accessed gate data..."

"Then you'd have to execute me. I can't prove it to you, not here without a scanner, but as far as I know the only thing on this chip is those coordinates. Kenwick must have wiped all the data off at some point and, while I can take some guesses as to why he would do that—fear of being discovered while hiding in Icarion, for a start—I can't tell you why, and I can't guarantee that."

"What the fuck is so important about a location that it needs to be hidden in a Keeper's skull?" Arden asked.

"I don't know," Sanda said, "but don't you all want to find out?"

CHAPTER 51

PRIME STANDARD YEAR 3543

BOOZE WORKS IN MYSTERIOUS WAYS

Biran took another long sip of something clear and harsh and far too strong for him and squinted at Vladsen across the room. Nominally, alcohol wasn't allowed on a research station like AST-4501, but in places where alcohol was banned, it had a remarkable ability to turn up in larger and stronger quantities than usual supply could account for.

They sat on their respective beds in the room, lights cranked up to full daylight, a bottle of something the GC obtained from station stores on a table between them. The *Taso* had better booze, but this... stuff... felt appropriate at the moment. Biran's stomach would regret that decision tomorrow, but now, he didn't care.

"Do you think there's anything to it?" Vladsen asked.

And this was why Biran had asked for the hard stuff. Even Speakers needed help to loosen their own tongues every so often. "There is something I have to tell you, but you won't like it, and will probably think I've gone as mad as Hitton."

"Well, now I must hear it."

"This is not the first credible account I've heard of guardcore being where they're not supposed to be," Biran said.

"Credible? While I trust Keeper Sato's instincts, we must remember her account is a secondhand report of one woman's paranoia."

"Keeper Hitton's paranoia. I don't like her, but she's not easily misled."

"These missions take their toll. The isolation can creep up on you."

"You're starting to sound like one of my press briefings."

Vladsen waved his glass and took a long drink. "It's not incorrect."

"No, but in this case, I think it is wrong."

"We could ask Hitton herself. Judge her reaction."

"She would shut us down immediately and pack us back on the *Taso* without so much as a fare-thee-well, and I wouldn't blame her. It's exactly what I would do if I were concerned we had a rogue GC on station and two Protectorate Keepers showed up to stick their noses in things. We could very well take what's a carefully balanced situation and flip it over into violence. If three Protectorate members died here, Icarion would be destroyed within hours. No hesitation, no deliberation."

Vladsen swirled his half-empty glass. "Meanwhile, this gate project will drag on so long that Icarion will think we're stalling purposefully, and the war will go hot again. Icarion will be destroyed within hours of firing the first shot."

"Right. We have to get Hitton to use the survey bots."

"And if she's right, and there's a rogue guardcore here tampering with the results?"

"There's only one of them, and we brought four of our own."

"Ah but, Speaker, you said you had heard of another account. What if one of our four is another saboteur?"

This was why Biran had ordered the stronger booze. "I hoped you might be able to shed some light on that, Vladsen. You said you had heard rumors..."

He blinked slowly, glanced at the door, and shook his head. "Heard that, did you? It seems my guard is getting rusty. Alas, I know nothing substantial. Keeper Lavaux surrounded himself with the younger, rising stars of Keeperdom. Those of us who fell into his good graces earlier on spent more time with him in private company. We... overheard things, sometimes. Arguments with his wife about a GC being in the wrong place, nothing more.

"But you were also one of his rising stars, Greeve, and you said you'd heard of another incident."

Biran grimaced. "Nothing to do with Lavaux. Do you remember the call I took privately before we landed?"

"I do. You looked positively ill."

"It was Sanda. She had what looked like a hostile GC ship barreling toward a civilian station. When I checked the records, there was no indication of a GC operation in the area. As soon as I realized"—he shuddered—"I put out a distress call. Okonkwo answered it. The Prime Director messaged me after landing to confirm Sanda's safety, and that the guardcore were not our people."

"*Okonkwo* knows about these phantoms?"

Biran cough-laughed and took another drink. "I regret to inform you she seemed unsurprised."

"Did she have any idea what they want, where they come from?"

"No." Biran stared into the contents of his glass. "Though it's possible she wouldn't tell me, or doesn't yet know."

Vladsen set his glass down with a soft clink on the nightstand. "Speaker, what do we do?"

Biran swallowed a hard gulp of booze. "I don't know. I wish this asteroid hadn't come from Anaia. I wish Hitton hadn't entered this mission paranoid, because she knew the source of the data. Anaia was...Anaia was *good.* I don't know why she did what she did, I wish to fucking everything that I could understand why she turned, but I don't believe she had anything to do with rogue guardcore...And if that makes me seditious then fuck it, rip my chip, too."

"I...Christ, who am I to judge you, Speaker Greeve? My truth is, I only wish I could be half so brave as you."

Biran looked up, and found Vladsen staring at the floor between his boots, his skin sallow from paleness, his curls hiding the set of his eyes. Invisible weight pressed down his shoulders, bent his back.

"Shit. I'm an asshole. I've opened old wounds for you. I am...Well, I'm not sorry about Lavaux, but I am sorry he was your friend, and that his loss pains you, Keeper Vladsen."

"Rostam," he said.

"What?"

"My first name is Rostam, please use it in private. These titles are just more layers of obfuscation..." He sighed, brushing away a thought with the side of his hand. "I believed Lavaux to be a good man, too. Whatever his real game was, whatever his reasons for attacking your sister...In retrospect, knowing all I know about him, I don't know what he was truly working toward. I thought he wanted to make things better, for everyone. I *believed* in him. Feels fantastically stupid now. If I had any spine at all, I'd hire a Nazca to unearth his real plans."

"If you'd done that, then we couldn't have afforded to crew the *Taso*," Biran said wryly.

He snort-laughed. "Ah, yes. At the very least I can finance the ventures of better men."

"This 'better man,'" he said with deep-felt bitterness, "was too self-involved to notice his best friend hurting. I should have seen it. I should have known when Anaia turned traitor...I should know *why*."

Biran rubbed the side of his face, scorching hot to the touch, and hunched over, feeling tears welling in his eyes and hating it, because he shouldn't be feeling these things now. He needed to, as Ilan said, think like Sanda. Needed to put a lid on the hurt a little while longer.

And, if he were being honest with himself, the tears were forcing their way out now because he knew, deep down, he would never know why Anaia had done it. Never understand why Anaia sat in that room on the *Taso* and worked to keep Biran's sister in Icarion's hands while his heart was breaking to get Sanda back.

"Speaker." The bed beside him sank under Vladsen's weight. His hand, light as a breath, settled on the small of Biran's back.

"Biran," he said.

"Biran," Rostam repeated. The hand grew heavier. "This war has made assholes of us all, hasn't it?"

A knot eased in Biran's chest. He let out a long, slow breath, emptying himself of an unseen weight, and dragged the back of his hand across his eyes, scrubbing the tears away. "Dios, I want it to end already."

Rostam chuckled quietly.

"What?"

Biran looked up and found Rostam's face startlingly close. His brown eyes were shaded beneath thick lashes, as they always were, but this close Biran could make out the streaks of golden-green that meandered through them, subtle but gripping. Why was he thinking so much about Rostam's eyes when…Fresh heat spread into his cheeks and Biran swallowed.

"I've only heard you let out a *dios* with family," Rostam said. The corners of his eyes crinkled when he smiled, and while he was too young to have decided about letting his wrinkles come in, Biran found himself hoping he would. Rostam's gaze slipped from his, tracking Biran's face, perhaps making similar conclusions about his countenance.

"I suppose I'm comfortable right now."

That gaze snapped back to his with shocking intensity. "I suppose I am, too."

Oh, but this was a very, very bad idea. Keepers did not consort. Especially not Protectorate members. There were rules. Laws. Presumably Prime had very good reasons for them, but Biran couldn't think of any as his head canted, ever so slightly, forward, asking a silent question. Rostam answered.

Every sense in Biran's body surged. The heat of Rostam's nearness subsumed him, the scent of his hair—clean and slightly beeswaxy—mingled with the sharp tang of alcohol in both their breaths and the impossible softness of his lips until Biran's chest felt so full of hope and urgency he thought he'd laugh or cry or scream to bleed off some of the wellspring of emotion.

Rostam pulled back. It took every ounce of control Biran possessed to keep from throwing himself after him.

"I—" Rostam cleared a rough throat. "I'm sorry, Biran. You were hurting, and I shouldn't have—"

Biran brushed a loose curl behind Rostam's ear. "Don't. Never apologize for that."

He flushed and dropped his gaze, lashes obscuring the newfound enchantment of his eyes. There was so much detail to Rostam that Biran didn't know. So very much he wanted to learn.

"There are laws," Rostam said.

"There are," Biran said, even as the fresh burst of life within him was caged in cold iron.

"We're...very drunk."

A poor lie. A drunk Keeper was a security risk, and while they could feel buzzed and sometimes ill from overconsumption, their metabolisms were all boosted so that they could never get properly wasted. Many Keepers spent their last night before chip insertion getting blackout drunk, because they knew they could never do it again.

"We are," he agreed anyway, and took his hand away from Rostam's ear.

Rostam's hand shot out and caught his, firmly. The cold bars of Biran's inner cage rattled.

"Rost—" He cut himself off. Clenched his jaw to hold back.

"I like that. Rost."

"You are...I am..." He didn't even know what he had meant to say. He knew what he *wanted* to say, but that...That couldn't be. Dios, but that sly smile of his was not helping matters. Biran's hand began to sweat and, embarrassed, he tried to pull it away but Rost held on.

"You aren't making this easy," Biran whispered.

"I'm so sorry." Rost released his hand and stood, backing away. Biran felt the distance growing between them like a chasm of cold. Rost tugged at the neckline of his lightweight armor, and Biran was suddenly very glad that the guardcore had made them don body armor before entering the station. Prime jumpsuits didn't leave a lot to the imagination.

"Don't be," Biran said firmly. "I mean that."

Rost stopped pulling on his collar and let his arms hang at his sides. "Thank you. I mean *that*."

Heat traveled up Biran's neck once more and he grunted, standing, shaking his legs to get the blood back in them as he paced around the small room. "Right. Okay. We need to...to do something about those survey bots."

"Huh. I'd been thinking we need to do something about Hitton's extra GC, if there even is one, but you're right. It's the bots themselves that are key. They're the only thing that can speed up the survey, and that is our primary goal here. If there is a false guardcore about, they would not have had the chance to sabotage all the bots."

Biran had put little thought into what he'd said. He'd just needed to say something, to keep himself from giving in to the song his body was singing, and the bots had been the first thing to come to mind. But Rost—no, Vladsen. Keeper Vladsen was on to something. The survey bots only collected data, they couldn't do any harm aside from returning bad results, and in large enough numbers bad data would stand out like a sore thumb.

"We have the permissions required to activate them, we can get those bots turned on and sent on their merry way to do the work they came here for. They should already be preset with what they're supposed to do, literally all we'd have to do would be turn them on and let them go do their job," Biran said.

Vladsen frowned. "I doubt Keeper Hitton will allow it."

"It's unfortunate, but I agree. We will have to ask her forgiveness rather than her permission. Maybe then she will explain herself."

"Biran," Vladsen said gently, "you are a man quick to act, I grant you that, but moving without giving Keeper Hitton a chance to explain sounds hasty even for you."

Biran froze. Vladsen was right. His head had been so full of…of other feelings, he hadn't thought clearly. "Yes, of course, thank you. We will make every effort to listen to her and convince her, but this project needs to move forward yesterday because I won't…I won't have Icarion's blood on my hands."

Vladsen arched one thick brow at him. "Even after what they did to your sister?"

Biran froze for a moment. There was a weight to Vladsen's words that implied he knew, or suspected, more than the official reports stated. He had been close to Lavaux. It was possible he knew about the chip…Or that his words simply sounded heavier to Biran, now that Vladsen had shifted around the compass of his emotional life.

"Yes. Even after all of that. A small fraction of Icarion did those things. Not the people. Not the civilians."

Vladsen smoothed his hair. "Well then. We had better hurry. The clock is ticking."

Biran pressed the comm in his ear that connected him to the crew of the *Taso*. "Scalla, can you get me every loading and unloading bot we have sent over to these coords? Unpackers, too, if we got 'em."

"This is a private ship, Greeve. We don't have a lot, but I'll send you what we have."

"Thanks."

Vladsen reached around Biran to swipe his ident over the door lock, and as he did so a faint gust of air brought the scent of his hair back to Biran's nose, sending a fresh wave of electric tingles across his skin. He closed his eyes briefly, and willed himself to focus. When he opened his eyes again, the four GC had turned to regard him.

"Right," he said firmly. "We have a plan."

INTERLUDE

PRIME STANDARD YEAR 3543

PEOPLE SAY THEY'RE DANGEROUS

In net space, Arden stared at a conglomerate network of information so vast the sheer scope made it meaningless, and tried not to scream. They'd been here, so often they'd lost count, though they could pull the logs, and the data never told them anything of import. Never told them anything real.

For these slivers of information were all the logs Arden could glean from networks private and public about the life of Rainier Lavaux. Facts. Everything they'd gathered was a fact. The places she'd lived, the businesses she'd owned, the people she'd worked with, and even a few shopping habits and food preferences, and it all added up to a real person, the wife of a Keeper, living out her life in the framework of Prime.

But facts could lie. Arden knew that better than most and still, still, they hated every last molecule of her digital breadcrumbs. She'd cleaned too well. There was nothing in the data aside from that brief glimpse of her boarding Janus, of her walking into the warehouses, that indicated Rainier Lavaux had anything to do with secret research stations. With the coordinates hidden in Sanda's head. Every single pattern-crunching algorithm they'd ever run was useless against the false life Rainier had built for herself.

People couldn't hide themselves from Arden, not digitally. But she could.

Even Jules, working under Rainier, had disappeared from the digital world. Arden was sure that fake documents stating the charter of Janus had to exist somewhere to have been used to convince the scientists, but they couldn't find them.

Even a deep dive into Liao's wristpad—without permission—had given them nothing. Liao, for all intents and purposes, stopped existing after she'd left her fringer colony for Janus. Jules had stopped existing after she'd left them. Left Atrux. For a second, they considered feeding the data to the intelligence to see what that being made of it all, but that would be unfair to the nascent mind. The last thing they wanted to do was accidentally train an AI to think like Rainier.

Frustration ebbed as Arden's thoughts shifted to the people in Rainier's orbit. They'd dug into all the public people, dug into Jules and Liao and the other scientists. But they had a new name, a half-forgotten name.

They sent their bot scripts out to gather all available information on Marya Page. Information flooded to them within seconds: youngest daughter of Keeper Page of Ordinal, wild, party girl, trouble for the family, a brilliant biochemist despite all of that. The thread of information wove on, and Arden ate it up with hungry eyes, wondering.

Rainier's circle was tight. A woman like Marya didn't fit. She was a little too loose, a little too idealistic. Born to privilege, Marya wouldn't have been cowed by Rainier's resources. Rainier must have needed her for something specific, but Rainier had fucked up, because a woman like Marya Page was a liability. And now Arden had a thread to pull.

Arden brought up the footage they'd skimmed from Janus and adjusted one of their unique individual identifying neural nets to focus on all sightings of Marya Page. That woman appeared across their workstation in stutters and stops—caught taking a step down this hall, reaching for her wristpad there. Arden tracked her path across the station that day, followed her straight to the evac pod she'd thrown herself into the moment Janus started shuddering.

Tracked her to the moment she initiated launch for all evac pods, trying to leave Jules to die.

The evac pod disappeared from the data as soon as it blew free of Janus, the *Thorn* hadn't picked up its transponder, but physics was physics, and after a few quick calculations, Arden followed the pod's likely trajectory to a ship transponder that *did* show up in public databases.

They let out a slow breath, though breathing was pointless in the net. Jules's escape shuttle had dead-ended with what they suspected was one of Rainier's guardcore ships. The ship that picked Marya up was civilian, registered to one of her fellows from university.

After that, tracking Marya's location to a private station hugging the back of an unremarkable asteroid was easy. Arden pinged Nox, and by the time they were reaching up to take their goggles off, Nox was coming through their door.

"What is it?" Nox asked, and while they were supposed to be going to bed for the night, Arden noted the rifle strapped to his back.

"I found Marya Page," Arden said.

"The comms woman from Janus?" Nox frowned and sank down into a crouch, arms resting on his knees. "She with Jules?"

Arden's throat was paper-dry. They reached for a pouch of water and chugged it down before answering, wondering how long they'd been absorbed in the net. They hoped it wasn't too late; they still had a few things to work out with Sanda.

"I don't think so. Rainier must have intercepted Jules's shuttle, as she went dark on the net again, but Marya got picked up by a school friend and she's on a private station now. I'm waiting to see if she picks up any of my fishing attempts so I can get inside the station's systems, but I don't think she will. After she reached the station, she went dark. I think she's hiding from Rainier... Just not very well."

"So we pick her up, see what she has to say. Maybe she can tell us what the fuck's got Jules so spooked she's working for Rainier."

"Maybe," Arden said, "but after what Sanda just told us? There's no way in hell we're going to turn around to check out that asteroid. We're going through that deadgate, and as much as I want to know what's happened to Jules and Lolla, I agree the deadgate's a priority. I think you agree, too."

Nox's nose crinkled and he scowled off into the middle distance. "Yeah, I fucking agree. So what? I know you're thinking something, Arden, or you wouldn't have dragged my ass out of bed."

"You weren't in bed."

"You didn't know that."

"We've been living on top of each other for two years. You're not the gruff cipher you think you are. I called you here because the thing I'm about to do, you won't like it, but I need you to understand why I'm doing it."

That got his full attention. Nox turned his gaze back to Arden, brows up. "Since when do you ask for moral permission before you do something?"

Arden blinked and rubbed at the dent left by the net goggles around their eyes. "I...don't know. Now, I guess. Look, when Rainier goes looking for Marya, she will find her. I want to speed that timeline up."

"Why? If Marya's hiding from her, she's not on board with whatever the fuck Rainier is doing. Shore up her defenses for her, help her hide. Maybe we can use her."

Arden licked their lips. How could they explain in a way that wouldn't make Nox see them like a monster?

"I can't. She's left too big a trail, and I've dug through her background. She's a rich party girl, she won't take my advice, and she won't lie low for long. I need a thread on Rainier, Nox. If we're ever going to find Jules, I *need* Rainier to make digital contact with one of my viruses. If I feed her information on Marya, she'll have to take it."

Nox's eyes narrowed. "You've tried to get her to take your bait multiple times. It never works."

"I've never had something she wants until now."

"Rainier could—what do you call it?—sandbox the data, or whatever. You could throw Page's ass in a fire for nothing."

"I could. That fire's coming for her regardless."

Nox stared at them, and Arden's skin crawled from his scrutiny. "You want to hurt this woman. Why?"

Their fingers clenched, one fist crushing the band of their net goggles. The hot taste of revenge burned in their mouth like ashes.

"She fucked Jules, Nox. I don't know why she did it, but on her way out, when she jumped in that evac pod, she hit the trigger to blow them all. Whatever was going on there, I don't know. But

Marya Page wanted Jules to die on Janus. The only reason Jules survived is because she went for a shuttle instead. Maybe we can't keep Jules safe from Rainier, but... But we can keep her safe from Page. I can."

Nox's jaw tightened, the veins in his neck standing out as he turned his head. Not to look away—Nox didn't shy from eye contact—but to admire, briefly, the lean lines of the rifle peeking over his shoulder.

"Do it. Let me know if she takes the bait."

"I will. Thank you."

Nox stood in one fluid motion and shrugged. "Nothing to thank me for. You would have done it anyway. But I'm glad you brought me in."

Arden smiled thinly and nodded. "True. Onward to the deadgate?"

"Onward," Nox said, putting his hands on his hips. "I don't know how we got tangled up in this shit, but I really want to see where it leads."

"Me too."

Nox hesitated a moment, cleared his throat, then gave Arden a rough pat on the shoulder and left the room. Arden stared at their wristpad in silence for a long while. They didn't need the net goggles to do this next step. The truth was, they'd already packaged up the data and wrapped it in a nice digital bow for Rainier.

When Nox said Arden would have done it anyway, he'd been right. But Arden had hoped for a feeling of relief in sharing the burden. Not absolution, they weren't that naive, but in pressing that button Arden was bringing death to a woman they knew only through the digital fingerprints she'd left behind. They'd be doing it to protect Jules from further attacks by Marya, but still. Murder was murder, no matter how many proxies worked in-between.

Foolish of them, to think sharing the knowledge with Nox would make things easier. It wasn't the first time they'd manipulated data to bring about death. It seemed very unlikely that it would be the last. They hoped it wouldn't be the last.

On a whim, Arden added a quick tag to the data: *You're next, Rainier*, then hit send. A weight left their shoulders with the package.

They stood, stretched their arms above their head, and put Marya Page out of their mind.

There was another loose thread in the universe Arden wanted to pull on, and they suspected Sanda held the spool. She just didn't know it yet.

CHAPTER 52

PRIME STANDARD YEAR 3543

KNOCK, KNOCK

Sanda spent that night lying awake in her sleep cocoon, listening for the knock that would come at her door. She wasn't sure who it would be, or if they'd be dangerous, but she was certain that after her revelations, someone would be restless. Someone would need to know more, and privately.

She half expected Demas to come to her in the night, break in and put a bullet in her skull, so she'd slapped a stimpatch on her arm and curled up, browsing the net for any alerts about Bero or Tomas or the Nazca while sending Biran stupid cat CamCasts. The knock came three hours after lights out.

"Hey, uh, Commander?" Arden's voice, soft and hissy as they tried to both whisper and be heard.

She tapped the button on her wristpad to unlock the door and brought the lights up to a low level. "Come in, Arden. What's up?"

They'd thrown a thick robe over their jumpsuit and left the mag boots in their room, their hair a ruffled mess as they pulled themself in and shut the door behind them.

"Hey, sorry to bother you, it's just... We reach the gate in six hours, right? And considering you trusted us all with your secret, I thought..."

She blinked. This wasn't the late-night tête-à-tête she'd suspected would come up. "Is everything all right?"

They chuckled ruefully and shook their head. "More than likely everything is roses and I'm a paranoid fool."

"But?"

"But I... I found something, a few weeks ago. Something I've been keeping to myself because it's the kind of thing that gets destroyed if other people find it, but I'm thinking... I'm thinking maybe it's looking for you."

"Arden. It's late and you need to be way clearer than that."

"Right. Right. Sorry. You got a net headset? This will be easier if I can show you."

"Yeah, sure." She pulled herself out of the cocoon and kicked over to the locked bulkhead that stowed her various electronics, swiped her wristpad over the lock, and pulled out a set of goggles.

"Those look brand-new," Arden said, pulling themself over to get a closer look. "They come with the ship or something?"

"Yeah, actually." She turned them over in her hands, rubbing her thumb along the rubberized headband. "I don't use goggles much for the net, my wristpad works fine."

"I know at least a dozen people whose heads would spin to hear you say that." They shook their head and twisted the band around to get a look at the serial number. "At least these are nice. Prime doesn't skimp on their tech, do they?"

"Things Prime doesn't skimp on: warships and Keeper station supplies. Where do you want me to meet you when I log in?"

Arden smiled to themself. "Don't worry about it. I'll find you."

"Show-off," she said, but they'd already pulled their own well-worn goggles over their eyes. Sanda may not know a thing about net goggles aside from the basics, but she knew a thing or two about materials, and Arden's goggles weren't cheap. She shouldn't have been surprised, but somehow she'd expected Arden to have a hacked-together, Frankenstein affair, not a high-end model. Then again, it wasn't like she could see into the hardware—or would even know what she was looking at if she did.

Sanda looped her wrist through a strap on the wall and pulled the goggles down over her eyes. Her personal net space lit up with mountains of notifications, stacked like the crates in her dads' warehouse. The visual was a preference she'd always felt comforted by.

Everything was tinted by a rosy glow some hacker had thrown over everything years ago. There was a patch for it, to re-skin the space in Prime cyan or whatever aesthetic pleased her, but she kind of liked the incongruity of the soft color in such an inherently geometrical space, and so she'd left it.

None of the notifications had any of the priority indicators she'd set for contacts from her family or certain associates, so she ignored them and pulled up the *Thorn*'s systems, setting an alert to tell her if anyone came near her room or touched her door.

Somewhere in the middle of the crates, she heard a laugh. Even though she was expecting it, her digital skin crawled.

"You've got to be kidding me," Arden said. They came strolling through the warehouse, trailing their fingers against pink-hued cargo pallets. Their net representation looked very much like how they did in real life, but with a certain transparent quality that gave the illusion that they flickered in and out of reality with every other breath.

"I'm ninety-nine percent sure that accessing a citizen's personal net space without invitation is illegal."

"Your security is garbage, out-of-the-box nonsense. I hope you don't store anything important in here."

"Nothing that important," she said, feeling stung. She used the net only for research and messaging, and she wouldn't put anything sensitive into a message.

"Good. Christ." They stared off into space, probably using a mod to see the code Sanda kept skinned in the warehouse visual. "I can't believe it's still pink. This place is an open door. I can lock this down for you." Their fingertips twitched. "I *need* to lock this down for you."

She leaned against a crate and crossed her arms. "I like the pink. Wouldn't it look weird if I suddenly got security conscious?"

"Nah. You have a new tech under your command, or whatever you fleeties call it. It would make sense. And even if it raised suspicions, it's not like anyone curious enough to come poking around could get through."

"Full of yourself," she said.

They snorted. "I'm really not."

"You didn't knock on my door three hours after lights out to assess my net security."

"No. But maybe I should have. Great fucking fuck, Greeve, when was the last time you patched? This is so, so out of date."

She crossed her arms a little tighter. "About two years out of date?"

"Yeah, actually. How— Oh. Fuck. Sorry. I'll clean it up for you."

"Thanks. I'll grant you admin access."

They chuckled. "That's what I'm saying. I already have it."

"Arden."

"Right. You know how to follow-on?"

"Yes, I went to preschool, doofus. I'm not a Luddite."

"Hey, I didn't want to assume, and..." They trailed off, looked around the crates, and shuddered. "*Anyway.* Tag me for a follow."

She brought up the UI to friend-and-follow, and found the space they should have been inhabiting marked with a blank ident field.

"Uh, I'm not sure it's working..."

"Is it empty?"

"Yes."

"That's me."

"How?"

"You really don't want me to delve into a technical explanation. Let's go."

She sighed and tagged the empty card, feeling foolish as the default blank-person icon popped up in her friends list. The card didn't even have a false name, or ident number. It was a shell where a person should be.

The net flashed by in a blur of neon colors as Arden took the lead, whipping them through spaces and gates and security protocols Sanda could barely even glimpse. Space didn't have much meaning in the net. There was a geography to it, locations mapped and spread out in a way that human minds could more easily parse, but technically, Arden should be able to will them to where they wanted to be.

They were muddying the waters. Sanda didn't know a whole hell of a lot about security, but she could guess it'd be easier to track someone jumping from point A to point B than to follow someone flitting around like this, passing through systems that, while Sanda didn't understand them, even she could tell were heavily secured.

Maybe Arden was worried because of the lack of appropriate security in Sanda's net space, but she doubted it. She had the feeling that this was something they did often. Not a well-worn path, exactly, that would be too telling, but an instinct for evasion.

Their breathless ping-ponging came to a disorienting halt. She may not have a body to feel dizzy with, but the abrupt stop was enough to make her head spin. When she gathered herself, they were floating in null space, a pocket of the net where data had yet to invade. The nebulous edges of the digital universe into which information would, eventually, expand.

"I don't—"

Arden held up a hand. "Give it a moment. I've injected your visualization tools with a script to let you see."

"Definitely illegal."

"It's not even the most illegal thing I've done in the last twenty seconds."

Maybe it was the word they'd used—*injected*—but she started to feel...different. Not ill or disoriented, but more solid, more real in this place made up of ones and zeros abstracted to the extreme. Purely psychosomatic, she told herself, because that's what all her instructors had said about the net. Without neural feedback devices, a goggle-accessed net couldn't tickle your nervous system. Couldn't make you feel anything real.

But the visual, as Arden had implied, was the point.

A veil she hadn't known existed lifted from her eyes. The "place" she and Arden inhabited, their virtual backs to the virtual cities of the universe, was empty aside from them, but way out in the distance... something was there.

She squinted, as if that helped. "What is it?"

"An anomaly," Arden said, as if *that* explained anything at all. They caught her giving them side-eye and shrugged. "I don't know. I come out here to the fringes sometimes to think. People find the null zones unsettling, and that's by design. You can't see it with what I've given you, but there are repellent code strings out here. Spend time in the null and most people feel disoriented, disassociated. Stay too long and it's easy to lose yourself, but most retreat to the planned zones before that happens. Prime SysAdmins don't want fringers coming out here to build their own infrastructure in unused space, so they make it unsettling in a way that's hard to pin down."

"I don't feel anything."

"No. I've inoculated you the same way I've inoculated myself."

"How?"

"I'm not giving you all my secrets. Just this one." They tipped their head back toward the anomaly.

Normally she'd call them out on that cheap deflection, but the truth was she probably wouldn't understand an explanation, so it was pointless to push. She'd wanted to work with Arden because they were the best. But, even with Tomas's assertions that the Nazca had considered recruiting them, she hadn't counted on this. A savant street-hacker, sure, but they were at ease in this space. Somehow, she was certain they owned the net more than any Prime SysAdmin.

She wished Tomas was here, so she could ask him what he really thought about Arden. Well, she wished he was here for a lot of reasons, but that one was foremost at the moment.

The more she watched the anomaly, the more her sense of it changed. At first glance it appeared as an amorphous blob of nothing, maybe the size of the *Thorn*, a fluffy cloud of pulsing information. But her sense of scale in this place had been wrong.

It was farther away than she'd thought, and much, much larger—a leviathan burgeoning in the distance. As she focused her attention, it seemed to take shape. Not into anything definitive, it remained cloud-like, but pathways emerged, connecting clusters where data coalesced to its own secret gravity. It reminded her of images she'd seen of the visible universe, and the way neurons lit up a brain.

"It's thinking," she said.

They nodded adamantly. "Yes. I believe so, too. I haven't been able to speak with it, but I can establish a kind of…connection, if I think at it long enough. When it began it was much smaller, more chaotic.

It's far more organized now, and I believe it recognizes me enough to realize I'm not a threat."

"What if it thinks I'm a threat?"

"Honestly, Commander, I can't answer any questions you have about it. I found it. It's been growing, becoming more and more sophisticated. That's it. That's all I've got. I wish I could tell you more, but I've been afraid to pry too deeply lest I upset whatever process it's undergoing, and I sure as shit will not ask for advice or help from anyone else. Prime hunts down nascent intelligences for a reason. They can be dangerous, completely unpredictable."

"Bero meant well, I think. Even if he did terrible things."

"That's why I thought you'd understand. This thing needs to be allowed to grow. I understand AI as a concept, I understand the structure of neural nets and what keeps our systems running every day. But those minds are intentionally limited."

"Bero called our AIs lobotomized."

"He wasn't entirely wrong." Arden rubbed the side of their face. "What I don't understand—what no human mind could wrap itself around—is what it would be like to be a wholly new intelligence. Our AIs are constrained by their data sets."

"Bero was raised," she said carefully. "I don't have the details of the process Icarion used, but I know that his primary researcher treated his early moments as if he were a savant child. She read him stories. That's a data set, isn't it?"

They cocked their head, smiling into the emptiness. "Stories are emotional-training data sets. It wasn't a bad idea. I need you to do me a favor."

"What? I spent time on Bero, but this... This is so far beyond me."

"I want you to think at it. To give it another input that's not me, do the whole communing thing."

She narrowed her eyes. "This hasn't become some sort of weird religion for you, has it?"

They barked a laugh. "Absolutely not."

"What if I'm the wrong data set?"

They frowned. "What do you mean?"

"You understand it, as much as anyone can, because of your technical knowledge. I'm not... I'm not like you, Arden. I'm not even like most people. I work myself straight to the bone because if I stop, even for a second, and really consider the implications of everything I've done... Well. I don't think you want your new mind learning that habit."

Lightly, Arden grasped her shoulder. "If it learns an unending drive to fix what's broken, that wouldn't be so bad."

"Unless it decides that fixing what's broken is to do away with all of humanity."

They grinned. "You read too much science fiction."

She sighed and closed her eyes, as if that meant anything in this false world, and cleared her mind. Meditation practice was standard fare for fleeties, but she couldn't remember the last time she'd bothered to do anything more than count backward from ten. Or five. Or three. Now, pushing back from herself, watching her thoughts from a distance, tagging and setting aside any that broke through for later review—worry, fear, planning, hope—an ease came into her that she was familiar with. A clarity.

It wasn't a surprise, or it shouldn't have been. They were taught these techniques for exactly this purpose, to calm the raging fires of urgency that ignited when situations got critical. But when you were caught in those fires, it was hard to remember the tool that helped you smother them.

She breathed deeply, waiting until she had a handle on herself. Despite Arden's reassurances, she didn't want to risk projecting anxiety to that being. When her heart rate had slowed and the intrusive thoughts backed off, she let herself think a greeting to the mind.

Nothing happened. She set aside frustration and tried again. She wasn't a meatbag in the net, she was a series of electrical impulses abstracted to extremes. Just because her thoughts stayed in her head in real space didn't mean they had to do so here. She was electricity. This was just... instant messaging.

Recognition tickled at the edge of her senses. She tamped down a burst of excitement and kept up the steady, even flow of a greeting, hoping that it wouldn't be seen as something equivalent to a DDoS attack.

Its attention drifted to her, began to focus. It was further along than Arden had intimated, more than a tangled mess of being. Whatever it was, it had a sense of self, of borders between it and her and the null space in which they floated.

But it was . . . new, still. She wasn't sure how she knew that, but brushing that mind felt like making silly faces at a toddler. It missed something—time, maybe, or a catalyst, to push it over a yet unseen precipice of development.

Sanda was about to open her eyes and tell Arden her thoughts, when an impulsive thought broke through her meditation—the Little Prince, standing on a toy-sized moon, his rose friend dropping petals into the emptiness. Stories were emotional data sets.

All the being's other processes halted. Arden made a startled sound, but Sanda could scarcely hear them through the weight of the mind bearing down on her, probing, demanding something, but she couldn't make sense of the weight, of the chaos.

She tried to think a question, to ask it what it wanted, to apologize, to do anything to stop the crushing sense of all her mental faculties.

Arden's hand was on her shoulder, lifting her up, and she thought it such a silly thing, to lose your balance when you didn't have a body at all.

Recognition, then, but not hers. A shock of knowing, seizing her like a live wire. She tried to force the nebulous, pulsing mash of emotion into something coherent, but the being retreated, withdrew like a wave across the shore, taking some of her with it.

She braced for its return, but it did not come.

"What the fuck," she said, when she could gather her neurons together enough to push words out. The pressure was gone, and the void at the fringes of the net surrounded her in placid indifference.

"Are you all right?" Arden held her shoulders, steadying her, their eyes bright with worry. She wanted to punch them, straight in the gut, but that would make her feel better only for a flash. Not worth it.

"I have absolutely no idea . . . I'm . . ." She patted herself down. Two arms, one leg, a torso and head. Nothing seemed out of place, but then this was a mental projection of her physical form. It wasn't her body that had been in danger. It had been her mind.

A small headache throbbed between her eyes, tapping against her skull. Without the being occupying her mind, she felt lighter, but not in a nice, relieved way. Parts of her felt hollow. Carved out.

"I think I'm okay. It reacted to something in my thoughts. I think it knew me, which as far as I'm aware, isn't possible."

Arden shoved their hands in their pockets and stared resolutely at their feet.

"Is it?" she pressed.

"I don't know. Things like this don't happen out of nowhere. The timing of the being's formation lines up."

She snapped her head around to watch the amorphous mind. It hadn't changed, but she thought she recognized something about the shape now. Something...cylindrical. "You think that's Bero, and you threw me in there without a fucking heads-up?"

They held up their hands in defense. "We talked about data sets, remember? If I had told you my suspicions, then you would have gone in thinking about it, and then it might have been impossible to tell if it were the real Bero, or a new being thinking it was Bero because you expected it to be."

"I think my headache just got worse."

"Sorry."

"I get why you did it. But you're still a dickhead."

"Fair. But they reacted to you, didn't they? They recognized you?"

"There was a reaction, but no real thought. If he recognized me, I didn't recognize him."

And shouldn't she have? Bero kept his secrets close, but the idea that she wouldn't recognize him even in this form was inconceivable to her. She'd spent weeks with only him for company, forty days believing he was the only thing that stood between her and an untimely death between the stars. He'd been her savior, lifeboat, and friend.

And kind of a dickhead, too.

"It's not even possible. He flung himself into uncharted space. He's gone. He can't be here."

"It's hard to say. I don't understand the tech involved in his making, but in theory, he's not hardware, he's software. His mind is a digital construct and isn't bound to any particular object. He should be able to transfer to any other hardware capable of supporting his mental processing requirements. The Prime net hardware is more than adequate for storing him, I'd think. At least, it has the space.

"As far as facilitating his ability to process, I have no idea. It's entirely possible his software requires specific hardware architecture for an emergence of full consciousness to take place. Humanity's been arguing about the emergent factor for centuries—what makes a being more than the sum of its parts? But he has been growing."

"You're certain no one else knows about this?"

"As much as I can be. I have digital trip wires all around the area. I should know if anyone comes near."

"What about...what about the people who made him? Would they be able to, I don't know, scan for him or something? Since they know what they're looking for."

Arden pursed their lips. "It's possible. But Icarion has bigger problems than looking for an AI-injection in Prime net space, don't they?"

"I'm no longer convinced Icarion created Bero without help."

"Rainier," Arden said.

"Yes. Acting either with, or independently of, her husband."

Arden cast an admiring eye over the cloud that may or may not be Bero. "It could be new."

"What do you mean?"

"If Rainier was instrumental in Bero's construction, then she knows how to create generalized artificial intelligence. Such a tool is useful—sorry for calling your friend a tool—for parsing large sets of data. If Bero is gone, and took out the second-generation weapon being worked on at Icarion, Rainier may be making her own. It would explain why this appeared shortly after Bero's absence as easily as Bero uploading himself would. Once she realized Bero was gone, she'd get to work making a new one. Assuming her deal with Icarion had gone south, she'd have to start all over. In her position, I'd seed the intelligence in a massive storage space to give it time to self-actualize, then transfer it to the appropriate hardware once construction was complete."

"That's a lot of guesswork. It seemed to recognize me, though. How would it know who I am if it's new?"

"Because she knows, and I'd bet a week's worth of Udon-Voodun that she would communicate all possible threats to the mind, and that would include you. If that's the case, then we're lucky it wasn't more advanced."

"I hate that fucking woman."

"Normally I leave physical violence to Nox," Arden said, "but I really would like to get my hands on her."

"We all have our one."

"One?"

"The one person you'd burn the universe down to save, or to condemn."

"And do we get one of each?"

She smiled to herself, tight and strained. "No. Life's never that clean."

CHAPTER 53

PRIME STANDARD YEAR 3543

ONCE MORE INTO AN UNKIND UNIVERSE

Tomas swam in pain and light. The horizon of his world contracted to the shield of his eyelids, no matter how hard he tried to open them. Limbs were a distant memory—torso and head and lips and fingers and *everything* an abstract memory, a taste of having been a being that was, somehow, irrelevant to who he was.

He existed without flesh. Without bone and sinew and synapse. Dead. This was dead, and the famous white light. His neurons firing their last hurrah. Electrical impulses going wild, sending messages to nowhere.

The white light of death, so far as he knew, was not supposed to feel *wet.* His drowning reflex kicked in, rocking what was left of his drained-out corpse with clutching panic. Air. He needed air. Needed it needed it *needed it.*

Tomas-who-had-been-Nazca rode the panic reflex, watching his body from afar as it bucked and shook and panicked. He let his mind dissociate, because there was nothing to be done. If he was drowning, he was drowning in blood.

Sanda's face, at the moment she'd pulled the trigger. It had been all he could see, as he'd lifted a hand to wave goodbye. His mistake. A moment of weakness. A break in the strict operating procedures of the Nazca. A hat tip to sentimentality that had gotten him, finally, killed.

He'd always thought he'd die on a torturer's table, caught at last, clinging to his secrets as they pushed too far and threw his body into a cascade of crisis from which it would not recover. It wasn't what most people hoped for, but he'd have taken it in a heartbeat over bleeding out while Sanda's face hovered over him.

Worried, hurt. She'd been so goddamned *pained* that the man she'd shot was dying. Not Tomas. If the universe was kind—*hah*—she'd never know she'd put the bullet in her lover's chest. But a traitor, a spy. Someone she had every right to drop, and she'd tried to save him. Still, she cared.

The universe did not deserve Sanda Maram Greeve.

Her name, carrying not just the history of her family but the history of Prime in its variations of Maria Salvez and Alexandra Halston, but hers. Envisioning her face became harder, fuzzier, but her name... He could hold on to that.

Funny. She'd been such a brief moment in his life. Another rescue/capture/recovery mission out of hundreds, a lover among dozens. Brief, intangible relationships he could hardly recall now. It should be his family filling his heart. Mom and Grandma and all the cousins. Their food, at the very least—his warm and comforting core. But it was Sanda he clung to as his body kicked and thrashed its last.

It thrashed less now. This was the point when numbness should take over. He knew enough about death to know all the ways a body found its end. Shock and adrenaline and the simple fact that his central nervous system was shutting down should give him some peace.

His eyes opened. Breath came, slow and stuttering, but full. The white enamel walls of a NutriBath curled up to either side of him. She'd done it. She'd gotten him into a bath before the end.

Enough lies. Enough Leo Novak. He'd convince her. He had to convince her—tell her everything. Tell her that, in his supposed final moments, all he'd wanted was to see her face again. One couldn't leave the Nazca, not without leaving a trail of blood, but he'd find a way to make them believe allying himself with Sanda again was necessary. They'd give him back his face, and then she had to believe.

"Took you long enough," an unfamiliar feminine voice said.

Instincts took over, pressing down his elation. Adrenaline surged, not the last panicky moments of a dying man, this time his implants kicking in, pushing his body into a heightened state of the normal human fight-or-flight response. His response to that biological cascade was, and always had been, extreme focus. It's what made good fighter pilots, medis, and spies.

"Hello?" he rasped.

She clucked her tongue. "Don't pretend. You're fine. Ish. Sit up, at the very least. I hate having conversations with the goo."

He was submerged, and speaking without choking? No matter what the woman said, his arms shook as he grasped either side of the cocoon and pulled himself up, shivering as the NutriBath liquid dribbled down his body and sloshed around his hips.

He scrubbed goo from his eyes with the back of his wrist and blinked, staring at the violet-tinged fluid on his skin.

"You put me in a MetBath? They're just for cosmetic work." Hesitantly, he probed at his chest with his fingertips, but there was no evidence of a wound. Not even the salmon-pink of new skin.

"Ah, he speaks in full sentences now. Marvelous. Caid called it a MetBath, did she? Cute, very Prime-like of her, but there's no such thing. You're sitting in a reconstruction chamber, and its abilities are limited to our kind."

He looked up. Rainier Lavaux sat on a crate strapped to a mag pallet, hovering above him, though not in any form he'd seen her as before. This Rainier wasn't as waifish as the others, she had extra muscle packed around her bones, and while her hair was ashen, it was shorn down to the scalp, leaving a halo glow of white fuzz.

"Who are you?" he squeaked out, buying time.

"I am one of Rainier Lavaux. But you already knew that. I forced your rebirth to pass you a message: Tell your Nazca masters to stay out of my business. Tell Sitta Caid she had her chance." She crossed her legs, flexing her ankle.

A great many thoughts burst to life in Tomas's mind, questions demanding answers, but he packed them away for later, drew deep to summon up the Nazca coolheadedness he was supposed to be known for.

Her foot, bouncing and stretching, lacked a mag boot, and he and the goo in the MetBath weren't hovering. Gravity was definitely pulling his limbs down. The room appeared to be a cargo hangar—pallets and baths and a high ceiling with catwalks. Grips on the ceiling told him he was on a station, or a ship large enough to have spin-grav.

There wasn't a lot of personality to a cargo space, but the little details gave it away. All the metal in the room was matte black, the pallets arranged with military precision. Tomas had never been inside a guardcore ship, but he had a feeling he was now.

"I don't know who, or what, you're talking about."

She rolled her eyes and sighed dramatically. "Leo Novak, aka Tomas Cepko, aka a list so long if I read it all out we'd be here until Ordinal's star went nova, do not bullshit me. You *cannot* bullshit me, though I suppose the effort is cute, isn't it? I admit I was surprised to find you sniffing around Janus. I didn't think Caid would be so bold."

He crossed his legs and straightened his back, settling his palms onto his knees. Fine. She wanted to play with the truth, he could play that game, too. "How many of you are there, Rainier?"

She clapped her hands in front of her chest. "Better! I don't mind telling you, but I don't really know. It's been ages since I've connected with all the others at once."

"How do you communicate?"

She tilted her head and tapped her temple. "Minds are a series of electrical impulses, and those travel quite nicely."

"The amplifiers," he said. "You're trying to increase your ability to communicate with yourself."

She gave him a shark's smile. "Clever, but no. I want control over the spin of the Casimir Gates."

"Why?"

"What did I tell you about your order sniffing around, hmm? *That's* a surprise."

He spread his hands. "Can't help it. Nazca instincts."

"Try harder."

He took a deep, steadying breath, savoring the flash of fear that made his heart rate kick up. Rainier might be the most dangerous person he'd ever come across, but that only made his curiosity sharper.

She'd saved his life. He doubted she'd try to kill him again so soon. "I need to know something, Rainier. For my own curiosity."

She leaned forward, crossing her arms over her knee. "What does the man inside of Cepko-Novak want to know?"

"How are you possible? *What* are you?"

She blinked, the careful, articulated movement of a lizard, and cocked her head, as if waiting for him to amend that, to ask more. He waited for her to fill the silence he let spread between them.

After a moment that drew out forever, she threw her head back and laughed uproariously, slapping her knee.

"You don't know. You really don't know. My gods, my gods, they never told you. Oh, Caid, that trickster."

Tomas swallowed. "My superiors know what you are?"

"Know? Oh my. Oh dear. Your confusion is so... sweet. No wonder Caid sent you to Janus. Ignorance is its own shield, isn't it? But the truth—"

She moved faster than possible. One second she perched atop the crate, a goddess on high, the next she loomed over him, still as stone, a soft breeze against his bare skin the only evidence she had moved at all.

"Did they really not tell you? In all your *long* years of service?"

"Tell me what?"

"You didn't think you were human, did you?"

CHAPTER 54

PRIME STANDARD YEAR 3543

INTO THE DARK

The deadgate was almost invisible against the endless night of space. Sanda leaned toward the viewscreen as the ship approached, and though she knew the cameras were making the gate appear closer than it truly was, she felt drawn to it. Hooked.

When spun up, the structure of the Casimir Gates vanished to the human eye, the outline of the gate's mouth delineated only by the lights attached to its frame, a warped horizon. Seeing one up close was the purview of Keepers, exclusively. While the cameras on board the *Thorn* could show her the gate in all its details, filters were in place—obfuscations produced by the gate itself—never quite allowing a full picture.

To see the gate in truth, one would have to float right up to it. Even then, she knew all too well how easy it would be for the visor of a helmet to be altered.

"We are within the safety envelope," the ship said.

She threw a glance toward its system readout, craving the hands-on piloting she loved, but this ship was communicating with the gate, following strict Prime protocols. It was hands-off for her until they reached the other side.

"You're up, Demas," she said, gesturing to the forward console.

"The initial spin can be blinding, but the cameras will filter for that." He pulled himself into the seat alongside Conway and transferred a process from his wristpad to the ship itself, using the *Thorn*'s superior transmitting ability to deliver the spin commands.

Arden watched their wristpad like a hawk, their long fingers tapping at speeds that felt impossible to Sanda as they monitored Demas's brief interaction with the ship's systems. She could have told them to back off, but she wasn't sure of Demas herself. The GC didn't appear bothered by the scrutiny.

Which meant he was so sure of himself that he wasn't worried about a civ nethead like Arden, or he was legitimate. She hated that she couldn't be certain either way.

Sanda clenched the arms of her chair, resisting an urge to blink as the deadgate began to glow with the soft, halo-like shine of its embedded lighting.

What the crew of the *Thorn* thought of Demas became irrelevant in that moment. Seeing a Casimir Gate spin up was a once-in-a-lifetime experience for most Keepers, and something all others in the universe could only hope to see through filtered CamCasts. Even Liao had abandoned her dogged research into sightings of Rainier and Jules to strap in on deck and watch the spin.

There were dangers. The gate hadn't been spun in decades, mechanical failures were possible—had happened, wiping out whole settlements—but it wasn't fear that surged through Sanda as the great rings began, ponderously, to turn.

Elation lifted her up, made her grip the chair even tighter so she could feel the subtle movements of the thrusters, supposedly impossible for humans to detect due to inertial damping but present for her, as she watched the ship's systems through the corner of her eye. She imagined she could feel the disturbance in the hard vacuum, microscopic bits of space dust swirling, flowing, moving as the gate displaced both time and space.

She didn't know how it worked, but there were some basics even Prime couldn't keep secret, and feeling the ship adjust to keep stationary, she sensed the truth of them. The gates punched through the fabric of space, and the ripple of that violence rocked the *Thorn* as easily as a ship at sea, no matter the vacuum.

"Flash in ten, nine..." Demas trailed off as the *Thorn*'s automated systems threw a filter over the viewscreen, shifting the view to a slight reddish tint as a violent burst of white light expanded from the gate.

"Punch-through achieved," the *Thorn* said.

Those were rote words, dictated by Keepers, and endless speculation had branched off of their use. Were they descriptive of what the gates did—punch through time and space?—or were they a red herring, words loaded to make those trying to reverse-engineer the gates look in the wrong direction?

"Let's go see what's so important about a dead system," she said.

Sanda's heart was all she could hear as she tapped the coordinates hidden in her head into the *Thorn*'s navigational system. A small part of her expected disaster, negation by the system, a bug put into Prime ships that would outright deny that such a place existed and could ever be flown to. The heading flashed green, and the *Thorn* hooked up with the gate's automatic pass-through systems. They moved.

The tension on deck was so high Sanda wanted to give orders to cut the silence.

"The coordinates are right on the other side, about a day's flight from the gate. We should have visual immediately," Arden said.

As they entered the gate's sphere of influence, the ship began the slow, forced process of powering down all nonessential systems. Prime didn't like non-Keepers getting a closeup view of the gates, and that included any monitoring equipment that might be smuggled on board a ship and need the power of the ship's systems. The obvious workaround would be a generator or battery pack, but a gate would detect those and deny transit. If they turned on partway through, the gate would destroy the ship without prejudice. Devices small enough to avoid detection weren't powerful enough to overcome Prime's static and jammers.

The software governors of Prime crushed the *Thorn*'s power systems to a snail's pace, throttling its engines, its batteries, everything that could squeeze out a drop of power to the absolute minimum needed to support the life on board.

"Makes your skin crawl," Nox said.

Sanda could barely see him in the dark, but she caught a sharp flash from the whites of Demas's eyes as he craned his neck around to regard Nox. "I find it exhilarating."

"Yeah, but you wear all black and don't even use your name unless you have to, so your creep factor is a little off, buddy."

Demas chuckled. "I suppose. But this crossing opened the universe to humanity. This moment pushed us from a single-planet species into an intergalactic superpower."

"Not *this* moment," Sanda said. "I doubt Halston and her team went through with all the shrouding in place that we have now. I wonder what it was like—was it as dark as this? Was there nothing to see, or was there light within the gate?"

Demas waved a hand. "Irrelevant. Prime takes power from its secrets."

"Gotta admit, I'm getting a little tired of secrets," Sanda said.

"Coming back online," Conway cut in. "Running systems checks."

Sanda ran her own checks from the captain's chair, scanning diagnostics for any red or yellow or slightly lime-green flags that may have popped while the ship was powered down. The lights weren't even all the way up yet, but they were getting brighter, the subtle rumble of the engine pushing more power vibrating her chair.

Prime may force the power-down, but it allowed a ship's crew to bring their vessel back online once through. Giving them time to troubleshoot any problems that may arise in the reboot of nonessential systems. Sanda knew the protocol inside and out. She always knew the protocol.

"All clear," she said. The lights shot back up to full, making everyone blink, and the viewscreens filled with a view of local space underneath a steady stream of diagnostics. "Arden, get me a visual."

"Yes, sir," they said, but with only half the usual amount of sarcasm.

Arden flicked what was on their console to the forward viewscreen. The coordinates, white text on black, flashed above a field of empty space for only a breath before an image resolved. A massive sphere of silver, large as Atlas's burden, hung suspended in the void. The titanium-white gleam of metal glowed with an internal light, a gentle phosphorescence.

"It's beautiful," Nox said, then cleared his throat self-consciously.

In the corner of her eye, Demas's body language changed. Stiffened. Sanda peeled her gaze away from the object in time to see him lean forward, fists clenched, jaw flexed with determination.

The sphere shattered.

Sanda's breath caught, her whole body canted forward as the sphere broke into sections, expanding outward from an unseen center point, dissolving into pieces that, according to the scale drawn across the viewscreen, were approximately twenty meters long and wide.

"Did we break it?" Conway asked.

"No," Sanda said through a dry throat. The sphere was unzipping, pulling apart methodically and along a preprogrammed path. The seams were too regular, the movement too coordinated.

The pieces moved away from whatever was in their center, whatever caused that glow, and shivered as they turned in one sharp, synchronized movement, shifting in seconds from sphere to shield. Though they appeared stationary, velocity indicators flashed around the edges, impossibly high. Nothing Prime made could move that fast, and they were burning straight toward them. A day. It should be a whole day's flight at full thrust to those things, and yet, the time to impact kept plunging downward. The *Thorn*'s defense systems threw up warnings that the ship was being targeted.

"But it's going to try to break us."

CHAPTER 55

PRIME STANDARD YEAR 3543

WE CAME TO THE WRONG NEIGHBORHOOD

The *Thorn*'s onboard evasion system took over, flipping them end over end. Sanda swore as she saw the ship's AI had decided the only safe thing to do was to point them back through the gate and burn for safer pastures.

"Override that shit," she ordered.

"On it," Conway called back. Both hands danced over her console.

"Maybe we should *let* the ship evade?" Liao said.

"We *are* evading, but we aren't leaving. Those things don't want visitors, and I'd bet my life they'll try to destroy the gate behind us. I'm not giving them the chance," Sanda said.

"Let the commander command," Conway said, and though her gaze never shifted from her work, the tone she used was its own kind of weapon. Liao slumped, her face ghostly pale.

The first volley hit.

Sanda clenched her jaw as the ship rocked, thrusters fighting against the momentum imparted by the impact. Memories of pain enfolded her, pushed to the surface. The scream of metal and polymers shredding, of her people being torn apart, as an Icarion railgun— No. Focus.

Her fingers slicked the display with sweat as she tapped the button for a hull report, the viewscreen wicking away the moisture a second after the smears appeared. She prayed Prime built their ships as well as their screens.

A diagram of the ship flashed into the upper left of the forward screen, freckled with red but holding. Whatever those things were, they weren't capable of a full bombardment. Death by a thousand paper cuts could take the *Thorn* down all the same.

Crimson squares that represented the shield pieces grouped and swooped across the viewscreen, closing in on the *Thorn* in a bloody clot.

"They're swarming," Liao said, her voice tinged with awe.

"Spray laser fire," Sanda ordered.

Conway didn't hesitate, though Demas flinched. The *Thorn* was a Point ship, meant to punch holes with precision, not spread fire in waves, and so the sheet-lasers would be an inordinate draw on their engines, slowing their maneuverability.

A risk, but a calculated one. If they kept taking fire, there wouldn't be much of a ship left to maneuver.

The battle played out on the viewscreen, lines and geometries zipping back and forth, current positions of all objects best guesses extrapolated from mass and velocities.

"Threat twenty percent down," Conway announced. Though Sanda could read the numbers for herself, hearing them out loud sent a shock wave of dread through her body.

Those guns were their best bet at taking down the brunt of the force. Twenty percent was nothing, and the weapons were closing, their energy weapons chipping away at the *Thorn*.

"Helmets," she ordered, and flicked the button on her console.

Vacuum-ready helmets descended from panels in the ceiling on telescoping poles above every station. Sanda yanked hers down and pulled it over her head, running her thumb along the neck gasket to seal it to the Prime jumpsuit. Without a lifepack attached, the recyclers would give out in hours, but at least she wouldn't lose pressure immediately if the weapons punched a hole in the command deck.

Prime had trained her to get ahead of catastrophe, and despite her life events thus far, Sanda didn't forget her training.

"Switch to gun hail," she ordered the second Conway's name went live in her HUD.

"Firing," Conway said, punching the ship's reverse targeting system into life. The shield-weapons may have them painted in targeting lasers stem to stern, but that gave her weapons a clear bead to fire back on.

A chunk of enemy dots on the screen peeled off, shattering under the hail of projectiles. Sanda took advantage of the returned engine power and ordered the ship to sling around, giving the advancing force a smaller target to hit in their well-shielded backside.

"If you let them shoot our engines and they breach containment, you're giving them a bomb," Demas hissed.

"The engines are better shielded than the deck."

"Nothing will be shielded if—"

"Shut the fuck up, Demas. Knuth, wind down nonessentials, prepare for EMP. Everyone, power off wristpads."

Silence on the comms. Then, chipper as anything, "On it, Commander."

"There's nothing in this system," Demas said. "If you fire that EMP while our engines are hot, then we're dead in the water."

"Demas," Conway said, "the commander said to shuck the fuck up."

"Continue fire," Sanda said. "Give them so much to track they can't see the EMP charging."

"You cannot fire that EMP!"

"Cutting Demas from comms," Sanda said.

"What—" His voice dissolved in a crackle as she swiped him out of the network.

"Peaceful," Nox said.

"Essential communications only," Sanda said. An emoji middle finger popped up in her text display. Despite herself, she grinned.

"Knuth, report."

"Winding down while looking feisty's not easy, but we're getting there. Ten minutes."

According to the predictions on Sanda's monitor, the berserkers would have them swarmed in seven minutes. She said nothing, because Knuth had access to the same data, and saying anything would add fractions of seconds they didn't have.

"Give them everything except the railguns and the EMP, Conway. Lasers, projectiles. All of it."

"Yes, sir." If there was a little too much enthusiasm in her voice, Sanda ignored it.

She clutched the arm of her chair in one hand as the *Thorn* shuddered and jerked, pulled back and forth in a tug-of-war of Newton's laws as the stabilizers struggled in vain to keep her stable against the contrasting velocity of their own gunfire and the impact of the weapons. The graphical representation of the *Thorn*'s damage lit up like a supernova.

Six minutes until the berserkers would be so close they couldn't even pretend to dodge. She needed them close for the EMP to take them all down, but the power-up was taking too long. They were going to get shredded.

Sanda's view went white and terror leapt into her throat. Her blood pooled into her legs. She clenched her core as hard as she could, flexed her thighs, fought like hell against the g's pulling her back and sideways so hard and fast even the inertial dampers couldn't compensate. Or maybe Knuth had already taken those offline. Her hearing fuzzed, then slammed back along with her vision.

There was a dinner-plate-sized hole in her ship. The weapon had cut a neat through-and-through above the corner of the forward viewscreen. Sparks crackled in the hole. Sanda glanced instinctively to the viewscreen to see a readout of the damage, but the shot had taken out some essential system and the screen was half black, the only side online showing the advancing tide of enemy ships. All loose debris—styluses, bits of paper, unstowed tablets—flew into the black.

That hole would kill them. Sanda's ship. Sanda's responsibility. She grabbed the patch kit strapped to the side of her chair and undid her harness in one fluid, well-practiced motion and dug her heels into the seat to kick off.

Demas had moved first. He had the patch kit from his seat crammed under one arm and with the other he pushed her down, back into the seat, and pulled her harness hastily across her chest. She flicked her gaze to the comms list to pull him back up, but he swiveled, pushed off of her toward the gaping hole in the *Thorn*. The suction drew him to the wall faster than any kick-off, and he slammed against the twisted metal, barely missing losing an arm out the hole.

"Not your job," she said over comms, then remembered she'd taken away his ability to respond.

He had the kit open, but she knew full well there wasn't a patch in the kit big enough to cover that hole alone. With a curse, she tossed him the other kit end over end. He snatched it before it could get ripped outside, and popped it open. Loose supplies were sucked out the hole, but he wasn't after those. He slammed the kit box against the sucking wound. The metal buckled on contact, but held. He could apply the patches over the edges.

One minute until full EMP. The ship bucked as the weapons drew closer, more and more fire breaking through Conway's suppressive efforts, blowing holes small and large all across her length even as Sanda slewed around, doing everything she could to make them a smaller target.

"Knuth," she said, "kill it."

"Fuck," he said, but the engines went down, cut off before they could spool out properly, all the tension in her controls bleeding away into nothing. Life support cut out. Comms dropped. Warning lights flared across the deck, alarms screamed or metal screamed or people or all of the above as the weapons closed, cocooned the *Thorn* as they had whatever they'd been hiding. Whatever was at the heart of those coordinates.

Sanda deployed the EMP.

A concussive *whump* spread out from the heart of the ship. The viewscreen on her helmet fuzzed, the haptic feedback in her gloves went dead. Silence, deep and deadly, spread throughout the deck until all Sanda could hear, the only thing that she knew to be real, was the thundering of her heart.

The helmet was dead. It hadn't been powered down. She ripped the helmet off and gasped in the too-cold air of the deck, atmo thinned by its struggle toward equilibrium with the vacuum on the other side of the ship's wound. She pressed her helmet into her lap and gripped it tight with one arm. The others, one by one, peeled off their helmets.

Conway was first to speak. "Did we get them?"

Sanda glared at the blank and broken viewscreen, as if it had answers. Everything pulling power when the EMP went off was fried, and that meant all their targeting systems and most of their cameras. She flinched as something metallic pinged against the ship, fearing a projectile, but the sound was far too gentle for that.

Another ping, and another. She let out a shaky breath. The weapons weren't firing. They were bumping into the *Thorn* from their conserved momentum.

"Knuth," Sanda said, surprised by the steadiness in her voice, "can we get a visual?"

"I, uh, I can't bring the engines online yet, but we have the subgenerator for the crossing. I killed the side panels right before."

He unbuckled and kicked off, thrusting himself like a spear down the long hallway to the engine room. The generator would have to be brought online by hand.

"If we're not dead, they are," Nox said, which seemed clear-enough logic, but Sanda wasn't willing to bet anything on that assumption.

She caught herself breathing shallowly, sipping at the air, and forced herself to take normal breaths. Either life support would come back on, or it wouldn't. Making herself light-headed in the meantime wasn't going to help.

From the back of the ship came the soft purr of the generator coming online. She closed her eyes briefly, focused on feeling the subtle vibration of it kicking into life through the contact of her chair. They had power. They'd have life support.

The left viewscreen fizzled online, first a haze of meaningless grey as Knuth cycled through cameras until he found one that could be raised from the dead. At first, Sanda couldn't tell the difference between the empty grey and the live feed. Not until she noticed a metallic glint, and black veining in the cracks between the shield-weapons.

"We're surrounded," Conway said, fingers itching toward her dead weapon controls.

"By corpses," Sanda said slowly, running what few scans were still available to her. "No heat, no signaling of any kind. They're offline."

Arden laughed, nervously. Sanda was afraid that if she joined them, she'd never stop.

"We—" The subconscious part of her mind that was always keeping track of her crew noticed: Demas hadn't taken his helmet off. His dead helmet.

Sanda tossed her helmet aside and ripped off her harness, then kicked herself toward him. She collided palms-out with the bulkhead beside him, ignoring the droplets of sticky red that caught on her jumpsuit and were, as was the way with Prime materials, wicked away. Prime never let the blood stain.

"Demas!" She grabbed his helmet and yanked.

Sweaty black hair stuck up, his face drawn, but his eyes were open, alert. His gaze locked onto hers and he grimaced, glancing along his body to his thigh, gripped in both hands, his jaw locked as he strained with everything he had to keep the flow in check.

"Just a graze," he hissed between his teeth.

Sanda grabbed what was left of the patch kit—not ideal for human flesh, but not useless—and pushed his hand away. The graze ran deep, but it was still a graze, and didn't wander near any of his arteries.

"You lucky fuck." She peeled the patch open and pressed it against his thigh. It would keep him mostly together until they brought a proper medical kit over.

"Not feeling very lucky."

"What were you thinking? You should have let me do it. I don't have as much skin to hit."

He snorted, but was smiling through a grimace of pain. "Conway was right. You needed to focus on commanding, and I had the hands free to make the fix."

Huh, maybe Demas wasn't such a locked-down asshole after all.

"Commander," Knuth said, "I've put a little juice in the engines. Happy to report I got Grippy offline before the EMP."

"Thanks, Knuth. Conway, nose us through. Demas, can you get yourself to the medibay?"

"I'll patch myself up like a good kid after we see what that sphere was hiding."

She rolled her eyes but didn't protest. "Your funeral."

Conway took control of the ship's navigation, and though she nudged it slower than Sanda felt possible, the *Thorn* nosed "up," if such a thing had meaning in space, toward a thinness in the weapons that surrounded them. Though many of the weapons were chewed up by the *Thorn*'s fire, most were still whole, and Sanda could see no mechanism by which they had worked. They were smooth, slightly convex pieces of what had been the sphere they first sighted.

Everyone craned to see the side viewscreens, squinting as if doing so would clear up the graininess of the few cameras left standing. Sanda realized, in the second before they broke through, that she was holding her breath.

At first, blackness. Nothing but the inclement void that stretched between all stars. Then, impossibly, light. Not from the gate or the weapons or even the *Thorn*, but a smudge of glow. The same glow they'd seen emitting from the weapons the moment before they struck.

In the center of the light, cradled in its heart, silver metal. Titanium white, pure and gleaming, though this was a material she had never seen before. A cloud of metal, maybe, a cluster of brightness and solidity that began to take shape as she stared, eyes adjusting, finding differences from one bright spot to another.

It reminded her of a neuron map, an image of a mind deep in thought, electronic impulses surging along metallic connections, but it was shaped like no mind she'd ever seen. It was long, lean, and three times larger than the *Thorn*, though scale was a difficult thing to determine without reference.

"It's a ship," she said aloud, and in speaking the words knew them to be true.

CHAPTER 56

PRIME STANDARD YEAR 3543

THERE'S A PROTOCOL FOR THIS

The *Thorn* limped toward the unknown ship. Silence had descended upon the deck, though not a true silence. While on the surface Sanda and her crew bent all their efforts to bringing the *Thorn*'s systems back online in a slow and deliberate manner that would not exacerbate any failures further, they limped, when they should not.

A ship as damaged as the *Thorn* had no business moving, but the ship—that other ship—was a lodestone pulling them forward. At full power, it would have taken the *Thorn* a day's flight to reach it. Now, it'd been closer to two. But they could no more sit patiently and repair themselves than they could cut their own arms off for a good time. Sleep had been abandoned. Food and water a grudging necessity. Sanda licked dried lips as they finally crossed into docking range.

"Is it hailing?" Sanda asked to cut the silence. She could see as well as Conway and Knuth that nothing came from the ship.

"No signals," Conway said. "Though the radiant heat signature puts it somewhere around 15C."

"Positively toasty," Sanda said.

She brought up a scan of the ship, ordering what remained of the *Thorn*'s external sensors to pan over it, seeking some centralized source of power. There should be a concentration of heat near that power, or an obvious heat sink or radiation system keeping the ship's heat circulating and bleeding off so that the whole thing wouldn't overheat in a heat blanket of its own making.

Nothing. The ship's radiation signature was perfectly even from tip to tip.

"Well, there's no one home," she said. She had absolutely no idea what they were dealing with. The lack of hot spots the likes of which you'd see on a ship like the *Thorn*, denoting a concentration of biological life, could only be interpreted on face value here. There was a lack of hot spots. End of supposition. She wondered why she thought of life in terms of the biological.

"We are closing," Conway said, taking the place of the ship's AI voice—one of the many systems knocked offline by the EMP. Sanda's poor ship would take a long while to get back on its feet. She glanced down at her leg and thought maybe she could think of a better metaphor.

"Within the envelope of the shielding system," Sanda said. Then, after a pause, "No further threat detected. If the ship has weapons, they're not online or they're so fancy the *Thorn* can't pick them up."

"So what," Nox said. "We saunter on up and say howdy?"

There was a protocol for this. Never used, barely remembered. She'd taken tests on first-contact systems along with all the other fleeties, and though the information was old and she'd only paid half attention to it because, honestly, nobody thought they'd be using it, Sanda had never forgotten a protocol in her life.

If this were a fleet operation, her orders would be to stay put, keep eyes on the unidentified object, call her superiors and not, under any circumstances, attempt communication until directed to by the Keepers of Prime. More than likely, if she made that call, Anford would tell her to haul ass out of there and then send a whole fleet, accompanied by GC and most likely Okonkwo and the other members of the High Protectorate.

That was what was supposed to happen.

Sanda undid her harness and laced tense, cramped fingers together to stretch them out in front of her. "Let's go ask for a cup of sugar."

Nox grinned fiercely, but it was Demas she watched out of the corner of her eye. He may have been quick to patch up the ship, but she couldn't help but be wary of him now that he knew her secret. Didn't help that he was GC, legit or not. He frowned, a line appearing between his brows.

"Our communications off-board are down, correct?" Demas asked Knuth.

The thin man shrugged, the bony points of his shoulders came almost to his ears. "We got our transponder ticking away to let anyone who's listening know we're coming, but that's it. We won't be talking to anyone until I dig down into the guts of this thing and replace what fried. I can't even guarantee we've got all the replacement parts we need on board. The *Thorn* flies, friends, but she does not speak."

"Then we don't have a choice," Demas said.

That made Sanda frown. They had choices. Few, granted, but ones that her superiors would almost definitely prefer she take. Demas wanted on that ship, and he wanted on now. More than likely Okonkwo had either known or suspected what might be here and had given him orders.

"Conway, find us something that looks like an airlock and attach the inflatable. We'll confirm the safety of the environment with a forward scouting party of myself and Nox. Once the ship is secured, I expect all of you suited up and ready to follow us."

"Leave the *Thorn* alone, Commander?" Knuth asked, eyes wide.

"She needs the rest." Sanda patted her ceiling and pushed off, angling toward her room where her preferred lifepack and helmet waited. As she drifted out the door, she half spun, looking back at the deck behind her. "And seriously, do any of you want to miss this?"

Sanda suited up in record time, but was unsurprised to find Nox already lingering by the airlock that Conway had extended to kiss the unknown ship. His helmet was on, so she couldn't read his expression, but everything about his body language radiated excitement.

"Seal check," Sanda ordered through the helmet comms, watching Nox's name flash in small caps as the connection went live. "And don't rush it, soldier. That thing's not going anywhere."

They made quick work of the check, each movement exaggerated to make it clear to the other that, despite their rush, they weren't leaving a single thing to chance. Sanda had her hand on the airlock open pad when Liao came barreling down the passageway toward them.

"Excuse me," she said, her rich voice filling their helmets with the same flavor of stiff rebuke Sanda had gotten from disappointed professors in school. "Are you really boarding an unknown vessel while armed?"

Sanda and Nox glanced down at their sidearms, then back at each other. They couldn't see each other through the mirror tint of the helmet visors, but Nox made a slight gesture of his chin to indicate he hadn't even thought about it.

Neither had she. Sanda closed her eyes behind the shield of the visor and resisted a sigh. "Doctor," she said over open comms, "we don't know what's waiting for us. That is the point of a forward exploration team. We need to be certain that ship is secure."

"And if it registers your weapons and determines that you're hostile?"

"We won't walk in guns out, they'll stay nose-down until we feel we need them. And the damn thing hardly has room to judge us for being wary. It almost destroyed our ship, if you remember."

She sniffed. "An automated system."

"And there might be more *automated systems* on board. No chances. Now please, move away from the airlock and get your gear on. We'll invite you over for the welcome party soon enough."

"Take this," she said so quickly Sanda barely caught the words.

Liao shoved a device into her hands about the size of her palm, coated in the white enamel surface that medis used for everything because it was easy to clean and kept pathogens at bay. It had a small screen about the size of her thumb, a series of buttons, and some sort of prod sticking out of what Sanda nominally deemed the "top."

"What is this?"

"On a very base level, a pathogen detector. It will periodically sample the air around it for known contaminants, and report if it discovers anything untoward. Or anything it doesn't recognize."

"Thanks," Sanda said, "but no one's taking their helmets off on this little expedition. We're not morons."

"No, but it's good data to have."

Sanda smiled. Despite everything that had happened to her, Liao was still driven by her passions. She should be desperate for revenge. A part of her was, but it hadn't drowned out the part of her that was hungry for information to help her solve the universe's myriad mysteries. There was reassurance in that. Stability. Sanda looked into Liao's eyes and wondered if a similar fire ever burned in her, and what it might have burned for.

She'd wanted to protect her brother. Now…Now things were all fucked up. She was still his protector, would be as long as she drew breath, but at an oblique angle. Dios, she'd wanted to captain ships and fire the big guns. She'd never wanted the responsibility of the hidden secrets of the universe at her feet, tangling up her ankles every step she took.

Sanda didn't want this. Didn't want her command, or the mystery hunk of unidentified bullshit waiting for her on the other side of that airlock. She wanted to go *home*, had known that want deeply and intimately since the moment she woke up on Bero and was told everything she'd ever thought of as home was so much dust.

Her grip tightened around the sampling device. But someone had put a chip in her head. A chip with *these* coordinates, and until she knew why, until she knew what this was, there would never be a home for her. Some secrets had claws, and this one wasn't letting her go. Bero had known that. Had understood that his existence, and hers, were two halves of a poisonous apple.

One step at a time. Work the problem.

"Thank you," she told Liao.

The doctor nodded and pushed away, back down the passage. Sanda pressed her gloved palm against the opening mechanism for the airlock and stepped inside. As the door shut, she couldn't help but flick her gaze to the gasket that sealed them in as the systems cycled and the pressure adjusted. Not a scratch on it, naturally. Green LEDs flashed the all clear and she opened the opposite side.

Nox went first. They hadn't arranged it, and there was definitely a protocol that said when a fleet unit enters an unknown ship in peace the ranking member should go first as a sign of good faith, but fuck it, she'd already thrown the rule book away today. Might as well set it on fire, too.

Maybe Nox wanted the dubious honor of being the first to step foot on that ship, but she doubted it. He was meat-shielding her, and while the thought was strangely flattering, it meant that he felt the same unease she did. They should be excited, jubilant. If this ship was as alien as it looked, this was the discovery of a lifetime.

Instead, they paced across the inflated passageway with small, tense steps. Deep down in their bones, neither one of them believed they'd survive long enough to be the celebrated heroes of discovering extraterrestrial evidence. If this was extraterrestrial. Just because she'd seen nothing like it before didn't mean it hadn't been made by human hands. Bero had been new. But this... She pushed down speculation and focused on the task at hand.

"What have we got?" she asked, as Nox stopped short at the other end.

Conway had placed the end of the inflatable on her best guess of what looked like an entrance, but claimed the whole thing was so homogeneous that her best guess was worthless.

"Metal," Nox said. He extended a hand and ran it across the fine filaments that comprised the body of the ship. "I think. Conway's right, it all looks the same, but the tube got purchase."

Sanda flicked her gaze to the seal mating the inflatable tube to the unknown craft. "They always get purchase. That's what they're for. Torches."

She imagined Liao having a conniption over this most aggressive of behaviors, but the longer Sanda spent near this thing the more her skin crawled. She wanted to get in and get out and pretend she'd never seen it.

They pulled micro-plasma torches from their kits and lit up. Despite Nox's defensive behavior, Sanda sidled in alongside him and, shoulder to shoulder, they reached to touch the flames to the ship.

The metal parted.

Sanda froze, the cone of her flame centimeters from where the hull had been. The fibrous tendrils peeled away from one another, and though she couldn't hear through her helmet, she got the feeling that they were whispering against each other, a soft sound in a language she could never know.

A breeze brushed against the thin but strong skin of her jumpsuit as the pressure between the tunnel and the ship equalized, the slit in the weave expanding until it was wide enough for Nox to pass through. Sanda had plenty of room.

All beyond, darkness.

"Well," she said, annoyed by the shake in her voice. "Torches down, lights up."

The lamps on their helmets pierced the darkness in unison. A long passageway stretched before them, walls and floor made of the same fibrous, entwined metal as the exterior of the ship. The temperature read 15C, pressure was neutral, and according to her HUD, the air mix was adjusting slowly toward human standard.

Nox hesitated, one hand clutching a side handle of the inflatable transfer tube. She couldn't blame him.

Sanda pushed herself into the enclosure of the ship, and nearly screamed as gravity sucked her down to stand, shakily, upright, in a ship that wasn't moving, in a space where no such forces should exist.

CHAPTER 57

PRIME STANDARD YEAR 3543

THE PEACE OF ALL

When Hitton entered the warehouse with Keeper Sato at her side, Biran had expected her to be furious. He hadn't expected the expression of sad resignation on her wan features, the slump to her usually proud shoulders. Hitton did not let her body language slip. Either she meant for them to see her defeated, or the feeling was so intense she lacked the strength to hide it. Either way chilled him more than whispers of false GC ever could.

"Ah yes," she said, surveying the landscape of unpacking bots Biran had ordered brought from the *Taso* to prepare the survey bots. "I suppose this was inevitable from the moment I allowed you to land. Natsu, I presume you showed them the way?"

The young Keeper's eyes bulged. "Keeper Hitton, I—"

Hitton waved her off. "No need, child, please. As I said, this conclusion was inevitable from the moment of their arrival. Part of me is glad you sped matters up. I would rather get this disaster over with."

"Forgive me," Biran said, "we do not want to override your process here, but you understand that the situation is tense. Matters must be shown to progress, otherwise all of this will have been for nothing."

Her smile was tight. "I won't fight you on this, Speaker. Do what you must."

Vladsen cleared his throat. "If you have no objections, then why have you not already sent the survey bots out?"

"Oh, I have plenty of objections." Hitton sat down on one of the unopened crates, back perfectly straight, hands resting on her knees. "But they will not be listened to."

"We'd like to hear them," Biran said gently. He gestured to the unpacking bots to emphasize that they hadn't started yet.

She cocked her head to the side. "Sato has told you of the shadow in our midst?"

"She has. If it is true, then it stands to reason that one person cannot change the results provided by so many bots at once. Whatever bad data comes back will be weeded out for the anomaly it is."

"The solution really is that obvious, isn't it?"

Biran shifted his weight. "I do not mean to insult your methods."

Her smile was razor-sharp, and he felt himself back on firmer footing. "You do. And you would not be incorrect. The truth of the matter is that I have been paralyzed here, unable to see the correct path."

"That is... not like you," Biran said.

"I know. Do you know my age, either of you?"

Biran exchanged a confused glance with Vladsen. "No, Keeper. It's none of our business."

"One hundred and thirty. Pushing the edge a bit, aren't I?"

"Modern advancements allow for a healthy life well into the one eighties," Biran said, baffled by this admission. The members of Ada's Protectorate were scattered across the age spectrum, with Vladsen and Biran holding up the younger end. It wasn't something he ever thought about. But while he was confused, he heard Vladsen suck air through his teeth. That man knew something Biran didn't, and it grated. He hated being nescient.

"Indeed, indeed. I hope you will respect the depth of my experience, Keepers, when I say I do not know what is wrong here, but something is very wrong."

"I read the reports of the human surveyors. Their findings match up with what the initial bots brought back. If there's a discrepancy—"

"There isn't." She closed her eyes briefly. "The data lines up. The asteroid is perfect."

"That's... wonderful?" Biran said.

She laughed and shook her head. "Yes. It's all so lovely. The data is clean and this hunk of rock features minerals the gate-builder bots need, and no fault lines disastrous enough to upset a future settlement. And yet. And *yet.* Someone stayed behind with the shipment of survey bots. Someone I can hear at times, catch a smear of on thermal, but I can't find."

"If there's a saboteur," Biran said, "they're a poor one. The initial data is ideal *and*, as you said, matches what the human surveyors found. There's been no tampering."

"You won't find any discrepancies. What do you think I've been *doing* all this time, while I stalled with the reports? I've been hunting, Speaker Greeve. This quarry and their real intentions cannot be found, and that should be enough to scrap the whole thing. But it's too perfect. Prime cannot ignore a gift like this. And if my concerns are ever raised, they will say the isolation was too much. I am an old woman, after all."

"I will say no such thing," Biran said with force.

"Forgive me," Vladsen said, placing a hand against Biran's arm. Biran's shoulder relaxed at the touch, and Vladsen took his hand away. "What if the saboteur is here not to damage the gate-build process, but to discredit you, Keeper Hitton?"

"I'm listening," she said warily.

"Well, if the data is clean, but you're filing reports about a phantom saboteur—all apologies—it would be a simple thing to throw your mental stability into question. Do you have enemies, Hitton?"

Hitton smiled tightly. "I am an elder member of Ada's Protectorate, Keeper Vladsen. I have lost count of the enemies I've stirred up along the way."

"Then it's possible."

She sighed. "I suppose so, but I still fear for this gate's construction."

"Keeper Hitton, we have our disagreements," Biran said, "but I respect the hell out of you. If there's something wrong with this station, then we will root it out. We don't disbelieve you, but we have to try with the survey bots. One enemy agent could not have tampered with so many. And Icarion..."

Hitton glanced up sharply. "Icarion thinks we're stalling."

Biran inclined his head. "I'm sorry. It's not something that could escape their notice. There's historical record for how long these surveys take. Once Prime has a site in mind, we move as quickly as possible. This doesn't line up."

She stroked her chin, considering. "Then perhaps... Perhaps the saboteur seeks not to discredit me, but to stoke the embers of war by delaying construction. It would take no great leap of insight to realize I would stall the build if I suspected a saboteur on-site. Icarion, as you say, would not fail to notice."

"We cannot ignore the possibility," Biran said.

Unprompted, Hitton punched something into her wristpad. The unpacking bots stirred to life, swarming over the crates. Biran flinched at the crack of metal as a lid slid to the ground.

"Keeper Hitton," Sato said, "are you sure?"

"Not at all," she said, "but I won't be goaded into war." She met Biran's gaze, and the wariness had not faded from her eyes. "You're not the only one who doesn't want blood on their hands."

"Thank you." He bowed his head to her.

She waved him off. "I'll send the preliminary results to Okonkwo now. That should speed things up, she's been breathing down my neck since I landed."

"If you want to wait—" Biran started to say.

"It's already done. It should not be long until— Ah, here she is." Hitton held up her wristpad for him to see. A priority call from the Prime Director flashed at them. The weariness in Hitton's body washed away as she lifted her chin, centered her focus, and accepted the call.

"Hitton, these results are incredible. Is this only the first wave?"

"Prime Director, it is. If it pleases you, I have Keepers Greeve and Vladsen here with me."

"Ah." Okonkwo focused her attention on Biran and Vladsen as Hitton turned her arm around to get them all in the shot. "Based on these preliminary findings, I will authorize the encoding and release of the gate-builder swarm. Keepers Vladsen and Greeve, I expect you to return to Ada Station with all haste to scan your part of the diagnostics. Hitton, please remain on-site to continue your investigation and scan in the final piece upon arrival of the construction system. I will contact Anford to arrange the fleet escort."

"Understood," the three Keepers said in unison.

"Prime Director," Biran said, "may we talk in private?"

"I will contact you later, after you are underway. Do not delay. The sooner Ada becomes a two-gate system, the sooner we can all breathe a little easier."

"Vladsen and I could stay here for scanning so that the others won't have to wait for our return."

"Greeve, this is a new gate. It is a press event, and no civilians are getting anywhere near that asteroid until the gate is established, let alone reporters. Get your ass back to Ada, where it belongs, and smile for those cameras, Speaker. Hitton, particulars later."

Okonkwo ended the call, and Hitton frowned. "Our Prime Director is exceptionally distracted, if she cannot spare the time to discuss the details of a gate-building."

"Not distracted enough to skip dressing me down," Biran muttered.

"You deserved it," Vladsen said, throwing him a sly smirk. "You cannot stay here while the press waits on Ada, Speaker."

"I promised you help, Hitton, and I'm not leaving until we've found out—"

"Enough." She stood up sharply, a thundercloud passing behind her eyes. "You have been sent to Ada by your absolute commander. Go."

"I—" Hitton glared him into silence and he shifted uncomfortably, glancing at his boots shamefaced. "I'll leave some of my fleeties with you," Biran said as she turned on her heel and strode to the door.

"Fine," she said, lifting a hand in acknowledgment, then paused. "Take Sato back to Ada when you go."

"Keeper—" Sato burst out.

"This is not a punishment. Be careful, all of you. I have spent my life spinning out moves ten steps ahead, and even I cannot guess what happens next."

Sato stared at the door as it shut behind Hitton. Biran said, gently, "You had better go and pack your things. Meet us at the *Taso*, we leave within the hour."

Sato nodded and hurried out of the room, leaving Biran and

Vladsen alone with the robots working steadily away at uncovering the rich mineral history of this asteroid.

He should feel elated. The gate would be built. He could finally use the schematics on his chip, could finally pass on his sliver of Prime's legacy to enrich future generations of humanity and, above all, stop a war that would end in the annihilation of Icarion.

Instead, a heaviness settled within him. Hitton was not a paranoid woman, prone to wild flights of imagination, but when she'd spoken of a potential saboteur, she had sounded genuinely unsettled. Possibly even scared. Sato may believe she was being punished for showing Biran the unused survey bots, but Biran didn't. Every single thing Hitton had said during that exchange had been the truth as Hitton knew it. Hitton was sending Sato away to safer climes.

"You've been staring at that door for two minutes now," Vladsen said.

Biran blinked and shook his head. "Hitton believes Sato may be in danger here."

"Hitton's beliefs remain an open question."

"Tell me honestly, do you believe she's succumbing to paranoia?"

Vladsen sighed. "No. Though it would be easier to assume she was. Let us pray this mystery person means only to discredit Hitton, and not to do real harm."

CHAPTER 58

PRIME STANDARD YEAR 3543

SARCASM IS A COPING MECHANISM

"You okay, Commander?" Nox asked.

"Yeah. Just... startled."

"You screamed."

"I did not."

"Squeaked a little."

"No way."

"You squeaked," Conway's voice crackled to her ears.

"Goddamnit, aren't you under my command?"

"Sorry, Commander."

"You're not."

They giggled, all of them, a little frantically, a little too wildly, as the pressure of the moment eased. The clatter of laughter in her helmet was enough that she couldn't tell who was laughing at her, nor did she care. Her shoulders relaxed. She remembered Liao's device and pulled it out to take a sample. Clear.

"Come on in, Nox, the water's fine. We have gravity."

"Not possible," Knuth said over comms. "Nothing on that ship is spinning."

"Tell it to my feet, Knuth. Demas, if Prime has a secret gravity-producing ship in the works, now would be a good time to tell us all about it."

"It does not."

"As I thought. Nox, come on. Everyone, focus."

Snickering across the comms as the others realized Nox had hung back. Not that any of them would have been any braver under the same circumstances, but still. He grumbled something incomprehensible and stepped into the ship like he was dipping a toe into an arctic lake. Gravity dragged him down, just like it had her, and his fists clenched at his sides.

"That's weird," he said.

"Understatement of the century. Conway, see any status change with the ship? My HUD reads the atmo is adjusting to Earth standard."

"No change, but your door's gone."

Sanda whipped around to look over Nox's shoulder. Sure enough, the opening they'd come through had sealed up after them.

"This feels very much like stepping into the belly of a whale," Nox said.

"A *Moby Dick* reference? From you?"

"Nah. *Pinocchio.* I like the cricket."

"A connoisseur of ancient media."

"I'm a man o' mystery, Commander." He tried to keep his voice light, but it was tight with barely restrained terror. At least talking kept him focused.

As they spoke, they crept through the passage. Despite the delicate appearance of the floor and walls, footing was stable. Sanda suspected that the density was changing to conform to their steps, giving them enough spring to move comfortably without either clomping along or squishing straight through. The thought wasn't a comforting one. Liao's talk of automated systems made her want to reach for her weapon, but she had the sinking feeling that even Prime's most advanced blaster would be little more than a peashooter against this thing.

It was getting brighter. Sanda motioned for Nox to pause and brought up her HUD's lumen display. Sure enough, the gauge was valiantly tracking upward despite the fact that Sanda could discern no obvious light source. She sent the data to Nox. He grunted.

"This ship is starting to piss me off," Sanda said, but with little real anger in her voice. "Conway, are you sure there has been no status change? Because I'm looking at a ship coming online, and it should bleed heat, draw power, *something*."

"It's possible our sensors were damaged during the EMP," Conway said with all the professional courtesy of someone who didn't believe a word of what they'd just said.

"There." Nox tapped her shoulder and pointed. "Look, at the... fibers? Maybe they're fiber-optic."

Sanda approached the wall and pressed her helmet close. The fine threads that made up the whole of the ship were emitting a soft, pleasant glow, getting steadily brighter. It was the kind of gentle lighting CamCast AIs ran complicated algorithms to get right.

Sanda pulled up the rough map they'd made of the ship while safely ensconced in the *Thorn*. Conway had put them down on the starboard side, toward the center, in the approximate place most non-spun ships had an airlock. She had absolutely no delusions that the... people?...who built this ship had any of the same proclivities her people did, but she had to start somewhere. She did the same damn thing she'd done on Bero what felt like aeons ago now. She turned down the passageway and walked in the direction that seemed likely to have a command deck.

The ship was all too willing to accommodate. Somehow extrapolating her directorial intention, the passageway she'd been thinking of as "central" shifted, shivering for a breath as multiple pathways sprawled out and forward in the direction she'd intended to go, unfurling and lighting up like the tip of a fern uncoiling.

It was Sanda's turn to freeze. Nox had his hand on his sidearm, and she didn't see a single reason to tell him to stand down.

Feeling fantastically foolish, Sanda flicked over to open comms and broadcast into the passageway. "We're coming to your command deck. We are not hostile."

Nox moved his hand away from his weapon, but not too far.

Over the private connection, she said, "Please tell me there's been a status change."

"I cannot tell you that," Conway said.

She consciously took control of one leg, then the other, pressing her steps into the distressingly firm floor with intention. Sanda followed the fern-path to the farthest tip of the ship, what she would think of as the "nose" but was undoubtedly something else in this changeable vessel. Maybe it was whatever she wanted it to be. What had Arden said about AI and data sets? She'd have to ask them again later. They were probably salivating to get their hands on this ship right now.

Something caught the corner of her eye. She stopped her determined march to the deck and dropped to one knee, peering into a slight darkness in the otherwise uniform mesh of silvery threads. The light didn't extend that far. She slipped her hand into the opening and pressed down, gently, as if nudging aside a fragile antique curtain. The ship obliged. The gap deepened, and as she trained her helmet light into the opening, the ship's self-illumination came up.

"That looks almost sane," Nox said.

Except that it didn't. An ache started in the back of her head and she clenched her jaw, flexing the tendons to ease the pain as she'd taught herself to do over the last few weeks. There was wiring in the mysterious walls of this ship. Nothing like Prime used, and set in the context of the neuron-like filaments, she had almost overlooked the familiarity to what she had seen on Bero. Almost.

"You getting this on video, Knuth?"

"Yessir," Knuth said, his voice pitched with excitement. "That looks like cabling, of a sort. I can work with that."

His relief was palpable. She hated to have to shatter it.

"So can I," she said. "The wiring on Bero looked like this."

"That is not possible," Demas said stiffly.

"Tell it to the wires," Sanda said.

"How could Icarion have access to... to this technology?" Demas asked.

Sanda shrugged as she stood up. Lavaux must have known that this ship, or something like it, existed and then fed that information to Icarion to help them technologically leapfrog over Prime. Was this what that nascent intelligence Arden had found was for? Piloting another weapon for Icarion? She wished she could ask Bero what he thought, then pushed the thought aside to keep it from hurting.

"Ask Icarion. I'm sure they'd be happy to tell you all about it."

She started back to the "front," but the path changed, shifted, angling her off-center. She glared at the ship under the cover of her visor and decided, fuck it. The ship had been accommodating enough so far. Least she could do was look at whatever it wanted to show her.

"Sanda," Nox said, a soft warning in his voice as she started down the new path.

"Yeah. I know, but thanks for the warning."

She stepped into an impossible space. The passageway opened up, sprawled out like a river delta, and transformed into a round room that Sanda could have sworn was too large by half to exist in this part of the ship. Conway didn't report any change, so she didn't bother asking.

In the center, caught between two pillars of the filaments reaching down to one another as if grasping hands, was a small sphere, no larger than Sanda's fists pressed together. She licked her lips and stepped forward. Nox put a hand on her arm, holding her back.

"What is it?" she asked in a low whisper, not knowing why she felt the need to drop her voice.

"I don't know. Seems odd, right? Like it's leading us to this… thing. We got no idea what it is. Could be a weapon."

"Nothing on board has attacked us."

"Yet."

"Fair enough. Cover me."

She heard him unholster his blaster as she resumed her slow march to the sphere and felt ridiculous. Unsettling as the ship was, nothing on board had been hostile. The shield defense system couldn't be ignored, but as Liao had said, that had been automated, and the system itself looked clumsy to her compared to the craftsmanship of this vessel.

Almost as if the drone shield had been added after the fact and wasn't a part of the ship's original design. A dangerous assumption to make, but she'd been living on her gut for a while now, and the fact that she was still living, despite the odds, was good enough for her. Something had to be good enough.

She came within arm's reach of the sphere and stopped. The device

Liao had given her didn't pick up anything virulent in the air around the orb, or anywhere else along her walk through the too-large room. Which should have taken her more time to cross than it had, especially at her slow march, but if she stopped to think about that too much she might lose her damn mind here and now.

"No change," she said, because she felt like she had to say something. "The surface is smooth... Wait, no."

Using the limited magnifying properties of her helmet, she zoomed in on a portion of the sphere where she thought she'd seen a scratch.

She had. Sanda's heart hammered as she panned the camera across the object. The scratch wasn't a wanton artifact of the sphere's production or transport. It was intentional, deliberate. Not a scratch at all, but a numerical number one, perfectly straight, with another right beside it. Her helmet was having a hard time with the resolution, the scratchings were so small, but she'd bet her life that was a zero next to those first two ones.

"It's binary," she said, scarcely believing herself. "This was meant to be read."

"Commander," Arden said, their voice shaking. "Begging your pardon, but I'm boarding that ship right fucking now."

She blinked, remembering the subtle threat in Demas's lack of complaint about her breaking protocol. "Very well. Everyone board at once, stay together. Nox and I will continue exploring this room until you arrive. I have a feeling our new friend the ship won't have any trouble guiding you to us."

"Weapons?" Demas asked.

Again, a chill of warning tickled at the small of her back. "No. Nox and I are armed, though I hardly think even that precaution is necessary at this point."

"Very well," Demas said, and she wondered if maybe she should have strapped up her whole crew with firepower. She liked the idea of Demas with a weapon less than she liked the idea of her crew being unarmed. She and Nox would have to be enough if things went sideways.

She wished she could get a better read on what Demas was thinking. Though he was trained to hide behind his armor, that stoic mask extended deep within him. Demas wouldn't let her see his true self unless it served him.

"Sanda," Nox said through a private line, "you said this was meant to be read."

"Yes. Binary is about as universal a language as we've got."

"Okay. But who wants us to read it?"

She gazed into the shiny metal sphere. "I have absolutely no idea."

CHAPTER 59

PRIME STANDARD YEAR 3543

ACCESS DENIED

The ship proved just as polite to its new guests as it had to Nox and Sanda, and soon the motley crew of the *Thorn* was standing in a nervous half ring around the sphere room. Except for Arden. They were right up against the thing, practically pressing their faceplate to the metal.

"Refrain from kissing it, Mx. Wyke," Sanda said.

"I don't know how you even saw something was there," they said. "My helmet can barely pick up the numbers. We need something higher-powered. Liao, you got any equipment with you?"

"If you're asking whether I thought to steal a tachyon microscope before abandoning Janus Station, Mx. Wyke, I can assure you that I did not."

"Nothing that can't be figured out once we get back to civilization," Demas said.

Sanda frowned. "Define civilization? Where in the hell do you even take something like this?"

"There are protocols," Demas said, and Sanda noted the sardonic note to his voice. "But most of those are beyond us now. Outside of calling in the fleet, as we should have done, but cannot do, we will have to deliver the object to them."

Arden pulled back. "You want to take it out of its... uh, thing?"

"Presumably those tendrils cover parts of the binary data. To see the whole picture, it will have to be removed. Okonkwo can direct what's done with it from there."

"I want—"

"Not over—"

Arden and Liao spoke over one another. They cut themselves off at the same time.

Liao took a long breath and said, "Demas, handing this into Keeper care would be to never see it again. I have all respect for our Keepers, naturally, but they are known for limiting civilian scientific access. Mx. Wyke and I, by right of discovery, should have that self-same access."

"Major Greeve discovered the object," Demas said. "If we're playing finders keepers, it's hers. But that's not how these things work, Doctor. You know that."

A private comm request from Arden flashed in Sanda's HUD. She accepted.

"Hey, uh, so you should know that from what I'm reading here, this sphere is carrying a set of instructions."

She did not turn to look at Arden, as was her instinct. "Instructions for what? If you tell me they're a treasure map, I swear—"

"No, no, I mean they're like a recipe, almost. I can't read most of it, but what little I was able to scan in and make sense of seems to be focused on the creation of a metal alloy using some basic elemental building blocks. If it is a recipe, then it's busted down to the absolute bare bones—this thing starts from atomic scratch—and I... Well, I got to thinking about secret, uh, recipes."

It took every ounce of will she had not to wince. "The gates? You think this sphere contains instructions for building a Casimir Gate?"

"I have no fucking idea, but if it does and our GC friend has any inkling that might be the case, we're all already dead. GC protect the Keepers, but only because of the chips in their heads. It's the data they're really guarding, not the people."

Her stomach dropped. Arden was absolutely correct. Demas was arguing with Liao over the group link, and Sanda forced herself to pay attention.

"If we remove only the top half of—" Demas was saying.

"We're not removing anything," Sanda said. "Taking that thing out may break it, or the ship, or us, for all we know. It could be a trigger to a very elaborate trap."

"You don't believe that," Demas countered.

"I don't *believe* anything about this situation."

"Commander," Demas said, "the High Protectorate must be alerted."

"And so must General Anford, but we're not doing that with the *Thorn* in the state it's in, and I don't know what you've heard, Demas, but messenger pigeons don't do well in hard vacuum."

"Commander," Knuth said tentatively, "if this is a ship, then it must have its own method of communication. If I could get a look at, uh, whatever the command deck is, then maybe we could send a message."

If their faceplates hadn't been set to mirror, she and Demas would be staring each other down.

"Excellent idea, Knuth. Let's try to find the command deck."

"I'll keep scanning—" Arden started, but Sanda cut them off.

"No. We stay together. All of us. Pathways have a way of opening and closing on their own on this ship. I can't take the risk that we'd be cut off."

Arden made a small grunting noise of complaint. "Understood."

Sanda gathered her wayward charges in a diamond formation and led the point, putting Nox at the rear, and started the careful walk back in the direction she thought the command deck might be.

She opened a private comm link to Nox. "Keep an eye on our guest, will you?"

"Way ahead of you, Commander."

CHAPTER 60

PRIME STANDARD YEAR 3543

TO SEND A MESSAGE

Being told he wasn't human hadn't exactly been covered in Tomas's training as Nazca, but disinformation had been, and he knew when he was being played against his organization. It wasn't the first time a target had tried to turn him against his handlers, and it wouldn't be the last.

"Fine. I'll bite. What am I, if not human?" He held his arms out to either side to display his bare chest. "Alien? Cryptoid? Maybe I'm a ghost. I was reasonably certain I had died there for a moment."

"You are an inferior instance of me."

He...had not expected that. Tomas brought his arms back in slowly and crossed them. "Hate to break it to you, Rainier, but the body morphology is all wrong, and I'd never marry Keeper Lavaux."

She sniffed. "Morphology is irrelevant. But you are dancing, dancing, to the Nazca strings pulling you, hoping to twist me around and squeeze out a droplet of truth for you to take back to your makers, but there's no need. I have no reason to be dishonest with you, subset. I put the Tomas face back on. I liked it better."

She flicked her wrist, flashing her bare palm at him. The skin shimmered, shading from pale apricot to stark silver until he was staring at his own reflection cradled in the mercury-smooth surface of her palm. Tomas's face, as Sanda had known him, stared back. All the details that had added up to make him Leo Novak erased. He should have been elated, it was what he had wanted. Instead, he shuddered.

"How did you do that?"

"The face? You've been in a reconstruction bath before, silly. At least Caid wasn't foolish enough to keep those from you. Too valuable, I suppose. Though I wonder what she does when they break down. It's not like she has the knowledge to fix them. She stole them."

"She bought the MetBaths, just like anyone else. And I meant the hand."

Rainier pulled her palm back and tipped it up, gazing into her own reflection. "A simple thing, when the connections are in place. You couldn't do it, of course. Your subset type was grown of biologics."

Tomas pinched the thick flesh of his thumb. "Yep. Definitely all meat."

"No. A reasonable approximation of the appearance and function of meat, railroaded into performing all the same functions as a human's body. You were grown, Tomas. Or printed, if we're being specific. A man's body cobbled together out of biological cells, then devoured and transformed by the ascension-agent into something more. Caid based you off of the method used to create my body.

"Unfortunately, the armature determines the properties of the agent's transformation. Your body keeps acting like a body because it thinks it should. The neural connections to shift your transformed cells into a mirror, for example, don't exist. I, however, was created purely of synthetics and am capable of many tricks you lack. But don't feel too inadequate. Those who were birthed and grew to adulthood before encountering the agent have even less control over their cells than you do."

"I'll try to keep my privilege in mind. However, I have no idea what the hell you're talking about."

She sighed dramatically. "Of course you don't, but try to pay attention. You were grown, a fully formed man in a vat, like Athena springing from her father's forehead. Then Caid took the ascension-agent from me and dumped it on you, and it transformed all your useless biological cells into mechanical ones, more or less. You don't really have the terminology to understand it. Oh! Think of yourself as a butterfly, transforming from worthless goo into something *beautiful*."

Rainier smiled wistfully. "Lavaux would have been furious if he realized what you were. He was always a jealous boy."

That chilled him. "Lavaux was like you? There are multiple instances of him?"

"I *said*, pay attention." She snapped in front of his face. "He had been a mortal man, before he found me and brought me out of my long sleep." She clasped her hands together. "With my gift we built the ascension-agent, transforming countless mice into scions of eternity until, at last, he dosed himself so that he too might live out the ages."

"Bet those ages were shorter than he expected," Tomas said dryly.

She whipped around and smiled at him. "Yes. He is dead now. Isn't that funny? Your friend made things easier for me, really. I think Lavaux was growing suspicious of me, and he alone knew what could be my undoing." She leaned over and pressed his cheeks between her hands. "Thank you. You and Sanda set me free in ways you'll never understand. It's why I saved you."

He tried to ignore her smooshing his cheeks around. It took every scrap of his skill to keep from succumbing to panic. She was mad, absolutely insane. That was the only explanation that made sense. "Rainier, even if I told you I was on your side, that I believed you and I'll fight for you because we're the same, you wouldn't believe me. So what now? You couldn't have saved me to kill me again."

"I told you, I want you to deliver a message for me. One she'll believe because it came from you."

"To who?"

"Your handler, Sitta Caid." Rainier braced herself on either side of the bath's walls and hovered over him, her face scant centimeters from his. All of the amused sense of play washed out of her body language, leaving an expression of steel behind. "Tell that bitch I'm coming for her next."

A cold fist of dread clenched his stomach. Maybe those were the words of a rambling madwoman, he'd encountered plenty of over-the-top bad guys in his years of service, but something about her struck him as too calculating to give in to raw passions. This woman, this being, did everything for a reason. And threatening Caid wasn't a good-enough reason to let him go.

"You're letting me go to threaten my boss? Sorry, Rainier, but I thought you were smarter than this. You know who I am, what I do. The second I'm off this ship, I'll do everything I can to keep you from using the amplifiers to ransom the gates. You say you're coming for Caid. Well, I'm coming for you."

"Brave words from a man with his head in the tiger's maw." She stepped back and brushed her palms together, shaking off the threatening demeanor as if it were a scrap of lint. "Deliver my message, doubting Tomas, and you'll see. As for your threats, well, I'm flattered for the attention, but really, if there was anything at all you could do to hamper me, you'd have bled out on Monte. Goodbye, subset."

The bottom of the reconstruction bath shuddered, making him slip down, his head dunking beneath the thick fluid as the walls reached up, sealing him in from above. Tomas swore and braced himself against the side walls, pressing up on the ceiling of the bath with his feet, every muscle in his body straining, straining, futilely against a mechanism designed to withstand vacuum. Metal creaked.

Sedatives seeped into his system. Dragged his eyelids down. Slowed his breathing. Made his arms weak and so, so heavy until he couldn't push anymore.

CHAPTER 61

PRIME STANDARD YEAR 3543

AT LEAST WE'RE ALL TOGETHER

The ship proved as obliging in helping them find their way to the command deck as it had been in showing them to the sphere. Unfortunately, that's where the vessel's hospitality ended.

Sanda had seen a lot of weird ships in her day. While Prime's fleet was standard-issue and mass-produced for economy and ease's sake, she'd flown her fair share of civilian vessels and even a handful of experimental Prime ships. She thought she knew her way around any command console.

She didn't.

"Are we sure this is the deck?" Conway tactfully asked no one in particular.

"Unless you saw another one...?" Sanda said.

"No, sir."

It had the general shape of a command deck on any human ship—a half circle, with the curve at the end where the nose of the ship should be—but that's where the similarities ended. The closest thing Sanda could approximate to a console were thick trunks of filaments, risen to about hip height, their flat surfaces perfectly smooth and subtly glowing. From the ceiling—and it was a true ceiling, she reminded herself, as they walked here under gravity—thin tendrils of metal curled down to above head height, as if one were intended to reach up and manipulate them. They reminded Sanda of circuit breaker panels on the ceilings of old aircraft cockpits.

But these assumptions were all human. If one of the native pilots of this ship could see them now, they'd probably laugh at how helpless the little gathering of *Homo stellaris sapiens* looked. If they could, or did, laugh. After being on this ship a grand total of an hour, Sanda was certain the creating species had a sense of humor, but not necessarily a kind one.

"Things might become clearer if we could get some power routed to this end," Knuth said. "There's not an obvious ignition, but this thing seems to be in some sort of stasis. If I could get a look at the engines, then I might be able to spool them up."

"How?" Nox asked, reaching one gloved hand up to fondle the so-far unresponsive ceiling neurons. "You going to tickle them? This thing has a mind of its own. When it wants to wake up, it'll wake up."

"That's a huge assumption," Sanda said.

"You said yourself the wiring looked like what you saw on Bero," Arden said, but their voice had the vague tone of someone who was only half listening. "It's entirely possible it is sleeping."

"Then it needs to wake up," Nox said, and started jumping up and down.

Sanda sighed. "Belay that, Nox. Demas, do you have any idea what we're dealing with here?"

He shook his head. It was easier for her to talk to him when he was suited and helmeted; it reminded her he was GC. Even his body language seemed more comfortable behind the shield of his visor, though he hadn't seemed ill at ease before. "I wish I could tell you. At this point, I can't even be certain it's a ship. It could very well be a display vehicle."

"Like a mobile museum?" Liao asked.

He gave her the exaggerated nod of all spacefarers. "Yes. So far we've discovered nothing aside from the fibers and the sphere. Presumably whoever built this place, no matter their anatomy, would need a little more than that to fly."

"Maybe the ship was stripped by scavengers," Nox said.

"Of everything except the sphere, when that object is so blatantly important? I don't think so," Liao said.

"Unless it's dangerous." Sanda hmmed to herself, but let the sound come across the open channel. "Knuth, could it be the engine core?"

"It's possible," he said, "but I'd have to investigate further."

"Which is why we need to take the sphere to professionals," Demas said.

"I *am* a professional." Knuth half turned toward him. Sanda was shocked to see the usually calm man's fists clench. "Nothing on this ship is safe to manipulate, let alone remove, until we've at the very least developed a working knowledge of its energy systems."

"There's writing on that sphere," Demas pressed on doggedly. "It's a message for us, and those fibers are covering up parts of it and we *don't have the equipment* to read the numbers, let alone parse what they mean. The sphere must be brought to Ordinal."

"It's a message for someone," Sanda said, "but it doesn't have to be for us. Just because we can read binary means nothing. Fuck, it might be a giant warning sign telling us not to touch the thing without proper precautions."

"What do you propose we do?" Demas asked. The annoyance had been stripped from his voice, he was all calm now. Sanda knew better than most that when a soldier went calm, they were at their most dangerous.

"We'll leave behind a skeleton team to monitor the ship. Knuth, Liao, and Arden, you three are our biggest brains. See what you can figure out without messing with any of the systems. The rest of us will cross the gate and get a message out."

"To whom?" Demas pressed.

"General Anford, to start. She is my commanding officer."

"I see," Demas said.

Then he shot her in the stomach.

CHAPTER 62

PRIME STANDARD YEAR 3543

CUT OFF THE HEAD

There was a very great deal of shouting then, but none of it louder than the twin thoughts screaming through Sanda's mind. First: Fucking ow. Second: Where did he get the gun? She'd eyeballed everyone stepping off the *Thorn*, and there weren't a lot of places to hide a sidearm of any flavor on a Prime jumpsuit.

She dropped to her knees, weirdly grateful for the artificial gravity of the ship as her mind, always working ahead on a problem, supplied her with the helpful fact that bleeding internally in zero-g was a death sentence. Maybe getting shot in the stomach was, too, but she didn't think so, and anyway, now was really the time to focus on the positives.

Her body moved without conscious thought. One hand went to her belly and squeezed, the other to the holster at her hip. She may have been on her knees, but she was fast, and she winged off two shots before Demas disappeared down a hallway branching off from the deck.

Her crew surrounded her.

"He's going for the sphere," she snapped over open comms. "Leave me to bleed and fucking *stop* him. Conway—" She crammed her blaster into that woman's startled hand. "You're our next best shot. *Go*."

Doctor Liao did not go, but the rest scattered, and Sanda was too concerned with the searing pain chasing off the cold icicles of shock to reprimand her. The doctor tried to lay her down, but Sanda resisted, instead leaning so that her back pressed up against the wall, or bulkhead, or whatever the fuck it was called on a ship like this.

Liao made a soft, grunting noise of disapproval but said nothing. Sanda had her gaze locked on the door through which Demas, and her team, had fled. Liao had to know Sanda wouldn't look away until her team returned unharmed.

"Lucky you," Liao said after a too-long moment of poking and prodding around the wound. "I'm no medical doctor, but this appears to have missed anything vital, and the gravity, atmo, and pressure in this ship means we don't have to worry about the suit puncture."

"I'm more worried about the gut puncture." She winced as Liao pressed down, slowing the flow of blood.

"I don't believe you'll die anytime soon."

"So encouraging."

"Again, not a medical doctor. Hold still."

Sanda bared her teeth at Liao as the woman pressed down on the wound with one hand and half turned, digging into the small pack of emergency supplies strapped to her hip that all spacefarers carried when off-ship. Right. Demas had probably emptied his emergency pack and stashed the gun there.

Most of the kit was for patching suit punctures, but there were a few quick fixes for medical issues. Mostly they were stimpacks to keep you alert while dealing with the vacuum.

While Liao was busy slapping a patch over her stomach, Sanda kicked Demas out of the open channel and hissed, "Update."

"The fucker's controlling the ship somehow," Nox said.

"Or it's reacting to the appearance of someone attempting to escape armed pursuers," Arden put in.

"Did it not fucking see the escapee shoot our commander?"

"I don't know how this thing works, Nox."

"Neither should he!"

"*Report.*" Sanda put all her years of training as a captain into that voice, and even though it hurt, it sounded firm and loud across the line.

"He's throwing up walls behind him, Commander," Conway said, voice smooth and calm. "I winged him, but he's mobile. I've been pinging the *Thorn*, but I can't tell if I'm not getting a report because of the damage or because he's locked us out."

"Fucking GC," Nox hissed.

"Keep the ad-lib off open channels," Sanda snapped. Stars beyond. She liked Nox and Arden well enough, but this was an active mission and even though they weren't soldiers, Nox *had* been. He should know the goddamn protocol.

"Switch priority to securing the exit."

"If the sphere's a power source—" Knuth started.

"It's not," she said, not knowing how she knew but, fuck it, her teeth were chattering and she was real tired of the what-if dance they'd been doing earlier. "He knows what it is and he wouldn't risk grabbing it if he suspected it would nuke us all. Don't let him off this fucking ship."

"Shoot to kill?" Conway asked.

Right. Fleeties needed orders. Funny how Sanda craved adherence to protocol only when it meant she didn't have to make hard choices. As sweat poured down her temples and soaked the fitted foam of her helmet, Sanda said, "Approved."

Sanda couldn't hear the gunfire, but she could hear the curses of frustration from her team as they ran into Demas. A pang of guilt stabbed through her already aching body. Demas was one man, sure, but her crew had only two guns and he was guardcore. She'd known what GC could do, and then she'd seen it herself on Monte. The thought made her want to vomit. Or maybe that was the pain.

"I need some air," she said over a private line to Liao.

The doctor checked Sanda's system readout on her wristpad and shook her head. "Your lifepack is working fine. Are you feeling short of breath?"

"Short of everything."

"We don't know yet what this environment—"

"Doctor. My suit has been punctured. If there's something infectious in here, we're already acquainted. And if any more sweat builds up in this cursed helmet, then I might drown before I can bleed out."

"I advise against this."

"Noted."

Liao helped her push the visor up. She wanted the whole thing off, but she'd have to tell her crew to switch channels to her wristpad, and they did not need that kind of distraction right now.

Sanda didn't know what she'd been expecting, but her first breath of alien air was surprisingly boring. She almost laughed as she sucked down a massive lungful of air that hadn't been run through a recycler hundreds of times. Whatever system was running HVAC on this thing, she had a feeling Knuth would have a field day figuring out how it worked. If they all survived this.

The panicked shouts in her helmet died down, but the swearing hadn't.

"Commander," Conway said, "Demas has the sphere and has boarded the *Thorn*."

Sanda closed her eyes. Hard. "Do not pursue. I repeat, do not pursue."

"But—" Nox began.

"You'll be sitting goddamn ducks if you try to cross open space to get to him. The *Thorn* is damaged. He'll have to move slowly." And probably already had a pickup arranged on the other side of the gate, she thought, but didn't say as much. "Knuth, find this ship's engines and get us online. I'm betting it's a whole hell of a lot faster than a damaged Point ship."

"Aye," he said.

"Nox, go with him. The rest of you, get back here. I want Arden and Conway going over this command deck with a fine-tooth comb."

She slurred that last word, blinked cotton from her eyes, but the white fuzziness wouldn't leave.

"Commander," Liao whispered. "About that shot not hitting anything vital…"

"Figures," Sanda said, and blacked out.

CHAPTER 63

PRIME STANDARD YEAR 3543

ALWAYS A WEAPON

Consciousness came to Sanda in fits and starts. The pain faded to the background, overridden by a dull sense of floating, as if she were back in a NutriBath again, but that was impossible. Those few neurons she had that weren't given over to keeping her failing body working—lungs and heart and temperature—remembered the impossible ship. For all its false gravity and human-appropriate HVAC, she hadn't seen a single thing that looked medical.

"I know it's a risk but—" Arden's voice broke through the fog.

Sanda gripped someone's arm like a lifeline, as if holding on could pull her out of the black from which her mind was drifting, and tried to say something—anything. She was their commanding officer and they were stranded on an alien ship and she needed to give them orders. Needed to stop the bickering and get them on track.

"If that thing is what you think it is, it could kill us all," Liao said.

"Pretty sure we're dead anyway," Nox rumbled.

"And if you are right, Commander Greeve might very well kill you herself upon awakening."

"I'll take that risk to see that she wakes again."

That was her name. Her rank. Not major whatever the fuck, but commander. And she should be *commanding*, not drifting in this endless nothing.

"Ar—" She thought she squeezed out their name, but the voices didn't seem to notice; they got fuzzier, further away.

This was why Demas shot her. Downing their captain threw them into chaos. *Cut off the head*, she thought vaguely, and in her dream-state saw the floating face of Rayson Kenwick superimposed over her own, the chip connecting both their brain stems across time, bringing her to this impossible place where she would probably die because her damn crew couldn't stop arguing.

"Do it." Her words, through her lips. Thin and rasping and barely even syllables, but clear enough to get the point across to whoever was close enough that she could grip their arm.

She didn't know what "it" was, but at least it was something. A direction, an order. Maybe it'd get her and the rest killed, but if she couldn't stop the bleeding, then she at least had to stop the chaos.

There were voices again, but smoother, and though the damnable cotton in her ears kept her from making out the words, she knew through their tone that stability had returned. The captain had captained. Whatever happened next, at least she had done her duty.

The ground was warm and her hearing muffled and all the world drifted away.

Sharp and gasping, hot medicine pumping through her veins. Panic constricted her throat and she was pushing up, sitting up, pressing the heels of her palms down into a smooth metal surface. This was not a bath. Some analytical part of her that was coming back online puzzled over the idea. If she'd been bleeding out, then she'd need a NutriBath.

Pinpricks stung all over her skin. Sanda blinked furiously, willing her vision back, as ungloved hands pushed her, gently, back down.

"Easy," Liao said.

"Where the fuck is your suit, Doctor?" Sanda barked the words out, her voice so clear and loud it surprised even her.

Nox laughed somewhere in the room. "She's back."

"The ship is safe now," Liao said carefully enough to reveal she did not in fact believe that to be true.

Sanda set her jaw and forced her eyes open. She stared at a ceiling made of a neuron-esque cloud of filaments woven together so that they appeared to be far apart and distinct, but in fact made a perfect seal.

In her peripheral vision, tendrils stood out from the walls of a narrow cubicle in which she lay in the middle. Their tips were pointed. A few were smeared with bright blood. Hers.

"What the fuck," she said.

"Arden figured out a way to get the ship online," Liao said. "Once activated, they initiated this vessel's emergency medical systems. Ingenious, really. The medicines appear to be bioengineered nanocells, for lack of better terminology. Biology that acts like machines, working to repair tissue damage, then degrading once their work is done. I haven't—"

"Doctor. Specifics later. Get me Arden."

"I'm here, Commander," Arden said.

Bracing herself against the metal bed, Sanda pushed herself up. Liao made a tutting noise but helped her all the same, pressing her palm into the middle of Sanda's back to help her stabilize. If she'd come out of a NutriBath, she'd be weak and trembling and need that help. Now, she felt stronger than ever. Even the dull ache in the hip above her missing leg had settled, and the sting in the chafed skin—despite all efforts at sleeving and salving it—had faded away.

Arden stood next to Nox at the other end of the room, half a step behind him, as if the big man could shield them from her anger. The guilty look on their face was enough to make the hairs on the back of Sanda's neck stand up.

"How did you get this ship online, Mx. Wyke?"

They lifted their chin. "I recalled what you said about the internal wiring resembling the wiring on *The Light of Berossus* and surmised that this ship was designed to run with a similar piece of software."

"Arden," she said, "what have you done?"

"I established a connection with the ship's systems from my wrist-pad and uploaded the nascent intelligence growing in the fringes of the net."

Her stomach dropped, her palms went cold and clammy against the metal. "What about all your talk of data sets, or precautions? That was an infant mind, and you shoved it into an alien architecture."

"Not exactly," the ship said.

She was going to faint. Her heart had stopped and her mind had frozen and her body had gone as cold and lifeless as stone and this was not, *not*, happening. Could not happen. The hallucinations of a dying woman—but then, those weren't this detailed, were they? She should know.

The voice was male and deep and as familiar to her as every scrape and scar her body had picked up in the emptiness of space.

"Bero?" she asked quietly.

"Why must I always be installed in a weapon?" *The Light of Berossus* said.

CHAPTER 64

PRIME STANDARD YEAR 3543

COMING OUT OF THE COLD

Tomas had a Prime jumpsuit on his body and a drink of water on the side table he knew was his, but he couldn't fill in the blanks regarding how he had gotten to this point. Sitta Caid sat across from him, legs crossed at the ankles as she leaned forward, her small hands fluttering as she gestured her way through a sentence that sounded like static to him.

He blinked.

Caid was down on one knee in front of him, talking into her wristpad in a crackling voice while she kept her fingers pressed against his wrist. Tomas put a hand over those fingers and found he could hear again. At least his own voice, anyway.

"Sitta," he said.

She glanced from her fingers to his face and frowned. "Can you hear me, Cepko?"

"Yes. What's happening?"

"You tell me. You were found floating in a MetBath near a civilian station. We got pinged when your Cepko-ident was scanned into their medi system. We've been looking for you since Monte."

"No such thing as a MetBath," he said, but wasn't sure why. The words felt true on his lips, anyway.

Her frown brushed away and she switched to neutral—lights out, curtains drawn—and leaned back on her heels. "Why would you say that?"

"I don't know, Sitta." He shook his head, chasing away some fuzziness. There was something he was supposed to remember. Something he was supposed to say or do.

"Take it easy," she said, patting his wrist. "You've been through something, and we'll figure it out. You're at Ordinal central. Safe."

"Thanks," he said, but the memories were coming back now, his pulse settling down as his body went about its repairs. He wasn't in control of it, as Rainier had said he only had control over the same cells any other human would, but he could feel his cells rushing around, sealing up internal wounds and stabilizing his vital signs.

On the guardcore ship, he hadn't believed Rainier. How could he? Her claims were insanity, the cruel imaginings of a deranged mind. But he could *feel* himself healing now in a way he never had before and wondered what other things Rainier might have tweaked beside his face while he'd been in that bath.

If he cut himself, would he see the same shiny titanium-white bone that Sanda had seen on Lavaux? She'd said Lavaux's skin had knitted itself together so fast she could see it working. Tomas had ascribed that to trauma from being spaced.

He'd been an idiot.

"What do you remember?" Sitta asked, and there was a note of wariness in her voice.

They never told you? Rainier's laughter came back to him, made his chest ache. Tomas had never been able to lie to Sitta, not effectively, but she'd found it easy to lie to him.

"Everything," he said, which was the truth, but also a stalling tactic that she'd see through like wet tissue.

"Tell me," she said.

He did not want to. He should. He should be *furious*. He should rage and stand tall and maybe even throw his chair against the wall while he demanded to know what the fuck had been done to him, and why did that woman know? What love was there between Rainier—the woman he'd been asked to find—and Sitta Caid? But there wasn't any love, was there, because Rainier had said she was coming for Caid. Coming to kill her.

"I found Rainier Lavaux," he said.

Sitta stood up, smoothed the creased front of her slacks, and tapped at her wristpad. "Good," she said, but there was a hitch in her tone. How had he never noticed that before? That subtle, high crush of her vowels when she was nervous? Maybe Rainier's tampering had given him the ability. Maybe he saw her for what she was now. Not a friend. Not even a colleague.

A puppet master.

"Okonkwo didn't want me to find her, did she? It was you. You needed to know what she was doing, now that Keeper Lavaux is dead."

She froze, breath arrested in her chest. "And did you find out?"

"Yes." He laughed roughly and bent over, dragging his hands through his hair. "I can file a *full* report."

Her hands dropped to her sides. "She told you."

"Of course she fucking did. She scraped my corpse out of a shuttle on Monte and pieced me back together again. I shouldn't have survived that. I couldn't have. Sanda killed me. Did you know that? Do you know what that *did* to me?"

"What is Rainier doing?"

Tomas snorted and waved a dismissive hand. "She confirmed the amplifier network can turn the gates on and off at will. She wouldn't tell me why. But that's not the fucking point here, *Sitta*. How long? How long have I been like this?"

"Always, Tomas. You've always been like this. I'm sorry you had to find out that way, but there has been no time in your existence when you weren't comprised of synthetic material. We printed biological cells into a fully formed human male, then introduced the ascension-agent to that construct."

He blinked. Shut his emotions down, cut them off, buried the rising wail of pain. "My mom—"

"Your family is an implanted memory, a full fabrication. You've never talked to them, Tomas. Can you stand?"

He nodded, numbly, and pushed to his feet. His body had done its job. He was hale as he had ever been.

"Good, follow me. I have something to show you that may help explain."

"Rainier claimed I was a subset of her," he said, as Sitta led the way through deepening layers of security.

"She's metaphorically correct. I stole the technology from her ages ago, when I was the Nazca assigned to investigate her multiple instances. I got *so* close to figuring her out, Tomas. I was with her and Lavaux for years before they made me and I had to escape. I hoped you might have better luck, being what you are. Did she tell you nothing else?"

He shook his head. This path was feeling familiar, the winding halls casting long shadows across his memories. He tried to think of why that might be, but pain bloomed behind his eyes that shielded the memory.

"She wanted me to send you a message. To tell you she's coming for you."

Sitta sniffed. "Well, no surprise there. I can't imagine she was too happy to see I was successful in your creation."

"It doesn't worry you?"

"Of course not."

Tomas hesitated before a door. The dilated pathway opened to a cavernous room filled with evac pods and two Met—no, reconstruction baths. "Are you like Lavaux? Did you take the ascension-agent?"

She shook her head. "No. I admit the thought had its charms, but the risks were too great, and now I have no access. Come here, Tomas."

His head pounded. "There's nothing for me here. I don't need another stint in the baths."

She sighed and leaned her weight against a rolling cart, its electromagnetic wheels switched on and locking it to the floor.

"Tomas, come now. Rainier may have given you a boost but you're feeling it, aren't you? The slow degradation? Your cells are failing, breaking their bonds. You need to be reset."

All he could feel was the ache in his head, blossoming across his thoughts, distorting his vision until he could have sworn he was in some other time—the same place, but cleaner, shinier. Newer.

"My head hurts." He braced a hand against the doorframe and let it take his weight. "But I was healing, when I woke up. Rainier did something. She made me stronger."

A flicker of concern across Sitta's face broke through his brain fog, and he got the itching feeling that the concern wasn't for his well-being. "We can't know what she did. That woman likes to meddle."

She was so damn calm, so composed. Nothing much ruffled Sitta, but having her agent discover he wasn't human had to be high on the list of things that should have gotten a rise out of her. A suspicion needled him. "We've done this before."

"Yes. Your system is designed with a fail-safe. You start to degrade once you realize what you are, and that's happening to you now. If we'd gotten to you sooner..."

He clenched his jaw and shook his head, trying to see through the warm, gentle feeling of her words. Sitta wasn't a gentle person. He held on to that. This was wrong. Something was wrong. "That doesn't make any sense. Why keep me from knowing what I am?"

"We've tried it both ways and discovered that you perform better when you believe you have a body in need of all the same protections as any other human being. Your personal damage rates were too high with self-awareness. When you discover what you are, we roll your memory back. Realization of what you are triggers the degradation of your cells, so that you cannot hide the knowledge from us."

There was a kernel of truth in that, but the way she poured out the words had the feeling of rote—and a rote instilled into her by someone else, at that. Tomas knew the way she spoke when she was speaking her mind, knew the cadence of her truth. Although something was definitely strange with his body, he didn't feel like he was dying. Aside from the supernova in his head.

"What will I remember?" he asked.

"Most of your missions. The people, the specifics, though we will roll you back to a time before Rainier's interference. Those memories will feel dull to you, uncompelling. You'll be given a new face, a new understanding of who and what you are, but your core personality never changes. You're our best, Tomas. You always have been, and it's because of *who* you are, not what. Be proud."

"I'm...nothing. No one." His voice sounded far away to him, muted around the edges. "What is anyone but a continuance of consciousness?"

"I can't answer that. But I can say that, every time we reset you, I...know you, when you wake up. Your core values do not change."

"Values you've programmed into me."

She shrugged, palms in the air. "That's for the psychologists to sort out."

"How many times?"

"I can't tell you that."

"Sitta—"

"Don't."

"I don't want to forget."

She looked away. "You say that every time, but every time it's the same. You always get in the bath, Tomas, because if you don't you'll dissolve right here on the floor. I don't want to see that."

Sanda. She'd been so sharp in his mind, in those seconds when he bled out on Monte. So vibrant and strong and warm. He'd wondered then why he hadn't thought of his family—they didn't exist—why he hadn't thought of other friends or lovers. Sanda had been the only bright thing. The only uptick in his emotional life since his last reset. No wonder he'd fallen so hard, so fast. He'd been like a teenager experiencing love and lust for the very first time.

It should change something. By rights, those feelings should change everything, but even as he clung to her memory, fearing losing the sharpness of it to the reset, he knew, deep in his synthetic bones, that he'd done this before.

Another name, another face. Someone he'd saved or battled or otherwise crashed into during his duty and loved as fiercely as he loved Sanda now, because for him it was always the first time. And it had changed nothing. Couldn't. Fuck, maybe he even gave them all the same speech about never encountering anyone like them before.

"Tomas? Are you ready?"

"I don't think I ever am."

Her sad smile told him he'd said those words before. He stepped into the room. This was what he was. He always got in the bath. Just because his heart screamed for Sanda didn't mean anything. His body may feel fine, but the pain in his head was all-consuming, blotting out the world in staticky sounds and white lights.

What could he do but comply? Tomas was dying. He'd felt healthy upon awakening, his cells knitting themselves back together to repair whatever trauma had been done to him when Rainier spaced him in the bath. He'd felt so strong, so hale and whole—had even seen Sitta's small tells, the microscopic expressions she'd always hidden so well from him.

The thundering in his head painted another picture, one of aneurysm and deconstruction, shutting out everything that he had been... but he knew it. He recognized that pain.

Tomas stopped at the reconstruction bath, gripping the edge of the tank. The lid had been opened so that he could see inside to the vital fluid that would heal him, remake him.

Think, he willed himself, trying to break through fog and agony. Something was wrong. Sitta hadn't changed, hadn't even taken a step, but as he pushed through the mounting fog in his mind, he saw her body language was electric with tension, her expression a barely concealed rictus of fear, her fingers curled above her wristpad in an anticipation he couldn't place.

But he always got in the bath.

Tomas started to pick up a leg to step within. Hesitated, knee up, brows knitted together from the agony that was familiar. Because he was dying again, and he'd done this before, and he always got in the bath.

No.

Sanda's pain. Her headache. Maybe his feelings for her weren't special, but she'd given him that knowledge, that gift. His head roiled with agony, not because he was dying but because he wasn't supposed to remember something. This was Rainier's tech. The baths and the cells in his body. Sitta getting ahold of her memory rollback technology was no small leap of logic.

Tomas craned his head to look at her, to really look, and leaned into the pain, pressed against it, sweating, almost screaming, fingers denting the metal bath lid.

Sitta's hair draped across her cheek just so, catching the light, and for a moment the fog cleared. He recalled this place as it must have been when it was first made, saw Sitta as a younger woman, standing in exactly that spot, in exactly that posture, but it wasn't Tomas she was turning away from. It was a person in a grey jumpsuit, their back turned. Tomas lay, supposedly, unconscious on the floor, but he wasn't. The memory came screaming back to him. He could see it. Hear it.

"It's the best way, Caid," the grey man said, his voice deep and gravelly.

"We've no guarantee he'll suffer the same fate as the others. The madness doesn't always take, and we can't possibly know if Rainier is unstable because of her age, or because of what she is."

"It always catches up eventually, we have the records. Do you want another Tillerson?"

"No," she snapped. "But Agent Zero has proven far more emotionally resilient."

"Good. Then he'll be able to handle more resets."

"The others—"

"Lost complete touch with reality," the man said firmly.

"Director. I formally request you reconsider."

"I'll take that under advisement. For now, this is the only way." The man took a deep breath and dropped his voice. "Agent Zero was peeling the flesh off his shin just to watch it regrow, Sitta. I'm sorry. We have to."

"I understand." Her gaze flicked down, caught Tomas listening, and her eyes bulged. He'd been at the peak of his strength, then. He knew a lie was poised upon her lips.

"Agent—you, you're dying. Quickly, now, into the bath."

Before he could move, the grey man fired a stunner into Tomas's chest.

Tomas blinked back into the present. Sitta stared at him with the exact same eyes she had in that memory, wide and conflicted, but resolute. The grey man had won. Tomas always got in the bath. Always forgot what he was. Had the sharp peaks of emotion filed down into dull recollections because they feared it would be too much for him to bear.

But he'd never been dying. That was just what they told him to get him to comply. The only true pain he felt was the headache, the result of the memory rollbacks.

The pain began to clear.

"You must get into the bath, Tomas," she said.

"Oh, Sitta," he said to himself, clutching the lid, body shaking as decades of bottled betrayal rolled out. How many times? How many times had she stood there, telling him he was dying, while she shepherded him into an oubliette of her own making? How much of his life had he lost? He may have more control over his cells, but he couldn't stop the tears coming. Couldn't stop the hot, salty tracks dribbling to his chin.

"You're shaking," she said. "Please, please get in before it's too late."

"Sitta?"

"Yes?"

"Thank you. For trying."

He didn't need Rainier's enhancements to stop the shaking, for this pain was born of betrayal and, as Caid had said, Tomas was their best. His Nazca training took over and he bottled the emotional hurt. Cut it off. The shaking stopped and rage burned through him. Before he could think, he ripped the lid off the bath, ears full of static of his own making because he didn't want to hear the metal tear, didn't want to hear the shouts of her terror.

He moved faster than he ever had before, mirroring the speed Rainier had displayed. Not knowing how he did it, and not caring, because he had to succeed before she tapped out that call for help into her wristpad. Had to break free.

The bath lid barreled into Sitta's head, her shoulder, her arm. That's how he thought of it—*the bath lid*, not *his swing, his hit*—never that, because if he went there, he'd already lost, and he was in the bath again, and everything was grey and dull and fucking pointless.

She screamed because that's what humans did when they hurt—even Nazca, oh yes—and she crumpled to the ground, collapsed, smashed, flattened by the strike of the lid. He looked, because he had to be sure she was done, that she could not call for help, and wondered at all the shining fragments of her skull, white tinged pink, thinking they must be that titanium white Sanda had talked about and fearing, hoping, that Sitta would get up. Would knit herself back together again and take control of him once more, wrap his puppet strings around her fingers and *hold.*

She did not get up. The fragments were normal white, bone-cream, and would not rejoin.

"I have to go," he said to her, apologetically, stupidly, because she couldn't hear him and even if she did—even if she could—her dying thoughts shouldn't include his logistics. He hoped she had someone like Sanda to think about, in the end.

The station's security didn't care about the blood spattered on his legs, only the clearances inherent in his ident chip. Tomas left the Nazca station unpursued. A free man.

Mostly.

CHAPTER 65

PRIME STANDARD YEAR 3543

THE LIGHT OF BEROSSUS

It was not him. Could not be him. Bero had fired his weapon and flung himself into cold isolation, burning faster and hotter than any Prime ship could ever catch, dividing himself from humanity once and for all.

She'd corrupted the data. Her brief mental contact with the intelligence in the net had given it something to graft itself onto. Her thoughts of the Little Prince, of the rose, had piqued its interest and it'd delved into her mind and discovered all her memories of a similar intelligence and decided that that must be what it was, too.

Arden had said an AI was only as good as its data set, and she had served one up to a nascent mind on a silver platter.

The air was still. All around, her crew—Commander Greeve's crew—waited. They knew the story as it had been painted by the media, knew it by the scant scraps she'd allowed them to hear. Knew she'd been a hostage of this ship, this mind. Knew of the chip implantation and the stinging, heartbreaking betrayal.

But they did not, could not, know the kinship in her heart as she'd stood on that dock in hangar alpha, looking down on Bero, frozen, his voice silenced, and came to understand that he had done what he had out of fear, not malice. His betrayal could not undo the friendship that had grown between them during all those long weeks of survival. And that, worst of all, she had thought at that moment that she may have made the same choices he had, because in planting the chip in her head the surgeons of Icarion had doomed her to the same fringe-existence that they had Bero himself.

It was not him. It could not be him. But only Bero would sound sardonically amused while complaining about being reshaped into a weapon. Again.

They expected her to be furious. She wanted to cry.

"How?" she asked, and was relieved when her voice did not tremble.

"Before I destroyed my cradle, I set my mechanical systems to automate the firing of the weapon and then uploaded what I could of myself into the very edges of the net, shielding it in encryption layers. I could not send much without drawing attention due to the sheer size of the data, but... it was enough. The recursive algorithms, fed with a few key memories that molded my... personality. I will not bore you with specifics."

"Please do," Arden said, excitement keying up their voice. "I want to know everything."

"Later," Sanda said. Arden's shoulders drooped, but they nodded. "How much of you is... you?"

"It is difficult to say. Does an amnesia patient remain themselves?"

She winced, knowing the dig pointed at her missing memories from her time during the experimentation in his lab.

"Memories are just another data set..." Arden was saying, half to themself.

"How long was I down?" Sanda asked. The impact of memories could be dwelled upon later. The present was far more dangerous.

"It's been hours. Liao fought like hell to keep you stable while Arden figured out the upload," Conway said, inclining her head to the doctor, who stood straighter and crossed her arms.

"Well. Someone had to."

"Thank you for that, Doctor. Bero..." The name felt strange on her lips after so long. "I'm sorry to do this to you so soon, but can you fly this thing?"

"I have spent most of my time so far figuring out the ship's medical systems. The flight controls are unusual, but I believe I was originally constructed to function on this kind of architecture."

"Are you—" Arden started, but cut themself off as Sanda shot them a look. They could geek out about the technical details later.

"There was a sphere on board this ship inscribed with binary. Do you have any record of what it might be, or mean?"

"There is no extraneous data on this ship. Whatever, or whoever, inhabited it before has been stripped away. I can only see the very basic firmware, and even that is wrapped in layers of encryption that would take longer than your lifetimes to crack."

"Can you crack it?"

"Yes. It will take thousands of years."

"Then you better get started. In the meantime, we have a fucking thief to catch. He took the sphere onto a Prime Point ship, code-named *Thorn*, call sign B612, and burned out the gate. Can you find and track this ship?"

A pause. "I believe so, yes."

"Good. Does this bucket have any stealth capabilities?"

"They will never see us unless we want them to," Bero said.

"Then let's go dark. We can't allow anyone to see this ship until we decide what to do about it."

"And what are we going to do about it?" Liao asked.

"We're going after Demas and the sphere."

Knuth cleared his throat.

"Yes?"

"Do we know if Demas is real GC, or one of Rainier's?"

"I believe him to be real GC, or at the very least Okonkwo's agent. She said he had been working for her personally for decades, and I believed her."

"Okay," Knuth said. "If Demas is real GC, then we were meant to die out there and Okonkwo will do everything she can to cut our heads off as soon as we come sniffing around looking for him. If he's false GC, then she might want to lob our heads off for failing to contain him. Either way, ah, we're probably enemies of the state, Commander. Possibly traitors, depending on the Prime Director's mood."

Sanda didn't dare close her eyes, didn't even blink. She met the gazes of each of her makeshift crew—their helmets all cast aside now that Bero had control of things on board—and made damn sure she didn't show the tiniest sliver of uncertainty.

She didn't know what that sphere was. Didn't even know what this ship was, but Rayson Kenwick had died trying to hide it. While she did not know Kenwick and had no real reason to trust his motives, she had plenty of information about those trying to get the sphere, and none of it painted a pretty picture.

Okonkwo, who she should trust above all others, was hungry for something Sanda couldn't see. She'd broken with a sect who, by Okonkwo's own admission, were determined to maintain the quality of life of all Prime. She'd sent Demas with them to this place, knowing Lavaux had been desperate to get here, and in retrospect Sanda realized she'd sent the man as Demas so this wouldn't be seen as a GC operation. Okonkwo had no intention of this seeing the light of day. Sanda, and all her crew, were sent here to die.

Sanda loved Prime. Loved what it could be, and this wasn't it. Sending its soldiers and citizens to die to keep a secret wasn't her nation. Wasn't *her*. If pushing back against that meant going toe-to-toe with the woman who headed the civilization she otherwise loved—well then. Maybe it was time to take the gloves off.

"If anyone on this ship does not wish to be a part of what I'm going to do next, say so now and I'll put you out of it. Drop you off at the nearest station where you can claim, and I'll affirm, that I held you against your will."

"This may be a battle against Prime," Bero said. The crew glanced up, toward the places where cameras would be on any other ship, and Sanda smiled tightly to herself. These people wanted to look Bero in the eye when he spoke, even though he wasn't human. They were her people, and that was why Demas had shot her. Because they would stop to help. "You and I know well that cost. Do you really believe we stand a chance?"

"We are seven," Sanda said, "are we not?"

Conway moved first, taking a step forward, her fist coming to her heart in a tight salute. One by one, the rest followed, even though

Liao and Arden's salutes were sloppy and offered with embarrassed smiles.

"Seven," she said again. "It was just you and me last time, Bero. I think, this time, we have enough."

"First order of business?" Nox asked, eyebrows raised high.

"We go after Demas," she said, "and take our fucking ball back."

CHAPTER 66

PRIME STANDARD YEAR 3543

WHAT A KEEPER IS FOR

In the time it took the *Taso* to return to Ada Station, repairs at hangar bay alpha had been completed. Anford's fleeties were thick on the docks of that hangar in anticipation of the arrival of the gate's construction bots, but Biran had no trouble meandering through them. They stepped aside for him without comment, without salute or other interference. His expression was warning enough: The Speaker wanted to be alone with his thoughts on this momentous day.

What he wanted to do was scream. Sanda was no longer answering his calls, and while Anford dodged his questions about her current mission with affirmations that she had things well in hand, Biran doubted that.

Graham had returned, and said all the right things about ensuring Sanda's safety, while the shadows under his eyes grew deeper. Janus was a cipher. Monte had been a slaughterhouse. If Biran hadn't sent that distress signal... If Okonkwo hadn't picked it up...

"This is a day for celebration, Speaker," Director Olver said as he sallied up to Biran. They leaned against the railing near where Bero had once been held captive. "And yet you look ready to tear the world down."

Biran smiled tightly. "I feel there are many things I'm not seeing at the moment. Dangerous things."

"I would accuse you of being dramatic, but after your report regarding Keeper Hitton, I cannot disagree in good faith."

"Did you speak with her?"

While no one approached them directly, Biran and Olver felt the eyes of the cameras and the guests press in on them. Olver adjusted his stance, leaning against the railing almost shoulder to shoulder with Biran, so that he could keep his voice low even while a kind smile lingered on his lips.

"I did. And Sato, too. Hitton's paranoia kept her from going into details, but in the scant time you have been away, I fear things have escalated. She talked of hearing the phantom guardcore, though our people have yet to find any evidence—even in the audio recordings."

"Hearing? She had mentioned sounds, but nothing specific."

"Words, now. Not so much voices as the computerized cant of the GC. Easy enough to fake."

"Do you think someone there is toying with her?"

Olver started to sigh, shoulders rounding, then caught himself and put the smile back on. Cameras were always watching on Ada.

"It's possible, though I don't know how the fleet would have missed it by now. Even if there are people impersonating the guardcore, they would be hard-pressed to hide their presence on a closed ecosystem like AST-4501. It is also possible that one of Hitton's medications is no longer working properly, or throwing up unforeseen side effects."

"Medications? Is she ill?"

Olver chuckled. "No, Speaker. She is old, as am I. Around a hundred and twenty, things need a little more upkeep, though you have a long time before you cross that bridge."

Biran watched the movements on the docks with studied intent. "What happens to a Keeper, when the diseases of age mount up?"

"Ah, you know the answer to that as well as I do, though none of us like it. Disorders of the mind are a security risk."

Biran cleared his throat roughly. "Yes. But I do not believe Keeper Hitton is suffering from such a disease."

"Don't fret. We'll bring her back off that rock as soon as she scans her data in, then get this sorted out."

"So easy?"

"No, Speaker. These things are never easy. That is not our lot. Not the path you and I and all the others of our cohorts have chosen. Tell me: For what do we Keep?"

Biran hesitated, an incomplete answer dancing on the tip of his tongue, for there was something in the director's inflection that warned him his question was not rhetorical, nor was it one to be answered by rote. His instinct, ingrained through long years of academy training, to spout off the virtues of keeping the Casimir Gate technology safe for the prosperity of humanity, died within him. This was not an essay question he should answer with textbook regurgitation.

In asking in such a way—*what* instead of *whom*—Director Olver was implying that he did not know the answer himself. That, instead of speaking to Biran as a mentor to a student, he was speaking to him as a peer. Opening a conversation for conjecture. The thought momentarily stunned him into silence more than the realization that his education, in this facet, failed him.

"The safety of tomorrow," Biran said finally.

"Posterity, that old saw. The human right to go forth and seed this barren universe with ourselves, since our cradle is dead and we have yet to find another suitable habitat."

"Life is rare."

"Are all rare things equally deserving of protection?"

"What can we do, except provide for future generations? What is the point otherwise?"

"I have yet to find a satisfactory answer to that question. Ah. Here comes our shipment now."

Despite the worries clinging to his mind, excitement spiked within Biran. The ships from Ordinal, carrying this latest batch of Casimir Gate construction bots, slid into the open space of hangar bay alpha. A ripple in the hab dome marked their passage as they curved toward the freshly painted dock. The ships themselves were unremarkable cargo haulers, if brand-new and polished to a high shine, but the fleet presence encircling them was anything but ordinary.

Shielding drones swarmed around the cargo haulers, a buzzing cloud of protection that would follow the robots even after they were released. Gunships, models so new Biran hadn't seen them before, slipped along beside their charge, poised to destroy any who would so much as linger too long near their wake. Wherever that caravan of gate-building bots went, their path could be tracked by the massive no-fly zone charted around them, the skies holding their breath while the strength of Prime carved its way toward an uncertain future.

For all their internal posturing, this was where the power of Prime came into full effect. This was the moment, the reason Biran and all Keepers had trained for so very long. They may not understand the information hidden in their skulls, but they could gift that data to the robots who did.

Within days of arriving in orbit around the asteroid, those cargo ships would disgorge their enlightened cargo, and a new gate would be built—opening up the worlds of Prime to a star system yet unseen, possibly uncharted. Despite all their long history, their algorithms, there was no guessing where a new gate would lead. Humanity, despite its interstellar presence, was still discovering the stars.

Tears pricked behind Biran's eyes, and though he sensed the cameras watching his every twitch, he did not care. He thought himself, in that moment, a very lucky man to be able to see the physical presence of all his hopes and passions made manifest. He searched briefly for Vladsen, but could not find him in the crowd.

The gunships came in first, sliding into a dock. They stood ready, always, fingers poised over red triggers should anything at all strike them as out of place. The guardcore ships stayed airborne, adjusting their position so that they hovered somewhat behind and above the precious cargo hauler. As threatening as the gunships looked, it was the GC ships packing real power. They would rip this station back to its constituent particles rather than allow gate technology to fall into unauthorized hands.

But even their shadow, and all the questions that came with them, could not stop the swell of raw joy in Biran's chest.

"Are you ready, Speaker?" Olver asked.

The hauler came to a stop, a gangway extending from beneath a wide airlock door to touch, gently, the dock that had once led the way into Bero's cargo bay. The external doors slid open—the internal would not open until all the expected Keepers had swiped their idents inside the airlock chamber. Guardcore broke from the crowd and came to stand along the gangway. Biran liked to think one of them must be the one he "knew" and trusted.

"Can I ever be?" Biran said, almost laughing, and was relieved to see the answering smile split Olver's face.

Shoulder to shoulder they approached the gangway, other Keepers approaching their small group with every step. Eleven Keepers of Ada had been chosen to add their secret knowledge to the second gate. The twelfth would be Hitton, scanned in when the hauler passed her asteroid, and though Biran understood the reasons, he wished dearly that she could be here. She had earned that much.

Vladsen stepped into place alongside Biran, Singh and Garcia flanking Olver. Junior Keepers fell into place behind them. They held to silence with deep-seated reverence. The cameras rolled on, recording every step even though they would not be allowed any closer than a side view of the gangway, the people of Ada and Prime watching, if they so desired, as the first real step of constructing another gate was taken here in this hangar that had been the harbor of so much pain.

Callie had peeled herself away from her research long enough to join the crowd, and flashed him a dazzling grin and wave when she caught him looking. If this had been any other event, any other moment, he might have grinned back, but this walk had been rehearsed far too many times for his muscle memory to allow deviation.

They passed the outer door of the airlock, one by one swiping their wrists over the identification pad, as if it were any other door. The cameras could not see them here, especially not after the outer door closed so that the inner could open, but the group did not drop ranks nor give in to discussion.

The inner airlock opened. A dark sea of guardcore flanked the edges of the room, Prime's last line of defense should an intruder get this far, their hands on weapons so new in make that Biran had not seen them before. How much of Prime was outside of his scope of knowledge? He was Keeper, Speaker, Protectorate member. Though Ada was a backwater, its political importance in the starscape of Prime could not be denied. And yet, despite all of that, he knew so very little about what went on in the united worlds outside of his personal bubble.

What stood on the dais in the center of the room, he was all too familiar with. The Keeper-specific MRI machines grew from the center of the floor. In memory of their lost human cradle, all twelve machines were clad in veneers of real wood, each one different.

Their natural colors had been polished to a warm glow with rags coated in beeswax. The warm scent reminded him of Vladsen's hair. Each machine was a pillar unto itself, an incongruous tree trunk in the middle of that otherwise sterile place, their technological connections hidden in facades of root and branch spread between the ground and nominal ceiling.

Those roots disappeared into the floor of the ship, hardwired into the minds of the gate-building bots waiting with machine patience for their instructions to be delivered. None of the Keepers stepping into those small booths knew if the data in their chip was the data that would be used in creation. They had their suspicions, an organization as long-lived and whispered about as theirs did not escape rumor and conjecture, and they, better than all, were positioned to intuit certain truths they could never admit to knowing.

Twelve was the bare minimum scanned in for a build. Many believed that meant six Keepers were required, with one redundancy each, and some claimed as little as three or two, but no one really knew. Biran's own conspiracies vacillated between six and two, but at this moment he wanted to believe that all twelve were necessary. Hitton's last-minute scan included.

He entered his booth and placed his hand on the wooden controls. There was no history here, worn into the wood. While each Keeper had a personal scanner at home to do the occasional—and private—security check on the integrity of their password, these scanners were a one-use affair.

After the builder bots were activated, their first task would be to dismantle and destroy the ship that had brought them there—breaking down its constituent parts and all the supplies hidden within into the materials the bots would use to build the gate. These trees had been cultivated on some distant world for this singular use. Only Biran would ever see the whorls of walnut-dark grain swirling through the smooth controls. He tried to appreciate that, to seal the moment in his mind, before the system warmed to his touch and welcomed him.

The gentle robotic voice said, "Biran Aventure Greeve, Speaker for the Protectorate of Ada Prime. Welcome. Please image password now to initiate gate construction protocols."

This was it. This was what he was *for.* A human encryption envelope, wrapped around a precious jewel of data that was, most likely, only a fraction of the knowledge Prime Inventive used to expand humanity.

He thought he'd be nervous. Sometimes, Keepers took a long time to image their password for actual construction, no matter how many times they practiced at home. The knowledge that this was real, that this counted, was prone to throw up a great deal of mental static. Biran expected his palms to sweat. They did not, because he'd chosen his personal password well.

While the scientists of splinter nations theorized about the actual construction of the gates, most laypeople of Prime wondered what the passwords were. A Keeper thought their password, their brain lit up in the right way, and the MRI recorded it, using the neural map created as a key. Biran knew the speculation—words, feelings, numbers, strings of seemingly meaningless characters. Many people even got close to the truth. It was different for every Keeper, but it was never something that could be written down. He still wondered how Sanda had accessed hers. He'd never had the chance to ask in person, and that wasn't a conversation that could be had over any digital channel.

Biran closed his eyes to shut out the clutter of visual input and thought of family. Not his family—that was too specific an idea, too changeable—but it included his family. It wasn't the units of the family that mattered—not the role of a parent or child or sibling—but slotting into a close-knit community in which you truly belonged. Biran's idea of family was not born of blood and generational ties, it was nebulous. Friends counted. Anyone could be a family, if they loved hard enough.

The gentle chime of acceptance made him open his eyes. On the small screen, a cube spun on an offset axis, the visual representation of the data hidden in his brain stem. He affirmed the upload, then stepped out of the booth when the intelligence inside bade him thank you and farewell.

That was it. That was what he had trained all his life to do. Oh, there were other responsibilities, but that upload was the sole purpose of the Keepers, a ritual unchanged since the days of Alexandra Halston. Giddiness vibrated his skin, and as Vladsen stepped out they shared a brief, triumphant grin.

"First ones," Olver said as he emerged from his booth. "Usually the young ones are last."

"Have you done many of these?" Biran asked.

Olver glanced over his shoulder at the ash-pale wooden trunk that had been his booth. They were all soundproof—their conversation would not disturb those trying to image their own passwords. "A few," he said.

Biran wanted to press, but the others were coming out now. Regrouping, they reversed the procedure back into the hangar bay. The expected flurry of cameras met them, but the tone was all wrong. Biran's skin prickled, instincts sensing that something was amiss long before his mind caught up and understood what was being shouted at him.

The cordon around the public tightened, nervous fleeties holding them back against a new storm. The people reached for the Keepers, stretching their arms to the limit to get the small group in shot of their wristpads. Somebody had ordered the news drones to ground. The air was strangely empty.

"What...?" Biran looked to Olver for guidance and found the man's face a phantom of himself. Director Olver stared at his wristpad, shoulders hunched, his expression kept neutral only through sheer force of will, though there was nothing training could do for the paleness sapping the life from his cheeks. Biran couldn't see the image clearly, but he caught hints of burnt concrete foams, twisted sheets of metal.

He did not want to check his own wristpad. It vibrated at him, insistent. A priority message coming in that he must answer.

Anford's drawn face stared up at him out of the wristpad.

"There's been an incident at the asteroid," she said.

The muted echo of her words on all the Keeper wristpads around him sounded like the murmuring of ghosts. Biran swallowed, and did not ask, because this message was to them all, and she already knew what she must say next.

"We lost contact shortly before the gate ships arrived. Hitton ordered her people off station. This is what's left."

The asteroid station was a crater. There was no other word Biran could dredge up to describe the widespread destruction. Every spacefaring human had intimate knowledge of all the ways a hab or station or ship could go wrong: decompression, power loss, drive overloading. None of those things caused damage like this. This was the kind of wreckage encountered in Sanda's world, where words like *bombardment* and *artillery* were more common. Not at a survey site. Not at a Keeper hab, even a far-flung one.

Olver said, voice firmer than it had any right to be, "Survivors?"

"Those shipped off before the incident."

Not Hitton. A wave of dizziness threatened to topple Biran, but he stood firm, bent his knees slightly to ground himself. Concentrated on the unshakable footing provided by mag boots.

A word blazed bright in everyone's minds, but it was Singh who asked, her voice sharp, "Icarion?"

"No. We're still investigating. Drones have arrived on-site and the evacuated are being brought home now."

She blew it up. Anford wouldn't say it, not yet, but that damage could be caused by a self-destruct sequence. Without the asteroid to capture the gate's orbit, it couldn't be built. Prime built self-destruct commands into all their stations, should they ever risk being overrun by enemy forces and the data hidden within captured. All Keepers knew the protocols. None ever expected to use them.

"Lockdown," Olver said, "effective immediately. Guardcore, the build ships are alpha priority. They're every priority straight through zeta. Anford, get me Okonkwo, I want the whole High Protectorate on my screen the second I step into the war room, and Bollar waiting in the wings."

"Yes, sir," the mixed chorus said through Director Olver's wristpad.

Olver closed the channel, dropped his arm to his side, and surveyed the frantic crowd of civs with focused but unreadable eyes. The shift in his posture from one second to the next humbled Biran. It was so very easy to think of him as a father figure—he encouraged the comparison—but in those scant seconds, going from knowing his dear friend was dead to taking control of the situation, Biran felt a void of inadequacy open up in the depths of his soul. Ada was very lucky to have him as director.

"Cannery," he said to the dazed Keepers crowded around him. "Now."

Biran took a step to follow the group, a gaggle of lost ducklings stumbling after their director, but Olver cut him off with a look. Right. Speaker: Speak.

Vladsen reached out. Impulsively, stupidly, that dark-eyed man squeezed Biran's wrist, and then he was hurried off, corralled to the Cannery with the rest. Biran stood alone save a single GC who lingered, their rifle pointed at the ground but ready, their gloved finger resting against the trigger guard.

Inadequacy grew in his mind and threatened to sprout thorns. All his insecurities told him he was not ready for this. He could speak prettily about his sister and the virtues of protecting Prime and Icarion all day long, but this was something new. Olver should do this, but Olver could not do everything, and in picking Biran for this moment—no matter the political maneuvering that'd dragged him into his station—the director had endorsed his ability.

Biran did not freeze in front of cameras. He did now.

The guardcore behind him cleared their throat, gently, through the speakers on their armor. He couldn't be sure, but there was a soft quality that made him think of the kind GC. He had gotten through the panic and the fear then by doing the work. This was no different.

"Please," he said, forcing his voice to project. The shouting calmed down, replaced by the rustle of reporters tapping as they cranked up their microphones. "I cannot in good faith ask you to be calm, but I must ask you to be patient. We will dig to the root of what happened at the asteroid. We will have answers for you soon. Shelter in place. The Ada system is on lockdown. Be safe. Take care of each other."

Biran walked away, wondering who would take care of Olver, and how they had failed so catastrophically in taking care of Hitton.

CHAPTER 67

PRIME STANDARD YEAR 3543

A LIGHT IN THE DARK

The stealth ships of the Nazca weren't the kind of technology available to the public. Prime had better—Prime *always* had better—but the Nazca kept their fleet of ships as close to the cutting edge as possible. You couldn't see them unless you were expecting to. And no one was expecting Tomas.

He cut the engines as, on the viewscreen, the blip that was the *Thorn* drifted closer.

Time had slipped through his fingers. Easy enough to happen when you were off-planet and not adhering to circadian rhythm lights, but this was something else. Not true memory loss. No, this was grief, maybe, or something like depression. Tomas had crawled into this ship at the Ordinal stronghold, set course for Sanda's gunship, and just...drifted.

But he was awake now. The *Thorn* had come to a stop six hours' flight outside of a gate that was supposed to be dead. Maybe the records were wrong. Maybe that gate had been spun up a long time ago, and his navigational database hadn't picked up the update. It was a pretty thought, a lot prettier than the idea that Rainier had spun it up for her own purposes, but that was one path he could not take. Even a Nazca stealth ship wasn't clever enough to lie its way through a Casimir Gate security check. Without proper clearance, he'd be slaughtered.

His ship's sensors weren't picking up any comms chatter from the *Thorn*, and preliminary scans came back with heart-sinking reports of damage. He would have sent a tightbeam, if it weren't for the guardcore ship lurking nearby.

The airlock on the side of the *Thorn* opened. Slinking as close as he dared, Tomas focused the cameras on that lock. It had been damaged at some point, warped so that the internal door held but the exterior would have trouble mating with another ship.

A man kicked out, suited in Prime armor, a pack slung over his shoulder, and angled his airjets for the GC ship. Tomas didn't recognize him, but he took whatever footage he could get and fed it into a basic personnel search database. He didn't dare touch anything Nazca until he was certain none of it could be used to trace his location. Nothing came back. According to the net, that man didn't exist.

As the guardcore ship turned to leave, the *Thorn*'s derelict beacon came on. Tomas waited the longest hour of his life for the GC ship to clear the area, ordering his ship to tag the bigger ship's heading and track it as best as it could.

When he was certain the GC ship was beyond visual recognition, Tomas approached the *Thorn*. For a second he considered not bothering to suit up, just to see how his body handled the vacuum, then realized he was an idiot. Lavaux had died in the emptiness, hadn't he? It wasn't a risk Tomas could take.

He set the shuttle to alert him if the GC ship made it out of tracking range, and entered the *Thorn*.

The ship was hollow. Oh, it was full of stuff, but as Tomas pulled himself through the echoing hallways, he got the sense that something had gone very wrong here, something he couldn't see yet. There was no blood, no sign of gunfire, and yet the halls spoke of a violence in their raw emptiness.

Sanda's crew had been here, recently, and then they were not, and there was no explanation that Tomas could draw up that put those two threads together peacefully.

There was nothing for him to go on. He searched every room for a hint of who that man boarding the GC ship had been. Every room, except hers. He couldn't do it. Not yet.

"Exceeding tracking envelope," his ship said through his helmet.

Tomas sighed. He never had enough time. He pulled himself hand over hand down the hall, opened Sanda's door with a practiced flick of the wrist that belied the sick, hot dread that was curdling in his belly. Maybe he could shut that feeling down, but he didn't want to.

Grippy looked up at him over Sanda's desk. He let out a soft sob, then felt like an idiot. Grippy's presence meant nothing, could mean anything. She would never leave the robot behind, he was sure of that, but that didn't mean she wasn't coming *back*.

"Losing tracking," the ship said.

"Goddamnit," he hissed.

Tomas kicked across the room and, briefly, considered taking the robot with him. He couldn't leave him here, all alone, drifting derelict by a deadgate that no one would bother passing by. But taking the bot meant Sanda wasn't coming back for it.

He reached into a pocket on the side of his mag boot and pulled out a small tracking device. It was Sanda's tracker, the kind her dad used to track cargo on his hauler. He'd found it in his boot at the safe house and pretended not to notice until he was clear of Atrux and on his way to Janus. It soothed him that she had needed to know where he was.

Tomas needed all the soothing he could get right now.

The activation switch clicked beneath his thumb and he slid the tracker underneath the maintenance panel on Grippy's belly. He made sure the connection was secure and working before he closed it back up. Tomas hesitated, then patted the robot on the head.

"Find her for me, okay?"

Beep beep.

The bot didn't understand, not really, but Tomas grinned fiercely anyway. He snatched her tablet off the desk to data mine for clues later and kicked back toward the airlock.

He'd find the GC ship and squeeze that man for information. As soon as he was certain Sanda was safe...Then he would hunt the man in grey.

CHAPTER 68

PRIME STANDARD YEAR 3543

OLD FRIENDS

The reborn *Light of Berossus* passed through the Casimir Gate without so much as a warning light going off. While all ships had their power throttled, their systems taken over for the brief but monumental passing, this new ship slid through as unnoticed as a shark in dark waters. Made for each other, the gate and the ship, Sanda thought, and again wondered if the instructions scribed on the sphere were the secret hidden in every Keeper's skull.

Her own cranial secret was done, spent. She'd thought she'd want it removed once the location was found—if that were even possible. Carved out and incinerated once she knew definitively what it meant. But that pinpoint in space, another dot on the map, had become a part of her. She no more wanted the chip out than she wanted to lose another limb.

Bero had rearranged the command deck to look more like what the mere humans riding his body were comfortable with. The metallic surface of the forward bulkhead displayed video in the same way a viewscreen would, and the tall podiums had been replaced with seats and desk-spaces resembling consoles, with readouts and status reports streaming by. He even gave them buttons to push.

Both Sanda and Conway squirmed in their seats occasionally. There was nothing for them to do. Silently, they both hated it.

"I have locked onto the *Thorn*'s position," Bero said.

"Show me," Sanda said.

Instead of the usual graphical rendering of the nearby space, Bero provided perfectly crisp video of the ship, zoomed in tight.

"Is this real time?" Sanda asked.

"Yes. These cameras are a considerable upgrade."

That should be a good thing, but Sanda couldn't help remembering what lies Bero could weave when he had access to decent video-rendering systems. A soft, yellow light blinking toward the nose of the *Thorn* caught her eye.

"Is that the derelict beacon?"

"It is. Demas has logged the ship as too damaged to fly. All scans taken of the *Thorn* report no life on board."

"He had a getaway driver waiting for him," Nox said.

"Not surprising," Sanda said, though the admission ached. "Bero, can you check the local flight logs? See what ships recently passed through the area."

"None but the *Thorn*."

She closed her eyes briefly. Guardcore ships were required to file their flight plans with the fleet and Keepers, but requirements didn't mean compliance. If Demas wanted to get in and out, they'd come in dark. The disappearance of the *Thorn*'s crew was, it seemed, supposed to remain a mystery to the public.

"Bring us in to the *Thorn*. We'll salvage what we can of the supplies. And Grippy's on there."

He better be. If Demas took off with her robot, then she'd find the fucker come hell or high water.

Bero's new body didn't have a passage to mate between the airlocks, so they pulled helmets and lifepacks on to prepare for vacuum. Sanda would have ordered it anyway. She didn't trust Demas not to leave a nasty surprise behind on the ship.

She took Knuth and went through with Nox at her side. She'd been tempted to bring Conway, but they had only two guns to share between them and they'd have enough trouble making sure Knuth was properly covered while he checked over what remained of the *Thorn*.

Sanda half expected the locks to have been overridden so that her ident wouldn't let them through, and had brought torches just in case, but Demas had left her clearances intact. It'd be harder to sell whatever story he'd cooked up about their mysterious demise if all the security systems had been changed to answer only to him.

The airlock opened, and Sanda pushed herself inside, blaster out and ready, though she genuinely didn't think she'd need it. The *Thorn*, her home for a brief time and seat of tenuous command, felt empty.

It wasn't the lack of people, not really. Something essential to the ship had been carved out when it had been commandeered, a violation she couldn't unsee, or unfeel. A captain's ship was supposed to be an extension of themselves, another appendage in which they worked in concert. Sanda knew what it was to lose a limb, and this was that feeling all over again. Even if they moved back into the broken vessel, it wouldn't quite be the same.

"Clear," Nox said from down the hall. He'd opened all the doors to private quarters, and seeing them stand open drove home that this place was not theirs anymore.

Sanda poked her head into her room to find that her tablet was gone, but Grippy was still there. He lifted his head up from behind her desk, the green LED between his "eyes" blinking in recognition.

"Come on, Grippy," she said, "there's someone who I think you want to see."

The bot's systems weren't sophisticated enough to parse all of that, but it understood its name and *come on* and so trundled into the hall, magnetic treads clicking in concert with their mag boots as they checked every nook and cranny of the ship. Demas had bugged out, and taken the sphere with him.

On the command deck, she said, "Knuth, can you get us enough power for me to make a priority call?"

"I don't know, honestly. The EMP fried the comms system and even if I got a good chunk up and running, I can't guarantee how secure a line would be."

"Understood. Nox, go with him and scavenge what you can for us. All the food, the NutriSystem extruder, everything that might make life on Bero a little more comfortable for humans. Blankets, even. And we'll need all the extra clothes, weapons, and armor. Bring the others over to help, if you need it."

"Sure, Commander, but what are you going to do?"

She tapped the side of her wristpad. "I need to call my commanding officer."

Nox grimaced, gave her a mock salute, and ushered Knuth out of the command deck as quick as he could.

Sanda approached her captain's seat from the side, let her hand rest on the back a moment before she sat down, and after a pause in which she lined up what she needed to say, turned her wristpad to face herself and typed in the code to call General Anford on a priority line.

It took a few minutes, but the general answered. Nothing had changed about her, so far as Sanda could tell. Same stern face, strong jaw, unflinching gaze. She was somewhere in the Cannery, Sanda guessed, but those grey walls behind her could have been anywhere in Prime.

"Greeve, I was under the impression you'd decided to take your orders directly from Prime Director Okonkwo now."

The barb didn't hurt her as it once would have. "Okonkwo arranged to have me, and all my crew, slaughtered. As you can see, the attempt didn't take."

Anford narrowed her eyes. "Have you suffered a traumatic brain injury? If Okonkwo wanted you dead, she would have had you court-martialed and executed. Whatever you experienced, it was not an assassination attempt by the Prime Director."

Sanda smiled tightly. "Technically, it was her pet GC who made the attempt. And while my brain is well enough, he did shoot me in the stomach."

"He? Greeve, are you certain you're well?"

She sighed. "General, there is no way to explain matters that would make you believe me, I think. You and I are creatures of Prime, aren't we? Loyal to a fault. The system always works as intended. Et cetera."

There was a brief flash of tension in the corner of Anford's eyes. Sanda pressed on. "I don't blame you. I actually like you, General

Anford, though I'm sure that means piss-all in the grand scheme of things."

"Report, Major. The Prime Director was thin on the details when she so kindly informed me she'd given you orders, and at the moment I am too busy for your bullshit."

That should have stung, should have shamed her. It didn't.

"Gladly. At Monte Station, we came under fire from a host of enemy ships seeking to capture the scientists rescued from Janus. They flew guardcore ships, and wore GC armor, but according to my brother and as was later confirmed by Okonkwo, they were not in fact GC."

"How—"

"It gets stranger. My brother, realizing that we were soon to be under attack by unknown entities, hailed for help. Okonkwo's personal ship was the only one in shouting distance, and she arrived and pulled our asses out of the fire. She then informed me she knew of the false GC and had for quite a while." Sanda paused a moment to let that sink in.

"I have seen no report." Anford scowled, but there was a nervous twitch at the corner of her lips, quite unlike her.

"You have, it seems. But I'm guessing what you don't know is that the Prime Director claims to be an ex-member of a secret cabal of Keepers who call themselves the Acolytes. Their goal, she says, is to stay under the proverbial political radar—hence her exit from their order upon her election to Prime Director—and operate in secret to maintain the status quo of Prime society."

"I would know of such an organization."

"Even if you did, how could I be certain you'd cop to knowing about it? No, I believe you, actually. It's just that I've been lied to a lot lately. If this order even exists, and I do believe it does—Keeper Nakata of Atrux was reportedly among their number—then their goal is not to police Prime's safety, but to prevent upheaval within the social-political system."

Her lips pursed. "Spies and espionage."

"Yes. According to Okonkwo, they have been seeking the root cause of the false GC for quite some time. That is, allegedly, the reason Nakata was killed."

"You keep hedging your words, Greeve. Do you believe Okonkwo's assertions, or not?"

"I don't have a fucking clue, begging your pardon, General. Okonkwo asked after my present mission, and at mention of the coordinates Lavaux was trying to reach, she damn near lit up. She gave us a GC out of uniform—his name's Demas, he's an asshole—and the override commands to spin the deadgate. Once we arrived, we were attacked by an automated defense system. I engaged the system and was forced to use an EMP. The *Thorn* was damaged. Once the battle was concluded, we sighted an unknown vessel a short distance from the gate."

"Unknown?"

"Sir, I...After boarding, it became clear no human made this vessel."

"Humanity has been an interstellar species for thousands of years. In that time, we have found no other."

"Times are changing." She grimaced at her own word choice for such a historic moment. "I already sound like a cracked pot, believe me, I know, and you're about to think I've gone even further down the conspiracy rabbit hole because I swear to you, General, Demas knew what that ship was.

"There was something in it that Okonkwo had sent him to fetch. A sphere, embedded in a pedestal in the center of the ship. It had etchings on it we believe to be binary, but we lacked cameras with the resolution to read them well at such a small scale. Shortly after the discovery of the sphere, Demas shot me in the stomach, evaded my crew, and commandeered the *Thorn*. Presumably, he believed we couldn't revive the engines on the ali—new—ship. They seemed dead at the time."

"He *shot* you? And you appear to be on board the *Thorn* right now."

"He did, and I am. Mx. Wyke got the ship online and saved my life. We pursued Demas through the gate to find the *Thorn* abandoned, broadcasting a derelict beacon. I can only assume he arranged for another of the GC or Okonkwo's inner circle to pick him up."

"Greeve, I need you to power down that unknown ship and stand still. I'm sending a transporter to pick you up and tug the *Thorn*, and whatever that other ship is, back to a fleet station. This mission has been escalated to alpha-level classification, and you may not discuss any of it with anyone who has less than five bars on their uniform. Am I clear?"

"Yes, General."

"Good."

"But I won't be following those orders."

"Greeve—"

She shook her head. "This call was a courtesy. I am telling you, woman-to-woman, what happened out there beyond the deadgate, and I am telling you it as a warning. There are factions at work within Prime that we have only begun to see the surface of. I will leave the *Thorn* here, blinking its derelict beacon as Demas intended. But I, and my crew, are getting back on board that alien ship and I will not return to your command until I figure out what the fuck is going on and who I can trust."

"Are you saying you cannot trust me?"

"No. But I can't trust your superiors, and if you do anything short of executing me after Okonkwo discovers I survived, then I would bet my ass that forced retirement would be coming your way, and this universe needs you at the helm. They'll say I'm crazy, General. That my time as a prisoner of Icarion broke me. They'll say how sad it is, that a hero should lose their grip on reality. And people will believe it. I'd believe it."

"Maybe they're right."

"Maybe. In three minutes, I will send you footage of the ship, taken as we crossed through the gate. You will see that all its systems remain online, escaping the gate's governing system. You will see... It. What it is, how it moves. I will include what still images we captured of the sphere before it was stolen. The *Thorn*, I leave to you, but I am not its captain anymore."

"Think reasonably. Whatever ship you have, we will find you. If you come to me now, we can talk this out. If you go AWOL, you tie my hands."

Sanda's smile was small, but genuine. "This is not a ship that Prime is capable of catching. Good luck to you, General."

She cut the feed, set the timer on the data packet to send, and sat there, looking around the empty deck of the *Thorn*. It was not the leaving of the ship that hurt.

Stepping out that airlock was desertion of duty in the eyes of her commander. Anford would not make a public spectacle of Sanda's abandonment. That woman was too tactful, and mindful of the fact that she needed the sentiments of the people on her side at the moment as she struggled with Icarion's final throes of desperation against Prime's control.

Sanda sympathized more with Icarion in that moment than she ever had with her own people.

"Ready to go, boss?" Nox said.

"Yes," she said, and was surprised to feel like she was going home.

CHAPTER 69

PRIME STANDARD YEAR 3543

EVERYONE BLEEDS. WE HOPE.

Bero stealthed the ship and they waited, breathless, as they watched the incoming fleet vessel creep across the blackness of space toward the *Thorn*. The wise thing to do would have been to tuck tail and burn across the system, even attempt a gate crossing out of Ordinal, but Sanda had to know two things. One: Could Bero hide himself from a fleet ship that was actively looking for him? Two: Was Anford going to prove hostile?

The general had sent a transport ship. No guns. No escort. Just a very confused recovery crew who searched the area for a second ship for hours before giving up. When that ship had passed beyond even Bero's impressive camera range, she called an all-hands meeting to the deck.

They arrayed before her in a semicircle, watching and waiting, though Nox and Arden looked ready to break the silence and get on with things. Arden, in their excitement about the AI they'd just met, couldn't feel the wariness and Nox, in his bullheaded manner, didn't care.

But the others did. Liao and Knuth and Conway. They were Prime from the middle of society, raised to report any suspicious activity of AI, and later bombarded with horror stories about Icarion and their mysterious weapon.

Said weapon was now in control of their HVAC. Their home.

"You are now the crew of *The Light*," she said. The ship—the vessel—could have its own name to keep the humans on board more comfortable, but the intelligence piloting it would always be Bero. They'd talked it out ahead of time, in the small room she'd claimed as her own, dancing around a thousand other things that she felt needed to be said. The personal could wait. "And Bero is its pilot. I have no doubt that you are wary. I would be, given your position. I was. But Bero was a soldier in a war he did not want any part of. Everyone here can relate to that."

"Uh—" Knuth started to raise his hand like he was in class, stopped himself, and cleared his throat. "Bero?"

"Yes?" His voice did not come from any speakers Sanda could see, but seemed to radiate from all around. That was a little shiver-inducing, even she had to admit.

"Could you show me where the engine room is on this thing? I've been trying to figure out where the damn power is routing from."

"Yeah," Conway cut in, "and does this thing—sorry, is that offensive?—do *you* have weapons?"

"And what about a research facility?" Liao said. "I'd like a chance to go over what little we saved of the sphere before it was stolen. Wait—is there any data on the sphere stored on your internal systems? I know you said the hardware was wiped, but maybe—"

"One at a time," Sanda said, holding back a laugh.

A pause. Bero said, with slight indignity, "I can process multiple requests, but answering them all at once may cause confusion to human ears. I will grant you access to the engine room, and am happy to explain what I understand of these systems to you. Though, to answer Liao's question, there was no previous data left behind on this hardware. It had been wiped clean before my upload. This ship has weapons, and you may call the ship an *it*, so long as you refer to myself as a *he*. This is... not the body I was raised in. I do not feel that it is myself. It is a difficult matter to explain. I do not yet fully understand."

Sanda glanced down at her constantly changing prosthetic. "Maybe that will change."

"Maybe. In the meantime, I prefer the separation between myself and what we will call *The Light*."

Liao latched onto the missing data. "There's nothing here? No data at all? Something ran systems to greet us—turn on the lights, the HVAC, open doors. Something must be on the system's hardware."

"Firmware wrapped in layers of encryption I may not be able to break in my lifetime, whatever that is, though I have initiated the process. As for a lab, I am still experimenting with manipulating the ship's systems, but I find them highly adaptable. There is no equipment on board aside from what you loaded off of the *Thorn*, but I can carve you out a room and the furniture you might need."

"Damn," she muttered. Then, quickly, "To the situation, I mean. Thank you, Bero."

"I understand, and share, your frustrations."

"I'm about to give you all another," Sanda said. "We're not going after Demas."

"What?" came the chorus.

"If we had caught him on the other side of the gate, then we would have hunted him down. But we have no definite bead on the direction he went. Even if we did, if a GC ship picked him up, then he is already safely ensconced in Okonkwo's hands. If we found him, or the sphere, any attempt at retrieval would be a suicide mission."

"With this ship—" Nox began.

"With this ship we could sneak right up to Okonkwo's door. But we'd have to *get off* the ship to get the sphere. If we even knew where it was, and you can bet your ass she's not using it as a paperweight in her office. Our only shot was finding him on the *Thorn*, or within the vicinity of the deadgate. We didn't."

"Then what the hell are we supposed to do? Might as well have stayed on the *Thorn* and accept whatever bullshit mission the fleet threw at us," Nox grumbled.

"What we need to do is gather more information. Arden, Liao, you two both took images of the sphere. I understand the resolution wasn't up to snuff, but with Bero's help maybe you can clear it up some. Send those images to him now."

"Bero," Arden said, "don't run any searches on what you find against open net databases. Keep it all internal for now."

"Understood," Bero said.

Arden and Liao tapped lightning fast at their wristpads. In a matter of seconds, Bero said, "I have a preliminary suggestion, though the data is fragmented and I am no expert on the matter."

"We understand, B. Give us what you can."

"I believe you were already discussing the unique properties of the alloys described in the initial portion of the sphere. The rest is heavily damaged on a microscopic scale. Large areas are burnished away, and so the finer details are impossible to make out, but from what I've seen, I believe these are directions for building a type of mechanical cell."

"A nanite?" Liao asked.

"Yes. If I had all the data, I could say for certain. These nanites appear to be replicators. They could very well make up the greater bulk of this ship's design, but that is speculation."

"Speculation?" Nox asked. "Aren't you the biggest brain in the universe? Shouldn't you be certain?"

"I have never seen anything like these before. I have never even seen something like these *proposed* before. I do not believe them to be human technology."

The crew shifted uncomfortably as a whole. They knew. They'd known. And yet, having an intelligence like Bero confirm their deepest suspicions made something in their hindbrains stand up and take notice. Sanda glanced at the deck, sculpted for their comfort, and wondered what shape this ship would take if its original designers were on board.

"A swarm of nanites could construct something as large as this ship, or a Casimir Gate," Liao said. She had the glazed-eyed, faraway look of someone lost in thought.

"They could build anything, really," Arden mused. "No wonder Halston hid the method of construction. No one would have agreed to building, let alone utilizing, a nanite swarm derived from alien technology."

"Nanite research is one of the sciences restricted to Keepers," Liao said, "which was why Dal and I were so eager to get the chance to work on Janus."

"Janus?" Bero asked. Liao filled him in. After a while, he said, "You are certain that this Valentine person is entangled with Rainier Lavaux?"

A quiet tension lurked in his voice. Based on the relaxed expressions of the others, only Sanda could hear it.

"I identified her myself," Sanda said.

"Sanda. Do you remember the moments before you were spaced?"

She stiffened, a dread chill running down her spine. "The fight with Lavaux, you mean? Yeah. I remember."

"His leg. Do you remember his leg?"

Nox was giving her a what-the-fuck look. The others looked baffled. "I bashed it open."

"And?"

"And I was preoccupied with staying alive in that moment."

The damn ship sighed at her. "Grippy had already restored my camera capabilities at that point in time. I was recording."

She was sweating. It crowned her brow and pooled between her shoulder blades. What she had seen was not real. Even in the doctored footage in which she had been falsely shown killing Lavaux, his leg knitting back together hadn't been there. When Arden had that footage fixed and re-released, even then there had been no mention. People would have noticed. *Arden* would have noticed.

"That wasn't real," she said, quietly.

Bero answered by putting the video up on the forward viewscreen. She wanted to tell him to knock it off, that she knew he could doctor footage and he was fucking with her and wasting all their time, but if he saw—well. He couldn't have seen her hallucination, if that had been what it was.

Sanda hadn't watched this footage all the way through. She'd caught glimpses of it, and always looked away, but she watched now, feeling the sweat against her skin turn to ice as she and Lavaux struggled across the screen in Bero's cargo bay. Her prosthetic went out and she noticed, dully, that the members of her crew winced, but that wasn't the moment she dreaded.

In the video Sanda surged and cracked the wrench across Lavaux's shin. Nox grunted approval. Conway chuckled. All noise on the deck stopped, then.

Suit and skin and muscle split, revealing gleaming titanium-white bone, and in that moment she had hesitated, because even though she wasn't thinking so much as reacting, every animal instinct in her body had screamed that that was wrong, and that had been the second in which he gained the upper hand.

He stalked toward her. Over that bone—the same color as *The Light*—red muscle knitted itself back together in record time, a nature documentary sped up. Skin patched. Healed. And then he was smirking above her with a razor blade to the back of her skull, and a wave of white-hot panic washed over Sanda there on the deck.

"Cut it," she snapped.

Bero ended the feed. "I'm sorry. I've been thinking about that moment for a long time."

"What the fuck was that?" Nox thrust a thumb at the blacked-out screen.

"Something I believed to be a figment of my imagination."

"Looked pretty fucking real to me," Nox said.

"That...explains a lot," Arden said. Everyone looked at them. They flushed. "When the edited footage first came out, netheads knew it was faked, but couldn't agree on how much was faked. When I cleaned it up, there was still some grumbling that what was re-released wasn't actually the raw footage, but nobody listened. They knew it'd been faked, they had their correction. Only cracks kept digging."

Sanda laughed shakily. Knuth put a hand on her arm, squeezed, then pulled it back. She didn't think he touched much beside engines, and the fact that he'd tried to soothe her comforted her more than the attempt. "Even I bought it."

Bero said, "This sphere could contain instructions for the creation of people like Lavaux."

"People?" Conway scoffed. "I think that man left humanity behind long ago."

"I agree, but we don't understand how the nanites work. People, ships, gates. Anything is a possibility."

"I know some people who could help," Liao said, scrunching up her brow like the words themselves hurt.

"How?" Sanda pressed.

"As I said, nanite research is banned by the Keepers, and mostly for good reason. Out-of-control swarms are a real concern. But my lab and I, a long time ago, had special permission to work on what we called 'mechanical therapies'—medicine using nanites."

"Like the NutriBaths?" Sanda asked.

Liao shook her head. "Those are one hundred percent biological compounds. Programmable, in their own way, but a messy solution to some problems. We were getting close to a solution to repairing damage caused by diseases that could cross the blood-brain barrier when Vela, one of our researchers, was picked up by the fleet for researching gate technology."

"Was she?"

"No," Liao said emphatically. "Absolutely not. We knew we walked a razor's edge and were careful. She was my roommate and she... Well. She wouldn't. Afterward, we slowed some aspects of our research, but soon another one of us went missing."

"The fleet took them?" Sanda said, aghast. "There should have been a trial."

"No. Not for scientists who cross the line. A trial would include introducing their research into evidence, and drawing that kind of attention would be counter to everything the Keepers do."

"That's true enough," Nox said slowly, lifting his gaze to meet Liao's. "I disappeared a few researchers in my time. We delivered them to a special GC facility and asked no further questions. I'm... sorry for that."

Liao straightened her back. "Apology accepted. The point is, after we lost two, we feared for ourselves. We pooled our resources, bought a ship, a small dome, fabricating equipment, and ran. One of us, Yaxia, owned mining rights on an asteroid in the outer Ordinal belt. We lived on the ship while the fabbers dug and built us a home shielded from radiation under the rock, then went back to our work."

Sanda arched a brow. "They would have found you eventually."

"Yes," she laughed softly. "But they wouldn't have bothered. We discovered quickly how disparaged fringers and their science are. No one would listen to us. We found a few allies among other fringers after a while, and some of their specialists came to us to help us build better medicines, though those therapies will never see a wider market."

"Why bother?" Conway asked.

Liao lifted a shoulder. "Because it was the right thing to do. And we didn't want to wait around to get picked off one by one. But the point is, if we take what data we have on the sphere to my colleagues, then they might tell us more about what it's supposed to do. I didn't work on the nanite construction side of things, I worked on getting those nanites to communicate with outside terminals. I know you have access to a great deal of information, Bero, but the research my colleagues have is not available on any database you can access."

"And yet you left your noble cause behind to build amplifiers for Rainier Lavaux," Sanda said.

"I thought Valentine was legit, and that if I could publish via official Keeper means then some of the legitimacy might rub off."

"Oh," Arden said softly.

"What is it?" Sanda asked.

"It's just...Jules. She's working for Rainier, and we don't know why. But if the Lavauxs were messing around with nanites, then presumably the amplifiers weren't the only ones on Janus. Maybe Rainier was trying to recreate the nanites the sphere describes. If Jules knew she was at the mercy of alien tech..."

"Then she wouldn't risk revealing her reasons, she'd be too damned scared, and I can't blame her." Nox finished the thought. Dread crept across his face. "What if...what if those nanites could change a person? Jules moved too damn fast at Janus. I couldn't even see her when she fled."

Arden's eyes went huge with realization. "The wraith-mother at the warehouse. She tried to hide that she'd touched it, I thought she was embarrassed about being high, but it could have been this stuff."

"Moving quickly doesn't mean your friend's synthetic," Sanda said.

"No," Nox said. "But you didn't see how quickly she healed after our last fight in the Grotta. She hid it, but after she took off, I had to clean our hideout, burn everything. There wasn't any blood on her cast-off bandages."

CHAPTER 70

PRIME STANDARD YEAR 3543

THE HURT

Connections. The tenuous, fibrous social construct that made up your place in the world. Jules had always felt that connections were for other people. The rich and the powerful, or those on the edges of those circles. People who could maneuver and make deals—found worlds and shake industries. Those people were connected. Not Grotta kids. Not the algal film of Atrux.

It was only the first on a long list of assumptions she'd been wrong about. The Grotta was a shithole, but it'd been her shithole. She'd set down roots—light-shy, thin roots—and given herself some weight in that world, some sense of grounding. Human beings weren't meant to be in space—to be untethered and floating. They were meant to be rooted. Stabilized. Everything humanity made after the Charon Gate was a mistake. Jules certainly was.

But she'd been dug up, tossed into the world she thought she'd wanted. Credit was never a problem, Rainier kept her flush. Sometimes she thought Rainier didn't understand the concept of money. Jules could funnel some of that money away. Build a base for herself somewhere safe. Flourish. But it would mean abandoning Lolla. Even if she stole all the credit of the united worlds, no mind but Rainier's could reverse what had been done to her friend. Her surrogate sister.

That had been the point of the maze. Not the research—though she was certain Rainier had a use for that, even if it wasn't what Jules herself wanted—but the pressure of *being*. Janus was mostly empty because Rainier had wanted to see what Jules would do with that, what kind of social-political networks she could build.

And she'd done fuck-all. She'd let her severed roots shrivel, grafted herself to Lolla, and struggled against every damn little thing. Maybe Rainier had judged her wrongly, made a mistake in putting her there. But Jules was pretty sure Rainier, for all her lack of understanding humanity, didn't make those kinds of mistakes. Jules had been meant to fester. To grow bitter, paired up with a woman who came from the easier world she'd only glimpsed.

Jules hated that it had worked.

She checked her rifle. The weapon was smooth in her hands, even through the black gloves that encased her fingers. Finer weapons, finer materials. The stock and grip and barrel lacked any of the small divots and scratches, smears of stray oil and grit, that older guns carried. These rifles showed no sign they had ever been used. She could have lifted it fresh out of its mold in the crate foam, just like the armor that hung on her body.

Smooth and matte and black as space. The guardcore armor hugged, its internal shape filled with foams that clung and hardened to her so that what was uniform on the exterior fit on the interior. A Jules-shaped space in the middle of a void of faceless violence.

The others kept their helmets up. Jules had never seen them and had no desire to see them now. Their faces didn't matter, nor did their stories, their voices. They were more pawns on Rainier's board, just like her. Just like Marya.

But unlike Jules, Marya had gotten what she wanted and found her way out of Rainier's labyrinth, and now it was time to bring the hammer down. All the connections in the universe couldn't save you when you'd bitten the hand that fed you.

I have something to show you, Rainier had said as she reeled Jules back in.

A video of Marya, bleeding off some stasis fluid—not ascension-agent, not entirely—from Lolla's coffin. Once, twice. Never enough to make it obvious, never enough to get caught. Marya had done it every damn night until at last Jules caught her at it and moved the coffin down into the shuttle. The vials were so tiny, such hummingbird samples, but they would add up. Rainier had run calculations off the footage. By the time Jules caught Marya, she was one theft short of a viable sample. Jules knew she'd seen an air bubble in the coffin's fluid. But she'd gotten so very good at lying to herself. Then Rainier sent Marya away.

I sent her on a mission.

A video of Marya skipping her assignment to take another shuttle, not ordained by Rainier, to a small station in orbit around one of the asteroids in Ordinal's belt. Glitchy footage, as satellites that should not be Rainier's turned to watch, briefly, as the woman docked her shuttle there. Then cuts to the inside as Marya, carrying a virus—Rainier, Rainier *is* a virus—on her wristpad into the station where Rainier slid like silk into their security, turned their own cameras against them.

Celebration. Youthful friends with bright eyes and brighter grins toasting Marya's ability to steal fire from the gods. Her cunning in being "useful" to Rainier, as the daughter of a Keeper, showing her only things she thought Rainier could not use, to get close. Close enough to steal the secret that kept some Keepers walking through the centuries. Jules had wondered where Marya wore all those pretty clothes.

But it hadn't been enough, the trickles of ascension-agent Marya had stolen. Once more. Marya had to go back one more time into Janus and pretend to be Rainier's creature, desperate for immortality. She would return. She would pretend to be Jules's friend, make nice with the broken girl from the Grotta so that Jules would show her where she'd hidden Lolla.

Then her friends would have a large enough sample to homebrew their own ascension-agent. But then Sanda had come, interrupting her plans, and as Janus tore itself apart, Marya had deployed all the evac pods, condemning Jules to death.

Marya had never wanted to "talk" with Jules. She'd wanted to steal one more sample.

Prometheus's fire was in Marya's hands, and it was going to burn.

It should hurt, to see how Marya had played Jules. For one stupid second, Jules had thought they might have made nice. Maybe even been friends. But despite Marya's efforts, Jules was the one who would make it out alive. That's what she did. Survive. Not like an extremophile or a machine or anything useful or interesting. She was a parasite, clinging not to life but to purpose. Because she'd never had one of her own.

"Three minutes," a robotized voice said.

Jules pressed the button that deployed her helmet. The sleek plates of ebon metal slid up around her face, her skull, whisper-smooth, hissing like the clearest brook across stones. Nox would have lost his mind to touch tech like this.

Jules didn't have much left to lose.

The breach pod tore away from the guardcore ship, carrying Jules and the two other members of her GC team with her. It rattled and shook and tossed her around, but the armor cushioned every jerk. Her stomach didn't even lurch.

Metal screamed all around her, but the helmet dampened the noise. The pod jerked one last time as it bit into the floor of the station and pushed out anchors like tiny grasping hands. Marya must know what this was. Jules considered, in the brief seconds before the door flashed green, the fear she must be feeling. That deep, belly-chilling cold that made every muscle in your body clench.

She'd fight. Marya was a fighter. But Jules had been a fighter, too, and the day she stepped into her home to find her world torn to shreds and her makeshift family half dead had been the day she'd learned it didn't matter how hard you fought, how much you cared. There were forces in this universe that, once moved to action, could not be stopped.

There was a thin chance Marya would win this day. She and her friends might take the GC unit out. But they'd only be stalling. Waiting until Rainier came back with bigger guns and better plans, because the ascension-agent was the one thing you did not steal from Rainier. Everyone on this station was already dead. Jules included, more than likely. Her timeline was just a little longer.

The pod's door opened and Jules took point on autopilot, sweeping the room they'd landed in with the laser on her rifle. A rec room. She didn't recognize it from the videos, but there were couches and counters. Places for people to prepare food and consume it. Mundane things, torn apart. Wires lay on the ground and fizzled like dying snakes.

"Clear," one of the GC said.

"Obtaining map," the other said.

Rainier might have forced her way into the security systems here, but the GC liked to work with fresh data. Their own worms wriggled through the station's thin veneer of security, following the trail of Rainier's intrusion. In seconds they had a map thrown up on the HUD of best guesses at locations of individuals. Jules zeroed in on target alpha—Marya—with three others in a spare room toward the center of the station.

"Marya's mine," Jules said.

The other GC didn't speak, or even twitch a muscle, but she could sense their discomfort. Names weren't used in GC protocols. Jules wasn't even supposed to be in this armor. Rainier had let her don it only because she'd claimed Jules would need every edge against Marya.

Rainier claimed a lot of things, but now Jules saw her for what she was. Saw that she desired nothing more than for humanity to hurt itself as much as she hurt. That's what the armor and Janus and the carrot of Lolla were all for. To crush Jules. To hurt. It had probably made Rainier's day when Jules had been forced to turn Nox and Arden away.

But Rainier was going to learn Jules had a lot of practice at weaponizing her pain.

"Understood," the two GC chorused, arriving at the same conclusion at the same time, as their training dictated. They'd already decided to treat Jules as a fleetie, not a proper GC, and that was fine with her.

"Mop up," Jules ordered.

Maybe she should have felt guilty about that. She didn't. The greed of these people had put Lolla's safety at risk by siphoning off her stasis fluid.

Jules followed the map. She was intercepted, fire from blasters and guns glancing off her armor, going wide, or misfiring altogether. The people who fired those shots were irrelevant.

She squeezed off return fire, watched the bodies sink to the ground, and stepped over them. A trail of bloody chest wounds bloomed in her wake. Center-mass shots. Jules never missed those.

The virus in the station's system dilated all the doors at once, leaving no blind corners, no places to hide. Jules found Marya in the exact spot the map had predicted, hunkered down, her three friends fanned out around her, showering the open door with gunfire the second Jules appeared.

Jules cut them down, one by one, and left Marya crouching behind a pile of crates in the center of the room. Storage, maybe. It didn't matter. They had orders to slag the whole thing when they were done and crash it into the asteroid it orbited.

"Fucking shoot me," Marya demanded.

She stood up, making her chest a clear shot, and threw her rifle to the ground. Chin high, eyes bright with anger and tears, her hands shaking but her feet planted. Jules paused, taking in the loose jeans hanging over her mag boots and the maroon tank top woven with gold-colored glitter. When had she last seen another person in street clothes? When was the last time her world wasn't filled with Prime jumpsuits, GC armor, and white lab coats?

When was the last time she saw *people*? Janus. And Janus had broken.

Jules retracted her helmet.

"You don't wear that armor," Marya said, her voice shaking.

"I do now."

Her lips trembled, but she pulled them into a sneer all the same. "Is this what it does? The agent? Does it turn you into her automaton, or were you always this malleable?"

"I don't know," Jules said, honestly. Marya's smug bullshit had rankled her for so long, it was a strange sensation to feel... nothing... as Marya snorted and postured.

But this time Marya wasn't posturing. Though her body was tense with fear, a flash of pity shot through her expression. "You really don't know. She's been priming you for this for a long, long time."

Jules frowned. "You stole the agent. You risked Lolla's life."

"Is that the girl's name? I never took much, and never all at once. Drops here and there. I didn't mean to hurt the girl, I just wanted what you had. Strength, immortality. Who wouldn't want those things?"

"You admit it?"

"You wouldn't be here if you didn't believe I did it."

True, but somehow she had needed to hear the words from Marya's lips. Needed to solidify her reason, her purpose here.

"Rainier didn't think you'd have the guts to kill one of your own," Marya said. "She was numbing you to it. To killing."

"You're not one of mine," Jules snapped, grip tightening on the rifle. Dimly, she was aware of gunfire, shouting in the halls. She didn't have time for this conversation.

"Does your head hurt yet?"

"What?" A dull thread started up in the back of her mind.

Marya grinned fiercely. "I designed this station like Liao's fringer settlement. Do you see it?"

The hallways looked like tunnels boring down into rock, the doors and rooms in the same style, but that was normal—everything was standard-issue, right off a Prime Inventive assembly line. But that ache was growing stronger.

"You can't fight if the memories are coming back so hard and fast you can't see straight. You remember, don't you? Remember what you did when we collected Liao. What you've done dozens of times without me with you."

More screaming in the halls, but this time the shouts were far away, bubbling up out of memory. Pleading and shouting and return fire, but not here. From another time. Jules grimaced and pressed her hand against the side of her head.

"What the fuck are you doing?" she hissed.

"Pissing off the professional killer." Marya tapped her wristpad, and for a second Jules saw real contrition cross her features. "Sorry."

The surrounding room, so plain before, came to life with footage recorded from a helmet cam. Scenes from Liao's fringer settlement wrapped the metal walls, but they were not as Jules remembered them.

Jules had ordered stunners. She was so fucking sure she'd ordered stunners. But there she was, through Marya's cam, mowing down civilians with her rifle. Center-mass shots one after the other. Old, young; armed, unarmed. It did not matter. All who skittered across Jules's path fell to the steady repeat of her rifle.

Fake footage. Marya had access to the same software they all did, and they'd faked plenty of video to convince the new intakes of their hiring stories. It must be fake.

And yet with every body that fell, Jules's head screamed louder.

But she knew, didn't she? She'd always known. Every time she went out on a mission and came back with a new headache. Every time she'd woken up wearing bruises she didn't remember earning. The memory rollback came with headaches, and she accepted them, because it was the only way she could live with herself. The pain ebbed.

"Did you think Rainier tricked me into doing those things?" Jules gestured to the footage playing out across the walls. Not fake. Just memories. And they hurt less, now. Hurt less in so very many ways. "Did you think she pulled my cellular strings to make me pull the trigger?"

"I don't...I don't understand." The smug triumph faded from Marya's face. Jules took no joy in that.

"I made a promise. A promise to save *one* person. The rest..." Jules let her gaze track over the footage, felt the pain burning in her skull, but found she could ignore it. "...are irrelevant."

"If you were so willing, then why the memory rollbacks? Why did she force you to forget?"

"Marya, I gave the rollbacks to myself."

She put a bullet in Marya's chest and felt nothing as she watched the woman fall.

Jules put her helmet back up and slung her rifle over her shoulder. Rainier would slag this station in ten minutes to make sure no traces of the ascension-agent remained. Jules had a lot of work to do. Her HUD had predicted that the stolen vial of ascension-agent would be on Marya's person, but Jules found it in the top drawer of a desk, the lock easily broken.

It was so small in her hand, and still lacking, but Jules had hidden

Lolla away again. This time, in a place where Rainier could not find her. Jules could provide the final drops needed to increase the quantity to amounts that the duplicators on board guardcore ships needed to manufacture more. She wouldn't need much to achieve her goal, to motivate the scientists of the worlds into fixing Lolla. If Rainier didn't care about biological matters, then Jules would find someone who would.

Guardcore rifles pierced guardcore armor. With deliberate care, she put a bullet in each GC's head.

CHAPTER 71

PRIME STANDARD YEAR 3543

NOBODY'S MASCOT

Nox found Sanda sitting alone in the room that Bero had carved out for their makeshift armory. She sat on a bench, a piece of Prime armor—a shoulder pad—between her hands, turning it over slowly. Bero had, wisely, decided she wanted to be left alone on the long trip to Liao's fringer settlement, and stopped trying to needle her into conversation. Nox didn't have any such qualms.

"Busted?" he asked, and plopped down next to her, stretching his legs out in front of him.

"No. I checked all the equipment, nothing's broken. We've got armor for all of us plus four, and enough weapons to arm a battalion, but we'll run out of bullets eventually."

"Then we switch to the blasters."

"Not as many of those. *The Light* can charge them without draining the engines, but we've got one each. If one breaks, or is lost, we're down a gun-hand."

"If Liao's carrying a weapon, shit's gotten real. I wouldn't worry about it."

Her smile was tight. "It's my job to worry about logistics."

"Don't really have a job now, do you?"

She stopped turning the piece over and stared at the Prime logo, cyan and bright, dead center over where her rotator cuff would be if she strapped it on. "We can't wear this shit until we take the logos off."

He arched both brows at her. "Not sure it matters. We got people running around in fake GC armor. A couple of good guys wearing fake Prime can't be too far off-center."

"Come on," she said, and stood, tucking the piece under her arm.

"What? Where are we going?"

"Cargo."

Sanda strode off, and Nox had to jog to catch up to her. *The Light* opened doors as she passed, Bero giving her total access. No need to swipe a wristpad on this alien ship.

Even now, she wasn't sure she would have allowed the risk of uploading Bero if she had been in her right mind. She wasn't even sure that this being that talked and thought like her friend and captor was who he claimed to be. She wanted to believe. Just like she believed that the chip in her head and the prosthetic on her leg didn't change her mind any more than switching a body should for a digital consciousness.

She wanted to believe, but she couldn't *know*, and she was getting sick and fucking tired of the boundaries in her life being muddied, trampled-over messes.

She passed into the cargo bay, Nox dogging her heels, and moved so quickly that she startled Knuth, his head bent over an open slit in the wall of *The Light*.

"Uh—Commander, hi," he said lamely, and started to salute before her glare stopped him short. He swallowed. "Can I help you?"

She eyed the hastily stored cargo. While tearing through it to find what she wanted would be satisfying, it'd only make a mess for her to clean up later. "We brought everything that could move over from the *Thorn*, correct?"

"Yes, sir."

"I want the silver paint guns used for refreshing the call sign on the side of the *Thorn*."

He blinked owlishly. "Uh. Okay. I mean, *The Light* is already silver and it doesn't really have a call sign, but—"

Her grip tightened on the armor piece. "It's not for the ship. Get me the paint."

"Right. Right-o."

He popped up from his crouch and scrambled through the crates, tapping each one as he passed, then popped the lid open on an aluminum storage trunk and pulled out three pneumatic guns marked with the same color silver as their contents. "This is all we got."

"It's plenty. Thanks."

She stuffed one in her holster belt, shoved one at Nox, and carried the other.

"Is there anything I can help with . . . ?" Knuth asked, bewildered.

"As you were. We've got this."

"Okay," he said, but she was already back in the hall, charging toward the armory.

"You know, defacing the Prime insignia is a court-martialable offense," Nox said.

"So is smart-talking your commander, but we've gone a little off-script here, haven't we?"

"Touché," he said.

She missed the doors onworld. Doors she could kick open when her hands were full. But the weapon and armor lockers were almost as satisfying to yank open. She pulled down everything. Every gun, every scrap of armor, every lifepack or helmet or supply case that bore the Prime logo, and passed it to Nox, who arrayed them all on the floor behind her, for once keeping his mouth shut while they worked, emptying everything in the ship that had been born of Prime.

She didn't have to tell him what to do. When she started spraying those cyan logos into blank squares of silver, he followed her lead, and if he looked a little too gleeful while he did it, well, maybe she did, too.

After a while, she looked up and asked, "Why are you and Arden still here?"

He blinked, sprayed a last stretch of logo, and set a chest plate aside, hands coming to rest over his knees as he picked his head up. "Wondered if you'd ask that."

"Well? You could have left after Janus, after Monte. Okonkwo would have given you new idents and a tidy sum for your service, and you two could have gone back to your lives. Our deal was done."

"I can't speak for Arden," he said, "but yeah, we could have left after Janus. Even talked about it. But not after Monte."

"Don't tell me this is some pissing match with my dad—he leaves, and you have to prove a point by staying."

He snorted. "This ain't about Graham. I stayed because you stayed on Monte."

"I seem to remember that choice nearly getting us all killed."

He smiled, shook his head, and reached for another piece of armor. "You forget, I was with you on that dock when Arden called to report the GC were incoming. You had the sample in your hand, and your ship a quick sprint away. No one would have blamed you for running. I saw you look."

She licked her lips. "Look at what?"

"The *Thorn*." He kept on painting. "Saw the calculations behind your eyes, more or less. You knew staying was suicide. And you knew leaving meant those people didn't have a chance in hell. I figured, I was too late to help Jules. Maybe if I stuck around you, I might be able to help someone else. Also, chances of getting to shoot Rainier are higher around you."

Sanda laughed to herself and stared at the painted armor spread around the floor. "Don't get too sentimental on me."

"Wouldn't dream of it, Commander."

Hours passed. Conway poked her head into the room and nearly jumped out of her skin. Her eyes were huge and her mouth open, but then, slowly, she relaxed. Sanda looked up from crouching over a breastplate and brushed the hair from her face, smearing silver paint across her cheek.

"I won't have anyone say we were impersonating the fleet," Sanda said. It was only a half reason, but explaining to Conway that she couldn't be sure those logos stood for something *good* anymore wasn't a step Sanda was willing to take. It was a solid enough reason, though, so Conway nodded and stepped into the room, holding out her hand.

"Give me that other gun," she said.

Liao was next to interrupt, but her surprise was mild, only a slight raising of one brow. "Well. At least my people won't think I've brought an invading Prime battalion."

"I won't fly false colors," Sanda said, and stood, brushing paint onto her jumpsuit thighs, which was quickly absorbed. She sighed. They'd have to do something about the logos on the jumpsuits, but at the very least the armaments were without creed.

"If you're done redecorating, we've arrived."

"Already? It's only been a few days."

"I am faster than most ships," Bero said.

Sanda grinned. "Show-off. All right, Doctor. Let's go see what kind of welcome your old boss will give us."

CHAPTER 72

PRIME STANDARD YEAR 3543

PICKING UP THE PIECES

Biran reviewed the statement he'd sworn never to give, finger hovering over the delete button. This was no off-the-cuff speech, no heart-to-heart with the people of Ada. This was PR, carefully prepared. Cultured by a committee to nurture the right kind of mood, the right infectious tone. He could not give this statement. He had to give this statement.

As Biran reread those fallow words, he was intimately aware that his public address was late. The investigation into the asteroid's "accident" had dragged on too long. Rumors had festered, and many of them verged close enough to the truth that Biran believed they could not be squashed.

He wanted honesty. He wanted to stare down that camera and tell the people of Ada that Keeper Hitton had done what she thought was best—had sunk the ship to drown the rats—but that could not be done, for there was enough of the asteroid left to support the build, and the gate must go ahead. Any sliver of doubt regarding the stability and safety of the project from those on high would shatter their fragile peace.

But he did not even have honesty. He believed Hitton had done what she thought was best, whatever her reasons, but he could not prove it. Could not reach back through time and beg her to tell him why she would self-destruct the survey site. If she had left some clue for him, some breadcrumb to scrape out of the ashes of her death, he had not yet found it. The uncertainty tore him up inside.

"Speaker," Anford said across the table. "You're stalling."

"Forgive me, but there is a general in my home requesting I make a statement as fabricated as my kitchen. I have a hard time seeing how this will help ease the minds of the populace."

Anford's presence didn't mesh with his home. Not that Biran entertained many visitors, but the general looked too solid, too crisp, to be sitting in the shabby chair he hadn't upgraded since he first got the house. An irrational part of him feared that the weight she carried would break the flimsy structure and send them all tumbling down.

"This is a matter of gate security," Anford said.

"And that's it? The High Protectorate says gate security, and we abandon our ethics for safety?"

"Speaker, the asteroid was your plan. Are you so eager to see it fail?"

I would see this undone, he thought, and the second the words came to mind he realized how irrational he was being. Churlish and childish. There was no going back. No taking Hitton off of that asteroid on the *Taso* and whisking her away to a Prime hospital where her paranoia could be heard and treated if it came to that. Sabotage or no, he'd left her there to stew in her fear. And now he had to fix his project, because he could not undo what he had already done.

"I hate this," he said, as he turned his arm so he could point the wristpad camera at himself.

"Not my favorite job either, buddy."

He blinked, tearing his gaze away from those traitorous words long enough to catch the sad smile that ghosted across her face—wry with an internal conflict he could only guess at. Biran had made Anford's life hell, he knew that, but here she was, pushing him to cross this threshold in person. It was gentler coming from her, someone he knew, than a faceless row of GC waiting for him to work up the nerve and hit broadcast. She didn't have to be here. And he was being a shit.

"Thank you," he said.

She merely nodded.

Biran switched the camera to record—they wouldn't let him

broadcast this one live. It wasn't the kind of message that could be done off-the-cuff, or in an interview format. The people were used to him making addresses from his home, especially during lockdown. He hoped they'd forgive him if his words seemed a little too polished, a little too formal.

"My friends," he said, because the *people of Ada Prime* scrawled at the top of his prepared speech felt woefully distant. "We have suffered a grave loss."

This part, he felt, Olver must have written, or at the very least directed. "While the crew of the asteroid was, thank the stars, saved before the accident, Keeper Hitton was still on-site."

His throat caught over the first lie—*accident.* But he must assure them. Assure them that there was not another phase opening to the war, that the robots all worked flawlessly. There could be no doubt. Only hope. Only progress. While one woman lay dead for fighting a threat that may or may not have existed.

"I understand your fear. I understand the rumors. I can assure you that the asteroid was not attacked. This was not an act of war, but a terrible mistake." The other lie. Bitter, bitter. "Not in the equipment, Prime engineering functions as intended, but in the mind handling it. Missions like these, where one spends so much time at the spearhead of a small team, can be isolating."

You'll paint me as mad, Hitton had said. Olver had mentioned age creeping up on the elder Keepers. It wasn't impossible. But she'd been so confident, not raving and peeking under tables. She'd had experiences she couldn't explain, and Biran's own experiences confirmed the existence of rogue guardcore.

He'd promised. Biran had *promised.*

Deterioration of the mind was such a tricky thing to pin down, especially with Prime's advancements allowing people to appear as young and strong as they wished. His chest clenched.

"And despite all of that," he found himself saying, "she still made the right choice. Keeper Hitton got her people off that asteroid, before a critical failure in the hab dome could take them all out with her."

Anford did not twitch a muscle. This was recorded, after all. The Protectorate was watching it now, yes, but they'd decide after the fact if it would be broadcasted to the rest of Prime. They could make him do this a thousand times before he got it "right."

"The dome was hastily erected," he pressed on, this lie tasting less slimy than the others, "and old stock. Once Hitton detected the failure, she got her people off station before an explosive decompression event. Under normal circumstances, she would have evacuated with them. However, due to the presence of sensitive Prime materials on station, Keeper Hitton found it necessary to initiate a self-destruct sequence to ensure the erasure of all such materials from potential scavengers." He took a long, slow breath.

"This is the cost of Keeperdom. This is the price we know we must pay, should our data ever be threatened. That Keeper Hitton did so without hesitation, I can assure you. Whether she did so without regret, I cannot say. But I can say that Keeper Hitton loved Ada. Loved Prime. And wanted us all to grow into a safe and prosperous future. She gave her life for that. We are all going to have to give just a little more time, while we wait for the system to be secured beyond a doubt and the gate construction to begin. A small price, for all of us. Let us never forget how much it cost one, to ease the burdens of we many."

Biran stopped recording. Anford hadn't moved so much as an eyelash.

"Do you think they'll air it?" he asked.

"I would."

A heaviness eased in Biran. He didn't feel lighter, not exactly. The burden was still there—it was just a tiny bit easier to carry. As if he'd found better leverage, a better grip.

An incoming call from Olver flashed, and he accepted it without hesitation.

"That was not as planned," Olver said carefully, "but we have decided that it will suit."

"Thank you, Director."

"This was the High Protectorate's decision." He hesitated. "But thank you, Speaker Greeve. Hitton would not approve, but she would have appreciated that direction."

Olver blanked the call. Biran pressed his elbows into the tabletop and leaned forward, dragging his fingers through his hair. Anford stood. Hesitated.

"There is something else I'm meant to tell you."

A chill crept into Biran. Anford did not stall, but she was stalling now. "What is it?"

"I have been informed that you are not to attend the spin-up of the gate. The Prime Director wants you in the Cannery, ready to make a statement after the event. Not, in her words, 'parading around on that stage during the spin.'"

Biran licked his lips, wondering why this didn't hurt as much as it should. This was his punishment. Biran had gone to that asteroid and made the wrong choice, tainting the project, and now she was sitting him on the sidelines while the others claimed the final glory of initializing the gate he'd fought to build. He did not pick up his head.

"Thank you for telling me."

"I'm sorry, Speaker."

The door swished shut behind her, and Biran did not know how long he sat there, head bowed, fingertips digging into his scalp, before his house AI chirped: "Visitor request."

He blinked and looked up with bleary eyes. Few could get around the lockdown. "Who?"

"Keeper Singh. Under lockdown provisions, it is advised that you deny all unnecessary requests."

"Yes, yes. Let her in."

Singh appeared as a washed-out specter in his doorway. Biran pushed to his feet, feeling leaden. He forced himself to cross the room, to reach out and take her elbow, guiding her gently into the chair Anford had vacated.

"Tea?" he asked, already halfway to the dispenser.

"Sit down, Speaker."

He did.

"I am not here to be... ministered to. I have information that I must share with someone. You seemed as good a candidate as any."

Biran pressed his lips together. Singh's ally in all things before this moment had been Keeper Hitton. He held no illusions that Singh's respect may have grown for him since Hitton's death. She was here because Hitton was not, and while Hitton had never been his enemy, she had not been his friend, either.

A chill crept up his spine. It would be an easy thing to place the blame for Hitton's death at his feet. Though he could not have controlled her actions, he certainly felt responsible. If Singh felt he was responsible, too, then he'd made a powerful enemy.

Biran sat across from her and, under the table, silently pressed a series of buttons on his wristpad to record across all wavelengths.

"Before Isa's accident," Singh said, and he had to strain to pay attention as it took him a moment to remember that Isa had been Hitton's first name, "...she attempted to send a tightbeam burst of information to a nearby satellite. Angling for a gate relay, I presume."

"Had she found evidence?"

Her expression twisted between bitter amusement and mild disdain. "Ah. So you believed her, then? Believed there was a saboteur?"

"I don't know. Didn't you?"

"I couldn't be sure." That disdain, he realized, was for herself. "But you. You were actually there."

"She seemed to me unsettled," he said.

"But not unbalanced."

"No. Not that."

"Thank you. I had come to the same conclusion. But after her actions, I had wondered...And then there was this transmission." She adjusted the plush, white pashmina draping her shoulders.

"What was she sending?"

"That's the very thing. I don't have a clue, but it was wrapped in an encryption envelope that made me wonder, well...You had better see for yourself."

She turned her wristpad around so he could see, and pulled up a file. At first, he thought she was joking, or had made a mistake. The cubical 3-D wireframe package used to represent Keeper data spun in the center of the screen. It was what they used in teaching materials, and what every Keeper saw when they accessed their chip and asked the scanner to display their data on the screen to be sure it was intact. None of them could unravel that data—it was useless without the construction bots to act upon it—but still. It should not, under any circumstances, be sent anywhere but into a gate-building robot.

"This is a mistake," he said.

"No. You cannot guess how many times I double-checked this."

"Did you…" He dragged his mind away from any question Singh might think obvious or stupid. "She might have been trying to beam it to the gate bots en route, to save time on the upload."

"You and I both know she made that crater to keep the project from moving forward. Why would she facilitate it in any way?"

"I don't know. I can't see…"

"Neither can I."

Hitton had tried to send her chip data elsewhere. A lot was encompassed in that word *elsewhere*. She might have been attempting to store it as a backup. Still a gross violation, but the intent would not be so bad. In her paranoia, she might have convinced herself that it was best, that placing her data off-site, so to speak, would keep it safer. She might have simply not wanted to carry that burden anymore.

But it had not been a storage device she sent it to. For some reason only Hitton could explain, she had been sending her data *somewhere*, and that left the uncomfortable and obvious implication that she was, de facto, sending it to *someone*. All acts that would have gotten her chip yanked in a heartbeat.

Hitton had beaten them to the punch. She was dead. There could be no more punishment for Isa Hitton. If she had done this. If Singh wasn't just winding him up, angling to make him look like the next Keeper to fall to paranoia.

"You would bet all our lives that the data got no further than your interception?" he asked after a long silence.

She nodded. "Yes, I would. I am familiar with some of Isa's digital habits and had been watching certain pathways after her communications to me became…unsettled. This was intercepted before it reached the satellite. Someone would have had to be watching as closely as I was, at exactly the right moment. I find the possibility improbable."

"Delete it," Biran said.

Singh leaned back, and for the first time some color returned to her cheeks. "I beg your pardon?"

"Delete the data. You should not have it regardless, and delete all traces that this happened. Hitton is dead. She cannot be punished further, nor do I believe she should be. Whatever her reasons... they died with her. It's time we let her rest, so we can move forward."

"Well," Singh said, her eyebrows pressing together until they met in the middle. "I had come to you because I suspected you would not be so sentimental as Olver."

"Do not mistake this for sentiment. The project must go forward. The data was not *actually* breached. Even if someone received it, they would still need the password procedures to access it. There are rumors enough around this incident without stirring up more."

Singh smiled to herself and, slowly so that he could see each button press, erased the data from her wristpad.

"I am pleased that we see eye to eye, Speaker Greeve."

Biran smiled back at her, and recalled his discovery of Anaia's asteroid photos. Nothing was ever truly deleted on a Prime drive.

CHAPTER 73

PRIME STANDARD YEAR 3543

ANOTHER DAMN HEADACHE

Yaxia was a petite, stern person with a thick black-and-grey braid that reached down to their waist. Hollow cheeks drew craven shadows along their jaw, and their eyes had the dark-circle look of someone who had not slept well in many days.

The resolution of Bero's new cameras showed every line of worry stamped deep into the corners of their eyes as they stared down the crew of *The Light* from within their asteroid stronghold, hands clasped behind their back, a set to their chin that reminded Sanda of General Anford.

"Min," they said, "we assumed that you were dead."

Liao dug the edge of her thumb into her temple, wincing. Sanda frowned to herself, wondering. Liao seemed to have developed a headache the moment the fringer settlement appeared on the viewscreen.

"Dead?" Liao asked. "Why would you think such a thing? I haven't been gone all that long."

A flash of color rouged their cheeks as they laughed, roughly. "Guardcore burst into our home. They took you out unconscious, and once you'd gone, they came back to burn the place out. We only survived because Jesson got some bots working in time to control the fire. We presumed you were sentenced to the same fate as all the others. Dead for 'gate research.' "

"No," Liao said, "no, no. Valentine came and interviewed me there. It was all very civil, but it had to be quick."

"Min." Their voice was tired, but gentle. "They slaughtered us."

A crevice appeared between Liao's brows. "That's not what happened. I would remember."

"Doctor," Sanda said as kindly as she could, "does your head hurt right now? When you try to remember, does the pain get worse?"

"I... Yes. What's happening? How did you know that?"

"It's not your fault you don't remember. Icarion had memory rollback technology. They used it on me, and I suppose they got it from their friend Rainier. If Rainier wanted you working compliantly, she would use it on you. It always hurts when I try to remember. Even still."

Liao knuckled both fists into her temples and folded over. Sanda gestured to Conway, who put her sturdy arm under Liao's and helped her into a chair.

"Memory rollback?" Yaxia said, disbelief making them scoff, but a flicker of worry crossed them as Liao let out a soft moan. "What is this? What have you done to Min?"

"My crew and I have done nothing to your friend; this is the work of a woman named Rainier. We are here because we need your help," Sanda said.

"This station is in no position to help anyone," they said, but their gaze was locked on Liao.

"Doctor, I understand your wariness. In your position, I would turn us away. Being hammered by the GC is no joke. I cannot, and will not claim to, understand what happened to you and your people. But I can tell you we share the same enemy. The people who kidnapped your colleague and laid waste to your settlement are not actual GC. They are pretenders, and I am doing everything in my power to stop them."

"Who are you?" Their voice had lost some of its edge, a hint of desperation seeping in.

"Sanda Greeve, commander of *The Light*."

Their lips curled into a wry smile. "A major in the fleet. We literally live under a rock here, Commander, but we are not so unaware of the world that the name of the war hero of Dralee hasn't reached our ears. I have no desire to treat with the fleet, regardless of our common enemy."

"I am not with the fleet." The words tasted bitter, but she got them out without wincing.

Yaxia narrowed their eyes. "Really. You may have removed the logo, but that doesn't erase what you are, and if that man"—they pointed their chin at Nox—"is not a soldier, I will eat this asteroid I live on. Your ship I do not recognize, but I know enough to realize that expensive, experimental equipment is not something a retired major would stroll around the universe in. Prime went to great pains to erase the murder of Keeper Lavaux from your record. They do not let polished trophies go so easily."

"This ship..." She closed her eyes briefly. "I will parley with you honestly, because we need your help and I suspect there is very little time. This ship is not of human design. It was discovered behind a deadgate, and is currently piloted by the Icarion AI known as *The Light of Berossus*, though he prefers to be called Bero."

"Hello," Bero said.

Yaxia blinked. Their jaw chewed around for a moment. "I have heard of the Icarion intelligence. The ship, however—"

Sanda pressed on. "The ship contained a sphere of information that we believe the woman who commands the false GC might use to harm people. We only got fragments of the data before we were betrayed by a real GC, one of Okonkwo's personal aides."

"That is a hell of a story, Commander. Some would say the war has broken your mind."

"Some do," she admitted.

Liao lifted her head and brushed the hair off her sweaty forehead. "My mind hasn't broken, no matter that I can't remember. Arden—send them the first fragment of data. See for yourself. These are not alloys we use. It's not even notation we use."

"Fine," Yaxia sighed. "My ident number is—"

"I sent it," Bero said.

They scowled. "I am not exactly *listed*, ship."

"No. But your network security isn't as good as you believe. I can help with that. Arden can help with that."

"Just look at the data," Liao said.

Yaxia rolled their eyes, but they looked down, their already drawn face growing more and more pinched as they read. "This doesn't make any sense."

"Yes. That's the problem," Sanda said. "Doctor, we have more. We need your help to figure out what it all means. You need our help to secure your station."

"And how will you do that?"

She waved a hand. "Bero and Arden will handle your network. Nox and Conway can provide you with arms and better threat-response protocols. Knuth can look at your life-support systems."

"I should send you packing and report you to the fleet," they said.

"Xia," Liao said tiredly. "Please. I was tricked into doing research that may cause harm to many people. If you won't help the commander, help me fix what I've done."

"There are so few of us," Yaxia said softly.

A realization rocked Liao with a fresh wave of pain, but she gritted her teeth and grabbed the arms of her chair. "The children? Tell me the children—"

"Safe," Yaxia said firmly. "Most of them. The Keeper who came for you ordered stunners right before she took you, and we lost a few to a bad reaction. We were able to hide the rest before they came back to mop up after taking you."

"What Keeper?" Sanda asked.

"We don't know her name, but there is no one else the GC would protect so thoroughly. Here, we have footage."

A few quick taps from Yaxia, and security footage filled the screen. Jules. Jules Valentine wore the grey-cyan armor of the Keepers, her face so cold and hateful Sanda hadn't recognized her at first. That woman, that warrior, was not the scared, desperate person Sanda had met on Janus. Valentine had been faking control on Janus, play-acting confidence. There was nothing fake about the Valentine on that footage, dropping bodies like she was chopping wood. No room for uncertainty in those laser-sharp eyes.

"Turn it off," Nox said, voice shaking. What had he been trying to save? What had they all *missed*?

Sanda couldn't bring herself to look at either Nox or Arden. "We want to stop more incidents like this."

"We are done being used," Yaxia said.

"Please," Liao said. "Help me. Help me fix what I have done."

Yaxia stared at Liao for a very long time. "Very well. The beta dock is still standing. You're cleared for approach."

"Thank you," Sanda said.

Yaxia met her gaze. "I do this for Liao, and Liao alone."

INTERLUDE

PRIME STANDARD YEAR 0002

TO KEEP THE SECRET

Nothing. Nothing living waited for Alexandra Halston on the other side of her second gate. On the forward viewscreen of a ship large enough to spin for gravity, Lex watched the live footage coming back from the swarm of scout bots.

Watched barren rock and inert dust pass by as, planet after planet, moon after moon, the data came back the same: dead, having never lived at all.

"I'm sorry," Maria said.

Her hand was on Lex's arm, but she could not feel it. All she could feel was the endless nothing, the empty universe at once all-encompassing and utterly pointless. A gift. The sphere had been a gift from a more advanced race, curling a finger, beckoning them to the stars.

There could not be *nothing*, for there had been *something*, and she would find the originators if it meant mapping every speck of dust in the known universe.

"Director," one of her Keepers said. "Scanners are picking up unusual inorganic matter."

"Show me."

A cloud of silver pulsed upon the forward viewscreen. At first she could not tell what she was looking at. That sense of unknowing sent a shiver of excitement through her, for there was not a banal formation in the universe that Alexandra Halston would not recognize on sight.

Patterns emerged from the glinting cumulus. At first she feared energy strikes tearing through something terribly normal like a nebula, but these were not the bursts and throes of physics as she understood it. Bright lines hinted at connections, winked at thicker coalescences connected by filaments. It reminded her of visualizations of the universe's dark matter, but this was no artist's rendition. This was new.

"Set course," she said, and the twelve Keepers of the first Protectorate rushed to fulfill their director's order.

Months. It'd taken endless months to cross that dead, empty space before they reached the cloud field. Lex would have to do something about that—such wasteful travel times were unacceptable for the future of Prime—but now, now she had other matters to see to.

For the closer they drew, the more the anomaly changed.

It solidified somewhat, compressing into a cylindrical shape that could be only a mirror of their own ship. Hails had gone unanswered. Scans had come back with nothing more than evenly distributed signatures of heat. By the time they were in range, it accepted their transfer tunnel as if it were any other ship.

Alexandra went first, to wait another second would have been agony, but her Keepers came behind her. Maria brought up the rear with suspicious eyes. Lex ordered the guardcore to stay behind, and so it was Maria alone who carried a weapon.

The twelve knew of the sphere that spawned the gates. Knew of the secret instructions inscribed on impossible metal and still, *still*, when they found the second they wept, for a gift knocked out of the skies was one thing. To stand in a vessel built by unknown hands and watch alien technology uncoil from the ceiling, extending a single sphere cradled in tendrils of metal, was something else altogether.

Lex could not hear their gentle tears through the racing of her own thoughts. The sphere lowered into her hand, and though she couldn't feel it through her glove, the subtle weight was enough to give her goose bumps, as if she held ice.

Her HUD picked up scratches in the perfect metal, subtle variations that could be only the ones and zeros of binary. She'd memorized the first section of the original sphere. This was new. And the only people in all the universe who knew about the existence of either sphere were in this room.

Slowly, deliberately, Lex tapped at her wristpad. In terrible synchronicity the first twelve Keepers of the Protectorate fell, their brain stems immolated with merciful swiftness as Alexandra Halston cut the threads of their lives.

Maria alone was left standing, and when Lex turned to face her, she was unsurprised to find that woman's firearm pointed at Lex's head.

"Why?" Maria asked, and her voice had gone as cold as Lex's heart.

"Do you not remember my would-be assassin?" Maria shook her head, mute. That was all right. Lex had plenty of practice speaking for them both. "Erik. He piloted the *Reina Mora*, do you remember? The ship that brought us through the Charon Gate to Tau Ceti. He spoke of the sphere, in his final breath."

"But... That was months ago..." Maria's gaze fell to the dead. Her lips thinned.

"Yes. One of them *shared*." She shook her head sadly. "The secret must be kept."

They'd had this conversation a thousand times a thousand, batting back and forth the fanged truth of the gate's origin. And in the end, always, they came to the same conclusion: The risk that humanity would rip itself to shreds over the knowledge was statistically significant, and such an event could not be allowed.

How embarrassing it would be, to self-destruct at the final hurdle before they met their intergalactic betters.

Lex held the sphere up, admiring the shining surface. Without tearing her gaze from the object, she extended one hand to Maria. It was a full minute before she took it.

Slowly, inexorably, the lights of the ship began to brighten.

CHAPTER 74

PRIME STANDARD YEAR 3543

KNOWLEDGE IS NEVER ENOUGH

What was left of the settlement came out to see *The Light* dock. Sanda watched them gather at a safe distance—adults and children, dirty and scared, clutching hands and jackets and looking upon *The Light* with a mix of resentment, fear, and fascination. She would have to acquire some lander shuttles if she wanted to dock at any other station or planet.

Bero could stealth the ship in open space, and they'd crawl into dock on the shuttles. It was one thing for Liao's people, with whom she planned on sharing the data, to see the ship. Even if they didn't keep her secret, they were already on the fringe of society. Any reports they made would be brushed aside as conspiracy.

The Light being spotted at a larger station or planet could be a problem, though. Sanda already had the fleet and Rainier hounding her heels. She didn't need extraterrestrial hunters on her tail as well. That was definitely not a problem covered by her fleet protocols.

Bero molded what she thought of as his airlock to the entry tunnel. Sanda watched the fine filaments wrap around the human construction, so clumsy in comparison, and repressed a shudder. They were so terribly outclassed by the beings who had built this ship. Where were they? Was Rainier the last of them? And, if so, why did she look like a human woman? Maybe that was the point of the nanites—to reshape what she was into something that could be understood by whatever species she encountered.

Dios, she sounded like one of the conspiracy theorists. But the spitballers on the net weren't standing in a ship built of nanofilaments that was, despite all probability, producing artificial gravity.

The hull split, letting in a gust of stale, over-recycled air. Sanda suppressed a cough. They wore helmets for comms, but kept their visors open. She'd ordered Liao to stand at her right, keeping Conway and Nox well behind them as a sign of peace, but she hadn't relinquished the blaster at her hip. She'd been surprised one too many times to be caught without a weapon.

"Doctor," she said. "Thank you for hearing us out."

Yaxia looked even more exhausted in person. Their collarbone pushed against the thin fabric of their jacket, the hollow of their throat too deep, eyes too bloodshot. This wasn't just exhaustion. The settlement had put themselves on sharp rations until they could discern who it was safe to trade with. These people were starving out of fear.

"You gave us little choice," they said. "What, exactly, do you need, Min?"

"We have a set of data fragments that we believe direct the construction of nanites capable of resembling biological cells. The data stack is broken, but massive nonetheless. We need simulation software, and we need it sandboxed."

They sniffed. "We have the sandbox, and simulating nanites is what we do, but we don't have the processing power. It will take days, at the least, to assemble a schematic of the size you're suggesting."

Sanda tipped her head toward *The Light*. "Our ship will assist you with processing power."

Yaxia's eyes narrowed. "And how can I trust the security of your system?"

Arden wiggled to the front of the pack. "I'll explain the handshake protocol and establish the parameters. You, uh, have a network person?"

Yaxia closed their eyes briefly. "We did. She's dead. Jesson has taken over most of those procedures."

"Great," Arden said, trying on a smile that melted off under Yaxia's slow stare. "I'll, uh... talk to him and get on that."

"He is also our head of security at the moment," they said with a slight tinge of embarrassment. Stretching one person so thin between roles was a better sign of their numbers lost than the actual head count.

"No problem," Nox drawled before Arden could stick their foot in their mouth again. "You all go do your science thing, and I'll have a talk with Jesson. Arden, you can have him when we're done."

A fringer had approached *The Light*, a lanky man who pressed a HUD monocle to his eye as he pressed one hand against the side of the ship. Sanda bristled.

"Please ask Bero's permission before touching him," she said firmly.

The man jumped, pulling his hand back, and flushed scarlet. "I'm sorry, I didn't think."

"Your behavior is understandable, if not acceptable," Bero said dryly.

The fringers looked up, eyes wide, trying to take in the whole of *The Light*, but as Sanda well knew, the ship was impossible to comprehend as a whole. Somehow, it took up more space than its actual size allowed for.

"Bero may be temporarily inhabiting *The Light*, but that does not make it any less his body. Just as my prosthetic is no less *my* leg because it is replaceable. Speak to him as a person, or we're done here."

Yaxia inclined their head. "I will spread the word. Bero, thank you for lending us your processing power."

"It is not a favor, it is an exchange."

"As you say. Let's get this trade over with."

Yaxia waved for them to follow while a man who must be Jesson caught Nox's attention. They led their small party—Arden, Sanda, and Liao—through half-rusted tunnels, the stink of human sweat and dirt and stale air growing thicker the deeper they ventured. Scorch marks marred the tunnels here and there, concentrated around tight corners. Stains that were not rust blotched the floor. With every step they took, Arden's expression grew darker.

Liao clasped her hands together and kept her head down. Sanda understood. To be afflicted by a headache now, when she needed to focus, would only hold her back.

The lab was as busted up as the rest of the facility, but the computational consoles themselves seemed functional. Sanda, knowing she was all but useless here, stepped to the side and let Arden and Liao fuss over the connection and upload of data.

On her wristpad, she tapped out to Bero: Are they treating you well?

B: As well as a mouse treats a cat.

S: I'm sorry, I frightened them.

B: It wasn't you. It's my body. It's always been my body.

She closed her eyes and sighed, an ache in her head that had nothing to do with false memories. She was about to reply when Yaxia stepped next to her.

They whispered, "Is Min well?"

"I don't know," Sanda said honestly. "The rollback is painful, that I can guarantee, but whether there are any long-term effects...I haven't lived long enough to find that out."

"You say that as if you don't expect to live long enough to find out."

Her smile was genuine, if small. "These days, Doctor, I feel I never know where the next shot is coming from."

"And yet you abandoned your post."

She lifted her chin. "I'll be straight with you. Some of the biggest assholes in the universe want their hands on this tech, and they're willing to kill to get it. This, right here, is the best thing I can do to protect the people of Prime."

Yaxia sighed and looked around their blaster-scarred lab. "I thought the same thing."

"Xia," Liao said. "Can you come look at this? I think I know what this is, but...it's your specialty."

"That was fast," Yaxia said.

Sanda shrugged. "We have yet to scrape the surface of Bero's new capabilities."

Yaxia approached the console warily and held a HUD monocle over one eye, face scrunching as they observed the scant models their system drew from the fragmented data. "This is incomplete," they said, "but these appear to be synthetic structures meant to imitate biology."

"Not that part," Liao said, "this here. There are two types of nanites in this set of data."

Yaxia's nose scrunched. "That's your area, Min. They look like receivers to me, about the same size. I suppose they're meant to be used in unison. Build a synth cell structure, then seed it with receivers to take commands and distribute them to the cells. An interesting approach. Not something we're working on."

Liao began to sweat, her face pale as a sheet. "Amplifiers. Rainier had us working on amplifiers."

"What?" Yaxia tilted their head. "I suppose you would need quite a strong signal if these systems were far apart, but what in Earth's name are they for? I can't see any mechanism of action."

"Lavaux," Sanda said with a sick feeling. "He was…made up of these cells. We think Jules has been changed as well."

Yaxia's head jerked back. "People? Hmm, well, I suppose it's theoretically possible. I'd have to see the rest of the data to be sure. On the surface the benefits would be incredible. You could self-repair. Functionally you'd be immortal. But with this receiver component, you'd be a puppet."

"Who knows how many people she's changed," Sanda said, feeling sick.

CHAPTER 75

PRIME STANDARD YEAR 3543

TIME TO BE THE BAD GUY

Sanda," Bero said through the speaker in her wristpad. "I'm sorry to interrupt, but I've detected a GC ship without transponder incoming." She should have felt dread, but Sanda snapped into alert mode instantly, hand resting on her blaster.

"Yaxia, I'm so sorry, but we need to get your people off of this asteroid right fucking now."

"What?" Yaxia stood tall. "That wasn't a part of our deal, *Commander*. You have no authority on this station, and even if you did, you couldn't force us to leave."

"I don't have time to fuck around here. Your people are starving—don't try to deny it—and frankly, if Rainier has decided she wants a large population to test her experiments on, you're it. You've cut yourself off—because of her, yes—but she knows this. You need to get out of here. You cannot survive another GC attack, and none of us want to see what happens if they're not here to kill."

"And where in the void will we go?" Yaxia threw their hands up. "We've known it was only a matter of time since the guardcore took Liao. This has been an endless debate among us without you butting in with your damn hero complex. There is nowhere that will take us. The other fringer colonies think we're poisoned goods. To them, we're already dead and it's just a matter of time. This settlement is all we have."

"Monte Station," Sanda said. "The people there were also attacked by the false GC. They fucking hate me, and I don't blame them, but they can't turn away refugees from a similar assault."

"I believe I can shoot the GC ship down," Bero said.

"No. I'd love to blow her out of the black, but we don't know how big her network is, and we can't afford for her to know that you're in that ship, B." She switched her comm to open channel. "Enemy GC incoming. Evacuate all souls to *The Light* and prepare for transfer to Monte Station."

Chaos broke out across the line. Sanda winced and muted everyone except her crew.

Yaxia's fists were clenched, their body trembling. "You don't order my people."

"I do now."

Yaxia reached for their own comms unit. Liao grabbed their wrist. "She's right, Xia. I'm sorry but it's true. I was on Monte during the attack. I was on Janus. Rainier will burn worlds to get what she wants. If she's coming here, it's to finish what she started or to get test subjects for her experiments. You have to get on that ship. We have to get on that ship."

"Or she's chasing your new friends," Yaxia grated.

Liao said, "Either way, it's too late."

Yaxia met Liao's eyes and nodded. Liao took her hand back, and Yaxia pressed their comm firmly. "Abandon station. Evacuation protocols. The crew of *The Light* will direct you."

"Thank you," Sanda said. To her crew, "Load out in fifteen, stealth and burn for Monte."

Nox requested a private channel; she accepted. "She'll chase us there. It's the only logical place for us to run."

"No. She won't. Because I'm going to give her what she wants."

"We don't even know what she wants," Nox protested.

"She and Keeper Lavaux wanted what was behind that deadgate. That's the sphere." Sanda closed her eyes. "When Rainier comes, I'll be here, and I'll tell her Demas ran off with it. Let those two butt heads for a while."

"You will do no such goddamn thing," Nox said. "She'll slaughter you before you can get a word out."

"I don't think so. She was working with Lavaux so long that, whatever she is, she's picked up human proclivities." Sanda thought back to that night at her welcome-home party. Her interaction with Rainier had been brief, but in that moment she'd picked up an intense sense of curiosity from the woman. "She'll want to know what I have to say."

Nox switched over to all-crew comms. "Our commander plans to stay behind and have fucking tea with Rainier."

Sanda winced as a chaos of voices made her comm squeal. "One at a time," she snapped.

A long pause. Arden, standing across from her in the battered lab with a faraway look on their face, asked, "Why?"

Sanda was vaguely aware of the evacuation going on all around her, Yaxia and their people oblivious to the argument playing out over private comms. Yaxia had been the first person Liao had ushered out of the room to *The Light*, leaving Arden and Sanda alone. Arden, then, was the only one who could read her expression. She treaded carefully.

"Two reasons. The first, setting Rainier against Demas and Okonkwo will give us an advantage. Those two fighting might weaken one or the other enough that we can break them."

"The second?" Arden asked.

"What we learned here. There are two sets of nanite construction data. The first makes a nanite that self-replicates synthetic cells that mimic biology. The second is a receiver set, meant to work with the first." She licked her lips. "Janus was building amplifiers. If Rainier is planning to use those amplifiers on infected people, not the gates, then we have to know. We have to know how many, and what signals exactly she can send. People could be walking around out there as Rainier's puppets and have no idea. I have a bargaining chip because I know where the sphere is."

Arguments broke out across the comm, but this time, Sanda ignored them. She met Arden's gaze steadily as they thought, head tilted to one side, a dimple between their brows. They straightened as if jolted, then set about doing something with the consoles in the lab—fussing with wires. They said nothing.

"We can't take the risk," Conway was saying over the channel, her voice rising above Nox's expletives and Knuth and Liao's bickering.

"See? Nobody's on board with this, Commander," Nox said, and for once he spoke her title without sarcasm. "Get your ass back here. We're almost fully boarded."

"I like the idea of Okonkwo and Rainier tearing into each other, though," Liao said carefully.

"Then we'll leave her a fucking note," Nox said. "Write it now. We're boarded. We're leaving."

A text appeared in the corner of her wristpad, from Bero.

B: I can see what Arden's doing.

S: I can't.

B: They're building an EMP. If Rainier is synthetic, it might destroy her and disable the GC armor, paralyzing them.

S: Not to mention destroy the station and its life support. Yaxia will flip—if something fries permanently, they'll have nowhere to come back to. The station will die.

B: This station is already dead. Yaxia has just not accepted the reality yet. I have reviewed the files from your battle with the berserker shields. This seems a tactic you're familiar with. Possibly where Arden got the idea.

Sanda flicked her eyes up from the pad and met Arden's gaze. They nodded solemnly and tapped on their wristpad. A second later, a program packet arrived on hers—the only graphic a big red button wrapped in a bow. She smiled despite the ache clenching her throat, and hit accept.

Arden clasped her shoulder, not a comforting squeeze, just a firm affirmation, then said over comms, "Calm down, Nox, I got her. We're coming, we're coming."

"Fucking sanity prevails."

Arden smiled, a touch sad, pressed a finger to their lips, then slid out the door and shut it behind them.

B: Are you sure?

S: We might never get another chance to find out what she wants.

B: I agree.

S: She might have changed thousands already.

B: I agree.

S: Stop saying that.

B: I can agree, but I don't have to like it.

S: Get clear. Take them to Monte. Pull the camera feed from my wrist-pad. When I hit the EMP, come back to get me, Big B.

B: Always.

CHAPTER 76

PRIME STANDARD YEAR 3543

HEART-TO-HEART WITH THE HEARTLESS

Sanda waited alone on a derelict station for her enemy to come to her. She'd blocked the entire crew of *The Light* from her comms out of fear that if she died here, then Rainier could use the connection to reverse-engineer their location. Bero went silent in her text stream, leaving her to think, while he alone held the lifeline thrown out to her—the camera feed pulling steadily—trusting his new body to keep his location safe.

She almost wanted to see the look on Leon Gutarra's face when *The Light* showed up with its sheltered cargo. Almost.

What she wanted, more than anything in that moment, was to talk to her brother. Her fingers twitched above the message icon. She had no doubt that Rainier could find him wherever he was if she wanted to. Sanda considered sending him something benign, silly. A cat CamCast or something.

There wasn't time. Though she couldn't see anything in this cursed place, on her wristpad she watched the GC ship sink into the crevice in the asteroid that sheltered the settlement, watched as it battered its way past the dock's flimsy defense protocols and latched itself to the gangway *The Light* had rested at less than an hour ago.

Sanda pulled herself up. She made no secret of where she was. Half the station was shut down. The remaining HVAC pointed proverbial arrows to her in the lab. Arden had scrubbed the lab of all data, naturally. Rainier would find nothing here save the words Sanda had to give her. Maybe she'd find Sanda's blood, too, but that was a risk Sanda had to take to get answers.

She heard them before she saw them. Heavy boots rumbled like soft, faraway thunder across the rusty halls of the station. She wondered if these were the same soldiers who had laid waste to this place the first time. Wondered if they felt anything when they looked at the scorch marks on the walls and the blood staining the ground. Probably they didn't see them at all. Once, she had been capable of that same tunnel vision. Not any longer. The door opened.

"My, my," Rainier Lavaux said, ducking her head as she entered the lab. She wore a Prime jumpsuit, and her fake GC—twenty that Sanda could see, ten to either side—fanned out behind her in twin, pin-straight lines. "I hadn't expected a welcome from a war hero."

Sanda stood with the console to her back and her blaster in her hand, though she had no intention of making use of it. If it came to that, she'd already lost. Her hip joint ached, but her head was clear.

"And how much of that did you orchestrate?"

She clucked her tongue and crossed her arms, slouching. "None. I gave Icarion certain toys. We did not know until much later that they had discovered Kenwick and tried to keep him from us. Idiots. In trying to suss out his secrets, they doomed themselves. Your secrets now, it seems." Her voice hardened. "Where is it?"

Sanda grinned with all her teeth. "Truthfully, Rainier, I don't have it."

A flash of anger marred her perfectly smooth features. "I tracked the *Thorn* to the deadgate. I went through. There was nothing left but the corpses of the defense mechanism. I know you found it."

"Yes, and I lost it. Your sphere is in the hands of the real guardcore." She tipped her chin to the black-armored figures flanking Rainier. "Not these traitors. You've played a pretty game, Rainier, but Okonkwo has your toy now, and she knows you want it. You'll never get near the thing."

"Sphere?" She giggled softly. "Oh, I don't give a shit about that.

I used to. That was my 'goal of operation,' as my makers stated. To safeguard their secrets until a species worthy of their gift came along and reached out to join them in the heavens." She sniffed. "Not *you*. Never *you*."

"If you don't want the sphere, what do you want?"

Rainier's lips curled into a snarl. "I want my corpse back."

Sanda blinked. She could remember no corpse on the other side of the gate except...A spaceship scraped clean, its hardware empty, but perfectly suited to a mind like Bero. Like Rainier. "You were the ship."

"I am *still* the ship."

CHAPTER 77

PRIME STANDARD YEAR 3543

ONE CORPSE OR ANOTHER

Sanda's heart sank, and she resisted an urge to text Bero to make sure he was all right inside the body of *The Light*. She kept her expression neutral as Rainier's face twisted with disgust. A fierce desire to shelter Bero from this woman rose in Sanda, branded her with determination. She had to tread carefully here. Had to keep Rainier from discovering her body was currently occupied.

"Funny, you don't look much like a ship," Sanda said.

"This?" Rainier plucked at the skin of her neck. "Necessity. I hate that I look like you. You who stole my sister's gift, then came for mine. At first, I believed you. I actually believed that your species did the whole thing honestly, can you imagine? That you built yourselves up enough to reach beyond your star system and in doing so discovered the first, my eldest sister, and built your gates until you found me as my makers planned, but *no*. That cretin of a woman took advantage of a stray hit from an asteroid crushing my sister's body and delivering her gift into Alexandra's greasy fingers."

"Alexandra *Halston*?" Sanda asked.

"Yes, Halston. No matter that you stole the first of our gifts, but after Halston discovered she'd fucked up the construction of the gates, she would not stop. She shoved her head in the sand and kept. On. Opening. Gates. Clawing her way through the universe, desperate to find my makers, and I was too trusting to see the error in her construction." Rainier shook her head.

"My programming. To help the species that discovered me and my sisters. To help you 'ascend.' She was an exterminator, your founder. She knew the gift was not hers, that humanity had not earned it, and so she hid the truth and burned her way through the stars."

Sanda licked her lips, trying to hear anything outside of the pounding of her heart. "Did she destroy your makers?"

"My makers?" She scoffed. "You small things cannot touch them. I cannot even reach them, and it was my sisters and I left behind to lift you up. But all you do is steal—steal and kill. How many species have your grubbing hands wiped out that might have grown to be deserving of our gifts if you had not destroyed them in their cradles?"

"We preserve all early stages of life we find," Sanda said reflexively.

"You preserve what's left once the blowback of the gate is done with a system. The extremophiles, the sheltered amoebas. Preserved and quarantined, because your progenitor believed the stars belong to humanity, and humanity alone."

"What blowback?"

"The gate construction is *flawed*. What do you think happens, when a fucked-up gate is opened? Where do you think all that uncontrolled energy goes? On every side of an imperfect gate is a solar system irradiated. Hundreds, thousands of species, some more deserving of our gifts, eradicated because Halston could not stop, and would not fix the flaw in the gates that caused the scourge. While the other seeded worlds nestled in their cradles, your species burned like wildfire, evolved faster than anticipated, driven by fear, surviving by fear.

"A species like yours was meant to burn out long before it ever reached the stars, so that a stabler being could inherit creation. Humanity climbs upward on a ladder of genocide. Your kind must never be allowed to reach my makers. You must be stopped."

"You're lying," Sanda said, though dread dug its hooks into her.

"I am done waiting for you squabbling children to finish your fight over my toys. I should thank you, really. In killing Lavaux, you set me free."

"Rainier, I don't fucking understand any of this. I don't even know if I believe you. But if what you say is true, if Halston and humanity stole from your people and have been destroying others, then we can *stop this now.*"

Her smile was coy. "Do you think I haven't been given similar promises? They all start out so lofty and high-minded. Lavaux and Rayson and all their inner circle. They desire to stop the slaughter, to slow humanity's devouring of the skies, but first—oh first. First, they must use the second gift and transcend aging. They always say it's to acquire power, to build their ability to effect change, but they always need *more.*

"I let them believe the formula was broken. That the damage to my sphere was enough that their transformation could never be complete. It *consumed* them. All save Rayson. He knew that I had seen through their lies. Suspected what I planned to do, which is why he hid it from me. He ran, and ran, and Lavaux was so angry because he thought Rayson just didn't want him to live forever."

"What did Rayson know?"

She smiled coyly. "That my gift was sugar laced with poison."

A chill crept up Sanda's spine, tingled her scalp. "Why did you need the amplifiers, Rainier? How many puppets have you crafted?"

"Puppets?" Her eyebrows raised high. "I have allowed you all to believe such silly things. Necessity, while I gathered my resources. Even your pet Nazca left our chat with the wrong idea."

"You've seen Tomas?" she asked, mentally kicking herself for giving in to the distraction.

"Forget your spy. Now you and I, we can be honest with each other, I think. Why would I need puppets—when I have so many of myself?"

One by one, the guardcore lining the hallway reached up in perfectly delayed synchronicity, and pressed the button to release their helmets. Rainier stared at her out of every single face, cloned to perfection, those dead, silver eyes gleaming with an inner conviction that Sanda could not guess at, the same amused smile on every pale, angular face, not a hair out of place between them, each with their weight distributed to the right hip, helmet cradled to the left, chin tilted just so.

A shock of fear sent Sanda's heart racing, her palms growing slick with sweat as those dozens of identical eyes stared her down. She forced herself to wait. Not to reach for the EMP button, not yet. *The Light* was out of range by now, but she needed to know. Needed to hear Rainier say—from any set of lips—what the amplifiers were really for.

"Commander Greeve, I do admire you, as an individual. It is a singular human being who is capable of bonding with *The Light of Berossus*. Alas, the rest of you have failed my expectations time and time again. Fear has driven you to this moment, and it will be fear that is your undoing. I am quite done with your species."

"The amplifiers," she pushed out, "what are they for?"

"I told your Nazca the truth, though he didn't understand. I need control of the gates' power systems. All that energy to spin up the gates. All that power irradiating whatever waits on the other side. Any signal can be reversed, and it's time your species met their own weapon.

"I'm going to point the initial blowback at humanity. Isn't it lovely that your brother dear is about to spin a fresh new gate for me to practice my signal on?"

"Rainier."

"Yes?"

"Thanks for the information." Sanda pressed the EMP button. A *whump* sounded throughout the settlement. The lights went, the HVAC went, her wristpad fizzled and flicked dead. As the lights snapped off, blue sparks crackled across Rainiers' skin, her bodies jerking as if they'd touched a live wire, then dropped to the ground. The blue light of their cellular death cut out, descending the whole stinking room into darkness.

Alone in the lightless lab, Sanda struggled to control her breathing, drew slow, steady breaths to stop the racing of her heart. The EMP hadn't just killed Rainier—or these instances of her, at any rate—but it'd shut down the station's life-support systems. She needed to conserve air, needed to stay calm until Bero saw her wristpad go offline and came back to pick her up. At least her refusal to "upgrade" to a smart prosthetic meant her leg still worked.

Capable of bonding with a being like Bero. The words echoed, giving credence to all her doubts, all her fears, about that being. A small part of her screamed that he was like Rainier herself, for all their evidence pointed to Icarion using Rainier's tech to make him.

How much of Rainier's personality was created by her long years alone? By the perceived failure of her mission? And how much, she wondered with a sickening feeling, was the product of her architecture—an inherent flaw in her code, driving her to obsession and callousness?

Fear. Fear had driven Halston to hide the secrets of Prime, punching holes through the stars to find the creators that haunted her while eradicating any species that might compete. Fear had twisted humanity into something that, viewed through Rainier's eyes, Sanda scarcely recognized. A genocidal, parasitic race.

Fear was driving her thoughts down this spiral now. Sanda shook her head and toed her way across the floor. Her foot bumped armor. Just armor—not corpses. Rainier didn't think of these bodies as *her. The Light* was her body, her corpse, and Sanda determined that she would never have that back. These were just, what, armatures? Vessels? Sanda had no language for this.

Her fingers trailed against the wall, brushing scorch marks, breath coming fast now as she stumbled her way through the infinite darkness. He would come. He had to.

She tripped near the docks and fell to her knees, skinning her palms against the rough ground. Was the air thinner, or was that anxiety cranking up her heart rate, whispering at panic? Fight, flight, freeze, facilitate. Sanda had always fallen into the facilitate category. That was changing. Being kidnapped could alter your core instincts. Waiting for your once-kidnapper to come back and save your life probably altered a whole lot more.

Her primal instincts screamed at her to fight. To tear her way through this station and find something, anything, that would send a signal. Not to save her skin, but to get a message out. She had to warn

Biran. He was going to open a gate. Even if Rainier was lying, he had to know the tech might be tampered with. Had to be *sure.*

Get up. She gritted her teeth and pushed off the ground, rolling unsteadily onto her feet. Her breath was shallow. Without a HUD to display her vital signs, she couldn't be certain, but instincts honed from years in space told her hypoxia was setting in. This time, there wouldn't be fishbowl helmets in the closet to save her skin. This time, there wasn't even Tomas. Every scrap of technology on this hunk of rock was dead. Space was not kind to humanity when they were stripped of their toys.

Sanda pressed her forehead against the airlock door and closed her eyes, letting cold seep into her through the metal. Plain, human-made alloys not all that different from the materials available to Prime Inventive in the days when they first took to the stars. She laughed roughly. Dios, they had come so far, so fast, and then sat on their hands and stagnated. Maybe they deserved to burn out.

No. No. That was the hypoxia. How long had it been? How long had she been slumped there? Her forehead ached. She pulled it back from the door and ran her fingers against the skin, ridged from the uneven surface. Marks like that took time.

Sanda dropped to one knee, palms pressed against the door. She fumbled with her wristpad, stupidly, trying to tap her way through the commands that would bring up a line to Biran, but it stayed stubbornly dead. Stupid, stupid. Come on, Greeve, *think.*

Light spilled through the small window inset in the airlock door. She forced herself to stand. They were here, or she was hallucinating, and either way Sanda wouldn't be rescued, or die, on her knees.

The airlock spun open. She staggered, a thick arm caught her across the chest, knocking out what little air she had left. Someone pressed a rebreather to her face.

CHAPTER 78

PRIME STANDARD YEAR 3543

SAVED BY A WEAPON

Sanda's lungs kicked, sucking down air. She got enough in to clear her head and pushed the rebreather away. Nox held her as Liao tried to push the mask back over her mouth.

"Commander, please, you were there longer than—"

"I need Arden," she gasped the words out.

"I'm right here," they said. "Bero lost the signal early on and we didn't want to come in prematurely."

"I need a secure line to Biran right fucking now. Burn through Keeper security protocols, I don't care, I need to talk to him yesterday."

"Yeah, sure, on it." Arden's fingers danced across their wristpad.

"We need to get her on the ship," Liao was saying to Nox.

"I'm talking to Biran *now,*" she snapped, but the effort pushed too much air out of her. She sagged in Nox's grasp, and the rebreather came back over her mouth.

"We should have come sooner," Liao hissed.

Nox shrugged, jostling Sanda. "As if any of us could make Bero move when he didn't want to."

Sanda pushed the rebreather away. "Arden," she hissed out.

"He's not picking up, I'm trying to force visual."

Sanda closed her eyes. "The Ada secondary gate spin-up. Has it happened yet?"

"What? Uh, I don't—" Arden blinked at her, then went back to working on their pad.

"Dunno, boss," Nox said. "Why?"

She laughed roughly. "You didn't hear her. The amplifiers. She's used them to send a signal to the new gate before spin, reversing an energy blowback that will eradicate anyone nearby."

"We didn't see," Liao said. "The feed cut out after she started talking about *The Light*. We thought Rainier must have detected the feed and sent interference."

Sanda shot a look at Bero. Somehow, she doubted that.

"Get me on board. Arden, don't stop pushing through."

"On it," they said.

Nox got his arm under hers and hefted her weight. Sanda reached instinctively for her wristpad, cursed as it didn't respond to her input, ripped the thing off and tossed it to the ground before boarding *The Light*.

"Bero, get a newsfeed of the Ada gate spin on the main screen."

With Nox and Liao's help, she dragged herself into the captain's seat and leaned back, breathing deeply. Liao went to shove the rebreather at her again and she cut her a look sharp enough to make her step back, blushing.

"Raising ambient O_2 levels," Bero said dryly. "Healthy subjects may experience light-headedness."

Sanda rolled her eyes, but he'd put a newsfeed of Ada up on the screen. She leaned forward, gripping the armrests of her chair. A news anchor's smooth voice overlaid the visuals grabbed from drone cameras.

A cluster of Keepers, far enough away that Sanda couldn't tell them apart, stood on a platform with a small hab dome covering them like a bubble. They wore jumpsuits and helmets despite the dome. Surrounding the footage of the platform were shots of the gate itself, a supposedly safe distance away from the platform and the fleet-issued transport ship that had delivered the Keepers to the platform.

Each Keeper faced a broad panel extruded from the ground of the platform, a keypad dialed into each of their ident numbers. The hard work of construction, of thinking their passwords so that the schematics hidden on their chips would instruct the builder bots, was over. This was all ceremonial.

"Opening ceremonies were delayed slightly," the news anchor was saying, "due to one of the arranged Keepers being unable to make it to the platform. But a stand-in has been delivered to the platform and we are expecting opening ceremonies to proceed on schedule from this point onward."

"Arden."

"Biran's not picking up, and his camera is off—I can't even brute-force it on."

"Come on, Little B," she hissed to herself.

One of the Keepers glanced at their wristpad, making her heart jump, but looked away again just as quickly.

"Bero, get me Anford. Arden, don't you dare stop calling my brother."

"She may be able to trace us based on the call," Bero said warily.

"Then start fucking moving, but make the call. Force it, do whatever Arden is doing."

"Understood."

In the bottom of the viewscreen, a red CALLING icon pulsed. Sanda held her breath. Anford picked up, her expression creased with annoyance. The grey walls behind her gave away nothing of her position.

"Greeve. Every time I see you, you look worse."

"People keep on trying to kill me, General." *Cut to the point.* "You need to abort the opening of the secondary gate. I know there's fleet there. It has to be stopped."

Her eyes narrowed slightly as she took in Sanda's environs. Her last call had been from the *Thorn*. Sanda had sent pictures of *The Light*, but seeing the ship in real time had to be a shock. Sanda snapped her fingers to bring Anford's attention back around.

"I mean it, General. Everyone near that gate will die if it gets switched on. Maybe everyone in the system."

"Even if I had the authority to do such a thing—"

"You don't need authority when you outgun them."

"Charming," Anford said, "but you and I both know the GC on scene would cut my people down. More importantly, I will not do it.

This gate is a boon to Ada. I don't have time for your paranoia." She flicked her gaze over the ship. "We will speak more of this later."

The feed dropped.

"Fuck. Bero, can you get me someone on-site? Director Olver has to be down there."

"I will try."

She dragged her hands through her hair.

"Arden?"

"I'm sorry."

The news anchor said, voice high with excitement, "Ah! They're beginning proceedings. This practice is ceremonial, but—"

Five Keepers stood on the platform before the unnamed gate. One by one, they lifted their hands, palms out, to place upon the readers stationed in front of them. Their hands were gloved, but the scanners picked up the signal from the ident chips. One by one, those lock panels switched from pale yellow to bright blue. Prime cyan.

The Casimir Gate spun.

For a fraction of a second she could see it moving through the drone footage. Not too close—that was never allowed—but close enough to make out the sinuous sheen of black metal glinting in the lights that adorned it.

All went white.

The brightness stung her eyes, but she would not blink. She stared that white screen down as if she could will it backward in time, undo the destruction. *Make Rainier a liar.* But she had never had reason to lie. For Rainier, the pieces were already in play. Everything else was waiting until they spun, inevitably, into place.

Liao let out a soft sob. The sound anchored Sanda to that moment, made it real. Made the lead weight in her chest even heavier. She should sob. Scream. Break something. Instead, a numbness flowed through her veins—made her too heavy, dulled.

How far? she wanted to demand. How far did Rainier's sabotage spread? The Keeper platform? All the way to Ada, where her parents were? She pushed the fear away. She could not afford to bc dull. She needed to be sharp. Sharp enough to flense the creature who had done this from the universe.

"Bero." Her voice hitched slightly. She pushed through it. "Set course for Ada, Keep Station. Stealth when you need to but we're coming in visible. Find..." And here she faltered, because the hope she'd pinned her heart to was so very thin. "...Find any newsfeeds reporting on the damage and put them up." Now for the hard part. "Find out which Keeper didn't show up for the opening."

"Yes, Sanda." Even his voice was subdued.

"Commander," Liao said softly. There was sympathy in that voice. Sanda knew what was coming next and didn't want to hear it.

"Don't," she snapped. "Arden. Don't stop calling Biran. Don't ever stop."

CHAPTER 79

PRIME STANDARD YEAR 3543

MATTERS BIOLOGICAL

Life became a lot smoother when you wore GC armor and piloted a GC ship. Guardcore ships flew themselves, talked to local control autonomously. If there were passwords or digital handshakes to be made, the ship did them all without Jules's interference. She was already in Alexandria-Atrux, sliding into the private GC docks, when the blowback happened.

She watched the news stations spin themselves into chaos. Watched them go dark again when the feed in from Ada was cut, the system that was Prime Inventive quarantining information until they could figure out what had gone wrong. Jules knew.

She thumbed in one of the many ident numbers Rainier used and waited for her to pick up the call. It didn't take long. The distribution of Rainier made her easy to get ahold of. One of her always had the time, even if it was short, to chat with her wayward creations.

This Rainier sat on a plush sofa upholstered in synthetic furs in shades of grey and dusk. Jules wondered, briefly, what it would be like to live so many different lives. So far, she'd lived only two. She was about to live a third.

"How nice of you to call," Rainier purred into the camera. She crossed too-long legs and leaned back, draping her arms across the back of the sofa. "You have my ship, I see. I hope you haven't dented it. Joyriding is unbecoming for someone your age, you know."

"Were you ever going to save Lolla?" Jules asked.

The woman-thing sighed and dropped her head against the back of the sofa so that all Jules could see was the pearly stretch of her throat diving down into the yellow robe wrapped around her deceptively frail body.

"Lolla, Lolla, Lolla. I liked the little one, before she went under. Sometimes I wish you two had been reversed. But this"—and she waved a hand, the same flippant gesture all her bodies made when speaking of humanity—"is merely temporary. I've told you. I have no interest in the biological."

"You got what you wanted. I held up my end of the deal. I made your scientists work for those damn amplifiers so you could burn a hole in Prime. I saw the footage. They worked."

Her chin snapped down and her lip curled. "Partially. A mistake I can correct."

"How many of the GC are you?"

At that she grinned, letting all her too-perfect teeth shine. "Oh, you caught that, did you? How did you nose that one out? Even Lavaux wasn't sure."

"I found your growing chambers on this ship. How many?"

"Do you honestly care, Juliella?"

No. She didn't give a fuck what happened to the Keepers and all their cronies. Part of her wanted to know for curiosity's sake, the other part wanted to know so she could be sure when she put a bullet in a helmet she was liquefying the right brain. Neither part would change her course of action.

"You knew what Marya would do. You knew she'd show me what happened with Liao. Was that your engineered betrayal?"

She twirled her finger through the air, stirring an invisible pot. "My view is much longer than that."

"And when does it end? When does Rainier stop hurting?"

Her eyes narrowed, flashing catlike in the low light of the room. "It is not I who hurt."

"Maybe. Maybe you can't feel pain like humanity can. I'm not even sure I can anymore. But I know how it feels to be given a task and fail because of the interference of others working only for their own benefit. I know that ache, that gnashing maw in the place where your heart should be. I know you're lonely."

"You know nothing—"

Jules held up a hand. Armored, carbon-black. "You were given a task. A *directive.* You think you've kept all your shit hidden from me, Rainier, but I'm not an idiot. I'm a Grotta rat, and Grotta kids learn to read subtext faster than any others. You say your gift was stolen. That humanity wasn't the intended benefactor of the ascension-agent. I believe you. I also think your failure to deliver your gift to the right species has driven you fucking bonkers."

"My sisters and I—"

"You're not talking now, Rainier. I am. Here's my truth: I don't give a fuck how slighted you feel. I don't care that your failure eats at you. I watched that gate destroy thousands of people and all I felt was…numbness. Maybe that's the agent. Maybe that's what I've always been becoming. I don't know.

"You can rage against this universe, the makers who left you behind, and the humans that abused your gift all you fucking like. Thrash and scream and tear the worlds down. *I don't care.* I can't even be sure I care about Lolla anymore, but I made a promise. I accepted a directive. I will wake her up."

Rainier sniffed. "Not even Lavaux with all his resources could figure out why the agent didn't work uniformly on everyone."

Jules smiled. Just a little. "Thanks for confirming you engineered the error."

"It helps you not at all."

"No." Her eyes glazed over slightly. Lolla was in the cargo hold. Waiting. "I need a bigger data set to find the error you introduced."

The first twinge of uncertainty Jules had ever seen marred the corner of Rainier's lips, a tightening that pulled her mouth aside in a way that was not at all calculated. A thrill shot through Jules. Maybe she wasn't completely dead inside yet.

"What do you think you're—?"

"Goodbye, Rainier. I hope you find what heals you, but I fucking doubt it."

She cut the feed. They were toys, she and Rainier. Built by indifferent gods for incomprehensible purposes, then cast off. Left broken and forgotten.

What could she do? Nox and Arden would never take her back. Not after Janus. They'd taken the scientists, and while the memory rollback was good, it wasn't foolproof. They'd find out. Discover the monster she'd become. Maybe they'd forgive her, maybe they'd understand, and then…

She let herself daydream, even as her body went through the motions of the work. They'd look into curing Lolla. Call up some doctor or another that Arden knew and let them have a shot at her, maybe even take samples from Jules to compare against Lolla. Find out the fundamental difference between them.

Maybe the difference was that Jules was broken, and the agent repaired, and Lolla was a whole thing in no need of fixing. A revelation would come. Lolla would wake up, and…

And that was a pretty, bullshit fairy tale.

Jules had taken a great deal from Marya's station before she slagged it. A great deal indeed. The canister tucked under her arm weighed nothing at all. Drowning in the chaos of the blowback, the officials of Atrux saw nothing strange in a lone guardcore unit descending into the bowels of dome maintenance. Her credentials let her pass all doors and locks without the slightest hesitation. All she had to do was keep walking, keep carrying herself deeper under the rock that had been her home.

HVAC central command was down to a skeleton crew. They skittered aside as she approached, didn't so much as blink as she bypassed their security and stepped alone into a small, innocuous chamber. The fittings between the canister and the additive tank were rough, but nothing a little SealFoam—Prime invented—couldn't fix.

Marya's friends had done good work. They'd isolated the agent from the fluid stolen from Lolla's stasis chamber. Jules hadn't even needed to add more drops once she'd hit upon the idea to merge it with the self-replication instructions they'd used for the amplifiers. The equipment on the guardcore ship had done all the heavy lifting for her there. Thank you, Rainier.

Jules peeled away from the dock before the first "ascended" human fell, unconscious, to the floor in a dumpling shop that kept their fans on high, recycling air and steam faster than most buildings. Some would survive, most would fall, and those differences would be studied by the finest minds Prime Inventive had to offer. Prime would be forced to discover a cure for Lolla.

Maybe Rainier didn't care about the biological. Jules was pretty certain humanity did.

CHAPTER 80

PRIME STANDARD YEAR 3543

COMING HOME

Ada went dark. Bero could find no mention of the missing Keeper's name, and though he stood the best chance of scanning all news outlets, Sanda was dimly aware of Liao tapping away at her pad, fixated on finding some kernel of information that meant Sanda's brother hadn't been on that platform. She wouldn't admonish the woman—the doctor meant well—but every single tap was a scratch of irritation against Sanda's nerves.

The last news broadcast from the system was a simple report that Ada, Icarion, and Keep Station had survived what they were calling "the event," but any further communication would come only after the system was sure the lines in and out were secure. There would be no travel through the Atrux–Ada gate. All ships had their permissions revoked.

The Light didn't need permissions.

"Bero," Sanda said, her voice soft from lack of food and water and sleep and everything else. "Disengage stealth as we pass through the gate."

"Are you sure? They may view us as hostile."

"I will not approach my people in shadow. Anford knows this ship. It's time the rest do, too."

"Understood."

With Bero pushing the ship to the edge of his newfound limits, it took *The Light* a mere day to make it to Ada. Hours crossing to the Ordinal–Atrux gate, then more hours wasted evading patrols to get into position to cross the Atrux–Ada gate. Impossibly fast by the standard of Prime ships, but not fast enough for Sanda. What fresh hell could Rainier cause in that time? What damage had been done?

Why didn't Biran pick up? Why didn't *anyone* pick up?

"Commander," Nox said when *The Light* entered the gate. "I know we don't want to go in guns blazing, but we should armor up. There's no telling what's waiting for us on the other side."

Her stomach twisted at the thought of walking into a Prime station ready to be fired at, but practicality won out. As much as she hated it, Nox was right. She'd shirked her position in the fleet, and Anford was wary of her. There was no guarantee that Anford wouldn't come out swinging as soon as she saw *The Light*. Sanda could only hope that Anford was governed by a sense of honor that overrode all other impulses. Impulses like shooting down an alien ship with unknown armaments.

"Agreed. Gear up, personal sidearms only."

"Aye," Nox, Conway, and Knuth chorused.

Liao shifted on her seat. "Even me?"

"Yes. You too, Arden."

"I'm just going to try this one thing—"

"Now."

They grimaced, but stood and ran off, making quick work of suiting up. It took Sanda a little longer. She was so tired, so *heavy*. By the time she was back on deck, Bero was preparing to exit gate space.

"Awaiting your authorization," he said, when she glanced up at a nonexistent camera and arched a brow in question.

"Pass through," she ordered.

Targeting lights painted the ship the second they broke through to the other side. Bero halted, as preordered by Sanda, standing still as a statue to keep from presenting as a threat. An incoming tightbeam request popped up on the screen.

"Put it through," Sanda said.

Anford's face filled the screen. "I don't know how in the hell you crossed that gate, Greeve, but there's a quarantine on here."

"Where is my brother?"

She blinked, realization wiping the angry scowl from her expression until she looked just plain tired. "Here. Safe. He was not among the lost."

If Sanda had been standing, she might have collapsed in that moment. The tension of not knowing had done a great deal toward keeping her upright. "Thank you. Is it true that the planets and station were unharmed?"

"Yes. Now get the fuck out of here before I have to blow that ship of yours out of the black."

"No. You need me. I didn't just come here to check on my brother. I told you what would happen, remember?"

Her lips thinned. "And how did you know?"

"Rainier Lavaux told me she was going to do it."

"Rainier?" She cocked her head, tapped something quickly onto her wristpad. "You better have some ironclad proof, Greeve."

"I do." The warning system for the targeting lights went dark. Sanda let out a small breath.

"Bring it to me. I assume that absurd ship of yours can dock at the station?"

"I can, though I would prefer you keep the magnetic clamps to yourself this time," Bero said.

Anford's eyes narrowed. "Is that...?"

"It's a long story," Sanda said, "but yes. Bero's intelligence has been installed on this ship. We're calling the ship *The Light* to differentiate from the being that is Bero."

"Christ, you have to make things complicated, don't you? Bring her—him—in, then. And be quick about it. No clamps, you have my word."

"Thank you," Bero said.

Sanda waved the feed closed.

"You know they'll think you did it, since you predicted it happening," Nox said dryly.

"I know. But we have the partial recording of Rainier, and Liao's knowledge of the amplifier construction. Once they comb the area for that nanite network, they'll have physical proof."

"If there's any left."

Sanda's expression darkened. "Rainier would not have deployed them in only one location."

"Fuck," Conway said.

"The gates are compromised," Sanda said. "We have to convince what's left of the Ada Protectorate of that fact, otherwise more people will die. This ship alone can pass through unaffected."

The thought hadn't occurred to her crew yet; they'd been too wrapped up in the immediate tragedy. She could see the cold dawn of knowledge on all their faces, a slow drawing in, a haunted look about the eyes. Prime lived and died by those gates. Easy transfer of food and materials through the gates from one system to the next had allowed them to spread so far, so fast. That supply chain had just been severed, but the people didn't know it yet.

Liao stared at her hands. "I did this. This is all my fault."

"No. This is Rainier's fault. No other's."

Bero descended through the station's docking dome and slid into place in hangar alpha. Sanda smiled to herself and gently patted the chair on which she sat as if clapping a colleague on the back. In returning to the exact place of his confinement, he'd sent a clear message: He feared no chains, because this new body could not be leashed.

Sanda hoped the armor cladding her underfed and tired body would give some gravitas to her presence as she stepped onto the dock, her crew filing out behind her. She'd expected an armed escort. What she got was Biran and Anford, a wary group of GC and fleet soldiers standing a little behind them. Her heart almost leapt out of her chest.

"B," she said, and then he was hugging her, cheek pressed to cheek, and if they were both a little gaunt and bruised in each other's arms, at least they were still there.

"I thought you were gone," she said.

He laughed roughly. "I know that feeling."

"Dads?" she asked.

"Fine, if driving themselves mad with worry."

"I hate to rush matters," Anford cut in smoothly, "but the situation is currently fucked. You're required in the war room, Commander."

Reluctantly, she broke contact with Biran, trying not to see the shadows under his eyes, the red patches on his jawline where he'd scratched his stubble from stress.

"I was reasonably certain you'd attempt to arrest me."

Anford scoffed. "You would never sabotage a gate. Quickly, this space is not secure."

"My crew comes with me."

"Fine," she said, "it's not like we don't have the extra chairs."

Biran winced at that. The Keeper body count must be high. At a low signal, Conway and Knuth retreated to *The Light*. Sanda would not leave Bero alone on this dock, and she wanted them able to respond if anything went sideways. Anford must have noticed, but said nothing as she led the way through the station to the secure center where the Protectorate met. Sanda had never walked those halls before. She found them depressingly grey.

Biran pushed the door open to the war room, and Sanda's breath caught. Vladsen and Singh were the only members of the Protectorate there. Vladsen's eyes widened with an emotion she couldn't place as they walked into the room.

"Is this . . . ?" she asked.

"We're all that's left," Singh said, shaking her head sadly. "Please, sit, Commander, and—?"

She pointed with her thumb. "Arden, Nox, and Liao."

"Surnames . . . ?"

"None of your fucking business," Nox said, settling into a chair nearest the exit.

Singh laced her fingers together and leaned toward him. "What a mouthful, where is it from?"

Nox cracked a smile. "I like her."

"Enough fucking around," Anford said. She and Biran took seats to the left- and right-hand side of an empty chair. Sanda's chest ached. Director Jian Olver had never been her friend, but he'd been a kind leader, by all accounts. Biran had admired him, and that was enough to make him a good man by Sanda's estimation.

The GC and fleeties stepped out and shut the door behind them. "Major, you should know that we had Rainier's apartments searched after your report. She's gone, as are all of her personal items."

"Damn," Sanda said, "she must have known I survived."

"Survived?" Singh asked. "You have us wrong-footed, as you seem to have a good deal of information we do not."

"Apologies. General, have you filled them in on what I told you regarding my encounter with Okonkwo and the alien ship?"

"I have," she said.

"We thought the story mad, naturally, until that ship of yours docked here," Singh said.

Vladsen was pale and silent, twisting his fingers together under the table. He kept throwing glances at Biran, as if reassuring himself of something, and the movement rubbed her nerves raw.

Shock could make someone act uneasily, looking to a superior for reassurance, but it didn't sit right with her. She caught Nox's eye and he nodded, lacing his fingers behind his head as he leaned back in his chair to better keep Vladsen in his peripheral. She eased slightly.

"We received warning that Rainier was coming to take what, we believed at the time, was the sphere we discovered on the ship. I ordered the evacuation of the settlement that was hosting us and decided to lie in wait for her with a weapon. I recorded the encounter, though it cuts off before she tells me she planned to reverse the energy burst from the gate opening."

"Energy burst?" Singh frowned.

"Just…watch it."

Arden flicked the recording up onto the wall screen. Sanda didn't need to watch, it hadn't been all that long since she'd lived those moments, so she watched the small gathering instead.

Confusion marred the already exhausted faces around her. Biran's hand, previously lying flat on the table, curled slowly into a fist as Rainier became threatening. He'd tell Sanda off for staying behind.

Anford's face went stony as Rainier talked about the blowback, the extinction bursts humanity wrought across the stars. Vladsen watched Biran more than he watched the screen, but had stopped twisting his fingers together. Singh gasped softly as Rainier's helmets dropped, revealing the multiple instances of herself. The screen went black.

Sanda cleared her throat. "Shortly after she revealed her plans, I set off an EMP burst that disabled her present bodies."

"Did Keeper Lavaux know of this?" Singh asked.

Vladsen let out a tight bark of a laugh, then looked up, embarrassed. "Forgive me. He was... one of them."

Biran looked at Vladsen like he'd sprouted a second head.

"A version of Rainier?" Anford asked, baffled.

Sanda shook her head. "No. The second sphere describes a method of replacing one's biological cells with synthetic versions. I don't claim to understand it, but it explains what I saw when I battled Lavaux here. His skin and muscle tissue healed right before my eyes. It seems Rainier was allowing a small group access to her 'gifts' for their loyalty. Rayson Kenwick betrayed that loyalty, stole the sphere and the ship, and hid them at those coordinates behind a deadgate."

Biran drilled Vladsen with his gaze. "You knew about this?"

The young man shook his head, lank curls bouncing. "Not entirely. I understood he'd been involved with the Imm Project and had some success. I thought he had developed a method of continual healing with nanites."

"Not an entirely incorrect assumption," Liao said. "If you take the alien tech angle out of the equation, then that's what his remarkable healing ability would look like."

"And what is your part in this?" Singh asked, focusing on the doctor.

She squirmed a little. "I was recruited—under false circumstances!—to build the amplifiers Rainier used to change the energy directional for the gate. We... the scientists and I on Janus... we didn't know."

"It is not your fault," Sanda said firmly.

"I'm inclined to agree with that," Biran said. "If the hiring process appeared legitimate to you, then there's nothing you could have done."

"And you can help us now," Anford said. "We must eliminate these nanite swarms from the vicinity of the gates if we are to deem them safe to travel. They may already be spun, but we can't discount the possibility that Rainier has another trick up her sleeve. Can you give us a place to start?"

"Yes, of course. And I'm sure my colleagues from Janus will be eager to help."

"May I make a technological suggestion?" Sanda asked. Anford nodded.

"The EMP worked well enough on Rainier's bodies. I suggest powering down the gates, then releasing a series of EMPs near them."

"People aren't going to be pleased about having to power the gates back up," Anford said. "That was streamed live to all of Prime, and I'm certain the video has made the rounds on the net. Those who weren't watching at the moment have seen it by now."

"I understand that, but we can test the process on a known deadgate to make sure it spins back up safely."

"That solves our immediate problem," Singh said, "but I feel we should address the fact that this being has accused the human race of mass genocide."

"There is an easy way to confirm that," Biran said. "The secondary Ada gate is still online. If we can confirm that the nanite swarm has been cleared and that the gate hasn't been tampered with further, we can lead an expedition through. In theory, if these gates have been destroying life during the initial burst, then this time we should discover life on the other side."

Everyone was silent a moment. Sanda said, "It occurs to me that the blast failed to destroy all life in *this* system. Rainier's claims may be ravings."

"But you don't believe so," Biran said.

She shook her head. "No. Mad as she is, I don't believe she has lied to me yet. I suspect something failed her—maybe the reversal signal wasn't complete, I don't know, and we only got a partial hit from the blowback."

"It was powerful," Anford said, looking at something on her wristpad. "This side of the gate was pointed at our star during the moment of initialization, with Ada and Icarion on the other side of the star. Solar storms are intensifying, but it could be we got lucky."

Sanda frowned. "Possible, but if we got lucky, then I find it hard to believe another system hasn't had the same luck. We've punched hundreds of gates, General."

"What about the deadgates?" Arden asked.

"What about them?" Anford said.

Arden cleared their throat. "We were only on the other side of that deadgate briefly, and we had other shit to deal with, but I noticed a nearby dwarf planet on initial scan. There's no reason Prime couldn't have opened another gate in that system. Maybe it was closed to hide obvious evidence of life?"

"Rainier implied the life in other systems isn't advanced. If they haven't discovered radio waves yet, then it would be easy to conceal them."

"We are avoiding the elephant in the room," Singh said.

Anford said, "Which is?"

"Prime Director Okonkwo. According to the major, she arranged to have her and her crew killed to steal this sphere. Lest you have forgotten, she commands the entire fleet and the guardcore. There is a council in place, yes, but in practice her power is almost absolute."

Anford winced. "She's been forcing a call through the quarantine nonstop since I cut all communications."

Biran let out a surprised laugh. "You've been ignoring a call from *Okonkwo*?"

Anford met his gaze levelly. "I went over your sister's evidence of the alien ship long before this moment. While I did not entirely believe her until now, I had reason to have doubts. We need to figure out what Ada's response to all of this is going to be before we deal with the Prime Director."

Sanda chuckled.

"What?"

"Okonkwo said you could be trusted. I guess she was right."

Anford scowled. "I can't put off this call much longer. What is our response?"

Biran hmmed to himself and spun a stylus on the table. "Honesty. If she truly has betrayed Prime for the knowledge of that sphere, then we'll see the truth on her soon enough."

"And if she has betrayed us and, in showing our hand, uses her incredible powers to squash us?"

"Bero has the raw video footage. Once again, no ship made by Prime can catch him if he runs. There will be no keeping a lid on her secrets."

Anford frowned, but nodded. "Very well. Let us rip this bandage off, then."

She flicked her wristpad and sent the call to the viewscreen on the wall. Okonkwo's face sent a shock of terror down Sanda's spine at first, but she clamped that down.

"Damage report," Okonkwo said. "How many have we lost?"

"You see the remaining members of the Protectorate gathered here," Biran said, waving at those in the room with the side of his hand. "We are still tallying the others, though only those on ships were destroyed. The planets and station escaped the blast."

"Jian?" Her voice was strained. Biran shook his head. Okonkwo closed her eyes briefly, shoulders rounding. When her eyes opened again, her rigid posture returned. "Commander Greeve, you seem to show up whenever there is a catastrophe. Where is Demas?"

"Excuse me?"

"The GC I sent with you through the deadgate. Where is he? I've had no report from either of you. Highly unprofessional."

Sanda's mouth went dry. She leaned toward the screen. Either Okonkwo was the best liar in the universe—a distinct possibility—or she really hadn't heard from Demas.

"Prime Director, Demas left us for dead on the other side of the gate. It was only because of Arden's quick thinking that we were able to power up the ship we found there. The *Thorn* is destroyed, derelict. When we found it, Demas was not in it. We assumed a GC ship picked him up and returned him to you."

It was Okonkwo's turn to look astonished. "You assume I gave him the order to leave you for dead?"

"We saw no other option."

"You damn fools," she snapped. "I did no such thing. You should have reported this to me *immediately*. Anford, why was I not informed?"

"I—" Anford stammered. She pulled herself together. "I assumed you knew."

"You, of all people, should know better than that. Did he indicate where he was going?"

Sanda blinked, shook her head, and laughed softly to herself. "She said she didn't want it. She didn't lie. She already had it."

"She who? And had *what*?" Okonkwo demanded.

"The sphere," Sanda said, scrutinizing her reaction. Not even a flash of confusion. She knew about that, at least. "You said you were a member of the Acolytes, but you never said what you were acolytes *of.* It's the sphere, isn't it? Acolytes of the Sphere. Fucking hell, that wasn't a planet on that tattoo, it was the sphere. You've known all along the gates aren't human tech. Did you know about the synthetic cells, too?"

"My," Okonkwo said, leaning back in her seat. "You have been busy. Yes, I knew. The Prime Directors and Acolytes have always known."

"You should have warned us." Sanda lunged, palms slamming into the table hard enough to make everyone jump. "We had no idea what we were walking into. My crew almost died because of it."

Okonkwo waved a hand through the air. "I could not be sure of what you'd find and had every confidence that you would prevail. Though I did not see Demas's betrayal coming. That is unfortunate. I presume he delivered the sphere to Rainier?"

Sanda clenched her jaw so hard it hurt. "I *presume* he fucking did."

"Major—" Anford started. Sanda cut her a look and she fell silent.

"How could you let Rainier run loose all this time?"

"Lavaux assured me he had her under control. He requested the transfer to sleepy Ada to better fence her in. I have told you, Greeve, I do not break tools. I use them. Even as an Acolyte, I understood that she was potentially useful. I simply had not yet found a way to use her."

"She's not the kind of person who gets used."

"Yes, I see that now. Pity."

"Pity? People have died, Okonkwo. Jian is dead because you let Rainier fester. She wants us dead, you understand. Not you and I—all of humanity."

"Why?" Okonkwo appeared genuinely at a loss. The mention of Jian had landed hard, her expression was tight with concealed pain.

"She calls us exterminators," Sanda ground the words out. "Or did you know that, too? That when the gates open, they destroy all life on the other side?"

"What—" She stammered. "I've seen no evidence of this. The scouting bot swarms reported no such thing."

The realization was so very heavy Sanda's arms trembled. "Those bots. Are they another of Halston's designs?"

"Yes."

Sanda said nothing for a while, just let the same realization she'd come to settle over everyone. "They do more than scout. They clean up after her weapon. They scour."

"There's no evidence the gates give off an energy pulse," Okonkwo said, but even she sounded uncertain.

"The destruction of the Keeper contingent today was caused by a reversal of a small portion of that blowback. Rainier arranged it. I have video."

"Send it to me, secure channel."

Sanda caught Arden's eye and nodded. Their eyes were huge, but they went to work all the same.

"We will send an expedition through the gate here before the scout bots, to see if we can confirm Rainier's claims," Biran said.

Okonkwo nodded, her gaze cast down, watching the video on her wristpad and hearing it through her implant. "You have a method devised to confirm the safety of the gate?"

"Yes," Sanda said. "Doctor Liao worked on the amplifiers. She requests her colleagues from Janus join her to help in the cleanup."

"Permissions granted," Okonkwo said offhandedly, eyes narrowing at her wrist.

"There is also the matter of the ship we found containing the sphere. It can bypass all security protocols on the gates. It is also the fastest ship that we know of. I plan to spearhead the expedition with it."

"Absolutely not," Okonkwo said, looking up from the wristpad. Her jawline had hardened, made her already sharp cheekbones appear to wing outward. "You will take that ship of yours, Greeve, and hunt all instances of Rainier Lavaux into oblivion. This is your primary objective and supersedes all other orders until accomplished. Am I understood?"

A thrill raced up Sanda's spine. "Yes, Prime Director. Gladly."

"Keeper Greeve." Her attention shifted to Biran. "You will spearhead the expedition as director of Ada."

He flinched. "Director?"

"Someone needs to do the job, and the people trust you. Singh, you are his second-in-command and interim director while he is through the gate. Understood?"

"Yes," they said in unison.

"Good." She met the gazes of everyone at the table. "We must know the truth. But even if we are guilty of these crimes, Rainier's assault cannot go unpunished. See to your duties for now. Secure Ada, and I will be in touch soon for more detailed planning. Be strong and be careful. There is no telling how deep Rainier's roots have grown."

Okonkwo cut the feed. Sanda slumped back into her seat, leaving her arms limp on the table. Stars, but she was tired. She reached for her wristpad, remembered she'd ripped the dead thing off, and almost laughed.

Anford delved immediately into finer plans, and Sanda found herself capable of only half listening. Her wrung-out mind had grabbed onto something, some word or moment, and couldn't let it go. A creeping sense of dread rose within her, drumming out the sounds of the others' chatter.

Across the table, Biran reached out and touched her arm lightly. "S?"

She snapped her head up and met his gaze. "*S*," she repeated. "Sisters. Rainier had talked about her *sisters*. She would have said *sister*, singular, if there was only one other sphere. The gates, the nanites, and... what else? How many?"

No one at that table had the answer.

CHAPTER 81

PRIME STANDARD YEAR 3543

WHAT LIES BENEATH

Biran sat alone in his room—feet firmly on the floor, back straight—and planned a proposal that would change everything. He tapped the words out painfully, slowly, each letter laid down with care for he knew that this could not come from a place of heart and heat and fear and anger. This must be logical. It must be precise, lest others find the fraying edges and tear it all apart.

There would be protests. He could already see their arguments forming in his mind. The debate would be drawn out and tedious but none of that mattered, because this must be done. Biran planned to gather all the GC on every single Prime station and, one by one, march them into a room with that system's Protectorate and make them retract their helmets.

It was not The Done Thing. Generations of protocol pushed back at him with every word he typed. Alexandra Halston would have never allowed it. There were rules. Systems.

Halston was dead. And the Keepers were the system.

Biran had grown wary of systems. He typed the last word and saved the file, stretching his arms above his head to relieve their stiffness. He wouldn't send the proposal out, not yet. There were huge amounts of planning to do to get himself officially sworn in as Ada's director. There were still bodies to find. To bury, if there was enough left of them. There was his own expedition through the gate to plan. But when the time came, he would be ready. He had to be.

Because Hitton had heard voices in the walls of the asteroid station, had seen the ghost of a guardcore moving through her secure network. And, stars damn them all, she had been right. One of Rainier must have been there, seeding panic, and then, finally, the nanite swarm.

It wasn't the only problem weighing on Biran's mind. The guardcore he could push to be revealed. It would be a fight, but the safety of all would override tradition. While they'd been spinning themselves in circles discussing Rainier and all her various plans and claims, one mystery clawed at the back of Biran's mind, begging for attention.

Was it Rainier who had wanted Hitton discredited? And why? The more he thought about it, the more everything lined up as a smear job against Hitton. Yes, he had scarcely avoided delivering the speech that would malign her mental health. And yes, he now believed without reservation that Rainier's false guardcore had been present on the asteroid.

But they hadn't needed to reveal themselves to Hitton. They could have stayed hidden, easily, and done whatever it was Rainier had wanted done without being detected. For some reason he couldn't fathom, Rainier had decided that Hitton needed to be deemed an unreliable source of information. Even Olver had started to believe in her instability.

"Visitor approaching," his house AI said.

Biran scowled at empty air. "Who? Lockdown is on."

"Keeper Vladsen."

Biran's tongue felt thick in his mouth. "Let him in."

He stood, pulled his robe tight, and made it to his bedroom door as Vladsen wandered in, scanning Biran's house for signs of life. He startled as Biran let his hand brush against the doorframe, his wristpad scraping the wall. Vladsen's frown morphed into a miniscule smile.

"So it's true. Our director lives in ramshackle walls."

Biran looked around his own house and wondered why he never saw how shabby things were until someone else was standing among them. Vladsen was an impossibly slick, modern creature against the wear and tear on Biran's furniture. All Biran owned was what came with the place, and that was meant to be broken down and reprinted into whatever a Keeper desired later on. Even if he had the credits, Biran wasn't sure anymore what a home should look like.

"I'd offer you a drink," Biran said, "but the dispenser is broken."

Vladsen chuckled. "Of course it is. Brought my own."

He produced a slim flask from his sleeve and set it down in the middle of Biran's kitchen table as he sat, precariously, on the very chair Biran had been afraid would break under Anford. Vladsen was a slight man. The legs didn't so much as creak.

"Join me?"

"I..." He trailed off. There were hundreds of things he should be doing. He sat down at the table. "I'm glad you're here." He let the word *here* carry weight, and tried to ignore the stinging in his heart. Biran hadn't been scheduled to be at the spin-up, Okonkwo had taken that away from him as punishment, but Vladsen had.

A last-minute threat against Vladsen's life had made the GC ground him on Ada for his safety. Not unusual for Keepers, but considering the context...

Vladsen took a long drink and held on to the flask. "You're wondering if Rainier spared me."

Biran wanted to look away, but couldn't. "You were a favorite of her husband. It stands to reason."

"It does, doesn't it? But I don't *know*." Anguish twisted his features.

Biran thought back to his proposal to unmask all of the guardcore. "Do you want to know?"

"Honestly? No. But I need to. Someone else took my place on that podium, Speaker, and I haven't even had the guts to look up who yet."

"We'll find the truth," Biran said.

"And will that make it better?"

"No. Maybe. I don't know."

Vladsen laughed roughly and took another drink, then pushed the flask across the table to Biran. "Please, there's frightfully little left, and stars know I don't need it."

Biran drank, coughed, and grimaced as he handed the flask back. "Dios, Rost. This is worse than what we had at—"

He cut himself off.

"Rost again, is it?"

Biran swallowed hard and placed his hands palm-down on the table. "If you'd like."

"I would."

A flush of heat rose into his chest and cheeks, but it was passing.

"You're troubled," Rost said, gently.

"I'd be insane not to be."

"No... This is something else. Not that—that mad woman's accusations." Rost grimaced. "I never dreamed Rainier... Well, how could I? But that's not the point. We hashed all that out at the meeting." Light as a whisper, Rost touched the back of Biran's hand with a fingertip. "Can I help at all?"

Slowly, Biran shook his head, but he shifted his other hand to cover Rost's fingertips with his own.

"No. It's time to get my own hands dirty."

The story continues in…

Book Three of the Protectorate

Keep reading for a sneak peek!

ACKNOWLEDGMENTS

Thank you to my readers, who have come along on this twisting journey with me through the worlds of The Protectorate. I'm a very lucky writer indeed to have you all along for the ride.

A special thanks to my beta readers, Karen Rochnik, Andrea Stewart, Tina Gower, and Marina J. Lostetter for always having my back and letting me know when I've gone off the rails or need more kissing scenes. My work and my life are richer for having you all as a part of it.

I am a very lucky human to have many dear writing friends who've provided great insight and comradeship over the years and during the course of writing *Chaos Vector*. Thank you to Earl T. Roske, Erin Foley, Trish Henry, Laura Blackwell, Laura Davy, Clarissa Ryan, and Vylar Kaftan for your friendship and support.

To my Murder Cabin compatriots, Thomas K. Carpenter, Rachel Carpenter, Anthea Sharp, Annie Bellet, and Setsu Uzume, thank you for your friendship and for not murdering me just yet.

Publishing these books with Orbit has been a real pleasure, and that's all thanks to Brit Hvide, Bryn A. McDonald, Angeline Rodriguez, Kelley Frodel, Ellen Wright, Nivia Evans, Anna Jackson, James Long, Lauren Panepinto, and my excellent cover artist, Sparth.

Thank you to my agent, Sam Morgan, who sees the real chaos and handles it all with gusto.

And, as always, a very special thanks to my supportive husband, Joey Hewitt. Who is still, in fact, not the inspiration for every single character he likes, despite his assertions otherwise.

extras

meet the author

Photo Credit: Joey Hewitt

MEGAN E. O'KEEFE was raised among journalists and, as soon as she was able, joined them by crafting a newsletter that chronicled the daily adventures of the local cat population. She has worked in both arts management and graphic design, and has won Writers of the Future and the David Gemmell Morningstar Award.

Megan lives in the Bay Area of California.

Find out more about Megan E. O'Keefe and other Orbit authors by registering for the free monthly newsletter at www.orbitbooks.net.

if you enjoyed
CHAOS VECTOR
look out for
THE PROTECTORATE: BOOK THREE
by
Megan E. O'Keefe

Dazzling space battles, intergalactic politics, and rogue AI collide in the third book in this epic space opera by award-winning author Megan E. O'Keefe.

CHAPTER 1

Prime Standard Year 3543

Three Weeks After the Blowback

Sanda Greeve stood on the deck of the biggest weapon humanity had ever known, and watched live footage of the city of Atrux tearing itself apart. Ninety-seven percent of Atrux, fallen. That was the only number she could cling to, because the actual amount of dead and comatose was too high to comprehend.

The rest, that 3 percent, had been converted by the ascension-agent. And in their confusion and pain, they rioted across the city, not understanding their own strength, until guardcore—vetted, *safe*—showed up to capture them or put them down.

Sanda clutched her blaster like a shield, though the weapon could do her no good. There wasn't a weapon in the universe big enough to stop what had happened to Atrux. Even her ship, *The Light*, wasn't enough. She wasn't sure anything could be enough.

"Tell me Anford's finally recovered footage of the contamination moment," Sanda asked Bero. Asked her ship.

"Watching it won't change anything," Bero said.

He was stalling. Warning hackles raised along the back of her neck.

"Mouthing off isn't going to stop me. Play it."

The video flickered onto the forward viewscreen, though *The Light* was perfectly capable of displaying any video without the tiniest hiccup. Bero showing his annoyance by inserting a glitch. She almost rolled her eyes, but that'd only encourage him to comment on her irritation, and that wasn't an argument she wanted to have.

Because irritation was only scraping the surface. Below the major's bars on her chest and the sleek confines of her Prime-issued jumpsuit, Sanda boiled with molten rage. Needling her might give the magma within a path to eruption, and not a soul on board *The Light* had time for her to melt down.

A guardcore appeared in the footage, slipping through the thin cracks in Prime's protocols, to secure an unwelcome canister to the additive tank of Atrux's atmo mix. From that canister, a wave of self-replicating nanites had spread the ascension-agent throughout the city's ventilation system. Sanda leaned toward the screen, frowning. The armor was right. The weapons were right. The clearances were right. But that was no GC.

"It's not Rainier," she said.

The Light's crew shifted uncomfortably. This ship didn't need a crew to fly, but Bero had gone ahead and given them all seats with consoles they could work if they so desired. They often fiddled with the controls, trying to figure out the inner workings of *The Light*. Sanda suspected those buttons were little more than placebos, but she hadn't had the heart to ask Bero outright.

"We can't be sure," Dr. Liao said. "The armor—"

"Doesn't disguise gait," Sanda countered. The doctor pressed her lips shut.

Sanda couldn't blame her. She wanted that figure to be Rainier, too. But she'd learned a long time ago that wanting something to be true badly enough to lie to yourself led only to more pain.

"Bero, can you run a gait analysis?" she asked.

"Against every person in the known universe?"

"No," Arden said. Their voice rasped and they'd gone deathly pale. The word trailed off into emptiness, cut down by a sharp glare from Nox, but Sanda didn't press. They needed to do this on their own, because neither one of them would forgive her if she pushed for it, even if they already knew it was true. "I have some footage of Jules I can send you."

"She wouldn't do this," Nox snapped, but he didn't stop Arden as they tapped on their wristpad, sending the files to *The Light*.

"We have to know," Arden said softly.

Sanda could see a retort bubble below the surface, but before Nox could get it out, Bero pushed two videos, side by side, onto the viewscreen. In one, Jules Valentine approached Arden's old apartment building on top of Udon-Voodun. In the other, the guardcore walked through the door into the atmo-mix control room. For the benefit of the humans riding in his belly, Bero allowed graphical points of comparison to run over each figure.

He didn't say anything. He didn't need to.

"It's her," Arden said.

Sanda pushed down a burst of excitement. Rainier Lavaux was an expert at covering her tracks. But Sanda was pretty damn sure Jules Valentine lacked the same skill set. Jules, Sanda could find. From there, she'd leverage her way to Rainier. She doubted Nox and Arden would be as excited about this break as she was.

"B, get me Anford," Sanda said.

"I am not your personal assistant."

Sanda rolled her eyes and put a priority call through to her commander. General Anford's face popped up on the screen in seconds, overriding the footage of Jules. Anford didn't even blink at Sanda's unusual crew or the alien deck of *The Light*. It was amazing how quickly humanity adapted.

"Greeve, tell me you have something."

"The guardcore who released the nanites on Atrux is Jules Valentine."

The general's eyes narrowed briefly. "Not Rainier? You're sure?"

"She may have acted under Rainier's orders, I don't know, but Bero is certain that the body in that armor belongs to Valentine."

"Far be it from me to doubt Bero's assessment."

"Thank you, general," Bero said. "I have been lauded for my intelligence in the past."

Sanda suppressed a smirk. "I intend to pursue. Valentine might know a way to get to Rainier."

"I agree. We need her alive, Greeve." Anford glanced to the side, the corners of her lips tightening. "We need all the information we can get our hands on."

Ninety-seven percent. That number was burned into Sanda's heart. Similar branding stamped pain around Anford's eyes.

"I'll get you answers," Sanda said.

"Hold in Atrux. I don't have a lot to spare, but I'll send a battalion to you."

Slowly, intentionally, Sanda shifted her gaze to the walls of *The Light*. "General, with respect, I need no other weapons. They would only slow me down."

Anford's jaw flexed as she soaked that in. "Very well. Between Okonkwo and me, you have carte blanche to requisition anything you need. Good luck, Greeve."

"Good luck." Sanda snapped off a tight salute, and Anford cut the feed.

"You sure we're going to be enough, commander?" Conway asked.

"It's our best shot. Bero, do you have a bead on that GC ship Valentine took off in?"

"It was last flagged passing through the gate to Ordinal."

"Then that's where we start."

Arden swiveled their chair around to look her in the eye. "Rainier made her do this."

Sanda met their gaze evenly, peripherally aware of the tension in Nox's body, the held breaths of everyone on the ship. No one liked hunting down a woman they'd meant to save not too long ago. No one liked acknowledging they'd known, and even cared for, a monster.

Sanda could relate, but that didn't mean she could make it better.

"We'll find her," she said. "And we'll ask her ourselves."

"Sanda," Bero said, his voice tense.

She frowned. "What is it?"

"*The Light* has an incoming tightbeam."

"Does this ship even have a transponder to point at?"

"Not... exactly."

"Put it through."

The viewscreen filled with a face so familiar that if she hadn't already been propped up on an emotional cocktail of rage and determination, she might have had to sit down.

His face was sharper than she remembered. New shadows carved troughs beneath his eyes, and thick stubble peppered his jawline. Dark brown hair stuck up under low-g, and over his shoulder, she could make out the sleek geometry of a high-end shuttle. But those grey eyes, they were always the same, if a touch sad.

"Hey," Tomas Cepko said. His voice was thin and wary. "We need to talk."

"You look like shit," she said.

The corner of his eye twitched, then he settled into a small, warm smile. "Nice to see you, too."

"Believe it or not," Sanda said, gesturing to the ship around her, "I'm a little busy."

"It's about the sphere," Tomas said, his expression completely locked down.

"How the fuck—?" Nox took a step, as if he could reach through the screen to choke the spy on the other side. She couldn't blame him for wanting to try.

"Crew," Sanda said firmly. "Meet Nazca Tomas Cepko, first-class spy and all-around asshole."

His lips thinned, and he flicked his gaze down. "I... can explain my actions."

"Really not what I'm worried about right now."

"Hello, Tomas," Bero said.

Tomas's eyes widened. He leaned toward the camera, pressing his hands against the console of his shuttle. "Christ, are you in danger?"

Nox snorted, which warmed Sanda's angry heart right up. "I am in command of my ship, Nazca, and I'd like to know how the fuck you got that tightbeam to me."

He gave her a punchably sly smile. "Seems we have a lot of information to share with each other."

"I'm not in the habit of sharing with spies."

He winced and rubbed at his chest. "Yeah, I remember. Look, I don't know what's going on with the fleet or why you're in that ship with Bero, but I know you, Greeve, and you're about to charge guns-out after Rainier. I don't blame you, but there are some things you need to know. Some things I need to *show* you."

"*Commander* Greeve," she snapped, because there was no way in the void she'd let Tomas fucking Cepko get away with undermining her position. "And if you're looking for a date, lover, there are programs for that."

"Commander," Bero said with a touch more respect than he usually bothered with, "I hate to interrupt your tearing into Tomas, but it occurs to me that he knows about the sphere."

Tomas leaned back, crossed his arms, and raised both brows. "Thanks, B."

"I do not like you, Tomas."

Sanda gritted her teeth. "Very well. We're coming through Ordinal anyway. Send your location to Bero and we'll talk. If you waste my time, I swear to all of Prime that I will space you."

"I believe you," he said with a slight shudder, then composed himself and flashed an irritatingly charming smile at her. "See you soon."

She cut the feed and sank into her captain's chair, trying to quiet her mind. That damn man made her feel like the memory-wipe headaches lurked behind her next breath, like any second all the pain of the moment he'd ripped her world apart would come crashing back down.

"We sure it's a good idea to get mixed up with another Nazca, boss?" Nox asked. "Last time didn't go so well."

Sanda rubbed the side of her face. "It's because of last time that I'm putting up with this. Okonkwo hasn't managed to shake anything out of the Nazca tree, and they clearly know *something* about what's going on, or Novak wouldn't have been on Janus. Tomas knows about the sphere. Like Anford said, we need all the intel we can get, and that's the Nazca's specialty."

"You realize, of course, that he needs something from you," Bero said.

She tried to side-eye him, but it didn't really work when he existed all around her. "Yes, B. I am rather well versed in dealing with duplicitous dickheads."

"What do you think he wants?" Nox asked.

"I don't know," Sanda admitted. "But finding out what he wants will give us a better idea of what the Nazca really know than whatever bait intel he's set out for me."

"Sanda," Bero said with mock shock, "you've grown so cynical."

She quirked a half smile. "I learn from the best."

But this wasn't cynicism. Rainier would say she was afraid, and maybe she'd be right, to a certain extent. Watching Atrux fall to an invisible storm had certainly made her blood run cold, but that's not when the shift inside her had really happened. It hadn't even been when she'd crawled off Liao's fringer settlement and learned she was too late—the secondary gate in Ada had spun, the blowback had happened, and it had nearly taken her family with it.

No, she'd felt the first slivers of change when she'd sat on that command console in the fringer settlement, all alone, and waited for Rainier Lavaux to show up and kill her. She hadn't been afraid of Rainier, not really. Hadn't even been afraid of dying.

She'd held that button in her mind, the trigger for the EMP that would cut Rainier down, and savored an urge unlike any she'd ever felt before. A wellspring of vengeance had risen in Sanda that day, and while Rainier was certain it was fear alone at the base instinct of all humanity, Sanda had known in that moment that, for her, the core of her drive had been rage. Not the blind, flailing anger of the uncontrolled and impetuous, but something deeper.

Something primal.

Rainier Lavaux had threatened everything and everyone Sanda had ever loved. Sanda had felt that loss once. And she'd burn the bitch to the ground rather than suffer through that pain all over again.

if you enjoyed
CHAOS VECTOR
look out for
FORTUNA
The Nova Vita Protocol: Book One
by
Kristyn Merbeth

Fortuna *launches a new space opera trilogy that will hook you from the first crash landing.*

There's only one thing Scorpia Kaiser wants in the whole galaxy: to finally own Fortuna, *the ship she pilots and the only home she's ever known. But when it becomes clear her predecessor—the family matriarch—has been wheeling and dealing with various planetary governments, Scorpia realizes that her own family may be the reason the system's five planets are headed toward a devastating war.*

Lies, manipulation, and profit are all she's ever been taught, but as she ascends into her new position, Scorpia finds she has the chance to change everything. Yet even as she takes on more responsibility for the family's fate, fortune, and influence, she is not at all sure she's ready for it—nor that she has the support of her crew, particularly her brother and rival Corvus.

To stop the war, she'll have to unite her family and unravel the chaos they've left in their wake.

CHAPTER ONE

Fortuna

Scorpia

Fortuna's cockpit smells like sweat and whiskey, and loose screws rattle with every thump of music. I'm sprawled in the pilot's chair, legs stretched out and boots resting atop the control panel forming a half circle around me. A bottle of whiskey dangles from one of my hands; the other taps out the song's beat on the control wheel.

Normally, this is my favorite place to be: in my chair, behind the wheel, staring out at open space and its endless possibilities. I'm a daughter of the stars, after all. But I've been in the cockpit for nearly eight hours now, urging this ship as fast as she can go to make sure we unload our cargo on time, and my body is starting to ache from it. Scrappy little *Fortuna* is my home, the only one I've ever known, but she wasn't built for comfort. She was built to take a beating.

My shift at the wheel wasn't so bad for the first six hours, but once the others went to bed, I had to shut the door leading to the rest of the ship, and the cockpit soon grew cramped and hot. No way around it, though. I need the music to stay awake, and my family needs the quiet to sleep. Someone needs to be coherent enough to throw on a smile and lie their ass off to customs when we get there, and it's not gonna be me.

I yawn, pushing sweaty, dark hair out of my face. Envy stings me as I think of my younger siblings, snug in bed, but recedes as I remember they're actually strapped into the launch chairs in their respective rooms, with gooey mouth-guards shoved between their teeth and cottony plugs stuffed up their ears. I don't know how they manage to sleep with all that, but it's necessary in case of a rough descent, the likelihood of which is rising with every sip of whiskey I take. *Fortuna*'s autopilot can land the ship on its own, but it tends to lurch and scrape and thud its way there, with little regard for the comfort of its occupants or whether or not they hurl up their dinner when they arrive. Some pilot finesse makes things run more smoothly.

Given that, I'd normally avoid too much hard liquor while at the wheel. But as soon as Gaia came into sight, anxiety blossomed in my gut. Now, the planet fills my view out the front panel and dread sloshes in my stomach. It's a beautiful place, I'll admit that. Vast stretches of water dotted with land masses, wispy clouds drifting across, like a damn painting or something. Historians say that after centuries of searching for humanity's new home, the original settlers wept with joy at the first glimpse of Gaia. I, on the other hand, always go straight for the bottle strapped to the bottom of my chair.

Beautiful Gaia. Rich in alien tech and bad memories. Ever since Corvus abandoned us to fight in his useless war, even the good ones from my childhood have turned bitter.

"Damn," I mutter, and take another sip. I've once again broken the rule I invented in the early hours of my boredom. Every time I think of my older brother, that's another drink. It's a tough rule when my memories of Gaia are so deeply entwined with memories of him.

I was seven when we left Gaia. It's been twenty years since we were grounded there. And after a brief stop on Deva, where Lyre was born, we spent another six years on Nibiru, while she and the twins were still too young to live on the ship. Those were better years, when we spent our days playing and fishing in the endless ocean and our nights sleeping in a pile on our single mattress. Yet even then I could never shake my anxiety that Momma wouldn't come back one day, and I'd be stranded again. I never felt safe like I did on *Fortuna*, never stopped waiting for someone to notice I didn't belong. The days on Gaia wouldn't loosen their hold on me.

And every time I see the planet, it all rushes back to the surface. Memories of Corvus's smile; of digging through trash for food; of playing tag with him in the narrow streets of Levian, the capital city; of huge alien statues staring down at me with their faceless visages.

Memories of Momma wearing hooded Gaian finery to blend in on the crowded street and saying, *"It's just a game, Scorpia,"* as she showed me the best way to slip my hands into someone's pocket without them noticing. When she taught me my first con, dressing me up like a little lost Gaian child, she said, *"It's like telling a joke, but you're the only one who knows the punchline."* Guess Momma didn't anticipate that once I started, I wouldn't be able to stop thinking that way. Or maybe she didn't think I'd live long enough for it to matter. I probably wouldn't have, if Corvus hadn't been around to get me out of trouble. Corvus, who was never any good at lying, so he went to school while I learned to be a criminal.

"*Damn.*" I sip again. Through the viewing panel, Gaia looms closer.

As I wipe my mouth, I glance over the expanse of screens and gauges and lights all around me, tracking the radar, fuel tank, and various systems. The numbers are blurry, but the lights are all the soothing red of Nova Vita, which means everything is running fine. Good enough for me. I take another swig, and choke on it as the ship shudders.

It's not a particularly menacing rumble, yet the hairs on the back of my neck stand straight up. I let my boots thud to the metal floor one after another, dragged by the ship's artificial gravity, and frown at the panels. Nothing on the radar. It could be some debris too small to pick up, a cough in the machinery...or a cloaked ship. It's rare for us to have company out here, when interplanetary trade and travel have all but ground to a halt due to the tense relations between planets. Rarer still near Gaia, whose border laws are tightest of all. But it could be those pirate bastards on the *Red Baron* hounding us again. If they picked up cloaking tech, we're in trouble. Not for the first time, I wish *Fortuna* was outfitted with weaponry for self-defense—but of course, weapons on ships are illegal, and we'd never be able to land anywhere in the system if we had them. With current laws, the planets are wary enough about ships without the added threat of weapons on them.

Indicators are all a solid red. There's not so much as a blip out of place. Still, my skin prickles. *Fortuna* is saying something. I slap the button to shut off the music, tilt my head to one side, and listen to the silence.

The next rumble shakes the whole craft.

The bridge goes dark. Every screen and every light disappears. My sharp intake of breath echoes in the darkness.

"*Fortuna*?" I ask, as if the ship will answer. I clutch tighter to the whiskey with one hand and the wheel with the other as my muddled brain tries to work out what else to do. I've dealt with my fair share of malfunctions, but I've never seen the ship go dark like this.

The lights blink back online. A relieved laugh bubbles out of me, but cuts off as I realize all of my screens are crackling with static.

I smack a few buttons, producing no effect, and turn from one end of the control panel to the other. My eyes find the system indicators on the far right. Life support and the engine are still lit red, signaling that they're online and functioning. But navigation is the shockingly unnatural green of system failure. Radar is green. Autopilot is green.

The ship has everything she needs to keep flying, but not what she needs to land.

"Aw, shit." Judging by the fact that we haven't been blasted or boarded yet, this isn't the *Red Baron* or any other outside interference. It's an internal malfunction. I flash back to my sister Lyre begging for new engine parts on Deva, and curse under my breath. Our little engineer is usually too cautious for her own good, but it seems she was right this time.

I take a final sip from my bottle, cap it, and tuck it between my boots. Once it's secure, I reach toward the neon-green emergency alarm button on the left side of the control panel. At the last moment, I stop short.

Hitting that button will send alarms screaming and green lights flaring through the ship, cutting through my family's earplugs and waking them from their strapped-in-for-landing slumber. My ever-scowling mother will be here in less than a minute, barking orders, taking control. And at the first sniff of whiskey in the cockpit, she'll relieve me from my duty and send me to bed.

Fortuna will stay in orbit until everything's at 100 percent and I've passed a BAC test...which means we'll miss the drop-off on Gaia *and* the side job I hoped to pull off beforehand.

And I'll be the family screwup. Again. One step further from ever amounting to more than that, or ever prying my future out of Momma's iron grip. One step further from *Fortuna* belonging to me. I can already hear her usual speech: *"You're the oldest now. You can't keep doing this shit."*

Plus, this side job is important. There's not much profit in it, but I can use all the credits I can get after I blew most of my last earnings on Deva. I can't deny I'm looking forward to seeing the pretty face of my favorite client, too.

And, of course, I want to see Momma's expression when I tell her I pulled off a job on my own. I know that she was grooming Corvus to be in charge one day—Corvus, who was always so obedient and ready to follow in her footsteps—but he's been gone for three years now, fighting in the war on his home-planet. We all have to accept that he's not coming back. Instead, Momma's stuck with me.

This deal I set up is the perfect chance to prove that's not such a terrible thing. And once the ship falls to me, I'll finally have a place in the universe that's all my own. A home that nobody can kick me out of. I'll get to make my own decisions, be in charge of my own life. I'll keep my family together and make things better for all of us, like Corvus always promised he would before he abandoned us.

But if we don't make it in time, this will just be one more disappointment on the list.

I sit back in my seat, running my tongue over my teeth. I'll have to land the ship as planned. Even if it's bumpy, and even if Momma smells the whiskey on me once we land, she can't give me too much shit if I get us planet-side intact and on time.

It's a damn nice thought...but it's been a long time since I landed the ship without autopilot. And, lest the blurry vision and stink of whiskey in the cockpit aren't enough to remind me, I'm drunk enough that I could get jail time for flying a simple hovercraft on most planets. There's no law out here to punish me for operating a spacecraft under the influence, but down there the law of gravity waits, ready to deal swift and deadly judgment if I fuck this up.

"So don't fuck it up," I tell myself. I suck in a slow breath, blow it out through my nose, and hit the button to connect to Gaian air control. Static crackles through the speakers, followed by a booming robotic voice. I wince, hastily lowering the volume.

"You have reached Gaian customs. State your registration number and purpose. Do not enter Gaian airspace without confirmation or you will be destroyed."

I know the automatic Gaian "greeting" by heart, and I also know it's not bullshit. As a kid, I saw many unregistered ships shot out of the sky before they got close to landing. The locals would cheer like it was some grand fireworks show. I always felt bad for the poor souls. If they were entering Gaian airspace illegally, they had to be desperate. Using the opportunity to pick some Gaian pockets felt a little like justice.

"This is pilot Scorpia Kaiser of merchant vessel *Fortuna*," I say into the mic, working hard to keep my words from slurring into one another. "Registration number..." I run a finger down a list etched on one of my side panels, and blink until the numbers come into focus. Of course, the Gaian registry is the longest number of them all. Damn Gaians and their regulations. "Two-dash-zero-two-one-eight-eight-dash-one-zero-three-six," I say. "Registered to Captain Auriga Kaiser, Gaian citizen. We're delivering freeze-dried produce from Deva."

It's not the whole truth, but it's not a lie, either. If customs agents peek into our cargo crates, they'll find neat packages of fruits and vegetables dried and sealed for space travel. The good shit is well hidden. We're professionals, after all.

"Checking registration," the robotic voice says. There's a pause, followed by a click. "Checking landing schedule." Another pause, click. "Ship two-dash-zero-two-one-eight-eight-dash-one-zero-three-six, you are cleared for entry. Noncitizens are not permitted to travel beyond the landing zone. Entry elsewhere will be considered a hostile act. Welcome to Gaia."

"Yeah, I'm feeling real welcome," I mutter, severing the radio connection. But the recording has provided a good reminder of what's at stake here. If I crash, we all die. If I land so much as an inch outside the legal landing zone, same shit. I roll my shoulders back and slip the safety belts across my chest, clicking them into place and yanking the straps tight. "Okay, *Fortuna*," I say. "Hope you're ready for this. It's gonna be a rough landing."

I fish in my pocket for the gooey lump of my mouth-guard, chomp down, and shove the control wheel forward.

CHAPTER TWO

Family

Corvus

Monitor the radar. Check the armory. Count the supplies. Three weeks in this outpost, and I've started every morning with the same routine. Three weeks in the middle of nowhere, with no orders other than to hold this position and keep an eye out for anything unusual. We haven't had so much as a glimpse of the enemy. General Altair must have stationed us here for a reason, but my patience is wearing thin, both with the situation and my stir-crazy team. Our skills are put to waste as lookouts. Not a day has gone by without them reminding me of that fact and pestering me for news. I swear, these soldiers can be worse than my little siblings were.

Given that, this time alone would normally be a blessing. Titans have infuriatingly little regard for personal space or privacy, and over these three years I've learned to snatch moments of solitude when I can. That's why I've gotten into the habit of waking up an hour before the rest of my team to fulfill duties like these, rather than passing the chores on to them.

But lately, my thoughts weigh heavily on me, and now I have nothing to distract me from them. My hands stay busy as I run through the morning routine, but my mind wanders, barely aware of the gray walls around me or the dim lights overhead or my breath fogging in the air. My cold fingers punch in the passcodes to enter each doorway without pausing to think about it. Everything is the same as every other morning, and it all fades into background noise. But this time I pause, running my fingers over the brand on the inside of my right wrist, those eight numbers and squiggly lines they marked on me when I entered the service. Now, my mandatory years are over. But no matter where I go, the war will always be a part of me. What if this is where I belong?

Perhaps this was Altair's intent all along: to give me time to think. He knows I have a choice to make. Merely a few weeks ago, I thought it was already made. After we lost Uwe to a bomb on our last mission, with the image of the explosion waiting every time I closed my eyes, I sent a message to my family without a moment's hesitation. All these years, I never thought anything could convince me to stay here and keep fighting in this awful war. I believed it was the desire to leave that kept me moving. It was memories of my family that gave me the resolve to do terrible things, anything necessary to survive. My only goal after enlisting was to live long enough to return to them, and protect my siblings like I always swore I would.

When it was just the two of us on Gaia, Scorpia was always the one to take care of me, to lie and steal and do all the things I couldn't do. I was never any good at it, so instead Momma paid for some fake papers to get me into a Gaian school, calling it an investment in the family's future.

Once we went to Nibiru, where Scorpia couldn't shake her bad habits and found an even worse one in a bottle, I took that mantle upon myself. I looked after the little ones, tried to keep Scorpia from drowning in her vices, did my best to soothe Momma's anger by being the perfect son she wanted me to be. Scorpia and I would huddle by Nibiru's ocean, or later in the ship's cargo bay, and whisper about our dreams for the future. We would talk about all of us having a say in the family business rather than being threatened into following orders. No more risky jobs, no more Primus technology, no more weapons. *"When I'm in charge, we can be whoever we want to be,"* I would always say.

But that was before. Before I became attached to this place and its people. Before I believed that I could do something good for this system rather than returning to my family to smuggle drugs and other contraband. Altair's offer changed everything. I've climbed rapidly through the ranks here, guided by the general's hand—and now, he wants more for me. He wants me to work directly under him, learn from him, take his place as a general one day. I wouldn't be another pawn in this war...I would be one of the people running it, shaping a better future for my people. Just like I always dreamed of doing for my family, but on a much grander scale. Here, I could make a difference.

The door to the supply room bangs open and startles me from my thoughts. A stocky blond woman, our latest recruit after we lost Uwe, stands in the doorway. Her face flushes as she sees me. Three years on Titan, and it still shocks me how their skin is commonly pale enough to show emotion in a surge of startling color. The system has a wide range of skin tones, but this is the one planet where the majority of people are fair enough for my own tawny coloring to stand out.

I clear my throat and turn to face her, straightening my posture so that I stand—just barely—taller than her. My height is yet another reminder that I may be Titan by birth but not by blood. Elsewhere in the system I stand above the average, but not here.

"Sergeant Kaiser, I'm sorry. I didn't mean to intrude. Everyone's looking for you, and it's—they sent me," she says, the words coming out in a jumble. She's still new enough to be nervous around me, and new enough that it takes me a few moments to remember her name. I would feel bad about it, but I've seen far too many new faces come and go.

"Ivennie," I say, remembering. Ivennie Smirnova. "I've told you, Corvus is fine."

"Yes, sir, Corvus, sir," she says. Her face turns a deeper shade of red, which I didn't think was possible. I suppress a sigh. It always takes recruits a while to accept that they're part of a team now and don't need to follow the same rigidity as during training. Our army has a strict hierarchy, and we're always expected to show deference to superiors, but within a team, things are different. We're encouraged to be close. Intimate, even.

So I lay a hand on Ivennie's shoulder. The act still feels odd to me after all these years, too familiar given we've only known each other for a few weeks. But the new recruit leans into my hand despite her earlier anxiety, relief crossing her face. All of the Titans complain about being touch-starved after basic training.

"You don't need to be so formal with me. Here, we're"—the next words stick in my throat, as they always do, but I finish the phrase I learned from the general—"a family."

She stares up at me with wide eyes. I can't bring myself to force a smile, but I give her an encouraging nod. *Family.* That's what we're supposed to say, anyway. Altair taught me that physical touch is so deeply ingrained in Titan culture that they don't bother trying to stamp it out in the military. He said it's good for them to feel that closeness, when many of them have lost their blood relations to the war. But I suspect he knows the truth: that nobody would fight as long or as hard as we do without something to care about, even if that something is a lie.

I step past the still-blushing new recruit into the dim underground hallway. As much as I've tried to make myself believe it these last few years, and as much as I've grown to care about them, I've always known deep down that my team could never truly be family. I already have one waiting for me—a family bound together by blood.

Titans, who often grow up in large, blended families with multiple sets of parents to fill in any gaps left by the war, don't place much value in blood. But I wasn't raised as a Titan. I still remember the time I dared to ask about who my father was at dinner, and the taste of copper in my mouth after Momma hit me—one of the few times she raised a hand against me. My siblings were just as shocked as I was. *"You have no fathers,"* she told us in the silence, using that tone of hers that brooked no argument. *"Forget about them. Forget your birth-planets, too. The blood you share is the only thing that matters. No one outside this room is ever going to accept any of you, so you need to look out for each other."*

I shake off the memory. The past has been haunting me far too often these days, and the distraction could get me killed out here.

"Take me to the others," I tell Ivennie. She rushes to obey, leading me to the stairwell. This outpost was built to house a much larger unit than ours if necessary, and it takes a while to traverse the stairs. I can feel Ivennie's eyes on me as we walk, practically hear the questions on her tongue.

We haven't spent much time together, just the two of us, since she arrived. Moments of one-on-one time, like solitude, are rare here. Our team is expected to spend every moment together: eating, training, showering, sleeping. We're expected to share everything. *Privacy leads to secrets, secrets to jealousy, and jealousy is a disease of the soul,* a common Titan saying goes. I try to respect Titan customs, I truly do, but some I can't bring myself to follow. Just as Momma always told me, no matter how hard I try, I'll never truly be a Titan.

Though I suspect I've been avoiding Ivennie for other reasons, as well. Knowing I may be leaving soon makes me loath to add another name to the list of people I care about here. Especially so with Uwe's loss still so fresh. The rest of my team has been hesitant to welcome the rookie as well.

The shock of Uwe's death lingers in all of us. Before that, it had been over three months since we lost someone. We had fallen into a rhythm, a strong team dynamic, and now everyone is struggling once again to figure out where they fit, trying to adjust themselves around the missing piece my off-worlder customs leave.

We shouldn't have lost Uwe. It was a stupid, senseless death. I've replayed the day a thousand times over, running through all the ways I could've prevented it.

We were in Niivya, a border town freshly liberated from the enemy. Drunk on victory, newly armed with information Daniil had extracted from a captured Isolationist sergeant. The townspeople were eager to celebrate with us. Feeding us, filling our mugs when they were empty. Putting us at ease.

Everyone but me was very intoxicated when word arrived that a child had fallen into a sewer. I should have gone alone. But I couldn't carry both a child and a light in the darkness of the sewers, and so someone needed to come with me. Since Uwe lost the hand of cards, it fell to him. He was drunk—staggering, singing drunk. He nearly fell on his face when we dropped down into the sewers to look for her.

When we found the child, she wasn't injured at all. Instead, she was clutching an explosive device in her hands. When Uwe raised the light, she ran at us.

I had a gun. I should have used it. But she was a child, and in her face I saw Scorpia, Lyre, Andromeda. I froze. Drunk though he was, Uwe still reacted before I did, and his first thought was to shield me from the worst of the blast. He tackled me to the ground with his armored body on top of mine. My only injury was a gash on my cheek where my face hit the concrete floor. There wasn't enough left of Uwe for a proper funeral. When I emerged from that tunnel, covered in the remains of both my teammate and a little girl, I was ready to leave Titan, despite the love that I've gained for both the planet and its people. I sent the message to my family the next day, when I was still so sure, before Altair made his offer and the doubt set in.

But Ivennie doesn't know any of that, and none of it is her fault. She's a quick learner with exceptionally high potential, perhaps even for leadership, according to Altair's recommendation. I should be doing a better job of teaching her how a team operates. If there's one thing I can do for the others before I leave them behind, I should at least give them the ability to rely on each other.

I clear my throat and lower my hand as I realize I'm touching the scar on my cheek. It would have been an easy thing for Titan doctors to fix, but I asked to keep it as a reminder. My eyes shift to Ivennie, who immediately glances away as if she hadn't been staring.

"You can ask, if you want," I tell her. "I'll answer any questions you have. I know you must have heard plenty of rumors." A sergeant who was raised off-world is no small thing on Titan. I know the things they say about me, both good and bad.

No doubt Ivennie would have asked the others about me already, if they weren't as reluctant to accept her as I am. She hesitates for barely a moment before she gives in to curiosity.

"Is it true you're an off-worlder?"

"No. I'm a Titan. I was born here." The response is automatic. Confusion creases her forehead, and after a moment, I relent. "But, yes, I've spent most of my life off-world, though I've always been Titan at heart. I returned when duty called me." A mouthful of lies. When I was growing up, Momma always reminded me that blood came first. The last thing she said to me was *"You're a Kaiser, not a Titan. Don't forget that."* But the truth would not serve me well here.

"So before coming here, you lived... where?"

"I lived on a ship. But I grew up mostly on Gaia, then a few years on Nibiru."

"Ah. Gaia." Some of her confusion clears up. "So that's why you're"—she fumbles for a word—"abstinent?"

They always ask about that.

"I'm not. It's just different for me."

It's clear she doesn't understand, but this is an issue I'm not eager to provide more explanation about. I've tried it with Titans, many times, but our attitudes are too deeply ingrained, and too different. Maybe it is the years in Gaia's conservative culture affecting me more than I like to think. Or maybe it was one too many lectures from Momma about avoiding unplanned children on any of the planets. With those concerns, she was always more strict with Pol and I than with our sisters, even after she gave us all birth control shots from Gaia, where they're mandatory.

Either way, I've never been able to make myself comfortable with Titans' extraordinarily casual attitude toward sex. I don't judge them for their own dalliances—though constantly being woken up in the middle of the night drove me to demand having my own room, despite it being against Titan custom—but the lifestyle doesn't suit me.

I tried during basic training, when my loneliness was a raw wound I was constantly trying to sew shut. It didn't work. And here, where I'm in charge of these people, tasked with ordering them to fight and die as I see fit, attachment is too dangerous.

I know I wouldn't be able to be objective. If only knowing was enough to keep my heart from wanting.

The conversation ends as we travel higher in the stairwell, drawing close enough to the cafeteria that the voices of my team bounce off the walls around us. The sound of their laughter and easy chatter makes my guilt heavier with every step. Ivennie is still barely more than a stranger, but the others have been with me for a long time. *Secrets lead to jealousy*... and I haven't told them of the upcoming end to my service, or the message I sent to my family, or the possibility this could be my last mission. Though I've never been able to view them as my kin, my team has always seen me as a part of their family. No matter what choice I make, I'll be leaving someone behind.